TABLE OF CONTENTS

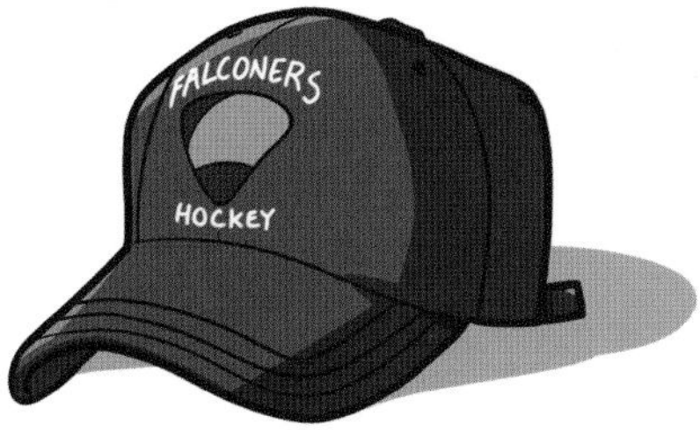
FALCONERS
HOCKEY

FOREWORD

ERIC BITTLE STARTED OFF as a ballpoint pen sketch in a college-ruled, spiral-bound notebook—a character in the margins with a speech bubble, a hockey jersey, and a pie. Five years, several chapters, and a slew of online comic updates later, he's as far from the margins as he'll ever be. He's the main character of the first graphic novel series I've ever written, and a person with a story.

If the first *Check, Please!* installment, *#Hockey*, was about Bitty discovering himself, then this book, *Sticks & Scones*, is about Bitty announcing himself. It's Eric Bittle reaching his full potential. It's about risk. It's about learning not to be afraid. And it's about realizing you were strong the whole time. We're a very long way away from the idea of "what if a figure skater (and baker!) joined a bro-y NCAA men's hockey team?" We're in Providence, Rhode Island, and Boston, Massachusetts, and Madison, Georgia; we're at center ice in a hockey stadium; and we're following Bitty to the end of Samwell, and into adulthood. We're a very long way from the margins.

This is the second and final *Check, Please!* book and I'm excited to share the end of this series. I will miss Samwell dearly. Just as Bitty discovered who he was in the Haus and in Faber and as a member of the Samwell men's ice hockey team, I learned so much about myself in the pages of this comic. I hope you discover a bit of yourself as well.

P.S. Oh, and please be sure to check out Bitty's tweets in the back of the book. B. "Shitty" Knight does in fact have a first name, and Bitty finally finds out what it is. (And so do we!)

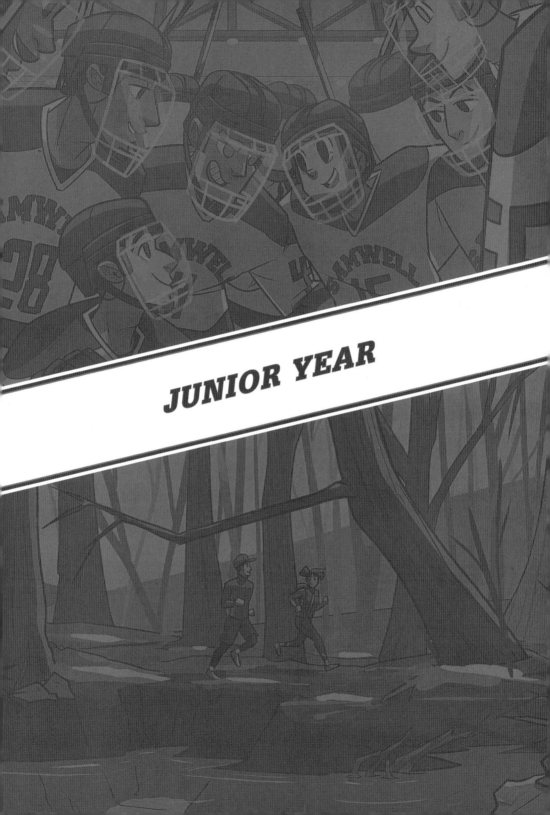

JUNIOR YEAR

1

WAG

HONEY, IT'S NOT LIKE I'M GONNA TELL THE WHOLE *WORLD*.
NOW LISTEN, HALF THIS VLOG POST IS ME RECOUNTING THAT JAM DISPUTE BETWEEN MY MAMA AND AUNT *ANYWAY*. WHICH–
OH, *HAR HAR*. YOU SNICKER BUT THIS IS TEARING THE PHELPSES AND BITTLES APART AT THE SEAMS!
HAHA!— OH *SHHH*! YOU SHUSH!!!
I SIGNED UP FOR THIS! I SIGNED UP FOR THIS CHIRPING.
JAM IS IMPORTANT.

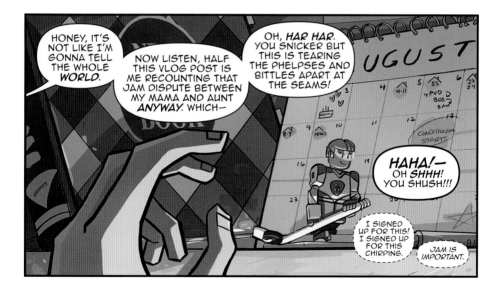

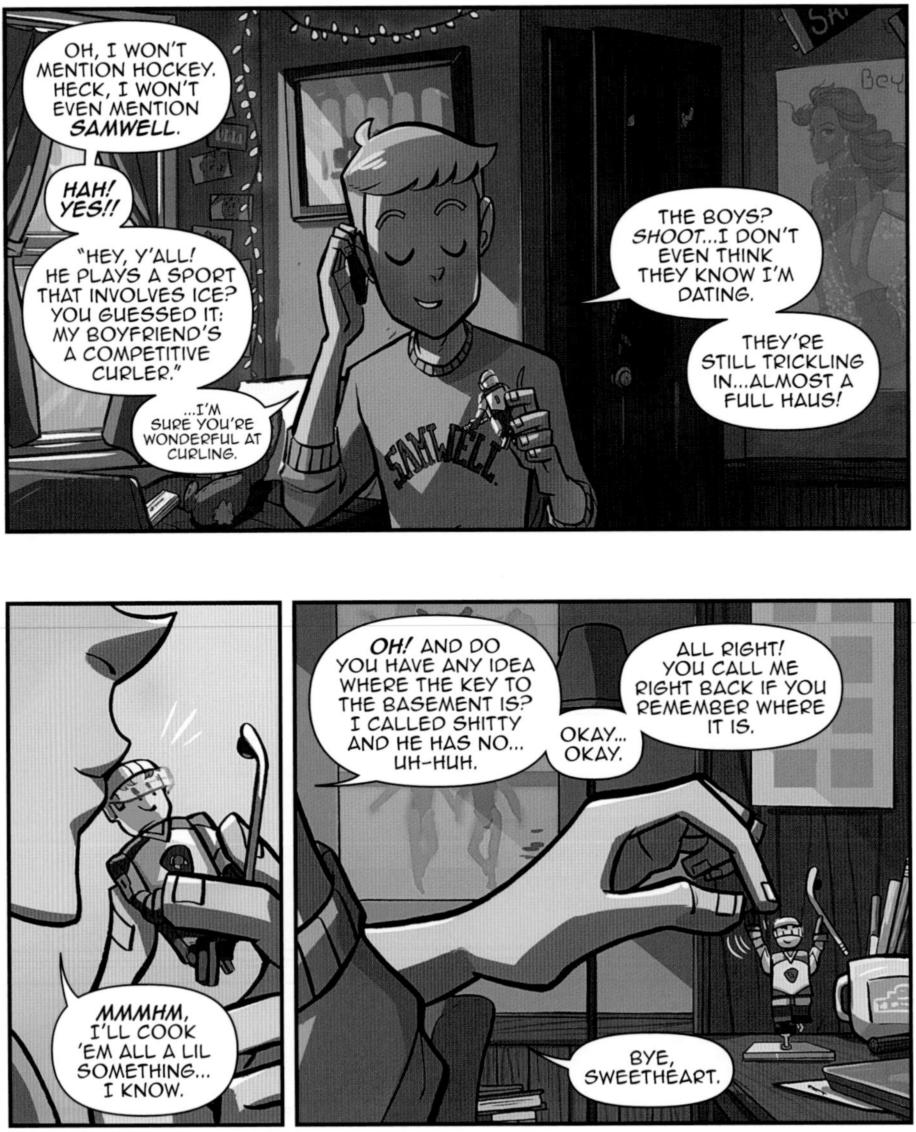
OH, I WON'T MENTION HOCKEY. HECK, I WON'T EVEN MENTION *SAMWELL*.
HAH! YES!!
"HEY, Y'ALL! HE PLAYS A SPORT THAT INVOLVES ICE? YOU GUESSED IT: MY BOYFRIEND'S A COMPETITIVE CURLER."
...I'M SURE YOU'RE WONDERFUL AT CURLING.
THE BOYS? *SHOOT*...I DON'T EVEN THINK THEY KNOW I'M DATING.
THEY'RE STILL TRICKLING IN...ALMOST A FULL HAUS!
MMMHM, I'LL COOK 'EM ALL A LIL SOMETHING... I KNOW.
OH! AND DO YOU HAVE ANY IDEA WHERE THE KEY TO THE BASEMENT IS? I CALLED SHITTY AND HE HAS NO... UH-HUH.
OKAY... OKAY.
ALL RIGHT! YOU CALL ME RIGHT BACK IF YOU REMEMBER WHERE IT IS.
BYE, SWEETHEART.

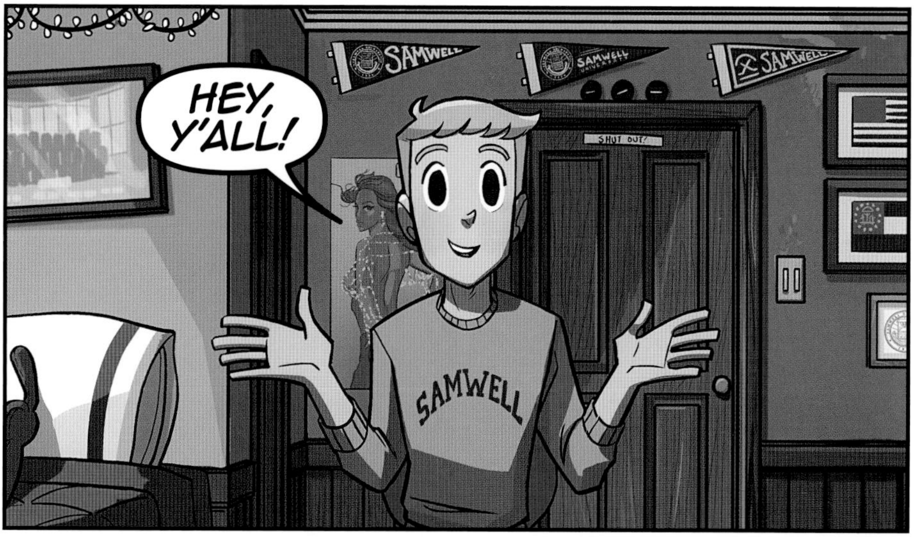
HEY, Y'ALL!
SAMWELL
SHUT OUT!

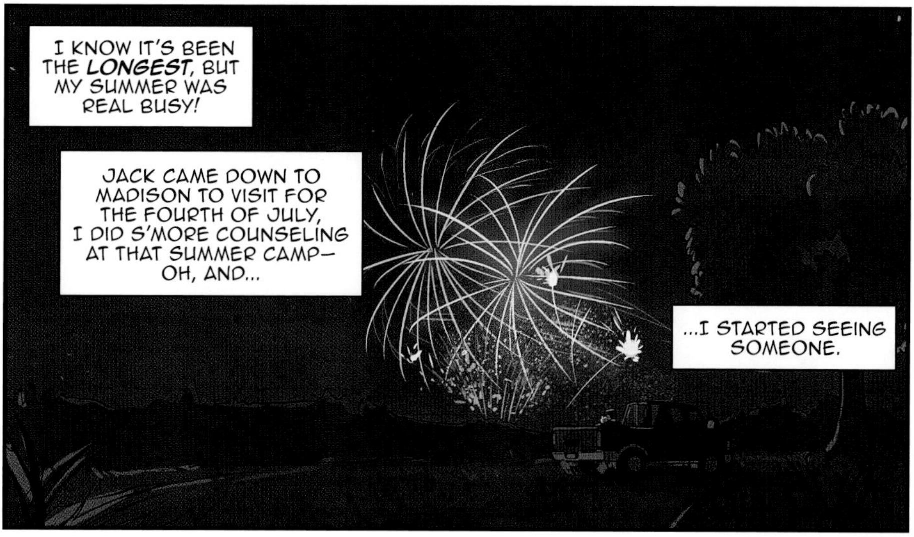
I KNOW IT'S BEEN THE ***LONGEST***, BUT MY SUMMER WAS REAL BUSY!
JACK CAME DOWN TO MADISON TO VISIT FOR THE FOURTH OF JULY, I DID S'MORE COUNSELING AT THAT SUMMER CAMP— OH, AND...
...I STARTED SEEING SOMEONE.

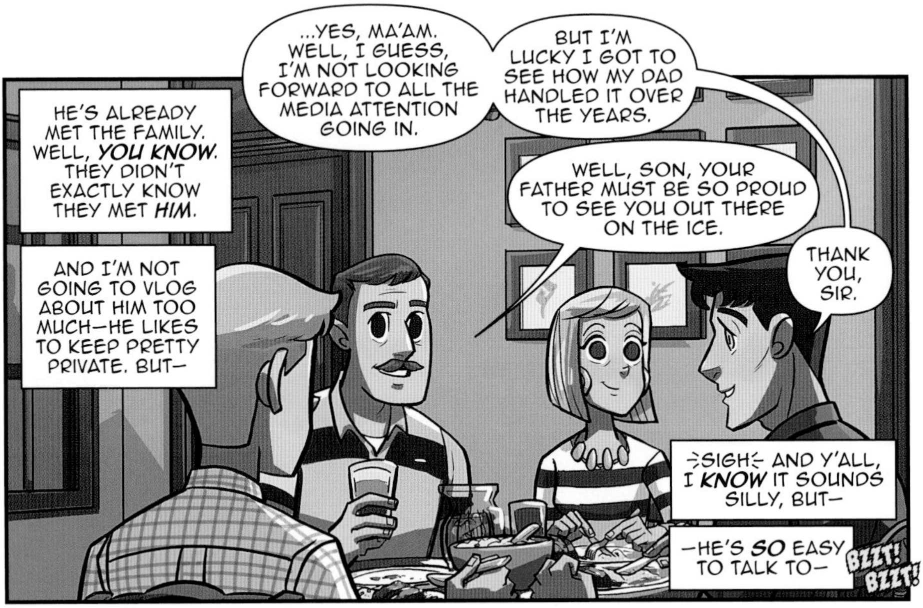
HE'S ALREADY MET THE FAMILY. WELL, ***YOU KNOW***. THEY DIDN'T EXACTLY KNOW THEY MET ***HIM***.
AND I'M NOT GOING TO VLOG ABOUT HIM TOO MUCH—HE LIKES TO KEEP PRETTY PRIVATE. BUT—
...YES, MA'AM. WELL, I GUESS, I'M NOT LOOKING FORWARD TO ALL THE MEDIA ATTENTION GOING IN.
BUT I'M LUCKY I GOT TO SEE HOW MY DAD HANDLED IT OVER THE YEARS.
WELL, SON, YOUR FATHER MUST BE SO PROUD TO SEE YOU OUT THERE ON THE ICE.
THANK YOU, SIR.
⇒SIGH⇐ AND Y'ALL, I ***KNOW*** IT SOUNDS SILLY, BUT—
—HE'S ***SO*** EASY TO TALK TO—
BZZT! BZZT!

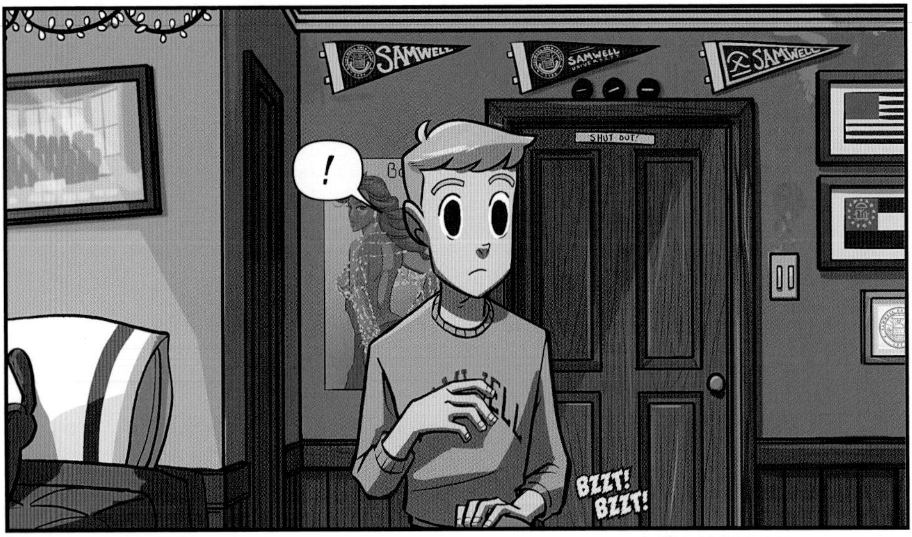
SAMWELL
SAMWELL UNIVERSITY
SAMWELL
SHUT OUT!
!
BZZT! BZZT!

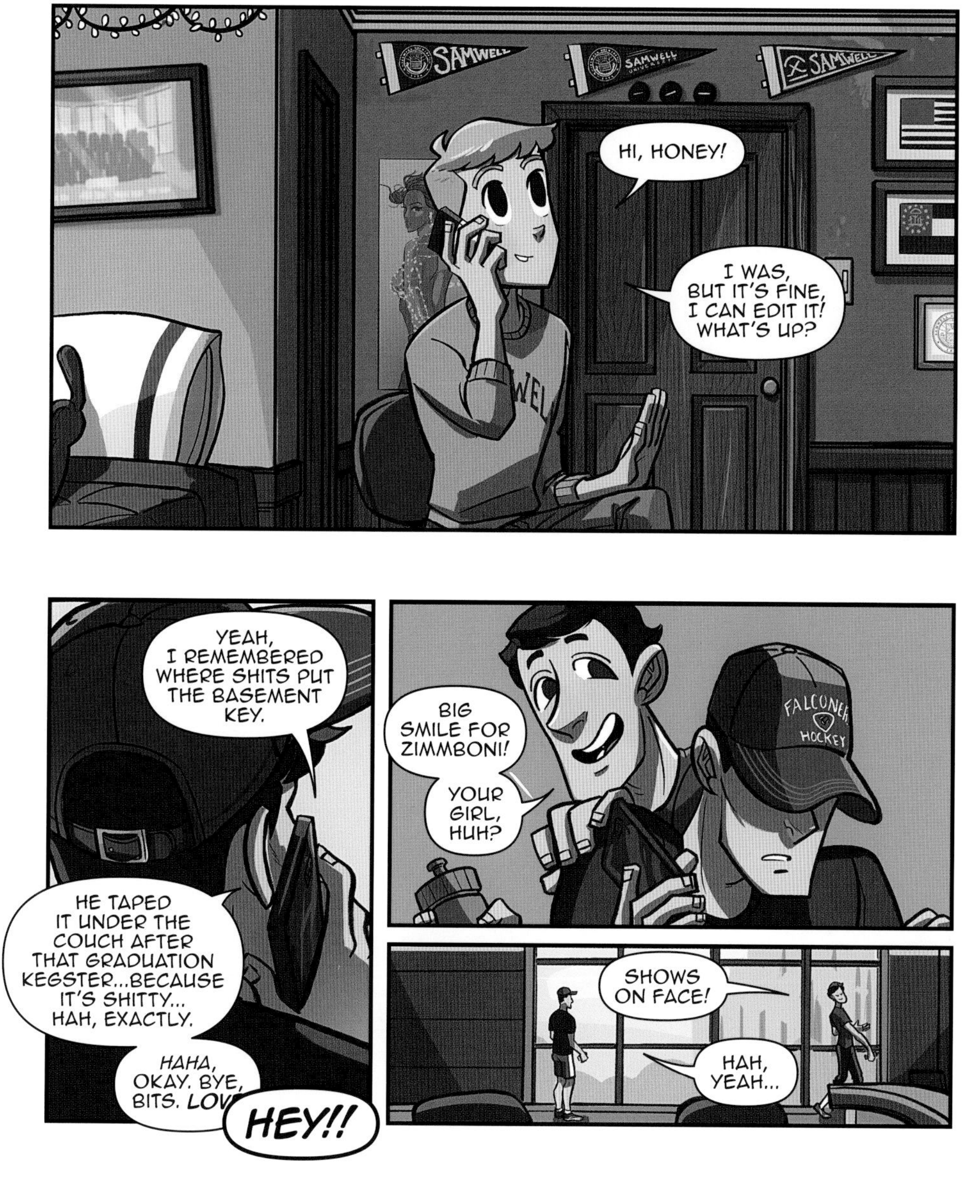
HI, HONEY!
I WAS, BUT IT'S FINE, I CAN EDIT IT! WHAT'S UP?
YEAH, I REMEMBERED WHERE SHITS PUT THE BASEMENT KEY.
HE TAPED IT UNDER THE COUCH AFTER THAT GRADUATION KEGSTER...BECAUSE IT'S SHITTY... HAH, EXACTLY.
HAHA, OKAY. BYE, BITS. LOV
HEY!!
BIG SMILE FOR ZIMMBONI!
YOUR GIRL, HUH?
FALCONERS HOCKEY
SHOWS ON FACE!
HAH, YEAH...

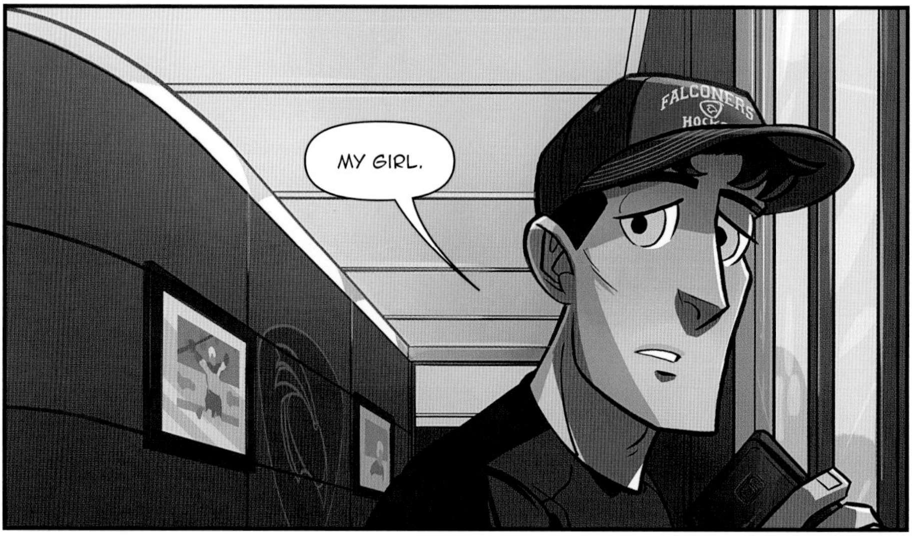
MY GIRL.
FALCONERS

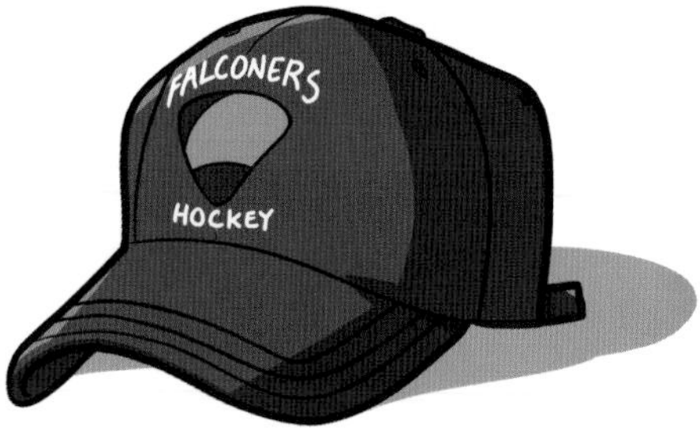
FALCONERS
HOCKEY

2

TADDY TOUR

GOOD MORNING, GENTLEMEN!
Y'ALL, THE NEWEST MEMBERS OF SAMWELL HOCKEY, HAVE THE WONDERFUL HONOR OF ENTERING FOR THE VERY FIRST TIME OUR TEAM'S HOME:
THE HAUS.
WE DO REGULARLY THROW KEGSTERS HERE—THAT'S PARTIES—AND THEY'RE FUN AS ALL GET OUT.
YOU'LL COME OUT OF MOST OF THEM UNSCATHED IF YOU KEEP YOUR HEAD ON STRAIGHT.
HAVE YOUR TEAMMATES' BACKS.
DON'T BITE OFF MORE THAN YOU CAN CHEW.
AND IF Y'ALL ARE EVER LOOKING FOR A QUIET PLACE TO STUDY, COME ON AROUND! LORD KNOWS I CAN'T EAT HALF OF WHAT I BAKE MYSELF!
NOW!
ANY QUESTIONS?

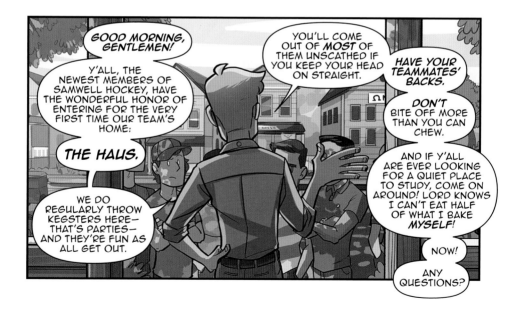

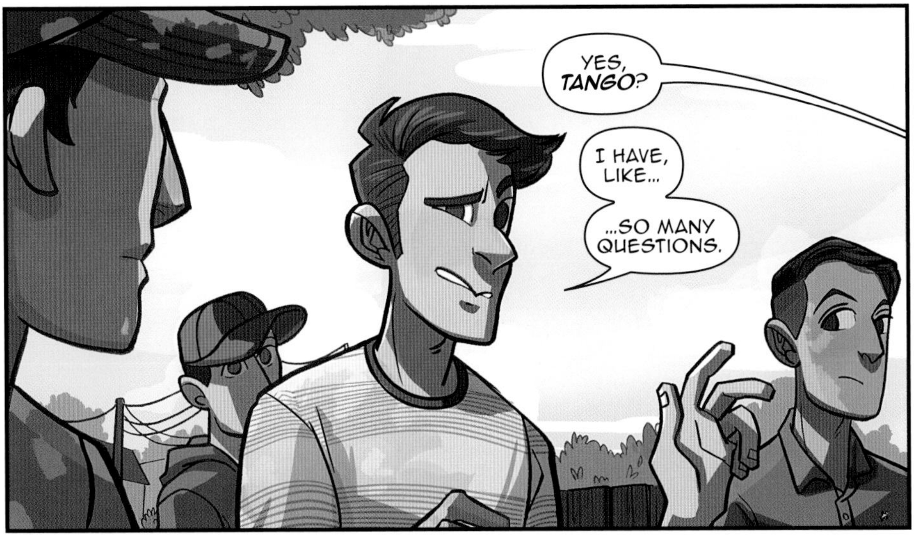
YES, TANGO?
I HAVE, LIKE...
...SO MANY QUESTIONS.

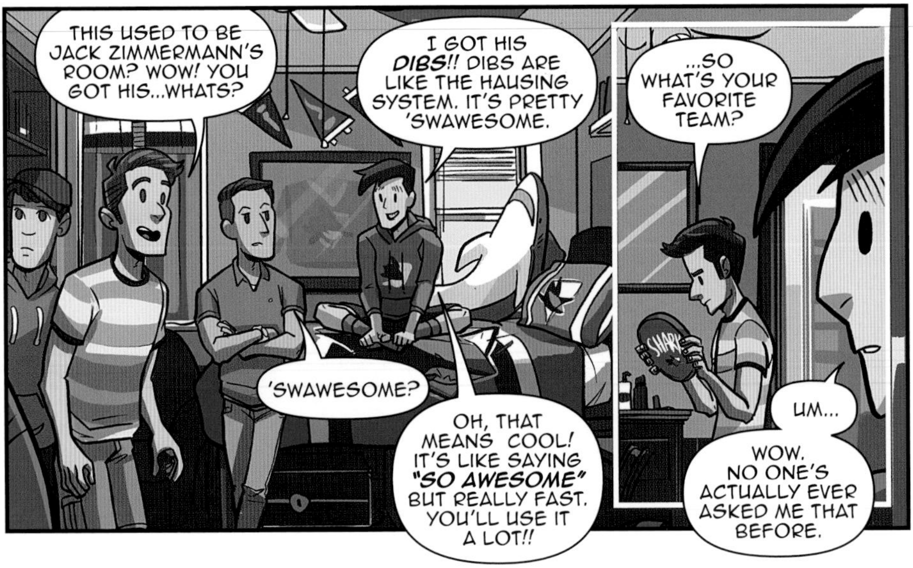
THIS USED TO BE JACK ZIMMERMANN'S ROOM? WOW! YOU GOT HIS...WHATS?
I GOT HIS DIBS!! DIBS ARE LIKE THE HAUSING SYSTEM. IT'S PRETTY 'SWAWESOME.
'SWAWESOME?
OH, THAT MEANS COOL! IT'S LIKE SAYING "SO AWESOME" BUT REALLY FAST. YOU'LL USE IT A LOT!!
...SO WHAT'S YOUR FAVORITE TEAM?
UM...
WOW. NO ONE'S ACTUALLY EVER ASKED ME THAT BEFORE.

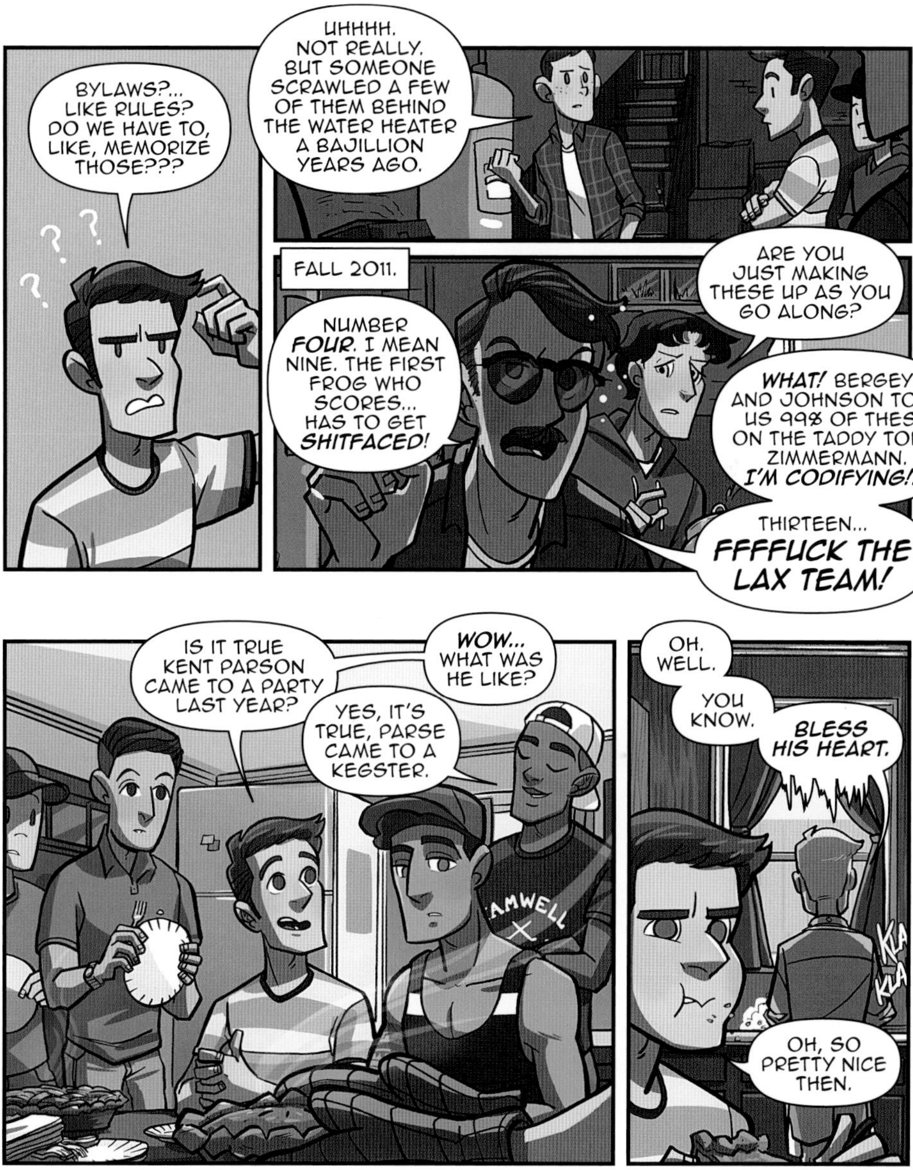
BYLAWS?... LIKE RULES? DO WE HAVE TO, LIKE, MEMORIZE THOSE???
UHHHH. NOT REALLY. BUT SOMEONE SCRAWLED A FEW OF THEM BEHIND THE WATER HEATER A BAJILLION YEARS AGO.
FALL 2011.
NUMBER FOUR. I MEAN NINE. THE FIRST FROG WHO SCORES... HAS TO GET SHITFACED!
ARE YOU JUST MAKING THESE UP AS YOU GO ALONG?
WHAT! BERGEY AND JOHNSON TOLD US 99% OF THESE ON THE TADDY TOUR, ZIMMERMANN. I'M CODIFYING!!!
THIRTEEN... FFFFUCK THE LAX TEAM!
IS IT TRUE KENT PARSON CAME TO A PARTY LAST YEAR?
WOW... WHAT WAS HE LIKE?
YES, IT'S TRUE, PARSE CAME TO A KEGSTER.
OH. WELL.
YOU KNOW.
BLESS HIS HEART.
KLA KLA
OH, SO PRETTY NICE THEN.

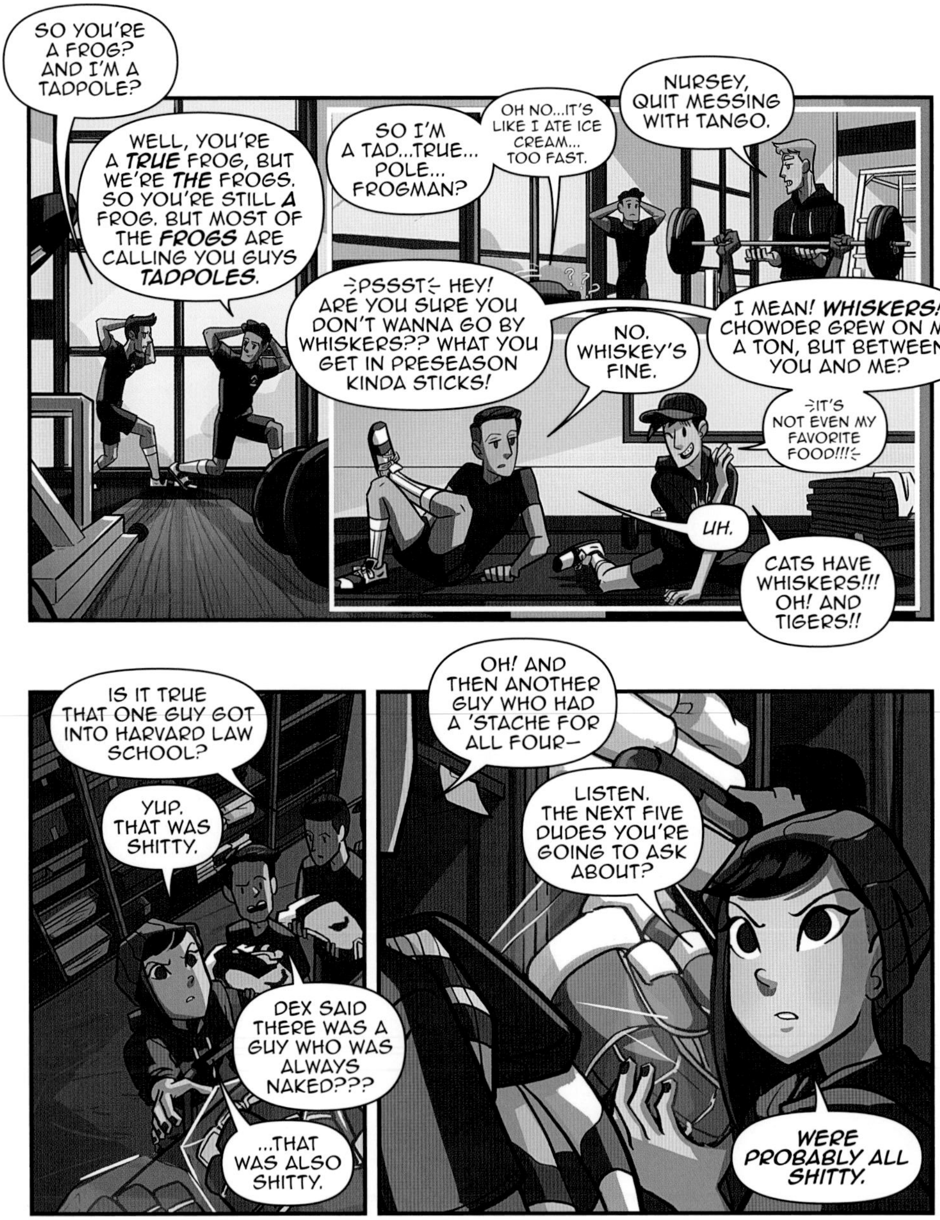
SO YOU'RE A FROG? AND I'M A TADPOLE?
WELL, YOU'RE A TRUE FROG, BUT WE'RE THE FROGS. SO YOU'RE STILL A FROG. BUT MOST OF THE FROGS ARE CALLING YOU GUYS TADPOLES.
SO I'M A TAD...TRUE... POLE... FROGMAN?
OH NO...IT'S LIKE I ATE ICE CREAM... TOO FAST.
NURSEY, QUIT MESSING WITH TANGO.
PSSST HEY! ARE YOU SURE YOU DON'T WANNA GO BY WHISKERS?? WHAT YOU GET IN PRESEASON KINDA STICKS!
NO. WHISKEY'S FINE.
I MEAN! WHISKERS! CHOWDER GREW ON ME A TON, BUT BETWEEN YOU AND ME?
IT'S NOT EVEN MY FAVORITE FOOD!!!
UH.
CATS HAVE WHISKERS!!! OH! AND TIGERS!!
IS IT TRUE THAT ONE GUY GOT INTO HARVARD LAW SCHOOL?
YUP. THAT WAS SHITTY.
DEX SAID THERE WAS A GUY WHO WAS ALWAYS NAKED???
...THAT WAS ALSO SHITTY.
OH! AND THEN ANOTHER GUY WHO HAD A 'STACHE FOR ALL FOUR—
LISTEN. THE NEXT FIVE DUDES YOU'RE GOING TO ASK ABOUT?
WERE PROBABLY ALL SHITTY.

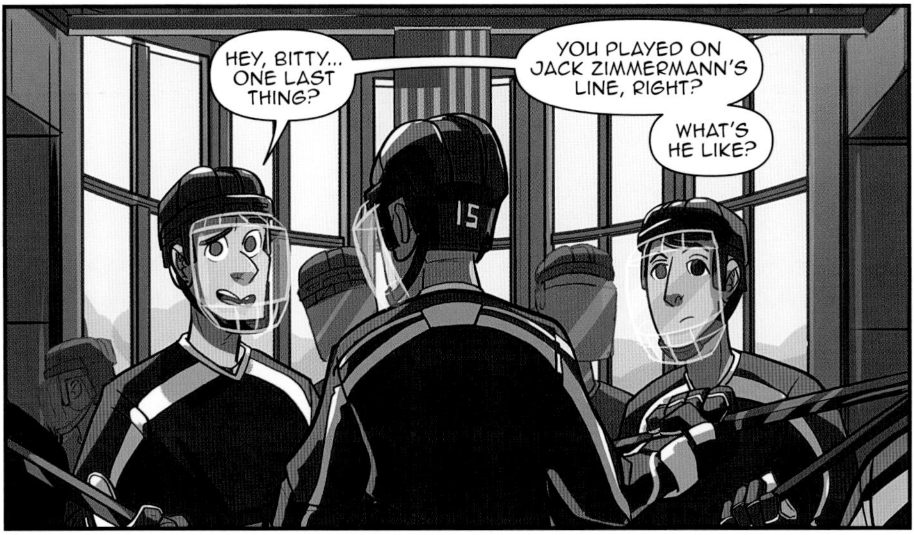
HEY, BITTY... ONE LAST THING?
YOU PLAYED ON JACK ZIMMERMANN'S LINE, RIGHT?
WHAT'S HE LIKE?

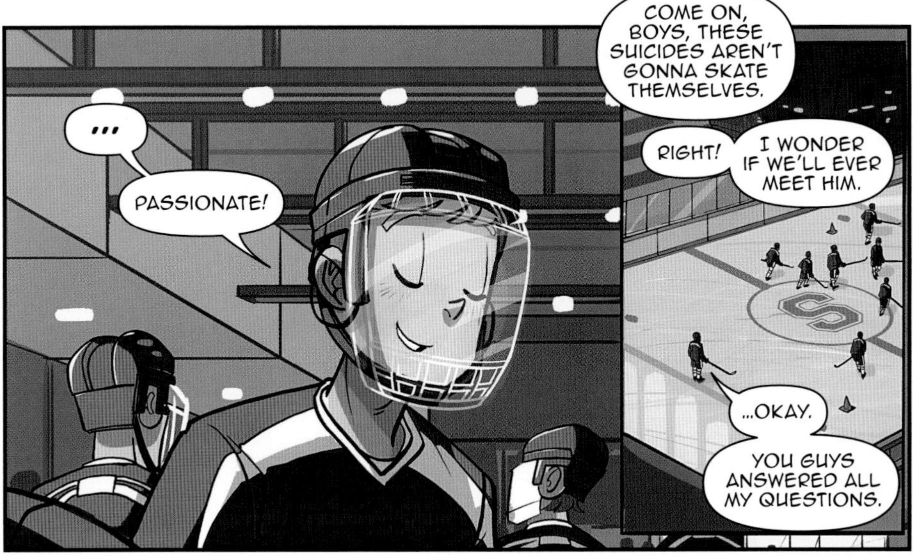
...
PASSIONATE!
COME ON, BOYS, THESE SUICIDES AREN'T GONNA SKATE THEMSELVES.
RIGHT!
I WONDER IF WE'LL EVER MEET HIM.
...OKAY.
YOU GUYS ANSWERED ALL MY QUESTIONS.

3

MEET THE FALCONERS

SAMWELL
SAMWELL UNIVERSITY
SAMWELL
SHUT OUT!
IF Y'ALL FOLLOW ME ON TWITTER, YOU KNOW I'M ALWAYS LINKING TO ALL THOSE FALCONERS VIDEO CLIPS THEIR PR PEOPLE PUT UP.
NHL TEAMS'LL DO THAT. GIVE YOU BEHIND-THE-SCENES STUFF SO YOU FEEL A LITTLE CLOSER TO THE PLAYERS.
SO IT'S KINDA **NEAT** WHEN ONE OF YOUR BEST FRIENDS STARTS HIS NHL CAREER AND **SHOWS UP** IN THESE CLIPS!
(WE USUALLY CHIRP JACK ABOUT IT ON GROUP TEXT.)

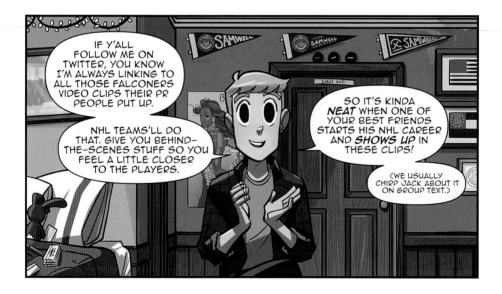

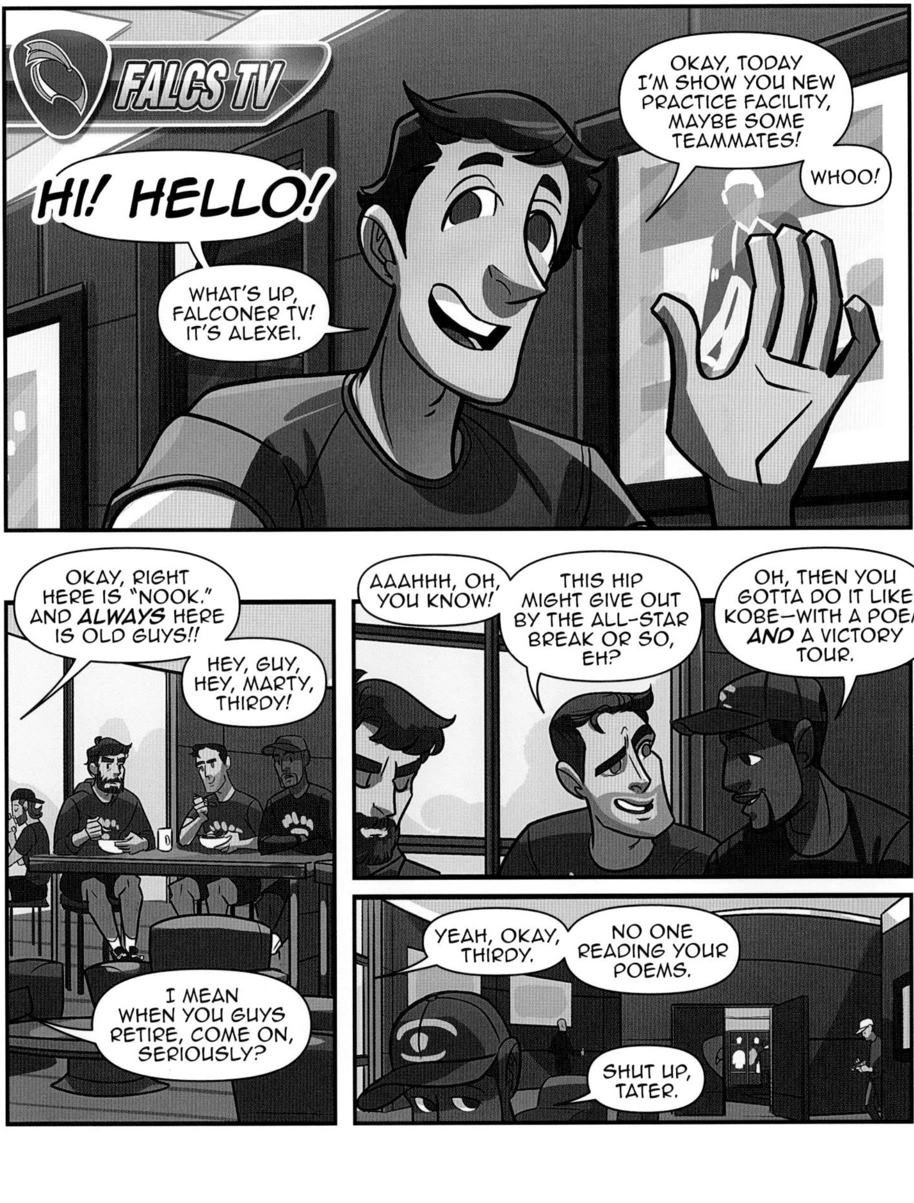
FALCS TV
HI! HELLO!
WHAT'S UP, FALCONER TV! IT'S ALEXEI.
OKAY, TODAY I'M SHOW YOU NEW PRACTICE FACILITY, MAYBE SOME TEAMMATES!
WHOO!
OKAY, RIGHT HERE IS "NOOK." AND ALWAYS HERE IS OLD GUYS!!
HEY, GUY, HEY, MARTY, THIRDY!
I MEAN WHEN YOU GUYS RETIRE, COME ON, SERIOUSLY?
AAAHHH, OH, YOU KNOW!
THIS HIP MIGHT GIVE OUT BY THE ALL-STAR BREAK OR SO, EH?
OH, THEN YOU GOTTA DO IT LIKE KOBE—WITH A POEM AND A VICTORY TOUR.
YEAH, OKAY, THIRDY.
NO ONE READING YOUR POEMS.
SHUT UP, TATER.

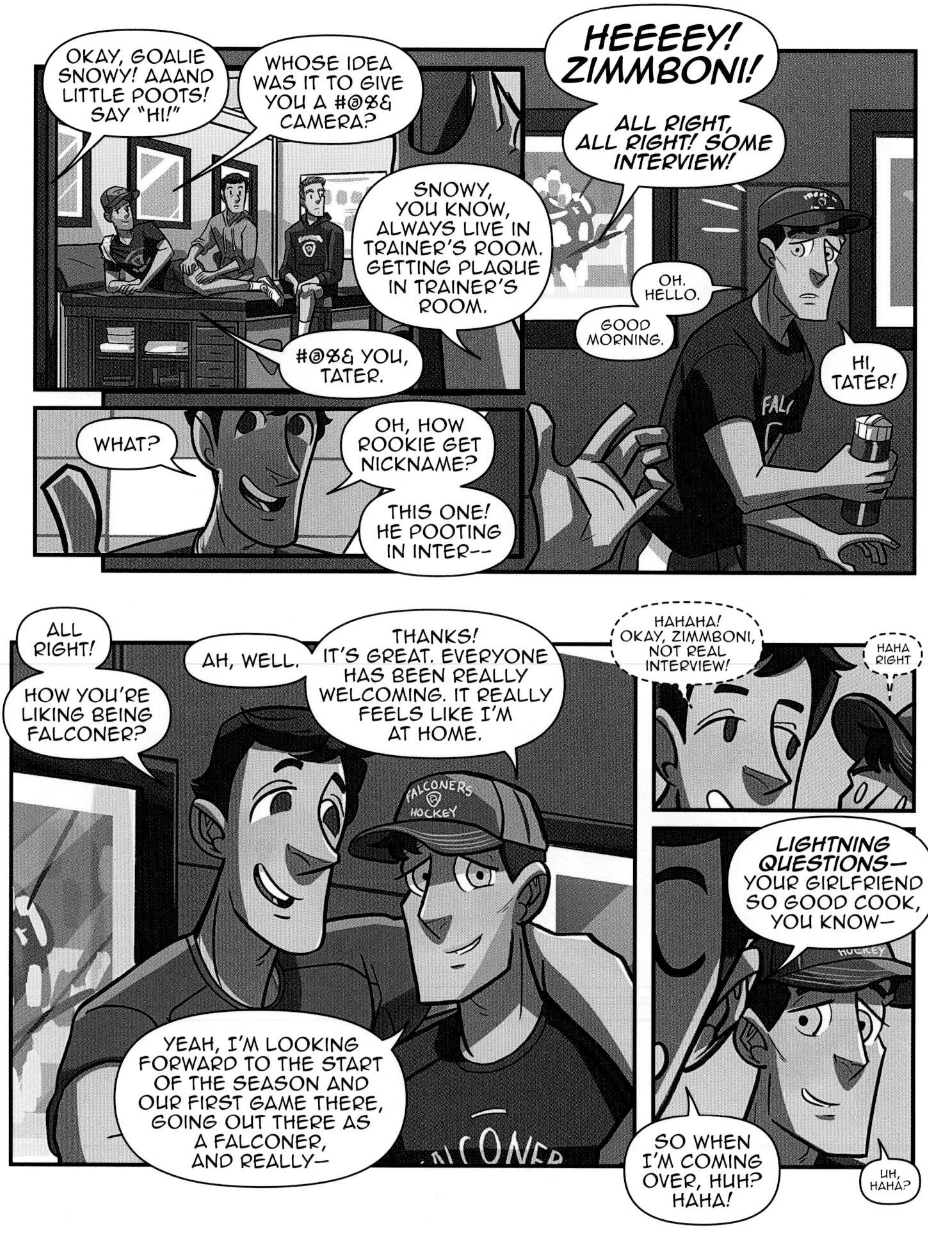
OKAY, GOALIE SNOWY! AAAND LITTLE POOTS! SAY "HI!"
WHOSE IDEA WAS IT TO GIVE YOU A #@%& CAMERA?
SNOWY, YOU KNOW, ALWAYS LIVE IN TRAINER'S ROOM. GETTING PLAQUE IN TRAINER'S ROOM.
#@%& YOU, TATER.
HEEEEY! ZIMMBONI!
ALL RIGHT, ALL RIGHT! SOME INTERVIEW!
OH. HELLO.
GOOD MORNING.
HI, TATER!
WHAT?
OH, HOW ROOKIE GET NICKNAME?
THIS ONE! HE POOTING IN INTER--
ALL RIGHT!
HOW YOU'RE LIKING BEING FALCONER?
AH, WELL.
THANKS! IT'S GREAT. EVERYONE HAS BEEN REALLY WELCOMING. IT REALLY FEELS LIKE I'M AT HOME.
YEAH, I'M LOOKING FORWARD TO THE START OF THE SEASON AND OUR FIRST GAME THERE, GOING OUT THERE AS A FALCONER, AND REALLY—
HAHAHA! OKAY, ZIMMBONI, NOT REAL INTERVIEW!
HAHA RIGHT
LIGHTNING QUESTIONS— YOUR GIRLFRIEND SO GOOD COOK, YOU KNOW—
SO WHEN I'M COMING OVER, HUH? HAHA!
UH, HAHA?

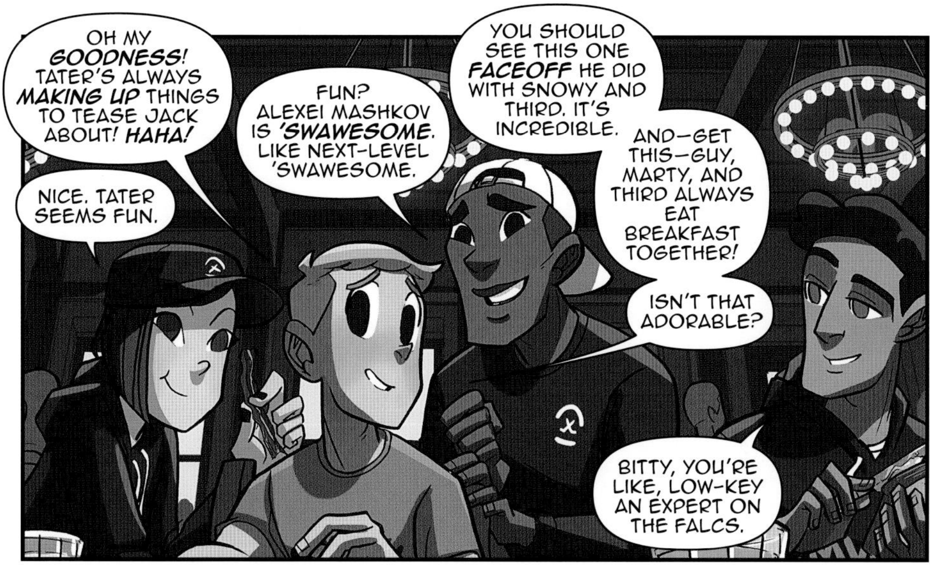
NICE. TATER SEEMS FUN.
OH MY GOODNESS! TATER'S ALWAYS MAKING UP THINGS TO TEASE JACK ABOUT! HAHA!
FUN? ALEXEI MASHKOV IS 'SWAWESOME. LIKE NEXT-LEVEL 'SWAWESOME.
YOU SHOULD SEE THIS ONE FACEOFF HE DID WITH SNOWY AND THIRD. IT'S INCREDIBLE.
AND—GET THIS—GUY, MARTY, AND THIRD ALWAYS EAT BREAKFAST TOGETHER!
ISN'T THAT ADORABLE?
BITTY, YOU'RE LIKE, LOW-KEY AN EXPERT ON THE FALCS.

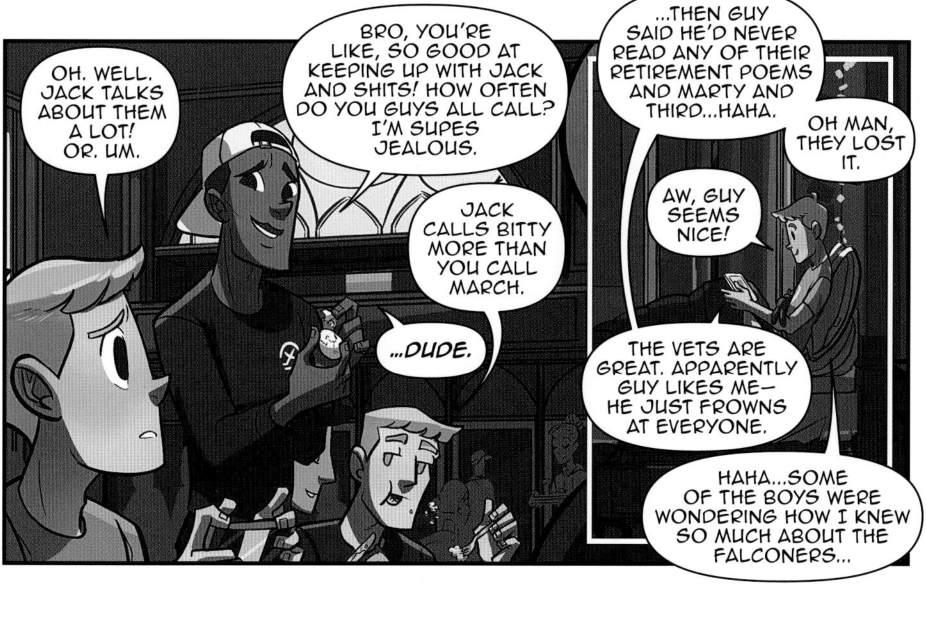
OH. WELL. JACK TALKS ABOUT THEM A LOT! OR. UM.
BRO, YOU'RE LIKE, SO GOOD AT KEEPING UP WITH JACK AND SHITS! HOW OFTEN DO YOU GUYS ALL CALL? I'M SUPES JEALOUS.
JACK CALLS BITTY MORE THAN YOU CALL MARCH.
...DUDE.
...THEN GUY SAID HE'D NEVER READ ANY OF THEIR RETIREMENT POEMS AND MARTY AND THIRD...HAHA.
OH MAN, THEY LOST IT.
AW, GUY SEEMS NICE!
THE VETS ARE GREAT. APPARENTLY GUY LIKES ME—HE JUST FROWNS AT EVERYONE.
HAHA...SOME OF THE BOYS WERE WONDERING HOW I KNEW SO MUCH ABOUT THE FALCONERS...

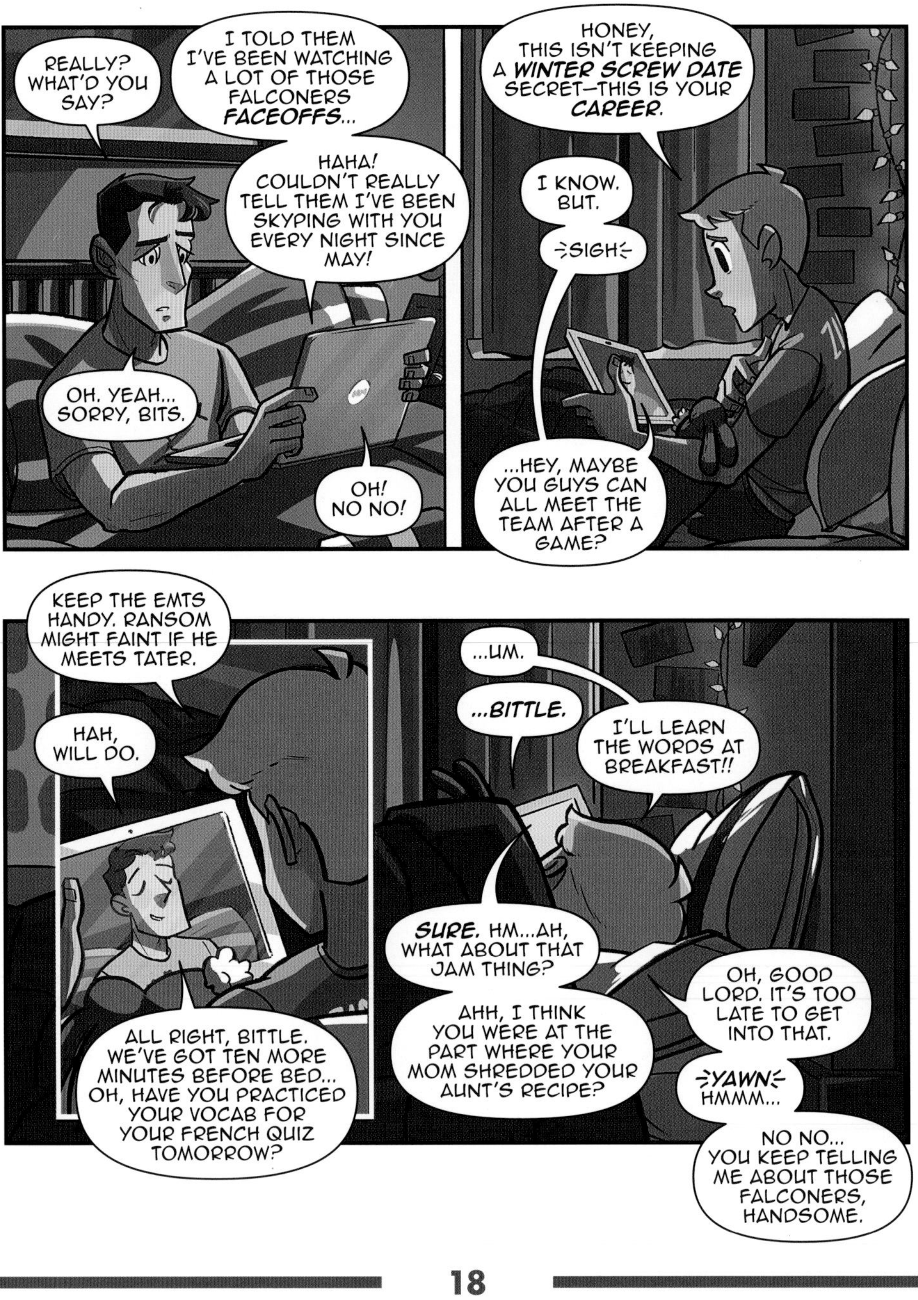
REALLY? WHAT'D YOU SAY?
I TOLD THEM I'VE BEEN WATCHING A LOT OF THOSE FALCONERS **FACEOFFS**...
HAHA! COULDN'T REALLY TELL THEM I'VE BEEN SKYPING WITH YOU EVERY NIGHT SINCE MAY!
OH. YEAH... SORRY, BITS.
OH! NO NO!
HONEY, THIS ISN'T KEEPING A ***WINTER SCREW DATE*** SECRET—THIS IS YOUR ***CAREER***.
I KNOW. BUT.
SIGH
...HEY, MAYBE YOU GUYS CAN ALL MEET THE TEAM AFTER A GAME?
KEEP THE EMTS HANDY. RANSOM MIGHT FAINT IF HE MEETS TATER.
HAH, WILL DO.
ALL RIGHT, BITTLE. WE'VE GOT TEN MORE MINUTES BEFORE BED... OH, HAVE YOU PRACTICED YOUR VOCAB FOR YOUR FRENCH QUIZ TOMORROW?
...UM.
...BITTLE.
I'LL LEARN THE WORDS AT BREAKFAST!!
SURE. HM...AH, WHAT ABOUT THAT JAM THING?
AHH, I THINK YOU WERE AT THE PART WHERE YOUR MOM SHREDDED YOUR AUNT'S RECIPE?
OH, GOOD LORD. IT'S TOO LATE TO GET INTO THAT.
YAWN HMMM...
NO NO... YOU KEEP TELLING ME ABOUT THOSE FALCONERS, HANDSOME.

4

HOME OPENER

HEY, Y'ALL! LIKE MY NEW ZIMMERMANN JERSEY? (IT'S SIGNED!)
WE'RE ALL GETTING ON THE TRAIN TO PROVIDENCE TO WATCH JACK'S FIRST GAME IN THE NHL.
IT'S STILL PRESEASON, BUT BELIEVE YOU ME— WE'RE SO EXCITED.
SECTIONS
SIGH
DO Y'ALL EVER JUST STOP AND LOOK AROUND... AND ASK YOURSELF "HOW IN HEAVEN DID I GET HERE?"
HAH! AND I'M NOT EVEN THE ONE WHO'S A PRO ATHLETE.
MMERMANN

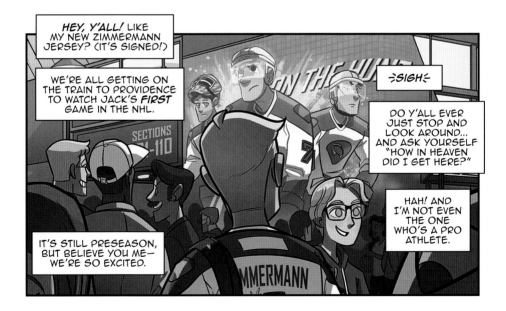

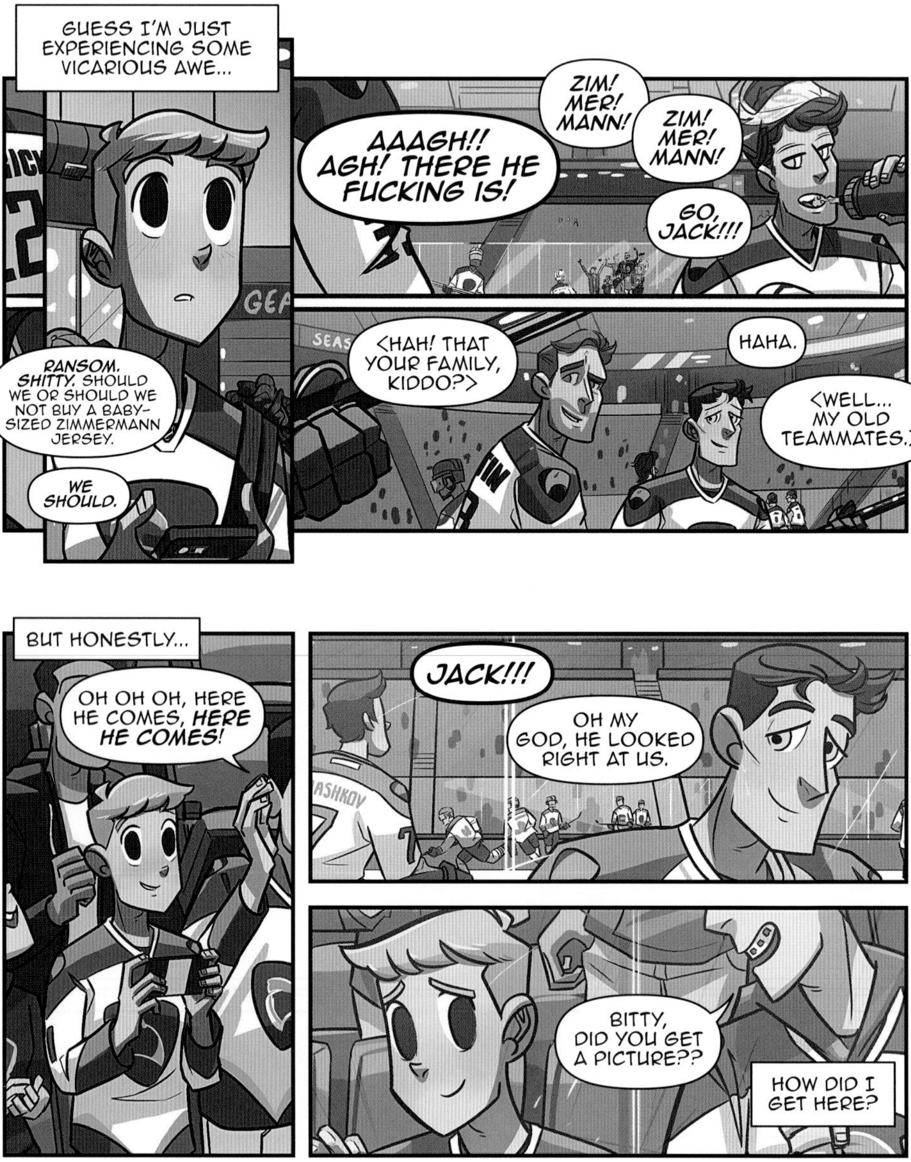
GUESS I'M JUST EXPERIENCING SOME VICARIOUS AWE...
AAAGH!! AGH! THERE HE FUCKING IS!
ZIM! MER! MANN!
ZIM! MER! MANN!
GO, JACK!!!
RANSOM. SHITTY. SHOULD WE OR SHOULD WE NOT BUY A BABY-SIZED ZIMMERMANN JERSEY.
WE SHOULD.
<HAH! THAT YOUR FAMILY, KIDDO?>
HAHA.
<WELL... MY OLD TEAMMATES.>
BUT HONESTLY...
OH OH OH, HERE HE COMES, HERE HE COMES!
JACK!!!
OH MY GOD, HE LOOKED RIGHT AT US.
BITTY, DID YOU GET A PICTURE??
HOW DID I GET HERE?

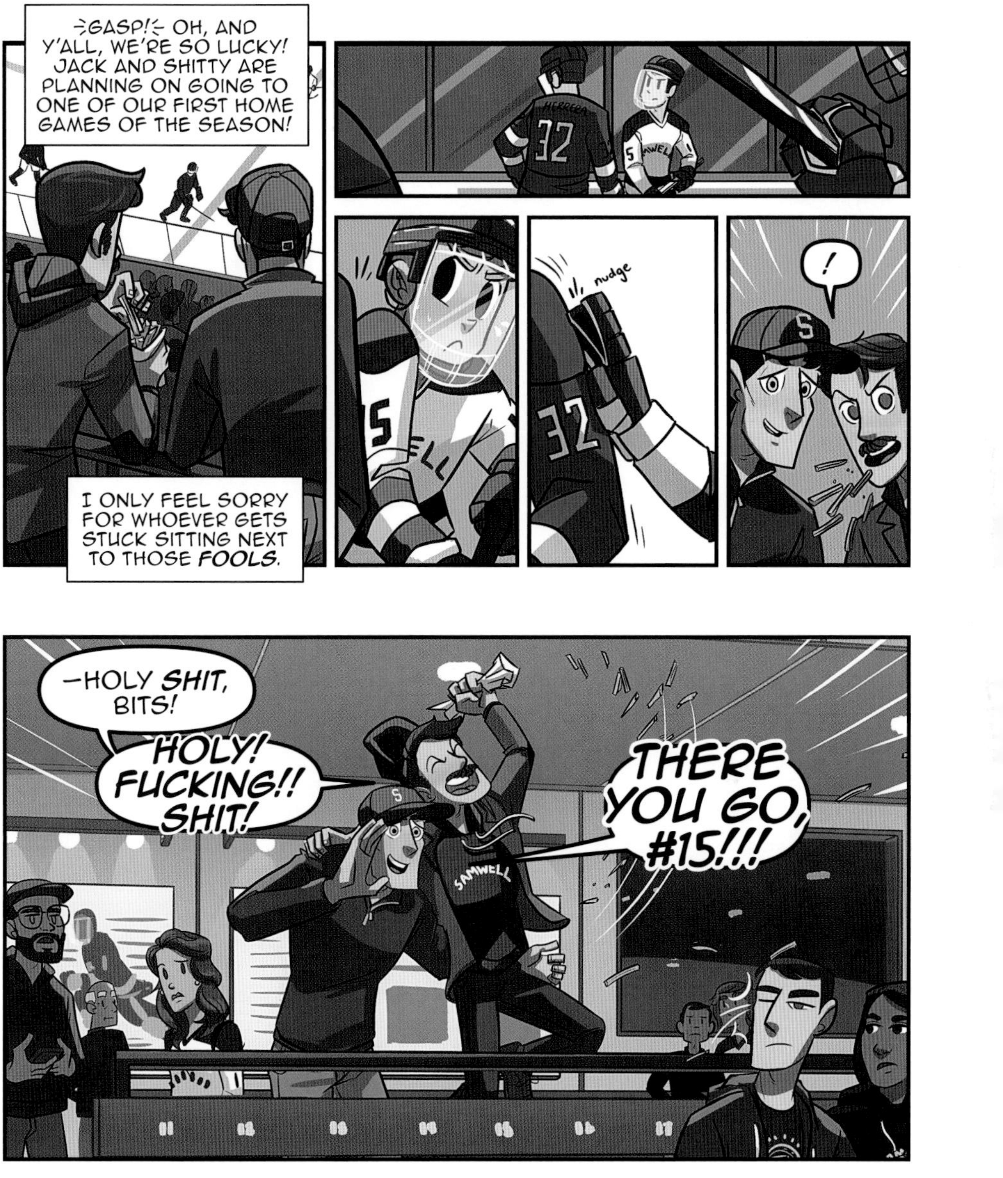
⇒GASP!⇐ OH, AND Y'ALL, WE'RE SO LUCKY! JACK AND SHITTY ARE PLANNING ON GOING TO ONE OF OUR FIRST HOME GAMES OF THE SEASON!
I ONLY FEEL SORRY FOR WHOEVER GETS STUCK SITTING NEXT TO THOSE *FOOLS*.
nudge
!
—HOLY *SHIT*, BITS!
HOLY! FUCKING!! SHIT!
THERE YOU GO, #15!!!
SAMWELL

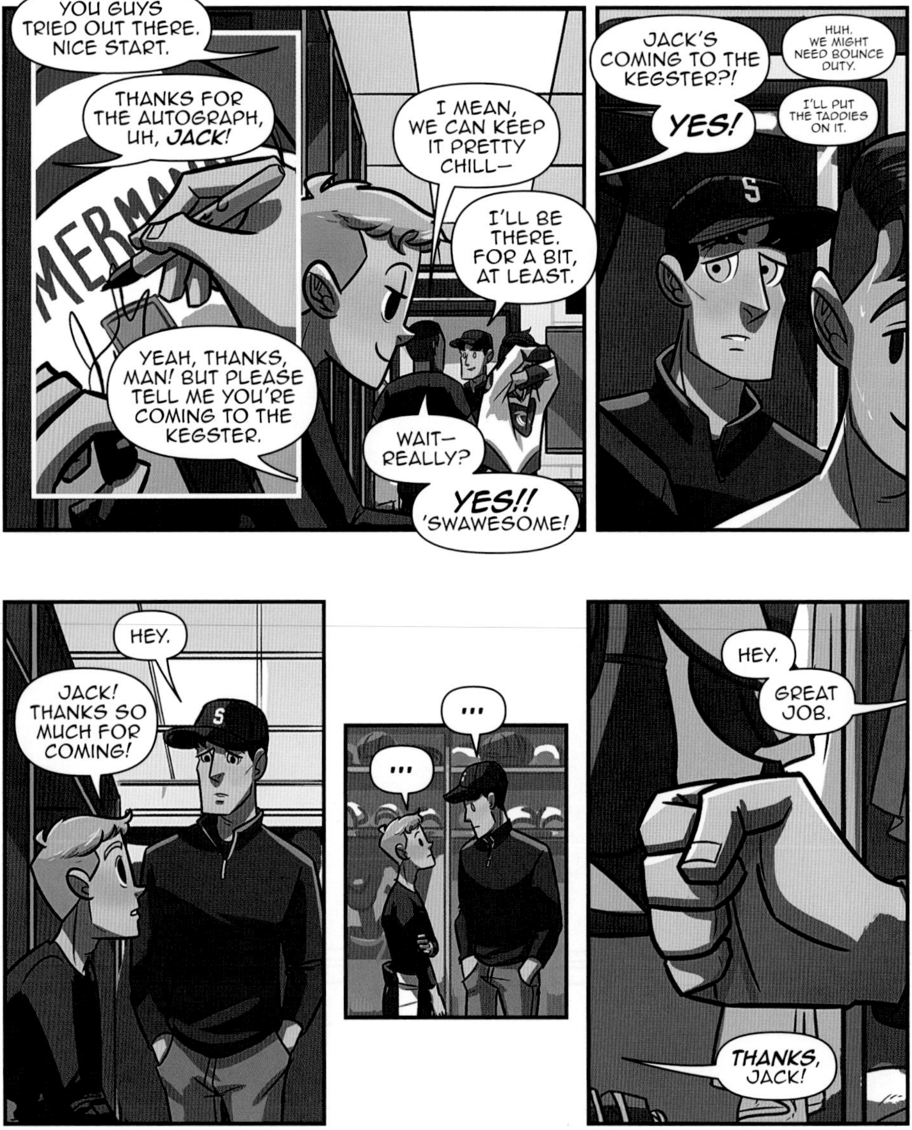
YOU GUYS TRIED OUT THERE. NICE START.
THANKS FOR THE AUTOGRAPH, UH, *JACK!*
YEAH, THANKS, MAN! BUT PLEASE TELL ME YOU'RE COMING TO THE KEGSTER.
I MEAN, WE CAN KEEP IT PRETTY CHILL—
I'LL BE THERE. FOR A BIT, AT LEAST.
WAIT— REALLY?
YES!! 'SWAWESOME!
JACK'S COMING TO THE KEGSTER?!
YES!
HUH. WE MIGHT NEED BOUNCE DUTY.
I'LL PUT THE TADDIES ON IT.
HEY.
JACK! THANKS SO MUCH FOR COMING!
...
...
HEY.
GREAT JOB.
THANKS, JACK!

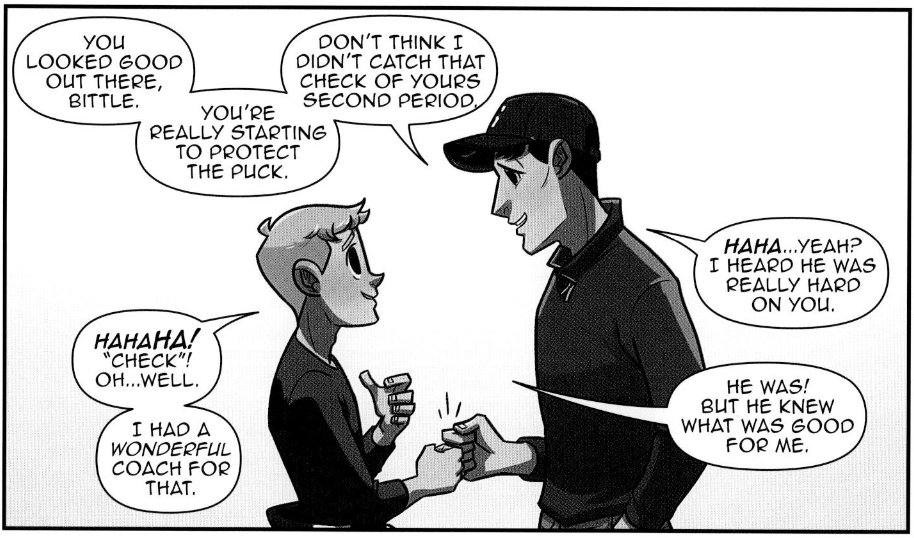
YOU LOOKED GOOD OUT THERE, BITTLE.
DON'T THINK I DIDN'T CATCH THAT CHECK OF YOURS SECOND PERIOD.
YOU'RE REALLY STARTING TO PROTECT THE PUCK.
HAHAHA! "CHECK"! OH...WELL.
I HAD A WONDERFUL COACH FOR THAT.
HAHA...YEAH? I HEARD HE WAS REALLY HARD ON YOU.
HE WAS! BUT HE KNEW WHAT WAS GOOD FOR ME.

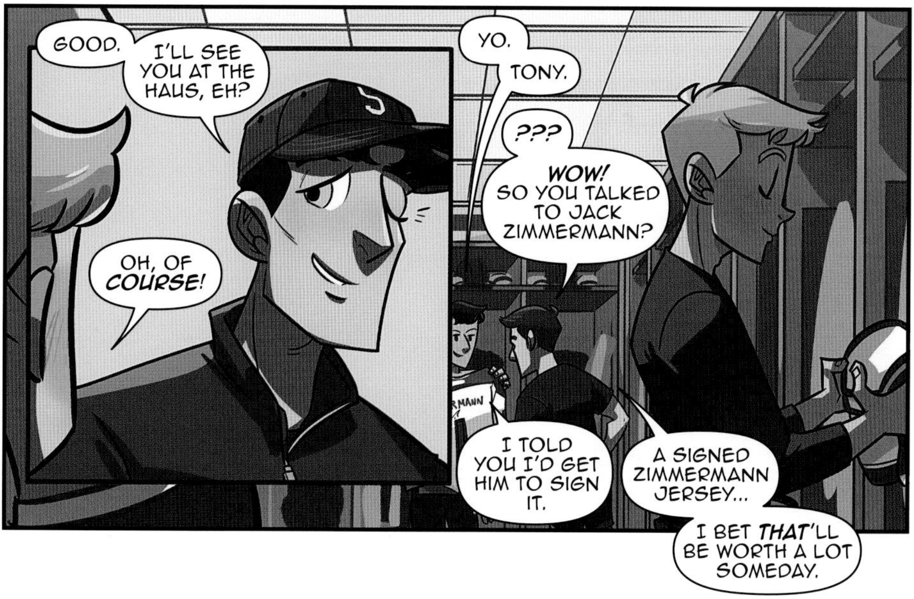
GOOD.
I'LL SEE YOU AT THE HAUS, EH?
OH, OF COURSE!
YO.
TONY.
???
WOW! SO YOU TALKED TO JACK ZIMMERMANN?
I TOLD YOU I'D GET HIM TO SIGN IT.
A SIGNED ZIMMERMANN JERSEY...
I BET THAT'LL BE WORTH A LOT SOMEDAY.

5

THE AFTER KEGSTER

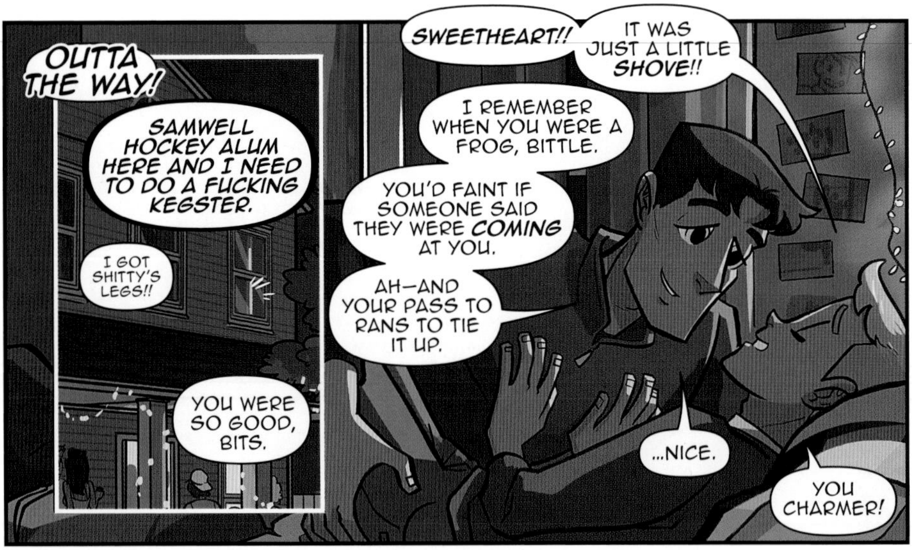

OUTTA THE WAY!
SAMWELL HOCKEY ALUM HERE AND I NEED TO DO A FUCKING KEGSTER.
I GOT SHITTY'S LEGS!!
YOU WERE SO GOOD, BITS.
SWEETHEART!!
IT WAS JUST A LITTLE SHOVE!!
I REMEMBER WHEN YOU WERE A FROG, BITTLE.
YOU'D FAINT IF SOMEONE SAID THEY WERE COMING AT YOU.
AH—AND YOUR PASS TO RANS TO TIE IT UP.
...NICE.
YOU CHARMER!

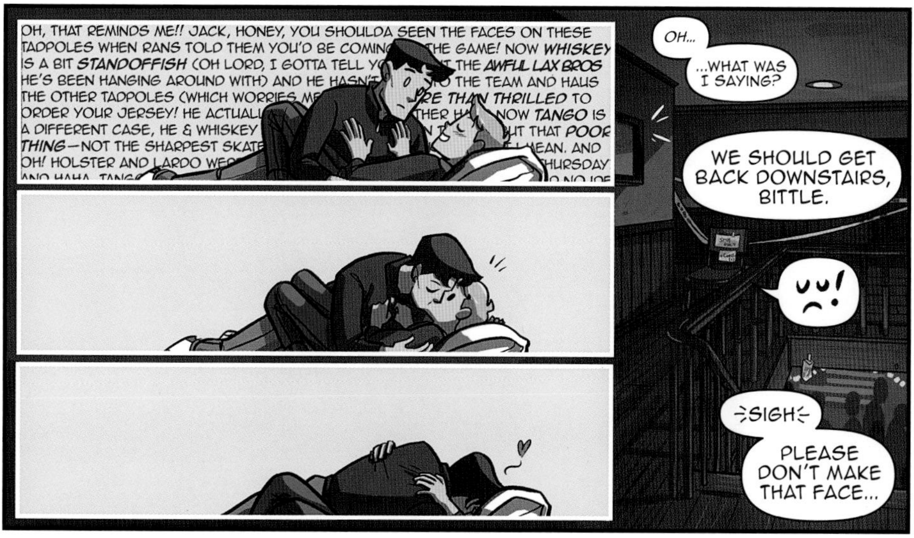
OH, THAT REMINDS ME!! JACK, HONEY, YOU SHOULDA SEEN THE FACES ON THESE
TADPOLES WHEN RANS TOLD THEM YOU'D BE COMING … THE GAME! NOW WHISKEY
IS A BIT STANDOFFISH (OH LORD, I GOTTA TELL Y… THE AWFUL LAX BROS
HE'S BEEN HANGING AROUND WITH) AND HE HASN'T … THE TEAM AND HAUS
THE OTHER TADPOLES (WHICH WORRIES ME … RE THAN THRILLED TO
ORDER YOUR JERSEY! HE ACTUALL… THER H… NOW TANGO IS
A DIFFERENT CASE, HE & WHISKEY … UT THAT POOR
THING—NOT THE SHARPEST SKAT… MEAN. AND
OH! HOLSTER AND LARDO WE… HURSDAY
OH...
...WHAT WAS I SAYING?
WE SHOULD GET BACK DOWNSTAIRS, BITTLE.
UU!
SIGH
PLEASE DON'T MAKE THAT FACE...

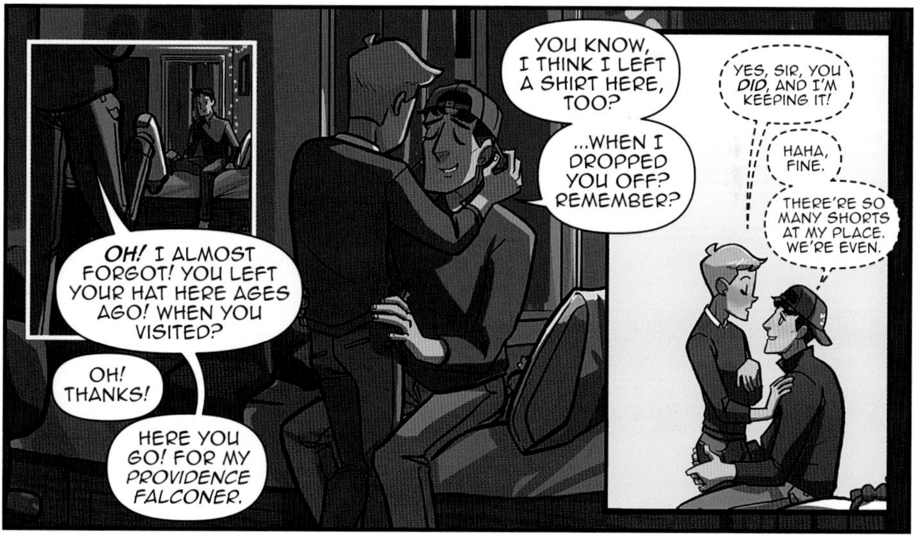
OH! I ALMOST FORGOT! YOU LEFT YOUR HAT HERE AGES AGO! WHEN YOU VISITED?
OH! THANKS!
HERE YOU GO! FOR MY PROVIDENCE FALCONER.
YOU KNOW, I THINK I LEFT A SHIRT HERE, TOO?
...WHEN I DROPPED YOU OFF? REMEMBER?
YES, SIR, YOU DID, AND I'M KEEPING IT!
HAHA, FINE.
THERE'RE SO MANY SHORTS AT MY PLACE. WE'RE EVEN.

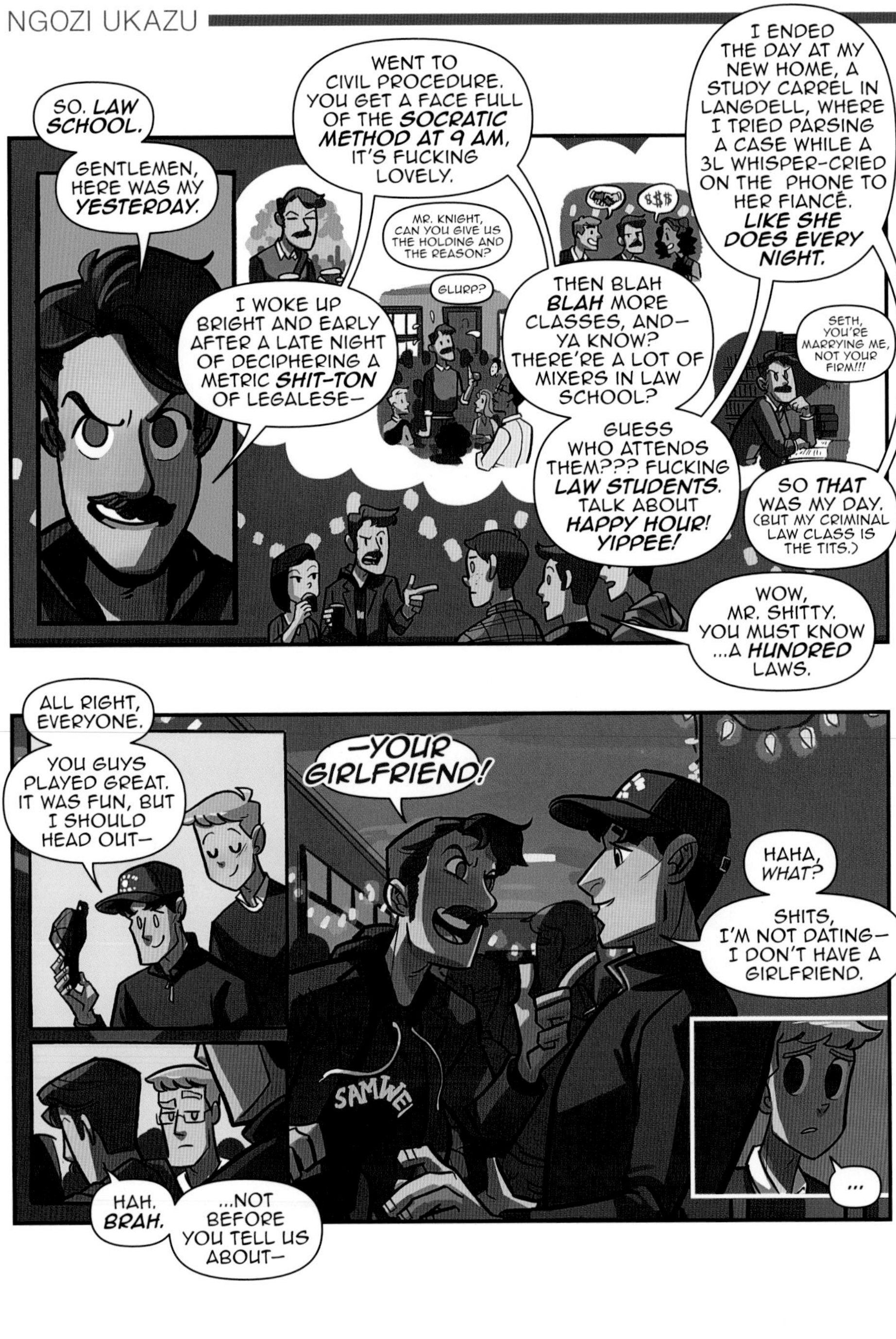
SO. LAW SCHOOL.
GENTLEMEN, HERE WAS MY YESTERDAY.
I WOKE UP BRIGHT AND EARLY AFTER A LATE NIGHT OF DECIPHERING A METRIC SHIT-TON OF LEGALESE—
WENT TO CIVIL PROCEDURE. YOU GET A FACE FULL OF THE SOCRATIC METHOD AT 9 AM, IT'S FUCKING LOVELY.
MR. KNIGHT, CAN YOU GIVE US THE HOLDING AND THE REASON?
GLURP?
THEN BLAH BLAH MORE CLASSES, AND— YA KNOW? THERE'RE A LOT OF MIXERS IN LAW SCHOOL?
GUESS WHO ATTENDS THEM??? FUCKING LAW STUDENTS. TALK ABOUT HAPPY HOUR! YIPPEE!
I ENDED THE DAY AT MY NEW HOME, A STUDY CARREL IN LANGDELL, WHERE I TRIED PARSING A CASE WHILE A 3L WHISPER-CRIED ON THE PHONE TO HER FIANCÉ. LIKE SHE DOES EVERY NIGHT.
SETH, YOU'RE MARRYING ME, NOT YOUR FIRM!!!
SO THAT WAS MY DAY. (BUT MY CRIMINAL LAW CLASS IS THE TITS.)
WOW, MR. SHITTY. YOU MUST KNOW ...A HUNDRED LAWS.
ALL RIGHT, EVERYONE.
YOU GUYS PLAYED GREAT. IT WAS FUN, BUT I SHOULD HEAD OUT—
HAH. BRAH.
...NOT BEFORE YOU TELL US ABOUT—
—YOUR GIRLFRIEND!
HAHA, WHAT?
SHITS, I'M NOT DATING— I DON'T HAVE A GIRLFRIEND.
...

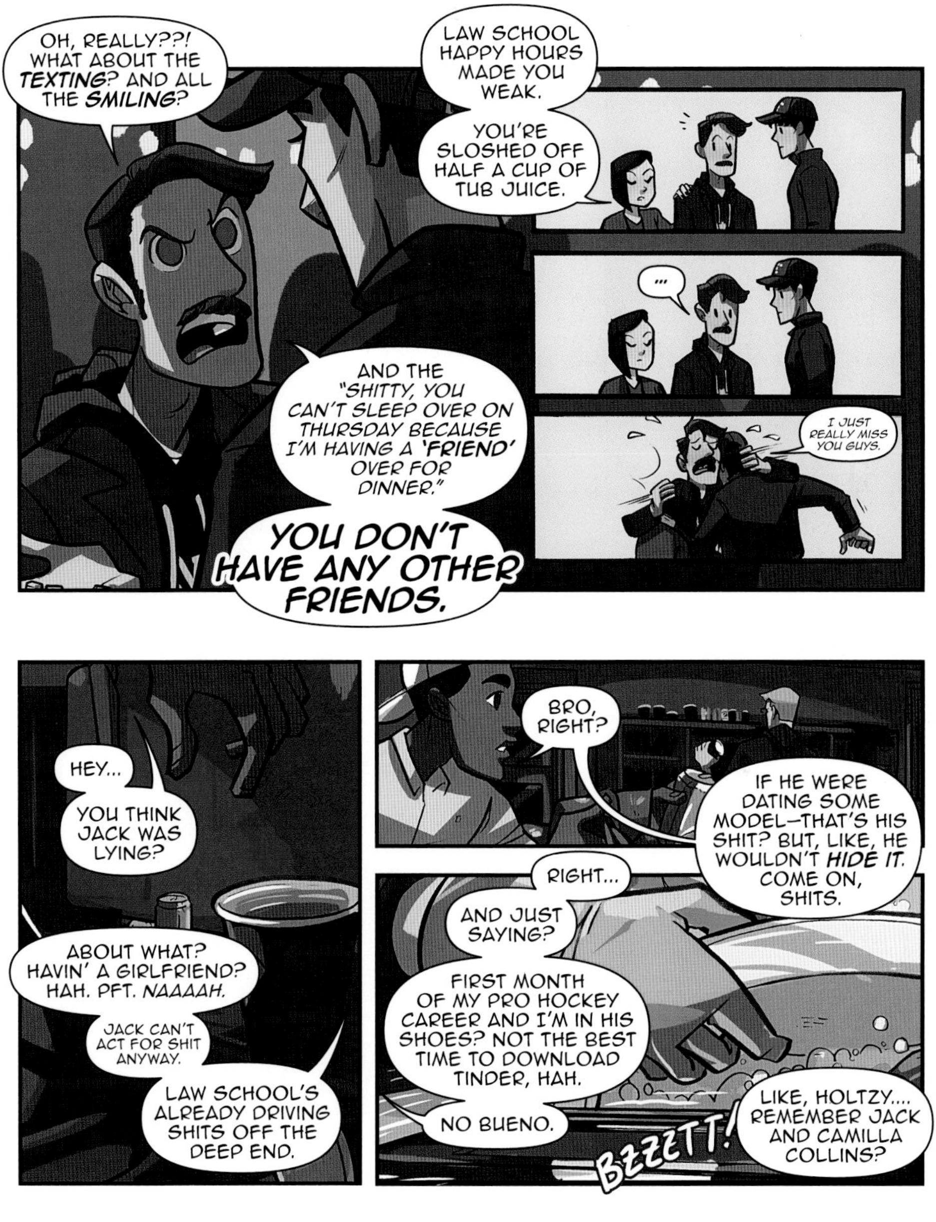
OH, REALLY??! WHAT ABOUT THE TEXTING? AND ALL THE SMILING?
LAW SCHOOL HAPPY HOURS MADE YOU WEAK.
YOU'RE SLOSHED OFF HALF A CUP OF TUB JUICE.
...
AND THE "SHITTY, YOU CAN'T SLEEP OVER ON THURSDAY BECAUSE I'M HAVING A 'FRIEND' OVER FOR DINNER."
YOU DON'T HAVE ANY OTHER FRIENDS.
I JUST REALLY MISS YOU GUYS.
HEY...
YOU THINK JACK WAS LYING?
ABOUT WHAT? HAVIN' A GIRLFRIEND? HAH. PFT. NAAAAH.
JACK CAN'T ACT FOR SHIT ANYWAY.
LAW SCHOOL'S ALREADY DRIVING SHITS OFF THE DEEP END.
BRO, RIGHT?
IF HE WERE DATING SOME MODEL—THAT'S HIS SHIT? BUT, LIKE, HE WOULDN'T HIDE IT. COME ON, SHITS.
RIGHT...
AND JUST SAYING?
FIRST MONTH OF MY PRO HOCKEY CAREER AND I'M IN HIS SHOES? NOT THE BEST TIME TO DOWNLOAD TINDER, HAH.
NO BUENO.
BZZZTT!
LIKE, HOLTZY.... REMEMBER JACK AND CAMILLA COLLINS?

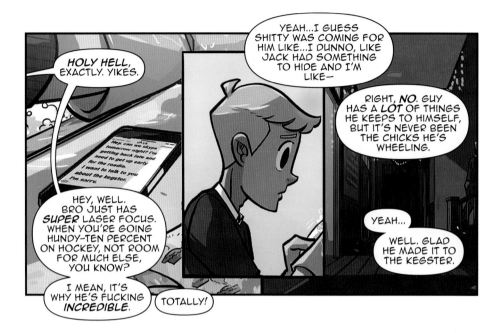

YEAH...I GUESS SHITTY WAS COMING FOR HIM LIKE...I DUNNO, LIKE JACK HAD SOMETHING TO HIDE AND I'M LIKE–
RIGHT, **NO**. GUY HAS A **LOT** OF THINGS HE KEEPS TO HIMSELF, BUT IT'S NEVER BEEN THE CHICKS HE'S WHEELING.
HOLY HELL, EXACTLY. YIKES.
JACK
Hey, can we skype tomorrow night? I'm getting back late and need to get up early for the roadie. I want to talk to you about the kegster. I'm sorry.
HEY, WELL. BRO JUST HAS ***SUPER*** LASER FOCUS. WHEN YOU'RE GOING HUNDY-TEN PERCENT ON HOCKEY, NOT ROOM FOR MUCH ELSE, YOU KNOW?
I MEAN, IT'S WHY HE'S FUCKING ***INCREDIBLE***.
TOTALLY!
YEAH...
WELL. GLAD HE MADE IT TO THE KEGSTER.

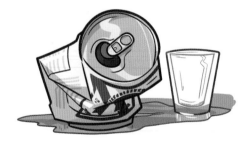

6

PB&J

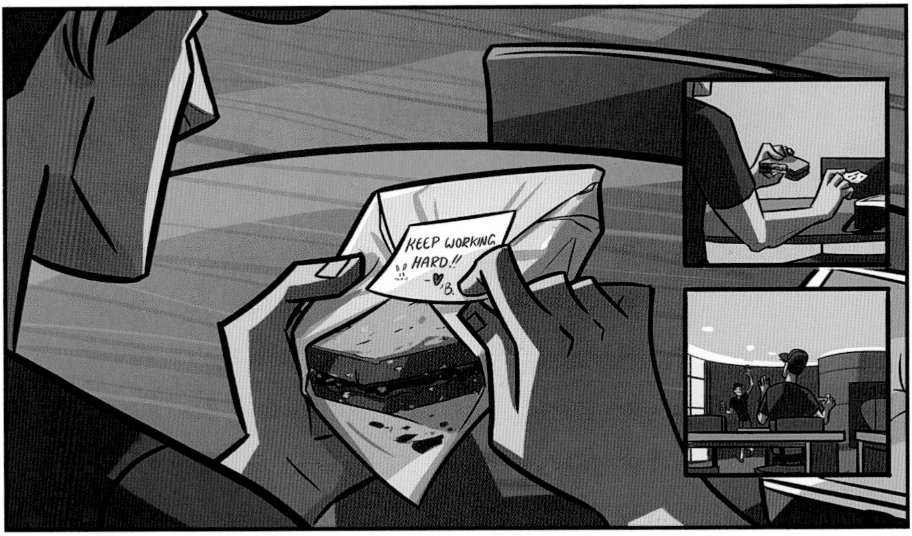
KEEP WORKING HARD!!
-B.

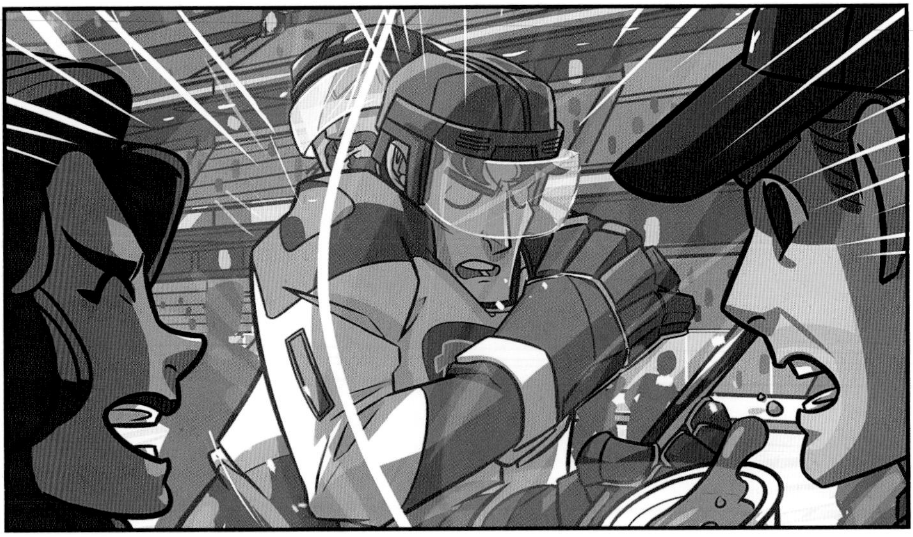

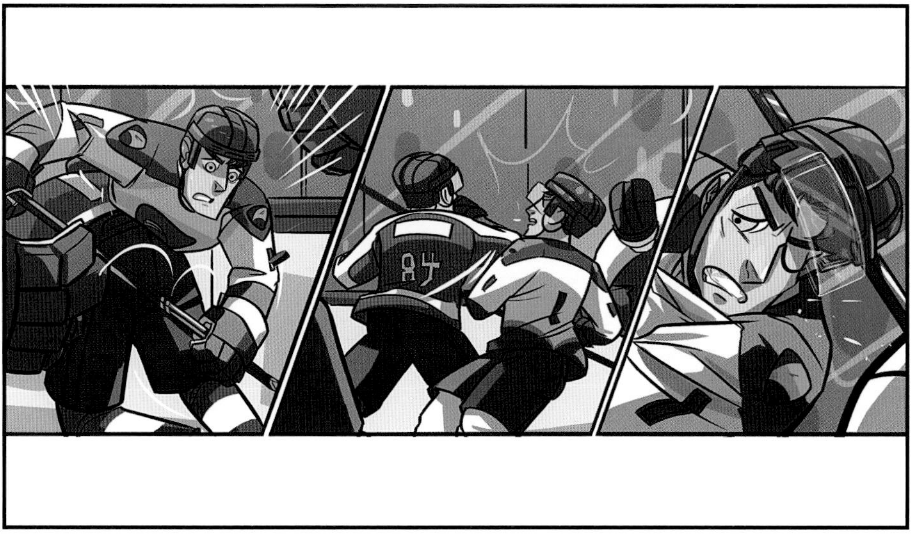
84

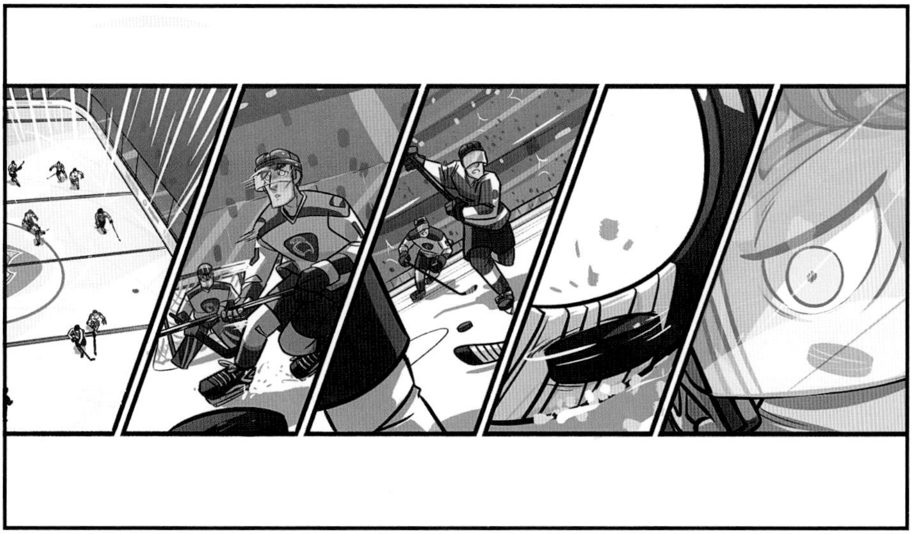

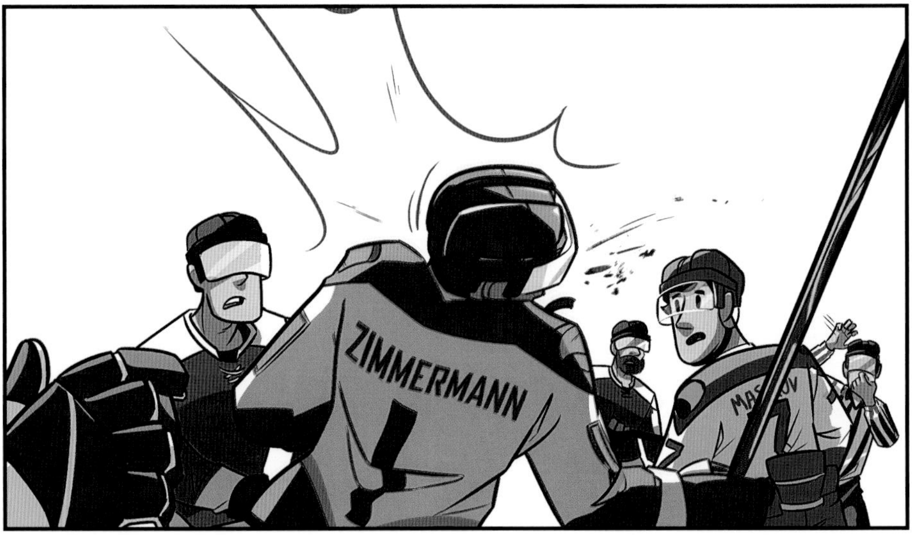
ZIMMERMANN

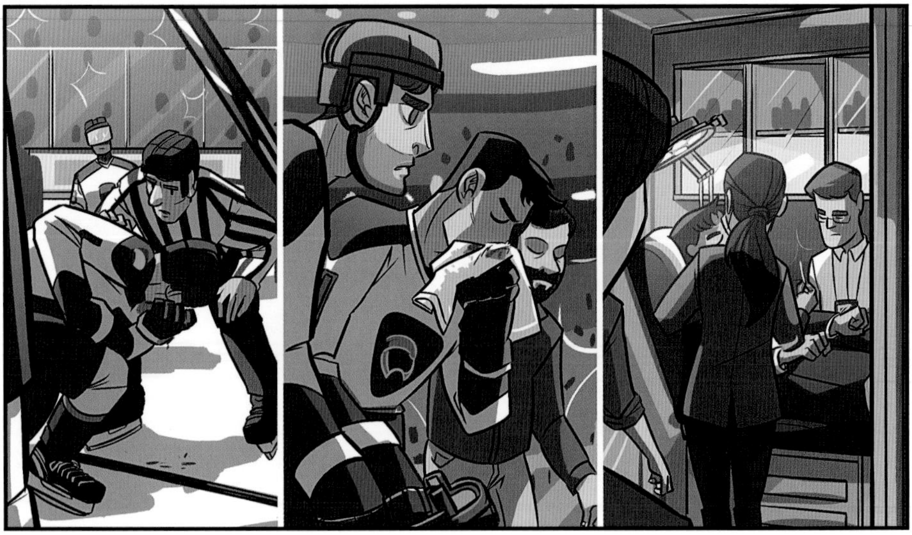

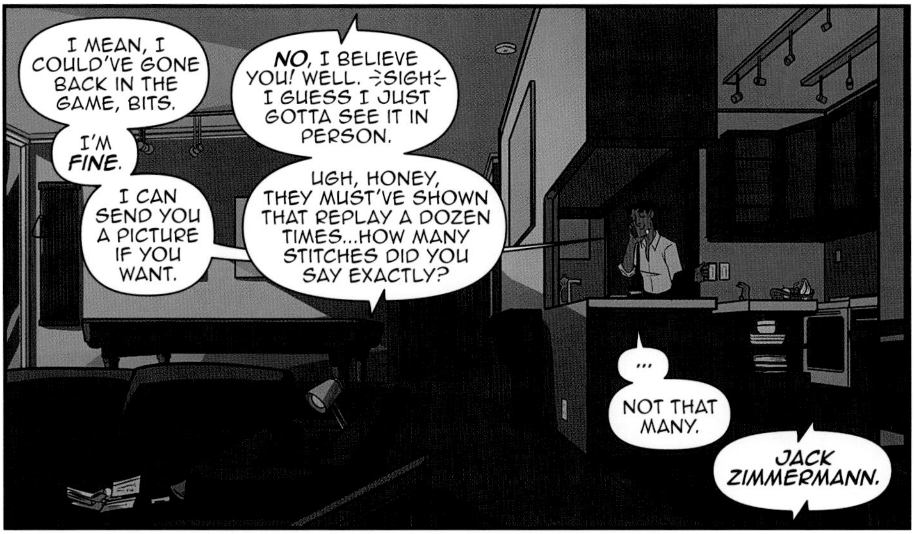
I MEAN, I COULD'VE GONE BACK IN THE GAME, BITS.
I'M FINE.
I CAN SEND YOU A PICTURE IF YOU WANT.
NO, I BELIEVE YOU! WELL. -SIGH- I GUESS I JUST GOTTA SEE IT IN PERSON.
UGH, HONEY, THEY MUST'VE SHOWN THAT REPLAY A DOZEN TIMES...HOW MANY STITCHES DID YOU SAY EXACTLY?
...
NOT THAT MANY.
JACK ZIMMERMANN.

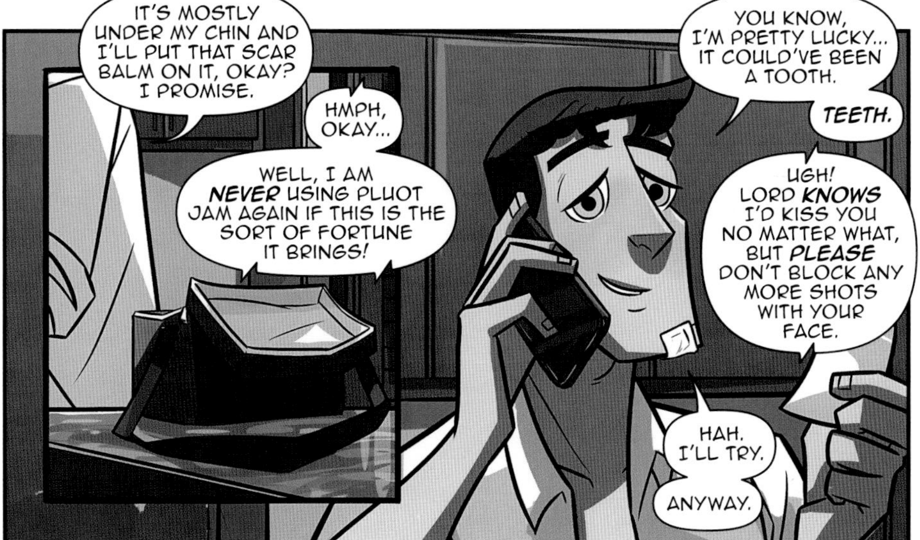
IT'S MOSTLY UNDER MY CHIN AND I'LL PUT THAT SCAR BALM ON IT, OKAY? I PROMISE.
HMPH, OKAY...
WELL, I AM NEVER USING PLUOT JAM AGAIN IF THIS IS THE SORT OF FORTUNE IT BRINGS!
YOU KNOW, I'M PRETTY LUCKY... IT COULD'VE BEEN A TOOTH.
TEETH.
UGH! LORD KNOWS I'D KISS YOU NO MATTER WHAT, BUT PLEASE DON'T BLOCK ANY MORE SHOTS WITH YOUR FACE.
HAH. I'LL TRY.
ANYWAY.

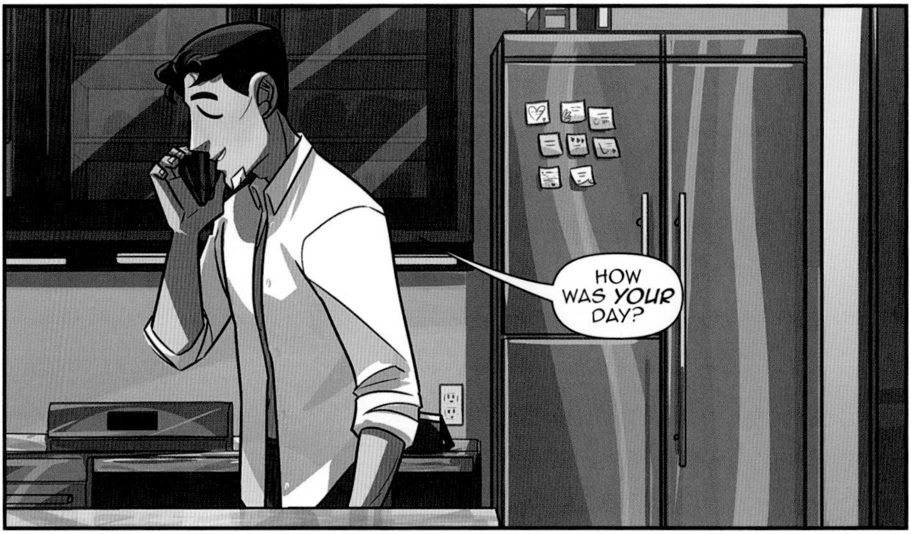
HOW WAS **YOUR** DAY?

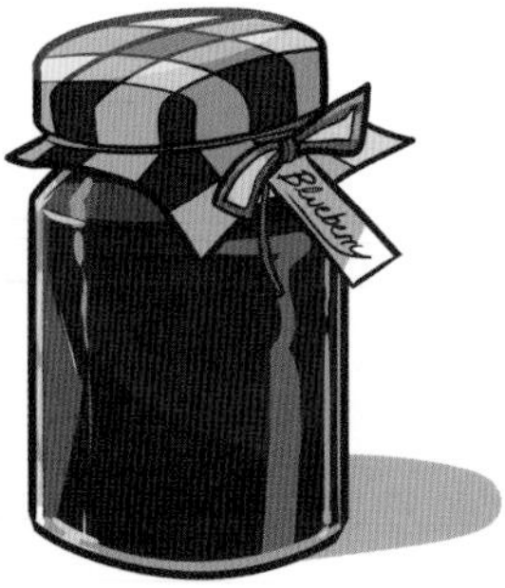
Blueberry

7

LVA @ PVD — I

OKAY, Y'ALL! I HOPE THAT TIP PROVIDES THAT PUNCH TO YOUR PECAN TARTS! NOW THIS NEXT QUESTION. HM.
...DOING ANYTHING DIFFERENTLY TO PREPARE FOR YOUR UPCOMING GAME AGAINST THE PROVIDENCE FALCONERS—
(I'VE ONLY HAD A BOYFRIEND FOR A MINUTE BUT Y'ALL ACT LIKE I'M A RELATIONSHIP GURU!)
SO ESTHER WRITES— "SHOULD I TALK TO MY BF ABOUT OUR HISTORIES? I'M WORRIED ONE OF US WILL GET JEALOUS."

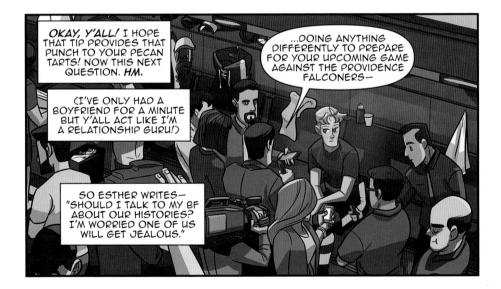

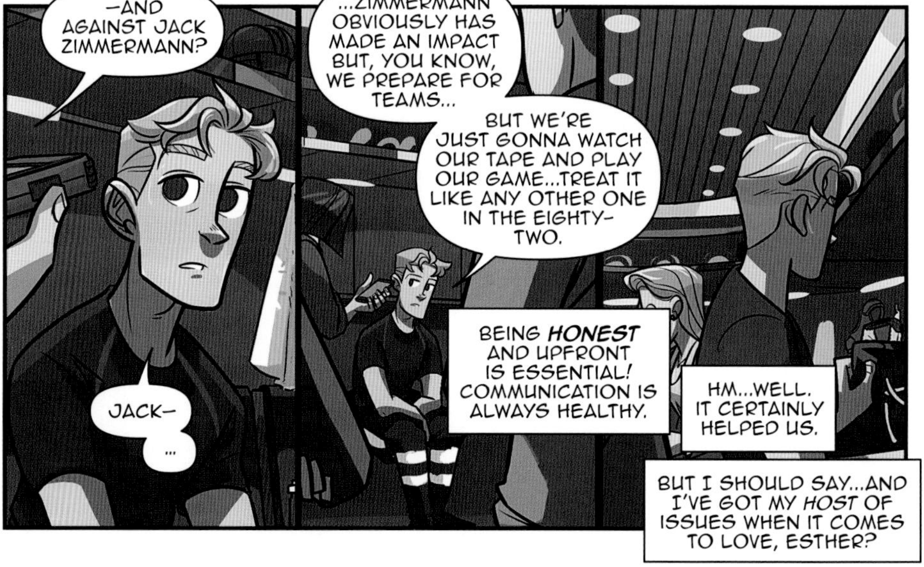
—AND AGAINST JACK ZIMMERMANN?
JACK—
...
...ZIMMERMANN OBVIOUSLY HAS MADE AN IMPACT BUT, YOU KNOW, WE PREPARE FOR TEAMS...
BUT WE'RE JUST GONNA WATCH OUR TAPE AND PLAY OUR GAME...TREAT IT LIKE ANY OTHER ONE IN THE EIGHTY-TWO.
BEING *HONEST* AND UPFRONT IS ESSENTIAL! COMMUNICATION IS ALWAYS HEALTHY.
HM...WELL. IT CERTAINLY HELPED US.
BUT I SHOULD SAY...AND I'VE GOT MY *HOST* OF ISSUES WHEN IT COMES TO LOVE, ESTHER?

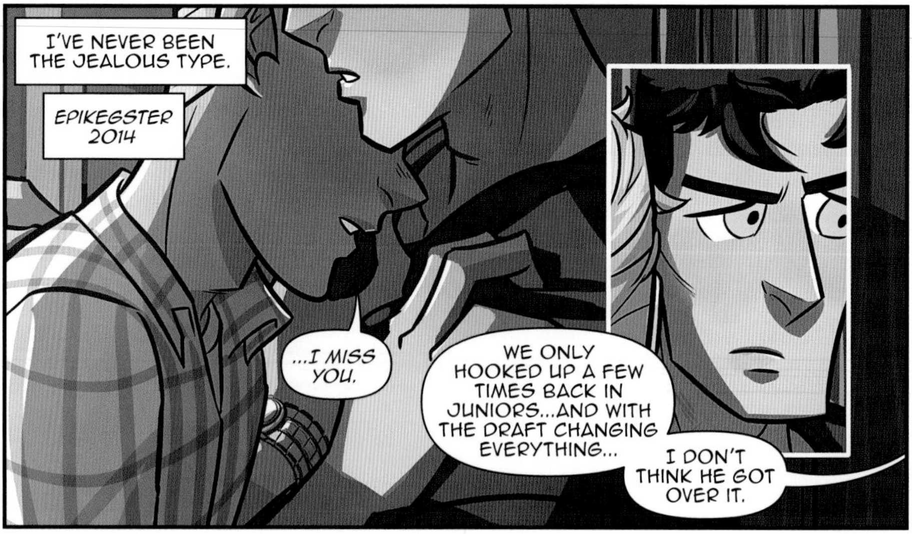
I'VE NEVER BEEN THE JEALOUS TYPE.
EPIKEGSTER 2014
...I MISS YOU.
WE ONLY HOOKED UP A FEW TIMES BACK IN JUNIORS...AND WITH THE DRAFT CHANGING EVERYTHING...
I DON'T THINK HE GOT OVER IT.

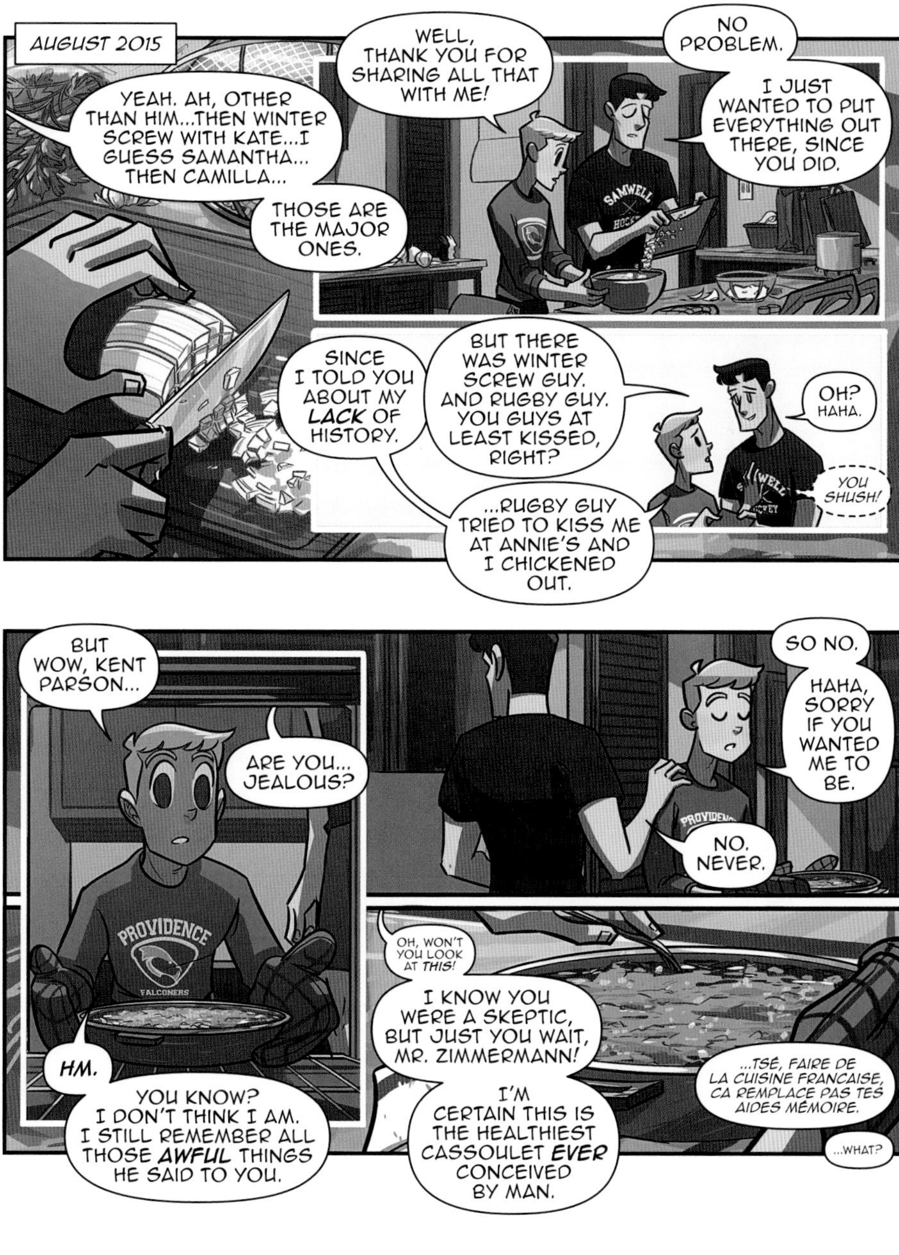
AUGUST 2015
YEAH. AH, OTHER THAN HIM...THEN WINTER SCREW WITH KATE...I GUESS SAMANTHA... THEN CAMILLA...
THOSE ARE THE MAJOR ONES.
WELL, THANK YOU FOR SHARING ALL THAT WITH ME!
NO PROBLEM.
I JUST WANTED TO PUT EVERYTHING OUT THERE, SINCE YOU DID.
SINCE I TOLD YOU ABOUT MY *LACK* OF HISTORY.
BUT THERE WAS WINTER SCREW GUY. AND RUGBY GUY. YOU GUYS AT LEAST KISSED, RIGHT?
OH? HAHA.
YOU SHUSH!
...RUGBY GUY TRIED TO KISS ME AT ANNIE'S AND I CHICKENED OUT.
BUT WOW, KENT PARSON...
ARE YOU... JEALOUS?
SO NO.
HAHA, SORRY IF YOU WANTED ME TO BE.
NO. NEVER.
HM.
YOU KNOW? I DON'T THINK I AM. I STILL REMEMBER ALL THOSE *AWFUL* THINGS HE SAID TO YOU.
OH, WON'T YOU LOOK AT *THIS*!
I KNOW YOU WERE A SKEPTIC, BUT JUST YOU WAIT, MR. ZIMMERMANN!
I'M CERTAIN THIS IS THE HEALTHIEST CASSOULET *EVER* CONCEIVED BY MAN.
...TSÉ, FAIRE DE LA CUISINE FRANCAISE, CA REMPLACE PAS TES AIDES MÉMOIRE.
...WHAT?

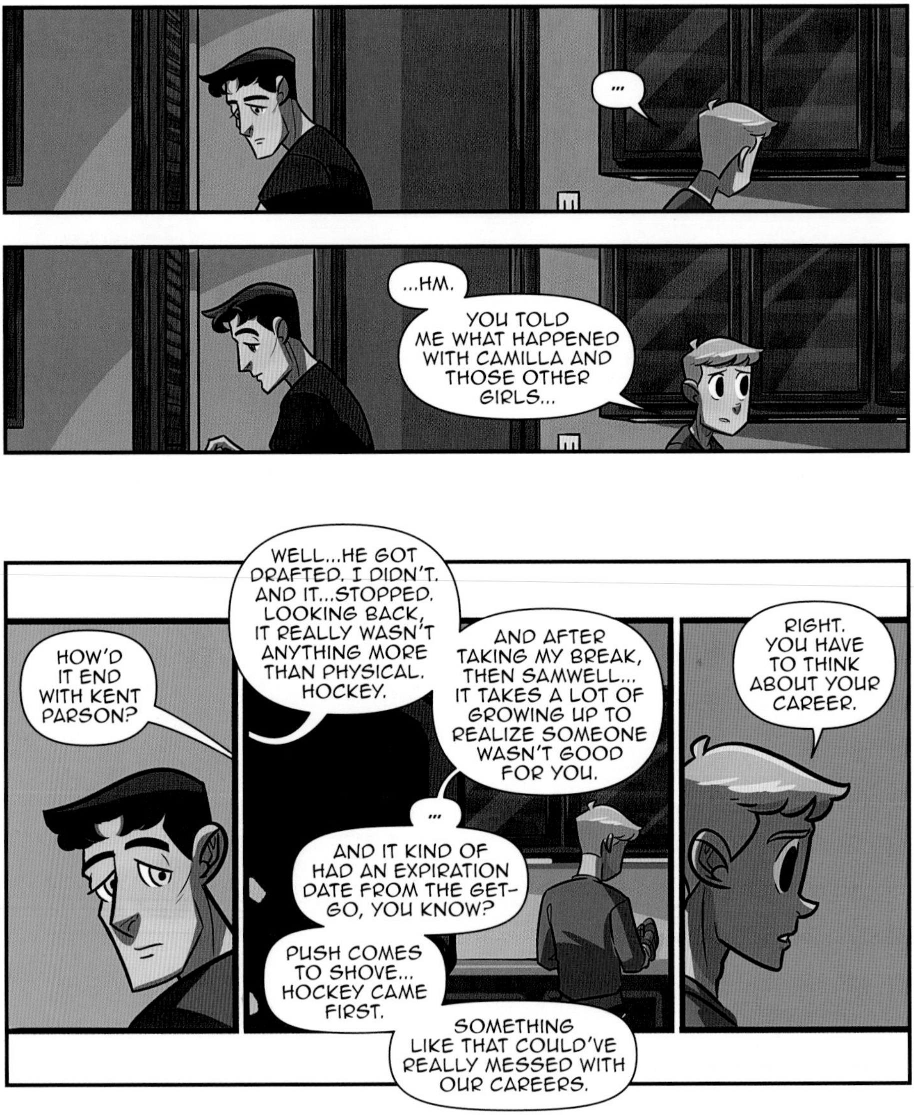
...
...HM.
YOU TOLD ME WHAT HAPPENED WITH CAMILLA AND THOSE OTHER GIRLS...
HOW'D IT END WITH KENT PARSON?
WELL...HE GOT DRAFTED. I DIDN'T. AND IT...STOPPED. LOOKING BACK, IT REALLY WASN'T ANYTHING MORE THAN PHYSICAL. HOCKEY.
AND AFTER TAKING MY BREAK, THEN SAMWELL... IT TAKES A LOT OF GROWING UP TO REALIZE SOMEONE WASN'T GOOD FOR YOU.
...
AND IT KIND OF HAD AN EXPIRATION DATE FROM THE GET-GO, YOU KNOW?
PUSH COMES TO SHOVE... HOCKEY CAME FIRST.
RIGHT. YOU HAVE TO THINK ABOUT YOUR CAREER.
SOMETHING LIKE THAT COULD'VE REALLY MESSED WITH OUR CAREERS.

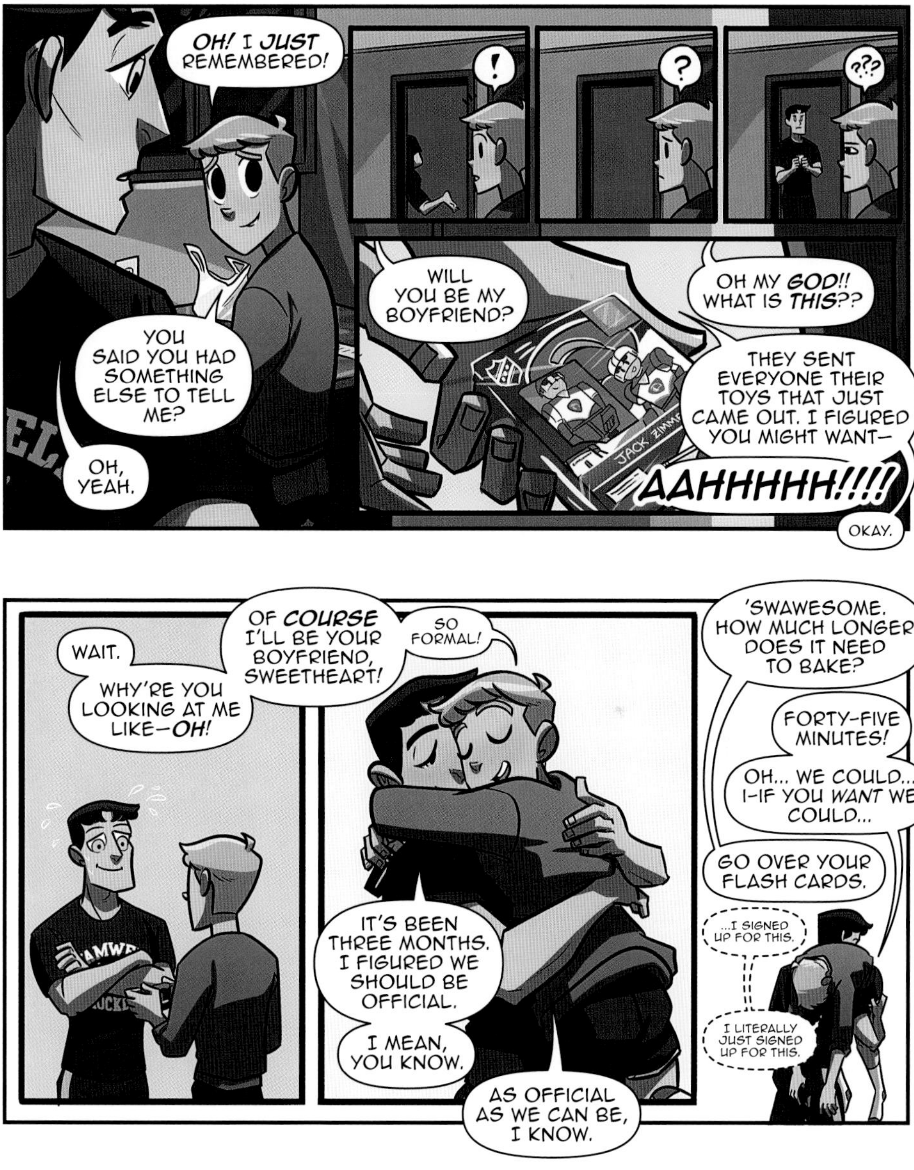
OH! I JUST REMEMBERED!
YOU SAID YOU HAD SOMETHING ELSE TO TELL ME?
OH, YEAH.
!
?
???
WILL YOU BE MY BOYFRIEND?
OH MY GOD!! WHAT IS THIS??
THEY SENT EVERYONE THEIR TOYS THAT JUST CAME OUT. I FIGURED YOU MIGHT WANT—
AAHHHHH!!!!
OKAY.
WAIT.
WHY'RE YOU LOOKING AT ME LIKE—OH!
OF COURSE I'LL BE YOUR BOYFRIEND, SWEETHEART!
SO FORMAL!
IT'S BEEN THREE MONTHS. I FIGURED WE SHOULD BE OFFICIAL.
I MEAN, YOU KNOW.
AS OFFICIAL AS WE CAN BE, I KNOW.
'SWAWESOME. HOW MUCH LONGER DOES IT NEED TO BAKE?
FORTY-FIVE MINUTES!
OH... WE COULD... I-IF YOU WANT WE COULD...
GO OVER YOUR FLASH CARDS.
...I SIGNED UP FOR THIS.
I LITERALLY JUST SIGNED UP FOR THIS.

JACK, HOW ARE YOU PREPARING FOR THE ACES NEXT WEEK?

AH, JUST, YOU KNOW— STICKING TO OUR GAME. WE'VE BEEN ON A GOOD RUN AT HOME.

BUT YOU AND KENT PARSON—

THIS IS YOUR FIRST ENCOUNTER IN A RINK SINCE YOU WON THE MEMORIAL CUP TOGETHER...

THERE'S A LOT OF HISTORY, ISN'T THERE?

YEAH.

BUT IT'S ALL IN THE PAST.

8

LVA @ PVD — II

'KAY, SO HERE'S A COMMENT FROM CLAIRE...
"IS IT STRESSFUL WATCHING YOUR FRIENDS PLAY HOCKEY ON TV??"
90

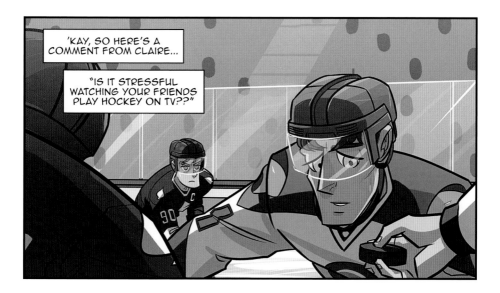

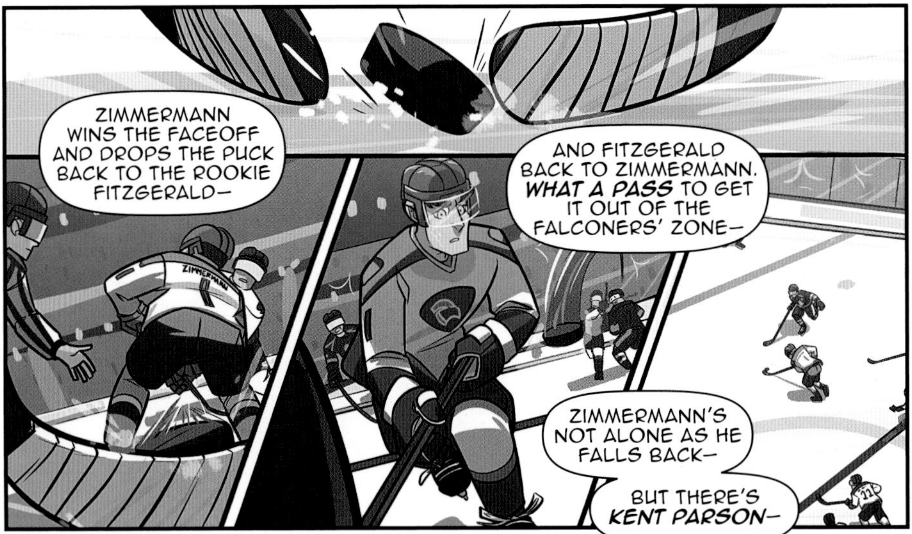
ZIMMERMANN WINS THE FACEOFF AND DROPS THE PUCK BACK TO THE ROOKIE FITZGERALD—
AND FITZGERALD BACK TO ZIMMERMANN. WHAT A PASS TO GET IT OUT OF THE FALCONERS' ZONE—
ZIMMERMANN'S NOT ALONE AS HE FALLS BACK—
BUT THERE'S KENT PARSON—

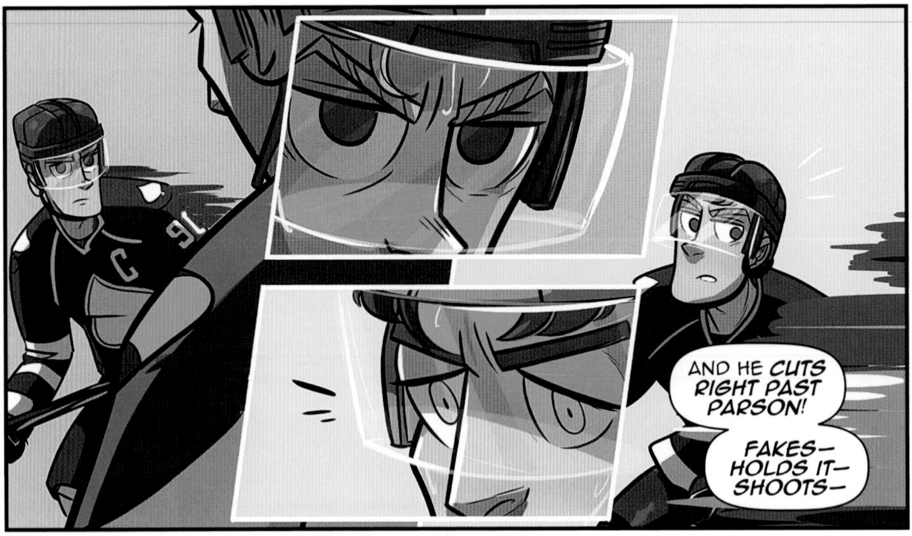
AND HE CUTS RIGHT PAST PARSON!
FAKES— HOLDS IT— SHOOTS—

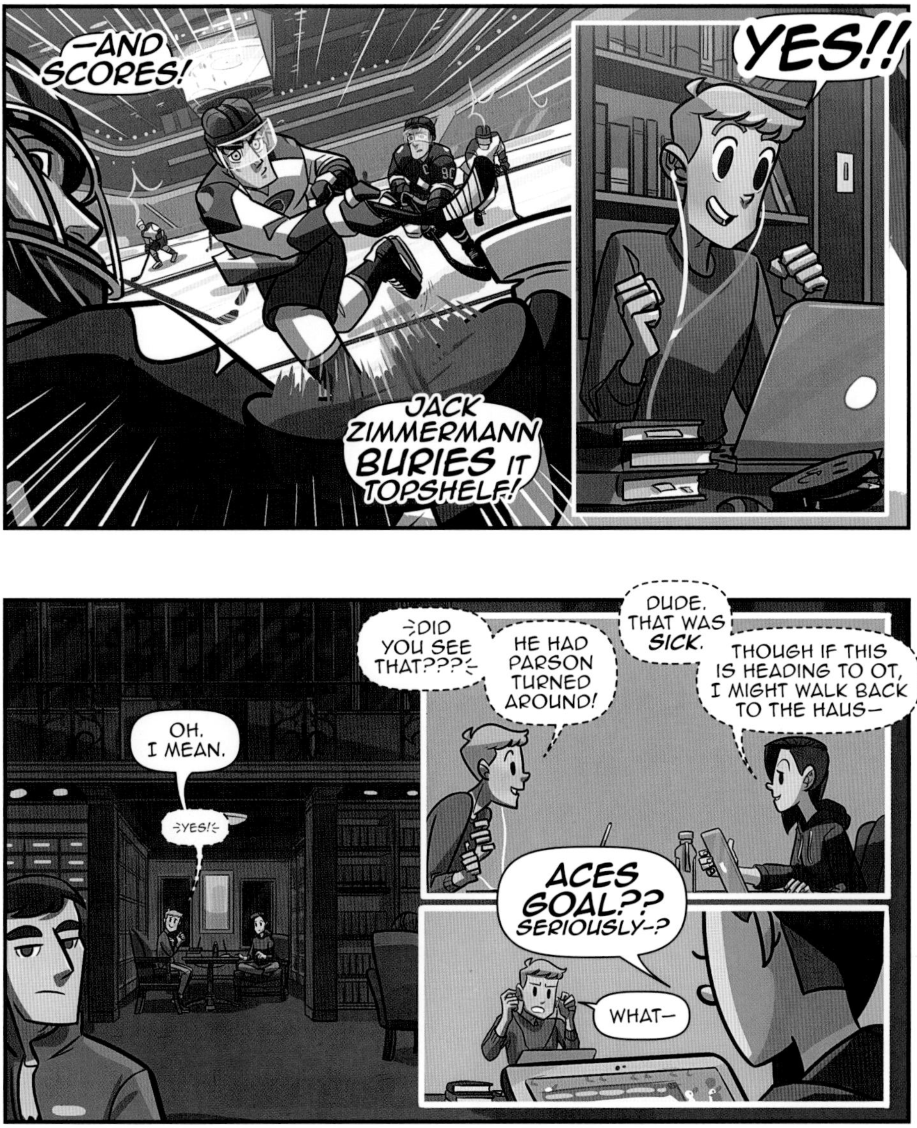
—AND SCORES!
JACK ZIMMERMANN BURIES IT TOPSHELF!
YES!!
OH. I MEAN.
YES!
DID YOU SEE THAT???
HE HAD PARSON TURNED AROUND!
DUDE. THAT WAS SICK.
THOUGH IF THIS IS HEADING TO OT, I MIGHT WALK BACK TO THE HAUS—
ACES GOAL?? SERIOUSLY-?
WHAT—

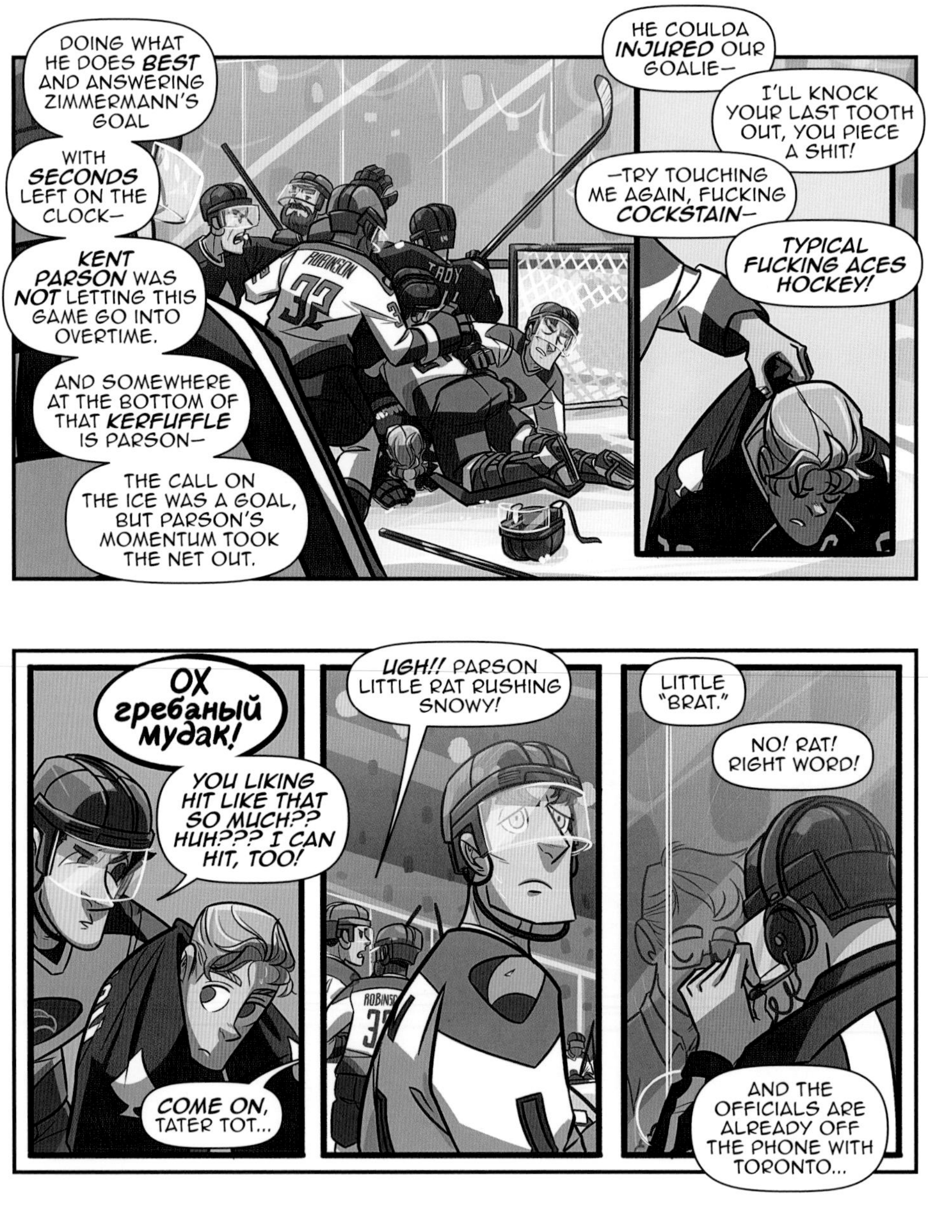
DOING WHAT HE DOES BEST AND ANSWERING ZIMMERMANN'S GOAL
WITH SECONDS LEFT ON THE CLOCK—
KENT PARSON WAS NOT LETTING THIS GAME GO INTO OVERTIME.
AND SOMEWHERE AT THE BOTTOM OF THAT KERFUFFLE IS PARSON—
THE CALL ON THE ICE WAS A GOAL, BUT PARSON'S MOMENTUM TOOK THE NET OUT.
ROBINSON
32
TADY
HE COULDA INJURED OUR GOALIE—
I'LL KNOCK YOUR LAST TOOTH OUT, YOU PIECE A SHIT!
—TRY TOUCHING ME AGAIN, FUCKING COCKSTAIN—
TYPICAL FUCKING ACES HOCKEY!
ОХ гребаный мудак!
YOU LIKING HIT LIKE THAT SO MUCH?? HUH??? I CAN HIT, TOO!
COME ON, TATER TOT...
UGH!! PARSON LITTLE RAT RUSHING SNOWY!
LITTLE "BRAT."
NO! RAT! RIGHT WORD!
AND THE OFFICIALS ARE ALREADY OFF THE PHONE WITH TORONTO...

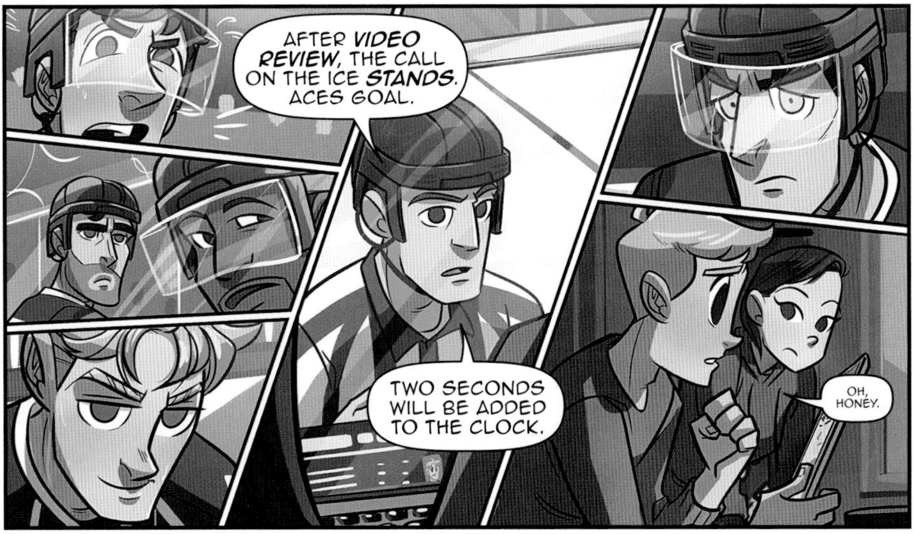
AFTER *VIDEO REVIEW*, THE CALL ON THE ICE *STANDS*. ACES GOAL.
TWO SECONDS WILL BE ADDED TO THE CLOCK.
OH, HONEY.

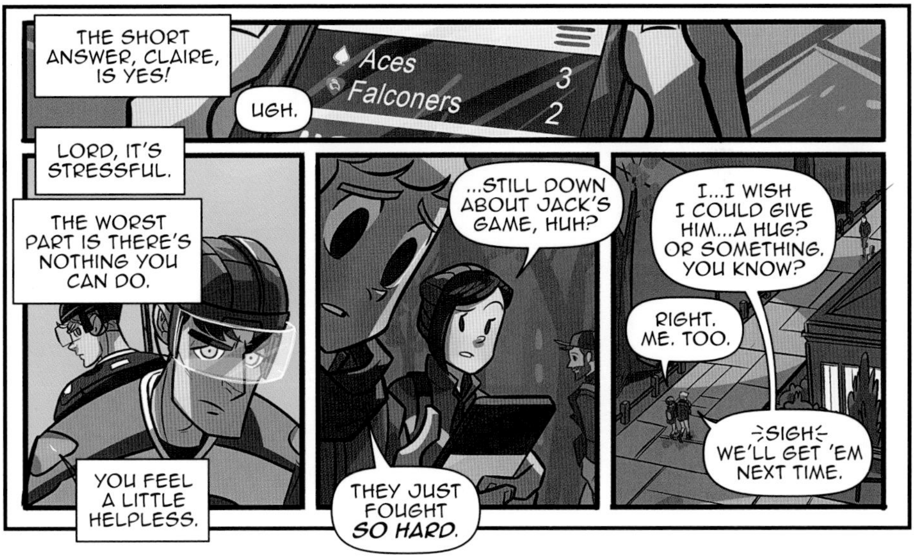
THE SHORT ANSWER, CLAIRE, IS YES!
Aces 3
Falconers 2
UGH.
LORD, IT'S STRESSFUL.
THE WORST PART IS THERE'S NOTHING YOU CAN DO.
YOU FEEL A LITTLE HELPLESS.
...STILL DOWN ABOUT JACK'S GAME, HUH?
THEY JUST FOUGHT *SO HARD*.
I...I WISH I COULD GIVE HIM...A HUG? OR SOMETHING. YOU KNOW?
RIGHT. ME. TOO.
SIGH
WE'LL GET 'EM NEXT TIME.

9

HI, HONEY — I

HI, HONEY.
⇉SNIFF⇇
I...I'M SORRY. I KNOW YOU JUST FINISHED A GAME...I SAW YOUR GOAL!
IT WAS *SO GOOD!* NURSEY SPILLED HIS PBR ALL OVER CHOWDER ON THE REPLAY. HAHA...
I KNOW YOU'RE PROBABLY ALREADY ON THE PLANE—

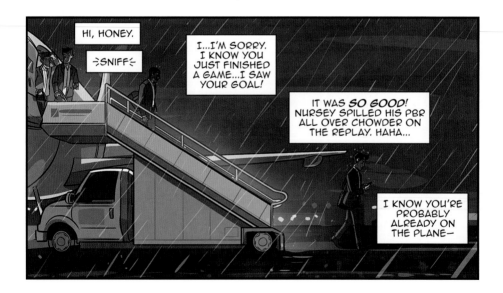

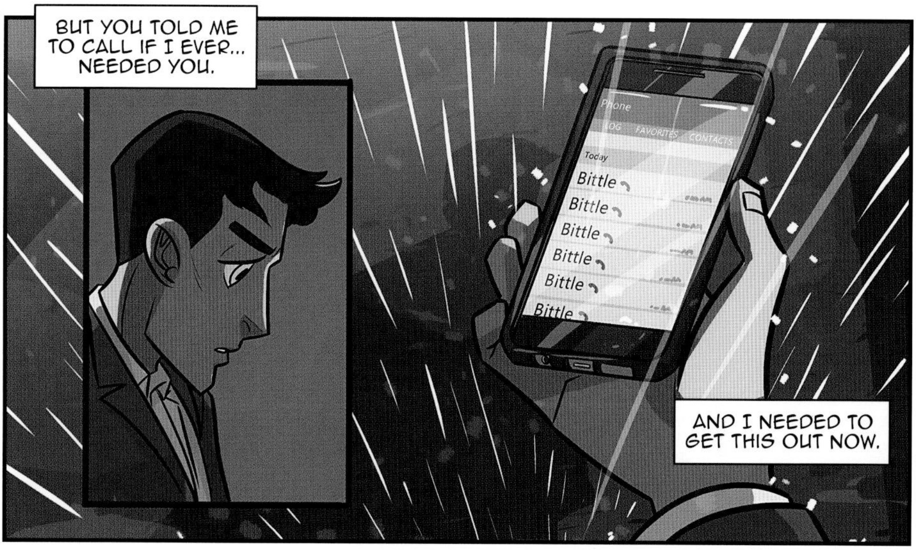
BUT YOU TOLD ME TO CALL IF I EVER... NEEDED YOU.
Phone
LOG FAVORITES CONTACTS
Today
Bittle
Bittle
Bittle
Bittle
Bittle
Bittle
AND I NEEDED TO GET THIS OUT NOW.

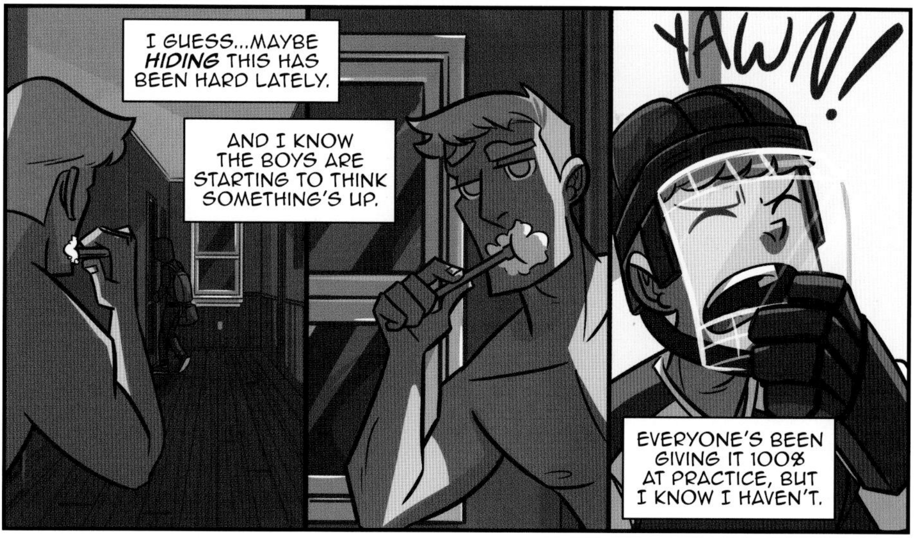
I GUESS...MAYBE *HIDING* THIS HAS BEEN HARD LATELY.
AND I KNOW THE BOYS ARE STARTING TO THINK SOMETHING'S UP.
YAWN!
EVERYONE'S BEEN GIVING IT 100% AT PRACTICE, BUT I KNOW I HAVEN'T.

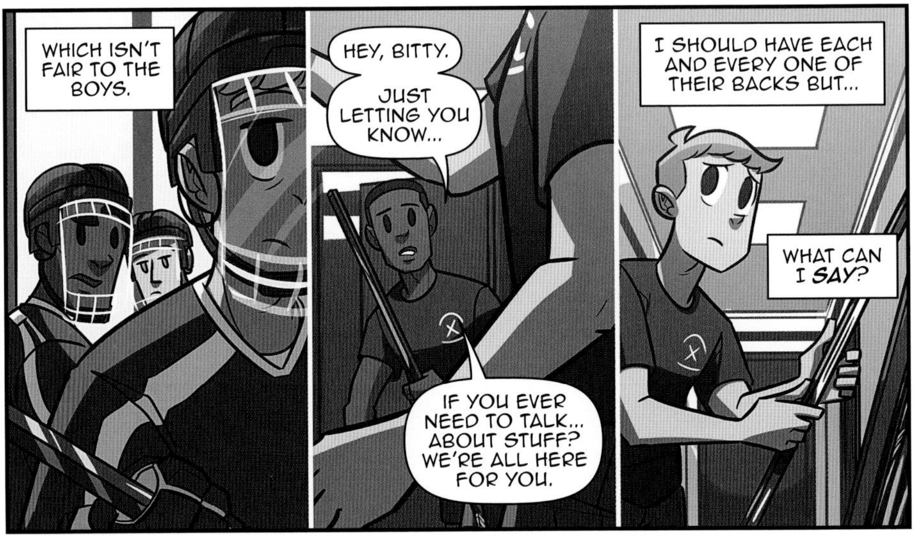
WHICH ISN'T FAIR TO THE BOYS.
HEY, BITTY.
JUST LETTING YOU KNOW...
IF YOU EVER NEED TO TALK... ABOUT STUFF? WE'RE ALL HERE FOR YOU.
I SHOULD HAVE EACH AND EVERY ONE OF THEIR BACKS BUT...
WHAT CAN I SAY?

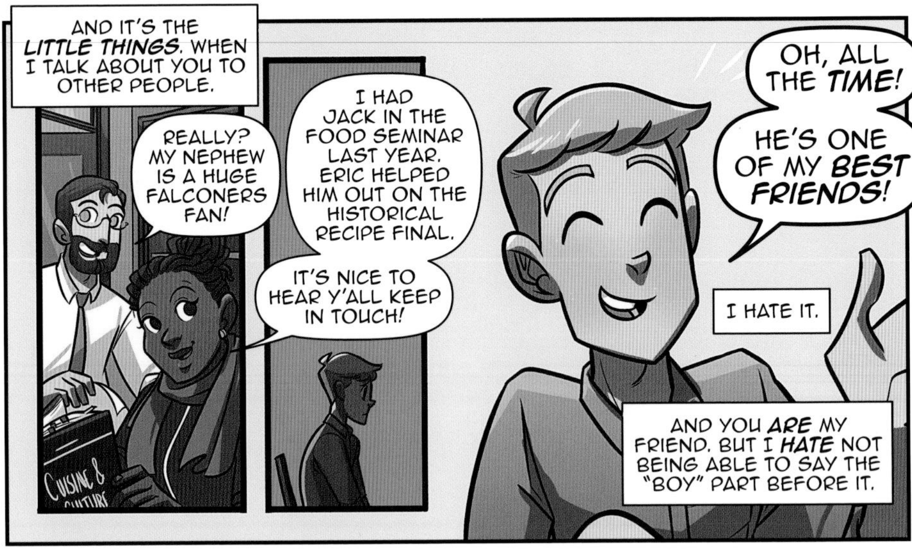
AND IT'S THE LITTLE THINGS. WHEN I TALK ABOUT YOU TO OTHER PEOPLE.
REALLY? MY NEPHEW IS A HUGE FALCONERS FAN!
I HAD JACK IN THE FOOD SEMINAR LAST YEAR. ERIC HELPED HIM OUT ON THE HISTORICAL RECIPE FINAL.
IT'S NICE TO HEAR Y'ALL KEEP IN TOUCH!
OH, ALL THE TIME!
HE'S ONE OF MY BEST FRIENDS!
I HATE IT.
AND YOU ARE MY FRIEND. BUT I HATE NOT BEING ABLE TO SAY THE "BOY" PART BEFORE IT.

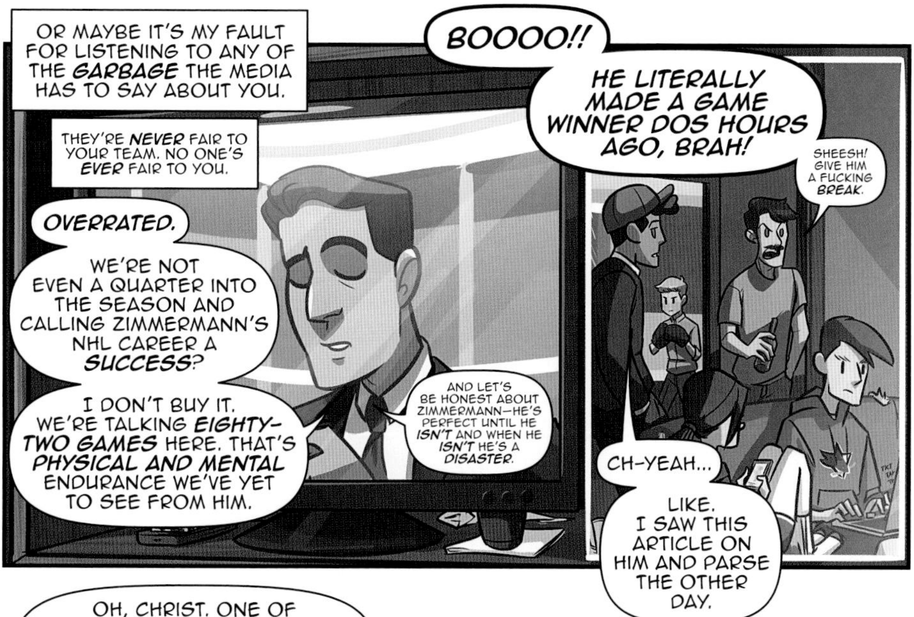
OR MAYBE IT'S MY FAULT FOR LISTENING TO ANY OF THE *GARBAGE* THE MEDIA HAS TO SAY ABOUT YOU.
THEY'RE *NEVER* FAIR TO YOUR TEAM. NO ONE'S *EVER* FAIR TO YOU.
OVERRATED.
WE'RE NOT EVEN A QUARTER INTO THE SEASON AND CALLING ZIMMERMANN'S NHL CAREER A *SUCCESS*?
I DON'T BUY IT. WE'RE TALKING *EIGHTY-TWO GAMES* HERE. THAT'S *PHYSICAL AND MENTAL* ENDURANCE WE'VE YET TO SEE FROM HIM.
AND LET'S BE HONEST ABOUT ZIMMERMANN—HE'S PERFECT UNTIL HE *ISN'T* AND WHEN HE *ISN'T* HE'S A *DISASTER*.
BOOOO!!
HE LITERALLY MADE A GAME WINNER DOS HOURS AGO, BRAH!
SHEESH! GIVE HIM A FUCKING *BREAK*.
CH-YEAH...
LIKE. I SAW THIS ARTICLE ON HIM AND PARSE THE OTHER DAY.

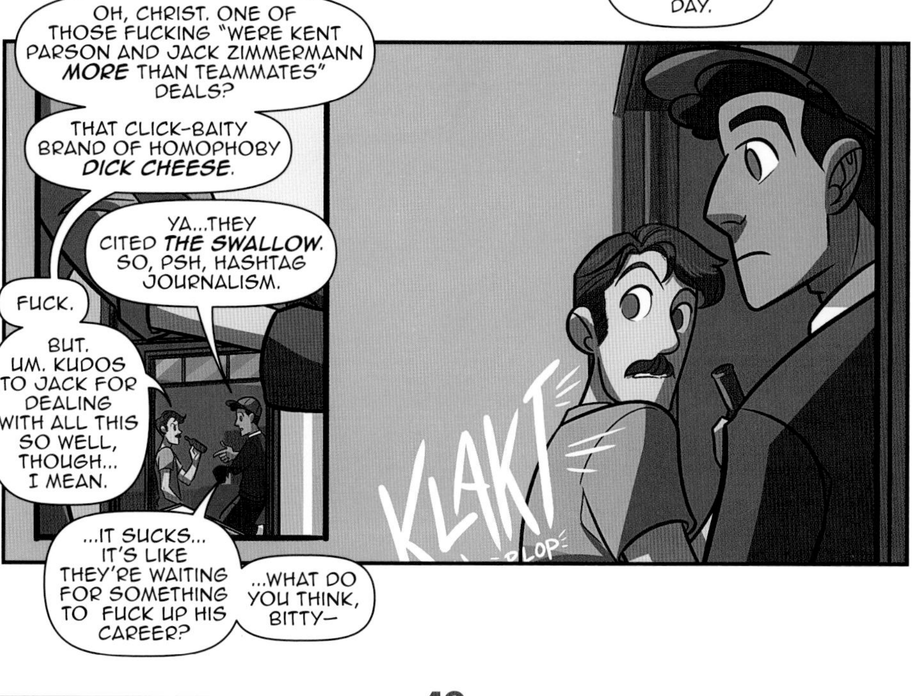
OH, CHRIST. ONE OF THOSE FUCKING "WERE KENT PARSON AND JACK ZIMMERMANN *MORE* THAN TEAMMATES" DEALS?
THAT CLICK-BAITY BRAND OF HOMOPHOBY *DICK CHEESE*.
YA...THEY CITED *THE SWALLOW*. SO, PSH, HASHTAG JOURNALISM.
FUCK.
BUT. UM. KUDOS TO JACK FOR DEALING WITH ALL THIS SO WELL, THOUGH... I MEAN.
...IT SUCKS... IT'S LIKE THEY'RE WAITING FOR SOMETHING TO FUCK UP HIS CAREER?
...WHAT DO YOU THINK, BITTY—
KLAKT
PLOP

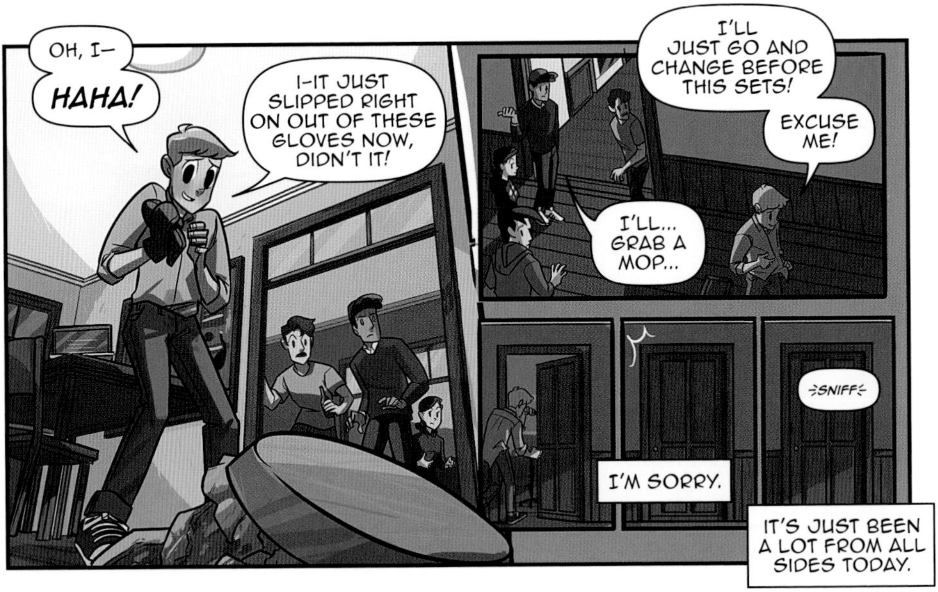
OH, I—
HAHA!
I-IT JUST SLIPPED RIGHT ON OUT OF THESE GLOVES NOW, DIDN'T IT!
I'LL JUST GO AND CHANGE BEFORE THIS SETS!
EXCUSE ME!
I'LL... GRAB A MOP...
SNIFF
I'M SORRY.
IT'S JUST BEEN A LOT FROM ALL SIDES TODAY.

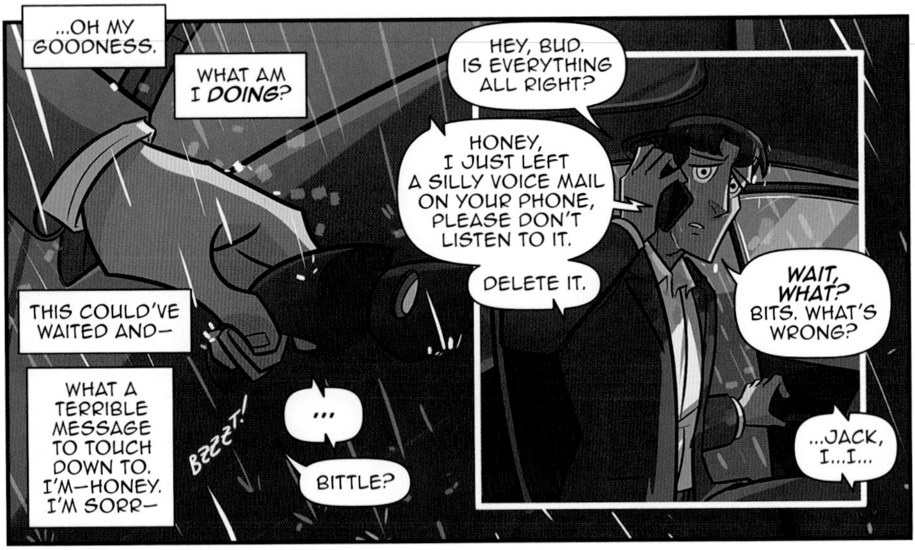
...OH MY GOODNESS.
WHAT AM I DOING?
HEY, BUD. IS EVERYTHING ALL RIGHT?
HONEY, I JUST LEFT A SILLY VOICE MAIL ON YOUR PHONE, PLEASE DON'T LISTEN TO IT.
DELETE IT.
WAIT, WHAT? BITS. WHAT'S WRONG?
THIS COULD'VE WAITED AND—
WHAT A TERRIBLE MESSAGE TO TOUCH DOWN TO. I'M—HONEY. I'M SORR—
BZZZT!
...
BITTLE?
...JACK, I...I...

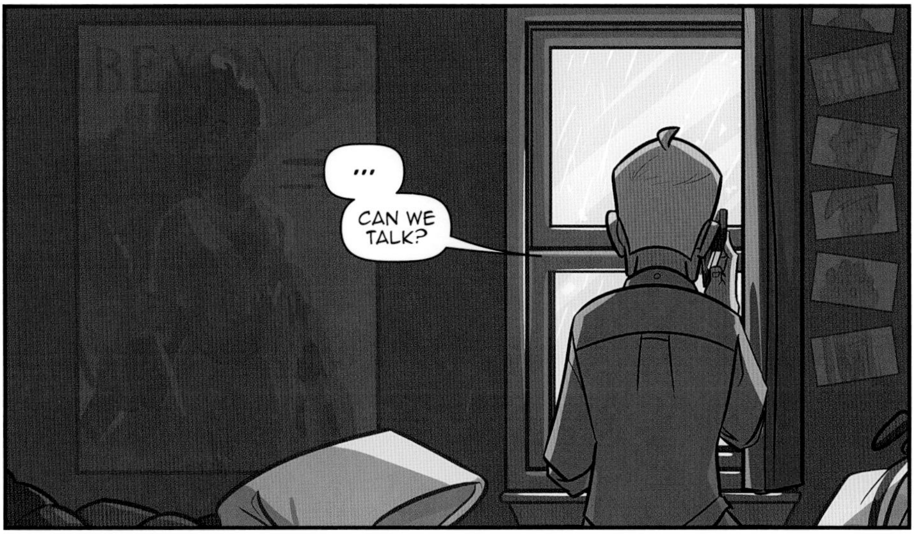
...
CAN WE TALK?

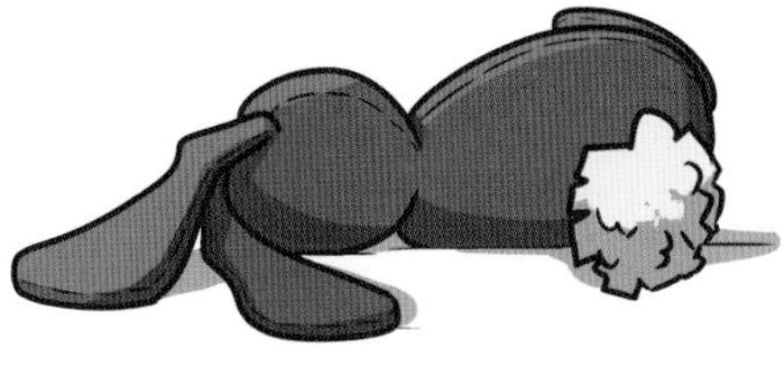

10

HI, HONEY — II

EVERYONE'S STILL DOWNSTAIRS...I'M SURE SHITTY'LL RUSH UP AND CHECK ON ME AFTER THEY MOP UP THAT PIE.
I JUST... IT'S BEEN SO ***HARD***, JACK.
KEEPING THIS FROM THE BOYS. FROM EVERYONE.
AND I KNOW... WE DON'T EVEN HAVE IT THAT BAD RIGHT NOW, BUT...
I JUST HATE THAT I CAN'T TALK ABOUT YOU... I HATE THAT I CAN'T BE PROUD OF YOU. AND—

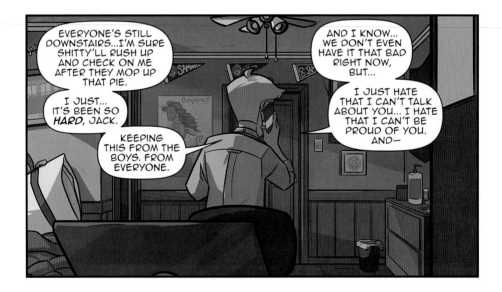

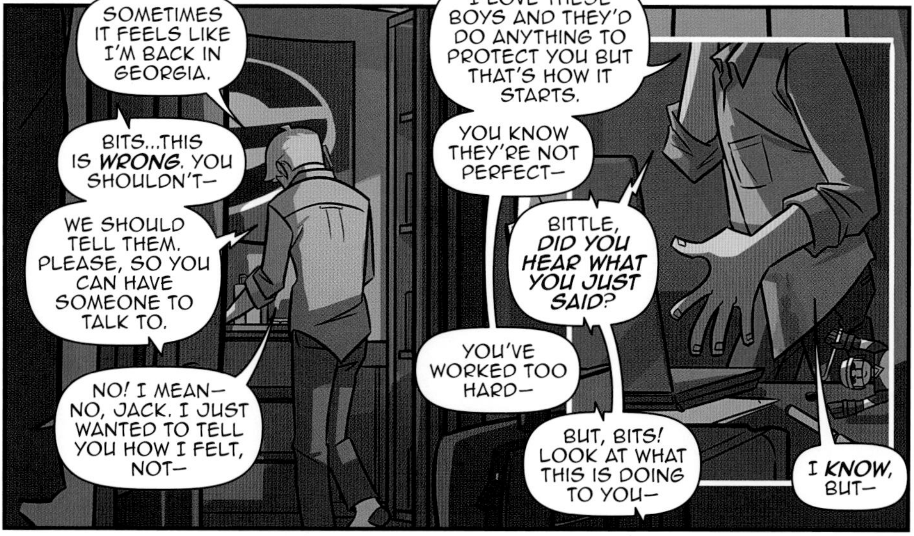
SOMETIMES IT FEELS LIKE I'M BACK IN GEORGIA.
BITS...THIS IS *WRONG*. YOU SHOULDN'T—
WE SHOULD TELL THEM. PLEASE, SO YOU CAN HAVE SOMEONE TO TALK TO.
NO! I MEAN— NO, JACK. I JUST WANTED TO TELL YOU HOW I FELT, NOT—
I LOVE THESE BOYS AND THEY'D DO ANYTHING TO PROTECT YOU BUT THAT'S HOW IT STARTS.
YOU KNOW THEY'RE NOT PERFECT—
BITTLE, *DID YOU HEAR WHAT YOU JUST SAID?*
YOU'VE WORKED TOO HARD—
BUT, BITS! LOOK AT WHAT THIS IS DOING TO YOU—
I *KNOW*, BUT—

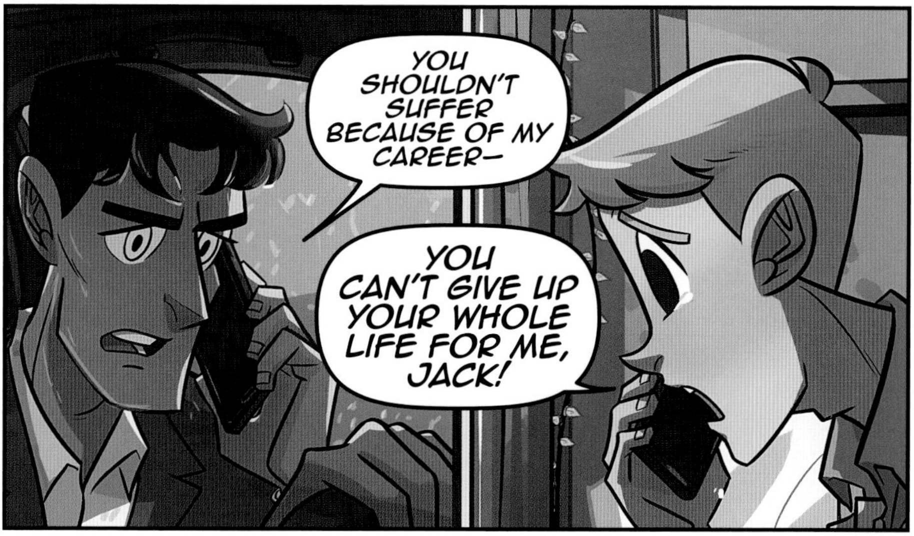
YOU SHOULDN'T SUFFER BECAUSE OF MY CAREER—
YOU CAN'T GIVE UP YOUR WHOLE LIFE FOR ME, JACK!

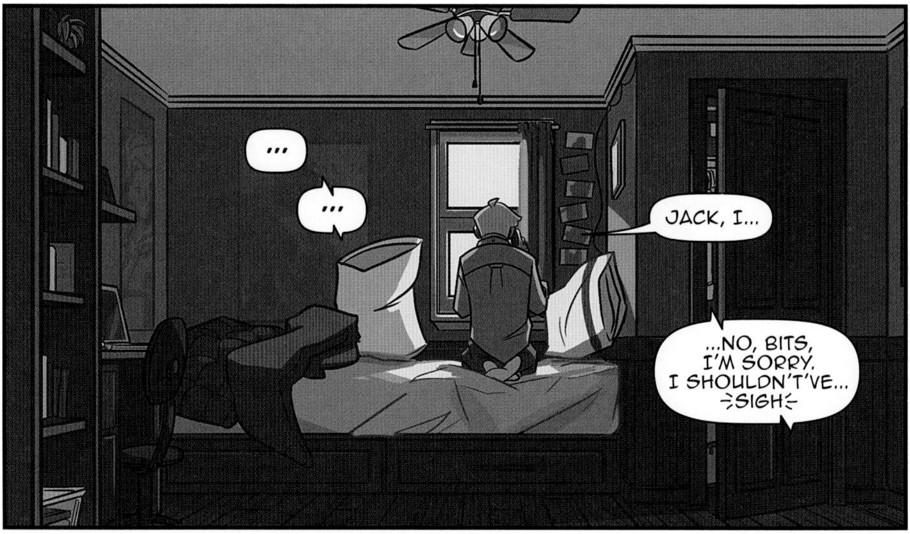
...
...
JACK, I...
...NO, BITS, I'M SORRY. I SHOULDN'T'VE... ⁓SIGH⁓

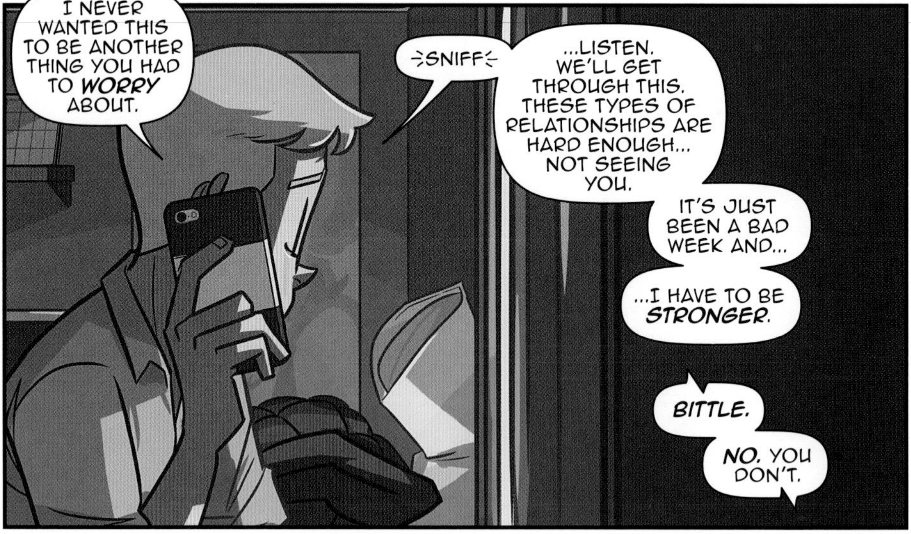
I NEVER WANTED THIS TO BE ANOTHER THING YOU HAD TO WORRY ABOUT.
⁓SNIFF⁓
...LISTEN. WE'LL GET THROUGH THIS. THESE TYPES OF RELATIONSHIPS ARE HARD ENOUGH... NOT SEEING YOU.
IT'S JUST BEEN A BAD WEEK AND...
...I HAVE TO BE STRONGER.
BITTLE.
NO. YOU DON'T.

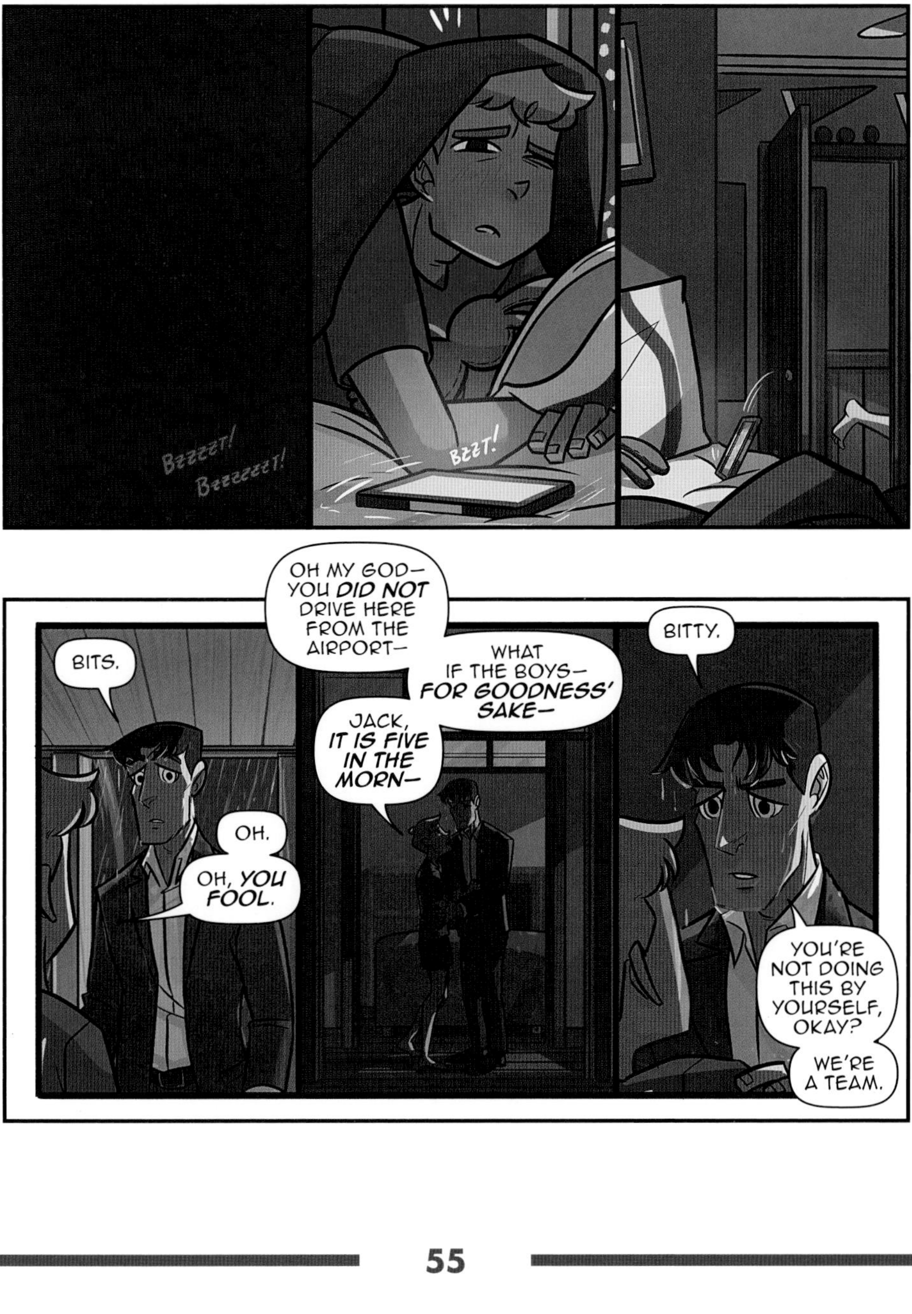
Bzzzzzt!
Bzzzzzzzt!
BZZT!
BITS.
OH MY GOD— YOU ***DID NOT*** DRIVE HERE FROM THE AIRPORT—
WHAT IF THE BOYS— ***FOR GOODNESS' SAKE—***
JACK, ***IT IS FIVE IN THE MORN—***
OH.
OH, ***YOU FOOL.***
BITTY.
YOU'RE NOT DOING THIS BY YOURSELF, OKAY?
WE'RE A TEAM.

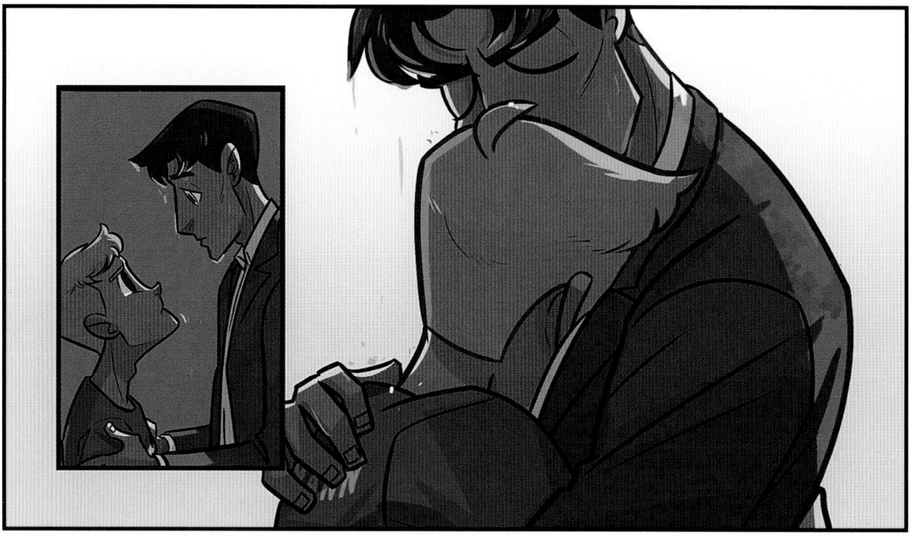

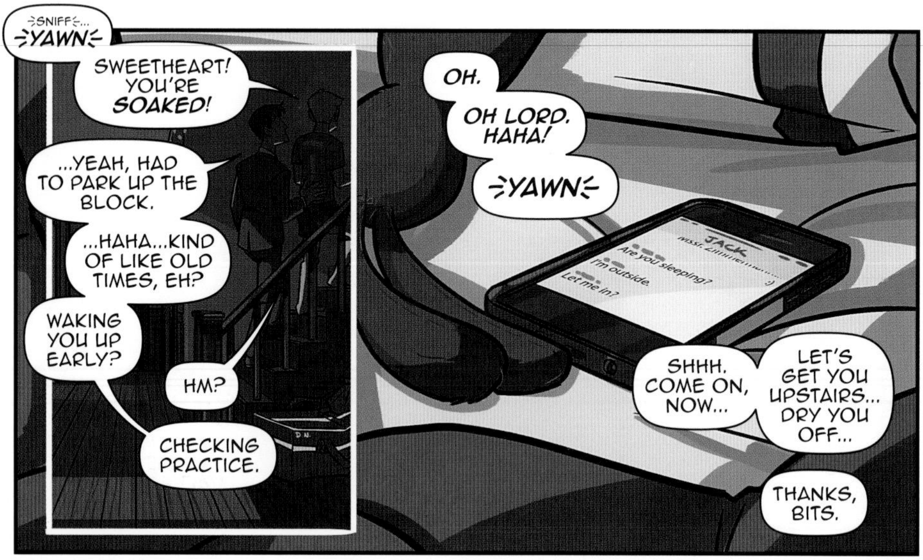
SNIFF...
YAWN
SWEETHEART! YOU'RE *SOAKED*!
...YEAH, HAD TO PARK UP THE BLOCK.
...HAHA...KIND OF LIKE OLD TIMES, EH?
WAKING YOU UP EARLY?
HM?
CHECKING PRACTICE.
OH.
OH LORD. HAHA!
YAWN
JACK
Are you sleeping?
I'm outside.
Let me in?
SHHH. COME ON, NOW...
LET'S GET YOU UPSTAIRS... DRY YOU OFF...
THANKS, BITS.

11

ME & JACK

ALL IT SAYS IS TO MEET HIM FOR BRUNCH AT JERRY'S IN TWENTY.
I DUNNO... SOUNDS, LIKE, KINDA SERIOUS?
DUDE, OF COURSE HE'S SERIOUS. MANDATORY AND IMPROMPTU BRUNCHES ARE BITTY'S TRADEMARK.
...MAN, HAVE YOU SEEN MY—
THEY'RE ON YOUR GAME THEORY BOOK, HOLTZY.
OH. THANKS. FUCK GLASSES.
I DIDN'T EVEN KNOW JERRY'S HAD BRUNCH...
PENITUS P

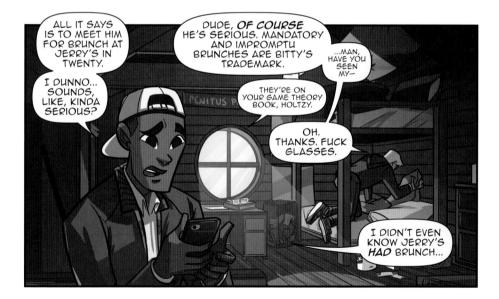

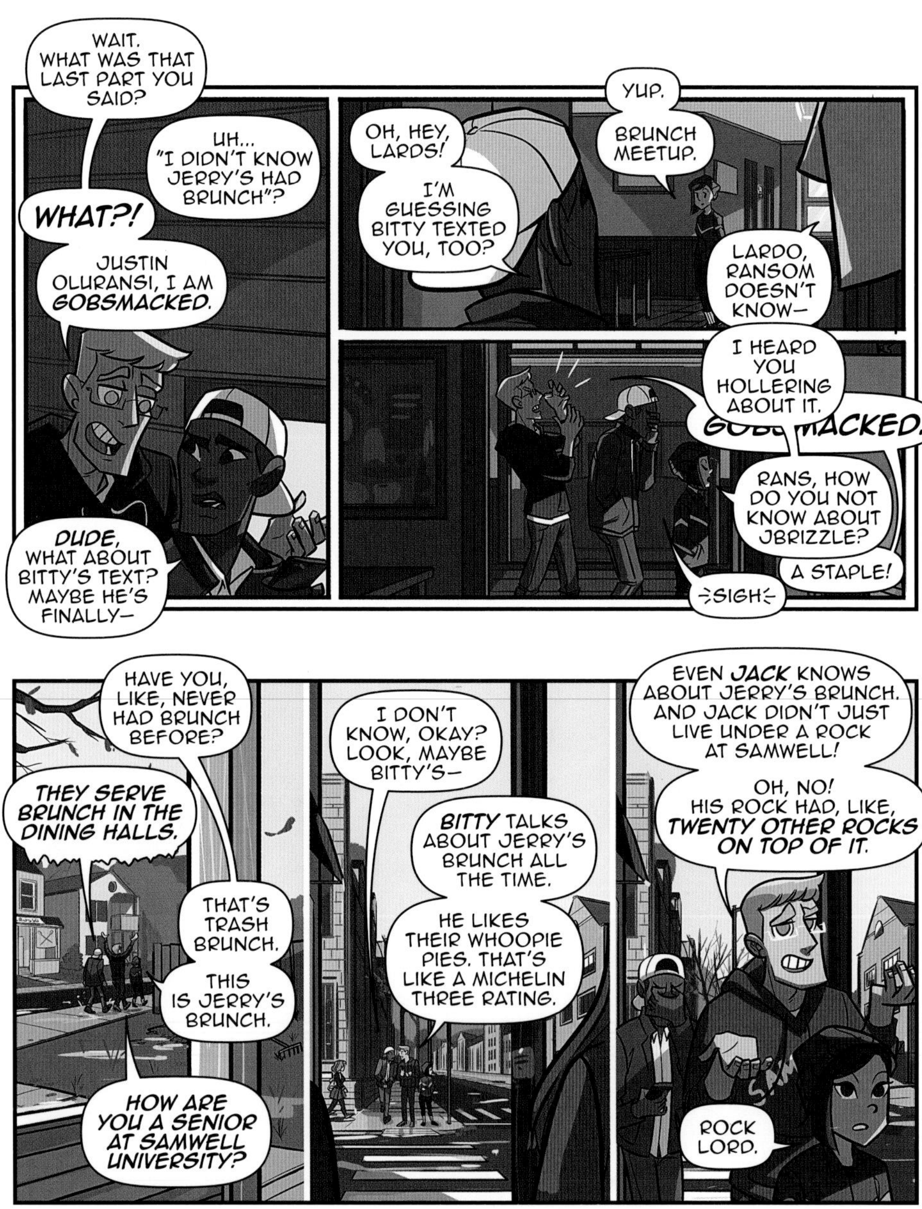
WAIT. WHAT WAS THAT LAST PART YOU SAID?
UH... "I DIDN'T KNOW JERRY'S HAD BRUNCH"?
WHAT?!
JUSTIN OLURANSI, I AM GOBSMACKED.
DUDE, WHAT ABOUT BITTY'S TEXT? MAYBE HE'S FINALLY—
OH, HEY, LARDS!
I'M GUESSING BITTY TEXTED YOU, TOO?
YUP.
BRUNCH MEETUP.
LARDO, RANSOM DOESN'T KNOW—
I HEARD YOU HOLLERING ABOUT IT.
GOBSMACKED.
RANS, HOW DO YOU NOT KNOW ABOUT JBRIZZLE?
A STAPLE!
SIGH
HAVE YOU, LIKE, NEVER HAD BRUNCH BEFORE?
THEY SERVE BRUNCH IN THE DINING HALLS.
THAT'S TRASH BRUNCH.
THIS IS JERRY'S BRUNCH.
HOW ARE YOU A SENIOR AT SAMWELL UNIVERSITY?
I DON'T KNOW, OKAY? LOOK, MAYBE BITTY'S—
BITTY TALKS ABOUT JERRY'S BRUNCH ALL THE TIME.
HE LIKES THEIR WHOOPIE PIES. THAT'S LIKE A MICHELIN THREE RATING.
EVEN JACK KNOWS ABOUT JERRY'S BRUNCH. AND JACK DIDN'T JUST LIVE UNDER A ROCK AT SAMWELL!
OH, NO! HIS ROCK HAD, LIKE, TWENTY OTHER ROCKS ON TOP OF IT.
ROCK LORD.

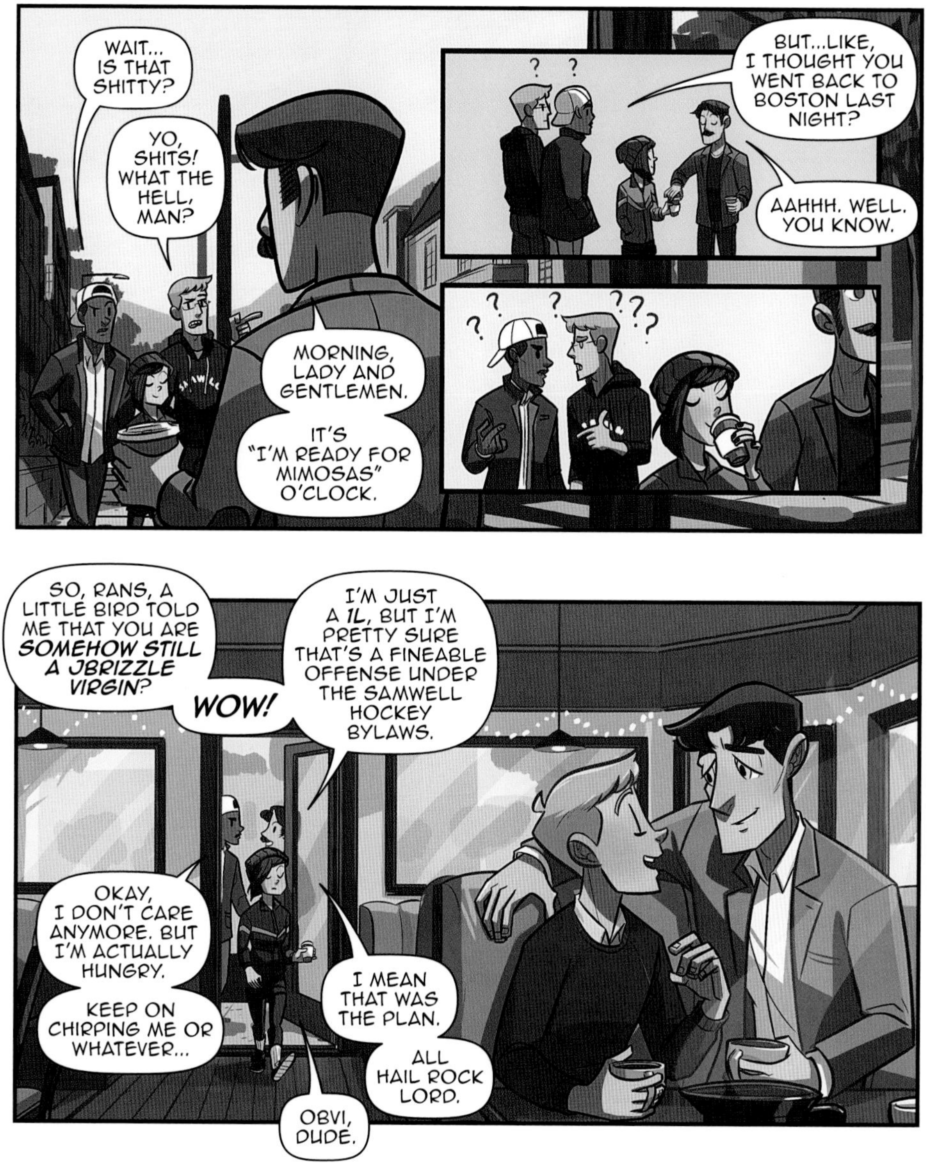
WAIT... IS THAT SHITTY?
YO, SHITS! WHAT THE HELL, MAN?
MORNING, LADY AND GENTLEMEN.
IT'S "I'M READY FOR MIMOSAS" O'CLOCK.
? ?
BUT...LIKE, I THOUGHT YOU WENT BACK TO BOSTON LAST NIGHT?
AAHHH. WELL. YOU KNOW.
? ? ??? ?
SO, RANS, A LITTLE BIRD TOLD ME THAT YOU ARE *SOMEHOW STILL A JBRIZZLE VIRGIN*?
WOW!
I'M JUST A *1L*, BUT I'M PRETTY SURE THAT'S A FINEABLE OFFENSE UNDER THE SAMWELL HOCKEY BYLAWS.
OKAY, I DON'T CARE ANYMORE. BUT I'M ACTUALLY HUNGRY.
KEEP ON CHIRPING ME OR WHATEVER...
I MEAN THAT WAS THE PLAN.
ALL HAIL ROCK LORD.
OBVI, DUDE.

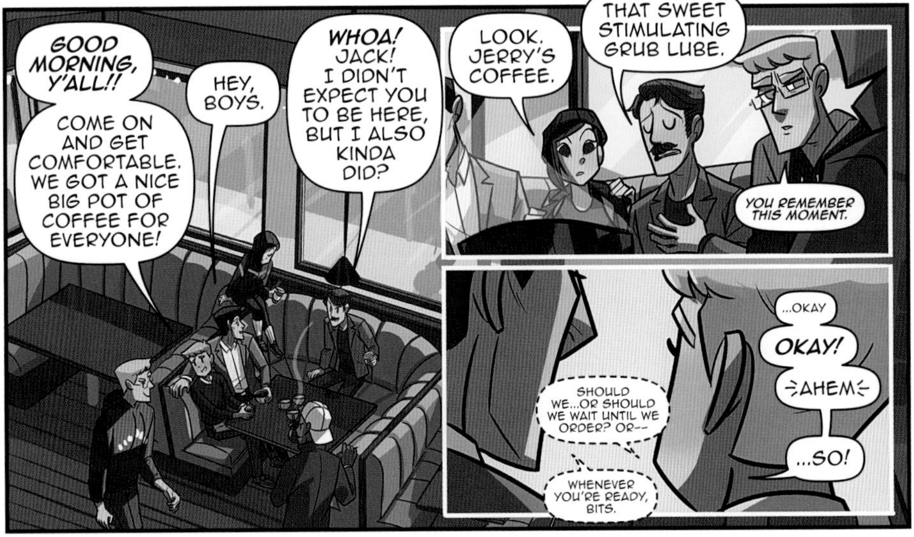
GOOD MORNING, Y'ALL!!
COME ON AND GET COMFORTABLE. WE GOT A NICE BIG POT OF COFFEE FOR EVERYONE!
HEY, BOYS.
WHOA! JACK! I DIDN'T EXPECT YOU TO BE HERE, BUT I ALSO KINDA DID?
LOOK. JERRY'S COFFEE.
THAT SWEET STIMULATING GRUB LUBE.
YOU REMEMBER THIS MOMENT.
...OKAY
OKAY!
AHEM
...SO!
SHOULD WE...OR SHOULD WE WAIT UNTIL WE ORDER? OR--
WHENEVER YOU'RE READY, BITS.

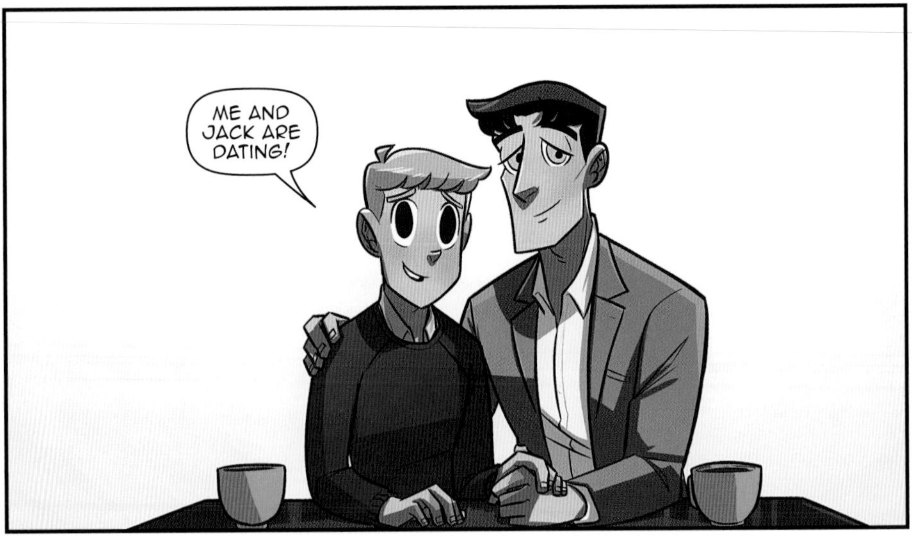
ME AND JACK ARE DATING!

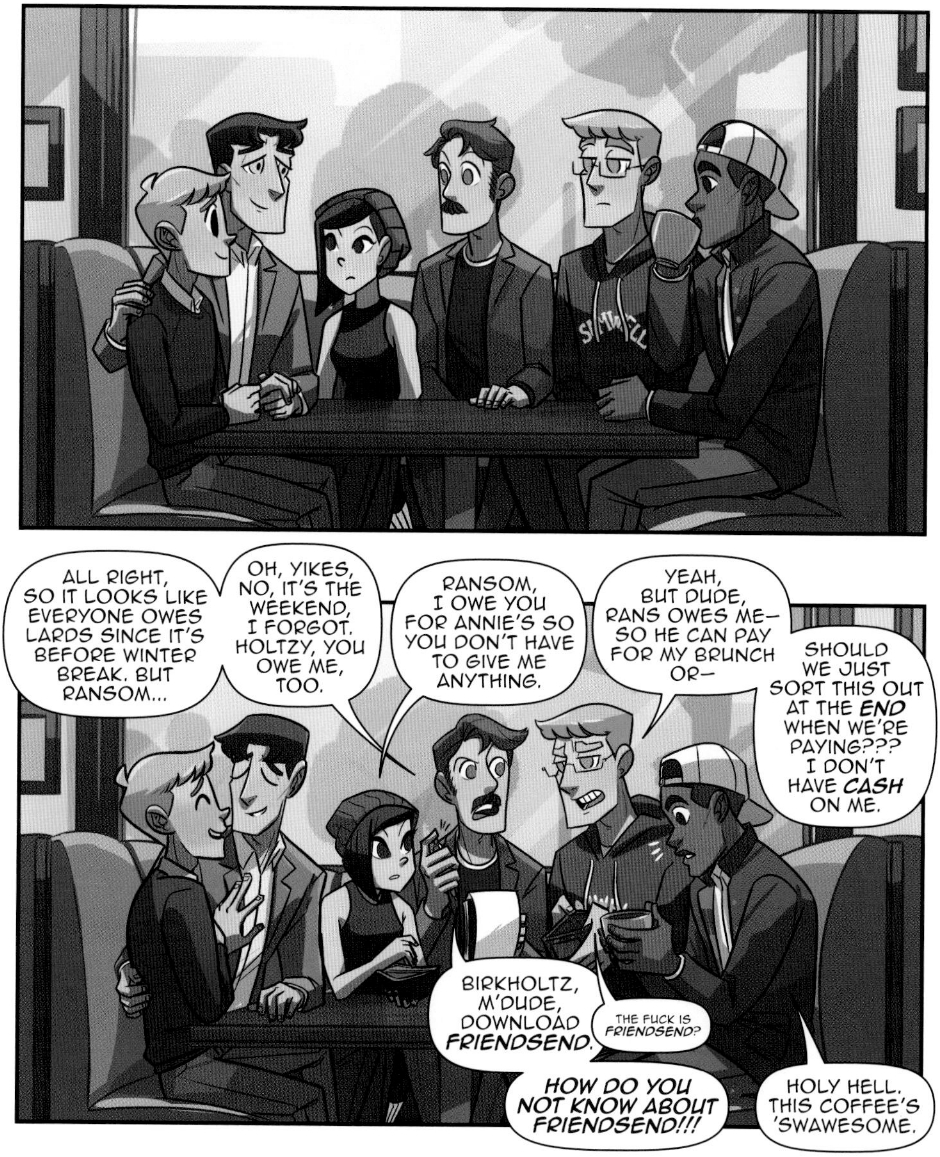
ALL RIGHT, SO IT LOOKS LIKE EVERYONE OWES LARDS SINCE IT'S BEFORE WINTER BREAK. BUT RANSOM...
OH, YIKES, NO, IT'S THE WEEKEND, I FORGOT. HOLTZY, YOU OWE ME, TOO.
RANSOM, I OWE YOU FOR ANNIE'S SO YOU DON'T HAVE TO GIVE ME ANYTHING.
YEAH, BUT DUDE, RANS OWES ME– SO HE CAN PAY FOR MY BRUNCH OR–
SHOULD WE JUST SORT THIS OUT AT THE END WHEN WE'RE PAYING??? I DON'T HAVE CASH ON ME.
BIRKHOLTZ, M'DUDE, DOWNLOAD FRIENDSEND.
THE FUCK IS FRIENDSEND?
HOW DO YOU NOT KNOW ABOUT FRIENDSEND!!!
HOLY HELL. THIS COFFEE'S 'SWAWESOME.

12

BITTY & I

AHEM!
SO! FIRST WE SHOULD SAY— THIS IS TOTALLY 'SWAWESOME!
YEAH. IT'S COOL THAT YOU GUYS ARE LETTING US KNOW, YOU KNOW?
Y'ALL ARE SWEET! THOUGH... IT'S. UM. CLEAR YOU HAD SOME INKLINGS.
...WELL, I GUESS ALL THAT SECRECY AROUND THE TEAM WAS FOR NOTHING.
NAW! DUDE, NOT FOR NOTHING! UH, THAT WAS PERFECT SECRECY.
FOR THE RECORD, BITS? I TOTALLY STILL BELIEVE YOU HAVE A COUSIN AT BROWN.

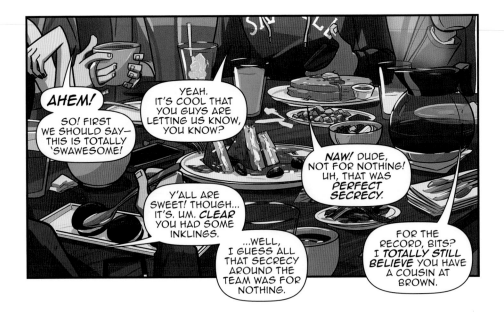

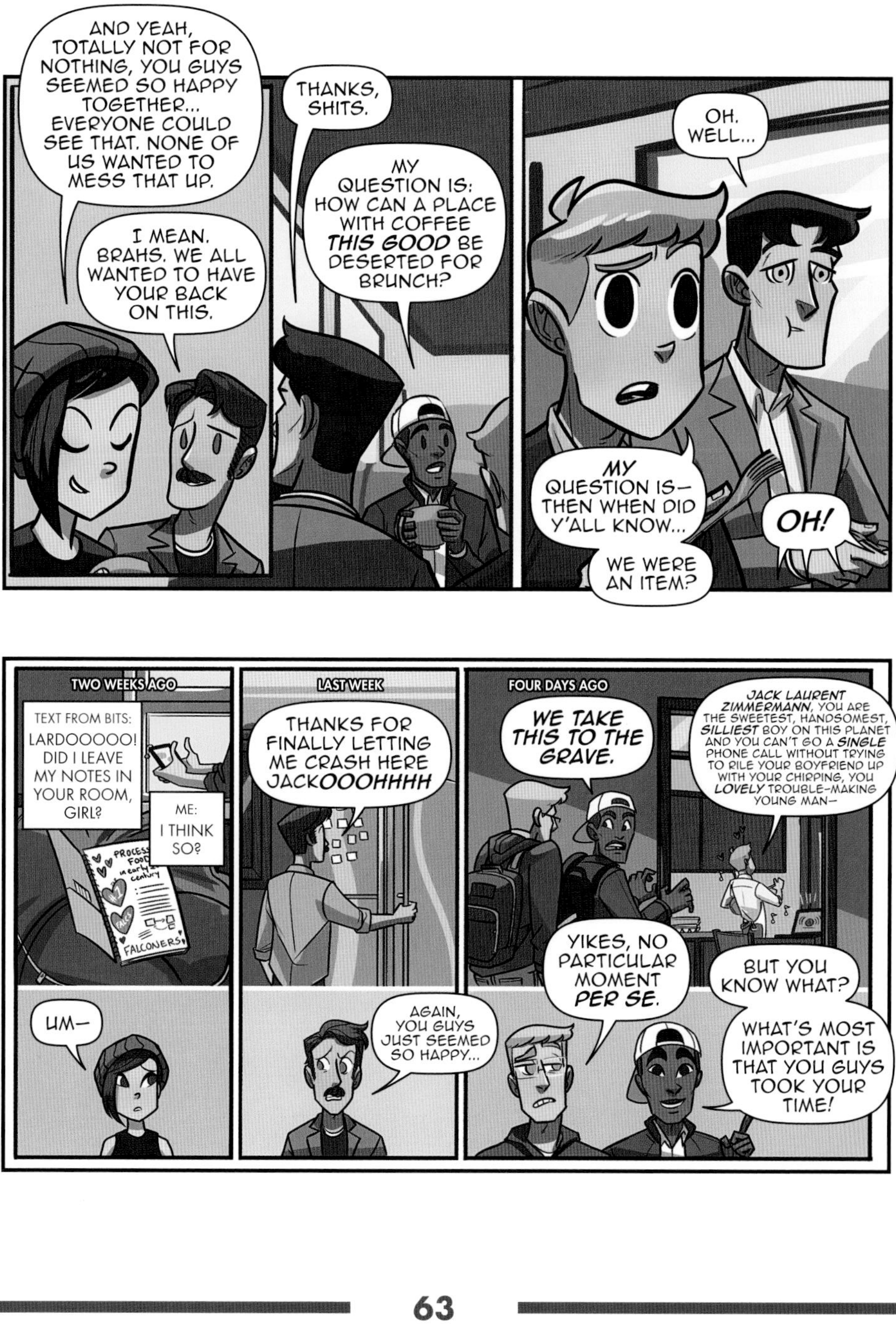
AND YEAH, TOTALLY NOT FOR NOTHING, YOU GUYS SEEMED SO HAPPY TOGETHER... EVERYONE COULD SEE THAT. NONE OF US WANTED TO MESS THAT UP.
I MEAN. BRAHS. WE ALL WANTED TO HAVE YOUR BACK ON THIS.
THANKS, SHITS.
MY QUESTION IS: HOW CAN A PLACE WITH COFFEE THIS GOOD BE DESERTED FOR BRUNCH?
OH. WELL...
MY QUESTION IS— THEN WHEN DID Y'ALL KNOW...
WE WERE AN ITEM?
OH!
TWO WEEKS AGO
TEXT FROM BITS: LARDOOOOO! DID I LEAVE MY NOTES IN YOUR ROOM, GIRL?
ME: I THINK SO?
UM—
LAST WEEK
THANKS FOR FINALLY LETTING ME CRASH HERE JACKOOOHHHH
AGAIN, YOU GUYS JUST SEEMED SO HAPPY...
FOUR DAYS AGO
WE TAKE THIS TO THE GRAVE.
JACK LAURENT ZIMMERMANN, YOU ARE THE SWEETEST, HANDSOMEST, SILLIEST BOY ON THIS PLANET AND YOU CAN'T GO A SINGLE PHONE CALL WITHOUT TRYING TO RILE YOUR BOYFRIEND UP WITH YOUR CHIRPING, YOU LOVELY TROUBLE-MAKING YOUNG MAN—
YIKES, NO PARTICULAR MOMENT PER SE.
BUT YOU KNOW WHAT?
WHAT'S MOST IMPORTANT IS THAT YOU GUYS TOOK YOUR TIME!

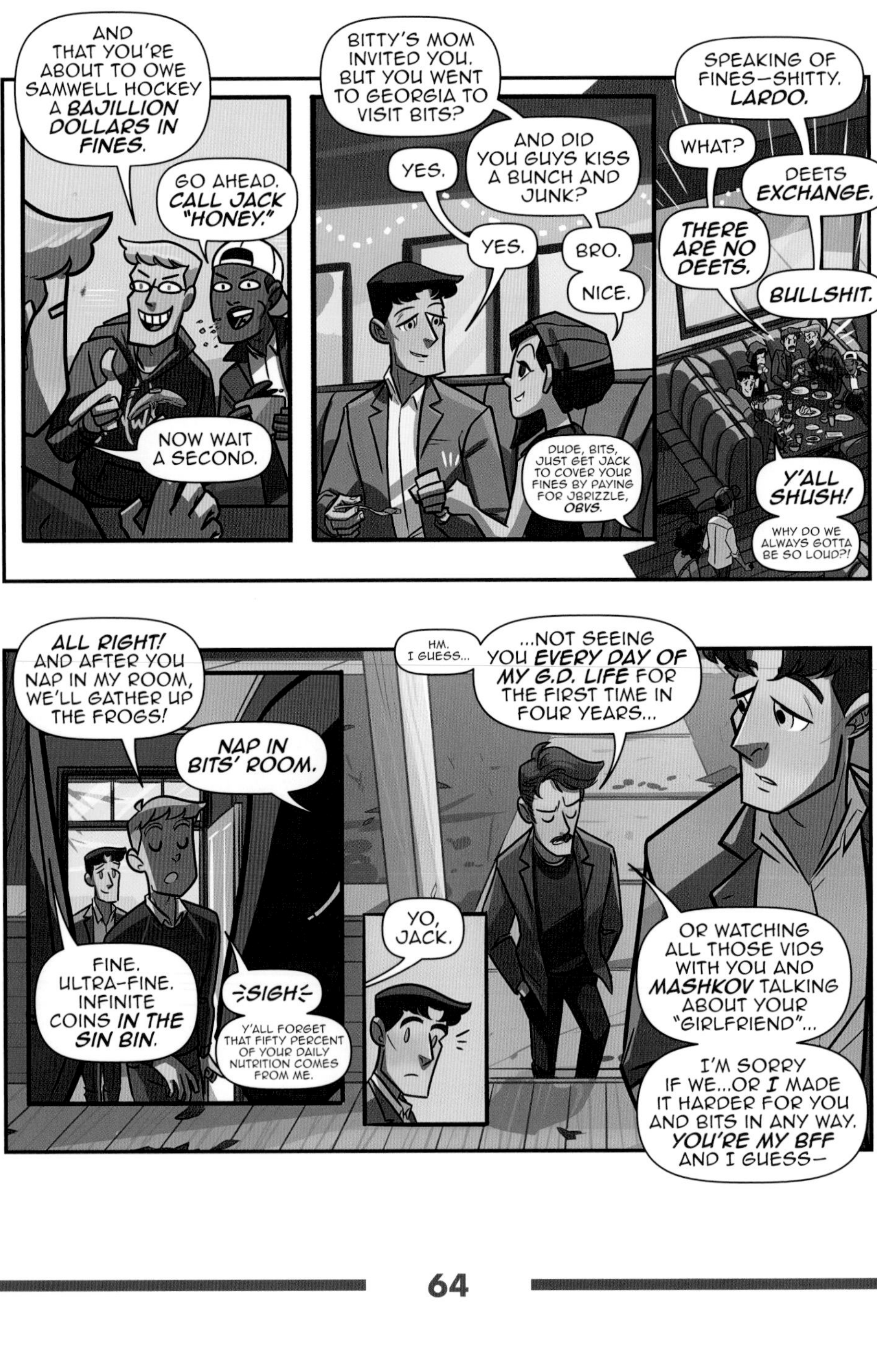
AND THAT YOU'RE ABOUT TO OWE SAMWELL HOCKEY A BAJILLION DOLLARS IN FINES.
GO AHEAD. CALL JACK "HONEY."
NOW WAIT A SECOND.
BITTY'S MOM INVITED YOU. BUT YOU WENT TO GEORGIA TO VISIT BITS?
YES.
AND DID YOU GUYS KISS A BUNCH AND JUNK?
YES.
BRO.
NICE.
DUDE, BITS, JUST GET JACK TO COVER YOUR FINES BY PAYING FOR JBRIZZLE, OBVS.
SPEAKING OF FINES—SHITTY. LARDO.
WHAT?
DEETS EXCHANGE.
THERE ARE NO DEETS.
BULLSHIT.
Y'ALL SHUSH!
WHY DO WE ALWAYS GOTTA BE SO LOUD?!
ALL RIGHT! AND AFTER YOU NAP IN MY ROOM, WE'LL GATHER UP THE FROGS!
NAP IN BITS' ROOM.
FINE. ULTRA-FINE. INFINITE COINS IN THE SIN BIN.
≈SIGH≈
Y'ALL FORGET THAT FIFTY PERCENT OF YOUR DAILY NUTRITION COMES FROM ME.
HM. I GUESS...
...NOT SEEING YOU EVERY DAY OF MY G.D. LIFE FOR THE FIRST TIME IN FOUR YEARS...
YO, JACK.
OR WATCHING ALL THOSE VIDS WITH YOU AND MASHKOV TALKING ABOUT YOUR "GIRLFRIEND"...
I'M SORRY IF WE...OR I MADE IT HARDER FOR YOU AND BITS IN ANY WAY. YOU'RE MY BFF AND I GUESS—

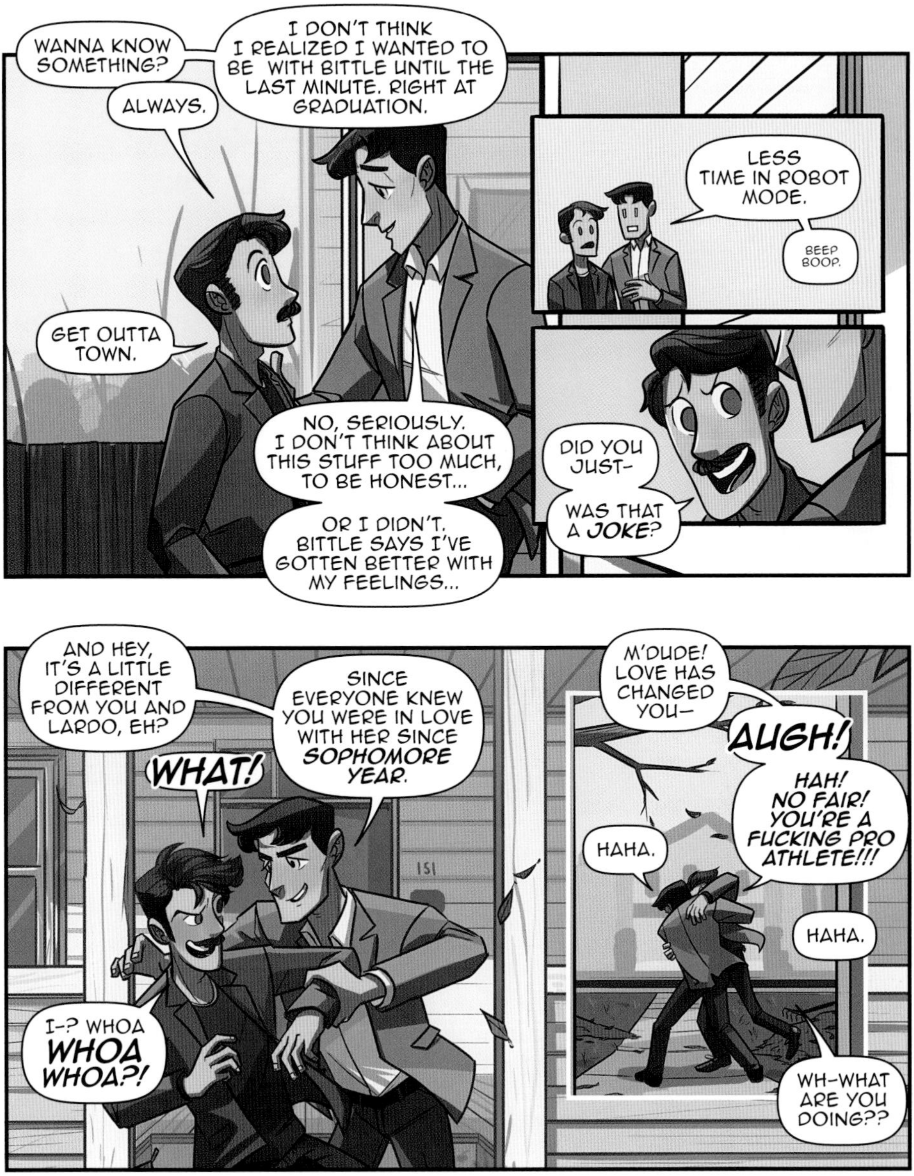
WANNA KNOW SOMETHING?
ALWAYS.
I DON'T THINK I REALIZED I WANTED TO BE WITH BITTLE UNTIL THE LAST MINUTE. RIGHT AT GRADUATION.
GET OUTTA TOWN.
NO, SERIOUSLY. I DON'T THINK ABOUT THIS STUFF TOO MUCH, TO BE HONEST...
OR I DIDN'T. BITTLE SAYS I'VE GOTTEN BETTER WITH MY FEELINGS...
LESS TIME IN ROBOT MODE.
BEEP BOOP.
DID YOU JUST-
WAS THAT A *JOKE*?
AND HEY, IT'S A LITTLE DIFFERENT FROM YOU AND LARDO, EH?
SINCE EVERYONE KNEW YOU WERE IN LOVE WITH HER SINCE *SOPHOMORE YEAR.*
WHAT!
I-? WHOA *WHOA WHOA?!*
M'DUDE! LOVE HAS CHANGED YOU-
AUGH!
HAH! NO FAIR! YOU'RE A FUCKING PRO ATHLETE!!!
HAHA.
HAHA.
WH-WHAT ARE YOU DOING??

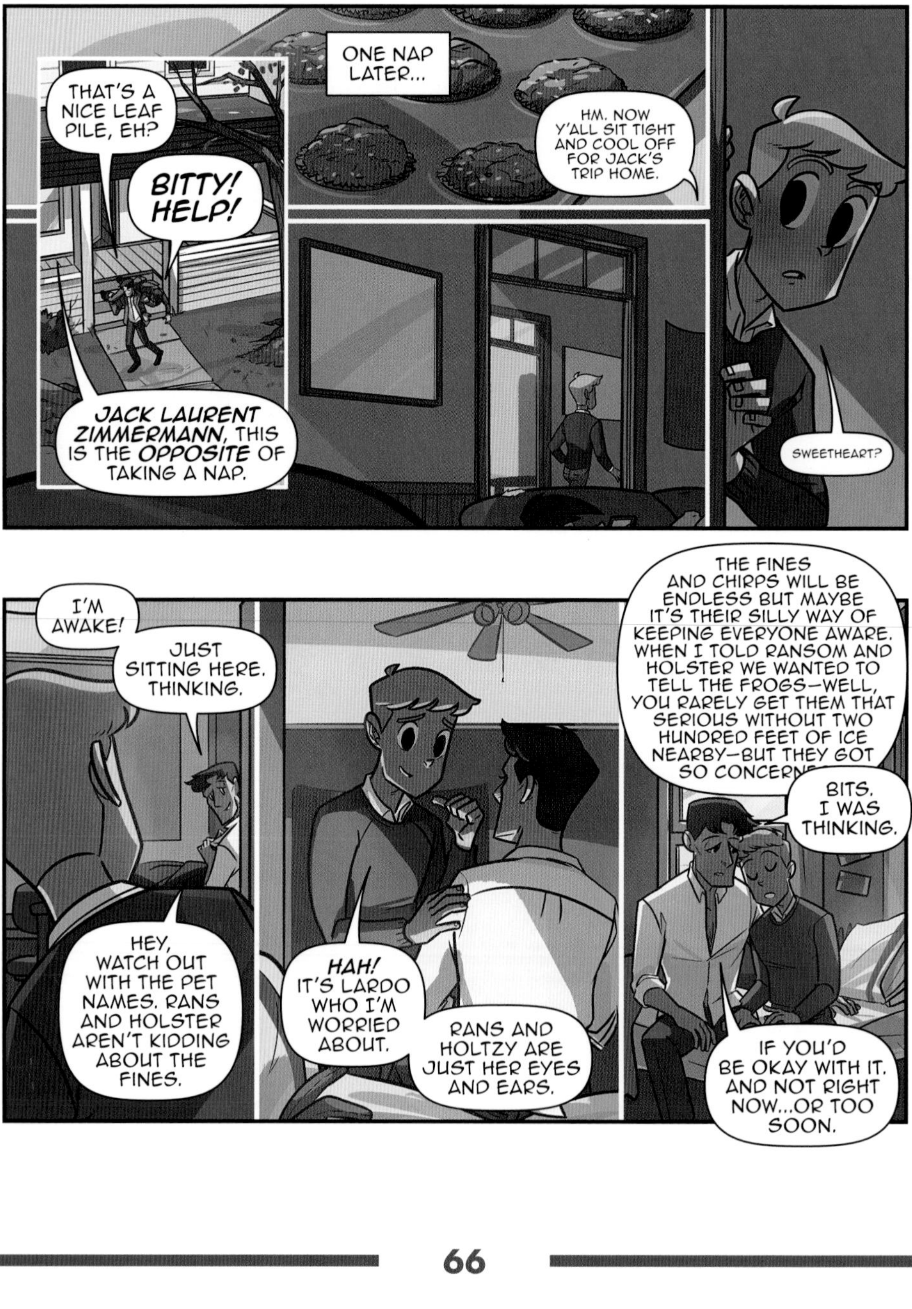
ONE NAP LATER...
HM. NOW Y'ALL SIT TIGHT AND COOL OFF FOR JACK'S TRIP HOME.
THAT'S A NICE LEAF PILE, EH?
BITTY! HELP!
JACK LAURENT ZIMMERMANN, THIS IS THE OPPOSITE OF TAKING A NAP.
SWEETHEART?
I'M AWAKE!
JUST SITTING HERE. THINKING.
HEY, WATCH OUT WITH THE PET NAMES. RANS AND HOLSTER AREN'T KIDDING ABOUT THE FINES.
HAH! IT'S LARDO WHO I'M WORRIED ABOUT.
RANS AND HOLTZY ARE JUST HER EYES AND EARS.
THE FINES AND CHIRPS WILL BE ENDLESS BUT MAYBE IT'S THEIR SILLY WAY OF KEEPING EVERYONE AWARE. WHEN I TOLD RANSOM AND HOLSTER WE WANTED TO TELL THE FROGS—WELL, YOU RARELY GET THEM THAT SERIOUS WITHOUT TWO HUNDRED FEET OF ICE NEARBY—BUT THEY GOT SO CONCERN
BITS. I WAS THINKING.
IF YOU'D BE OKAY WITH IT. AND NOT RIGHT NOW...OR TOO SOON.

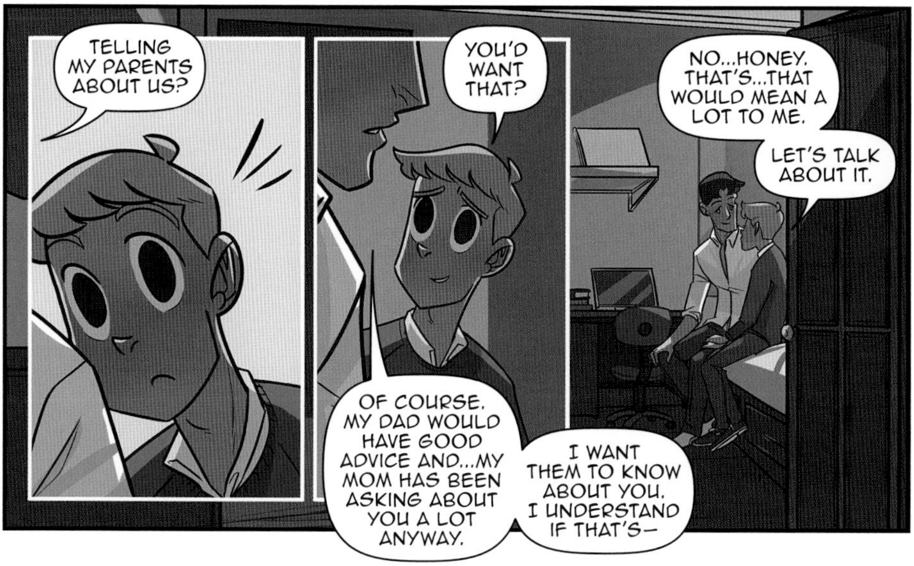
TELLING MY PARENTS ABOUT US?
YOU'D WANT THAT?
OF COURSE. MY DAD WOULD HAVE GOOD ADVICE AND...MY MOM HAS BEEN ASKING ABOUT YOU A LOT ANYWAY.
I WANT THEM TO KNOW ABOUT YOU. I UNDERSTAND IF THAT'S—
NO...HONEY. THAT'S...THAT WOULD MEAN A LOT TO ME.
LET'S TALK ABOUT IT.

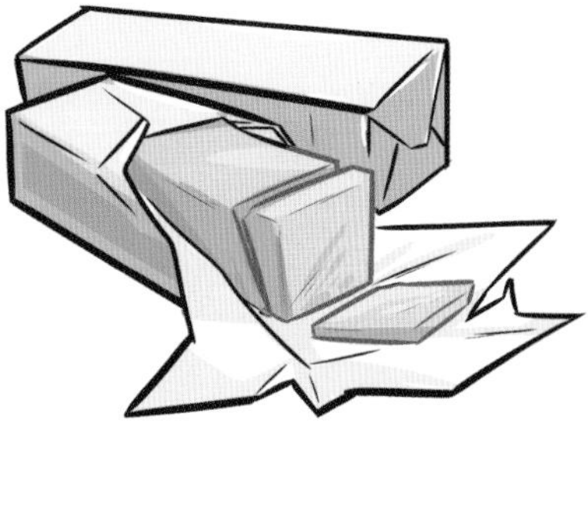

13

RIVERSIDE

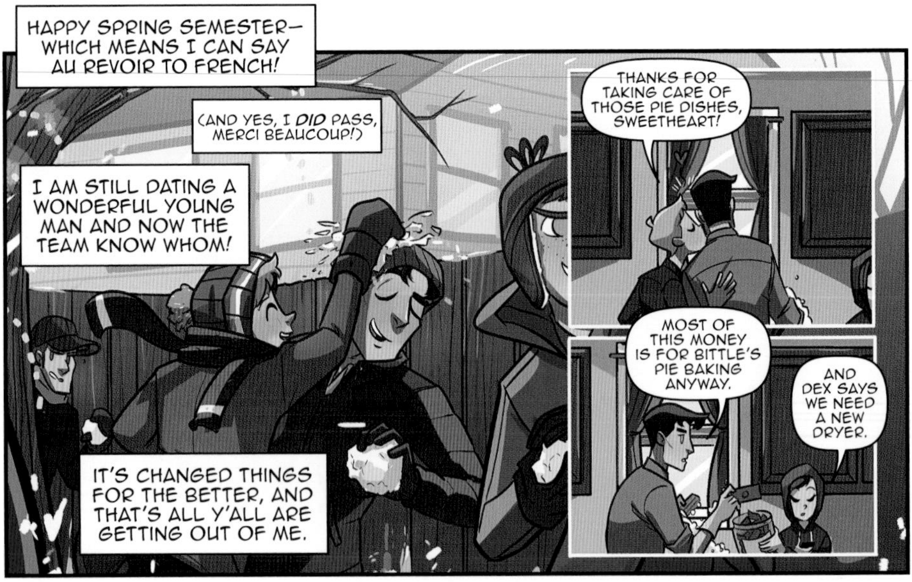

HAPPY SPRING SEMESTER—WHICH MEANS I CAN SAY AU REVOIR TO FRENCH!
(AND YES, I *DID* PASS, MERCI BEAUCOUP!)
I AM STILL DATING A WONDERFUL YOUNG MAN AND NOW THE TEAM KNOW WHOM!
IT'S CHANGED THINGS FOR THE BETTER, AND THAT'S ALL Y'ALL ARE GETTING OUT OF ME.
THANKS FOR TAKING CARE OF THOSE PIE DISHES, SWEETHEART!
MOST OF THIS MONEY IS FOR BITTLE'S PIE BAKING ANYWAY.
AND DEX SAYS WE NEED A NEW DRYER.

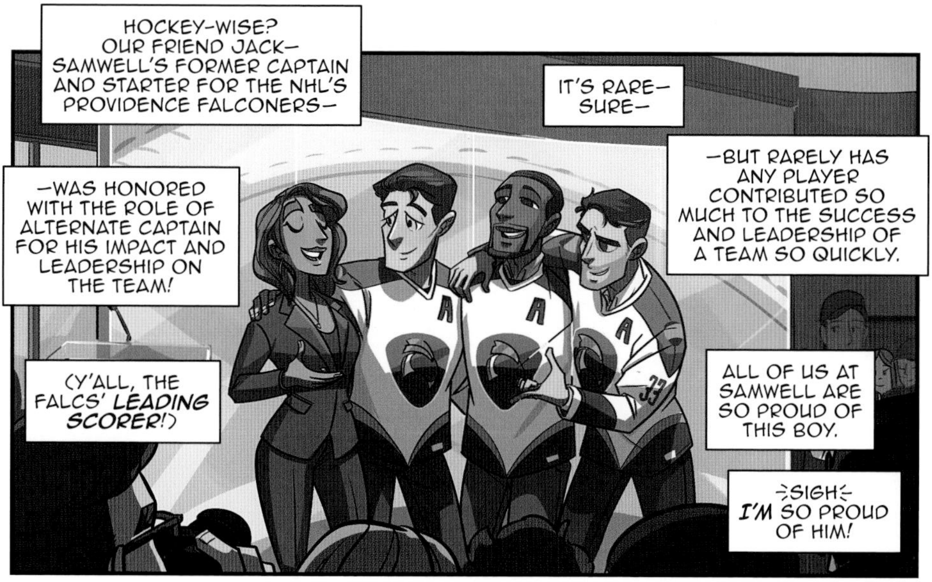
HOCKEY-WISE? OUR FRIEND JACK—SAMWELL'S FORMER CAPTAIN AND STARTER FOR THE NHL'S PROVIDENCE FALCONERS—
—WAS HONORED WITH THE ROLE OF ALTERNATE CAPTAIN FOR HIS IMPACT AND LEADERSHIP ON THE TEAM!
(Y'ALL, THE FALCS' **LEADING SCORER!**)
IT'S RARE—SURE—
—BUT RARELY HAS ANY PLAYER CONTRIBUTED SO MUCH TO THE SUCCESS AND LEADERSHIP OF A TEAM SO QUICKLY.
ALL OF US AT SAMWELL ARE SO PROUD OF THIS BOY.
SIGH
I'M SO PROUD OF HIM!

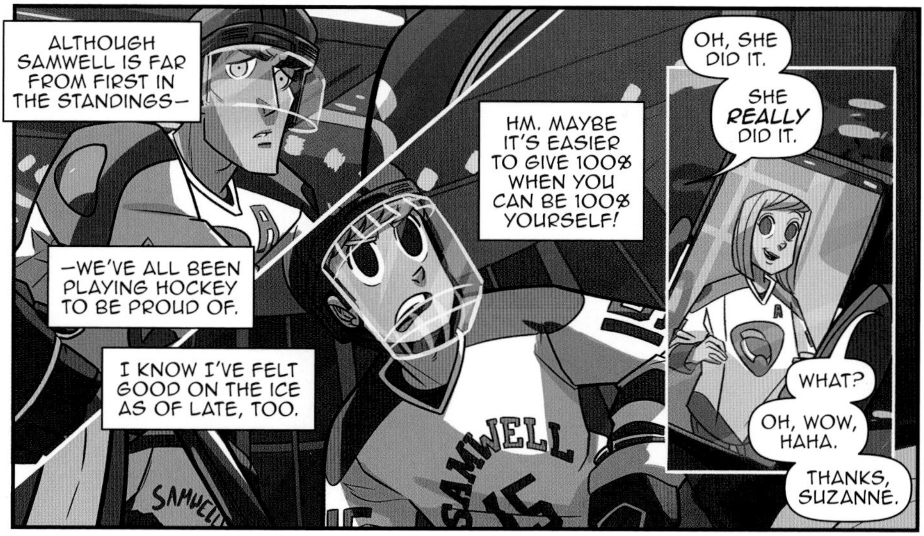
ALTHOUGH SAMWELL IS FAR FROM FIRST IN THE STANDINGS—
—WE'VE ALL BEEN PLAYING HOCKEY TO BE PROUD OF.
I KNOW I'VE FELT GOOD ON THE ICE AS OF LATE, TOO.
HM. MAYBE IT'S EASIER TO GIVE 100% WHEN YOU CAN BE 100% YOURSELF!
OH, SHE DID IT.
SHE **REALLY** DID IT.
WHAT?
OH, WOW, HAHA.
THANKS, SUZANNE.
SAMWELL

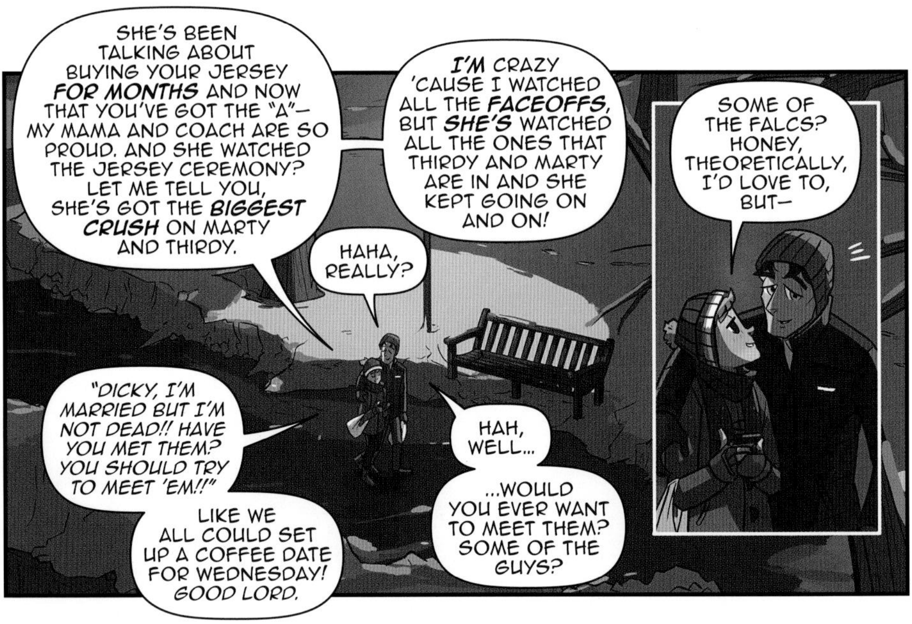
SHE'S BEEN TALKING ABOUT BUYING YOUR JERSEY FOR MONTHS AND NOW THAT YOU'VE GOT THE "A"— MY MAMA AND COACH ARE SO PROUD. AND SHE WATCHED THE JERSEY CEREMONY? LET ME TELL YOU, SHE'S GOT THE BIGGEST CRUSH ON MARTY AND THIRDY.
HAHA, REALLY?
I'M CRAZY 'CAUSE I WATCHED ALL THE FACEOFFS, BUT SHE'S WATCHED ALL THE ONES THAT THIRDY AND MARTY ARE IN AND SHE KEPT GOING ON AND ON!
"DICKY, I'M MARRIED BUT I'M NOT DEAD!! HAVE YOU MET THEM? YOU SHOULD TRY TO MEET 'EM!!"
LIKE WE ALL COULD SET UP A COFFEE DATE FOR WEDNESDAY! GOOD LORD.
HAH, WELL...
...WOULD YOU EVER WANT TO MEET THEM? SOME OF THE GUYS?
SOME OF THE FALCS? HONEY, THEORETICALLY, I'D LOVE TO, BUT—

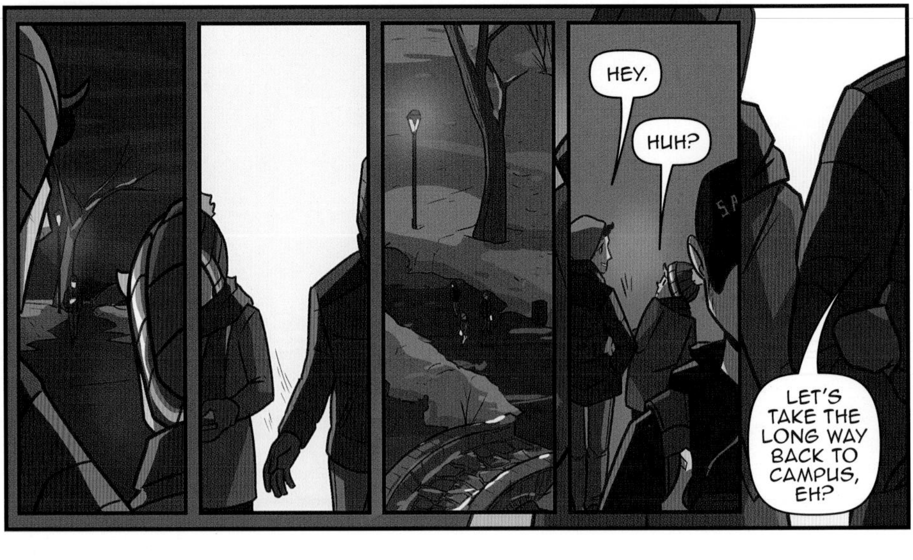
HEY.
HUH?
LET'S TAKE THE LONG WAY BACK TO CAMPUS, EH?

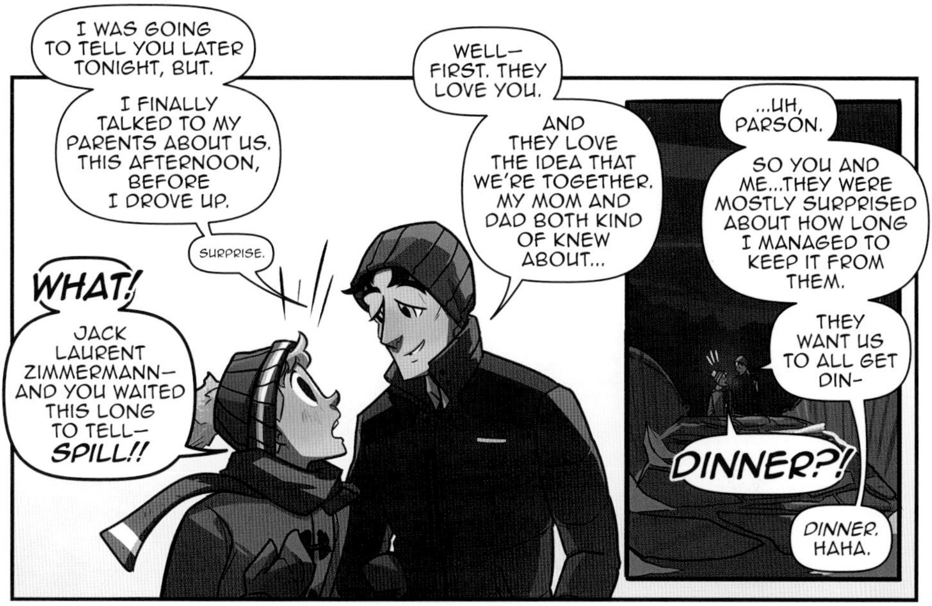
I WAS GOING TO TELL YOU LATER TONIGHT, BUT.
I FINALLY TALKED TO MY PARENTS ABOUT US. THIS AFTERNOON, BEFORE I DROVE UP.
SURPRISE.
WHAT!
JACK LAURENT ZIMMERMANN— AND YOU WAITED THIS LONG TO TELL— SPILL!!
WELL— FIRST. THEY LOVE YOU.
AND THEY LOVE THE IDEA THAT WE'RE TOGETHER. MY MOM AND DAD BOTH KIND OF KNEW ABOUT...
...UH, PARSON.
SO YOU AND ME...THEY WERE MOSTLY SURPRISED ABOUT HOW LONG I MANAGED TO KEEP IT FROM THEM.
THEY WANT US TO ALL GET DIN-
DINNER?!
DINNER. HAHA.

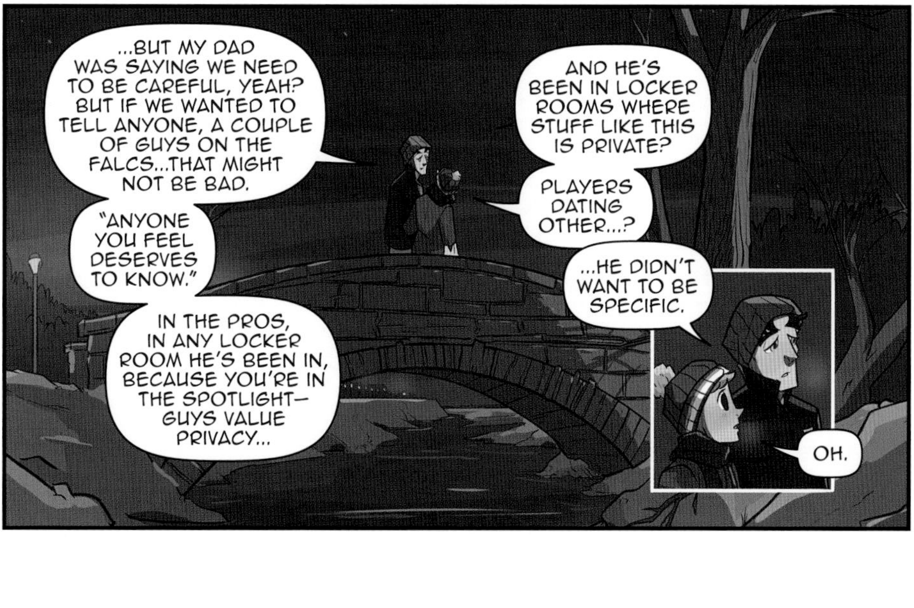
...BUT MY DAD WAS SAYING WE NEED TO BE CAREFUL, YEAH? BUT IF WE WANTED TO TELL ANYONE, A COUPLE OF GUYS ON THE FALCS...THAT MIGHT NOT BE BAD.
"ANYONE YOU FEEL DESERVES TO KNOW."
IN THE PROS, IN ANY LOCKER ROOM HE'S BEEN IN, BECAUSE YOU'RE IN THE SPOTLIGHT— GUYS VALUE PRIVACY...
AND HE'S BEEN IN LOCKER ROOMS WHERE STUFF LIKE THIS IS PRIVATE?
PLAYERS DATING OTHER...?
...HE DIDN'T WANT TO BE SPECIFIC.
OH.

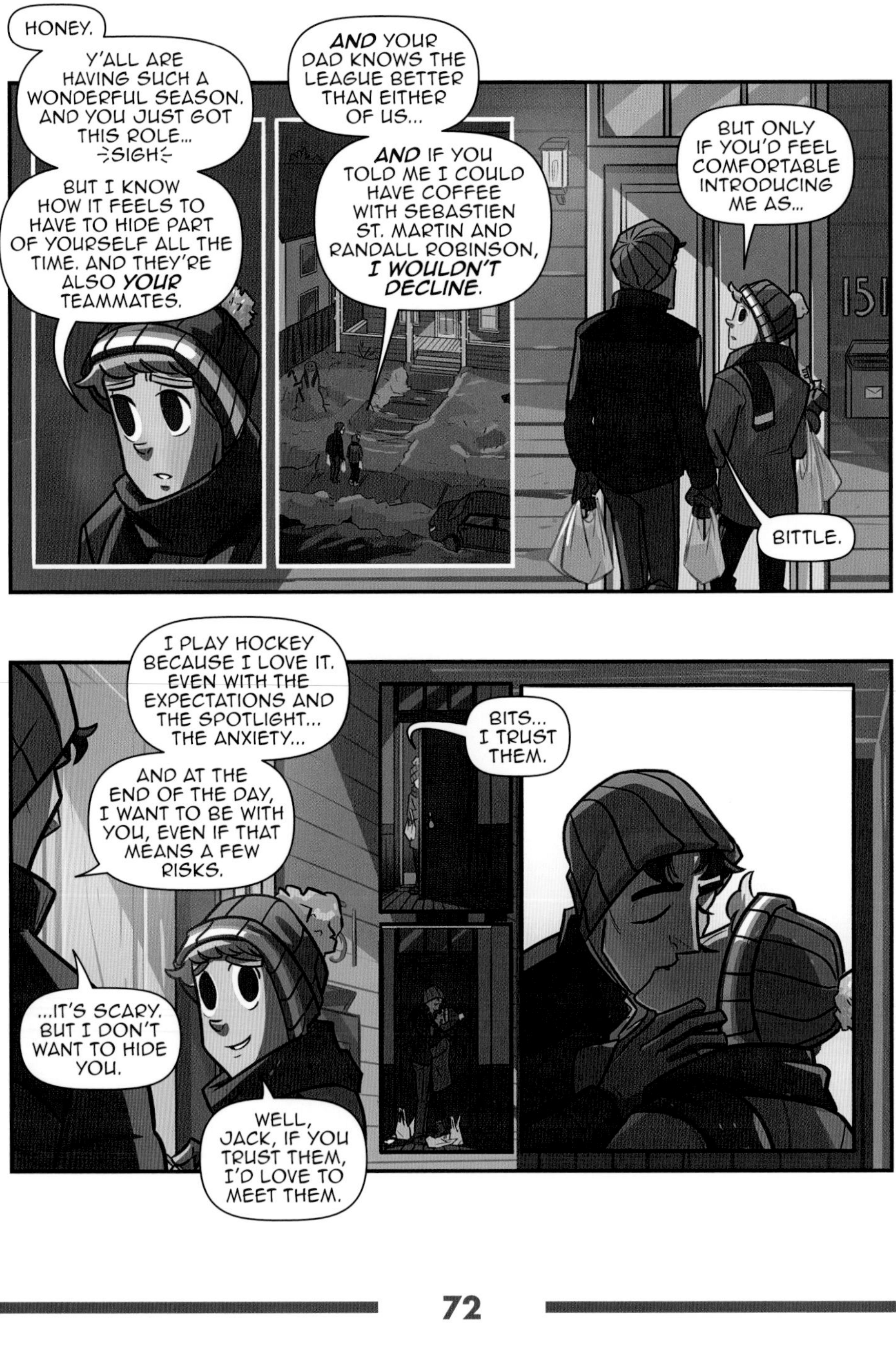
HONEY.
Y'ALL ARE HAVING SUCH A WONDERFUL SEASON. AND YOU JUST GOT THIS ROLE... *SIGH*
BUT I KNOW HOW IT FEELS TO HAVE TO HIDE PART OF YOURSELF ALL THE TIME. AND THEY'RE ALSO *YOUR* TEAMMATES.
AND YOUR DAD KNOWS THE LEAGUE BETTER THAN EITHER OF US...
AND IF YOU TOLD ME I COULD HAVE COFFEE WITH SEBASTIEN ST. MARTIN AND RANDALL ROBINSON, ***I WOULDN'T DECLINE.***
BUT ONLY IF YOU'D FEEL COMFORTABLE INTRODUCING ME AS...
BITTLE.
I PLAY HOCKEY BECAUSE I LOVE IT. EVEN WITH THE EXPECTATIONS AND THE SPOTLIGHT... THE ANXIETY...
AND AT THE END OF THE DAY, I WANT TO BE WITH YOU, EVEN IF THAT MEANS A FEW RISKS.
...IT'S SCARY. BUT I DON'T WANT TO HIDE YOU.
WELL, JACK, IF YOU TRUST THEM, I'D LOVE TO MEET THEM.
BITS... I TRUST THEM.

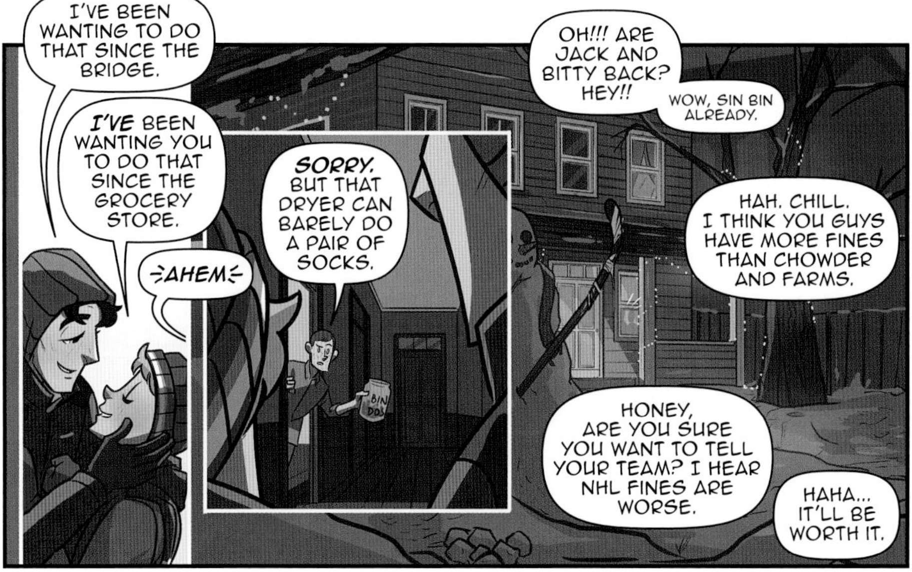
I'VE BEEN WANTING TO DO THAT SINCE THE BRIDGE.
I'VE BEEN WANTING YOU TO DO THAT SINCE THE GROCERY STORE.
AHEM
SORRY. BUT THAT DRYER CAN BARELY DO A PAIR OF SOCKS.
OH!!! ARE JACK AND BITTY BACK? HEY!!
WOW, SIN BIN ALREADY.
HAH. CHILL. I THINK YOU GUYS HAVE MORE FINES THAN CHOWDER AND FARMS.
HONEY, ARE YOU SURE YOU WANT TO TELL YOUR TEAM? I HEAR NHL FINES ARE WORSE.
HAHA... IT'LL BE WORTH IT.

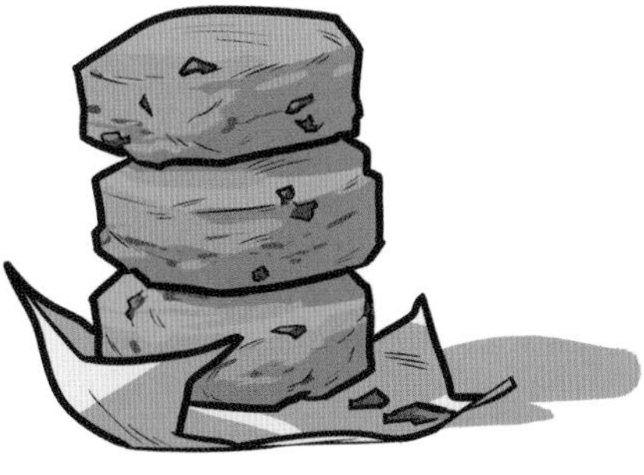

14

MONDAY IN THE PARK
WITH GEORGE

I CAN *STILL* CALL THIS A BAKING VLOG SINCE THE RELATIONSHIP QUESTIONS HAVEN'T OUTNUMBERED THE RECIPES.

TELLING PEOPLE ABOUT WHO YOU'RE DATING OR WHO YOU ARE—IT'S NOT A *ONE-AND-DONE* TYPE OF THING!

THE PERSONAL STORIES HAVEN'T OUTPACED THE PIE? (MORE LOAF TALK THAN LOVE TALK?)

BUT THAT IS A GOOD QUESTION.

HM. THE THING IS... IT'S DIFFERENT FOR EVERYONE. AND IT'S DIFFERENT EVERY TIME.

IT'S SOMETHING YOU'LL LIKELY HAVE TO DO OVER AND OVER (AND OVER AND OVER).

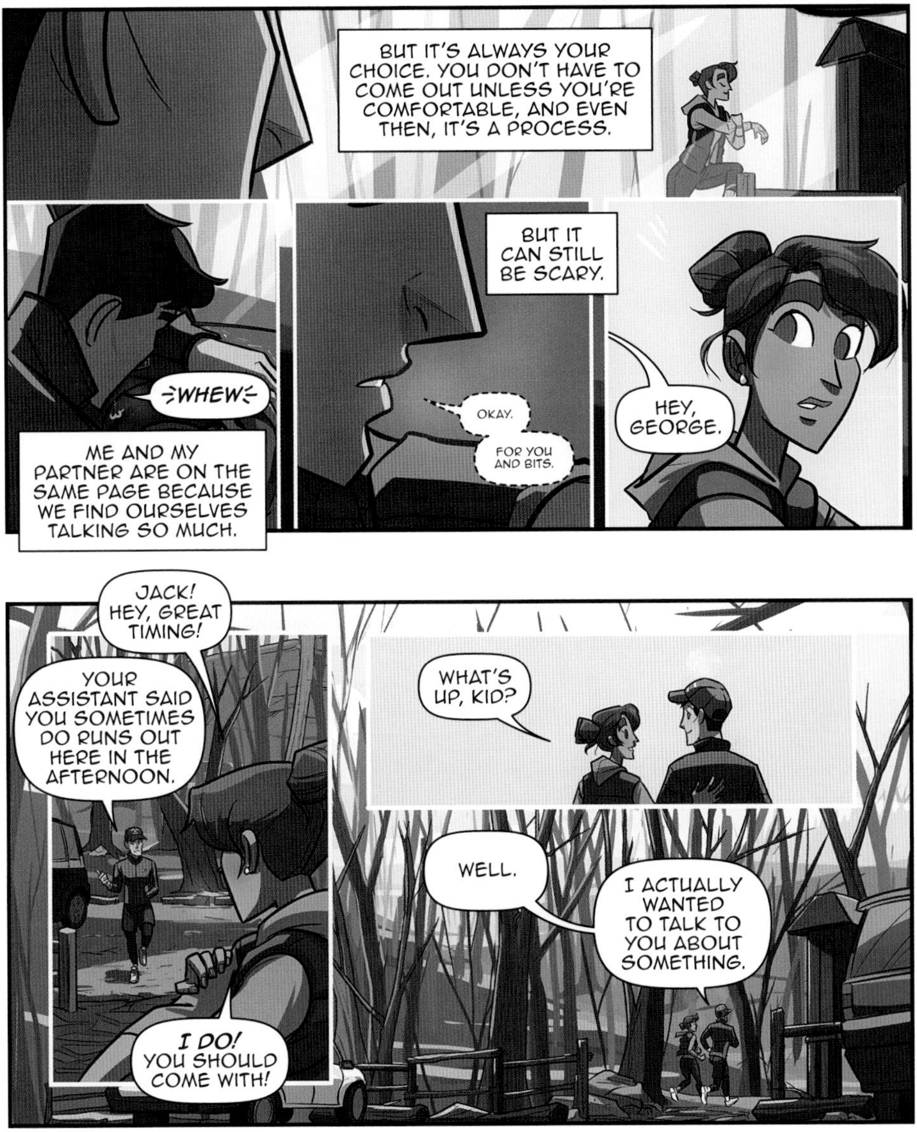
BUT IT'S ALWAYS YOUR CHOICE. YOU DON'T HAVE TO COME OUT UNLESS YOU'RE COMFORTABLE, AND EVEN THEN, IT'S A PROCESS.
WHEW
ME AND MY PARTNER ARE ON THE SAME PAGE BECAUSE WE FIND OURSELVES TALKING SO MUCH.
BUT IT CAN STILL BE SCARY.
OKAY.
FOR YOU AND BITS.
HEY, GEORGE.
JACK! HEY, GREAT TIMING!
YOUR ASSISTANT SAID YOU SOMETIMES DO RUNS OUT HERE IN THE AFTERNOON.
I DO! YOU SHOULD COME WITH!
WHAT'S UP, KID?
WELL.
I ACTUALLY WANTED TO TALK TO YOU ABOUT SOMETHING.

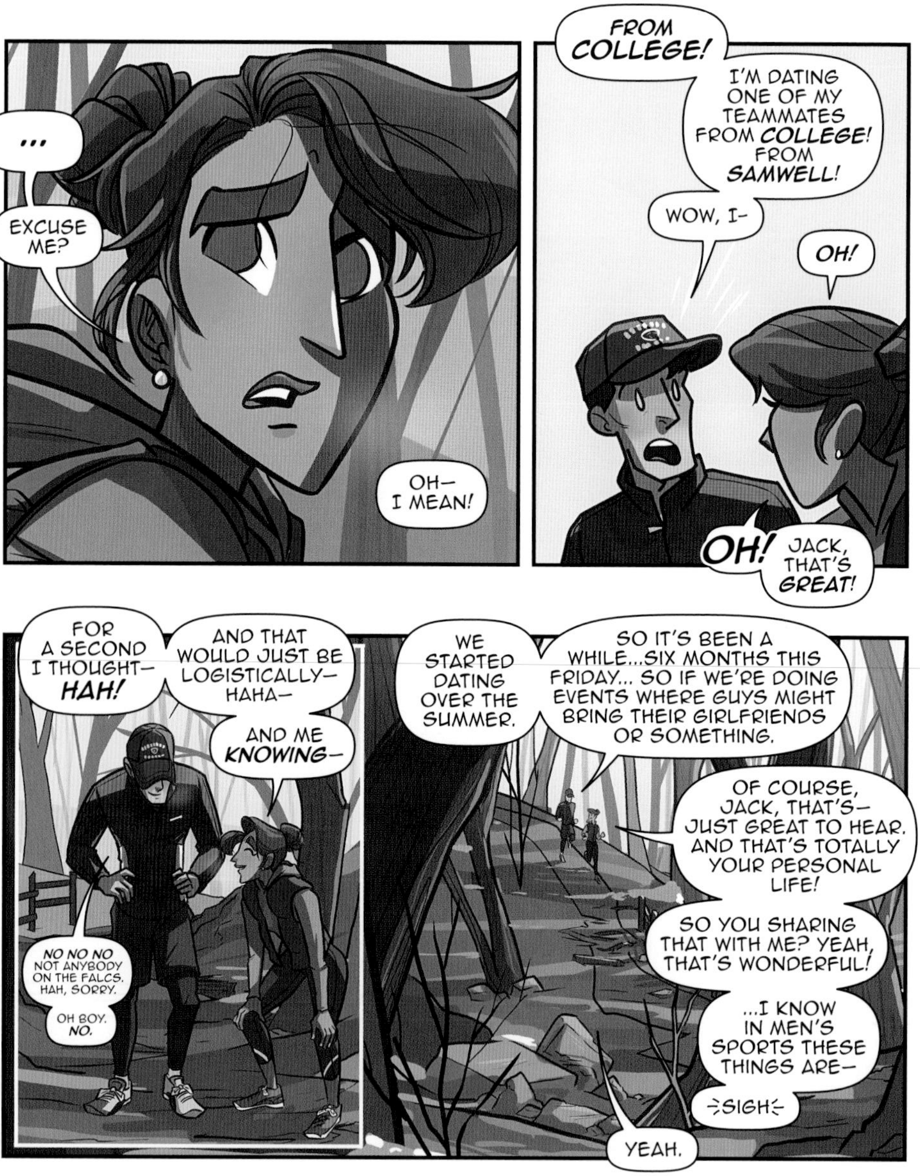
...
EXCUSE ME?
OH— I MEAN!
FROM COLLEGE!
I'M DATING ONE OF MY TEAMMATES FROM COLLEGE! FROM SAMWELL!
WOW, I-
OH!
OH!
JACK, THAT'S GREAT!
FOR A SECOND I THOUGHT— HAH!
AND THAT WOULD JUST BE LOGISTICALLY— HAHA—
AND ME KNOWING—
NO NO NO NOT ANYBODY ON THE FALCS. HAH, SORRY.
OH BOY. NO.
WE STARTED DATING OVER THE SUMMER.
SO IT'S BEEN A WHILE...SIX MONTHS THIS FRIDAY... SO IF WE'RE DOING EVENTS WHERE GUYS MIGHT BRING THEIR GIRLFRIENDS OR SOMETHING.
OF COURSE, JACK, THAT'S— JUST GREAT TO HEAR. AND THAT'S TOTALLY YOUR PERSONAL LIFE!
SO YOU SHARING THAT WITH ME? YEAH, THAT'S WONDERFUL!
...I KNOW IN MEN'S SPORTS THESE THINGS ARE—
-SIGH-
YEAH.

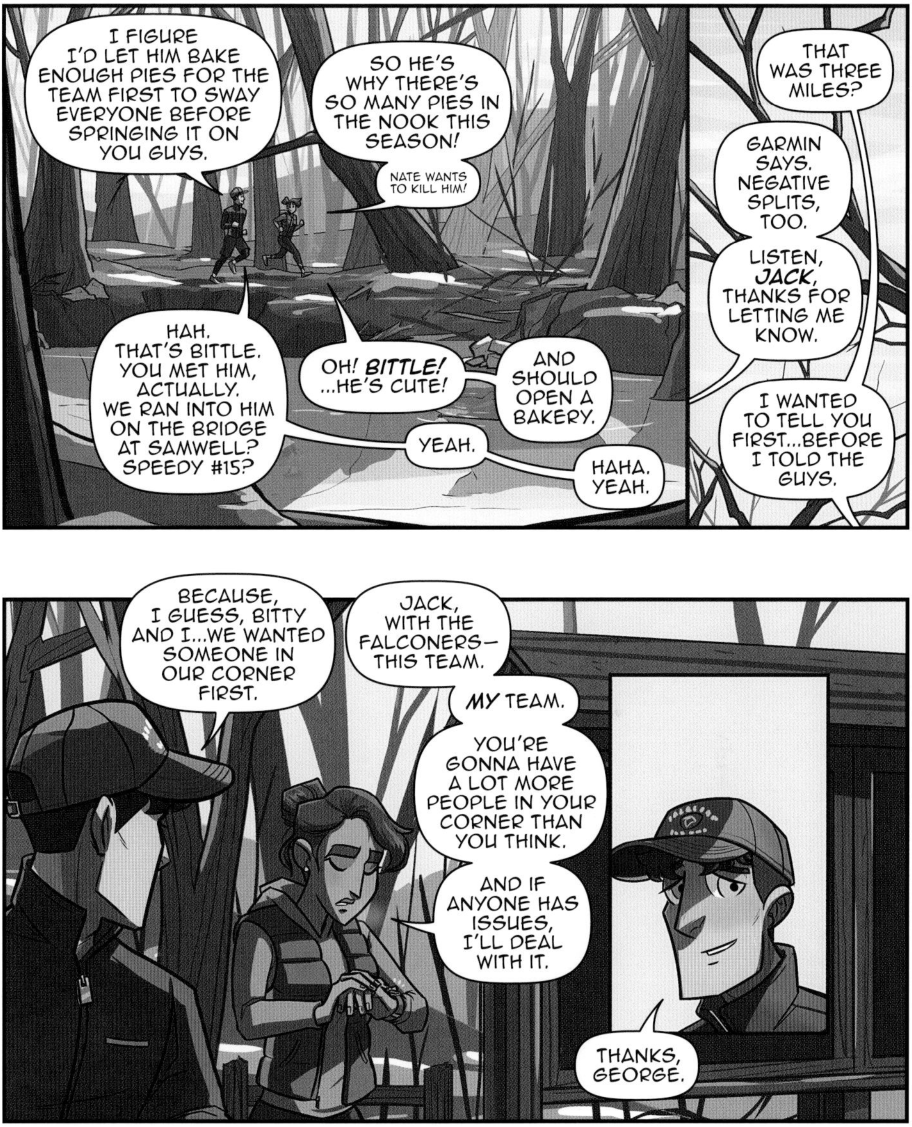
I FIGURE I'D LET HIM BAKE ENOUGH PIES FOR THE TEAM FIRST TO SWAY EVERYONE BEFORE SPRINGING IT ON YOU GUYS.
SO HE'S WHY THERE'S SO MANY PIES IN THE NOOK THIS SEASON!
NATE WANTS TO KILL HIM!
HAH. THAT'S BITTLE. YOU MET HIM, ACTUALLY. WE RAN INTO HIM ON THE BRIDGE AT SAMWELL? SPEEDY #15?
OH! BITTLE! ...HE'S CUTE!
AND SHOULD OPEN A BAKERY.
YEAH.
HAHA. YEAH.
THAT WAS THREE MILES?
GARMIN SAYS. NEGATIVE SPLITS, TOO.
LISTEN, JACK, THANKS FOR LETTING ME KNOW.
I WANTED TO TELL YOU FIRST...BEFORE I TOLD THE GUYS.
BECAUSE, I GUESS, BITTY AND I...WE WANTED SOMEONE IN OUR CORNER FIRST.
JACK, WITH THE FALCONERS—THIS TEAM.
MY TEAM.
YOU'RE GONNA HAVE A LOT MORE PEOPLE IN YOUR CORNER THAN YOU THINK.
AND IF ANYONE HAS ISSUES, I'LL DEAL WITH IT.
THANKS, GEORGE.

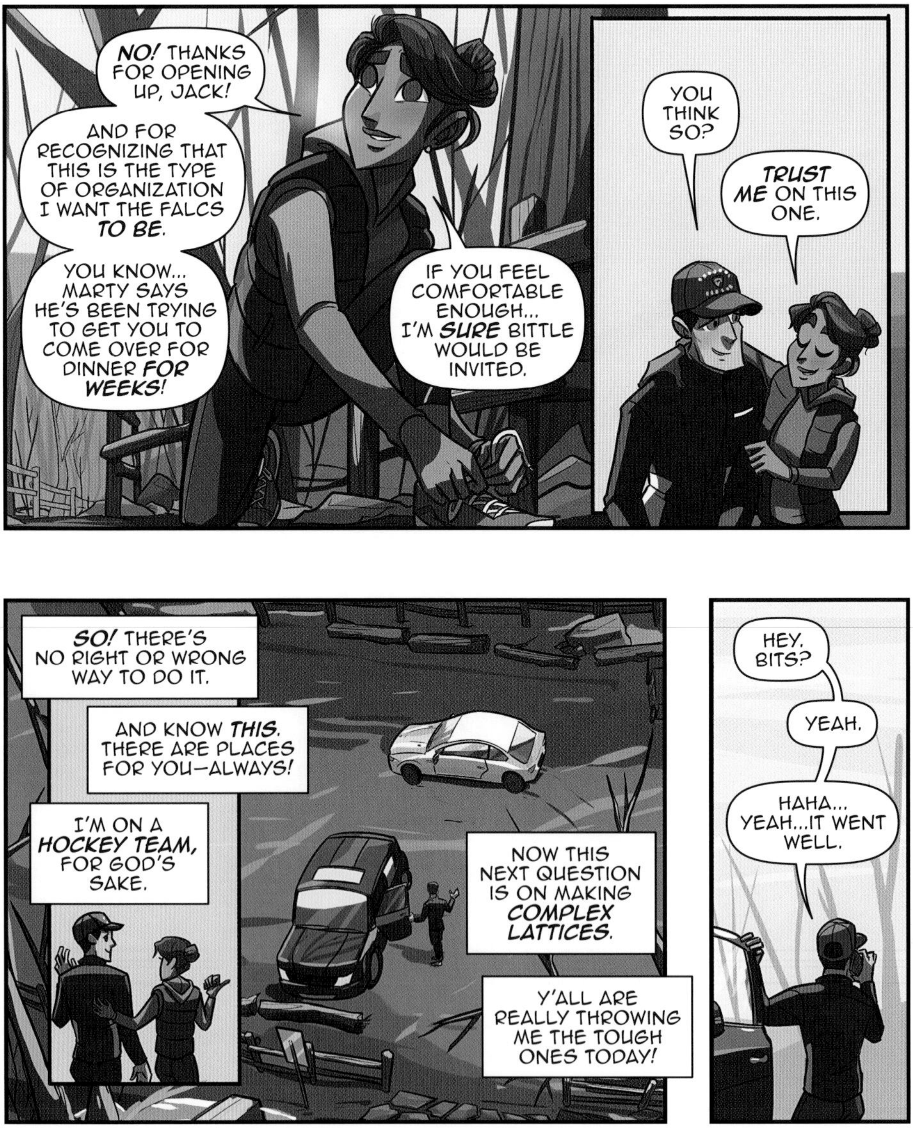
NO! THANKS FOR OPENING UP, JACK!
AND FOR RECOGNIZING THAT THIS IS THE TYPE OF ORGANIZATION I WANT THE FALCS TO BE.
YOU KNOW... MARTY SAYS HE'S BEEN TRYING TO GET YOU TO COME OVER FOR DINNER FOR WEEKS!
IF YOU FEEL COMFORTABLE ENOUGH... I'M SURE BITTLE WOULD BE INVITED.
YOU THINK SO?
TRUST ME ON THIS ONE.
SO! THERE'S NO RIGHT OR WRONG WAY TO DO IT.
AND KNOW THIS. THERE ARE PLACES FOR YOU—ALWAYS!
I'M ON A HOCKEY TEAM, FOR GOD'S SAKE.
NOW THIS NEXT QUESTION IS ON MAKING COMPLEX LATTICES.
Y'ALL ARE REALLY THROWING ME THE TOUGH ONES TODAY!
HEY. BITS?
YEAH.
HAHA... YEAH...IT WENT WELL.

15

DINNER AT MARTY'S?

WELL, I FIND OUT TODAY IF I'M HAVING DINNER WITH MY SIGNIFICANT OTHER'S COWORKER!
HE'S TRYING TO SET EVERYTHING UP. *HE'S* SO BUSY AND *I'M* SO BUSY—BUT IT'S NOT SO MUCH ABOUT FINDING A TIME...
15
TEXT FROM MAMA: Good luck on your game, dicky!! <3
TEXT FROM COACH: get em tonight jr
IT'S ABOUT MAKING THAT COMMITMENT.

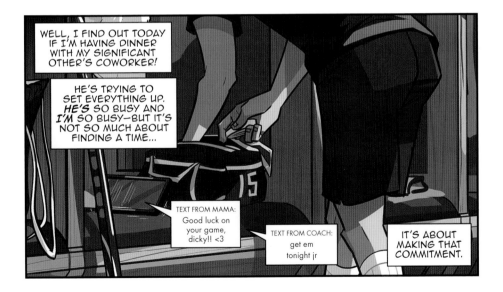

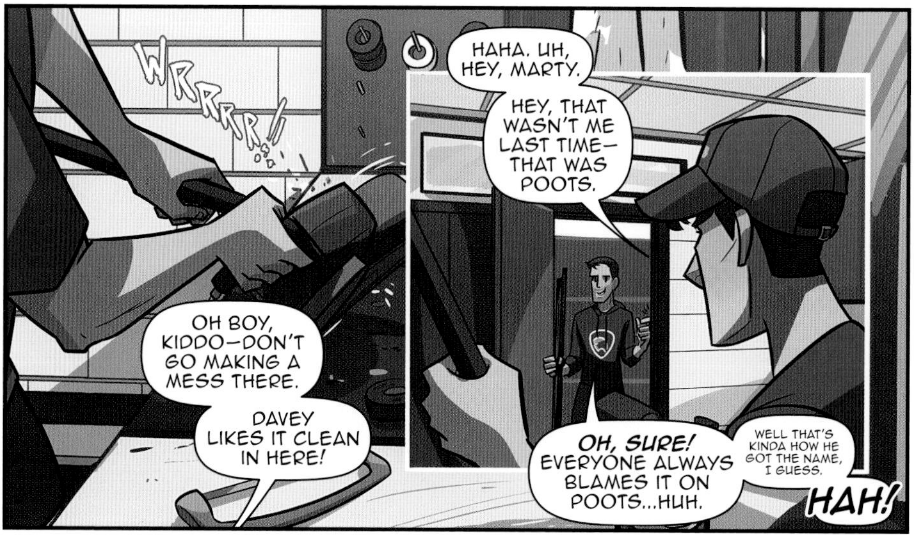
WRRRR!!
HAHA. UH, HEY, MARTY.
HEY, THAT WASN'T ME LAST TIME—THAT WAS POOTS.
OH BOY, KIDDO—DON'T GO MAKING A MESS THERE.
DAVEY LIKES IT CLEAN IN HERE!
OH, SURE! EVERYONE ALWAYS BLAMES IT ON POOTS...HUH.
WELL THAT'S KINDA HOW HE GOT THE NAME, I GUESS.
HAH!

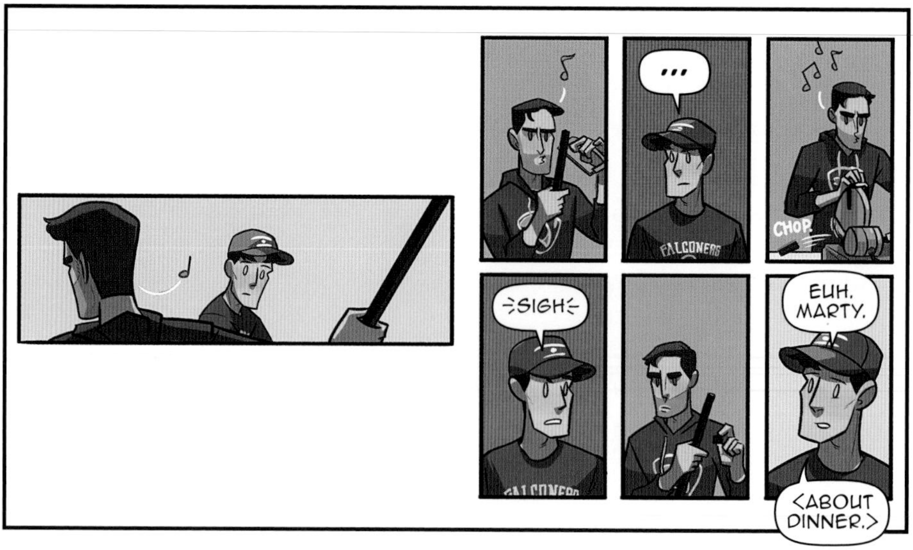
...
CHOP
⇉SIGH⇇
EUH. MARTY.
<ABOUT DINNER.>

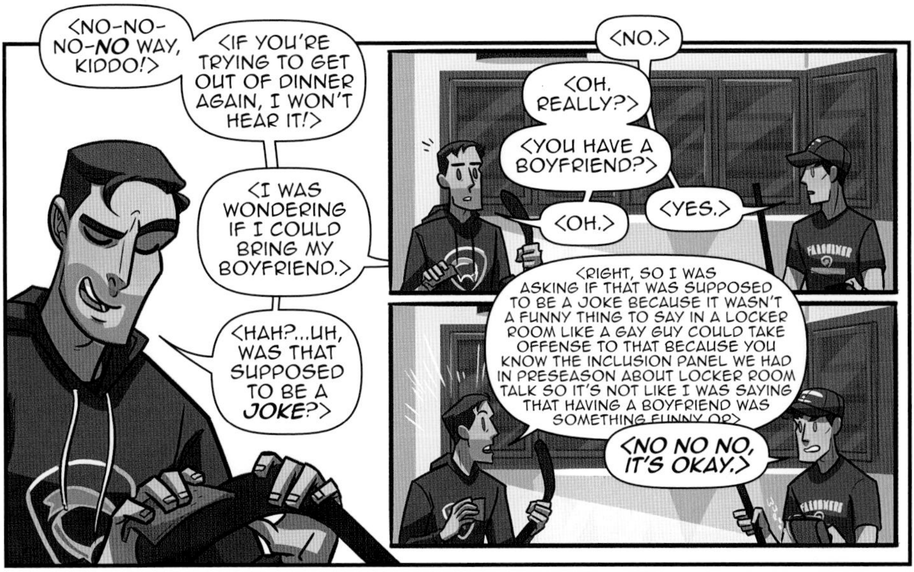
<NO-NO-NO-NO WAY, KIDDO!>
<IF YOU'RE TRYING TO GET OUT OF DINNER AGAIN, I WON'T HEAR IT!>
<I WAS WONDERING IF I COULD BRING MY BOYFRIEND.>
<HAH?...UH, WAS THAT SUPPOSED TO BE A JOKE?>
<NO.>
<OH. REALLY?>
<YOU HAVE A BOYFRIEND?>
<YES.>
<OH.>
<RIGHT, SO I WAS ASKING IF THAT WAS SUPPOSED TO BE A JOKE BECAUSE IT WASN'T A FUNNY THING TO SAY IN A LOCKER ROOM LIKE A GAY GUY COULD TAKE OFFENSE TO THAT BECAUSE YOU KNOW THE INCLUSION PANEL WE HAD IN PRESEASON ABOUT LOCKER ROOM TALK SO IT'S NOT LIKE I WAS SAYING THAT HAVING A BOYFRIEND WAS SOMETHING FUNNY OR>
<NO NO NO, IT'S OKAY.>

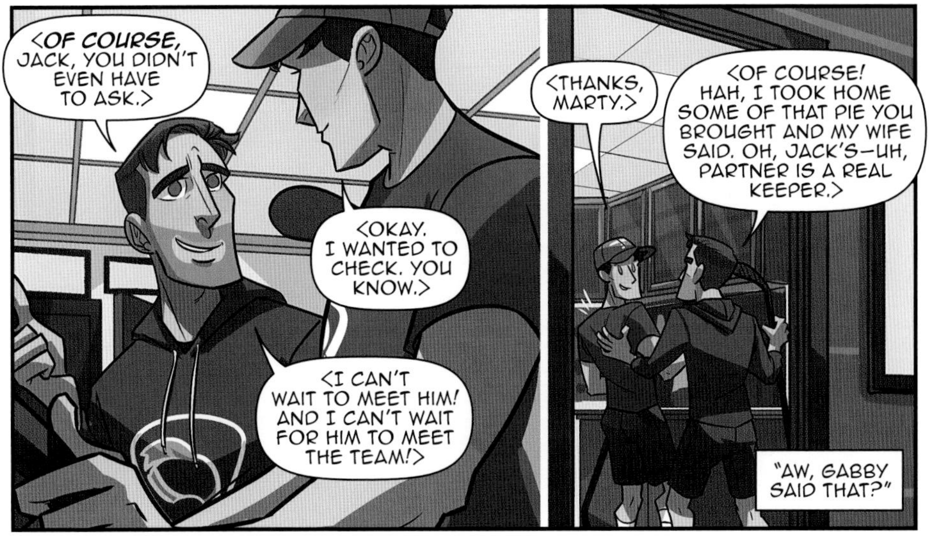
<OF COURSE, JACK, YOU DIDN'T EVEN HAVE TO ASK.>
<OKAY. I WANTED TO CHECK. YOU KNOW.>
<I CAN'T WAIT TO MEET HIM! AND I CAN'T WAIT FOR HIM TO MEET THE TEAM!>
<THANKS, MARTY.>
<OF COURSE! HAH, I TOOK HOME SOME OF THAT PIE YOU BROUGHT AND MY WIFE SAID. OH, JACK'S—UH, PARTNER IS A REAL KEEPER.>
"AW, GABBY SAID THAT?"

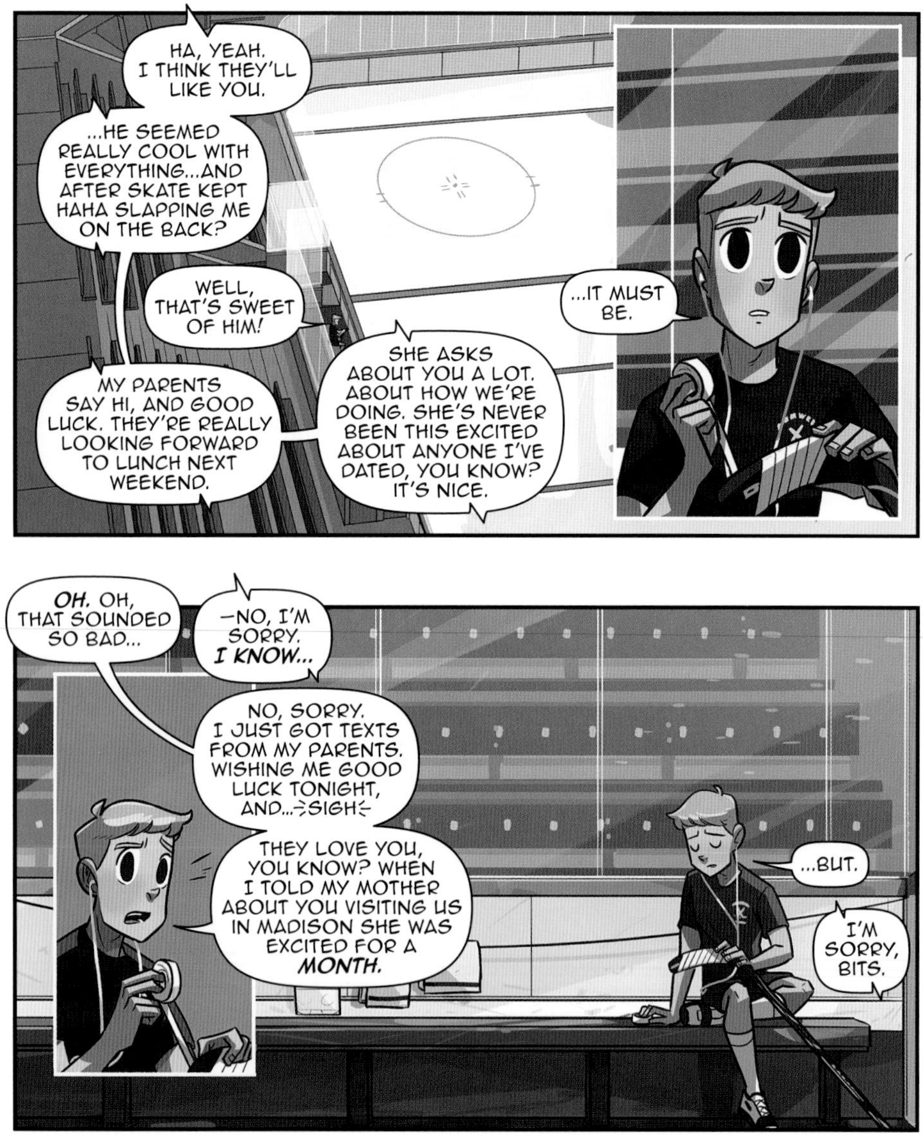
HA, YEAH. I THINK THEY'LL LIKE YOU.
...HE SEEMED REALLY COOL WITH EVERYTHING...AND AFTER SKATE KEPT HAHA SLAPPING ME ON THE BACK?
WELL, THAT'S SWEET OF HIM!
MY PARENTS SAY HI, AND GOOD LUCK. THEY'RE REALLY LOOKING FORWARD TO LUNCH NEXT WEEKEND.
SHE ASKS ABOUT YOU A LOT. ABOUT HOW WE'RE DOING. SHE'S NEVER BEEN THIS EXCITED ABOUT ANYONE I'VE DATED, YOU KNOW? IT'S NICE.
...IT MUST BE.
OH. OH, THAT SOUNDED SO BAD...
—NO, I'M SORRY. I KNOW...
NO, SORRY. I JUST GOT TEXTS FROM MY PARENTS. WISHING ME GOOD LUCK TONIGHT, AND...⇉SIGH⇇
THEY LOVE YOU, YOU KNOW? WHEN I TOLD MY MOTHER ABOUT YOU VISITING US IN MADISON SHE WAS EXCITED FOR A MONTH.
...BUT.
I'M SORRY, BITS.

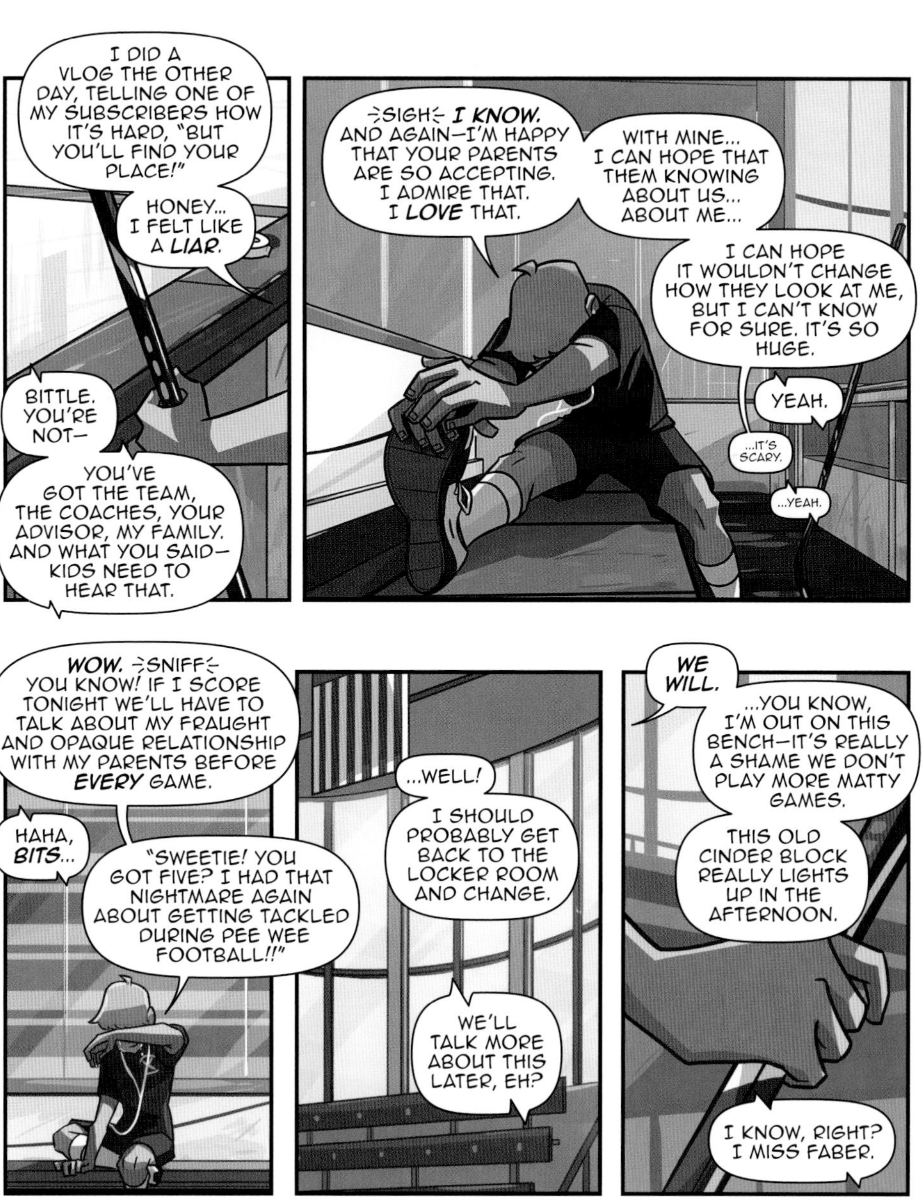
I DID A VLOG THE OTHER DAY, TELLING ONE OF MY SUBSCRIBERS HOW IT'S HARD, "BUT YOU'LL FIND YOUR PLACE!"
HONEY... I FELT LIKE A *LIAR*.
BITTLE. YOU'RE NOT–
YOU'VE GOT THE TEAM, THE COACHES, YOUR ADVISOR, MY FAMILY. AND WHAT YOU SAID– KIDS NEED TO HEAR THAT.
⇉SIGH⇇ *I KNOW.* AND AGAIN–I'M HAPPY THAT YOUR PARENTS ARE SO ACCEPTING. I ADMIRE THAT. I *LOVE* THAT.
WITH MINE... I CAN HOPE THAT THEM KNOWING ABOUT US... ABOUT ME...
I CAN HOPE IT WOULDN'T CHANGE HOW THEY LOOK AT ME, BUT I CAN'T KNOW FOR SURE. IT'S SO HUGE.
YEAH.
...IT'S SCARY.
...YEAH.
WOW. ⇉SNIFF⇇ YOU KNOW! IF I SCORE TONIGHT WE'LL HAVE TO TALK ABOUT MY FRAUGHT AND OPAQUE RELATIONSHIP WITH MY PARENTS BEFORE *EVERY* GAME.
HAHA, *BITS*...
"SWEETIE! YOU GOT FIVE? I HAD THAT NIGHTMARE AGAIN ABOUT GETTING TACKLED DURING PEE WEE FOOTBALL!!"
...WELL!
I SHOULD PROBABLY GET BACK TO THE LOCKER ROOM AND CHANGE.
WE'LL TALK MORE ABOUT THIS LATER, EH?
WE WILL.
...YOU KNOW, I'M OUT ON THIS BENCH–IT'S REALLY A SHAME WE DON'T PLAY MORE MATTY GAMES.
THIS OLD CINDER BLOCK REALLY LIGHTS UP IN THE AFTERNOON.
I KNOW, RIGHT? I MISS FABER.

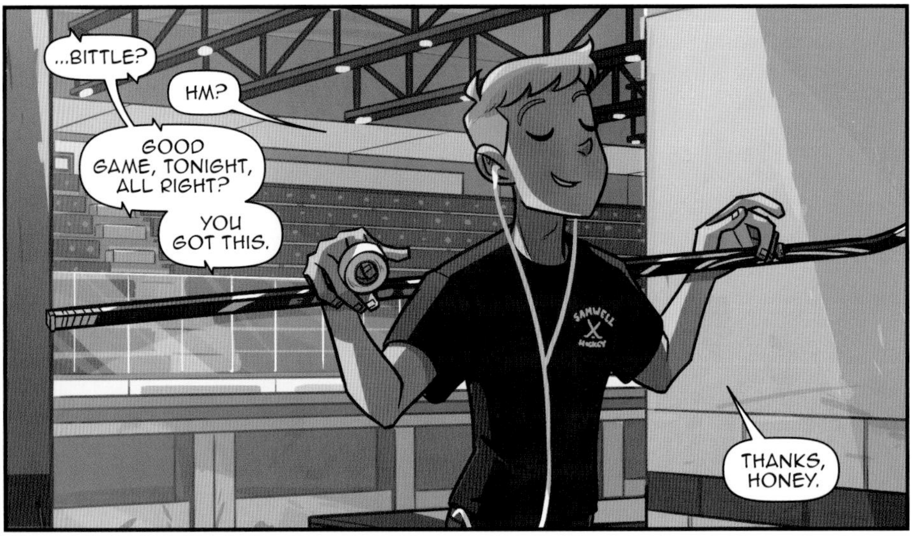
...BITTLE?
HM?
GOOD GAME, TONIGHT, ALL RIGHT?
YOU GOT THIS.
THANKS, HONEY.

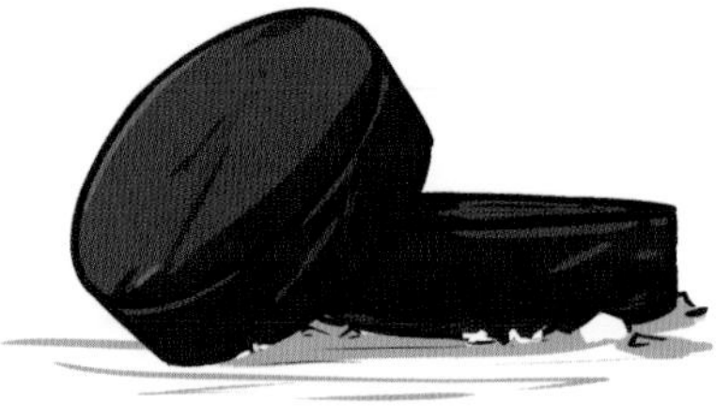

16

HELP WANTED

HEY, Y'ALL! IT FEELS LIKE WE JUST STARTED SPRING SEMESTER YESTERDAY, BUT BELIEVE IT OR NOT, OUR SENIORS ARE GEARING UP FOR GRADUATION AND LIFE AFTER SAMWELL.
THAT MEANS LARDO, RANSOM, AND HOLSTER ARE LOOKING FOR JOBS AND MAKING, ER, HASTY POST-BACCALAUREATE PLANS.
BUT LORD, LARDO! SHE WASN'T KIDDING WHEN SHE SAID SHE KEEPS THE BOYS RUNNING. AS I RECORD THIS VLOG, WE'RE ALL SCRAMBLING TO FIND HER REPLACEMENT.
WE'RE LOOKING FOR SOMEONE CRAZY ENOUGH TO MANAGE A BUNCH OF LOUD, RAUCOUS, PIE-EATING HOCKEY PLAYERS.
Y'ALL, WE'VE GOT A REPUTATION ON THIS CAMPUS.
SAMWELL

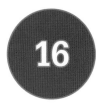

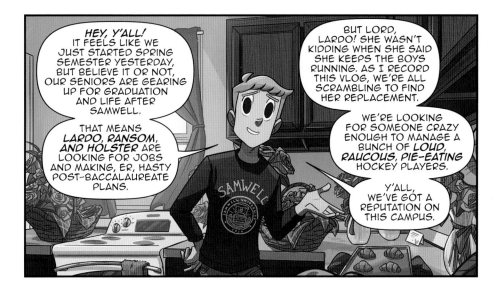

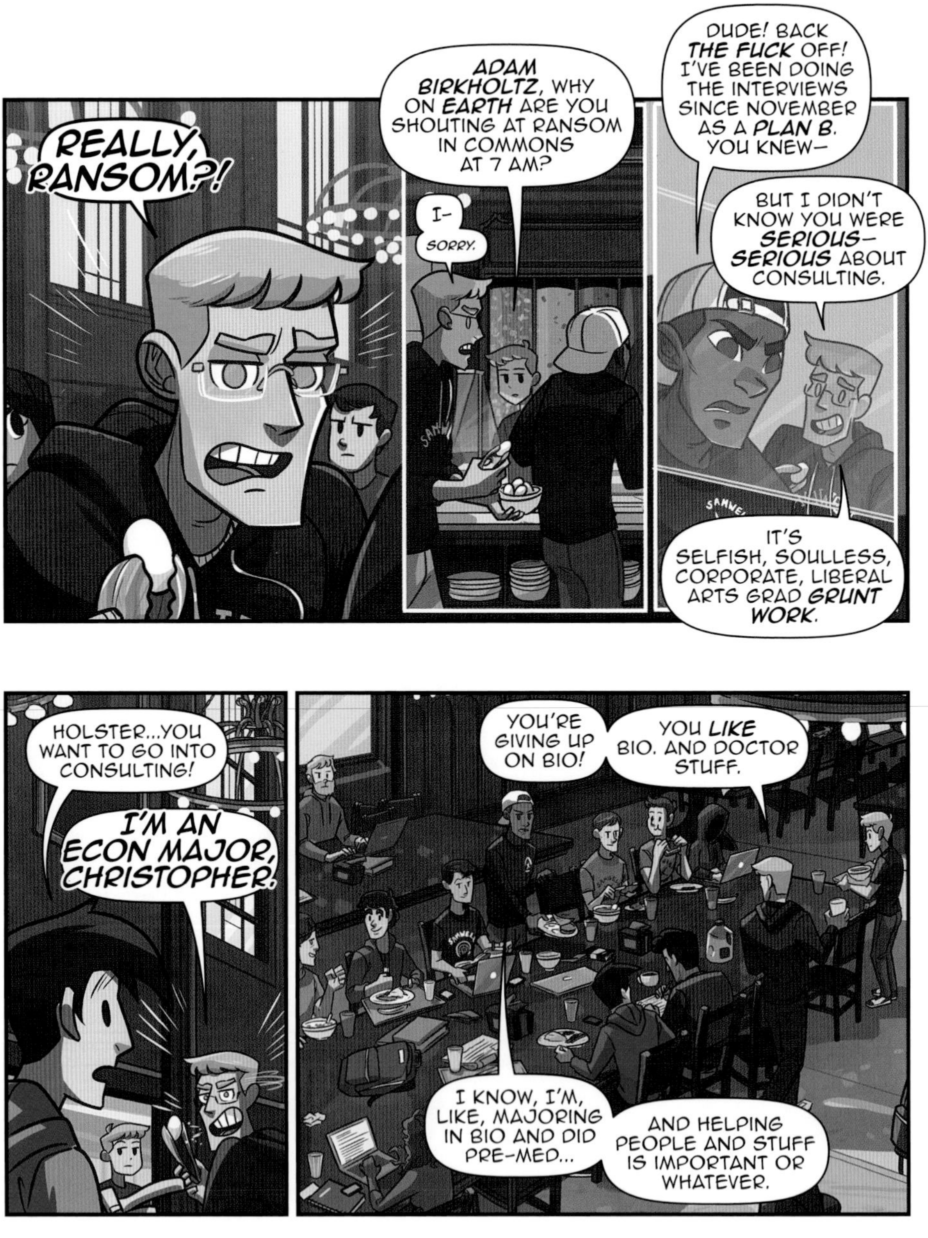
REALLY, RANSOM?!
ADAM BIRKHOLTZ, WHY ON EARTH ARE YOU SHOUTING AT RANSOM IN COMMONS AT 7 AM?
I-
SORRY.
DUDE! BACK THE FUCK OFF! I'VE BEEN DOING THE INTERVIEWS SINCE NOVEMBER AS A PLAN B. YOU KNEW—
BUT I DIDN'T KNOW YOU WERE SERIOUS-SERIOUS ABOUT CONSULTING.
IT'S SELFISH, SOULLESS, CORPORATE, LIBERAL ARTS GRAD GRUNT WORK.
HOLSTER...YOU WANT TO GO INTO CONSULTING!
I'M AN ECON MAJOR, CHRISTOPHER.
YOU'RE GIVING UP ON BIO!
YOU LIKE BIO. AND DOCTOR STUFF.
I KNOW, I'M, LIKE, MAJORING IN BIO AND DID PRE-MED...
AND HELPING PEOPLE AND STUFF IS IMPORTANT OR WHATEVER.

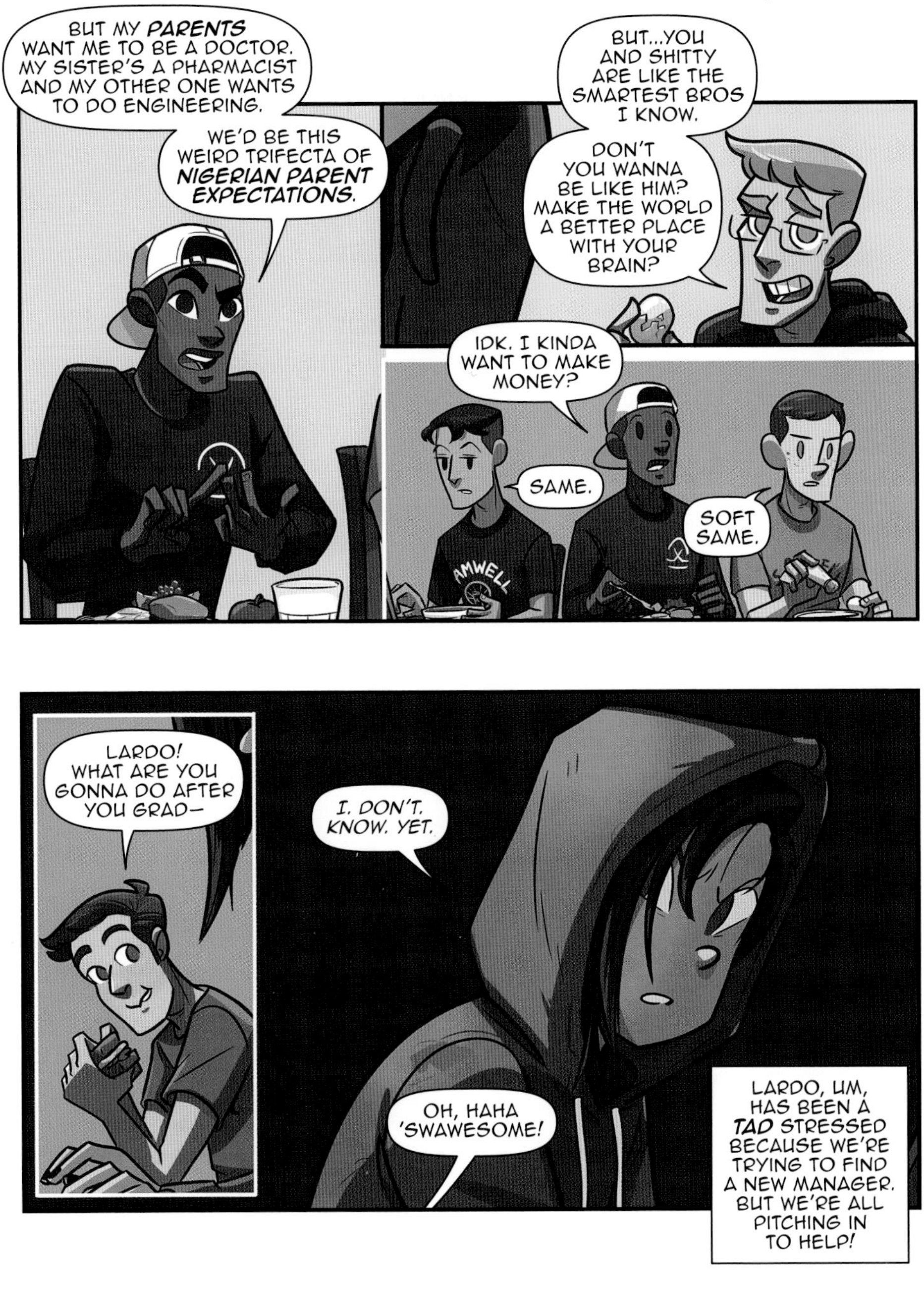
BUT MY *PARENTS* WANT ME TO BE A DOCTOR. MY SISTER'S A PHARMACIST AND MY OTHER ONE WANTS TO DO ENGINEERING.
WE'D BE THIS WEIRD TRIFECTA OF ***NIGERIAN PARENT EXPECTATIONS***.
BUT...YOU AND SHITTY ARE LIKE THE SMARTEST BROS I KNOW.
DON'T YOU WANNA BE LIKE HIM? MAKE THE WORLD A BETTER PLACE WITH YOUR BRAIN?
IDK. I KINDA WANT TO MAKE MONEY?
SAME.
SOFT SAME.
AMWELL
LARDO! WHAT ARE YOU GONNA DO AFTER YOU GRAD—
I. DON'T. KNOW. YET.
OH, HAHA 'SWAWESOME!
LARDO, UM, HAS BEEN A ***TAD*** STRESSED BECAUSE WE'RE TRYING TO FIND A NEW MANAGER. BUT WE'RE ALL PITCHING IN TO HELP!

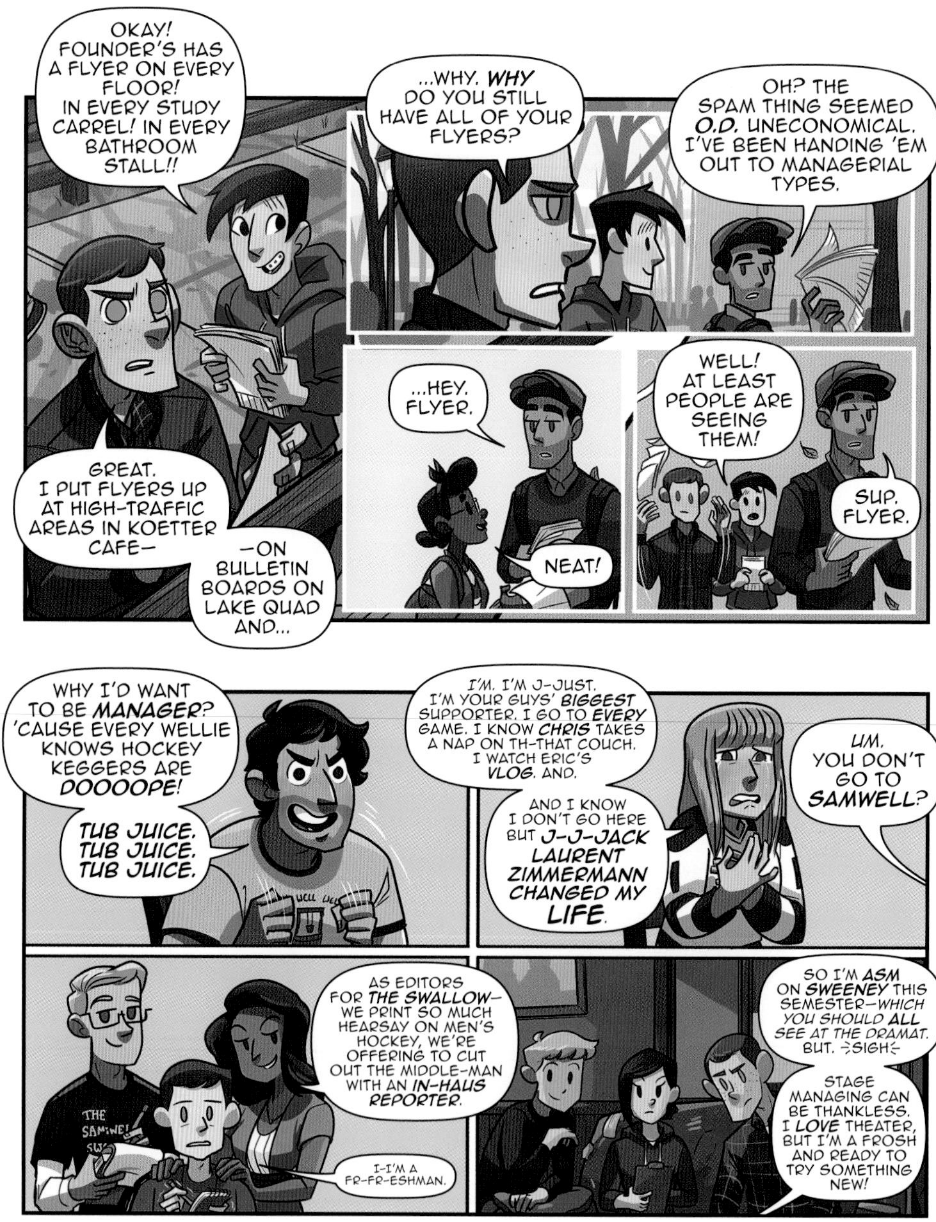
OKAY! FOUNDER'S HAS A FLYER ON EVERY FLOOR! IN EVERY STUDY CARREL! IN EVERY BATHROOM STALL!!
GREAT. I PUT FLYERS UP AT HIGH-TRAFFIC AREAS IN KOETTER CAFE—
—ON BULLETIN BOARDS ON LAKE QUAD AND...
...WHY. WHY DO YOU STILL HAVE ALL OF YOUR FLYERS?
OH? THE SPAM THING SEEMED O.D. UNECONOMICAL. I'VE BEEN HANDING 'EM OUT TO MANAGERIAL TYPES.
...HEY. FLYER.
NEAT!
WELL! AT LEAST PEOPLE ARE SEEING THEM!
SUP. FLYER.
WHY I'D WANT TO BE MANAGER? 'CAUSE EVERY WELLIE KNOWS HOCKEY KEGGERS ARE DOOOOPE!
TUB JUICE. TUB JUICE. TUB JUICE.
I'M. I'M J-JUST. I'M YOUR GUYS' BIGGEST SUPPORTER. I GO TO EVERY GAME. I KNOW CHRIS TAKES A NAP ON TH-THAT COUCH. I WATCH ERIC'S VLOG. AND.
AND I KNOW I DON'T GO HERE BUT J-J-JACK LAURENT ZIMMERMANN CHANGED MY LIFE.
UM. YOU DON'T GO TO SAMWELL?
AS EDITORS FOR THE SWALLOW— WE PRINT SO MUCH HEARSAY ON MEN'S HOCKEY, WE'RE OFFERING TO CUT OUT THE MIDDLE-MAN WITH AN IN-HAUS REPORTER.
I-I'M A FR-FR-ESHMAN.
SO I'M ASM ON SWEENEY THIS SEMESTER—WHICH YOU SHOULD ALL SEE AT THE DRAMAT. BUT. ⪡SIGH⪢
STAGE MANAGING CAN BE THANKLESS. I LOVE THEATER, BUT I'M A FROSH AND READY TO TRY SOMETHING NEW!

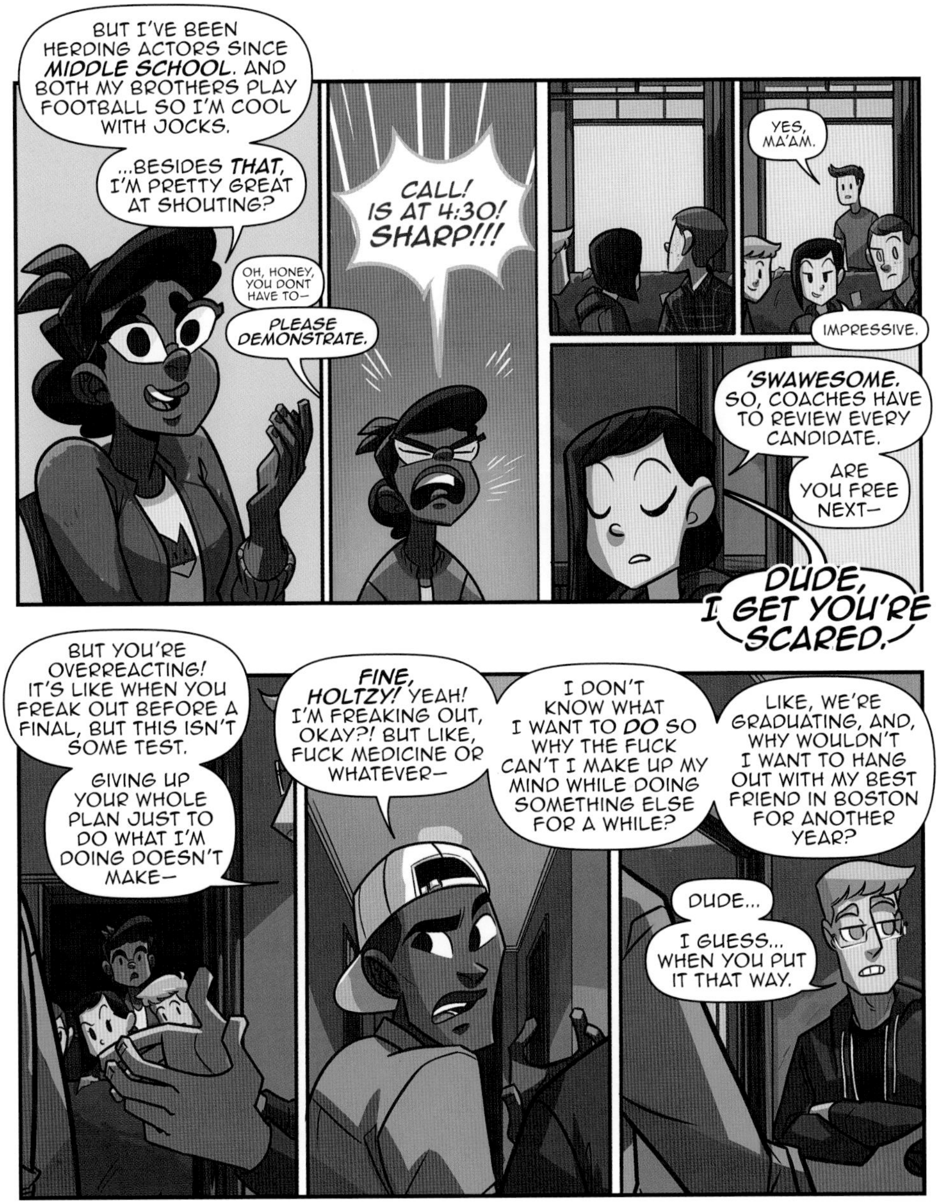
BUT I'VE BEEN HERDING ACTORS SINCE MIDDLE SCHOOL. AND BOTH MY BROTHERS PLAY FOOTBALL SO I'M COOL WITH JOCKS.
...BESIDES THAT, I'M PRETTY GREAT AT SHOUTING?
OH, HONEY, YOU DONT HAVE TO—
PLEASE DEMONSTRATE.
CALL! IS AT 4:30! SHARP!!!
YES, MA'AM.
IMPRESSIVE.
'SWAWESOME. SO, COACHES HAVE TO REVIEW EVERY CANDIDATE.
ARE YOU FREE NEXT—
DUDE, I GET YOU'RE SCARED.
BUT YOU'RE OVERREACTING! IT'S LIKE WHEN YOU FREAK OUT BEFORE A FINAL, BUT THIS ISN'T SOME TEST.
GIVING UP YOUR WHOLE PLAN JUST TO DO WHAT I'M DOING DOESN'T MAKE—
FINE, HOLTZY! YEAH! I'M FREAKING OUT, OKAY?! BUT LIKE, FUCK MEDICINE OR WHATEVER—
I DON'T KNOW WHAT I WANT TO DO SO WHY THE FUCK CAN'T I MAKE UP MY MIND WHILE DOING SOMETHING ELSE FOR A WHILE?
LIKE, WE'RE GRADUATING, AND, WHY WOULDN'T I WANT TO HANG OUT WITH MY BEST FRIEND IN BOSTON FOR ANOTHER YEAR?
DUDE...
I GUESS... WHEN YOU PUT IT THAT WAY.

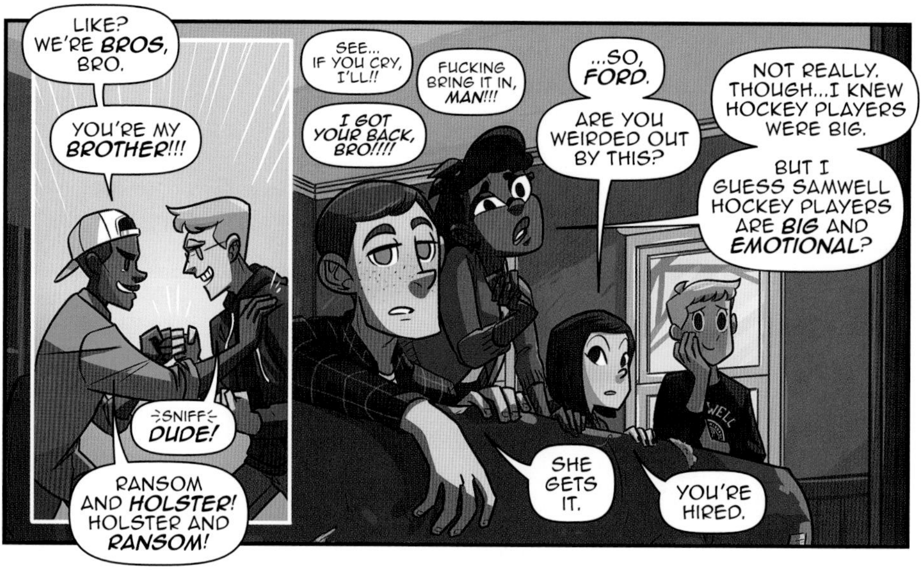
LIKE? WE'RE BROS, BRO.
YOU'RE MY BROTHER!!!
SNIFF DUDE!
RANSOM AND HOLSTER! HOLSTER AND RANSOM!
SEE... IF YOU CRY, I'LL!!
FUCKING BRING IT IN, MAN!!!
I GOT YOUR BACK, BRO!!!!
...SO, FORD.
ARE YOU WEIRDED OUT BY THIS?
NOT REALLY. THOUGH...I KNEW HOCKEY PLAYERS WERE BIG.
BUT I GUESS SAMWELL HOCKEY PLAYERS ARE BIG AND EMOTIONAL?
SHE GETS IT.
YOU'RE HIRED.

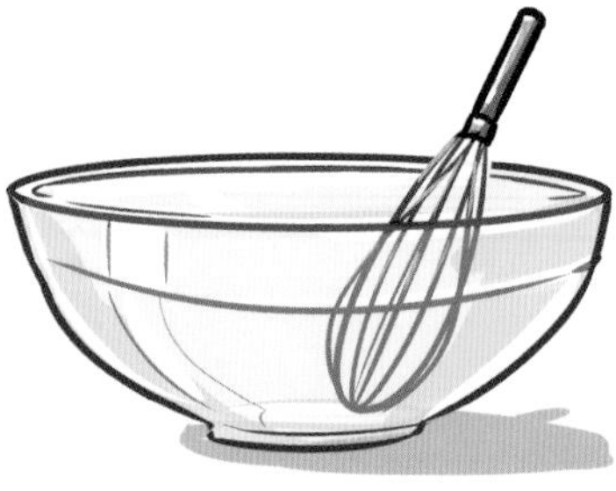

17

DIB FLIP

NOW, MOST OF Y'ALL WHO WERE CLAMORING FOR THIS JAM TUTORIAL SAID YOU WERE NEW, **SO**.
I'M GONNA SHOW YOU HOW MY AUNT JUDY STERILIZES JARS FIRST, WHICH TAKES A BIT MORE TIME BUT IS FAIL PROOF.
BUT FIRST. WE GOTTA GO OVER THE DIFFERENCE BETWEEN JAM, JELLY, MARMALADE, AND PRESERVES
WHAT?!
SIGH
DEAR LORD, HOW'S A BOY SUPPOSED TO MAKE **PRESERVES** IN THIS **GOD**FORSAKEN—

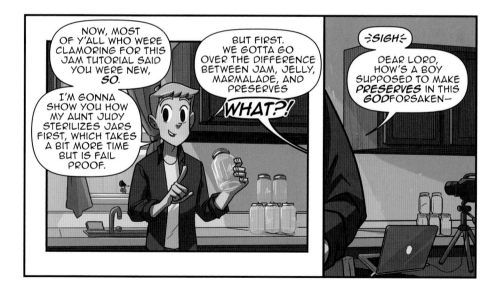

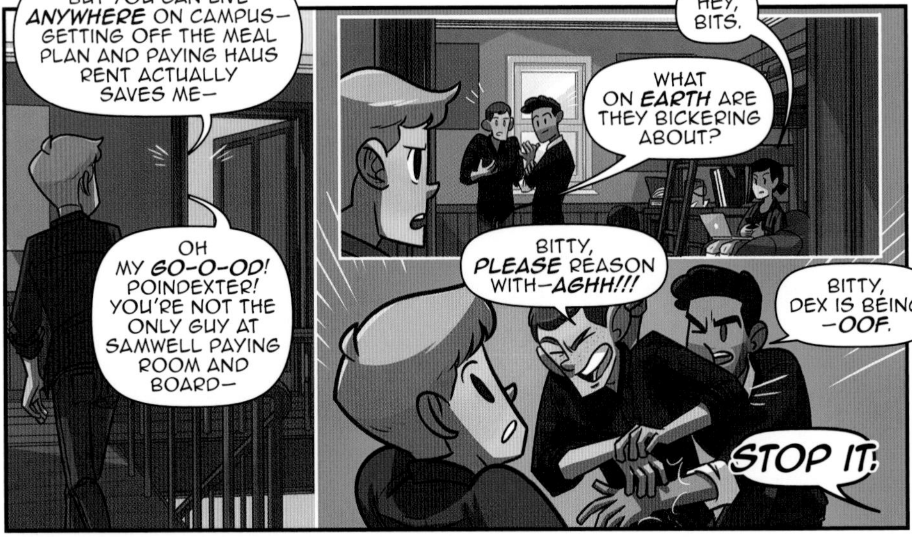
YEAH, BUT YOU CAN LIVE *ANYWHERE* ON CAMPUS— GETTING OFF THE MEAL PLAN AND PAYING HAUS RENT ACTUALLY SAVES ME—
OH MY *GO-O-OD*! POINDEXTER! YOU'RE NOT THE ONLY GUY AT SAMWELL PAYING ROOM AND BOARD—
HEY, BITS.
WHAT ON *EARTH* ARE THEY BICKERING ABOUT?
BITTY, *PLEASE* REASON WITH—*AGHH!!!*
BITTY, DEX IS BEING —*OOF*.
STOP IT.

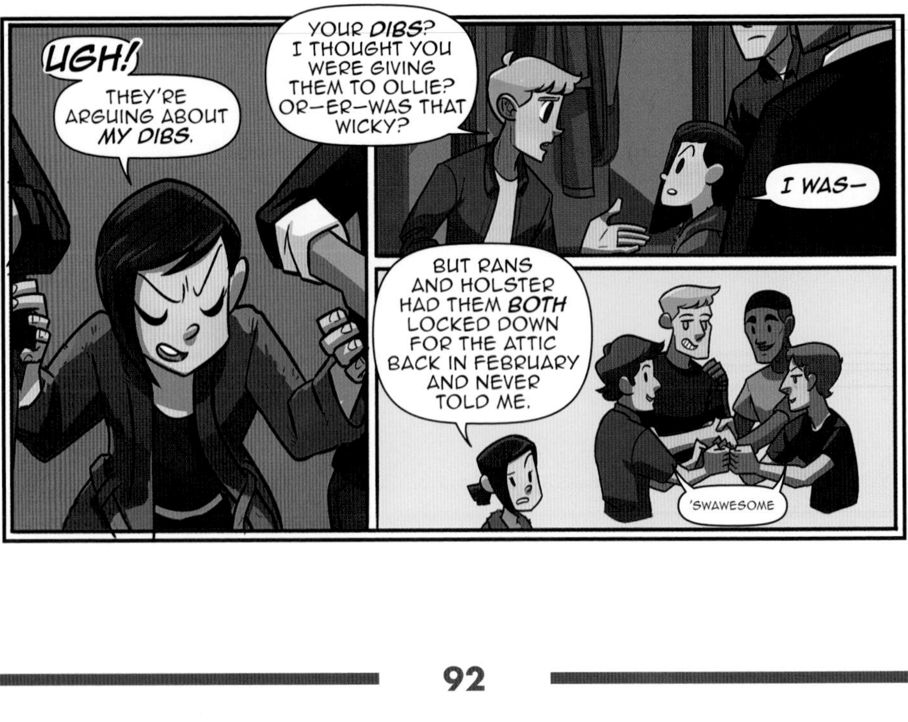
UGH!
THEY'RE ARGUING ABOUT *MY DIBS*.
YOUR *DIBS*? I THOUGHT YOU WERE GIVING THEM TO OLLIE? OR—ER—WAS THAT WICKY?
I WAS—
BUT RANS AND HOLSTER HAD THEM *BOTH* LOCKED DOWN FOR THE ATTIC BACK IN FEBRUARY AND NEVER TOLD ME.
'SWAWESOME

THESE TWO *DUMMIES* FOUND OUT FROM OLLIE THIS MORNING. AND IF THEY DON'T SHUT UP I'M GIVING MY ROOM TO *TANGO.*

IT'S NOT THAT YOU DON'T DESERVE DIBS, DEX—BUT I WAS BANKING ON YOU GETTING THE AT—

YOU WERE *BANKING*?!

ENOUGH. FULL TEAM LOTTERY. ONLY FAIR.

SORRY, BUT *HOW* DOES NURSEY DESERVE DIBS?

DEX. I KNOW YOU FIXED A TON OF STUFF IN THE HAUS THIS YEAR. BUT NURSEY PROOFREAD EVERY ART CRITICISM RESPONSE I TURNED IN THIS SEMESTER.

HE PRACTICALLY WROTE MY SENIOR THESIS.

AND HE GETS A WEIRD KICK OUT OF FIXING BIBLIOGRAPHIES.

THAT LAST PART'S FAKE.

LADY AND GENTLEMEN.

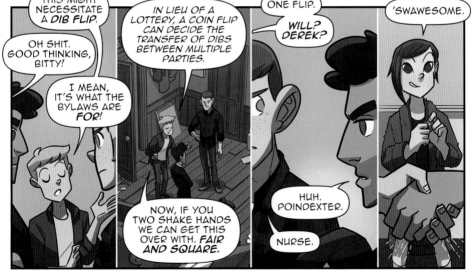

THIS MIGHT NECESSITATE A *DIB FLIP.*

OH SHIT. GOOD THINKING, BITTY!

I MEAN, IT'S WHAT THE BYLAWS ARE *FOR!*

IN LIEU OF A LOTTERY, A COIN FLIP CAN DECIDE THE TRANSFER OF DIBS BETWEEN MULTIPLE PARTIES.

NOW, IF YOU TWO SHAKE HANDS WE CAN GET THIS OVER WITH. *FAIR AND SQUARE.*

ONE FLIP.

WILL? DEREK?

HUH. POINDEXTER.

NURSE.

'SWAWESOME.

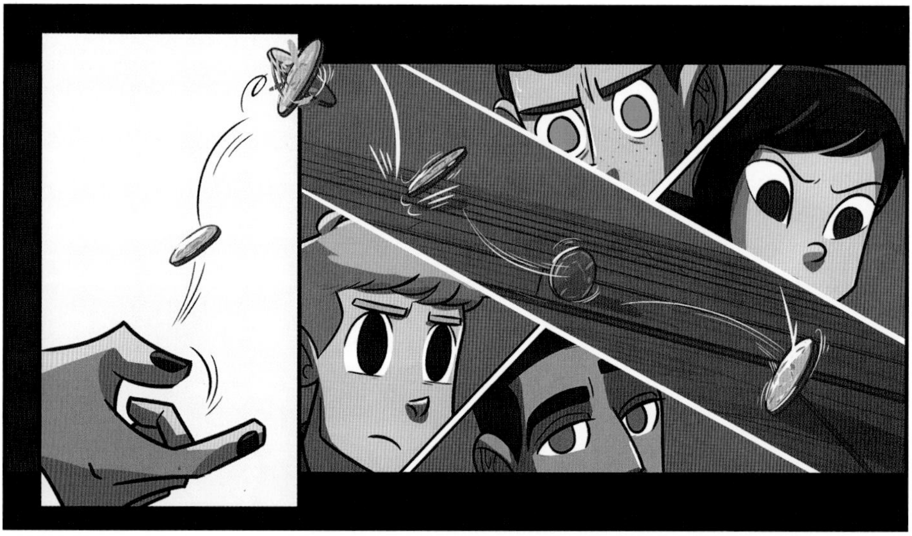

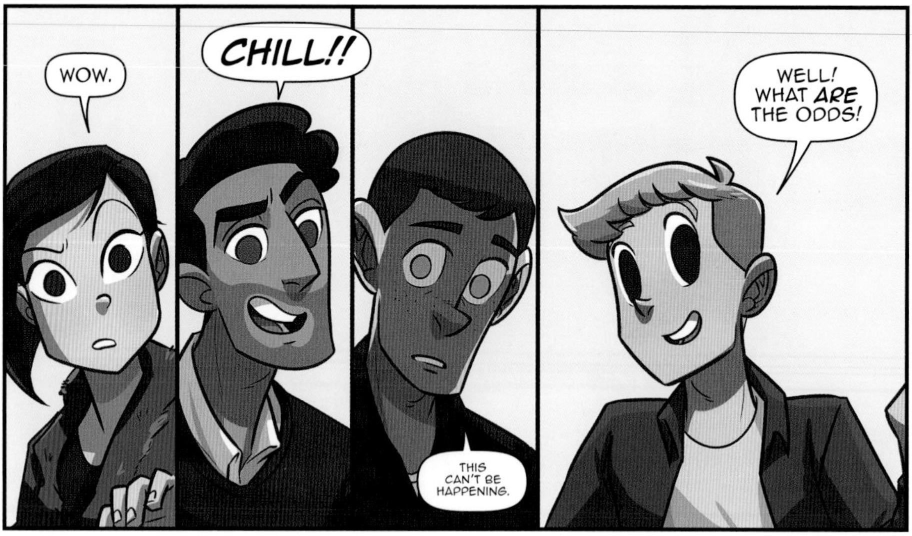
WOW.
CHILL!!
THIS CAN'T BE HAPPENING.
WELL! WHAT **ARE** THE ODDS!

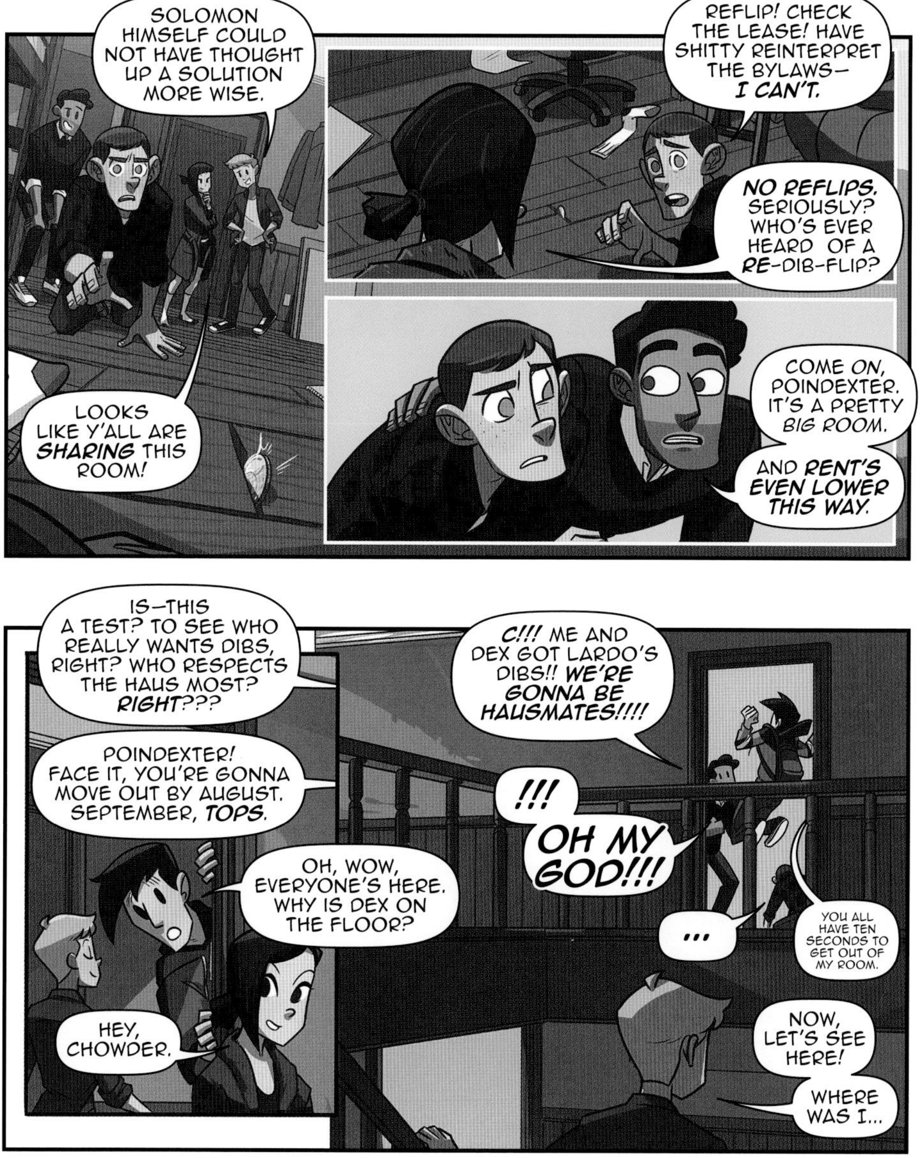
SOLOMON HIMSELF COULD NOT HAVE THOUGHT UP A SOLUTION MORE WISE.
LOOKS LIKE Y'ALL ARE SHARING THIS ROOM!
REFLIP! CHECK THE LEASE! HAVE SHITTY REINTERPRET THE BYLAWS— I CAN'T.
NO REFLIPS. SERIOUSLY? WHO'S EVER HEARD OF A RE-DIB-FLIP?
COME ON, POINDEXTER. IT'S A PRETTY BIG ROOM.
AND RENT'S EVEN LOWER THIS WAY.
IS—THIS A TEST? TO SEE WHO REALLY WANTS DIBS, RIGHT? WHO RESPECTS THE HAUS MOST? RIGHT???
POINDEXTER! FACE IT, YOU'RE GONNA MOVE OUT BY AUGUST. SEPTEMBER, TOPS.
OH, WOW, EVERYONE'S HERE. WHY IS DEX ON THE FLOOR?
HEY, CHOWDER.
C!!! ME AND DEX GOT LARDO'S DIBS!! WE'RE GONNA BE HAUSMATES!!!!
!!!
OH MY GOD!!!
...
YOU ALL HAVE TEN SECONDS TO GET OUT OF MY ROOM.
NOW, LET'S SEE HERE!
WHERE WAS I...

18

FAMILY SKATE

HEY, Y'ALL!! IF I SEEM A LITTLE JITTERY IT'S BECAUSE TONIGHT? I'M MEETING A BUNCH OF MY BOYFRIEND'S COWORKERS.

AND THEY'RE ALL NICE AND WONDERFUL, AND HE'S TALKED ABOUT ME BEFORE. *BUT...*

UH. SO THIS NEXT VIDEO IS GONNA BE ON CHOOSING A FOUR-PIE COMBO THAT WILL WIN STRANGERS OVER AND MAKE THEM NOT HATE YOU!

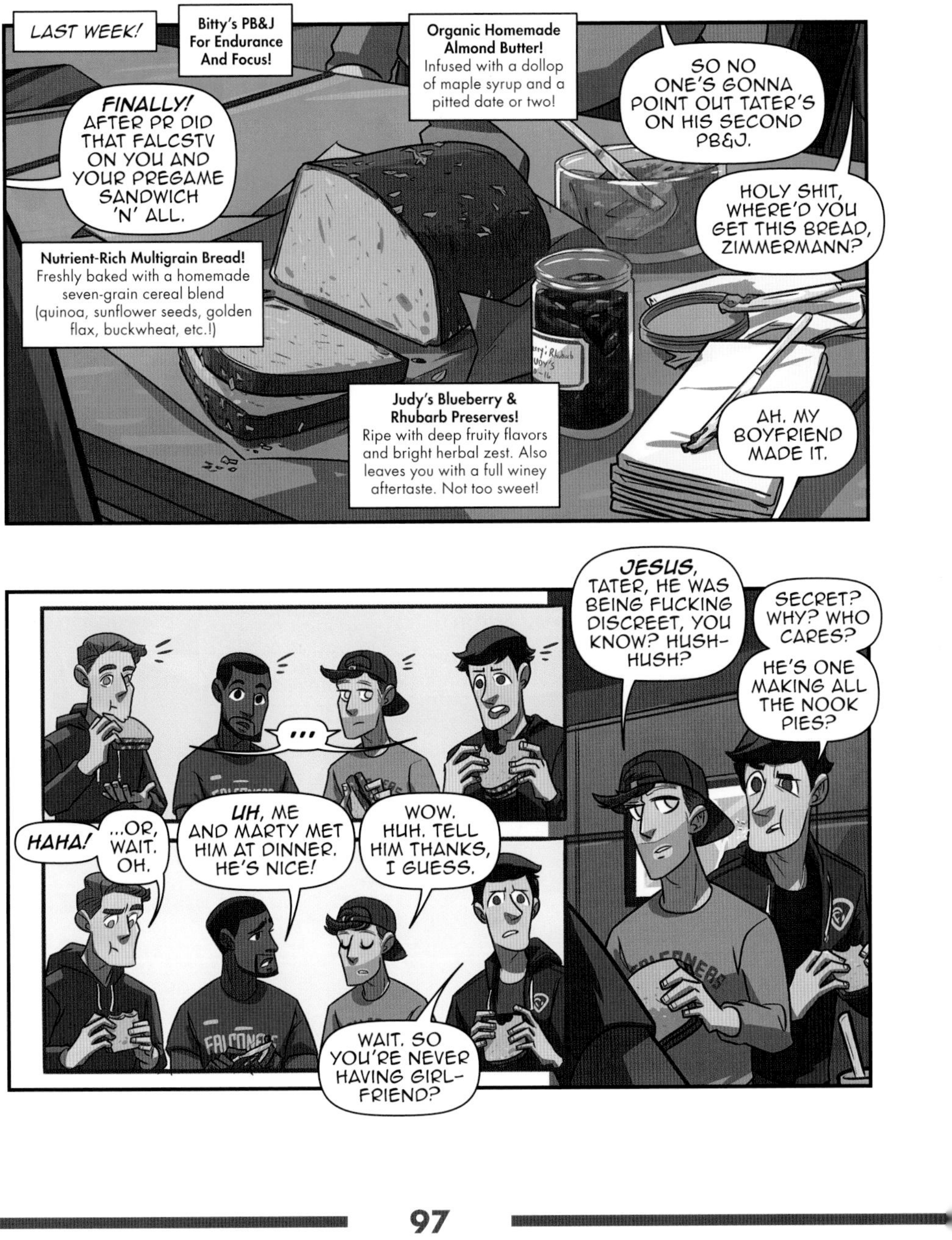
LAST WEEK!
Bitty's PB&J For Endurance And Focus!
FINALLY! AFTER PR DID THAT FALCSTV ON YOU AND YOUR PREGAME SANDWICH 'N' ALL.
Organic Homemade Almond Butter! Infused with a dollop of maple syrup and a pitted date or two!
SO NO ONE'S GONNA POINT OUT TATER'S ON HIS SECOND PB&J.
HOLY SHIT, WHERE'D YOU GET THIS BREAD, ZIMMERMANN?
Nutrient-Rich Multigrain Bread! Freshly baked with a homemade seven-grain cereal blend (quinoa, sunflower seeds, golden flax, buckwheat, etc.!)
Judy's Blueberry & Rhubarb Preserves! Ripe with deep fruity flavors and bright herbal zest. Also leaves you with a full winey aftertaste. Not too sweet!
AH. MY BOYFRIEND MADE IT.
...
HAHA!
...OR, WAIT. OH.
UH, ME AND MARTY MET HIM AT DINNER. HE'S NICE!
WOW. HUH. TELL HIM THANKS, I GUESS.
WAIT. SO YOU'RE NEVER HAVING GIRL-FRIEND?
JESUS, TATER, HE WAS BEING FUCKING DISCREET, YOU KNOW? HUSH-HUSH?
SECRET? WHY? WHO CARES?
HE'S ONE MAKING ALL THE NOOK PIES?

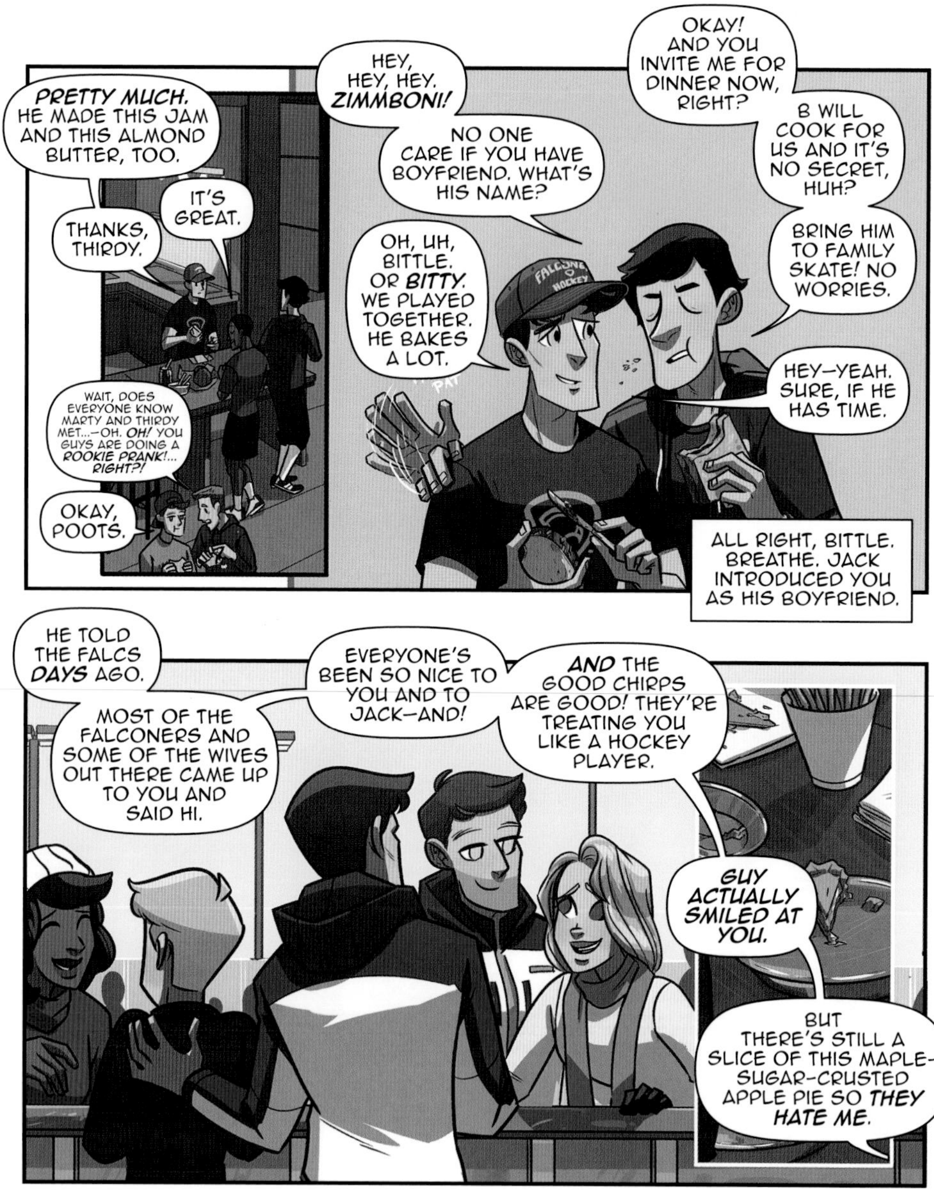
PRETTY MUCH. HE MADE THIS JAM AND THIS ALMOND BUTTER, TOO.
THANKS, THIRDY.
IT'S GREAT.
WAIT, DOES EVERYONE KNOW MARTY AND THIRDY MET...—OH. OH! YOU GUYS ARE DOING A ROOKIE PRANK!... RIGHT?!
OKAY, POOTS.
HEY, HEY, HEY. ZIMMBONI!
NO ONE CARE IF YOU HAVE BOYFRIEND. WHAT'S HIS NAME?
OH, UH, BITTLE. OR BITTY. WE PLAYED TOGETHER. HE BAKES A LOT.
PAT
OKAY! AND YOU INVITE ME FOR DINNER NOW, RIGHT?
B WILL COOK FOR US AND IT'S NO SECRET, HUH?
BRING HIM TO FAMILY SKATE! NO WORRIES.
HEY—YEAH. SURE, IF HE HAS TIME.
ALL RIGHT, BITTLE. BREATHE. JACK INTRODUCED YOU AS HIS BOYFRIEND.
HE TOLD THE FALCS DAYS AGO.
MOST OF THE FALCONERS AND SOME OF THE WIVES OUT THERE CAME UP TO YOU AND SAID HI.
EVERYONE'S BEEN SO NICE TO YOU AND TO JACK—AND!
AND THE GOOD CHIRPS ARE GOOD! THEY'RE TREATING YOU LIKE A HOCKEY PLAYER.
GUY ACTUALLY SMILED AT YOU.
BUT THERE'S STILL A SLICE OF THIS MAPLE-SUGAR-CRUSTED APPLE PIE SO THEY HATE ME.

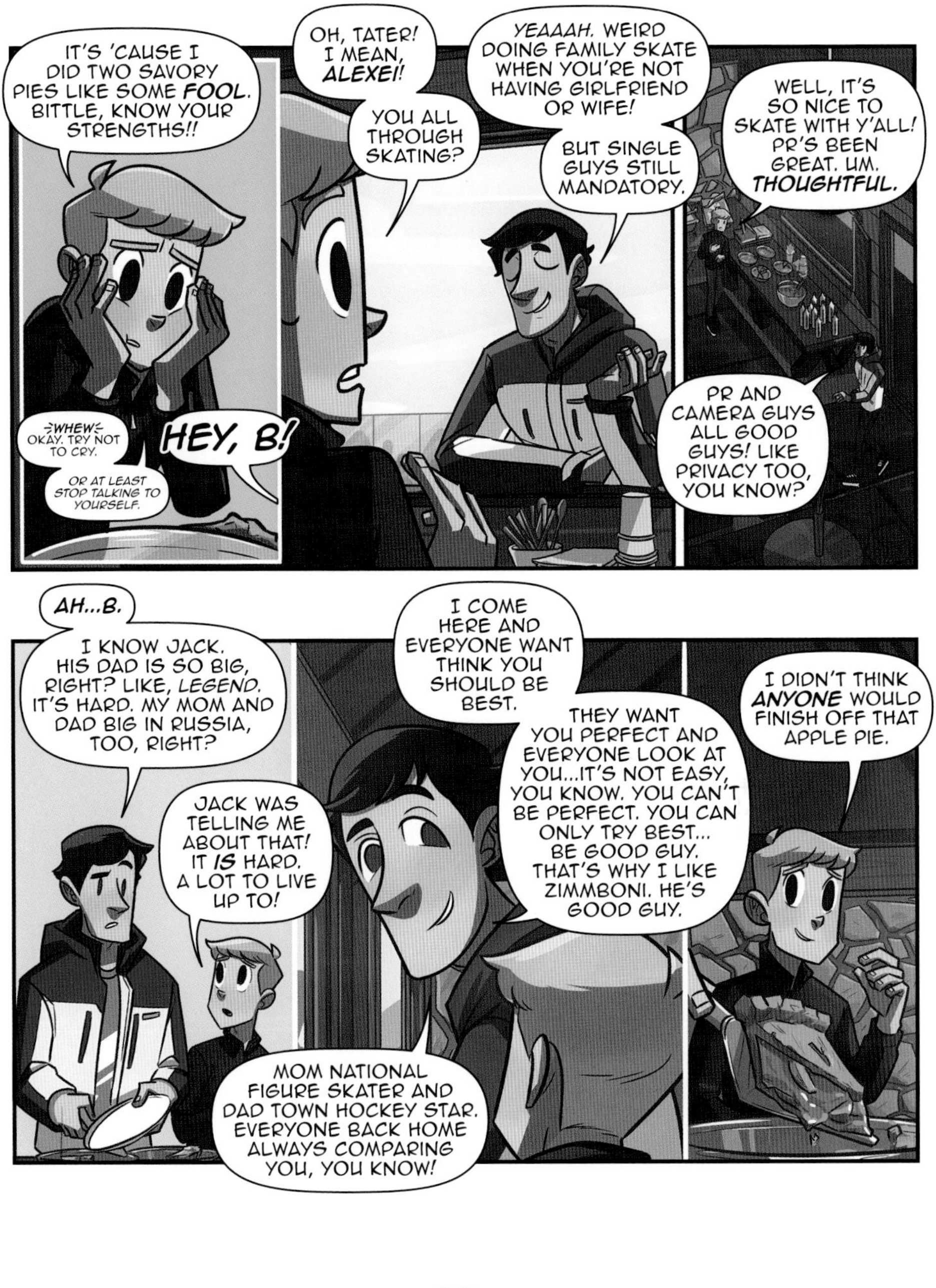
IT'S 'CAUSE I DID TWO SAVORY PIES LIKE SOME FOOL. BITTLE, KNOW YOUR STRENGTHS!!
WHEW OKAY. TRY NOT TO CRY.
OR AT LEAST STOP TALKING TO YOURSELF.
HEY, B!
OH, TATER! I MEAN, ALEXEI!
YOU ALL THROUGH SKATING?
YEAAAH. WEIRD DOING FAMILY SKATE WHEN YOU'RE NOT HAVING GIRLFRIEND OR WIFE!
BUT SINGLE GUYS STILL MANDATORY.
WELL, IT'S SO NICE TO SKATE WITH Y'ALL! PR'S BEEN GREAT. UM. THOUGHTFUL.
PR AND CAMERA GUYS ALL GOOD GUYS! LIKE PRIVACY TOO, YOU KNOW?
AH...B.
I KNOW JACK. HIS DAD IS SO BIG, RIGHT? LIKE, LEGEND. IT'S HARD. MY MOM AND DAD BIG IN RUSSIA, TOO, RIGHT?
JACK WAS TELLING ME ABOUT THAT! IT IS HARD. A LOT TO LIVE UP TO!
MOM NATIONAL FIGURE SKATER AND DAD TOWN HOCKEY STAR. EVERYONE BACK HOME ALWAYS COMPARING YOU, YOU KNOW!
I COME HERE AND EVERYONE WANT THINK YOU SHOULD BE BEST.
THEY WANT YOU PERFECT AND EVERYONE LOOK AT YOU...IT'S NOT EASY, YOU KNOW. YOU CAN'T BE PERFECT. YOU CAN ONLY TRY BEST... BE GOOD GUY. THAT'S WHY I LIKE ZIMMBONI. HE'S GOOD GUY.
I DIDN'T THINK ANYONE WOULD FINISH OFF THAT APPLE PIE.

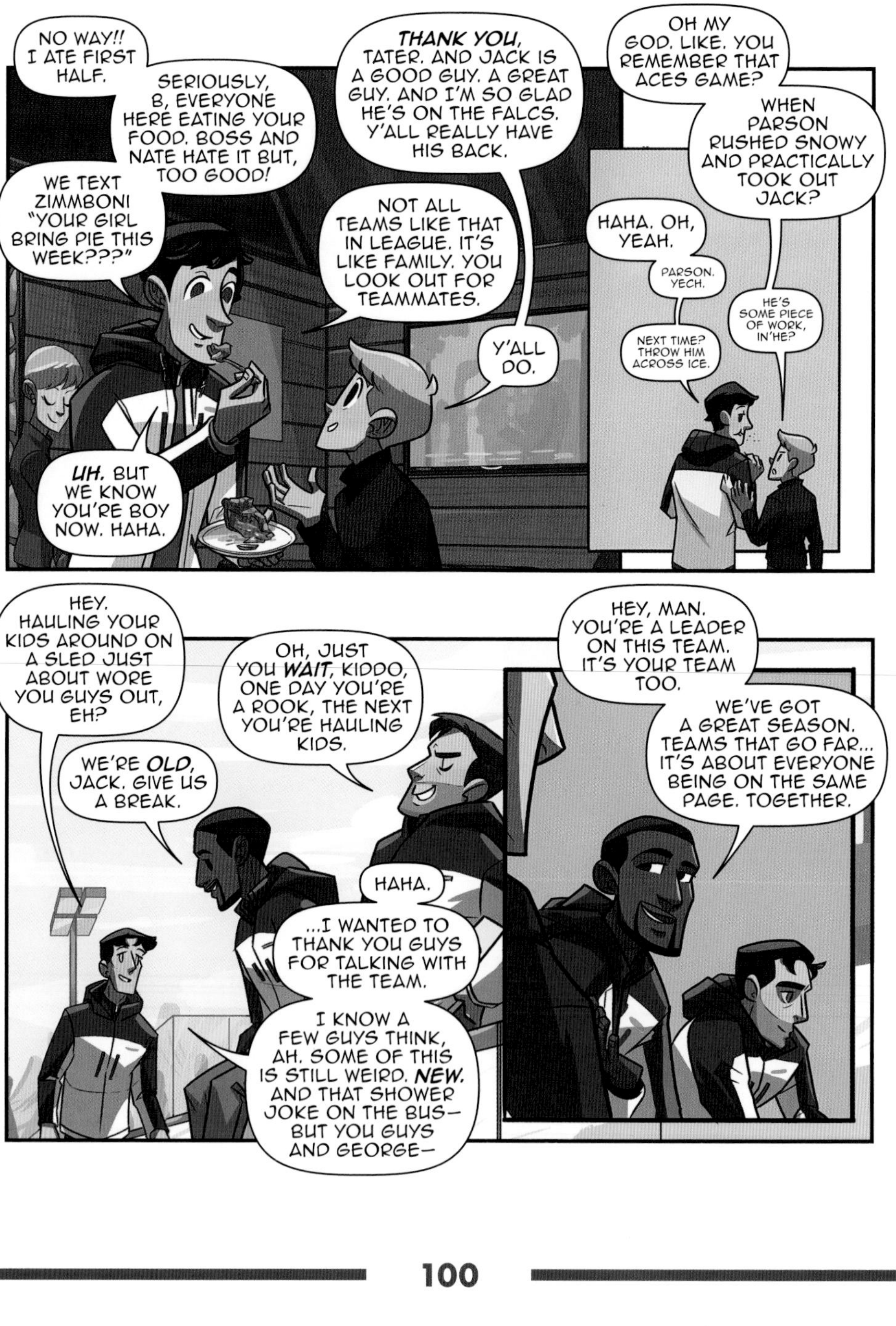
NO WAY!! I ATE FIRST HALF.
SERIOUSLY, B, EVERYONE HERE EATING YOUR FOOD. BOSS AND NATE HATE IT BUT, TOO GOOD!
WE TEXT ZIMMBONI "YOUR GIRL BRING PIE THIS WEEK???"
UH. BUT WE KNOW YOU'RE BOY NOW. HAHA.
THANK YOU, TATER. AND JACK IS A GOOD GUY. A GREAT GUY. AND I'M SO GLAD HE'S ON THE FALCS. Y'ALL REALLY HAVE HIS BACK.
NOT ALL TEAMS LIKE THAT IN LEAGUE. IT'S LIKE FAMILY. YOU LOOK OUT FOR TEAMMATES.
Y'ALL DO.
OH MY GOD. LIKE. YOU REMEMBER THAT ACES GAME?
WHEN PARSON RUSHED SNOWY AND PRACTICALLY TOOK OUT JACK?
HAHA. OH, YEAH.
PARSON. YECH.
NEXT TIME? THROW HIM ACROSS ICE.
HE'S SOME PIECE OF WORK, IN'HE?
HEY. HAULING YOUR KIDS AROUND ON A SLED JUST ABOUT WORE YOU GUYS OUT, EH?
WE'RE OLD, JACK. GIVE US A BREAK.
OH, JUST YOU WAIT, KIDDO, ONE DAY YOU'RE A ROOK, THE NEXT YOU'RE HAULING KIDS.
HAHA.
...I WANTED TO THANK YOU GUYS FOR TALKING WITH THE TEAM.
I KNOW A FEW GUYS THINK, AH. SOME OF THIS IS STILL WEIRD. NEW. AND THAT SHOWER JOKE ON THE BUS— BUT YOU GUYS AND GEORGE—
HEY, MAN. YOU'RE A LEADER ON THIS TEAM. IT'S YOUR TEAM TOO.
WE'VE GOT A GREAT SEASON. TEAMS THAT GO FAR... IT'S ABOUT EVERYONE BEING ON THE SAME PAGE. TOGETHER.

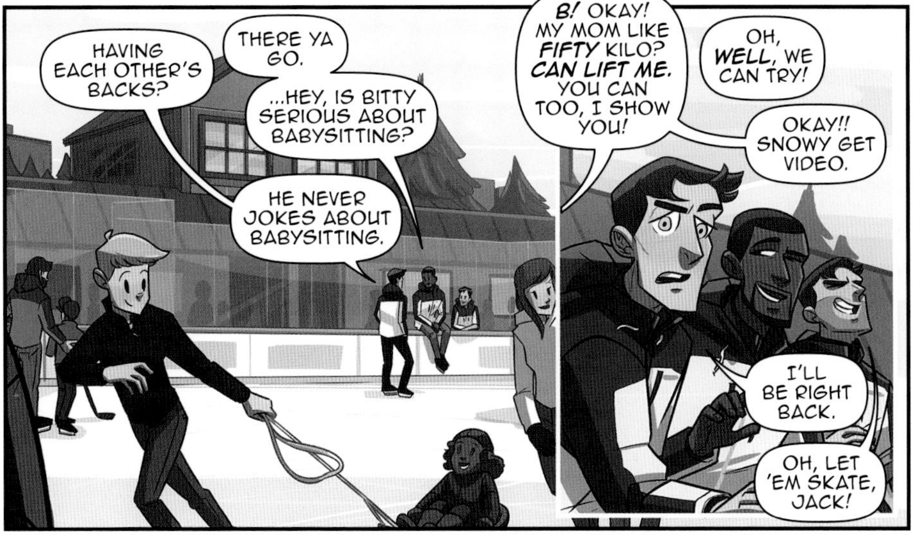
HAVING EACH OTHER'S BACKS?
THERE YA GO.
...HEY, IS BITTY SERIOUS ABOUT BABYSITTING?
HE NEVER JOKES ABOUT BABYSITTING.
B! OKAY! MY MOM LIKE FIFTY KILO? CAN LIFT ME. YOU CAN TOO, I SHOW YOU!
OH, WELL, WE CAN TRY!
OKAY!! SNOWY GET VIDEO.
I'LL BE RIGHT BACK.
OH, LET 'EM SKATE, JACK!

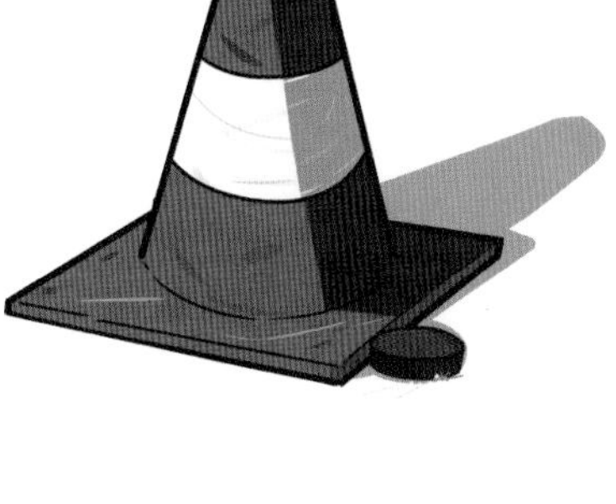

19

KEAGSTER

HEY, Y'ALL...
SIGH
SO. OUR SEASON IS OVER.
SOMETIMES THEY END WITH A BANG, AND OTHER TIMES... WELL.
FOR THE FIRST TIME IN FOUR YEARS, SAMWELL DIDN'T MAKE IT PAST THE FIRST ROUND IN THE ECAC PLAYOFFS.
IT'S KIND OF HARD WITHOUT ONE OF THE NHL'S CURRENT TOP SCORERS ON OUR ROSTER, BUT...
OUR CAPTAINS SHOULD HAVE ZERO REGRETS.
TANGREDI
13
BIRKHOLTZ
4
OLURANSI
11

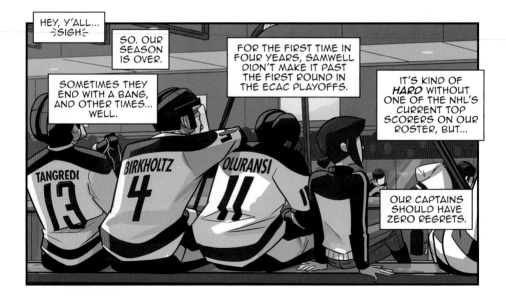

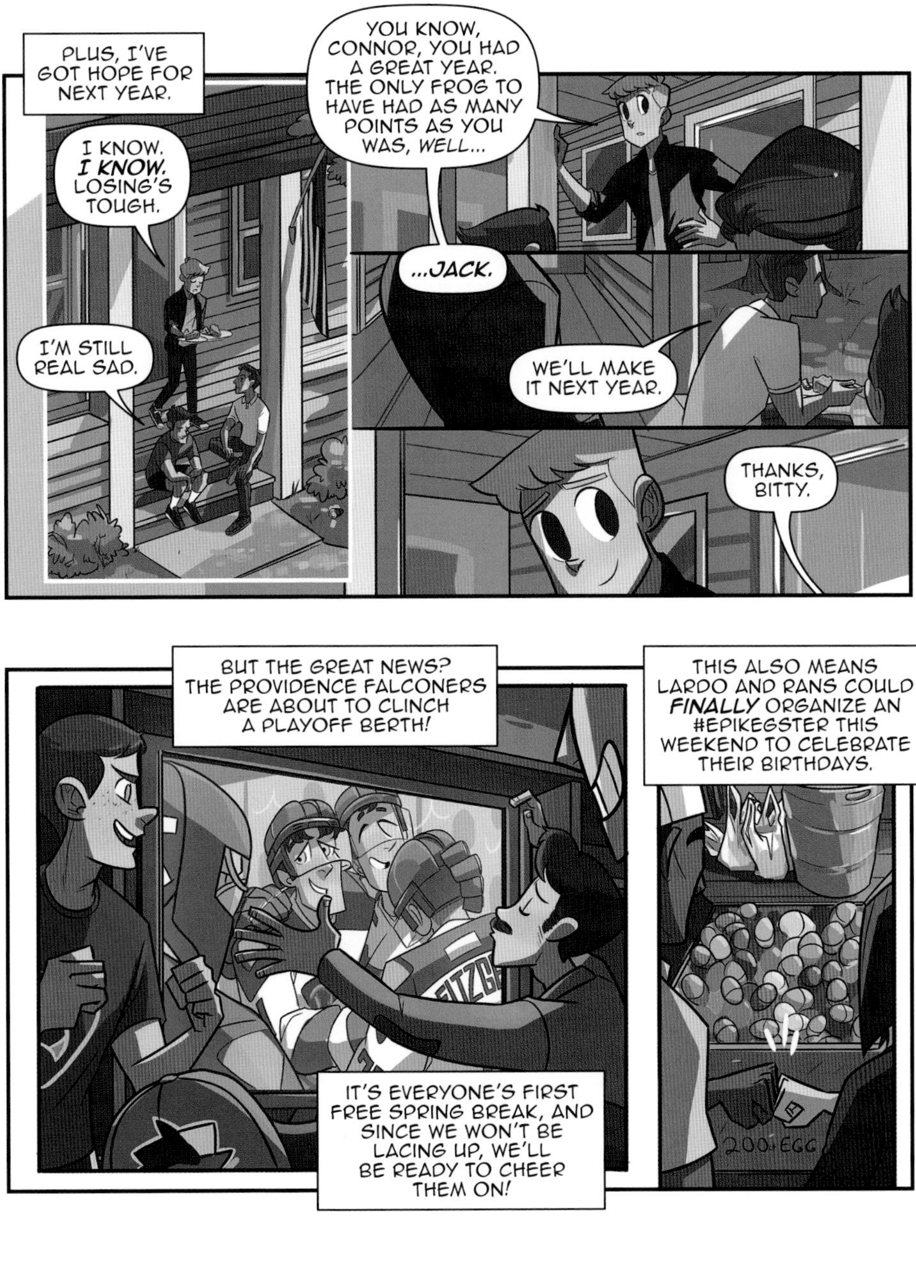
PLUS, I'VE GOT HOPE FOR NEXT YEAR.
I KNOW. I KNOW. LOSING'S TOUGH.
I'M STILL REAL SAD.
YOU KNOW, CONNOR, YOU HAD A GREAT YEAR. THE ONLY FROG TO HAVE HAD AS MANY POINTS AS YOU WAS, WELL...
...JACK.
WE'LL MAKE IT NEXT YEAR.
THANKS, BITTY.
BUT THE GREAT NEWS? THE PROVIDENCE FALCONERS ARE ABOUT TO CLINCH A PLAYOFF BERTH!
IT'S EVERYONE'S FIRST FREE SPRING BREAK, AND SINCE WE WON'T BE LACING UP, WE'LL BE READY TO CHEER THEM ON!
THIS ALSO MEANS LARDO AND RANS COULD FINALLY ORGANIZE AN #EPIKEGSTER THIS WEEKEND TO CELEBRATE THEIR BIRTHDAYS.
200+ EGG

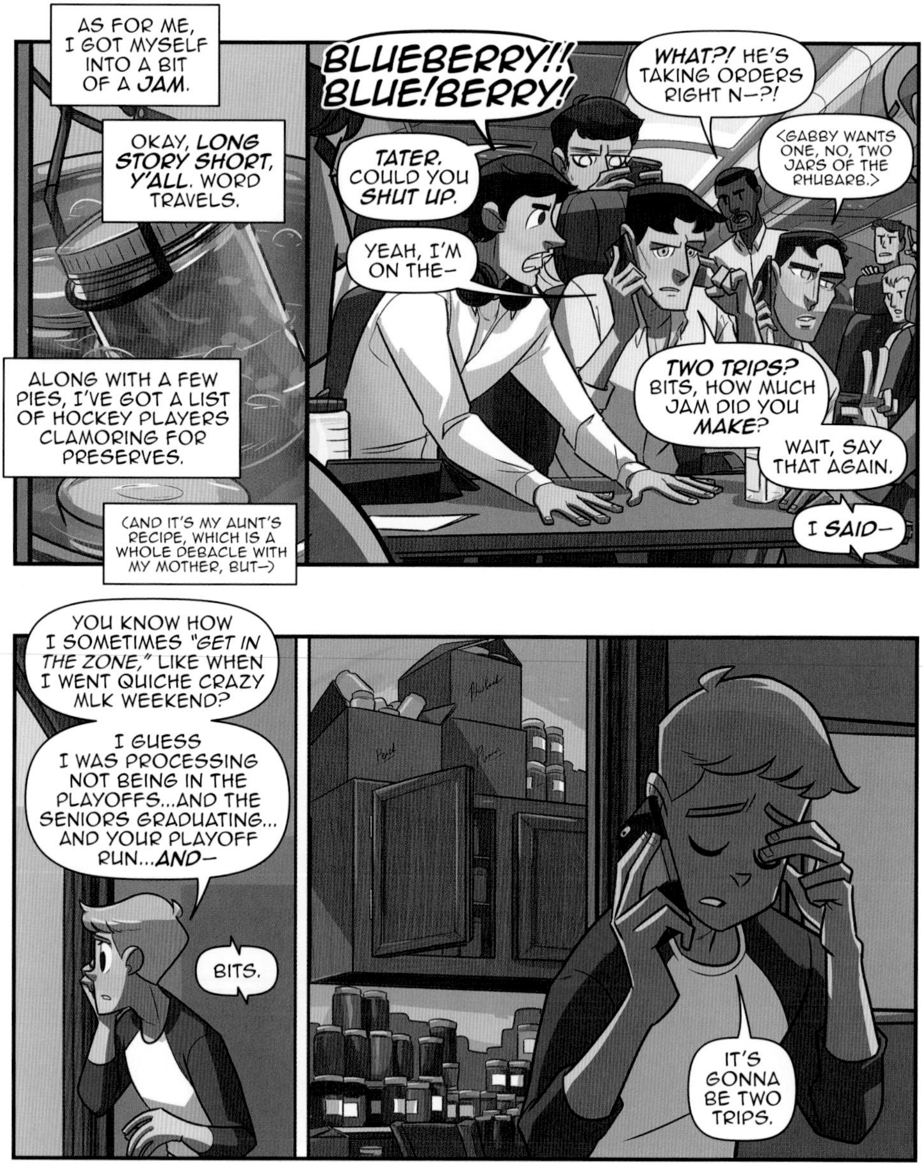
AS FOR ME, I GOT MYSELF INTO A BIT OF A JAM.
OKAY, LONG STORY SHORT, Y'ALL. WORD TRAVELS.
ALONG WITH A FEW PIES, I'VE GOT A LIST OF HOCKEY PLAYERS CLAMORING FOR PRESERVES.
(AND IT'S MY AUNT'S RECIPE, WHICH IS A WHOLE DEBACLE WITH MY MOTHER, BUT–)
BLUEBERRY!! BLUE!BERRY!
TATER. COULD YOU SHUT UP.
YEAH, I'M ON THE–
WHAT?! HE'S TAKING ORDERS RIGHT N–?!
<GABBY WANTS ONE, NO, TWO JARS OF THE RHUBARB.>
TWO TRIPS? BITS, HOW MUCH JAM DID YOU MAKE?
WAIT, SAY THAT AGAIN.
I SAID–
YOU KNOW HOW I SOMETIMES "GET IN THE ZONE," LIKE WHEN I WENT QUICHE CRAZY MLK WEEKEND?
I GUESS I WAS PROCESSING NOT BEING IN THE PLAYOFFS...AND THE SENIORS GRADUATING... AND YOUR PLAYOFF RUN...AND–
BITS.
IT'S GONNA BE TWO TRIPS.

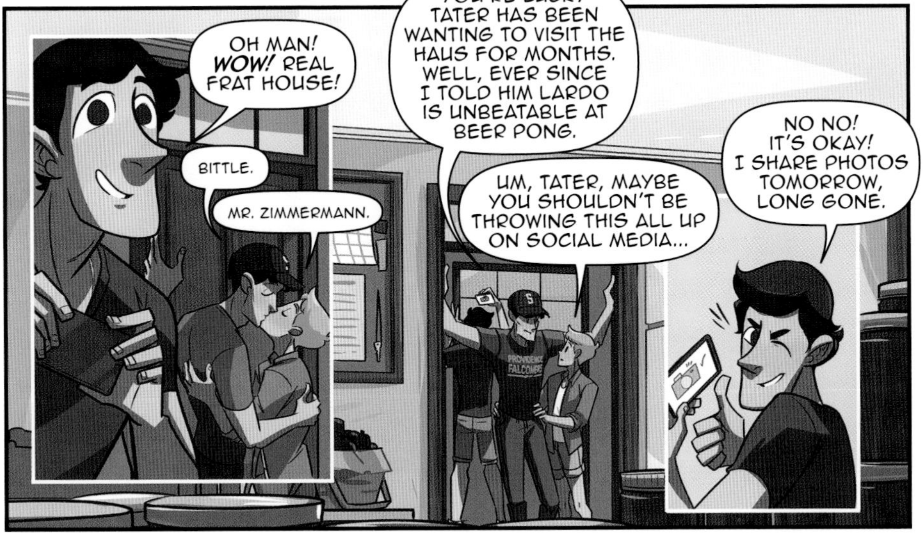
OH MAN! WOW! REAL FRAT HOUSE!
BITTLE.
MR. ZIMMERMANN.
YOU'RE LUCKY TATER HAS BEEN WANTING TO VISIT THE HAUS FOR MONTHS. WELL, EVER SINCE I TOLD HIM LARDO IS UNBEATABLE AT BEER PONG.
UM, TATER, MAYBE YOU SHOULDN'T BE THROWING THIS ALL UP ON SOCIAL MEDIA...
NO NO! IT'S OKAY! I SHARE PHOTOS TOMORROW, LONG GONE.

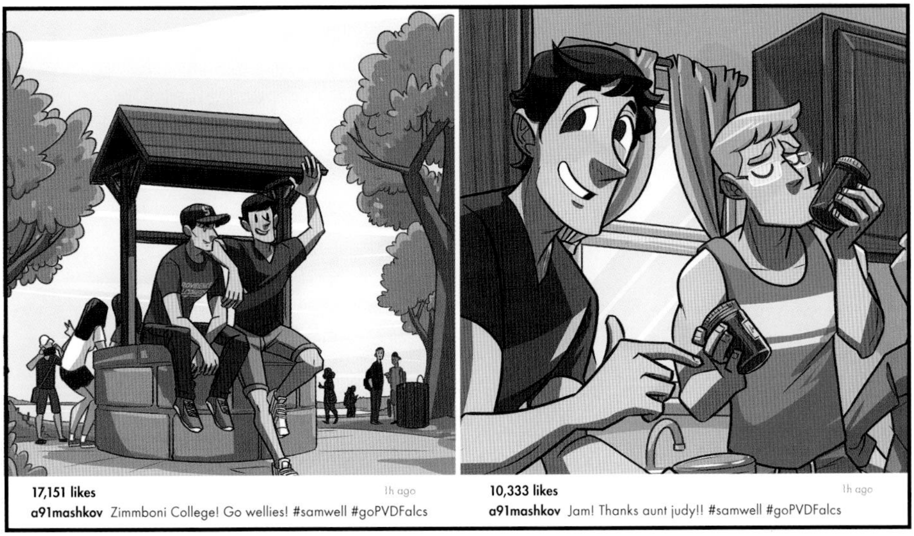
17,151 likes
1h ago
a91mashkov Zimmboni College! Go wellies! #samwell #goPVDFalcs
10,333 likes
1h ago
a91mashkov Jam! Thanks aunt judy!! #samwell #goPVDFalcs

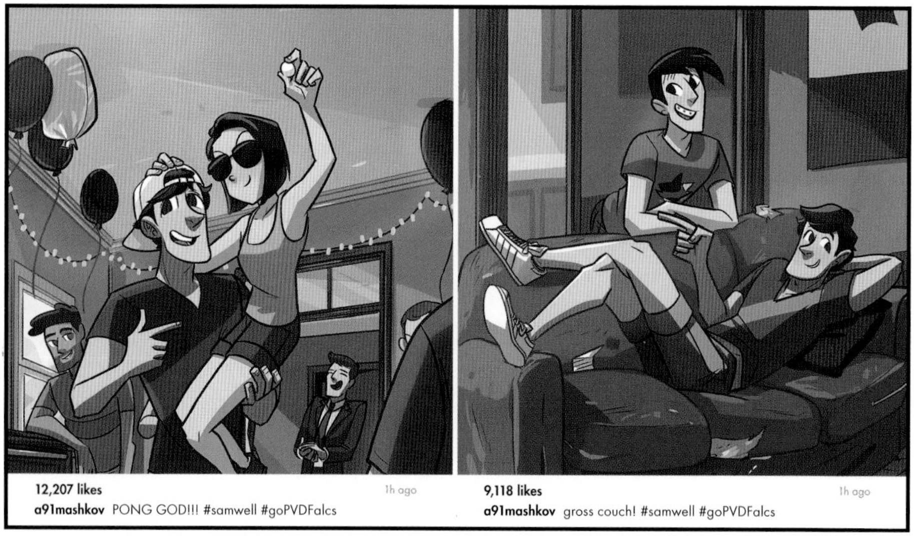
12,207 likes
1h ago
a91mashkov PONG GOD!!! #samwell #goPVDFalcs
9,118 likes
1h ago
a91mashkov gross couch! #samwell #goPVDFalcs

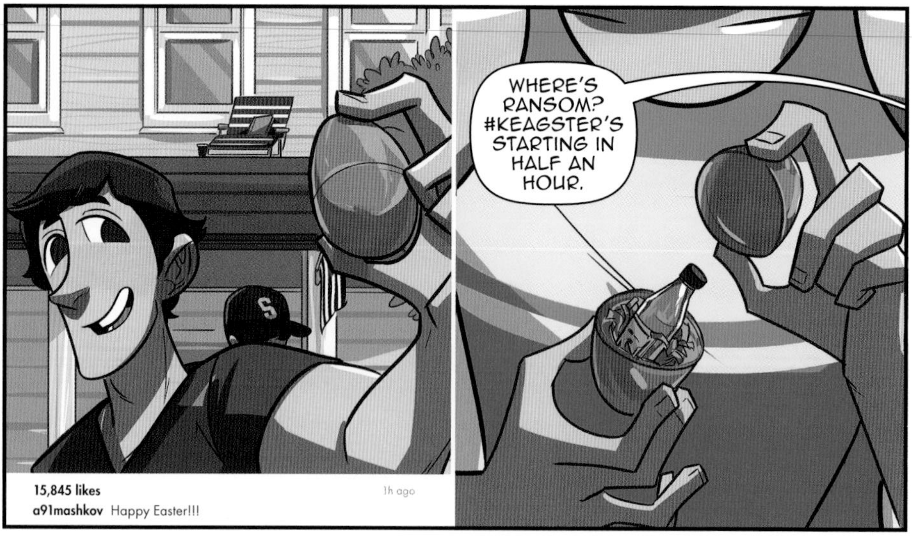
15,845 likes
1h ago
a91mashkov Happy Easter!!!
WHERE'S RANSOM? #KEAGSTER'S STARTING IN HALF AN HOUR.

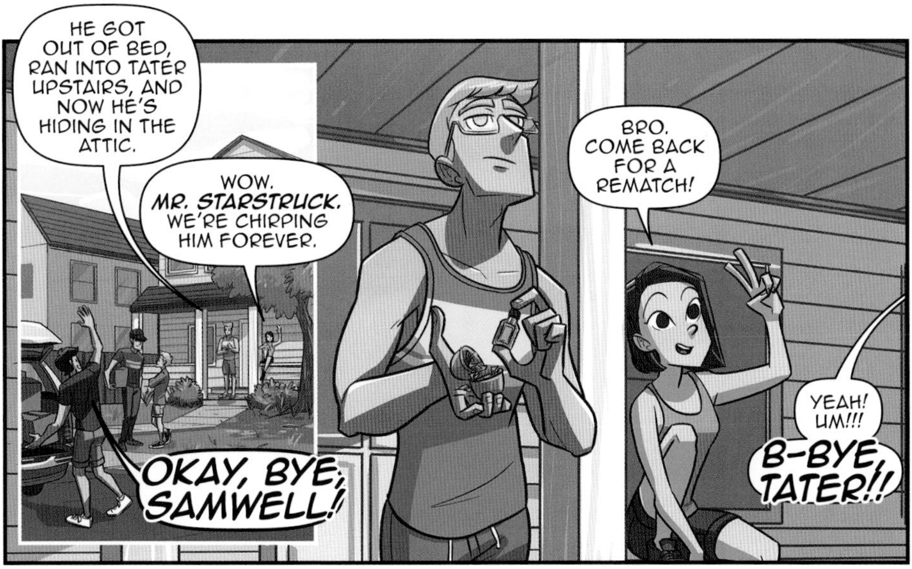
HE GOT OUT OF BED, RAN INTO TATER UPSTAIRS, AND NOW HE'S HIDING IN THE ATTIC.
WOW. MR. STARSTRUCK. WE'RE CHIRPING HIM FOREVER.
OKAY, BYE, SAMWELL!
BRO. COME BACK FOR A REMATCH!
YEAH! UM!!!
B-BYE TATER!!

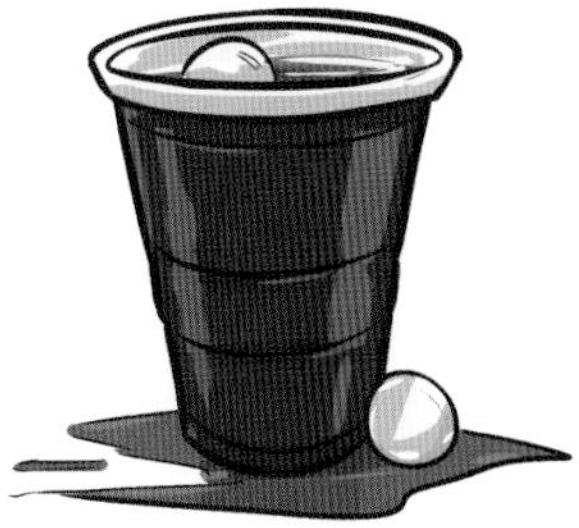

20

C

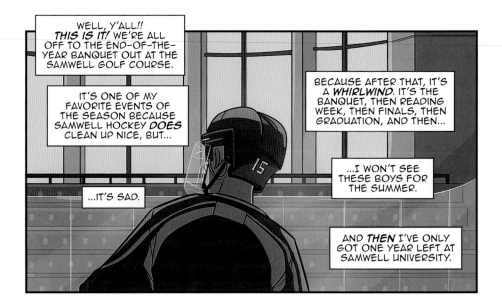

WELL, Y'ALL!! *THIS IS IT!* WE'RE ALL OFF TO THE END-OF-THE-YEAR BANQUET OUT AT THE SAMWELL GOLF COURSE.

IT'S ONE OF MY FAVORITE EVENTS OF THE SEASON BECAUSE SAMWELL HOCKEY *DOES* CLEAN UP NICE, BUT...

...IT'S SAD.

BECAUSE AFTER THAT, IT'S A *WHIRLWIND.* IT'S THE BANQUET, THEN READING WEEK, THEN FINALS, THEN GRADUATION, AND THEN...

...I WON'T SEE THESE BOYS FOR THE SUMMER.

AND *THEN* I'VE ONLY GOT ONE YEAR LEFT AT SAMWELL UNIVERSITY.

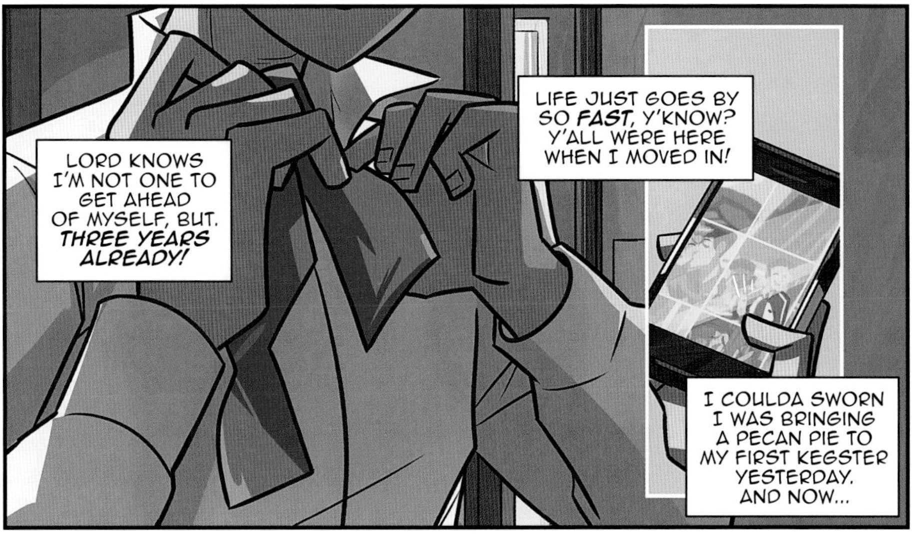
LORD KNOWS I'M NOT ONE TO GET AHEAD OF MYSELF, BUT. THREE YEARS ALREADY!
LIFE JUST GOES BY SO FAST, Y'KNOW? Y'ALL WERE HERE WHEN I MOVED IN!
I COULDA SWORN I WAS BRINGING A PECAN PIE TO MY FIRST KEGSTER YESTERDAY. AND NOW...

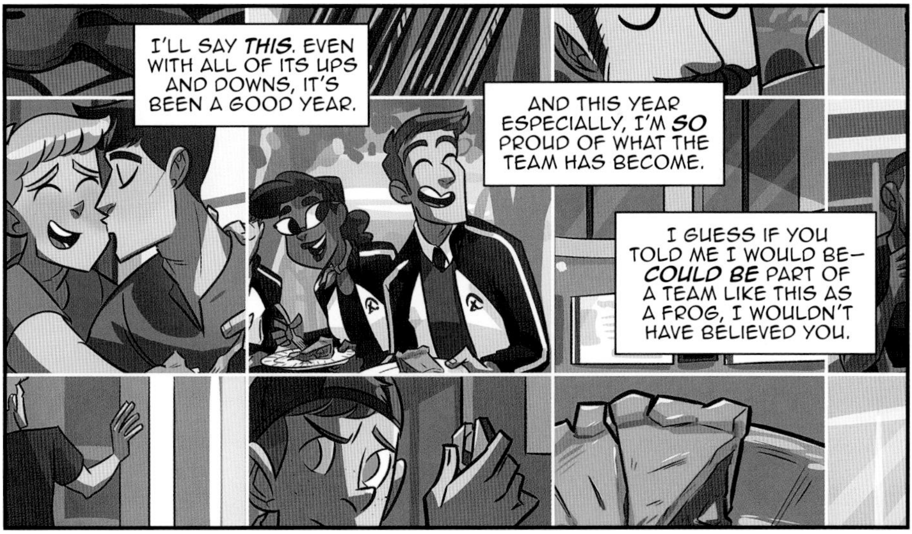
I'LL SAY THIS. EVEN WITH ALL OF ITS UPS AND DOWNS, IT'S BEEN A GOOD YEAR.
AND THIS YEAR ESPECIALLY, I'M SO PROUD OF WHAT THE TEAM HAS BECOME.
I GUESS IF YOU TOLD ME I WOULD BE— COULD BE PART OF A TEAM LIKE THIS AS A FROG, I WOULDN'T HAVE BELIEVED YOU.

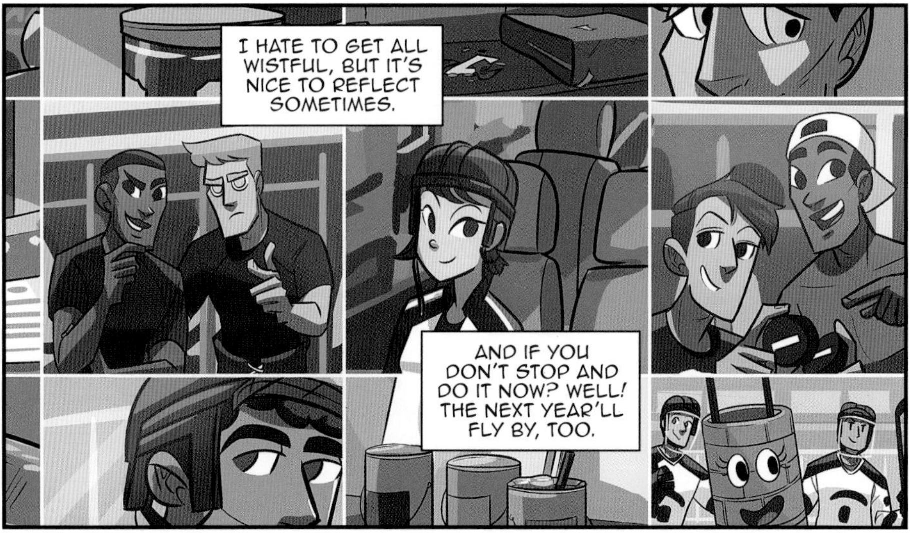
I HATE TO GET ALL WISTFUL, BUT IT'S NICE TO REFLECT SOMETIMES.
AND IF YOU DON'T STOP AND DO IT NOW? WELL! THE NEXT YEAR'LL FLY BY, TOO.

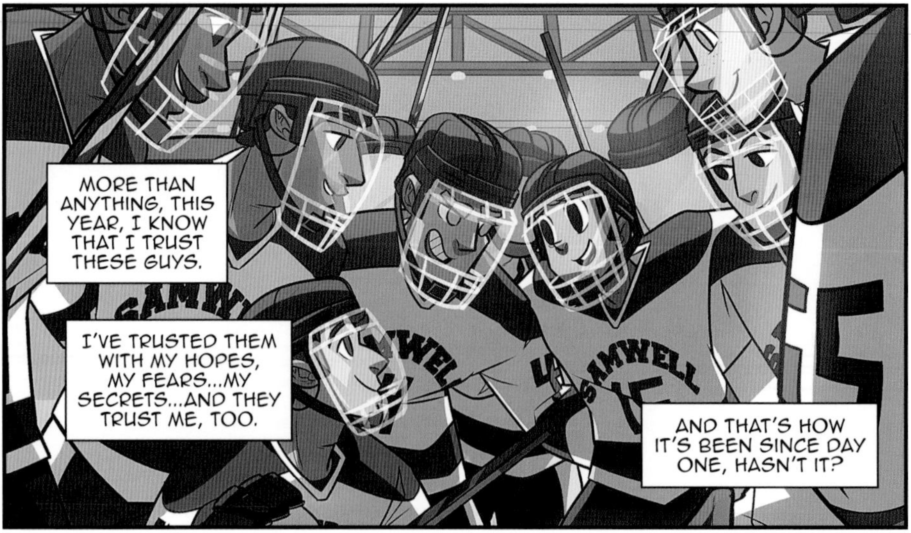
MORE THAN ANYTHING, THIS YEAR, I KNOW THAT I TRUST THESE GUYS.
I'VE TRUSTED THEM WITH MY HOPES, MY FEARS...MY SECRETS...AND THEY TRUST ME, TOO.
AND THAT'S HOW IT'S BEEN SINCE DAY ONE, HASN'T IT?

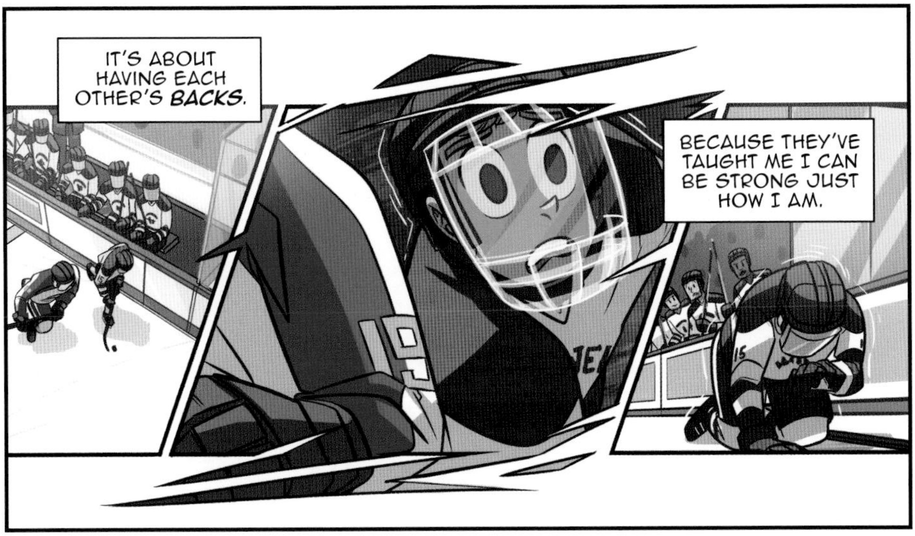
IT'S ABOUT HAVING EACH OTHER'S *BACKS*.
BECAUSE THEY'VE TAUGHT ME I CAN BE STRONG JUST HOW I AM.

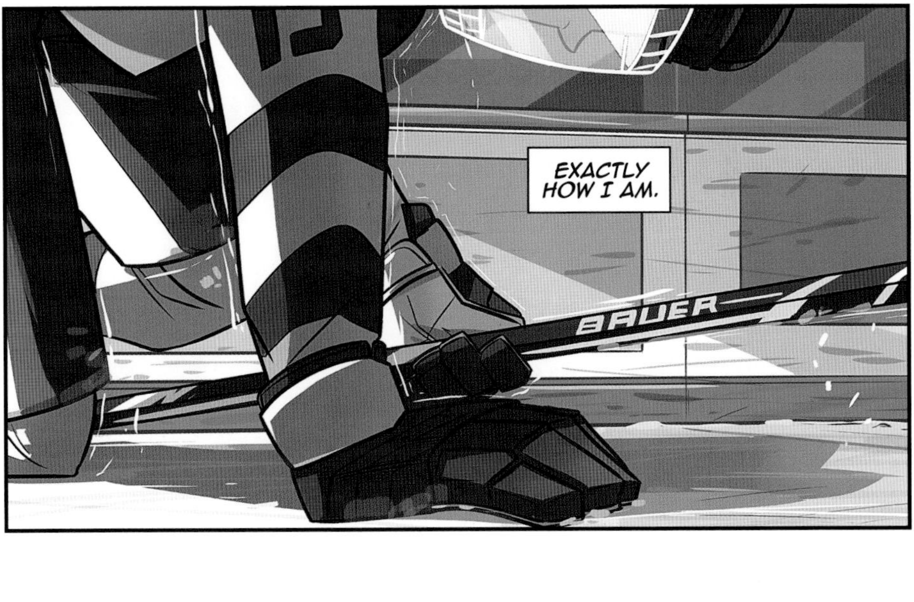
EXACTLY HOW I AM.
BAUER

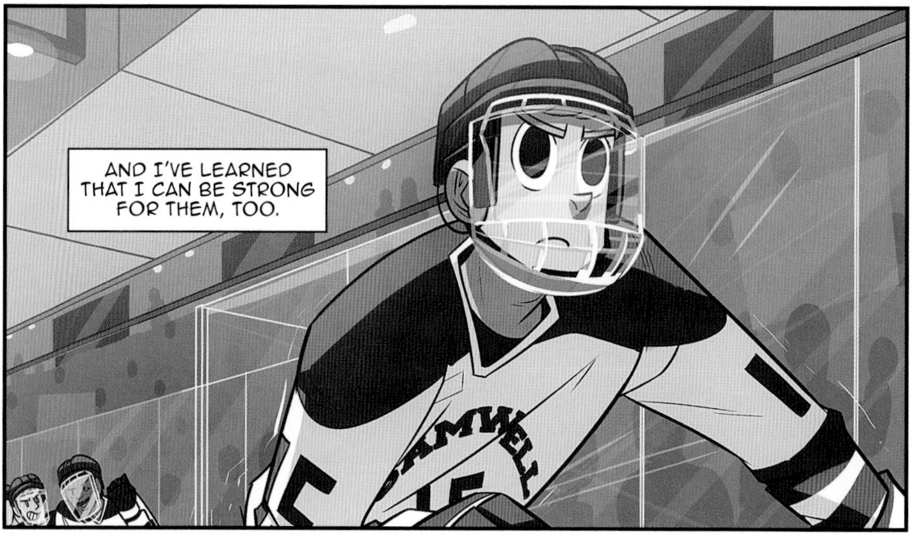
AND I'VE LEARNED THAT I CAN BE STRONG FOR THEM, TOO.
SAMWELL

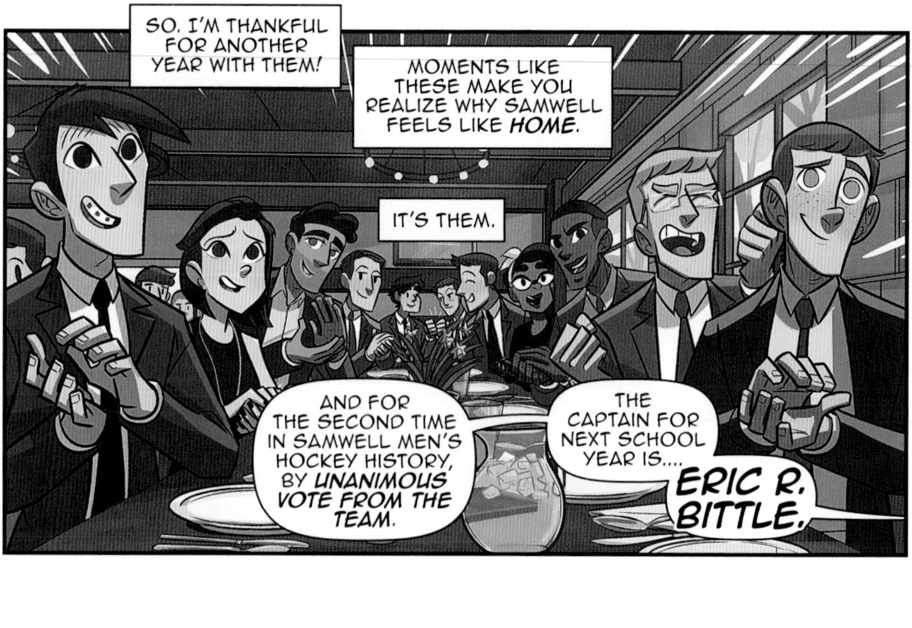
SO. I'M THANKFUL FOR ANOTHER YEAR WITH THEM!
MOMENTS LIKE THESE MAKE YOU REALIZE WHY SAMWELL FEELS LIKE *HOME*.
IT'S THEM.
AND FOR THE SECOND TIME IN SAMWELL MEN'S HOCKEY HISTORY, BY *UNANIMOUS VOTE FROM THE TEAM*.
THE CAPTAIN FOR NEXT SCHOOL YEAR IS.... *ERIC R. BITTLE.*

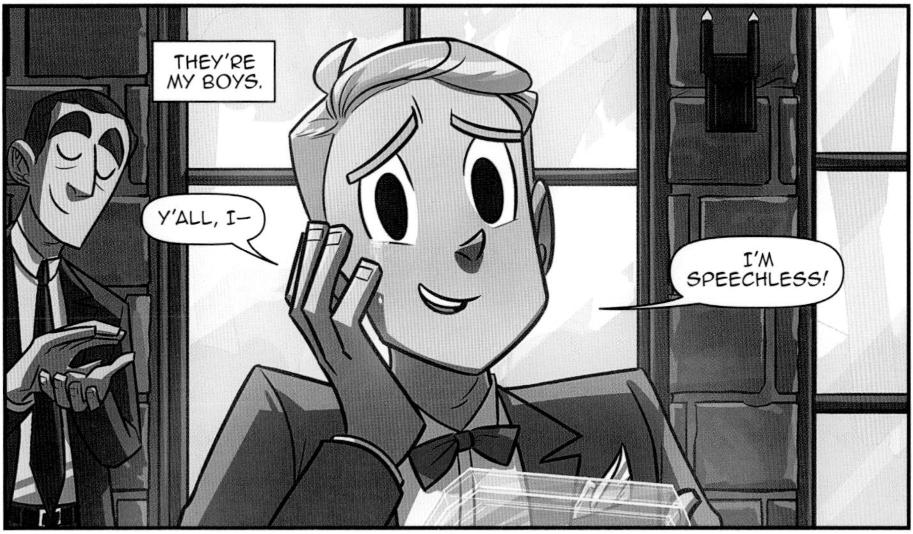
THEY'RE MY BOYS.
Y'ALL, I—
I'M SPEECHLESS!

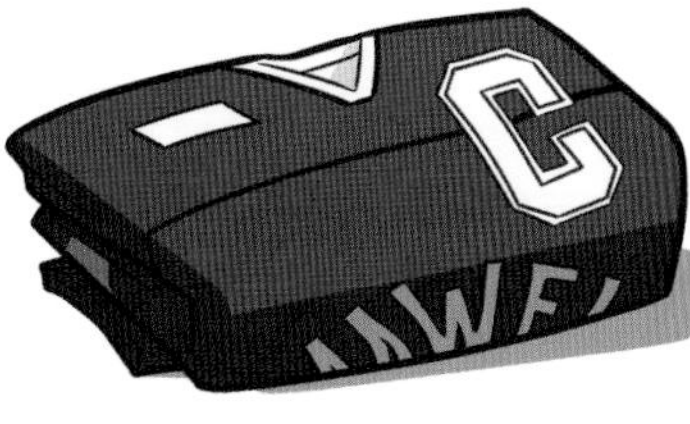

21

MOVING OUT

CONGRATULATIONS TO THE SAMWELL MEN'S HOCKEY SENIOR CLASS!!
GRADUATION WAS A BLAST!
...AND OF COURSE, BITTERSWEET.
BUT THEY'VE HAD THEIR GOODBYE KEGSTERS AND KISSED THE ICE.
OUR SENIORS ARE READY TO GO.

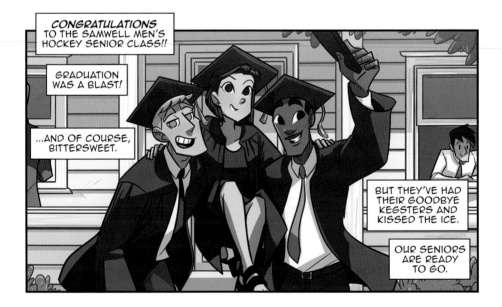

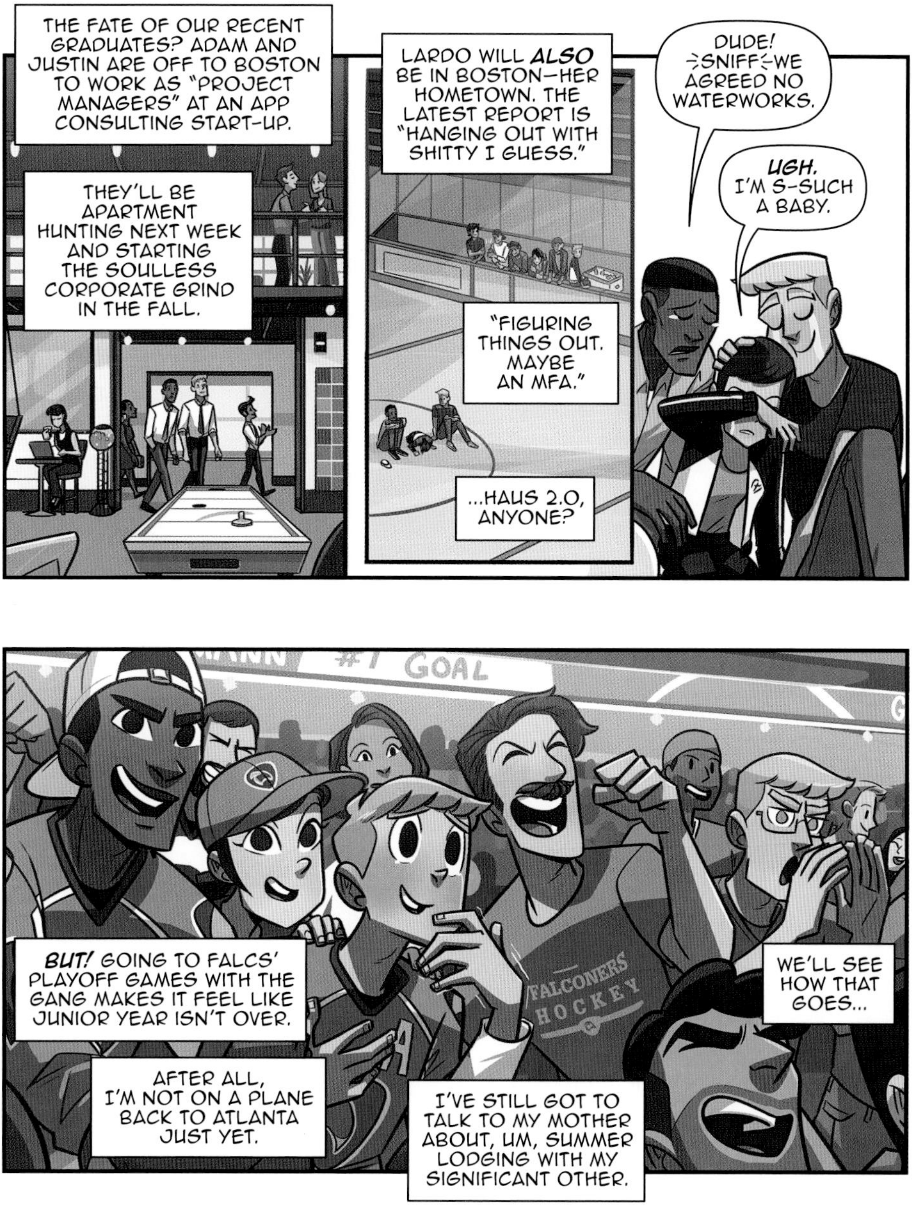
THE FATE OF OUR RECENT GRADUATES? ADAM AND JUSTIN ARE OFF TO BOSTON TO WORK AS "PROJECT MANAGERS" AT AN APP CONSULTING START-UP.
THEY'LL BE APARTMENT HUNTING NEXT WEEK AND STARTING THE SOULLESS CORPORATE GRIND IN THE FALL.
LARDO WILL ALSO BE IN BOSTON—HER HOMETOWN. THE LATEST REPORT IS "HANGING OUT WITH SHITTY I GUESS."
"FIGURING THINGS OUT. MAYBE AN MFA."
...HAUS 2.0, ANYONE?
DUDE! SNIFF WE AGREED NO WATERWORKS.
UGH. I'M S-SUCH A BABY.
#1 GOAL
FALCONERS HOCKEY
BUT! GOING TO FALCS' PLAYOFF GAMES WITH THE GANG MAKES IT FEEL LIKE JUNIOR YEAR ISN'T OVER.
AFTER ALL, I'M NOT ON A PLANE BACK TO ATLANTA JUST YET.
I'VE STILL GOT TO TALK TO MY MOTHER ABOUT, UM, SUMMER LODGING WITH MY SIGNIFICANT OTHER.
WE'LL SEE HOW THAT GOES...

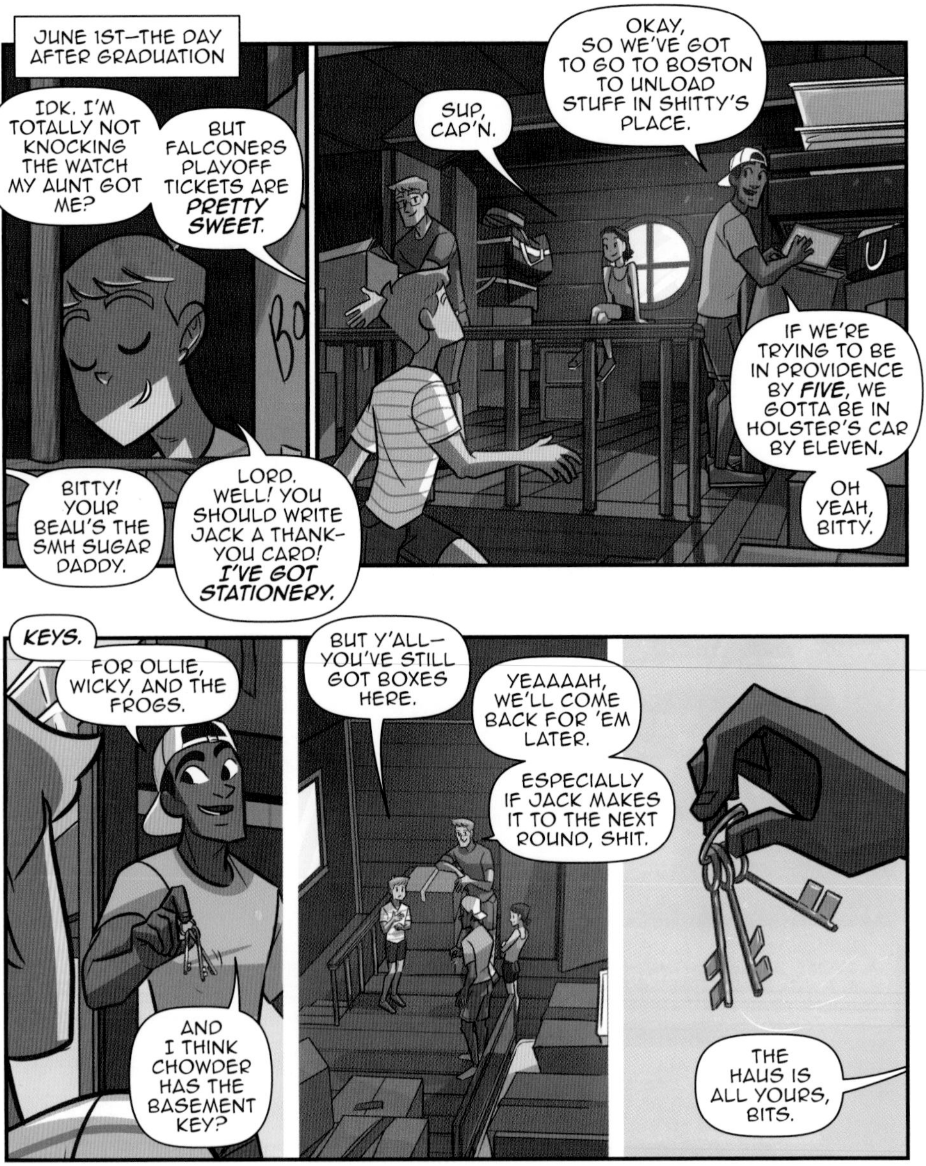
JUNE 1ST—THE DAY AFTER GRADUATION
IDK. I'M TOTALLY NOT KNOCKING THE WATCH MY AUNT GOT ME?
BUT FALCONERS PLAYOFF TICKETS ARE PRETTY SWEET.
BITTY! YOUR BEAU'S THE SMH SUGAR DADDY.
LORD. WELL! YOU SHOULD WRITE JACK A THANK-YOU CARD! I'VE GOT STATIONERY.
SUP, CAP'N.
OKAY, SO WE'VE GOT TO GO TO BOSTON TO UNLOAD STUFF IN SHITTY'S PLACE.
IF WE'RE TRYING TO BE IN PROVIDENCE BY FIVE, WE GOTTA BE IN HOLSTER'S CAR BY ELEVEN.
OH YEAH, BITTY.
KEYS.
FOR OLLIE, WICKY, AND THE FROGS.
AND I THINK CHOWDER HAS THE BASEMENT KEY?
BUT Y'ALL— YOU'VE STILL GOT BOXES HERE.
YEAAAAH, WE'LL COME BACK FOR 'EM LATER.
ESPECIALLY IF JACK MAKES IT TO THE NEXT ROUND, SHIT.
THE HAUS IS ALL YOURS, BITS.

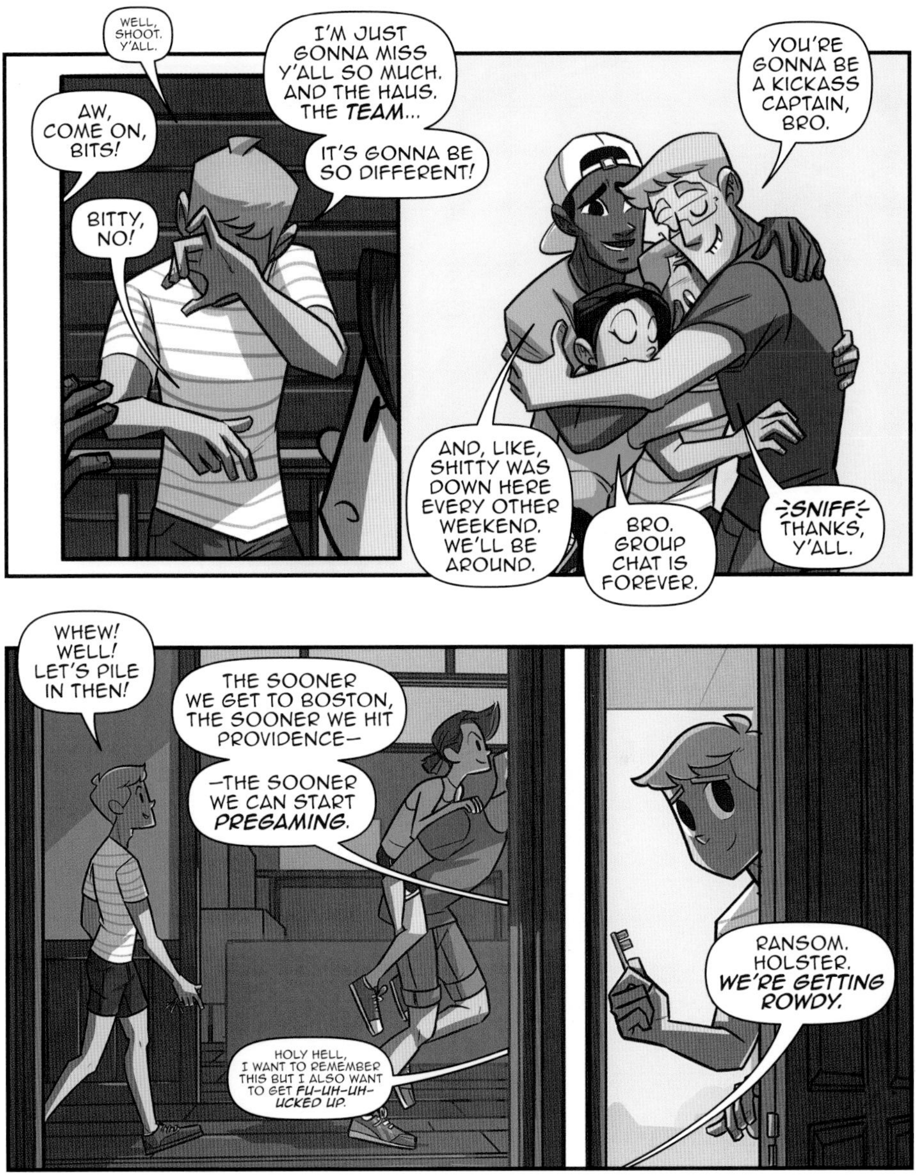
WELL, SHOOT. Y'ALL.
AW, COME ON, BITS!
I'M JUST GONNA MISS Y'ALL SO MUCH. AND THE HAUS. THE *TEAM*...
IT'S GONNA BE SO DIFFERENT!
BITTY, NO!
YOU'RE GONNA BE A KICKASS CAPTAIN, BRO.
AND, LIKE, SHITTY WAS DOWN HERE EVERY OTHER WEEKEND. WE'LL BE AROUND.
BRO. GROUP CHAT IS FOREVER.
SNIFF THANKS, Y'ALL.
WHEW! WELL! LET'S PILE IN THEN!
THE SOONER WE GET TO BOSTON, THE SOONER WE HIT PROVIDENCE—
—THE SOONER WE CAN START **PREGAMING**.
HOLY HELL, I WANT TO REMEMBER THIS BUT I ALSO WANT TO GET *FU-UH-UH-UCKED UP*.
RANSOM. HOLSTER. ***WE'RE GETTING ROWDY.***

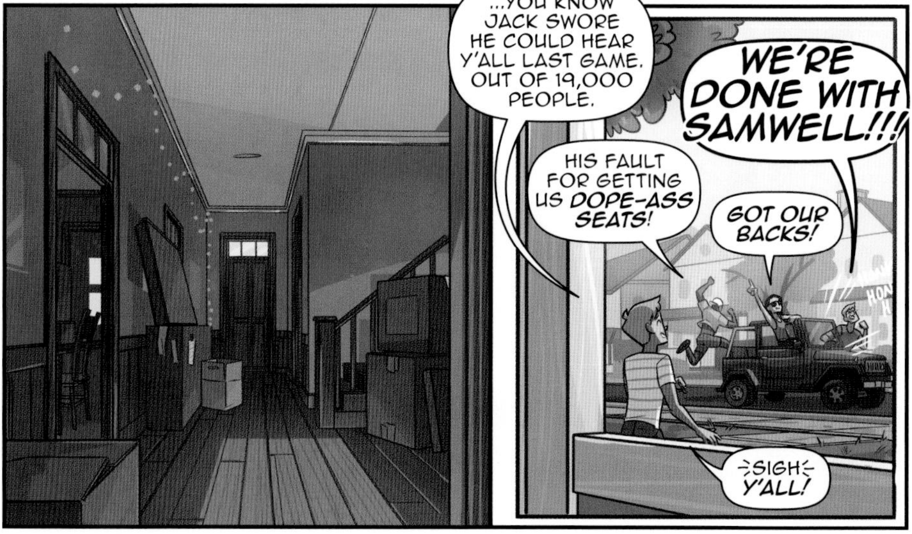
...YOU KNOW JACK SWORE HE COULD HEAR Y'ALL LAST GAME. OUT OF 19,000 PEOPLE.
WE'RE DONE WITH SAMWELL!!!
HIS FAULT FOR GETTING US DOPE-ASS SEATS!
GOT OUR BACKS!
SIGH Y'ALL!

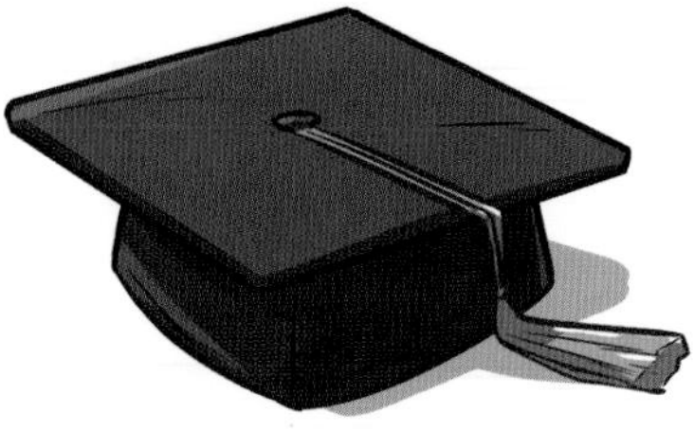

22

CUP I — PLAYOFFS

Y'ALL—AND I'M KNOCKING ON EVERY AVAILABLE WOODEN SURFACE AS I SAY THIS—
—BUT THE FALCONERS ARE SO CLOSE TO THE LAST ROUND. ONE GAME.
IF THEY WIN THIS NEXT ONE? GAME FIVE? IT'S A NEAR SWEEP, AND THEN IT'S FOUR WINS TO...
LORD, I KNOW THESE PLAYERS, AND I STILL CAN'T EVEN FATHOM HOW THIS FEELS.
BUT THEY SEEM AS COOL AS CUCUMBERS!

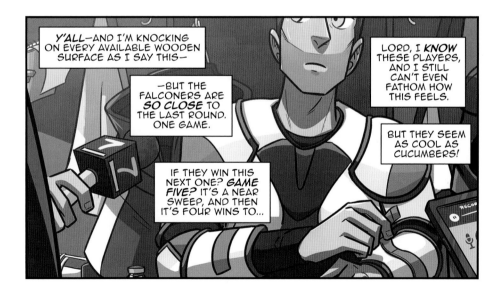

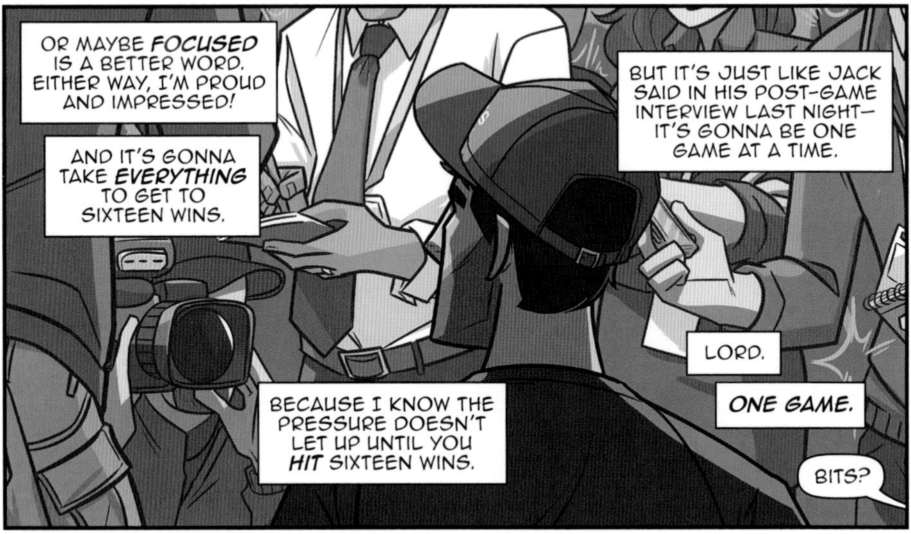
OR MAYBE FOCUSED IS A BETTER WORD. EITHER WAY, I'M PROUD AND IMPRESSED!
AND IT'S GONNA TAKE EVERYTHING TO GET TO SIXTEEN WINS.
BECAUSE I KNOW THE PRESSURE DOESN'T LET UP UNTIL YOU HIT SIXTEEN WINS.
BUT IT'S JUST LIKE JACK SAID IN HIS POST-GAME INTERVIEW LAST NIGHT— IT'S GONNA BE ONE GAME AT A TIME.
LORD.
ONE GAME.
BITS?

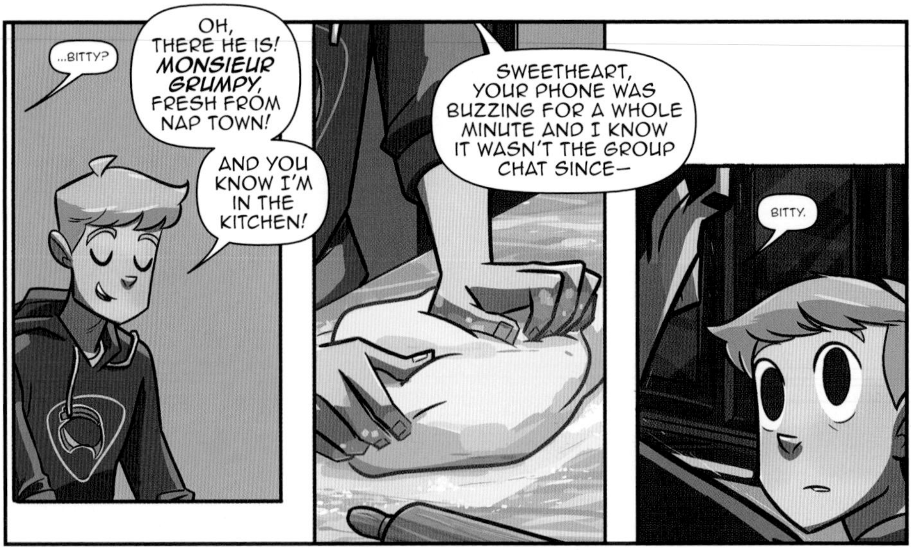
...BITTY?
OH, THERE HE IS! MONSIEUR GRUMPY, FRESH FROM NAP TOWN!
AND YOU KNOW I'M IN THE KITCHEN!
SWEETHEART, YOUR PHONE WAS BUZZING FOR A WHOLE MINUTE AND I KNOW IT WASN'T THE GROUP CHAT SINCE—
BITTY.

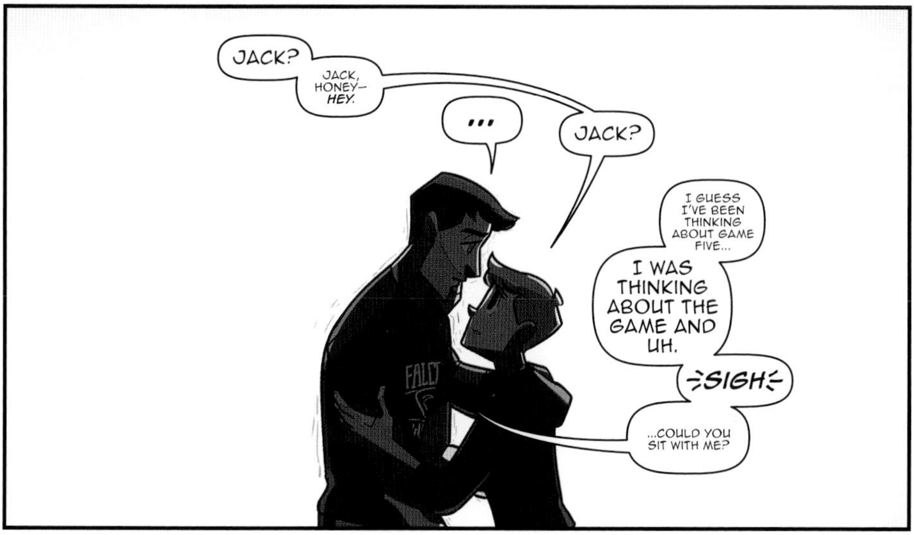
JACK?
JACK, HONEY— HEY.
...
JACK?
I GUESS I'VE BEEN THINKING ABOUT GAME FIVE...
I WAS THINKING ABOUT THE GAME AND UH.
SIGH
...COULD YOU SIT WITH ME?

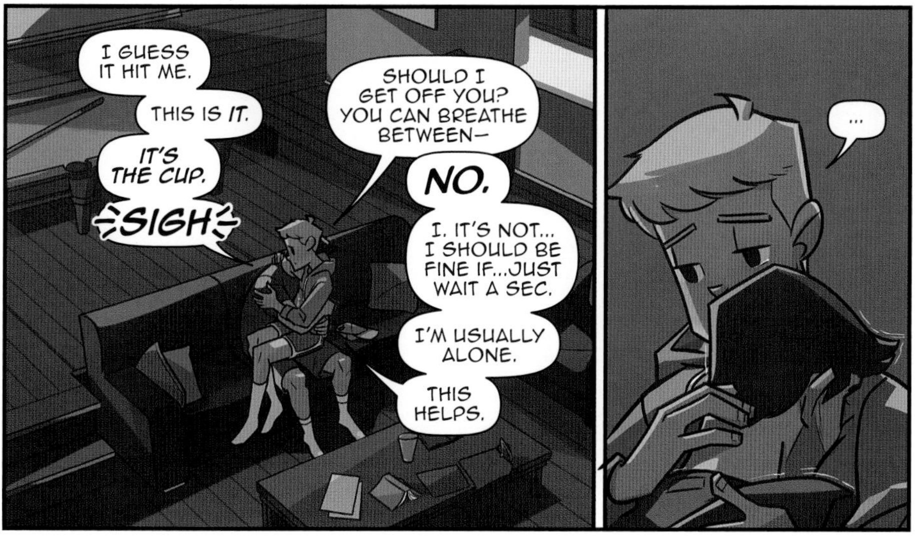
I GUESS IT HIT ME.
THIS IS IT.
IT'S THE CUP.
SIGH
SHOULD I GET OFF YOU? YOU CAN BREATHE BETWEEN—
NO.
I, IT'S NOT... I SHOULD BE FINE IF...JUST WAIT A SEC.
I'M USUALLY ALONE.
THIS HELPS.
...

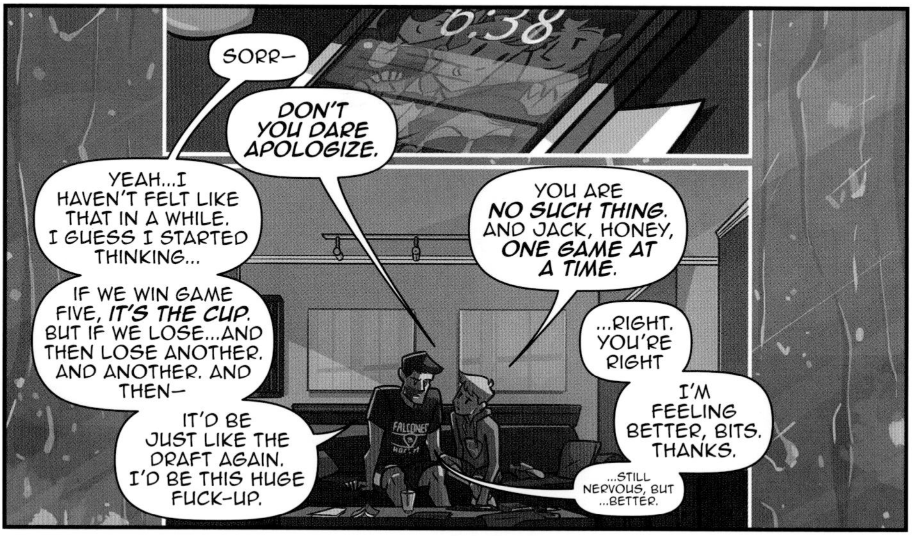
SORR—
DON'T YOU DARE APOLOGIZE.
YEAH...I HAVEN'T FELT LIKE THAT IN A WHILE. I GUESS I STARTED THINKING...
IF WE WIN GAME FIVE, IT'S THE CUP. BUT IF WE LOSE...AND THEN LOSE ANOTHER. AND ANOTHER. AND THEN—
IT'D BE JUST LIKE THE DRAFT AGAIN. I'D BE THIS HUGE FUCK-UP.
YOU ARE NO SUCH THING. AND JACK, HONEY, ONE GAME AT A TIME.
...RIGHT. YOU'RE RIGHT
I'M FEELING BETTER, BITS. THANKS.
...STILL NERVOUS, BUT ...BETTER.

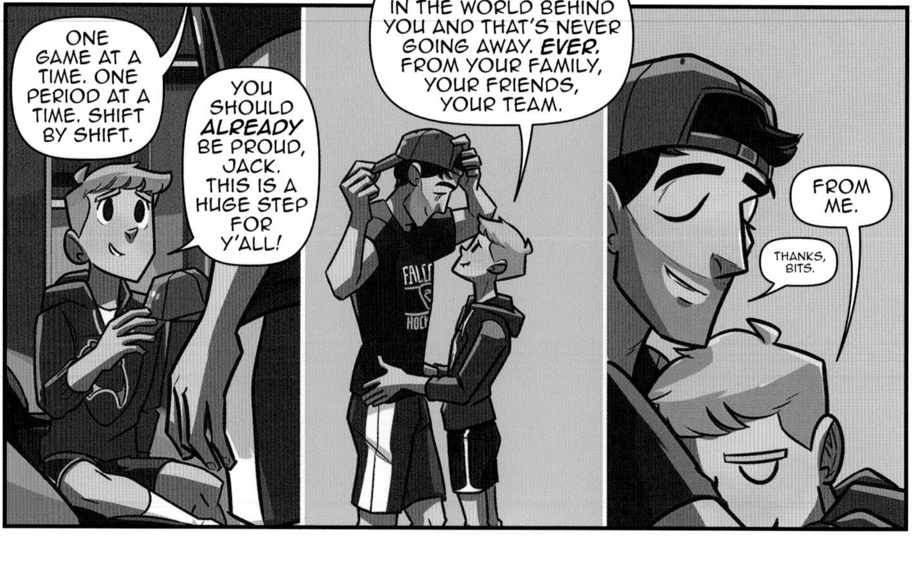
ONE GAME AT A TIME. ONE PERIOD AT A TIME. SHIFT BY SHIFT.
YOU SHOULD ALREADY BE PROUD, JACK. THIS IS A HUGE STEP FOR Y'ALL!
YOU GOT ALL THE SUPPORT IN THE WORLD BEHIND YOU AND THAT'S NEVER GOING AWAY. EVER. FROM YOUR FAMILY, YOUR FRIENDS, YOUR TEAM.
FROM ME.
THANKS, BITS.

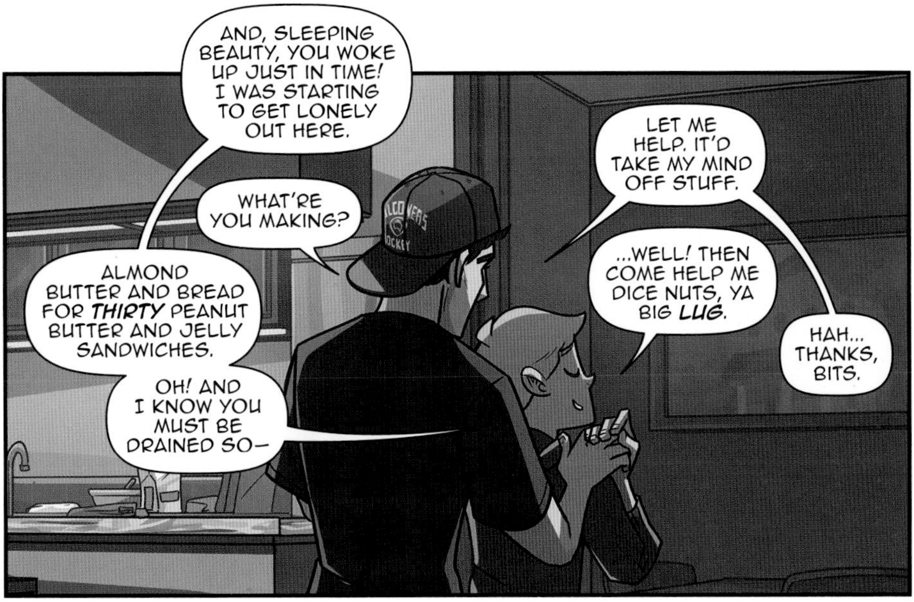
AND, SLEEPING BEAUTY, YOU WOKE UP JUST IN TIME! I WAS STARTING TO GET LONELY OUT HERE.
WHAT'RE YOU MAKING?
ALMOND BUTTER AND BREAD FOR *THIRTY* PEANUT BUTTER AND JELLY SANDWICHES.
OH! AND I KNOW YOU MUST BE DRAINED SO—
LET ME HELP. IT'D TAKE MY MIND OFF STUFF.
...WELL! THEN COME HELP ME DICE NUTS, YA BIG *LUG*.
HAH... THANKS, BITS.

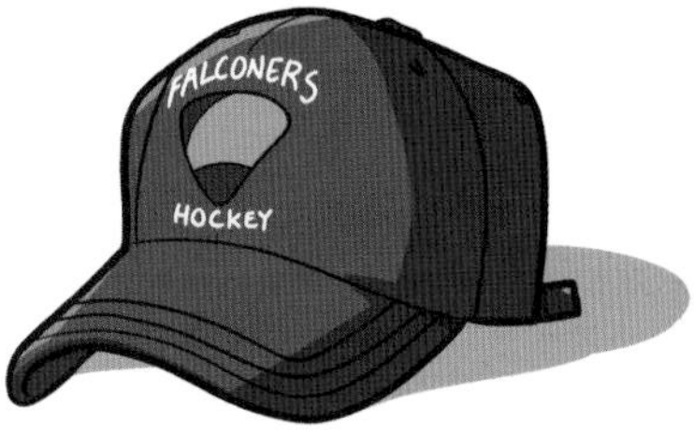
FALCONERS
HOCKEY

23

CUP II — SUMMER WITH JACK

WHO'S MY FAVORITE PERSON TO BAKE WITH?
OH, Y'ALL, THAT'S *EASY*. HANDS DOWN, MY MOTHER!
FALCONERS HOCKEY

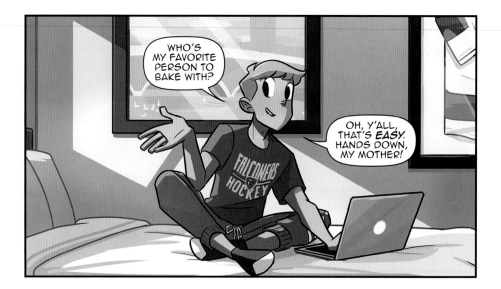

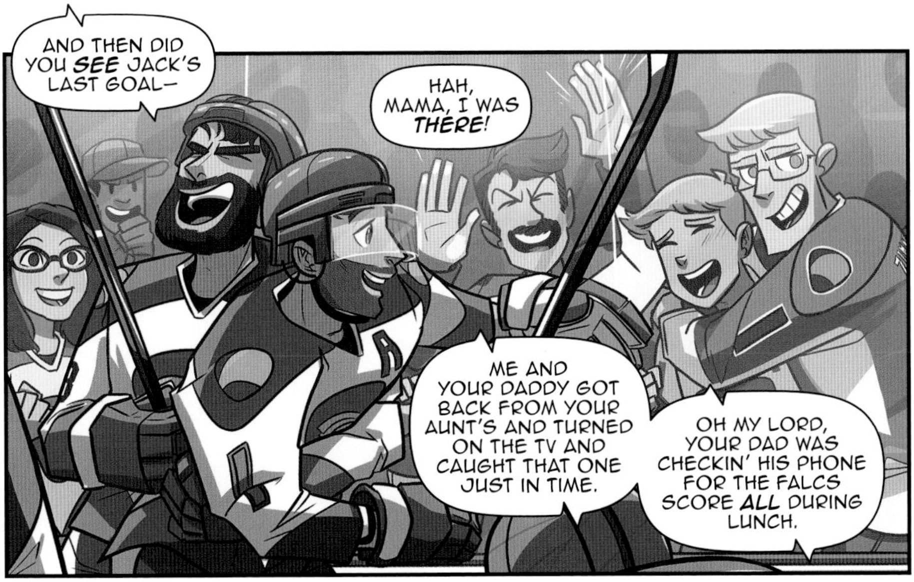
AND THEN DID YOU **SEE** JACK'S LAST GOAL—
HAH, MAMA, I WAS **THERE**!
ME AND YOUR DADDY GOT BACK FROM YOUR AUNT'S AND TURNED ON THE TV AND CAUGHT THAT ONE JUST IN TIME.
OH MY LORD, YOUR DAD WAS CHECKIN' HIS PHONE FOR THE FALCS SCORE **ALL** DURING LUNCH.

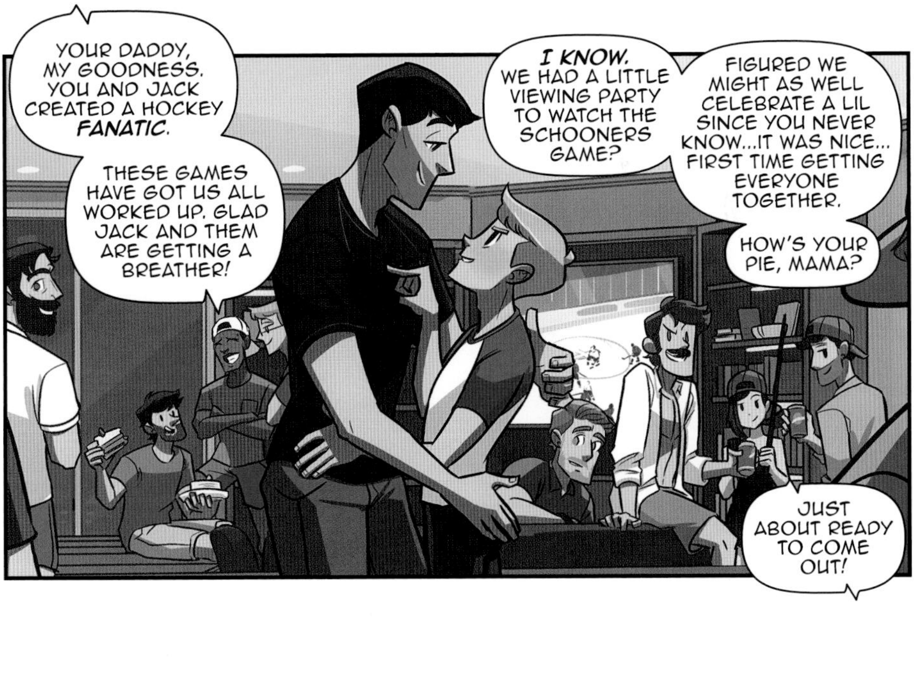
YOUR DADDY, MY GOODNESS. YOU AND JACK CREATED A HOCKEY **FANATIC**.
THESE GAMES HAVE GOT US ALL WORKED UP. GLAD JACK AND THEM ARE GETTING A BREATHER!
I KNOW. WE HAD A LITTLE VIEWING PARTY TO WATCH THE SCHOONERS GAME?
FIGURED WE MIGHT AS WELL CELEBRATE A LIL SINCE YOU NEVER KNOW...IT WAS NICE... FIRST TIME GETTING EVERYONE TOGETHER.
HOW'S YOUR PIE, MAMA?
JUST ABOUT READY TO COME OUT!

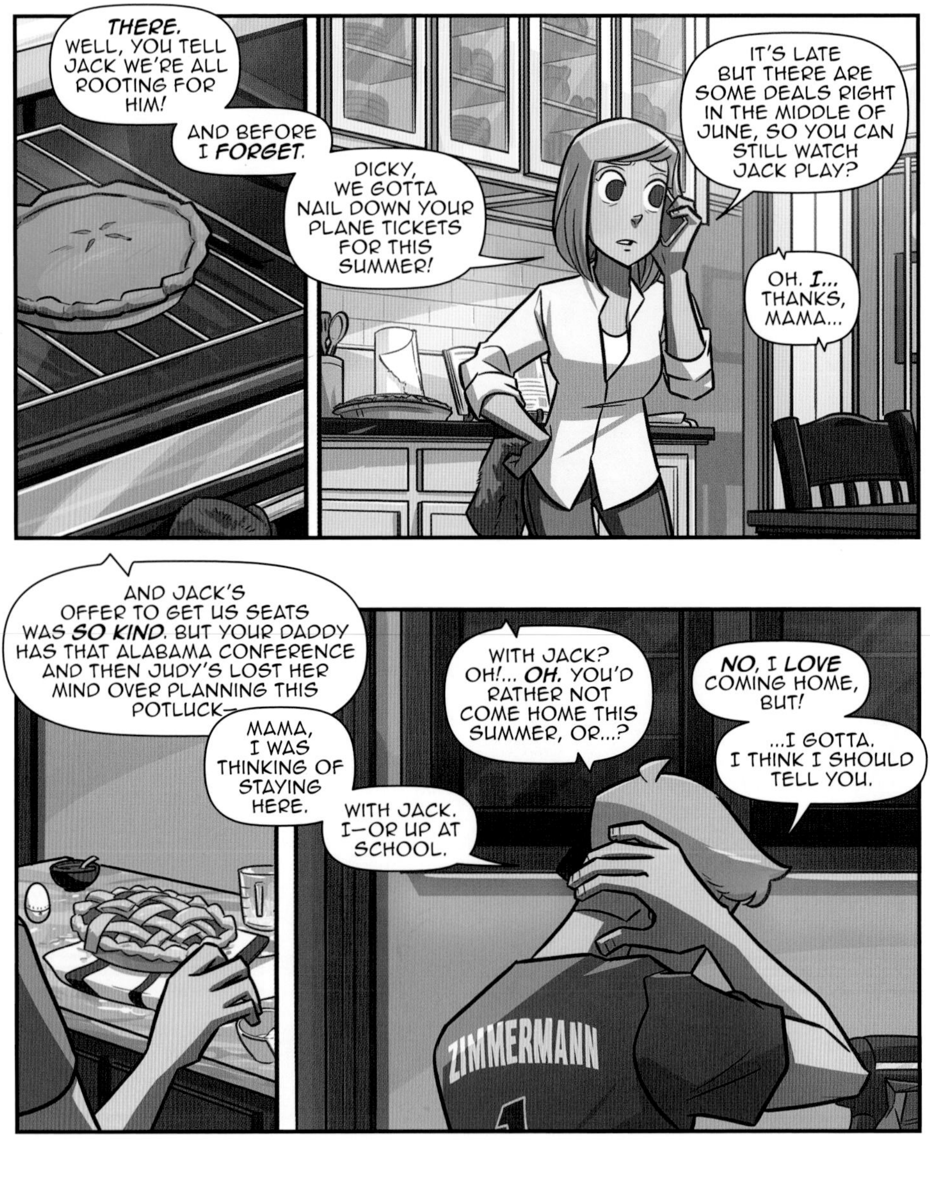
THERE. WELL, YOU TELL JACK WE'RE ALL ROOTING FOR HIM!
AND BEFORE I FORGET.
DICKY, WE GOTTA NAIL DOWN YOUR PLANE TICKETS FOR THIS SUMMER!
IT'S LATE BUT THERE ARE SOME DEALS RIGHT IN THE MIDDLE OF JUNE, SO YOU CAN STILL WATCH JACK PLAY?
OH. I... THANKS, MAMA...
AND JACK'S OFFER TO GET US SEATS WAS SO KIND. BUT YOUR DADDY HAS THAT ALABAMA CONFERENCE AND THEN JUDY'S LOST HER MIND OVER PLANNING THIS POTLUCK—
MAMA, I WAS THINKING OF STAYING HERE.
WITH JACK. I—OR UP AT SCHOOL.
WITH JACK? OH!... OH. YOU'D RATHER NOT COME HOME THIS SUMMER, OR...?
NO, I LOVE COMING HOME, BUT!
...I GOTTA. I THINK I SHOULD TELL YOU.
ZIMMERMANN

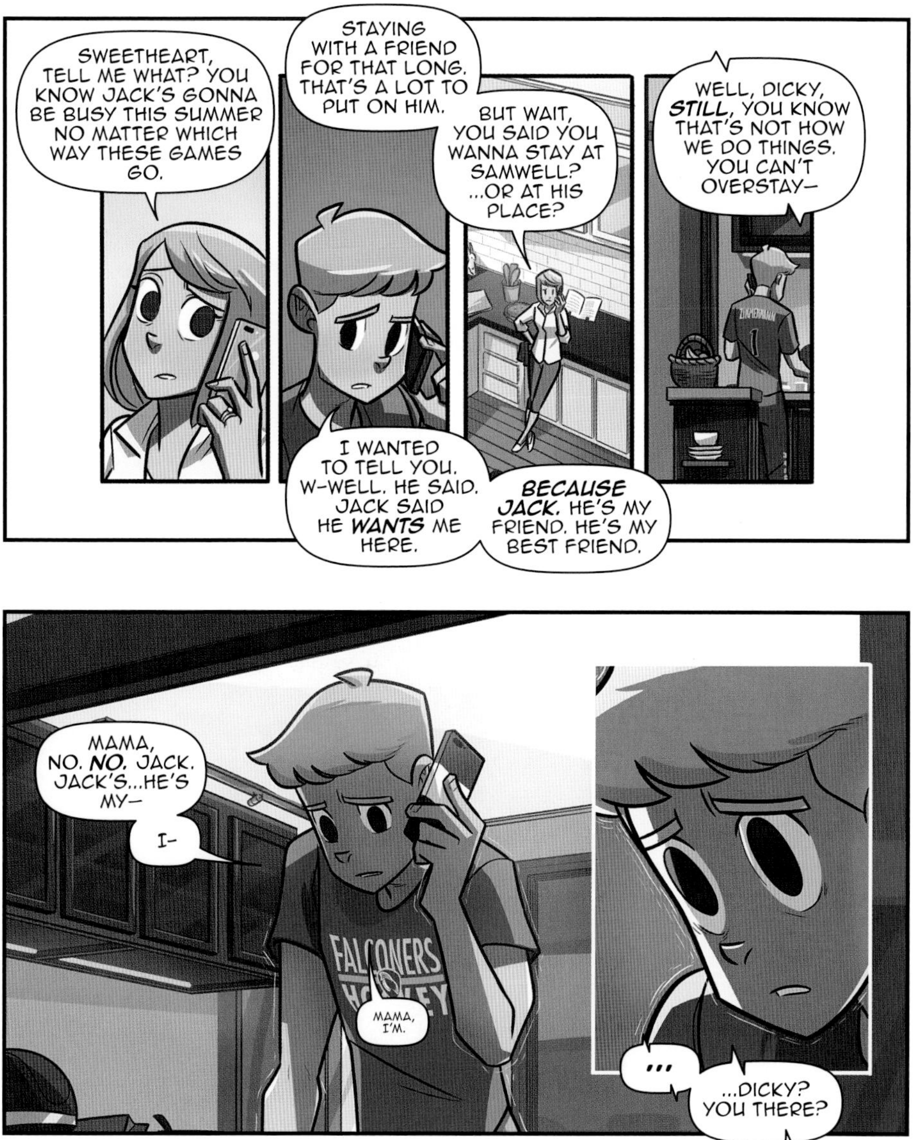
SWEETHEART, TELL ME WHAT? YOU KNOW JACK'S GONNA BE BUSY THIS SUMMER NO MATTER WHICH WAY THESE GAMES GO.
STAYING WITH A FRIEND FOR THAT LONG. THAT'S A LOT TO PUT ON HIM.
I WANTED TO TELL YOU. W-WELL. HE SAID. JACK SAID HE **WANTS** ME HERE.
BUT WAIT, YOU SAID YOU WANNA STAY AT SAMWELL? ...OR AT HIS PLACE?
BECAUSE JACK. HE'S MY FRIEND. HE'S MY BEST FRIEND.
WELL, DICKY, **STILL**, YOU KNOW THAT'S NOT HOW WE DO THINGS. YOU CAN'T OVERSTAY—
ZIMMERMANN 1
MAMA, NO. **NO.** JACK. JACK'S...HE'S MY—
I-
FALCONERS HOCKEY
MAMA, I'M.
...
...DICKY? YOU THERE?

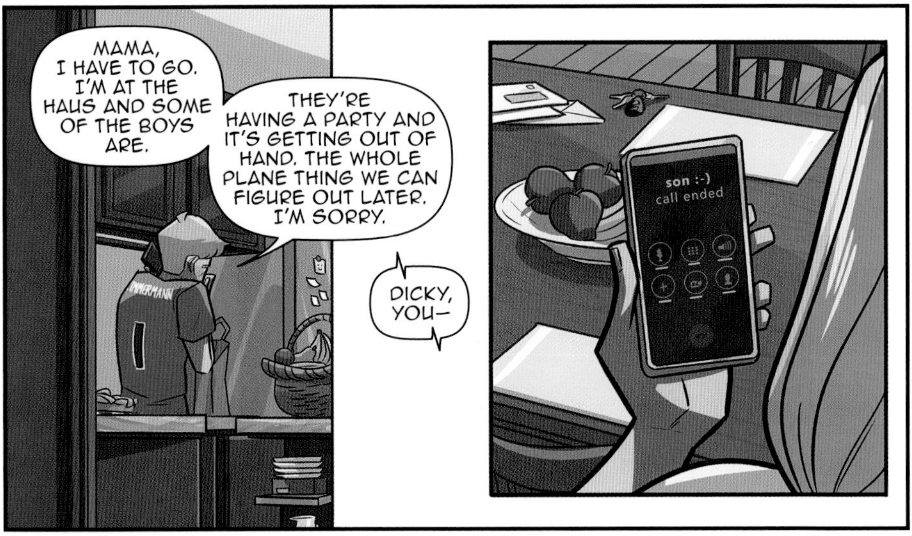
MAMA, I HAVE TO GO. I'M AT THE HAUS AND SOME OF THE BOYS ARE.
THEY'RE HAVING A PARTY AND IT'S GETTING OUT OF HAND. THE WHOLE PLANE THING WE CAN FIGURE OUT LATER. I'M SORRY.
DICKY, YOU–
son :-)
call ended

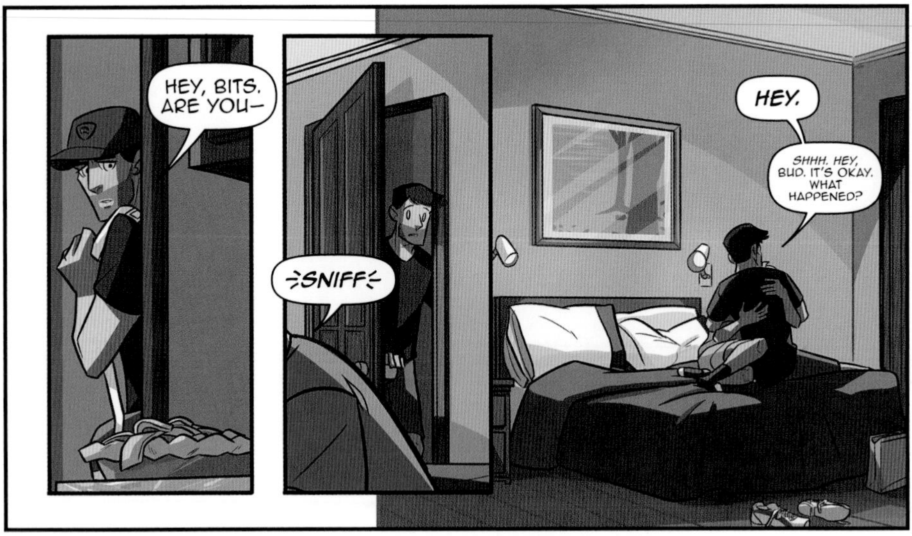
HEY, BITS. ARE YOU–
-SNIFF-
HEY.
SHHH. HEY, BUD. IT'S OKAY. WHAT HAPPENED?

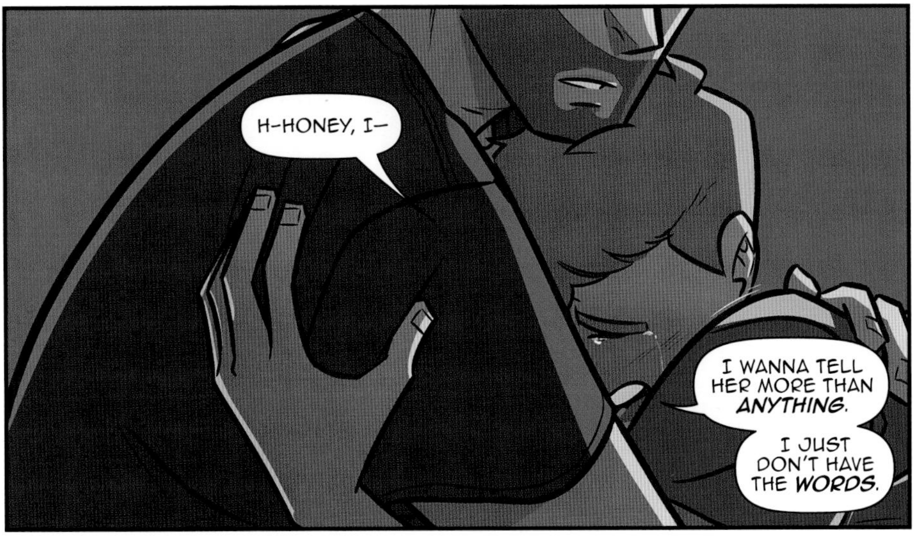
H-HONEY, I–
I WANNA TELL HER MORE THAN *ANYTHING*.
I JUST DON'T HAVE THE *WORDS*.

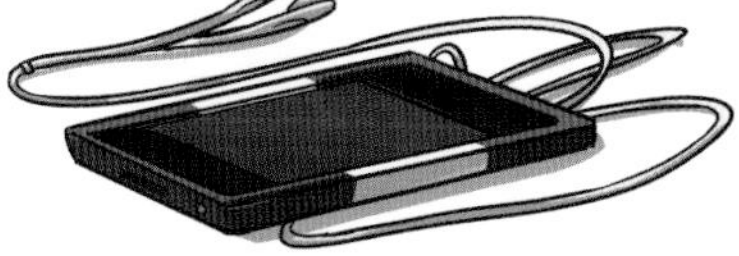

24

CUP III —
7 GAMES

Game 1

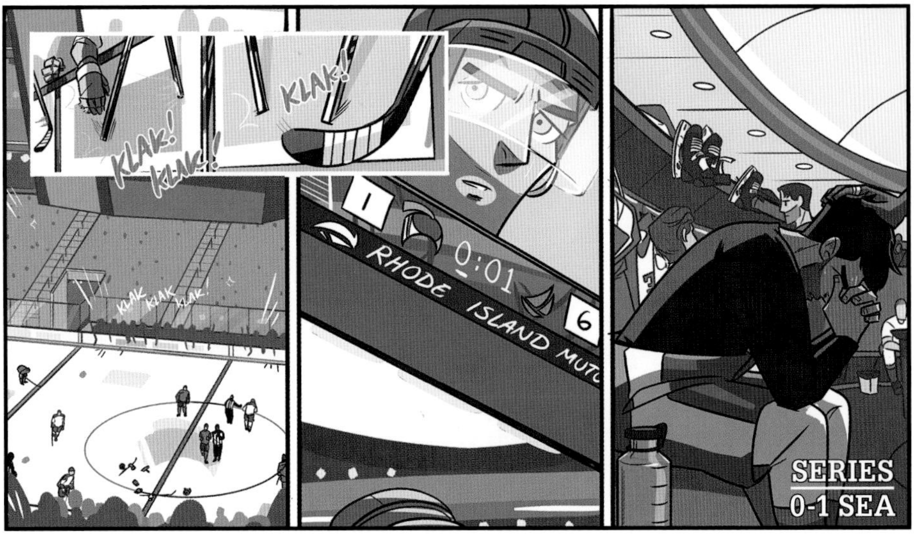
KLAK!
KLAK!
KLAK!
KLAK KLAK KLAK!
1
0:01
RHODE ISLAND MUTU
6
SERIES
0-1 SEA

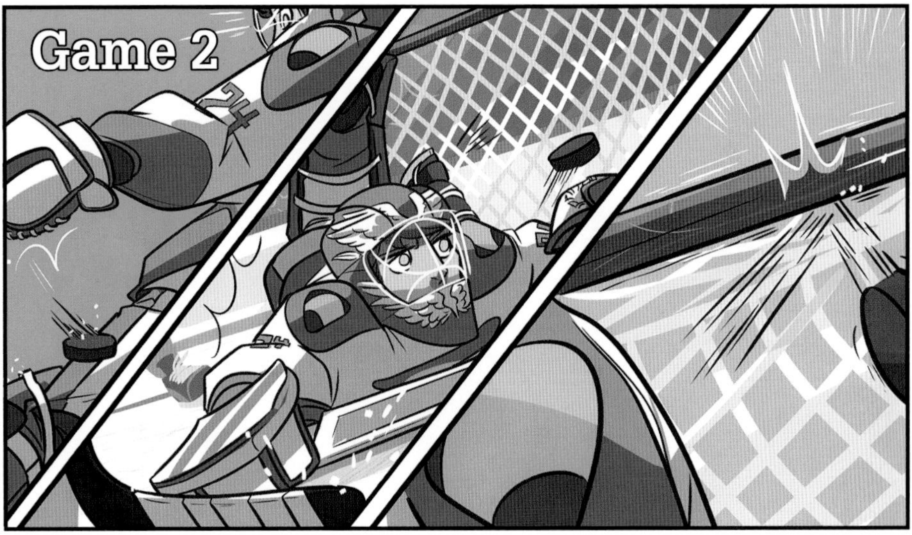
Game 2

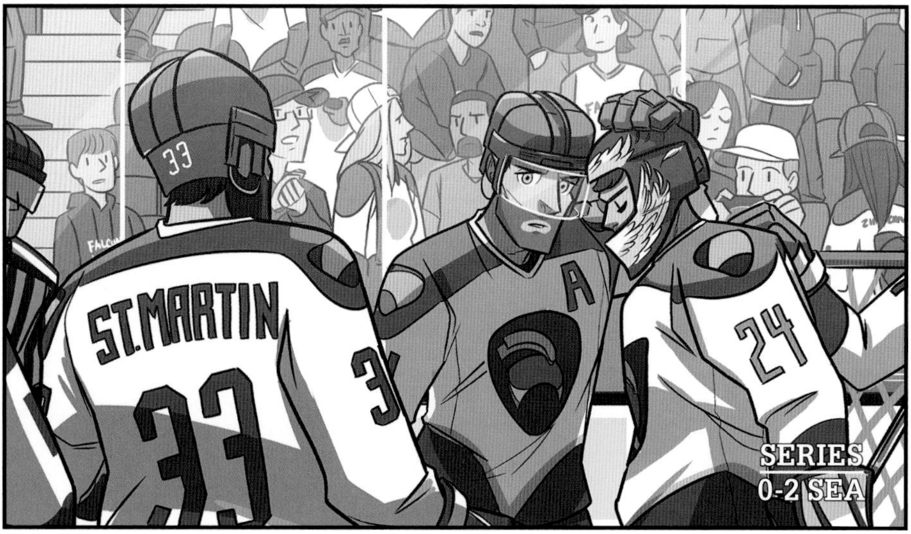
33
ST.MARTIN
33
24
SERIES
0-2 SEA

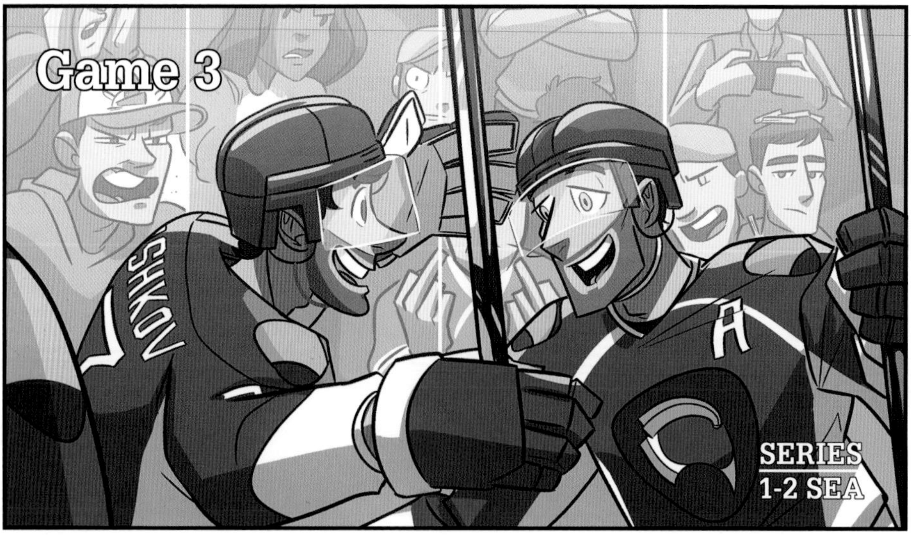
Game 3
SHKOV
A
SERIES
1-2 SEA

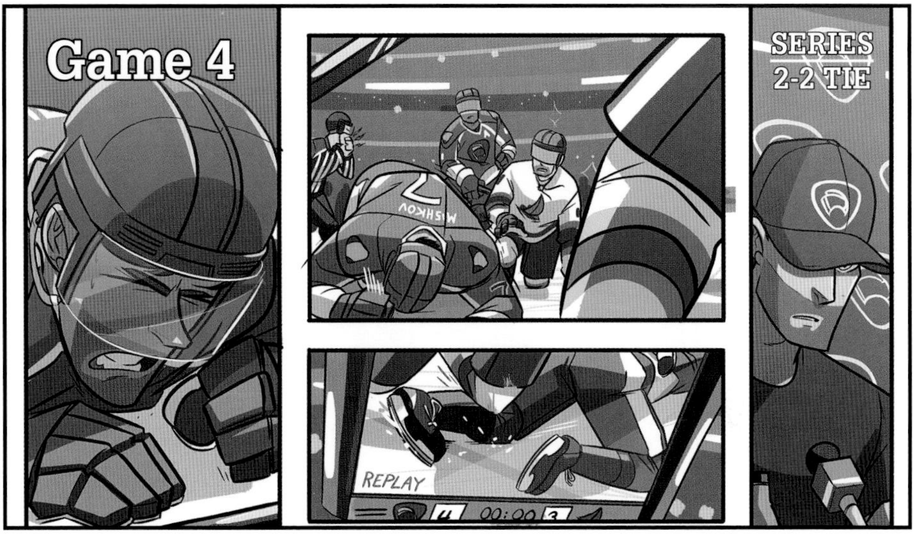
Game 4
REPLAY
SERIES
2-2 TIE

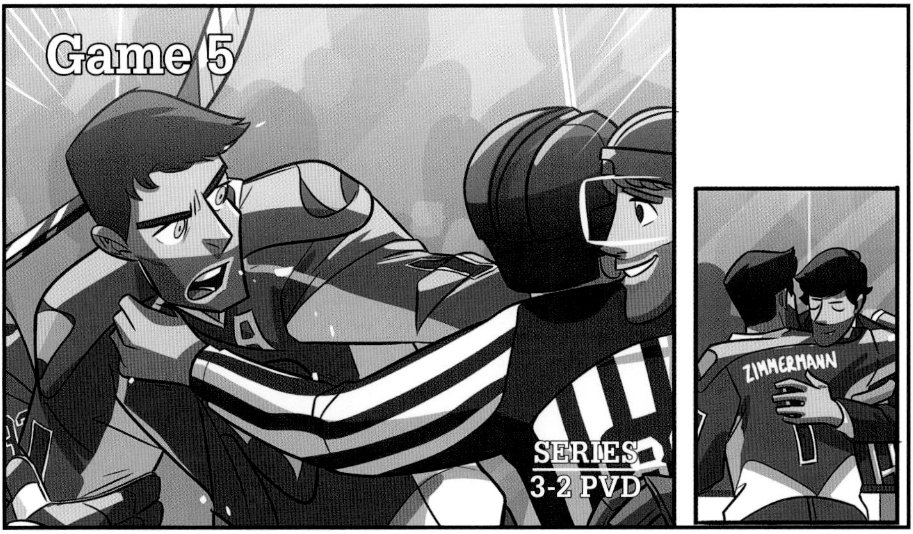
Game 5
SERIES
3-2 PVD
ZIMMERMANN

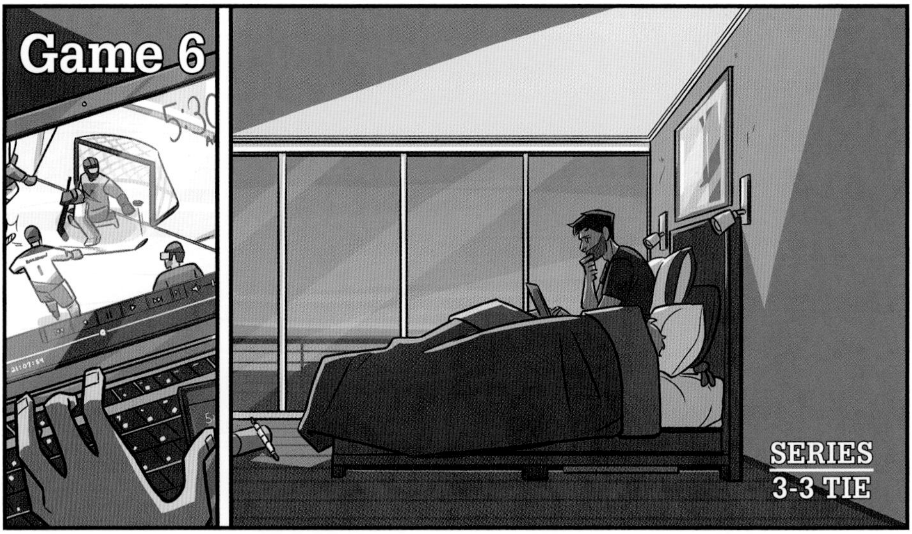
Game 6
SERIES
3-3 TIE

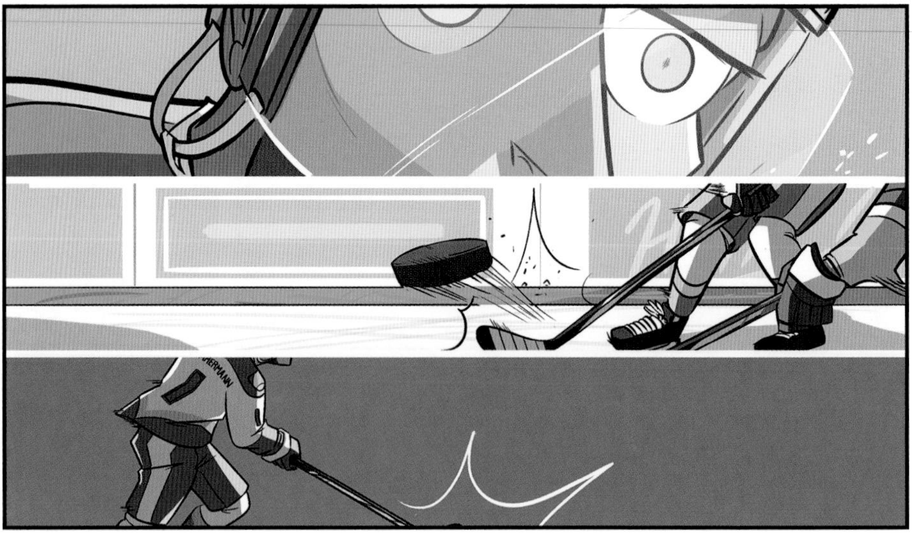

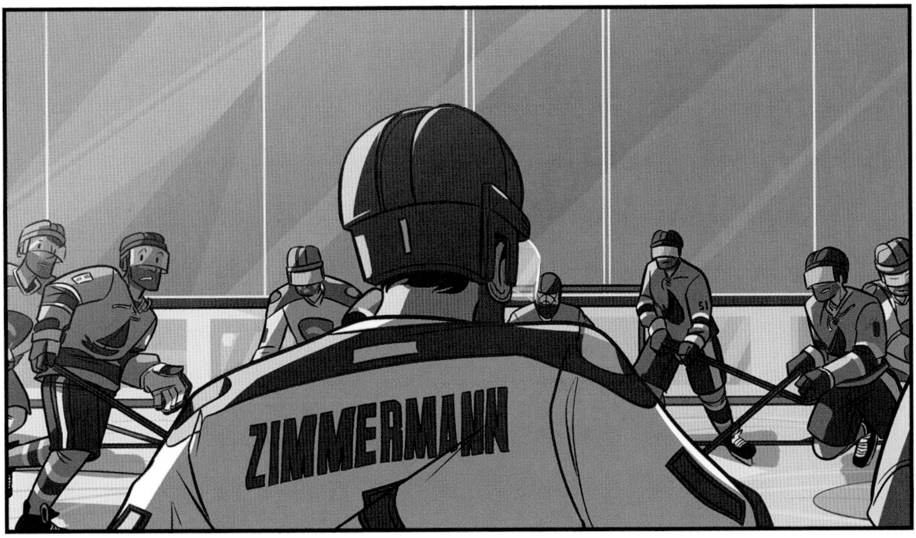
ZIMMERMANN

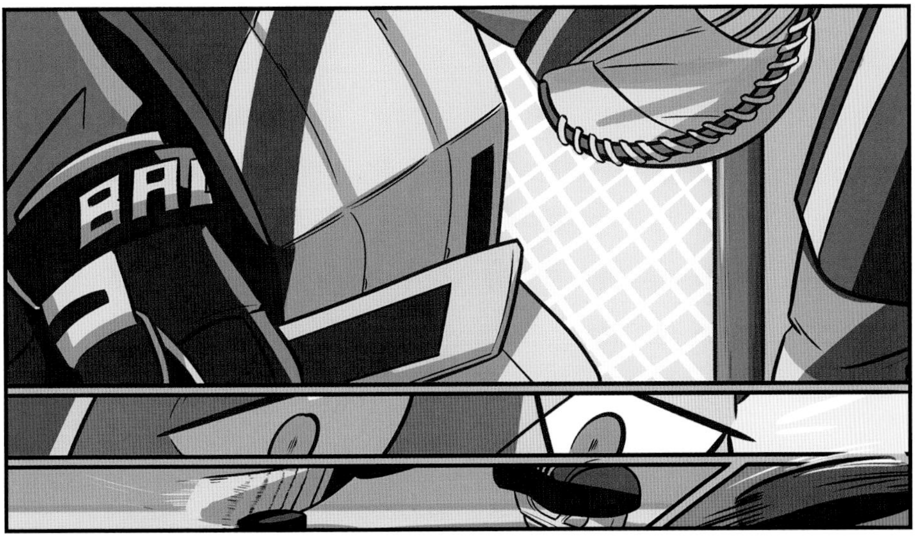
BA

Game 7

25

CUP IV — CENTER ICE

AUGUST BEFORE JUNIOR YEAR...
HAH.
YOU THINK THESE'LL HELP MY GAME?
MR. ZIMMERMANN, I'M *SURE* OF IT.
...OH, GOSH. HAHA.

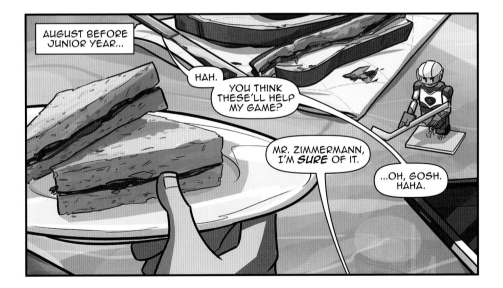

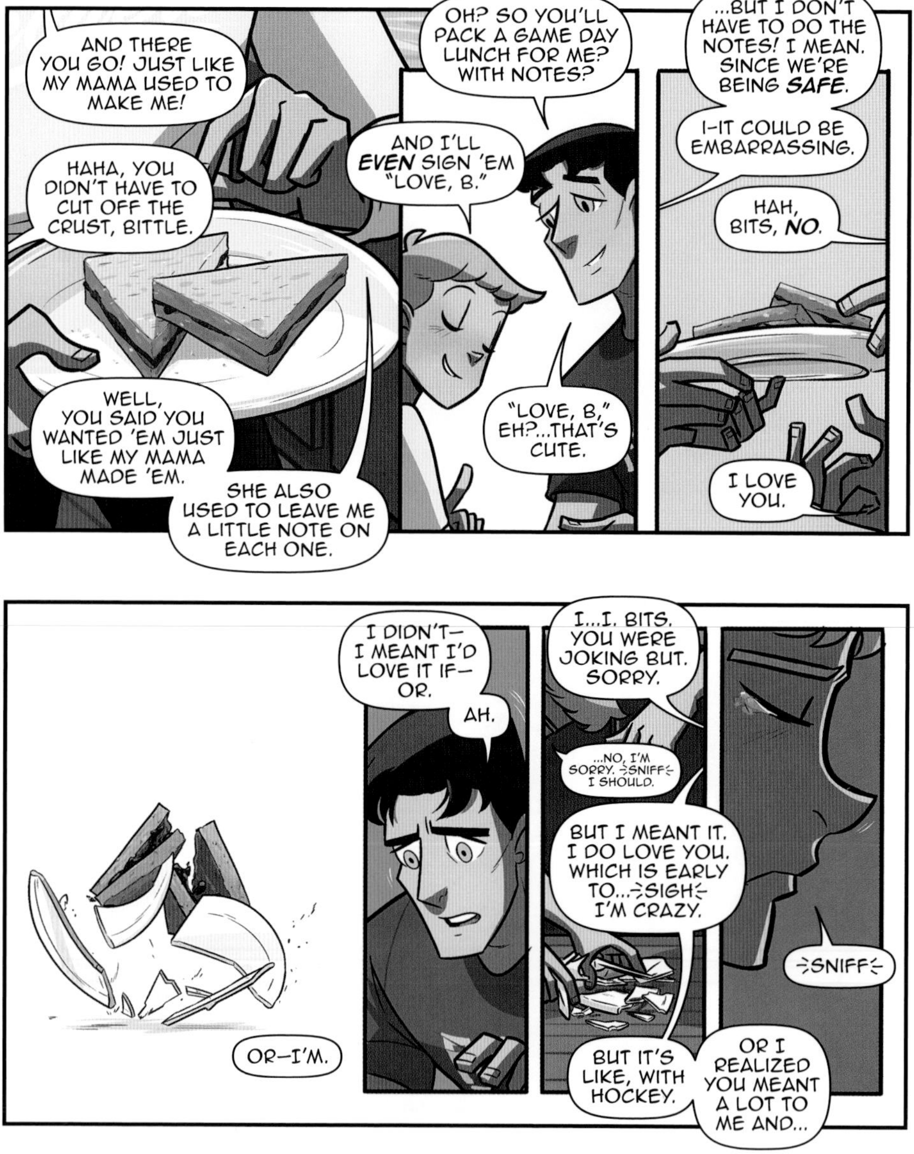
AND THERE YOU GO! JUST LIKE MY MAMA USED TO MAKE ME!
HAHA, YOU DIDN'T HAVE TO CUT OFF THE CRUST, BITTLE.
WELL, YOU SAID YOU WANTED 'EM JUST LIKE MY MAMA MADE 'EM.
SHE ALSO USED TO LEAVE ME A LITTLE NOTE ON EACH ONE.
OH? SO YOU'LL PACK A GAME DAY LUNCH FOR ME? WITH NOTES?
AND I'LL *EVEN* SIGN 'EM "LOVE, B."
"LOVE, B," EH?...THAT'S CUTE.
...BUT I DON'T HAVE TO DO THE NOTES! I MEAN. SINCE WE'RE BEING ***SAFE***.
I-IT COULD BE EMBARRASSING.
HAH, BITS, **NO**.
I LOVE YOU.
OR—I'M.
I DIDN'T— I MEANT I'D LOVE IT IF— OR.
AH.
I...I. BITS. YOU WERE JOKING BUT. SORRY.
...NO, I'M SORRY. SNIFF I SHOULD.
BUT I MEANT IT. I DO LOVE YOU. WHICH IS EARLY TO... SIGH I'M CRAZY.
BUT IT'S LIKE, WITH HOCKEY.
OR I REALIZED YOU MEANT A LOT TO ME AND...
SNIFF

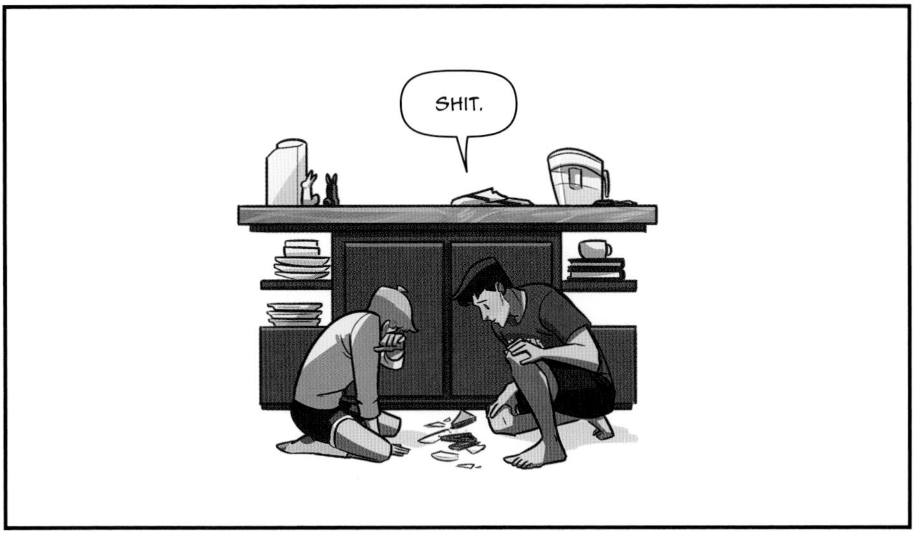
SHIT.

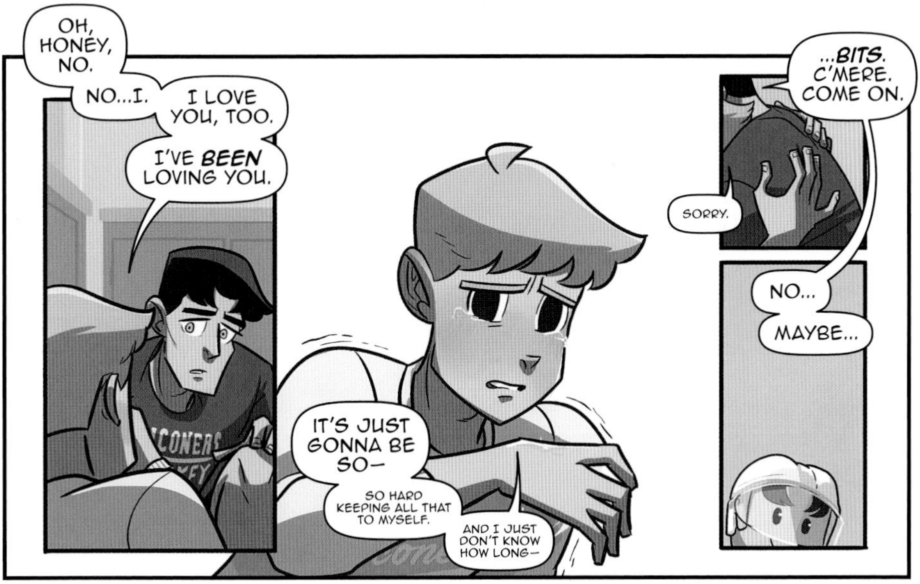
OH, HONEY, NO.
NO...I.
I LOVE YOU, TOO.
I'VE **BEEN** LOVING YOU.
IT'S JUST GONNA BE SO—
SO HARD KEEPING ALL THAT TO MYSELF.
AND I JUST DON'T KNOW HOW LONG—
...**BITS**. C'MERE. COME ON.
SORRY.
NO...
MAYBE...

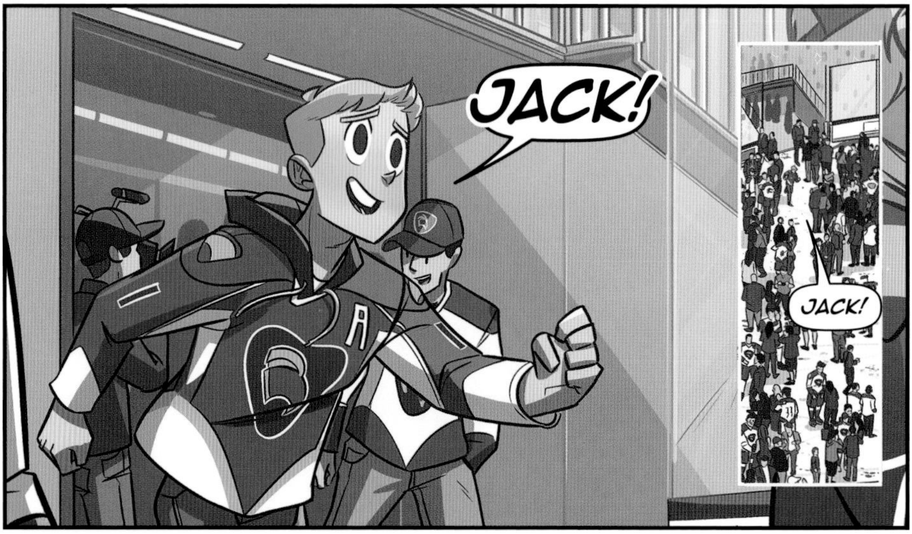
JACK!
JACK!

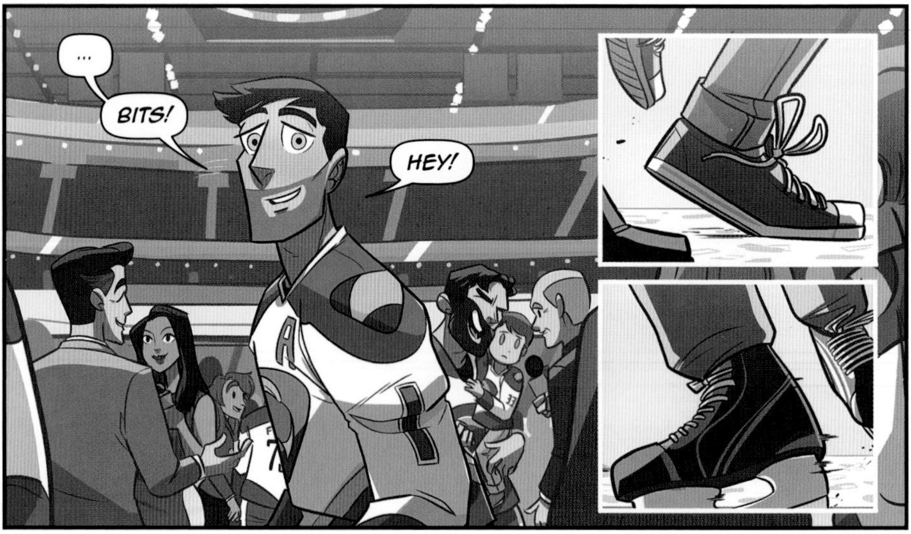
...
BITS!
HEY!

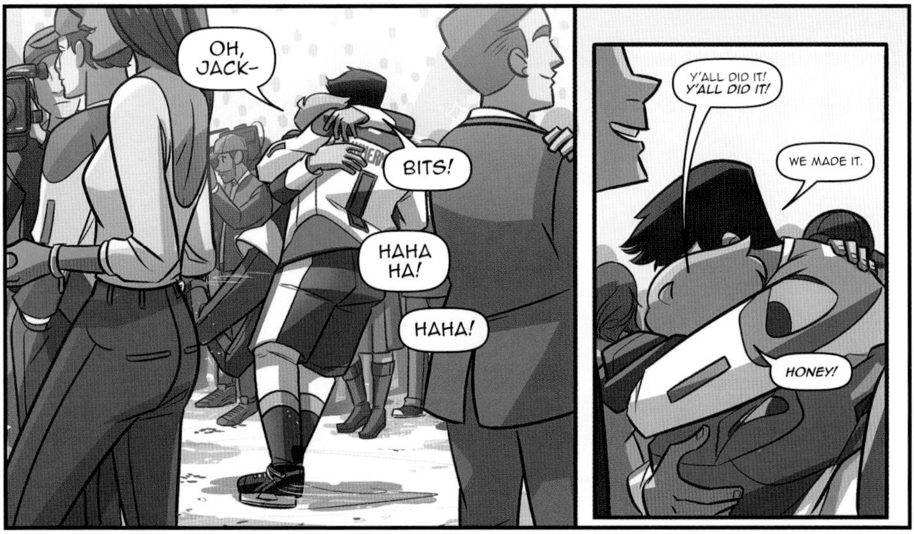
OH, JACK-
BITS!
HAHA HA!
HAHA!
Y'ALL DID IT! Y'ALL DID IT!
WE MADE IT.
HONEY!

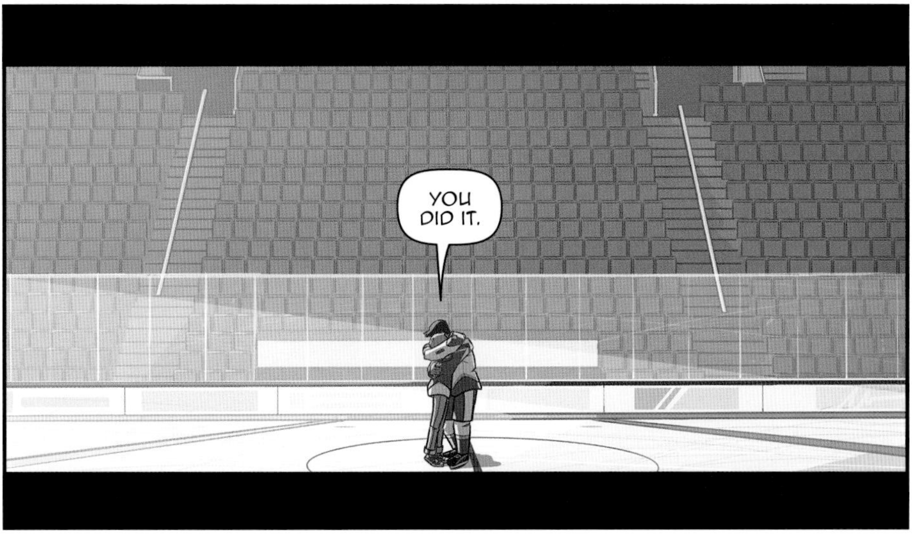
YOU DID IT.

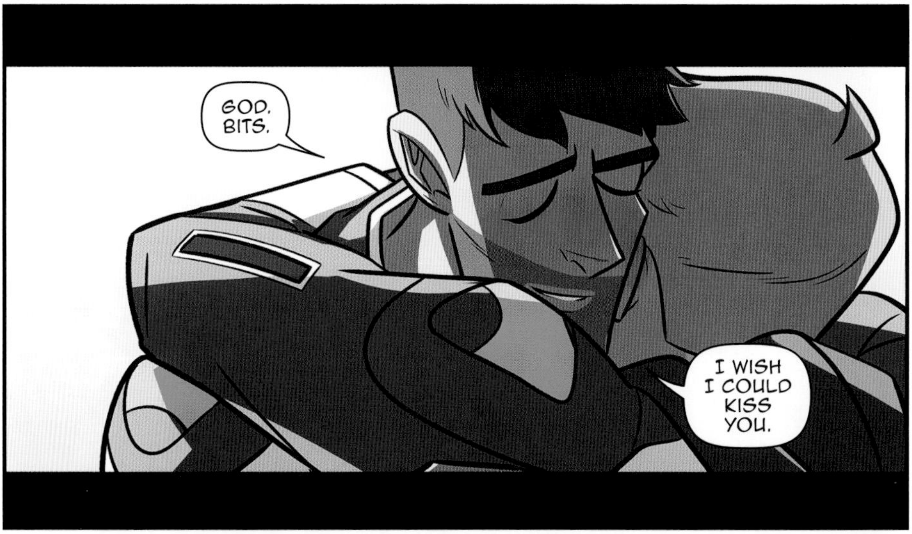
GOD. BITS.
I WISH I COULD KISS YOU.

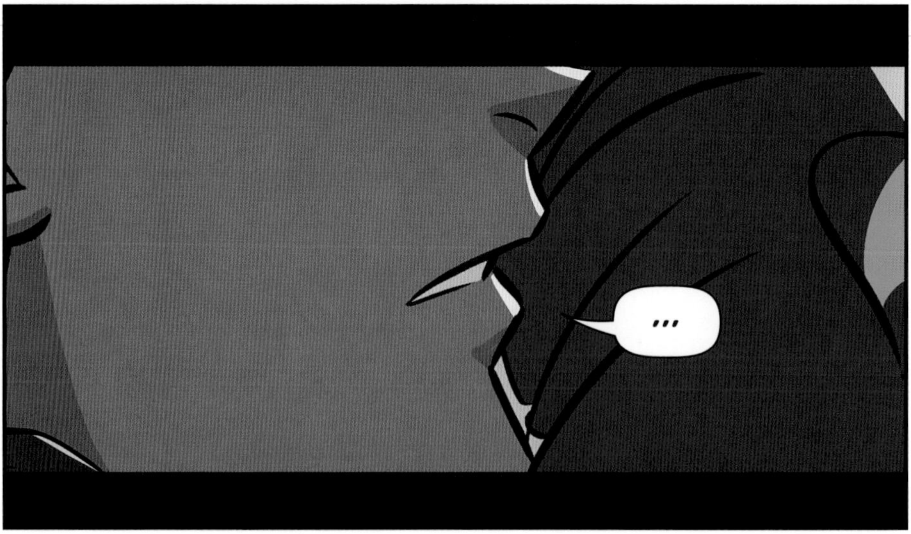
...

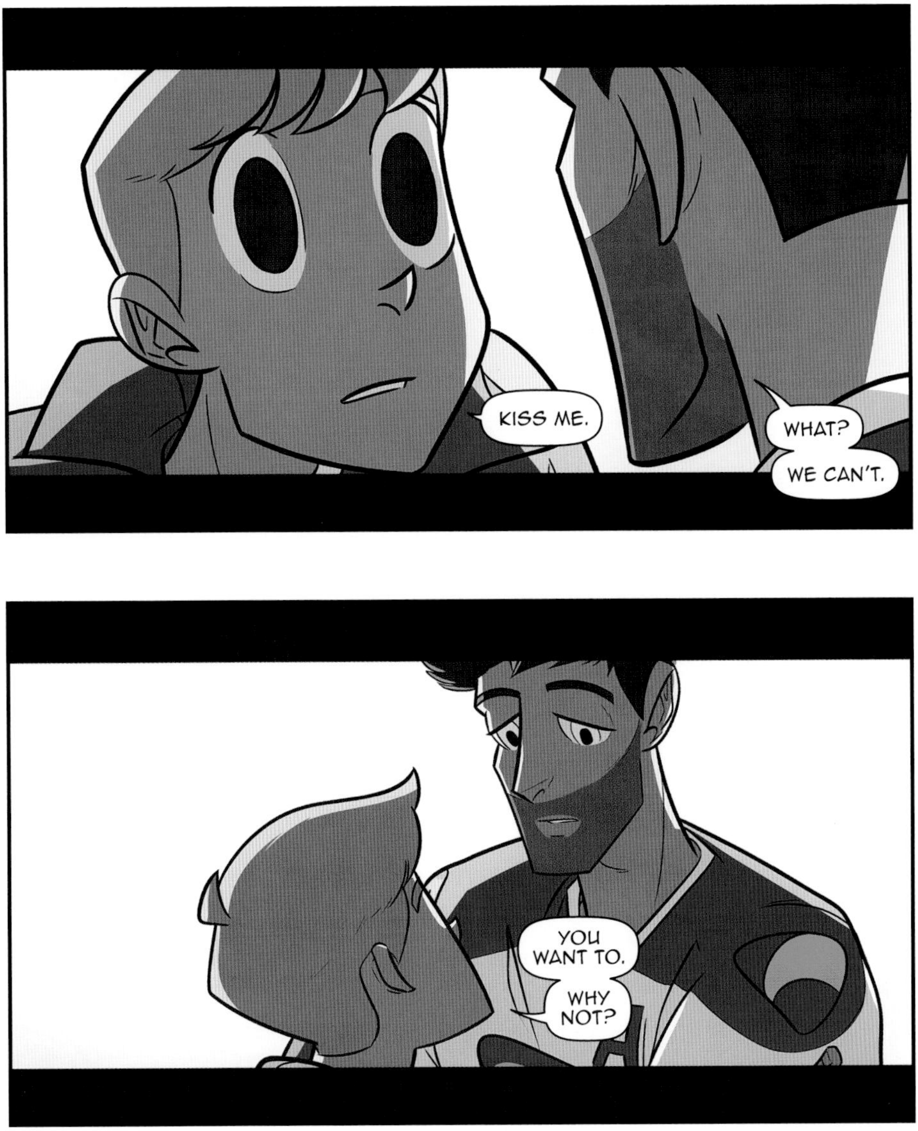
KISS ME.
WHAT?
WE CAN'T.
YOU WANT TO.
WHY NOT?

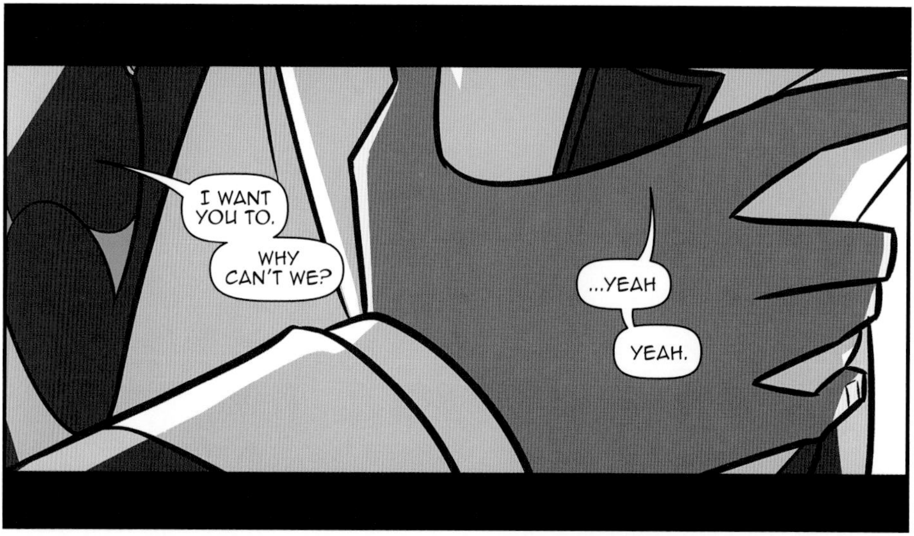
I WANT YOU TO.
WHY CAN'T WE?
...YEAH
YEAH.

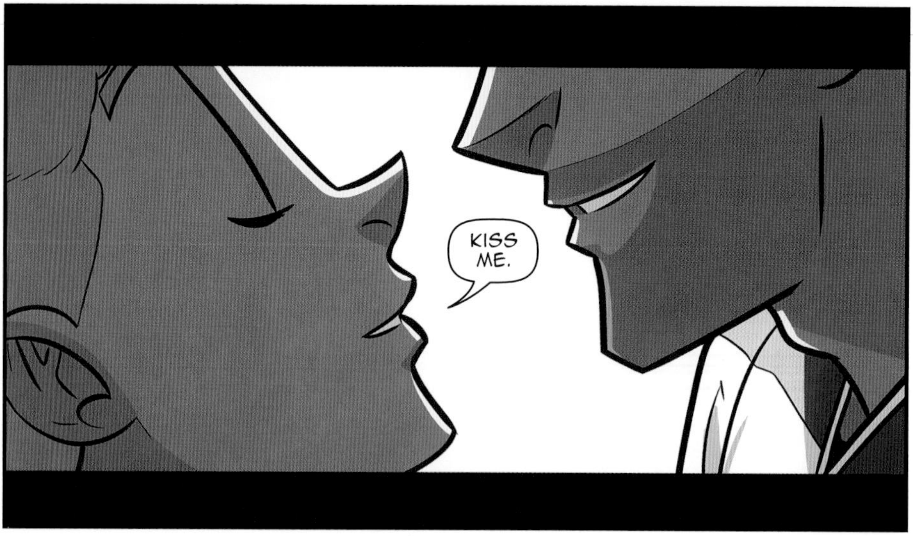
KISS ME.

26

CUP V — POST

NOON. THE DAY AFTER THE CUP.
UGH.
Bzzzt
Bzzzzt
UGHH.
FUCKING CHRIST.

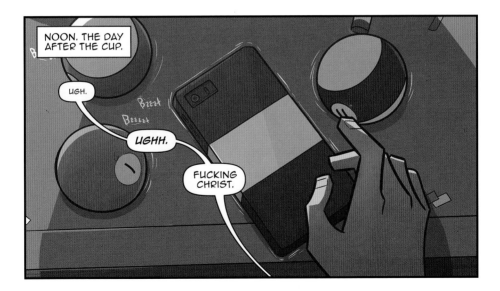

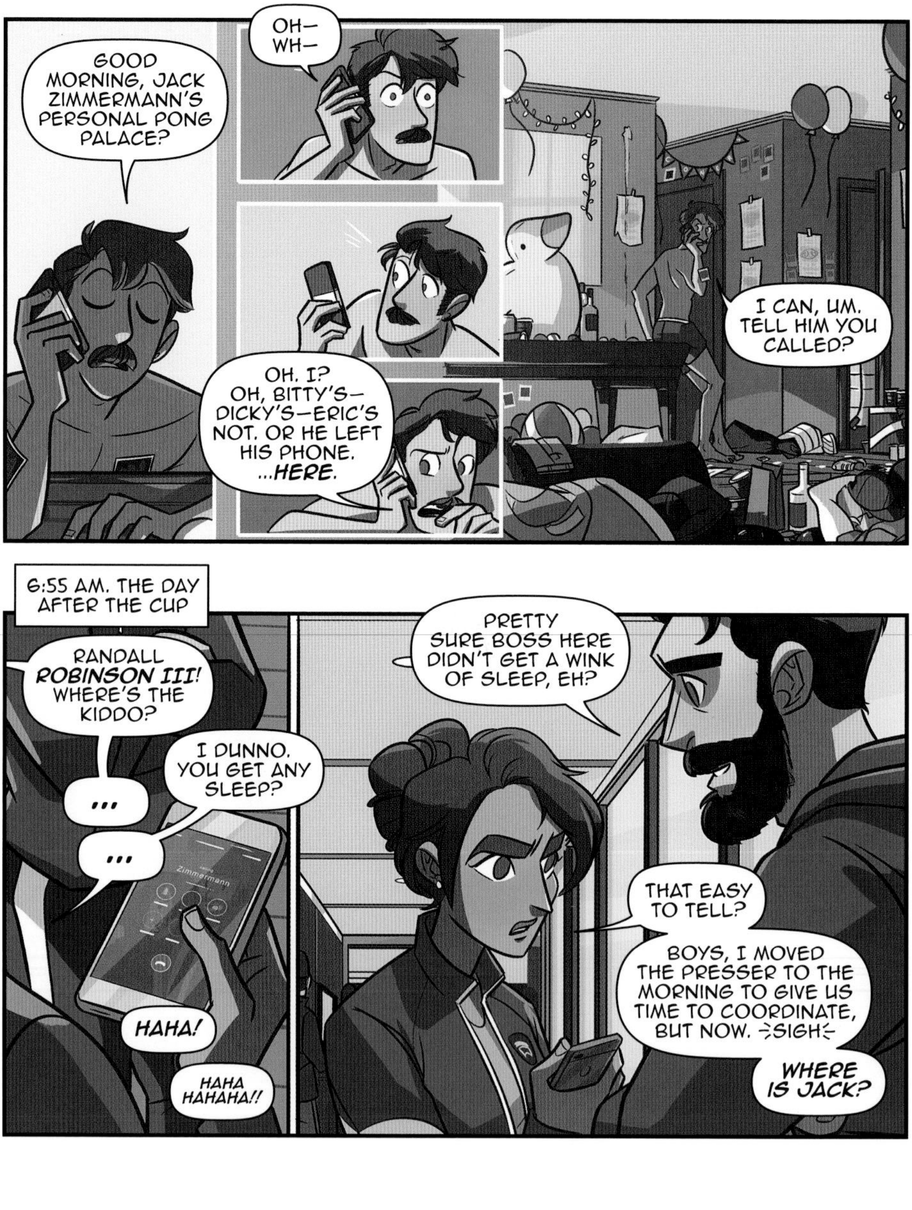
GOOD MORNING, JACK ZIMMERMANN'S PERSONAL PONG PALACE?
OH— WH—
OH. I? OH, BITTY'S—DICKY'S—ERIC'S NOT. OR HE LEFT HIS PHONE. ...HERE.
I CAN, UM. TELL HIM YOU CALLED?
6:55 AM. THE DAY AFTER THE CUP
RANDALL ROBINSON III! WHERE'S THE KIDDO?
...
...
I DUNNO. YOU GET ANY SLEEP?
HAHA!
HAHA HAHAHA!!
PRETTY SURE BOSS HERE DIDN'T GET A WINK OF SLEEP, EH?
THAT EASY TO TELL?
BOYS, I MOVED THE PRESSER TO THE MORNING TO GIVE US TIME TO COORDINATE, BUT NOW. ⇲SIGH⇱
WHERE IS JACK?

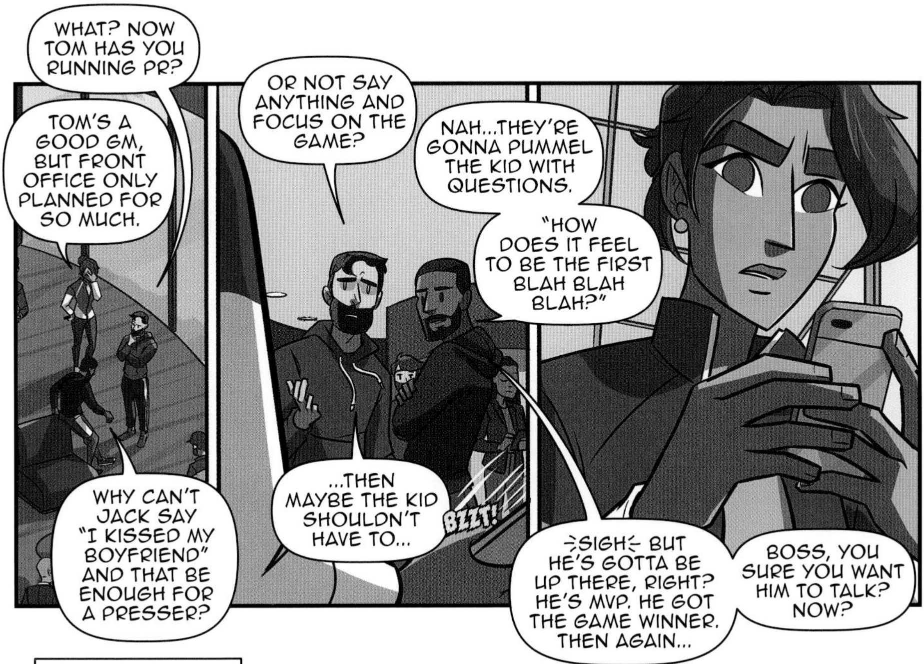
WHAT? NOW TOM HAS YOU RUNNING PR?
TOM'S A GOOD GM, BUT FRONT OFFICE ONLY PLANNED FOR SO MUCH.
WHY CAN'T JACK SAY "I KISSED MY BOYFRIEND" AND THAT BE ENOUGH FOR A PRESSER?
OR NOT SAY ANYTHING AND FOCUS ON THE GAME?
...THEN MAYBE THE KID SHOULDN'T HAVE TO...
BZZT!
NAH...THEY'RE GONNA PUMMEL THE KID WITH QUESTIONS.
"HOW DOES IT FEEL TO BE THE FIRST BLAH BLAH BLAH?"
BOSS, YOU SURE YOU WANT HIM TO TALK? NOW?
⸗SIGH⸗ BUT HE'S GOTTA BE UP THERE, RIGHT? HE'S MVP. HE GOT THE GAME WINNER. THEN AGAIN...

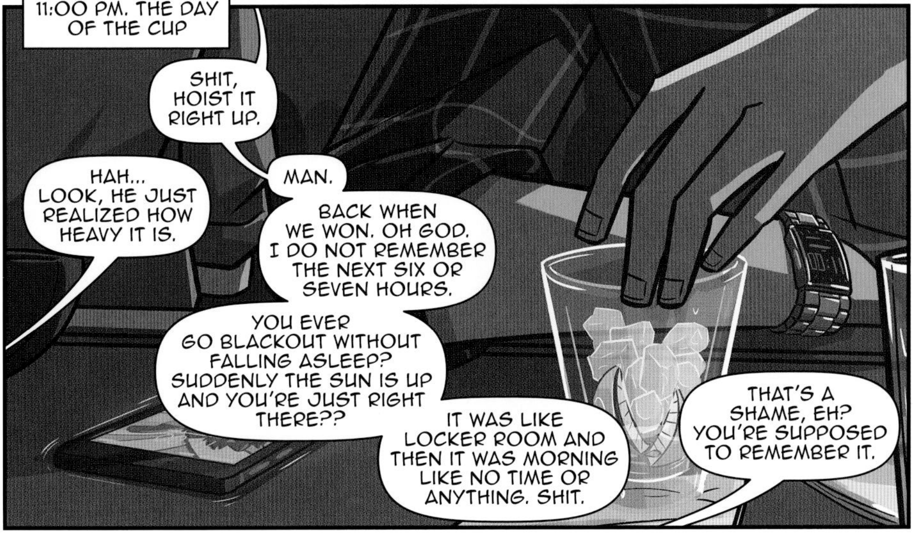
11:00 PM. THE DAY OF THE CUP
SHIT, HOIST IT RIGHT UP.
MAN.
HAH... LOOK, HE JUST REALIZED HOW HEAVY IT IS.
BACK WHEN WE WON. OH GOD. I DO NOT REMEMBER THE NEXT SIX OR SEVEN HOURS.
YOU EVER GO BLACKOUT WITHOUT FALLING ASLEEP? SUDDENLY THE SUN IS UP AND YOU'RE JUST RIGHT THERE??
IT WAS LIKE LOCKER ROOM AND THEN IT WAS MORNING LIKE NO TIME OR ANYTHING. SHIT.
THAT'S A SHAME, EH? YOU'RE SUPPOSED TO REMEMBER IT.

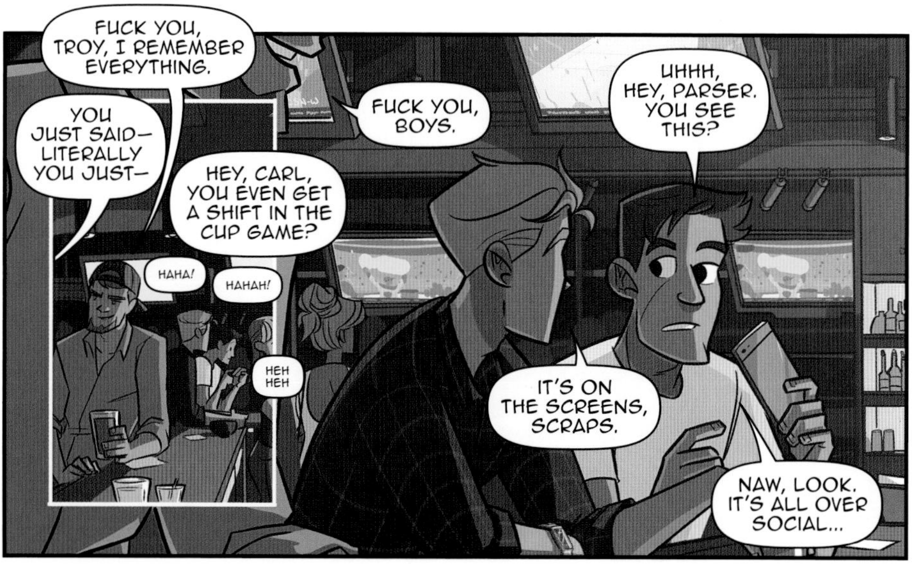
FUCK YOU, TROY, I REMEMBER EVERYTHING.
YOU JUST SAID— LITERALLY YOU JUST—
FUCK YOU, BOYS.
HEY, CARL, YOU EVEN GET A SHIFT IN THE CUP GAME?
HAHA!
HAHAH!
HEH HEH
UHHH, HEY, PARSER. YOU SEE THIS?
IT'S ON THE SCREENS, SCRAPS.
NAW, LOOK. IT'S ALL OVER SOCIAL...

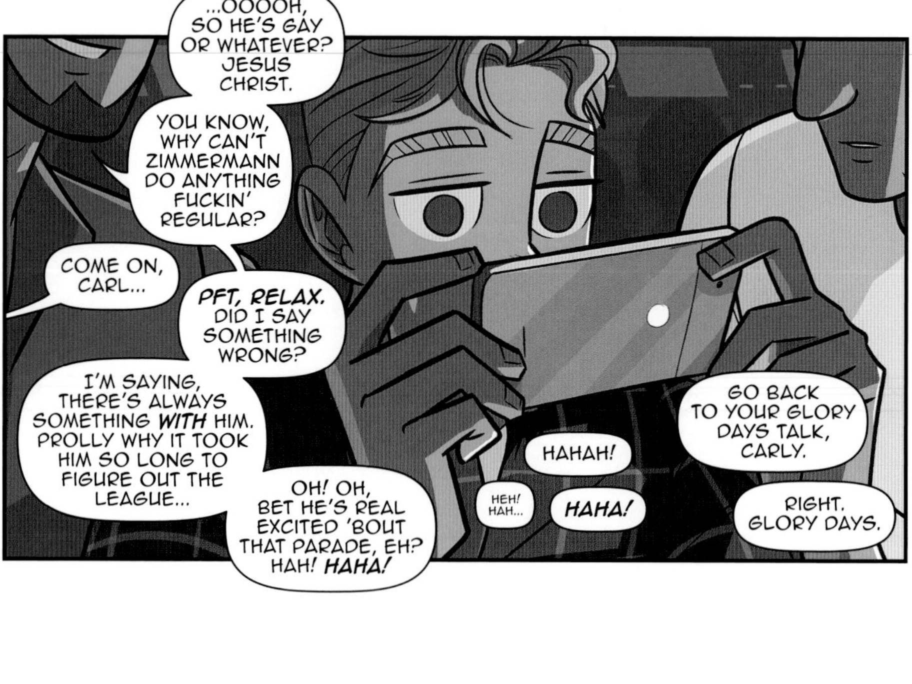
...OOOOH, SO HE'S GAY OR WHATEVER? JESUS CHRIST.
YOU KNOW, WHY CAN'T ZIMMERMANN DO ANYTHING FUCKIN' REGULAR?
COME ON, CARL...
PFT, RELAX. DID I SAY SOMETHING WRONG?
I'M SAYING, THERE'S ALWAYS SOMETHING WITH HIM. PROLLY WHY IT TOOK HIM SO LONG TO FIGURE OUT THE LEAGUE...
OH! OH, BET HE'S REAL EXCITED 'BOUT THAT PARADE, EH? HAH! HAHA!
HAHAH!
HEH! HAH...
HAHA!
GO BACK TO YOUR GLORY DAYS TALK, CARLY.
RIGHT. GLORY DAYS.

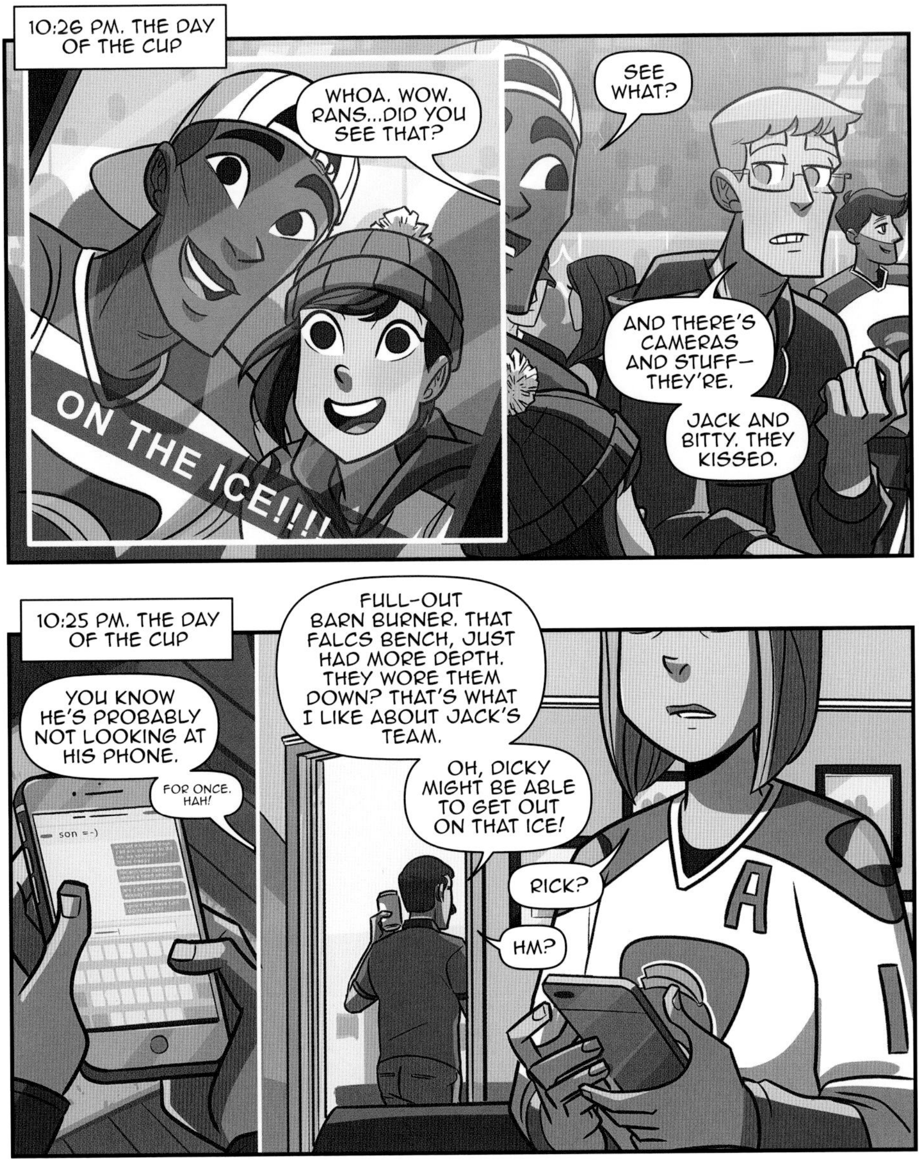
10:26 PM. THE DAY OF THE CUP
WHOA. WOW. RANS...DID YOU SEE THAT?
ON THE ICE!!!!
SEE WHAT?
AND THERE'S CAMERAS AND STUFF—THEY'RE.
JACK AND BITTY. THEY KISSED.
10:25 PM. THE DAY OF THE CUP
YOU KNOW HE'S PROBABLY NOT LOOKING AT HIS PHONE.
FOR ONCE. HAH!
son =-)
FULL-OUT BARN BURNER. THAT FALCS BENCH, JUST HAD MORE DEPTH. THEY WORE THEM DOWN? THAT'S WHAT I LIKE ABOUT JACK'S TEAM.
OH, DICKY MIGHT BE ABLE TO GET OUT ON THAT ICE!
RICK?
HM?
A

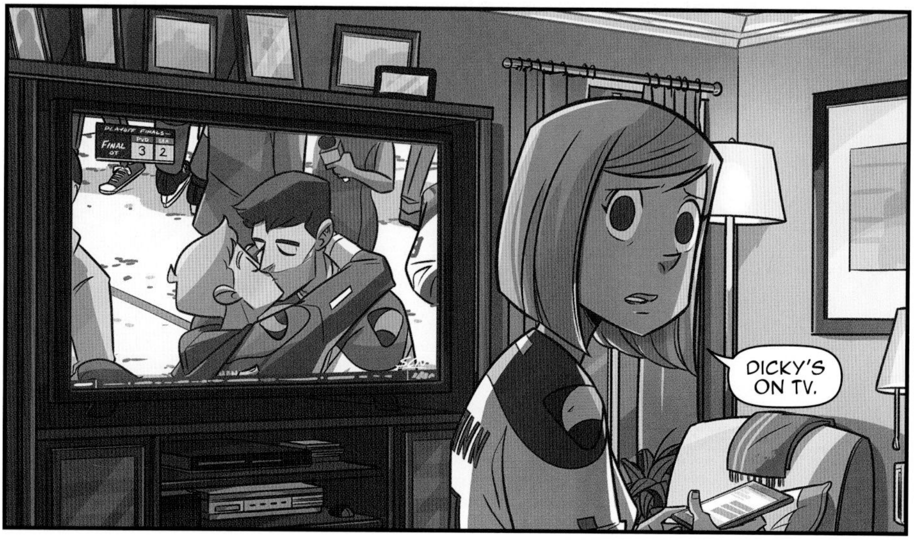
PLAYOFF FINALS
FINAL
OT
3
2
DICKY'S ON TV.

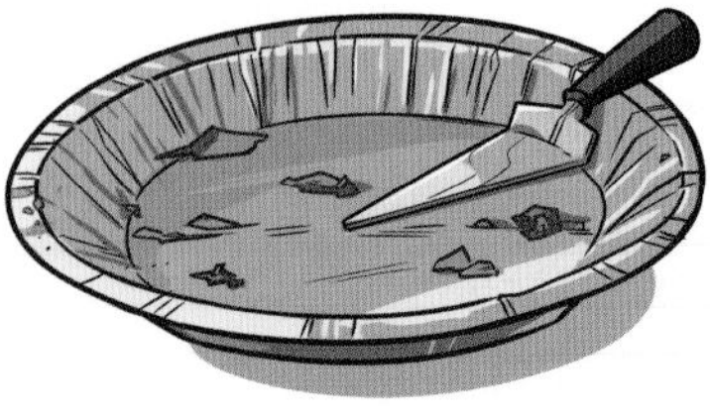

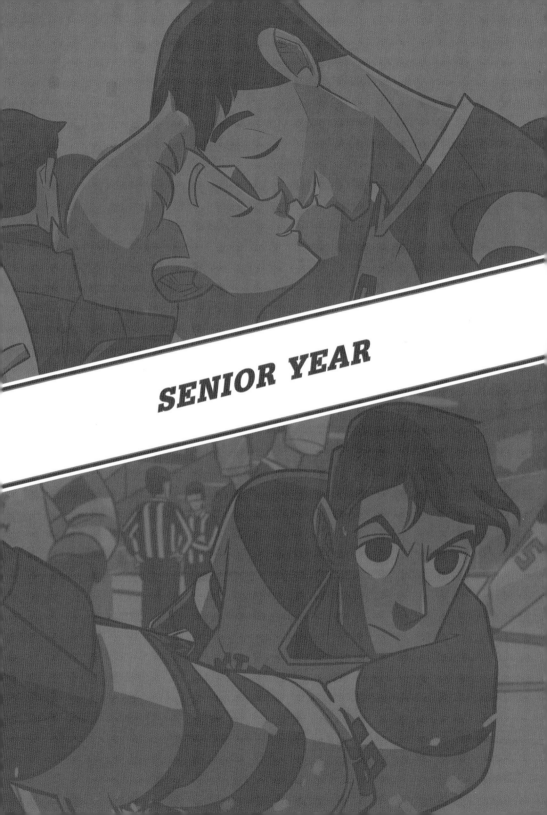

SENIOR YEAR

1

WAKE-UP CALL

M-MAMA... MAMA, I'M NOT SURE I CAN PLAY ANYMORE.
OH, DICKY. SWEETHEART. WHAT'S WRONG?

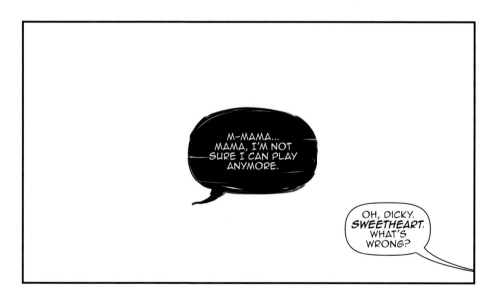

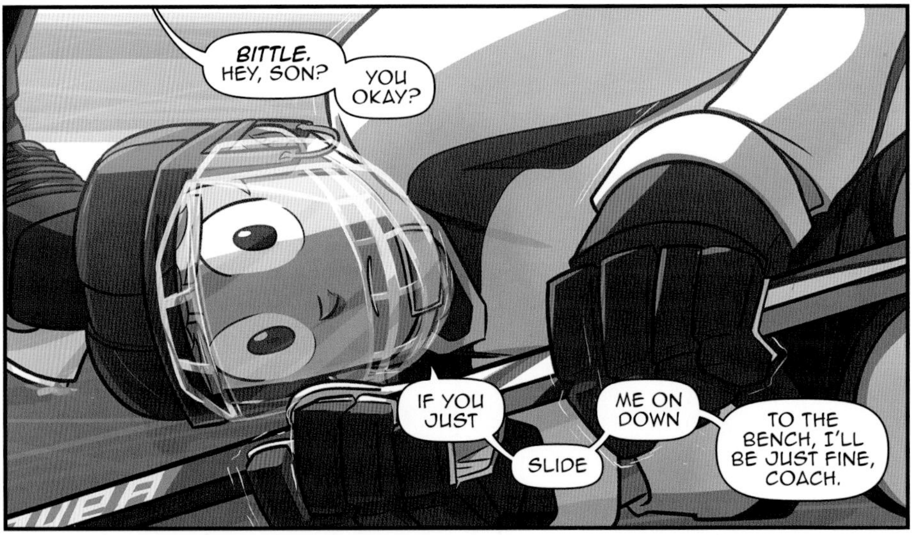
BITTLE. HEY, SON?
YOU OKAY?
IF YOU JUST
SLIDE
ME ON DOWN
TO THE BENCH, I'LL BE JUST FINE, COACH.

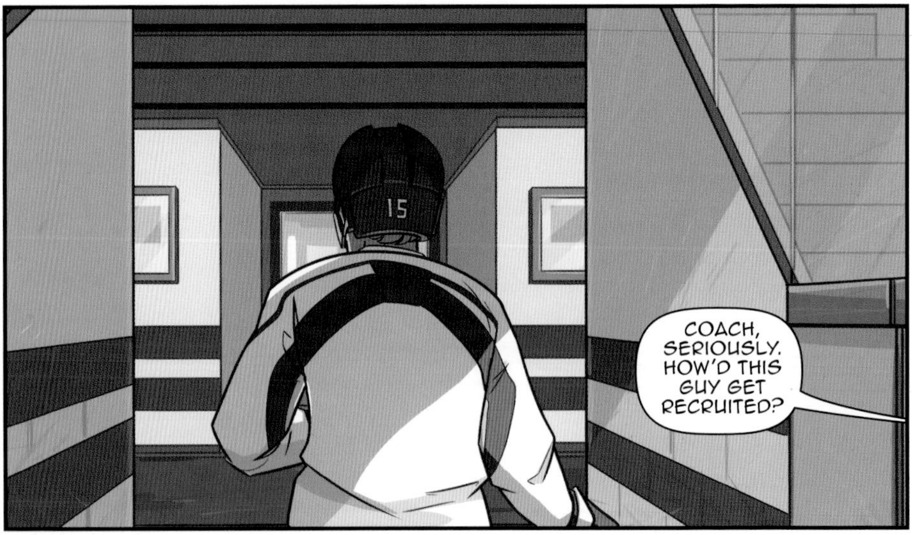
COACH, SERIOUSLY. HOW'D THIS GUY GET RECRUITED?

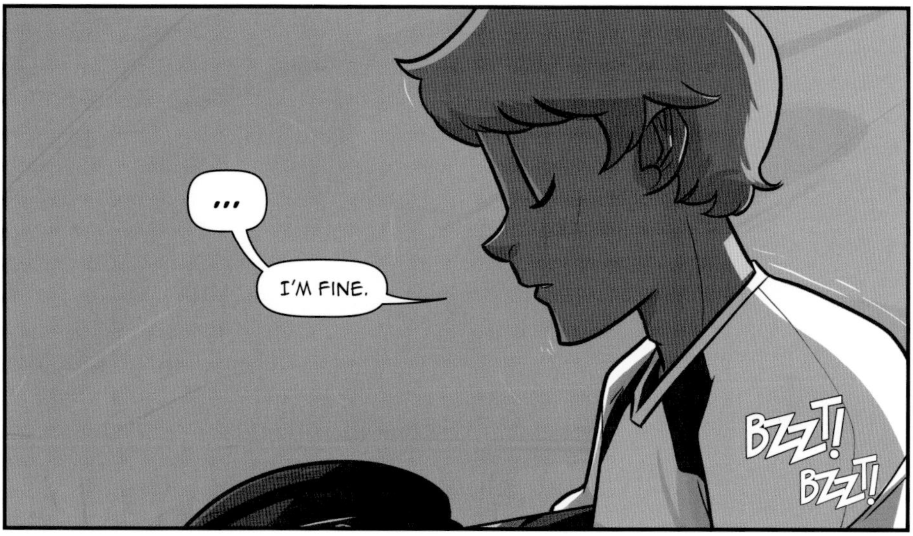
...
I'M FINE.
BZZT!
BZZT!

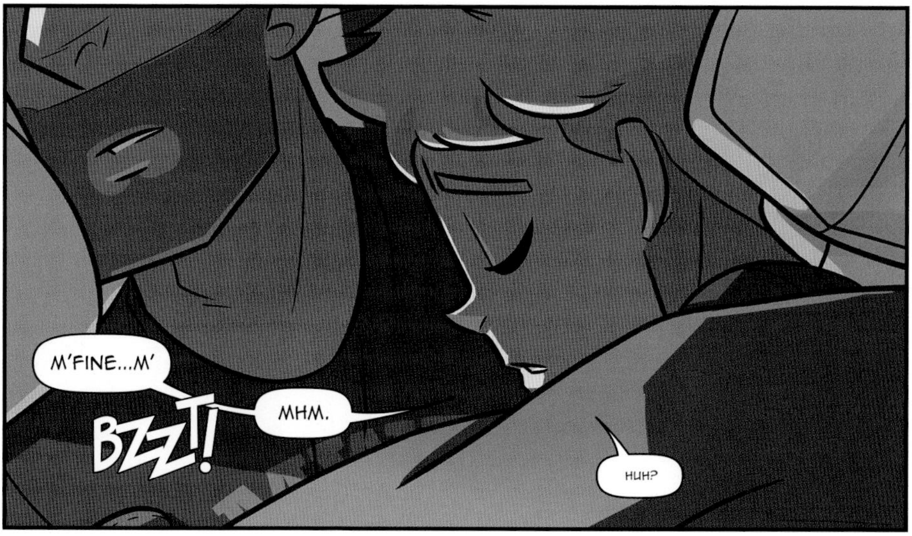
M'FINE...M'
BZZT!
MHM.
HUH?

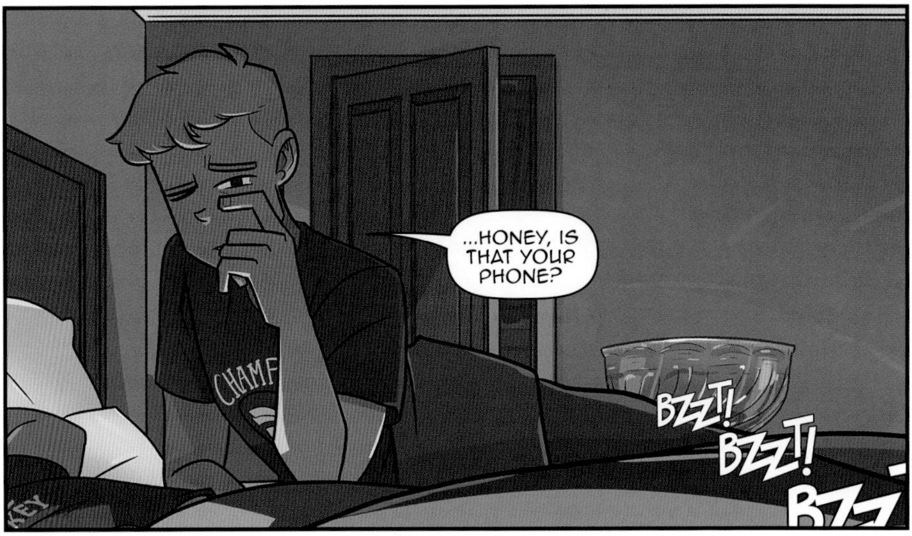
...HONEY, IS THAT YOUR PHONE?
CHAMP
BZZT!
BZZT!

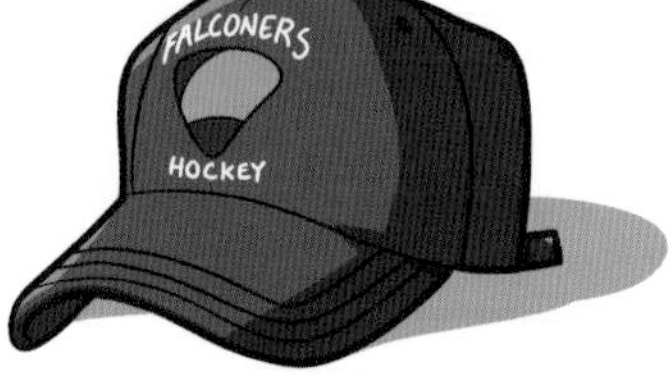
FALCONERS
HOCKEY

2

NONSTOP CELLY

HEY!!
JACK! BITS!
CAPITANES!!

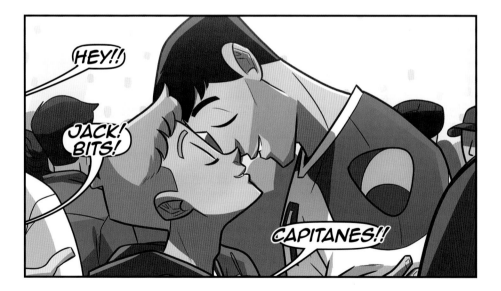

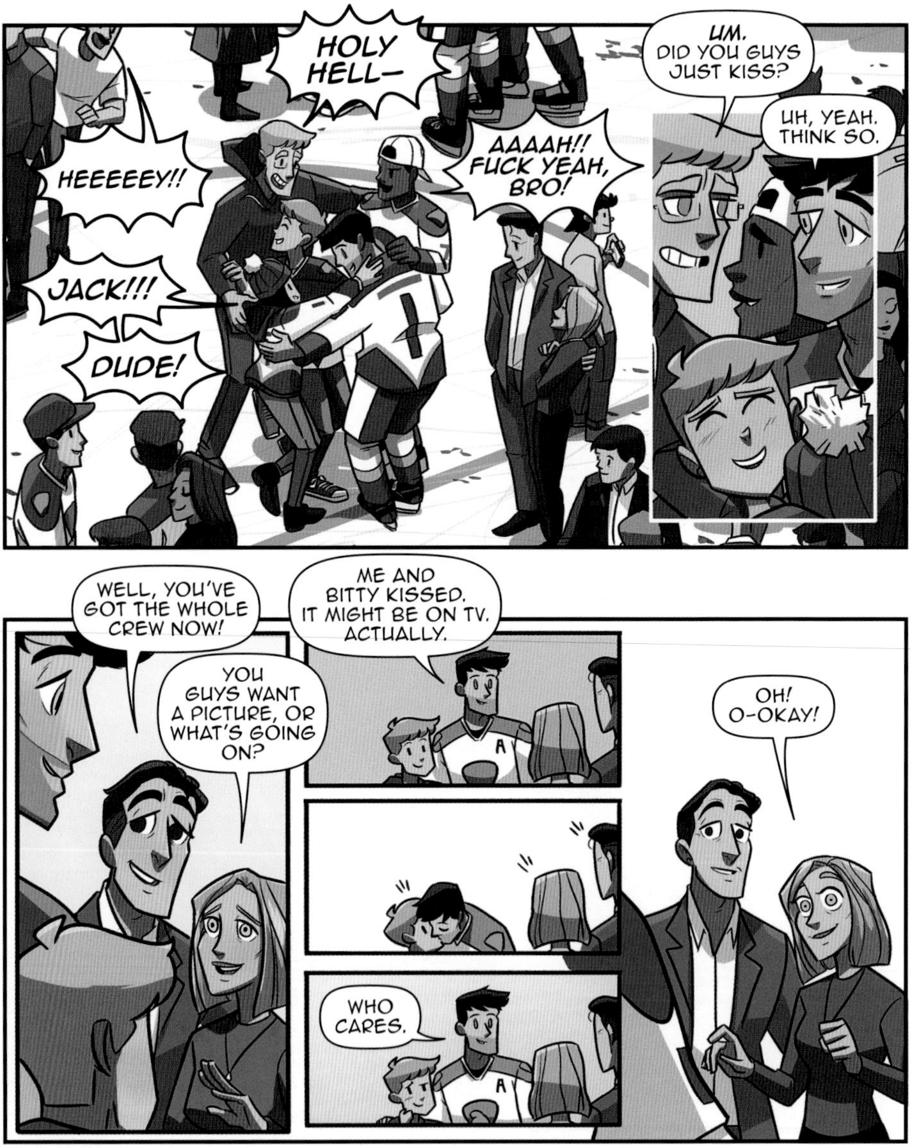
HOLY HELL–
HEEEEEY!!
JACK!!!
DUDE!
AAAAH!! FUCK YEAH, BRO!
UM. DID YOU GUYS JUST KISS?
UH, YEAH. THINK SO.
WELL, YOU'VE GOT THE WHOLE CREW NOW!
YOU GUYS WANT A PICTURE, OR WHAT'S GOING ON?
ME AND BITTY KISSED. IT MIGHT BE ON TV. ACTUALLY.
WHO CARES.
OH! O-OKAY!

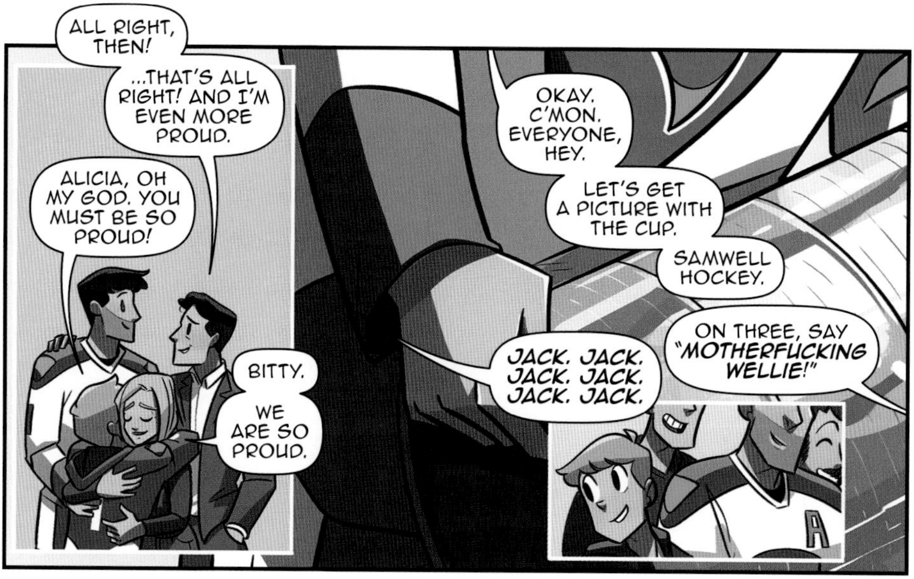
ALL RIGHT, THEN!
...THAT'S ALL RIGHT! AND I'M EVEN MORE PROUD.
ALICIA, OH MY GOD. YOU MUST BE SO PROUD!
BITTY.
WE ARE SO PROUD.
OKAY. C'MON. EVERYONE, HEY.
LET'S GET A PICTURE WITH THE CUP.
SAMWELL HOCKEY.
ON THREE, SAY "MOTHERFUCKING WELLIE!"
JACK. JACK. JACK. JACK. JACK. JACK.

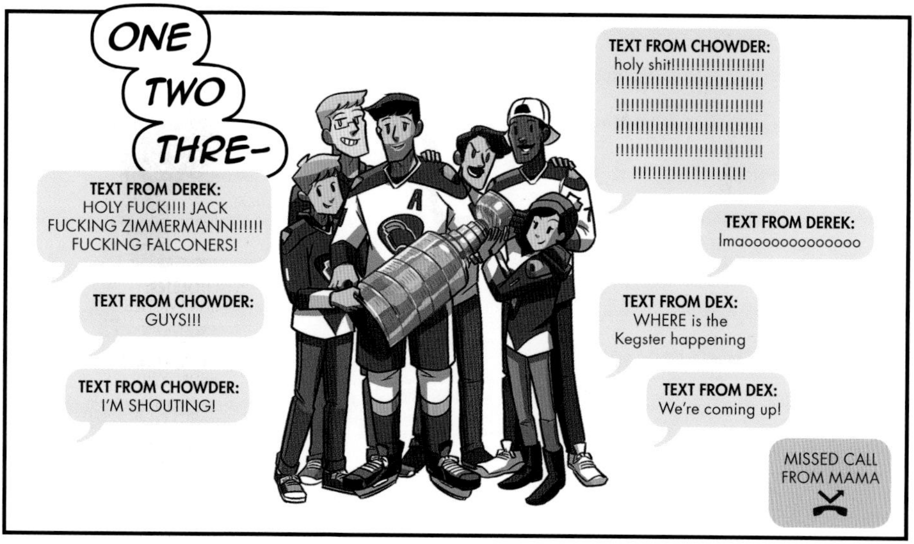
ONE
TWO
THRE-
TEXT FROM DEREK: HOLY FUCK!!!! JACK FUCKING ZIMMERMANN!!!!!! FUCKING FALCONERS!
TEXT FROM CHOWDER: GUYS!!!
TEXT FROM CHOWDER: I'M SHOUTING!
TEXT FROM CHOWDER: holy shit!!
TEXT FROM DEREK: lmaoooooooooooo
TEXT FROM DEX: WHERE is the Kegster happening
TEXT FROM DEX: We're coming up!
MISSED CALL FROM MAMA

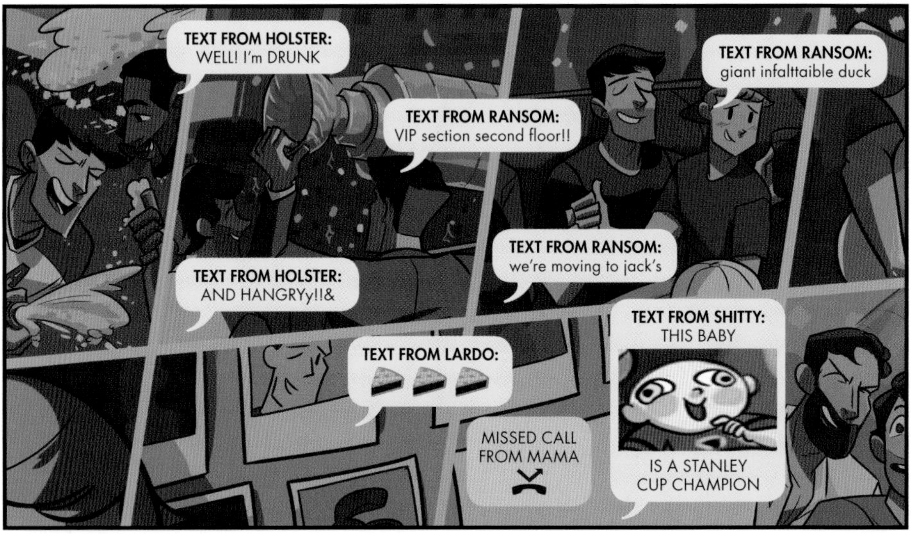
TEXT FROM HOLSTER:
WELL! I'm DRUNK
TEXT FROM RANSOM:
VIP section second floor!!
TEXT FROM RANSOM:
giant infalttaible duck
TEXT FROM HOLSTER:
AND HANGRYy!!&
TEXT FROM RANSOM:
we're moving to jack's
TEXT FROM LARDO:
MISSED CALL FROM MAMA
TEXT FROM SHITTY:
THIS BABY
IS A STANLEY CUP CHAMPION

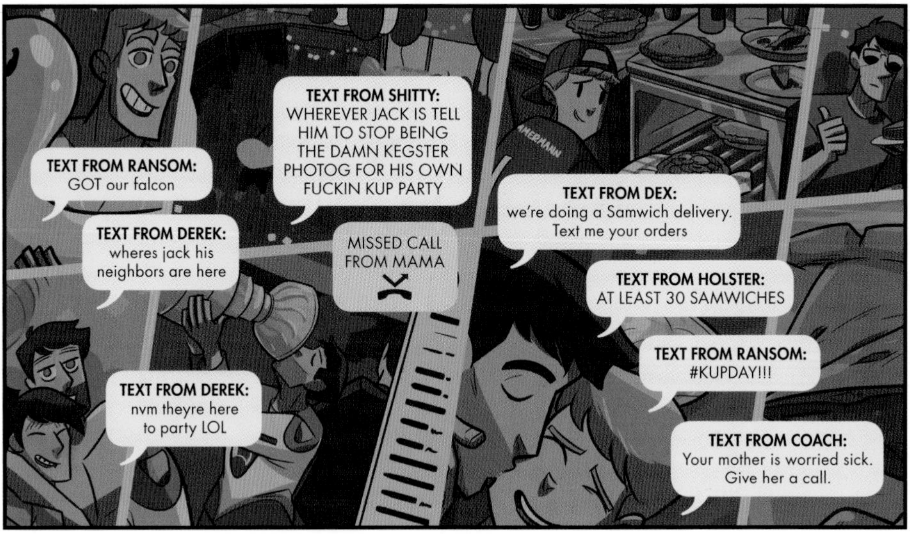
TEXT FROM RANSOM:
GOT our falcon
TEXT FROM SHITTY:
WHEREVER JACK IS TELL HIM TO STOP BEING THE DAMN KEGSTER PHOTOG FOR HIS OWN FUCKIN KUP PARTY
TEXT FROM DEREK:
wheres jack his neighbors are here
MISSED CALL FROM MAMA
TEXT FROM DEX:
we're doing a Samwich delivery. Text me your orders
TEXT FROM HOLSTER:
AT LEAST 30 SAMWICHES
TEXT FROM DEREK:
nvm theyre here to party LOL
TEXT FROM RANSOM:
#KUPDAY!!!
TEXT FROM COACH:
Your mother is worried sick. Give her a call.

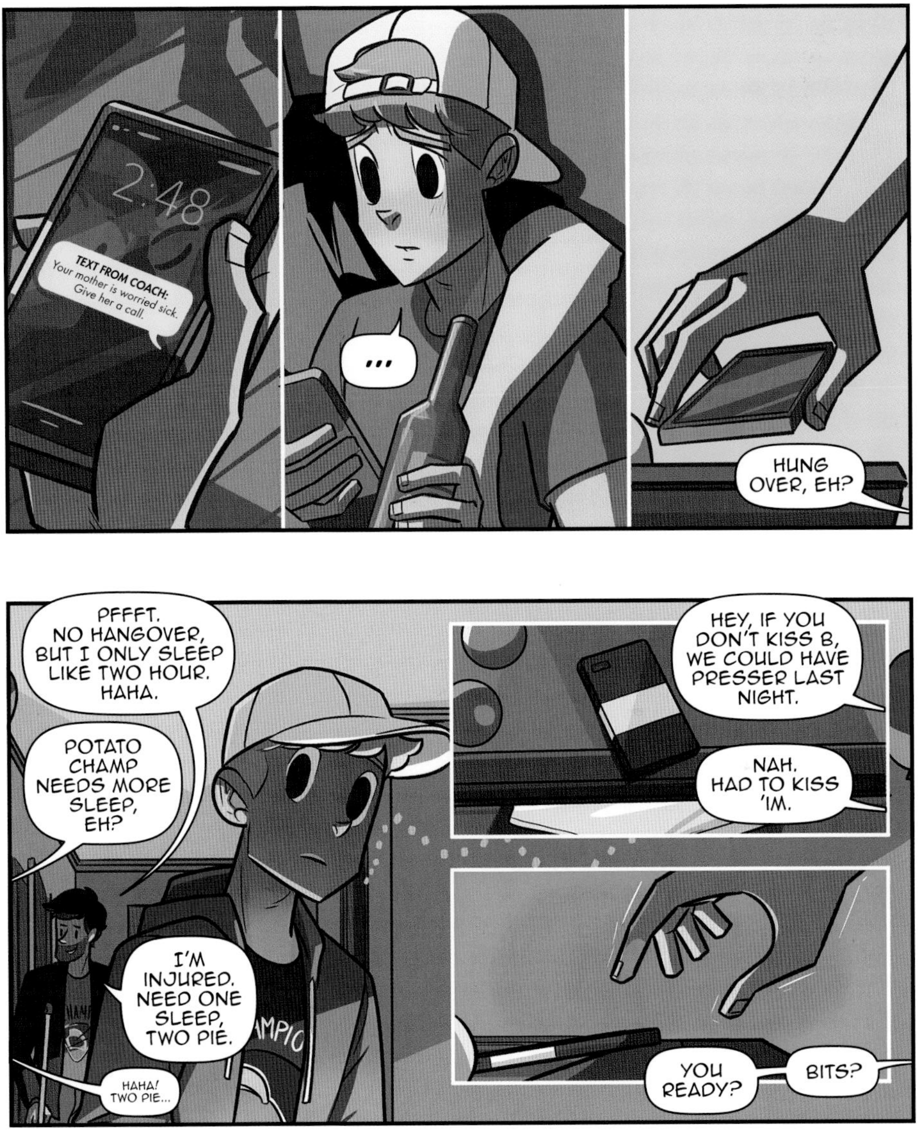
2:48
TEXT FROM COACH:
Your mother is worried sick. Give her a call.
...
HUNG OVER, EH?
PFFFT. NO HANGOVER, BUT I ONLY SLEEP LIKE TWO HOUR. HAHA.
POTATO CHAMP NEEDS MORE SLEEP, EH?
I'M INJURED. NEED ONE SLEEP, TWO PIE.
HAHA! TWO PIE...
HEY, IF YOU DON'T KISS B, WE COULD HAVE PRESSER LAST NIGHT.
NAH. HAD TO KISS 'IM.
YOU READY?
BITS?

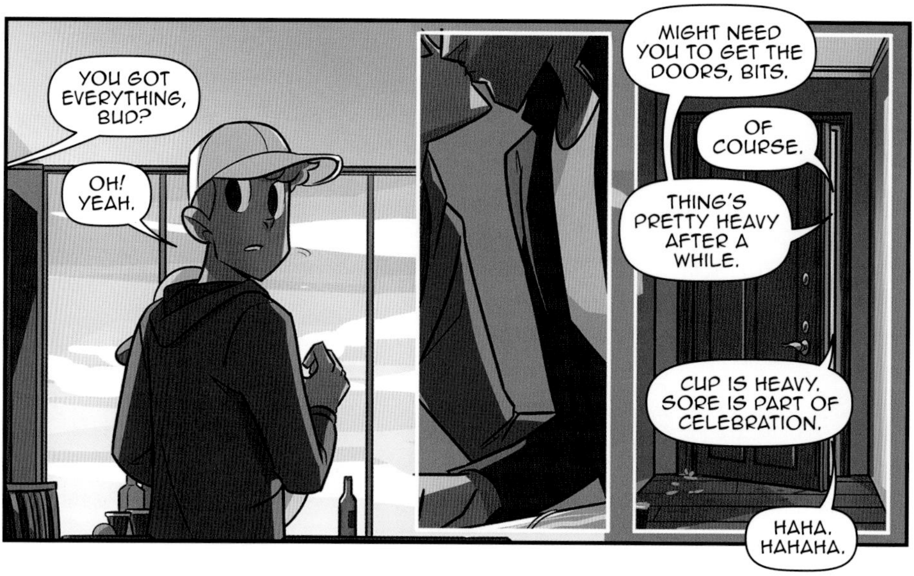
YOU GOT EVERYTHING, BUD?
OH! YEAH.
MIGHT NEED YOU TO GET THE DOORS, BITS.
OF COURSE.
THING'S PRETTY HEAVY AFTER A WHILE.
CUP IS HEAVY. SORE IS PART OF CELEBRATION.
HAHA. HAHAHA.

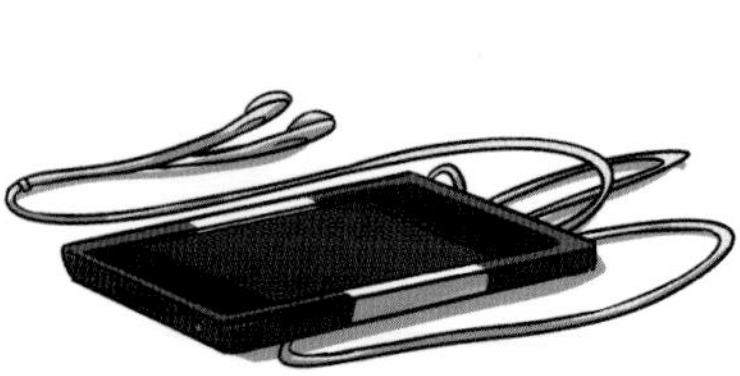

3

PRESSER

HOLY SHIT, THAT'S A CROWD.
PROBABLY ALL HERE FOR THE KID, LEMME SEE—
OH GOD. WHEEEWF.
G-GREAT! NOW I'M NERVOUS!!
I KNOW IT'S THE CUP BUT HOW MANY OF THOSE JOURNOS ARE ACTUALLY COVERING HOCKEY?
HOW MANY OF THEM BOOKED IT UP 95 ON A LAST-MINUTE ASSIGNMENT??
WOW, YEAH, LIKE, ONE BEAT JOURNO?!
WE RELEASED A STATEMENT, SO ALL YOU NEED TO DO IS TALK HOCKEY.
...BUT, IF YOU HAVE SOMETHING YOU WANT TO SAY—
GEORGE... I DIDN'T WIN A STANLEY CUP. OUR TEAM DID. THAT'S WHY WE'RE ALL GOING UP THERE, RIGHT?
AND THAT'S THE GAME PLAN. FOCUS ON THE TEAM.
IF WE STICK TO THAT, I THINK THIS'LL BE A NORMAL PRESSER.

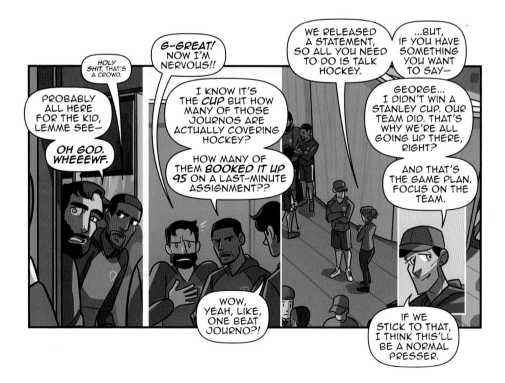

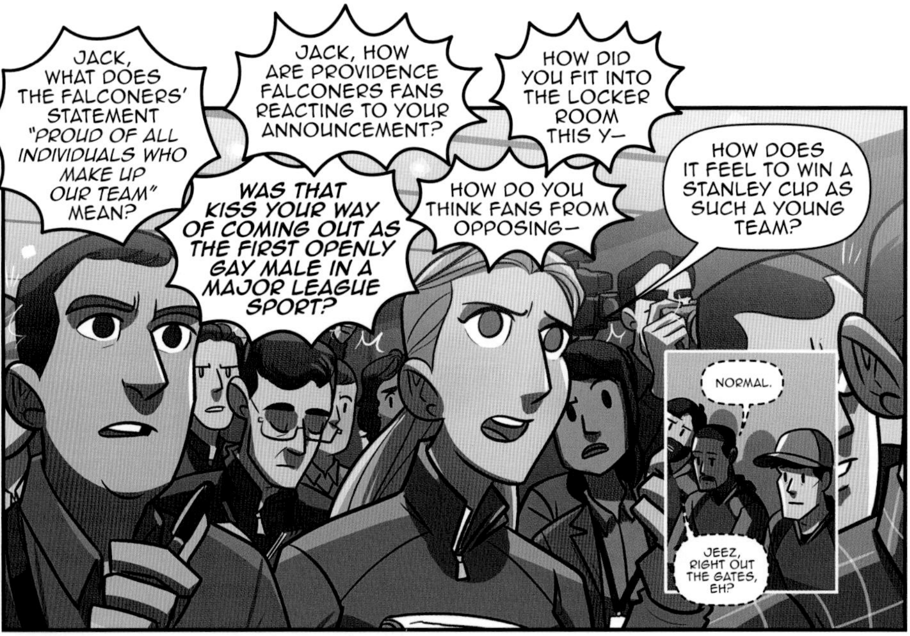
JACK, WHAT DOES THE FALCONERS' STATEMENT "PROUD OF ALL INDIVIDUALS WHO MAKE UP OUR TEAM" MEAN?
JACK, HOW ARE PROVIDENCE FALCONERS FANS REACTING TO YOUR ANNOUNCEMENT?
HOW DID YOU FIT INTO THE LOCKER ROOM THIS Y—
WAS THAT KISS YOUR WAY OF COMING OUT AS THE FIRST OPENLY GAY MALE IN A MAJOR LEAGUE SPORT?
HOW DO YOU THINK FANS FROM OPPOSING—
HOW DOES IT FEEL TO WIN A STANLEY CUP AS SUCH A YOUNG TEAM?
NORMAL.
JEEZ, RIGHT OUT THE GATES, EH?

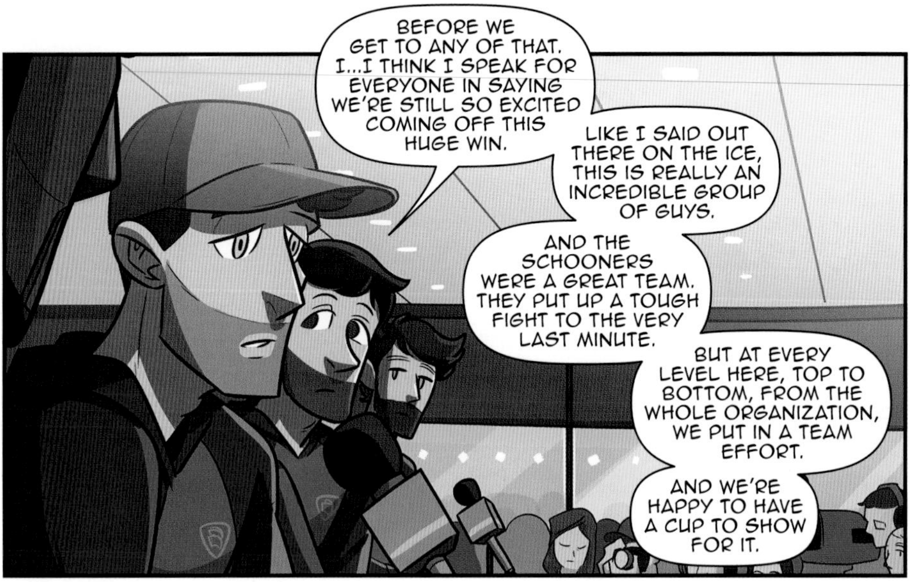
BEFORE WE GET TO ANY OF THAT. I...I THINK I SPEAK FOR EVERYONE IN SAYING WE'RE STILL SO EXCITED COMING OFF THIS HUGE WIN.
LIKE I SAID OUT THERE ON THE ICE, THIS IS REALLY AN INCREDIBLE GROUP OF GUYS.
AND THE SCHOONERS WERE A GREAT TEAM. THEY PUT UP A TOUGH FIGHT TO THE VERY LAST MINUTE.
BUT AT EVERY LEVEL HERE, TOP TO BOTTOM, FROM THE WHOLE ORGANIZATION, WE PUT IN A TEAM EFFORT.
AND WE'RE HAPPY TO HAVE A CUP TO SHOW FOR IT.

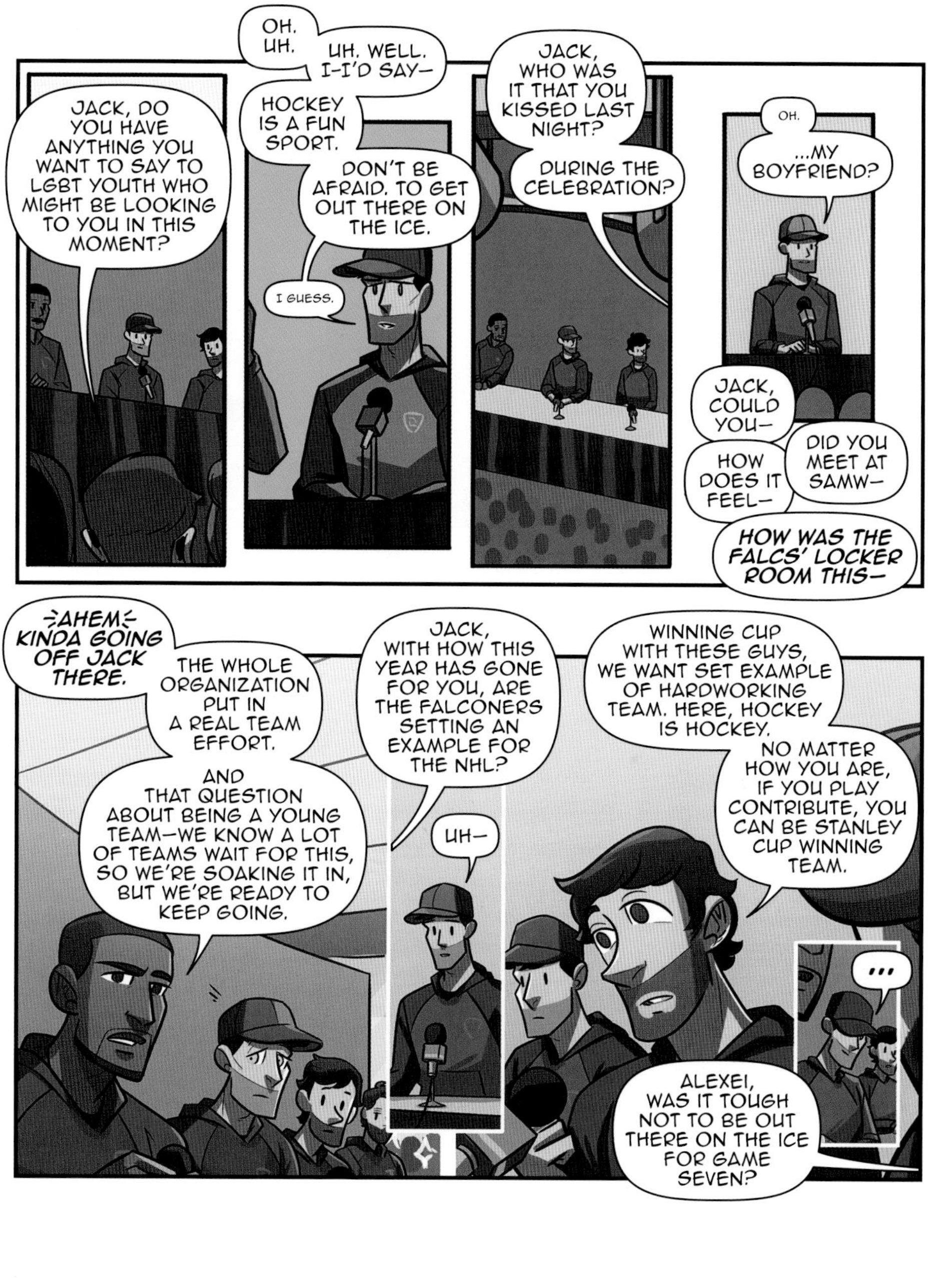
JACK, DO YOU HAVE ANYTHING YOU WANT TO SAY TO LGBT YOUTH WHO MIGHT BE LOOKING TO YOU IN THIS MOMENT?
OH. UH.
UH. WELL. I-I'D SAY—
HOCKEY IS A FUN SPORT.
DON'T BE AFRAID. TO GET OUT THERE ON THE ICE.
I GUESS.
JACK, WHO WAS IT THAT YOU KISSED LAST NIGHT?
DURING THE CELEBRATION?
OH.
...MY BOYFRIEND?
JACK, COULD YOU—
HOW DOES IT FEEL—
DID YOU MEET AT SAMW—
HOW WAS THE FALCS' LOCKER ROOM THIS—
-AHEM- KINDA GOING OFF JACK THERE.
THE WHOLE ORGANIZATION PUT IN A REAL TEAM EFFORT.
AND THAT QUESTION ABOUT BEING A YOUNG TEAM—WE KNOW A LOT OF TEAMS WAIT FOR THIS, SO WE'RE SOAKING IT IN, BUT WE'RE READY TO KEEP GOING.
JACK, WITH HOW THIS YEAR HAS GONE FOR YOU, ARE THE FALCONERS SETTING AN EXAMPLE FOR THE NHL?
UH—
WINNING CUP WITH THESE GUYS, WE WANT SET EXAMPLE OF HARDWORKING TEAM. HERE, HOCKEY IS HOCKEY.
NO MATTER HOW YOU ARE, IF YOU PLAY CONTRIBUTE, YOU CAN BE STANLEY CUP WINNING TEAM.
...
ALEXEI, WAS IT TOUGH NOT TO BE OUT THERE ON THE ICE FOR GAME SEVEN?

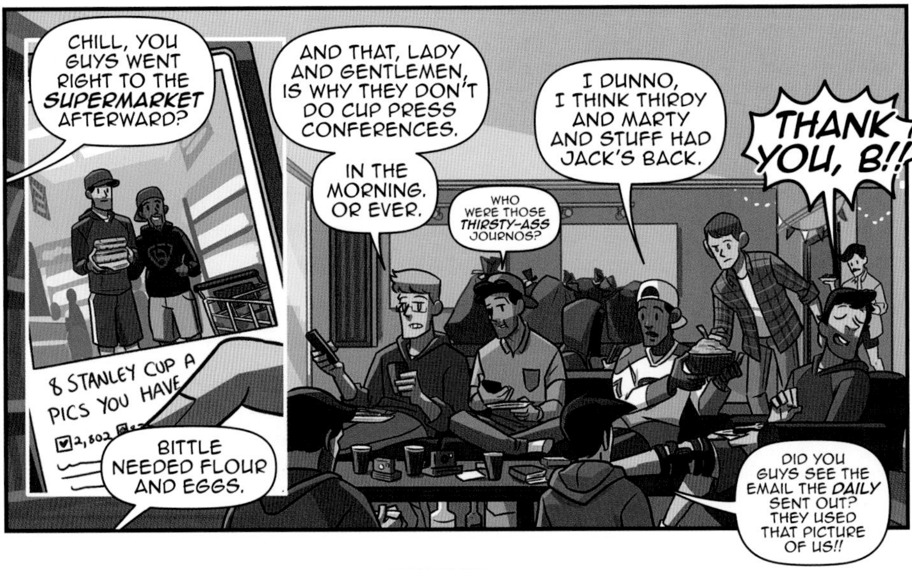
CHILL, YOU GUYS WENT RIGHT TO THE *SUPERMARKET* AFTERWARD?
8 STANLEY CUP A
PICS YOU HAVE
2,802
BITTLE NEEDED FLOUR AND EGGS.
AND THAT, LADY AND GENTLEMEN, IS WHY THEY DON'T DO CUP PRESS CONFERENCES.
IN THE MORNING. OR EVER.
WHO WERE THOSE *THIRSTY-ASS* JOURNOS?
I DUNNO, I THINK THIRDY AND MARTY AND STUFF HAD JACK'S BACK.
THANK YOU, B!!
DID YOU GUYS SEE THE EMAIL THE *DAILY* SENT OUT? THEY USED THAT PICTURE OF US!!

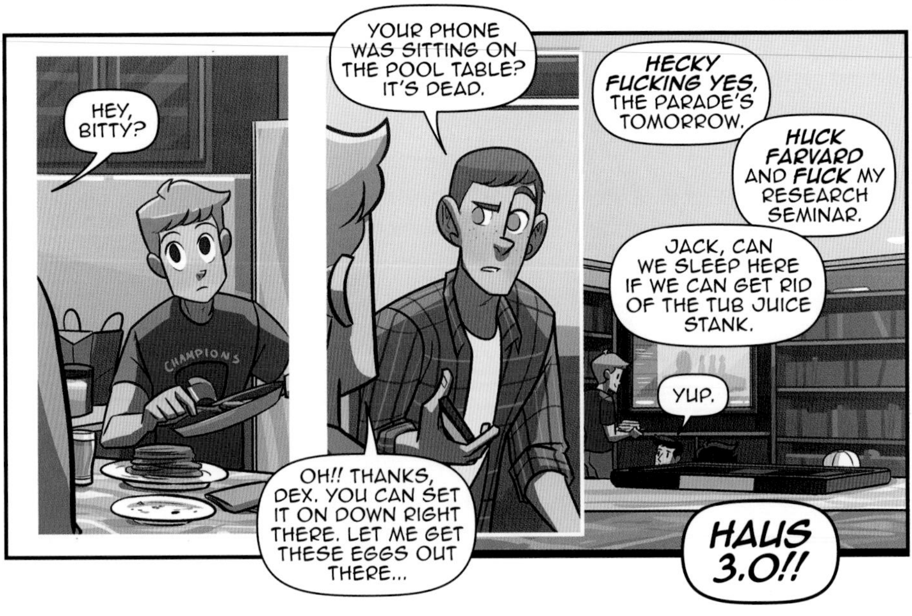
HEY, BITTY?
YOUR PHONE WAS SITTING ON THE POOL TABLE? IT'S DEAD.
OH!! THANKS, DEX. YOU CAN SET IT ON DOWN RIGHT THERE. LET ME GET THESE EGGS OUT THERE...
CHAMPIONS
HECKY FUCKING YES, THE PARADE'S TOMORROW.
HUCK FARVARD AND *FUCK* MY RESEARCH SEMINAR.
JACK, CAN WE SLEEP HERE IF WE CAN GET RID OF THE TUB JUICE STANK.
YUP.
HAUS 3.0!!

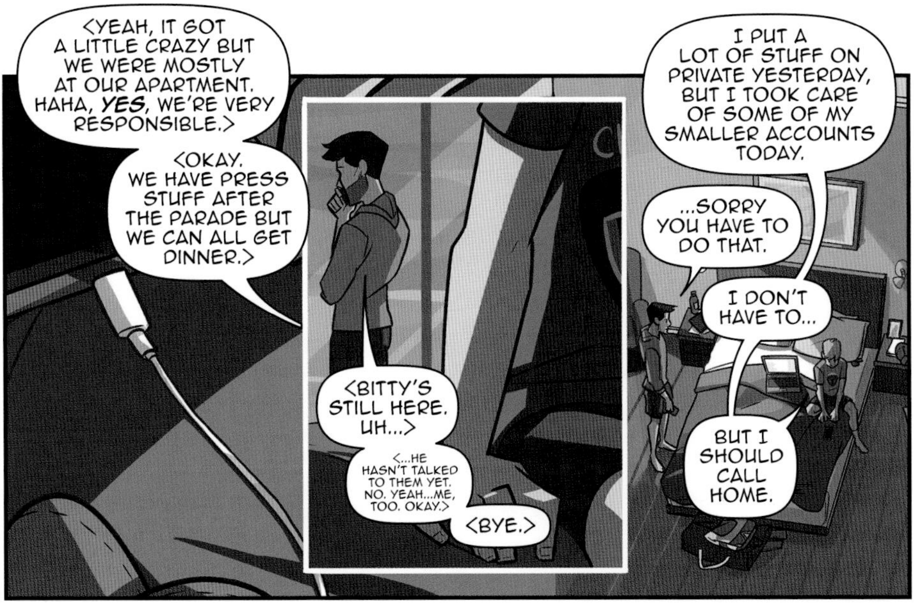
<YEAH, IT GOT A LITTLE CRAZY BUT WE WERE MOSTLY AT OUR APARTMENT. HAHA, *YES*, WE'RE VERY RESPONSIBLE.>
<OKAY. WE HAVE PRESS STUFF AFTER THE PARADE BUT WE CAN ALL GET DINNER.>
<BITTY'S STILL HERE. UH...>
<...HE HASN'T TALKED TO THEM YET. NO. YEAH...ME, TOO. OKAY.>
<BYE.>
I PUT A LOT OF STUFF ON PRIVATE YESTERDAY, BUT I TOOK CARE OF SOME OF MY SMALLER ACCOUNTS TODAY.
...SORRY YOU HAVE TO DO THAT.
I DON'T HAVE TO...
BUT I SHOULD CALL HOME.

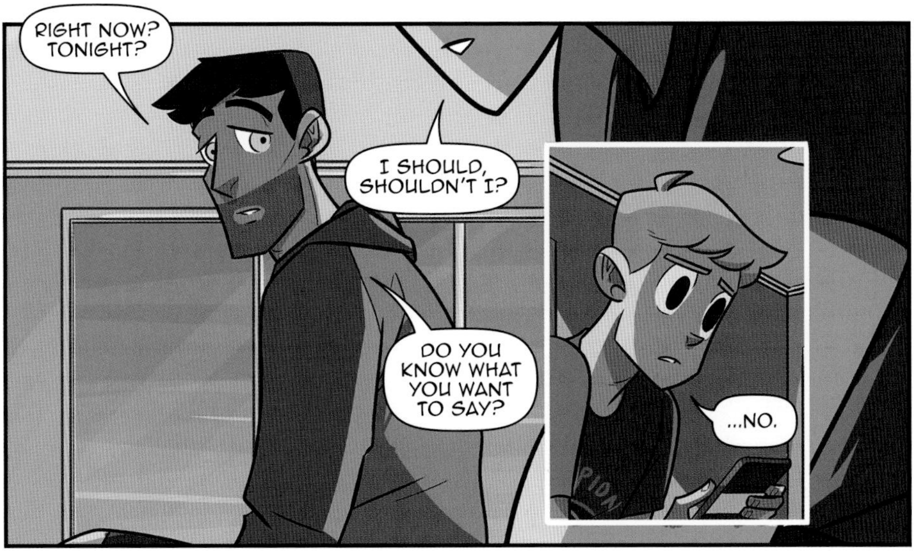
RIGHT NOW? TONIGHT?
I SHOULD, SHOULDN'T I?
DO YOU KNOW WHAT YOU WANT TO SAY?
...NO.

4

CALLING HOME

HI, MAMA.
...DICKY?

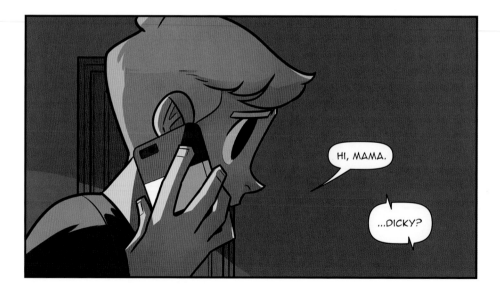

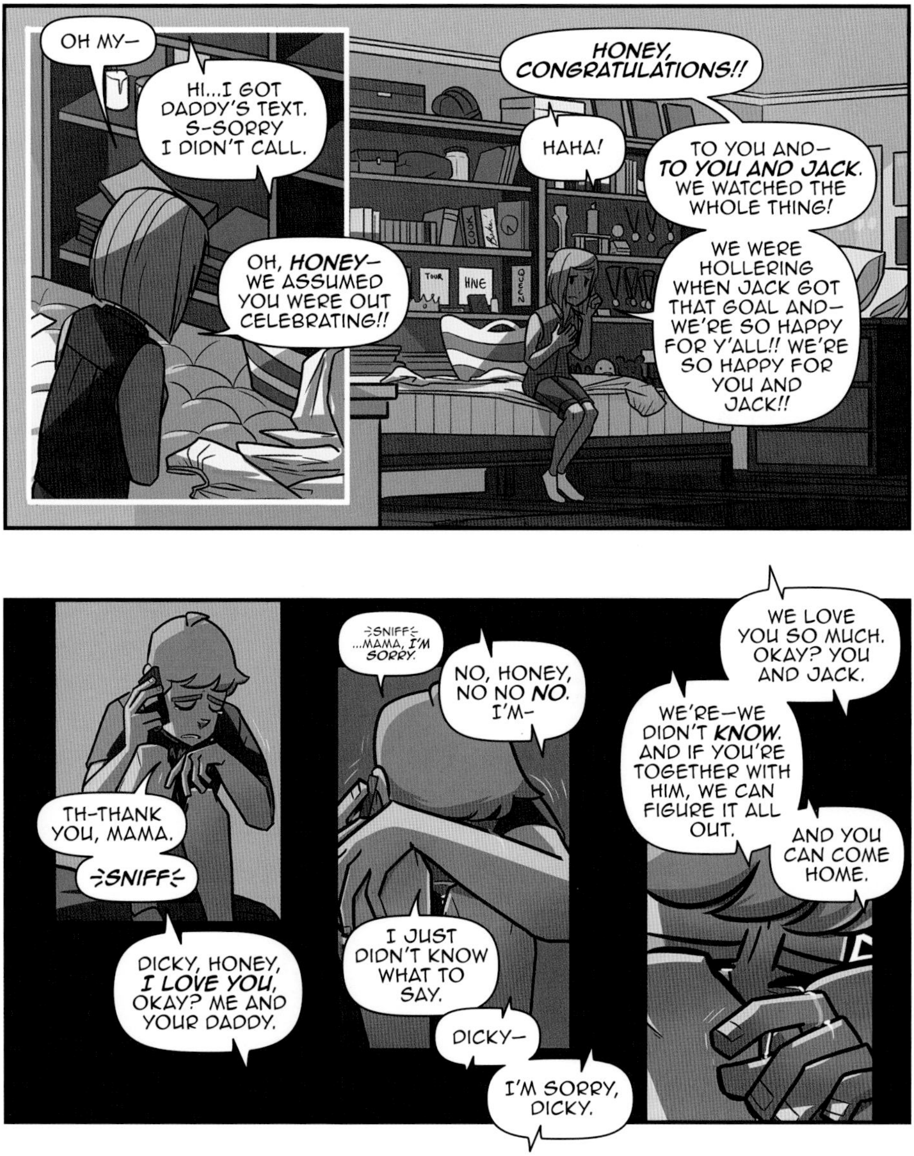
OH MY—
HI...I GOT DADDY'S TEXT. S-SORRY I DIDN'T CALL.
OH, *HONEY*— WE ASSUMED YOU WERE OUT CELEBRATING!!
HONEY, CONGRATULATIONS!!
HAHA!
TO YOU AND— *TO YOU AND JACK*. WE WATCHED THE WHOLE THING!
WE WERE HOLLERING WHEN JACK GOT THAT GOAL AND— WE'RE SO HAPPY FOR Y'ALL!! WE'RE SO HAPPY FOR YOU AND JACK!!
TH-THANK YOU, MAMA.
SNIFF
DICKY, HONEY, *I LOVE YOU*, OKAY? ME AND YOUR DADDY.
SNIFF ...MAMA, *I'M SORRY.*
NO, HONEY, NO NO *NO*. I'M—
I JUST DIDN'T KNOW WHAT TO SAY.
DICKY—
I'M SORRY, DICKY.
WE LOVE YOU SO MUCH. OKAY? YOU AND JACK.
WE'RE—WE DIDN'T *KNOW*. AND IF YOU'RE TOGETHER WITH HIM, WE CAN FIGURE IT ALL OUT.
AND YOU CAN COME HOME.

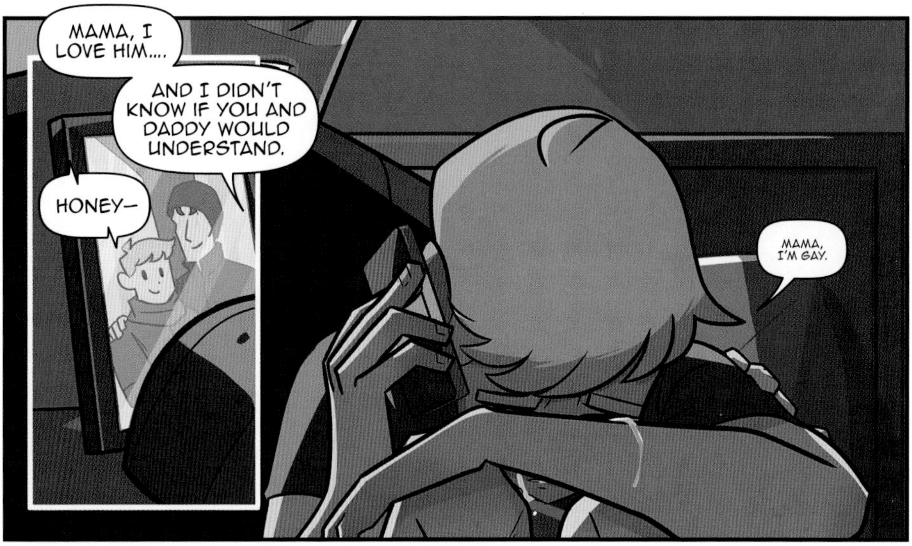
MAMA, I'M GAY.
MAMA, I LOVE HIM....
AND I DIDN'T KNOW IF YOU AND DADDY WOULD UNDERSTAND.
HONEY—

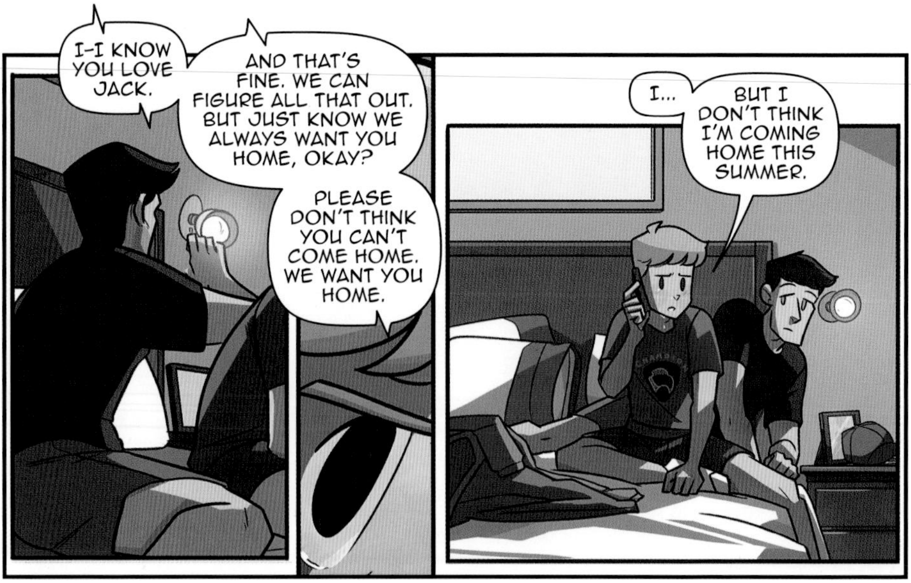
I-I KNOW YOU LOVE JACK.
AND THAT'S FINE. WE CAN FIGURE ALL THAT OUT. BUT JUST KNOW WE ALWAYS WANT YOU HOME, OKAY?
PLEASE DON'T THINK YOU CAN'T COME HOME. WE WANT YOU HOME.
I...
BUT I DON'T THINK I'M COMING HOME THIS SUMMER.

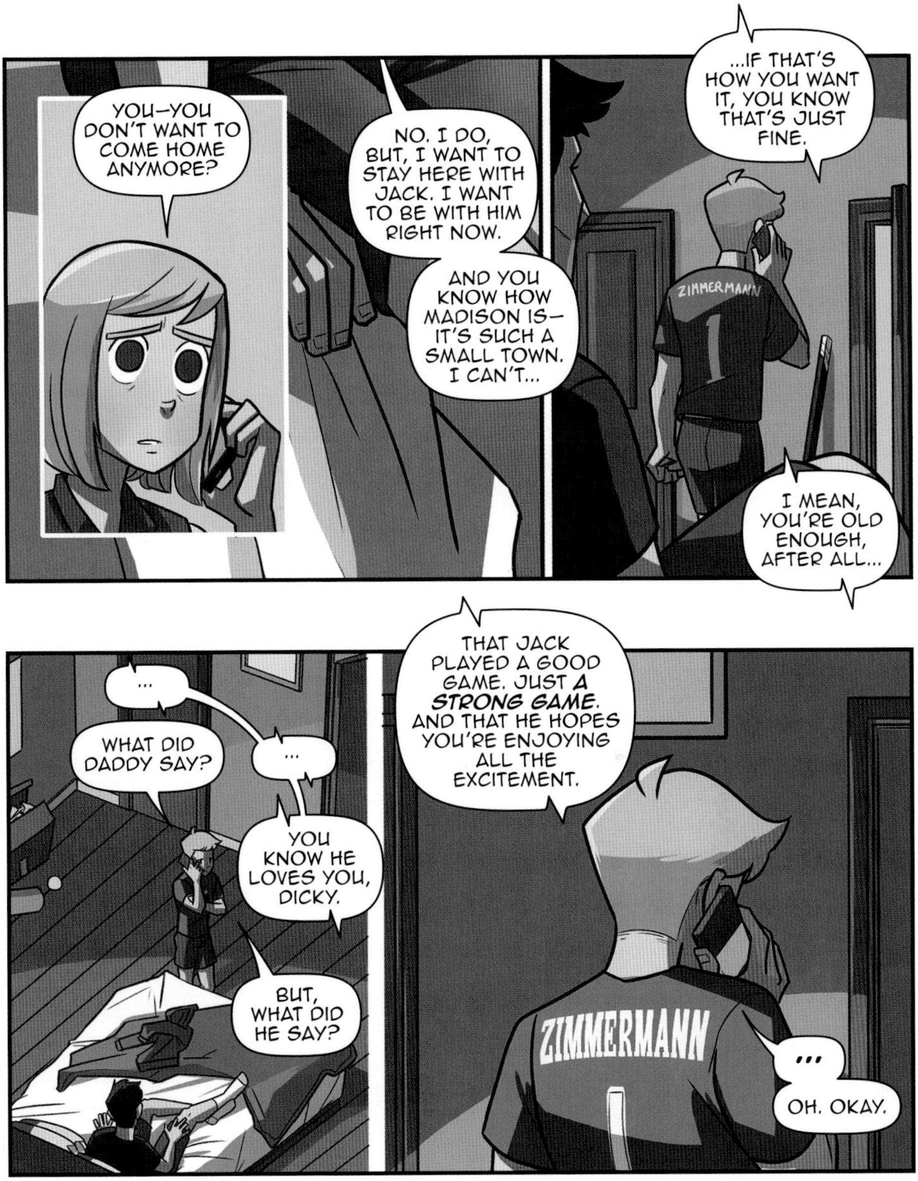
YOU—YOU DON'T WANT TO COME HOME ANYMORE?
NO. I DO, BUT, I WANT TO STAY HERE WITH JACK. I WANT TO BE WITH HIM RIGHT NOW.
AND YOU KNOW HOW MADISON IS— IT'S SUCH A SMALL TOWN. I CAN'T...
...IF THAT'S HOW YOU WANT IT, YOU KNOW THAT'S JUST FINE.
ZIMMERMANN
1
I MEAN, YOU'RE OLD ENOUGH, AFTER ALL...
...
WHAT DID DADDY SAY?
...
YOU KNOW HE LOVES YOU, DICKY.
BUT, WHAT DID HE SAY?
THAT JACK PLAYED A GOOD GAME. JUST A STRONG GAME. AND THAT HE HOPES YOU'RE ENJOYING ALL THE EXCITEMENT.
ZIMMERMANN
...
OH. OKAY.

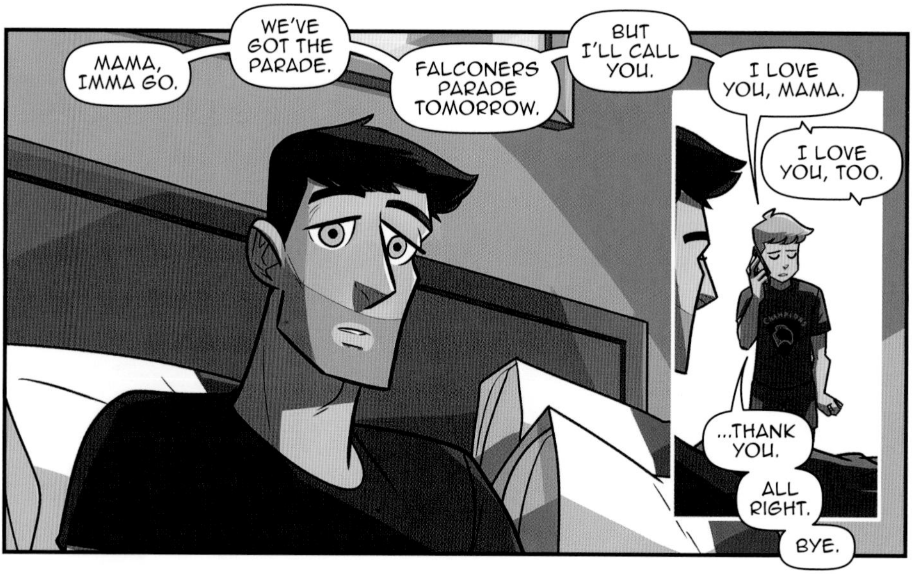
MAMA, IMMA GO.
WE'VE GOT THE PARADE.
FALCONERS PARADE TOMORROW.
BUT I'LL CALL YOU.
I LOVE YOU, MAMA.
I LOVE YOU, TOO.
...THANK YOU.
ALL RIGHT.
BYE.

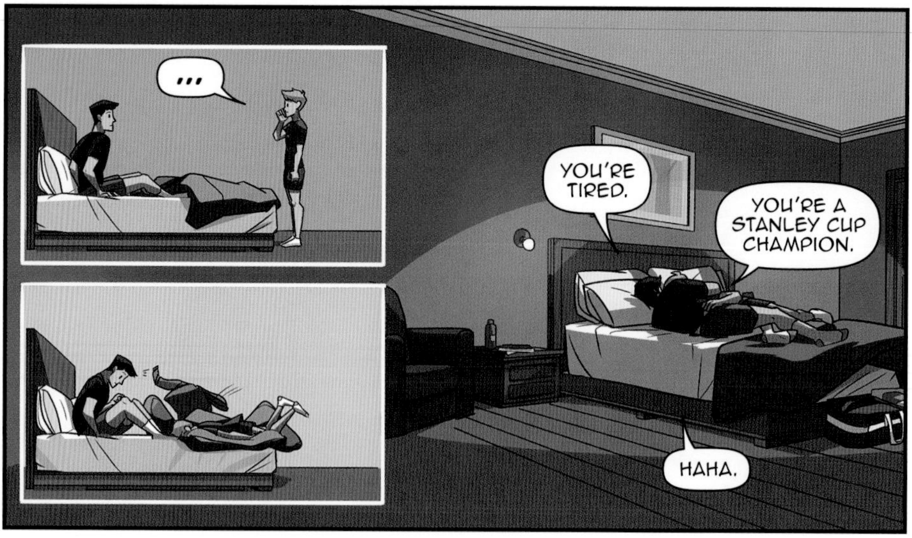
...
YOU'RE TIRED.
YOU'RE A STANLEY CUP CHAMPION.
HAHA.

5

#KUPDAY

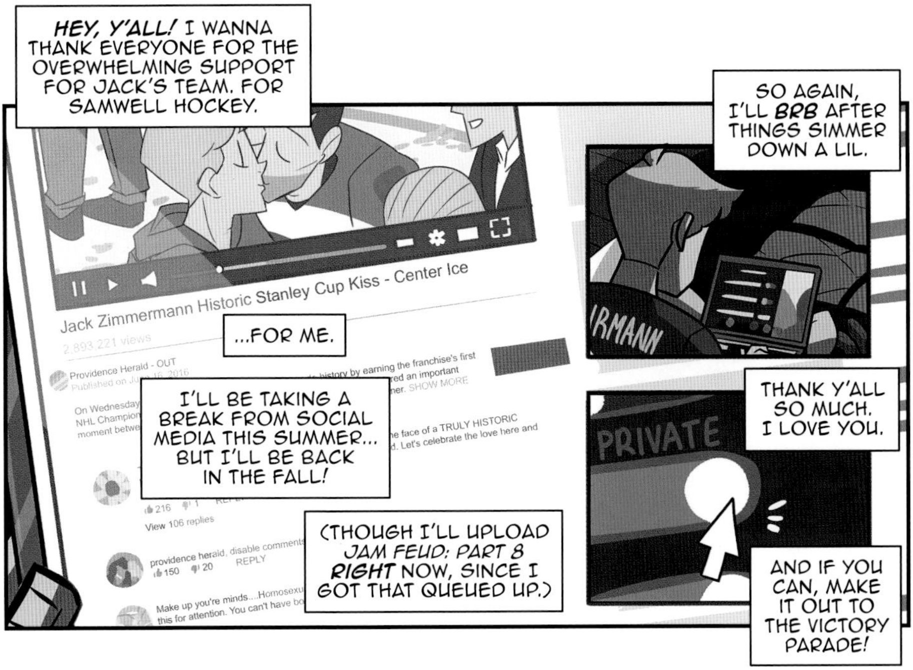

HEY, Y'ALL! I WANNA THANK EVERYONE FOR THE OVERWHELMING SUPPORT FOR JACK'S TEAM. FOR SAMWELL HOCKEY.
...FOR ME.
I'LL BE TAKING A BREAK FROM SOCIAL MEDIA THIS SUMMER... BUT I'LL BE BACK IN THE FALL!
(THOUGH I'LL UPLOAD JAM FEUD: PART 8 RIGHT NOW, SINCE I GOT THAT QUEUED UP.)
SO AGAIN, I'LL BRB AFTER THINGS SIMMER DOWN A LIL.
THANK Y'ALL SO MUCH. I LOVE YOU.
AND IF YOU CAN, MAKE IT OUT TO THE VICTORY PARADE!
Jack Zimmermann Historic Stanley Cup Kiss - Center Ice
Providence Herald - OUT
View 106 replies
providence herald, disable comments
REPLY
RMANN
PRIVATE

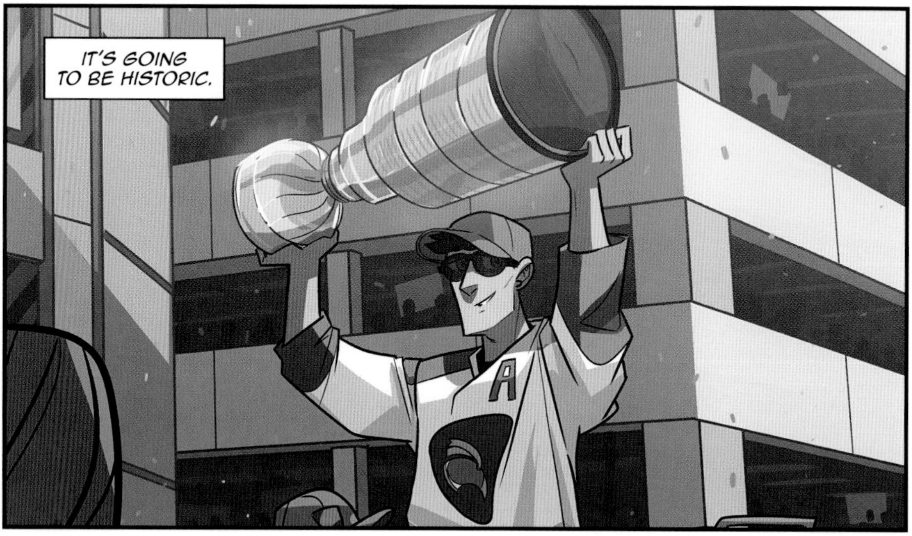
IT'S GOING TO BE HISTORIC.

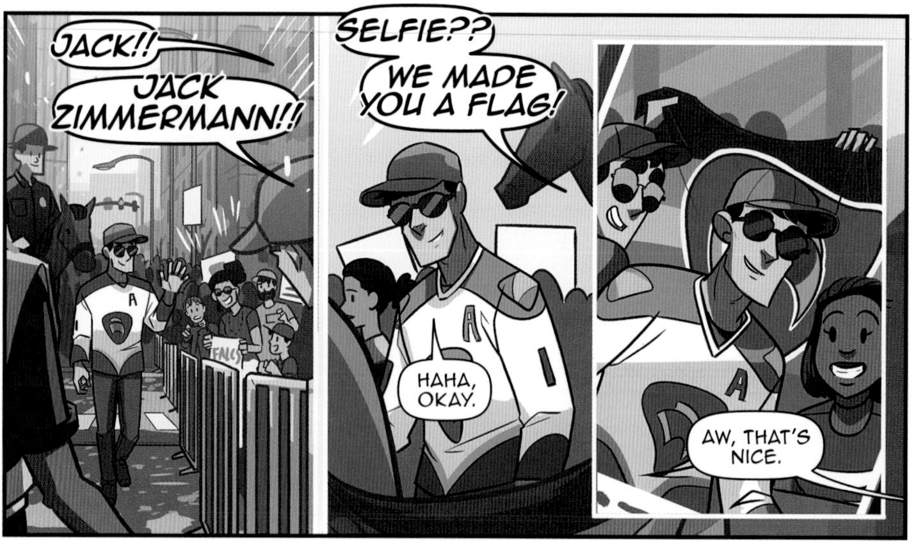
JACK!!
JACK ZIMMERMANN!!
SELFIE??
WE MADE YOU A FLAG!
HAHA, OKAY.
AW, THAT'S NICE.

YEAH, YOU GOTTA GIVE THAT TO PR! THAT'S A GREAT PIC.
YOU KNOW, WITH HOW ALL THIS WENT, I'M A LITTLE LESS WORRIED ABOUT MY DAY WITH THE CUP?
YOU WERE WORRIED?
HAH, ONLY A LITTLE.
I'M TAKING THE CUP BACK TO SAMWELL FOR AN EVENING AND THEN SPENDING THE MORNING WITH MY PARENTS.
BUT BASED OFF THIS PARADE, IT SHOULD BE A PRETTY QUIET NIGHT WITH THE TEAM!
FALCS

The Samwell Swallow

The Samwell Swallow Online | Volume 26 | Summer Edition 2

A REAL BARN BURNER!!!

STANLEY CUP CELLY LEAVES SAMWELL SCORCHING

SPECIAL EDITION | SUMMER SCANDAL

ATTENDEES CALL IT "HISTORIC" | HOCKEY TEAM WILL NOT DISCLOSE SOURCE OF FIRE | "HOTTEST RAGER SAMWELL HAS HAD IN 10 YRS LITERALLY" | "I HOOKED UP WITH 3 HOCKEY PLAYERS AND ONLY ONE OF THEM WENT TO SAMWELL"

SPOTTED: FALCS, BRUINS, THAT ONE GUY FROM THAT NETFLIX SHOW, SEXY FIREMEN, YOUR BELOVED SWALLOW EDITORS, A REPREHENSIBLE COUCH!

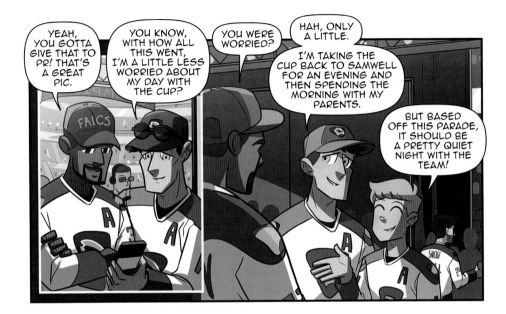

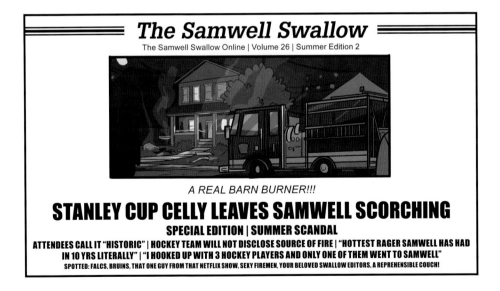

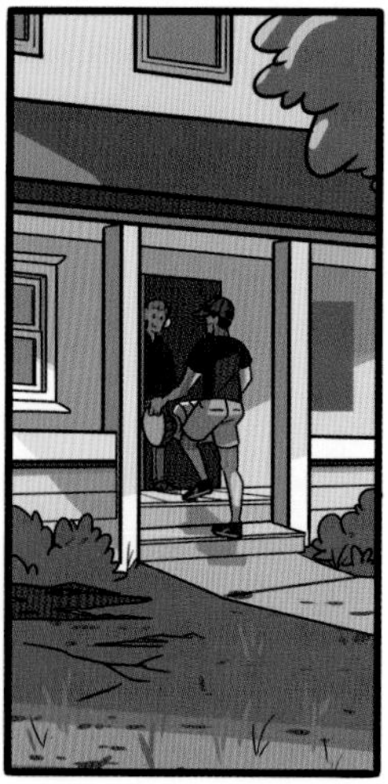

OUR SWEATY NIGHT WITH STANLEY

We here at the *Swallow* remain dedicated to providing you, dear reader, with reports on the juiciest Wellie gossip and coverage on the raunchiest Samwell orgies. Imagine how *beside ourselves* we were, when we learned our favorite (and now gayest!!) alum of our favorite (far from the gayest!!) athletics cult was coming home with the STANLEY CUP.

That's right! **JACK ZIMMERMANN '15**, newly proud and historic gay of the NHL, angst boy, and a **Swallow's 50 Most Gold Star**, returned with some serious hardware. We know most Wellies only watch sports by accident, but even the most reclusive Adderall-riddled biochem major knows that JACK ZIMMERMANN came out on national TV after the Super Bowl. (Basically.)

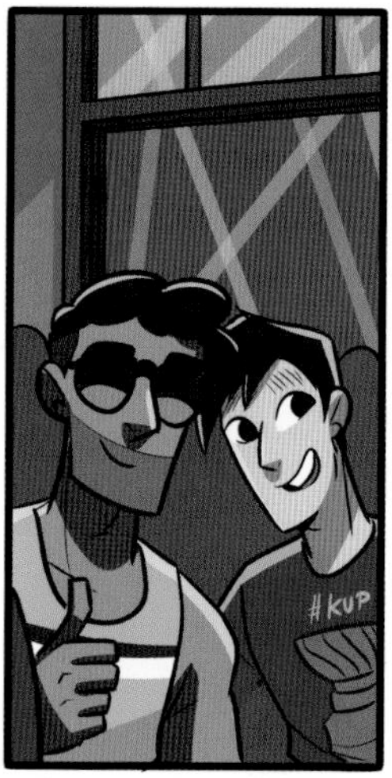
#KUP

Our staffers caught several glimpses of the famed Hockey Cup amidst all of the grinding and binge-drinking, and even spotted current hockey captain **ERIC BITTLE '17** with his beau before the two mysteriously disappeared—with the Stanley Cup. Only Lord Stanley knows how his trophy was later *defiled!* Hopefully, not reenacting Jack's first brush with the trophy??? *(...Yuck!)*

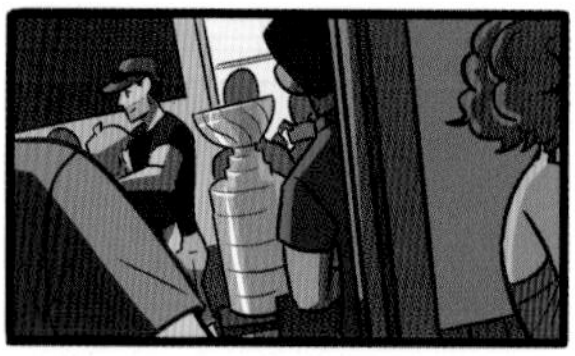

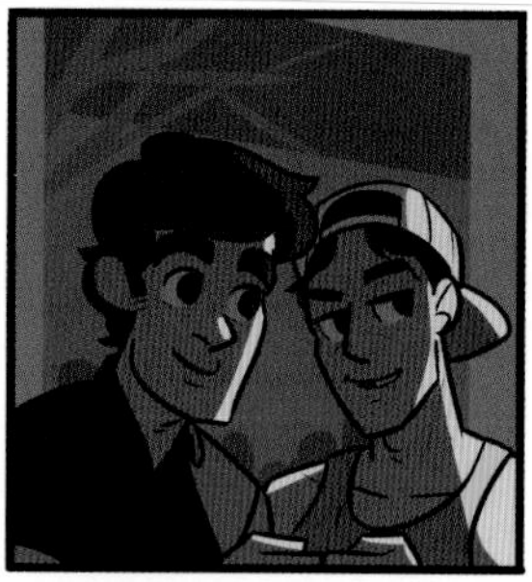

We at the *Swallow* are professional gossipmongers. By the time that one pap showed up, the bacchanalia was over.

Covering college parties? *Well, you're our kind of garbage*, but SMH is our beat, fuck you very much!!

Anonymous Hockey Player Tells All!

"Uh, well, I've been here all summer cuttin' grass and stuff at the golf course?? So it's cool that Jack Zimmermann came by with the Cup and stuff. I got to, like, touch it and stuff??? It's real cool...

"Well, it's cold because it's metal. ***I think.*** But yeah... then the Kegster kinda just happened. There's my team...the Falcs...I think a lot of these kids go to other schools???

"...Wait, uh, is that a fire on the porch?

"Uh-oh...BITTY-"

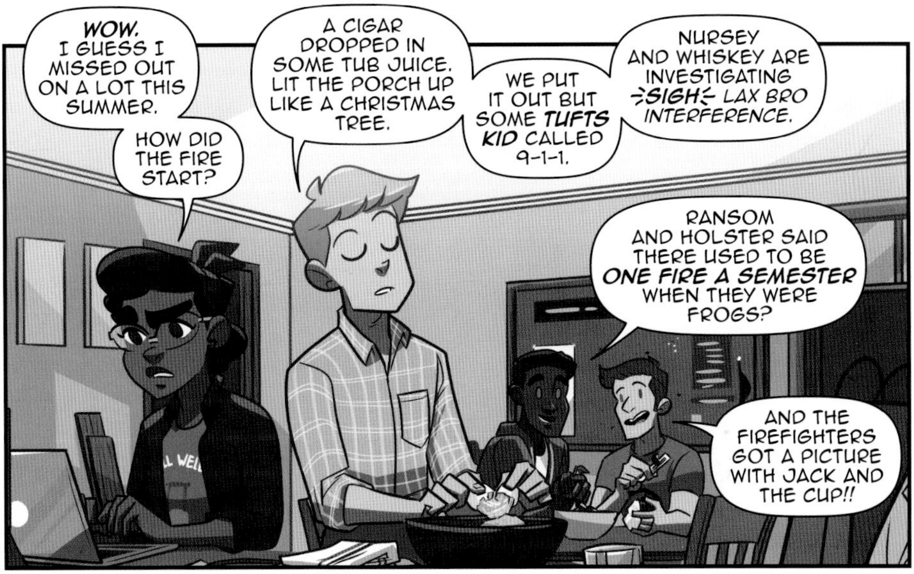
WOW. I GUESS I MISSED OUT ON A LOT THIS SUMMER.
HOW DID THE FIRE START?
A CIGAR DROPPED IN SOME TUB JUICE. LIT THE PORCH UP LIKE A CHRISTMAS TREE.
WE PUT IT OUT BUT SOME TUFTS KID CALLED 9-1-1.
NURSEY AND WHISKEY ARE INVESTIGATING *SIGH* LAX BRO INTERFERENCE.
RANSOM AND HOLSTER SAID THERE USED TO BE ONE FIRE A SEMESTER WHEN THEY WERE FROGS?
AND THE FIREFIGHTERS GOT A PICTURE WITH JACK AND THE CUP!!

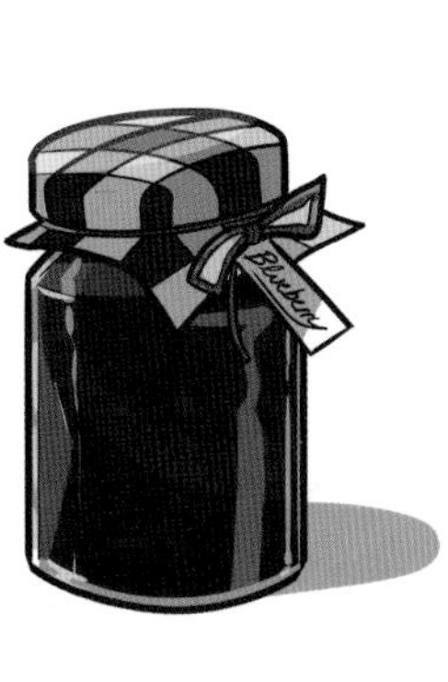

6

VARSITY CAPTAINS

HEY, Y'ALL!
IT'S BEEN A LONG SUMMER, BUT I'M BACK AT SAMWELL!
(AND I'M BACK TO VLOGGING! THANK YOU SO MUCH FOR YOUR PATIENCE!!)
≥AHEM≤ BACK FOR MY LAST YEAR AT SAMWELL. YES-I'M-IN-DENIAL-BUT-THAT-COULD-BE-AN-ENTIRE-VLOG-IN-ITSELF. HAHA.
SAMWELL
SAMWELL
SAMWELL
SHUT OUT!
ANYWAY! THINGS HAVE SUFFICIENTLY DIED DOWN SINCE THE CUP, AND IT'S BEEN... A RELIEF.
I ONLY DID ONE INTERVIEW AND THAT WAS WITH THE SAMWELL DAILY. AND NO, NO ONE HAS CAMPED OUT ON THE HAUS' FRONT LAWN. WELL, OTHER THAN THE SWALLOW.

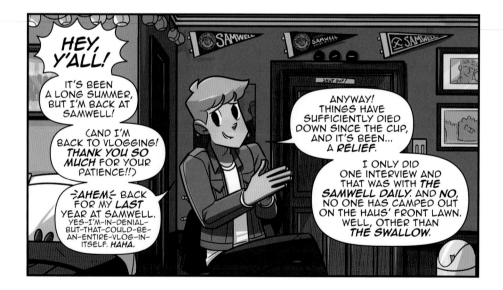

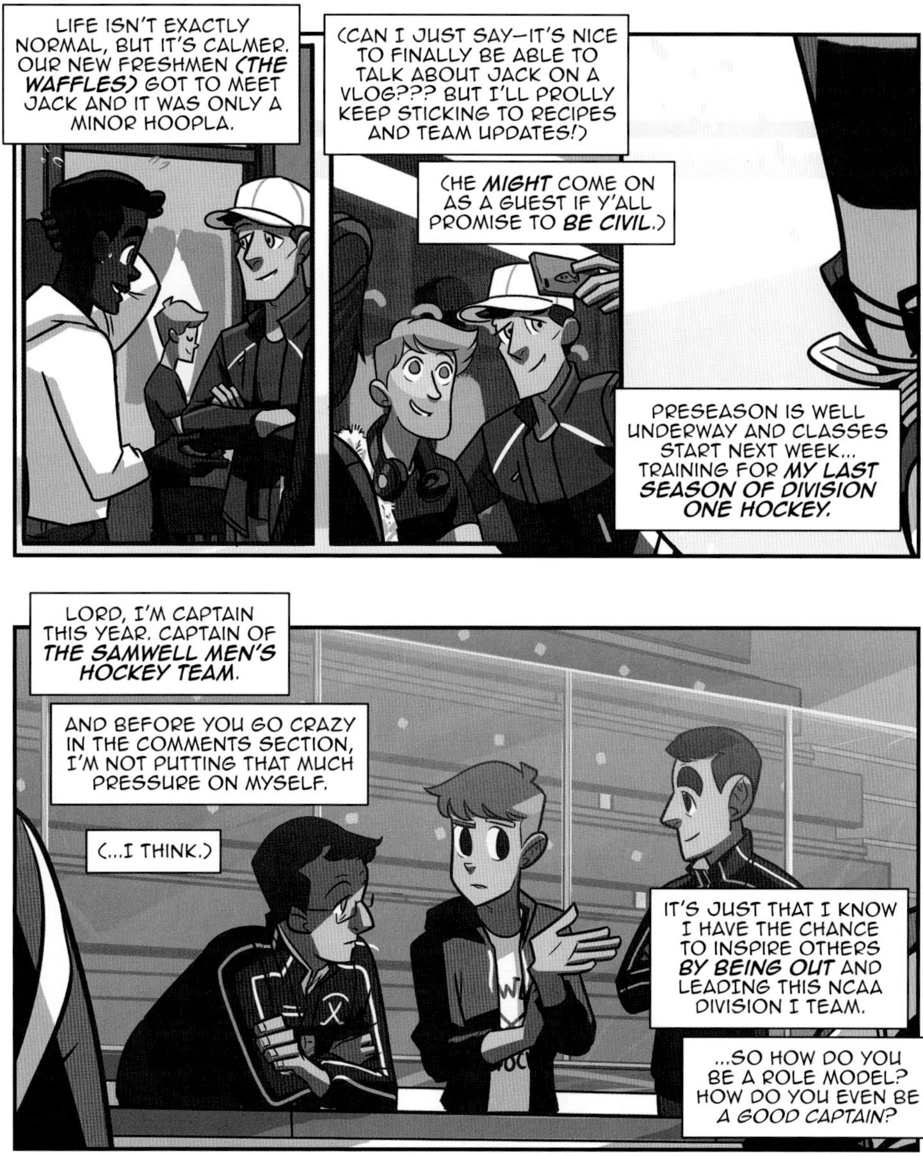
LIFE ISN'T EXACTLY NORMAL, BUT IT'S CALMER. OUR NEW FRESHMEN *(THE WAFFLES)* GOT TO MEET JACK AND IT WAS ONLY A MINOR HOOPLA.
(CAN I JUST SAY—IT'S NICE TO FINALLY BE ABLE TO TALK ABOUT JACK ON A VLOG??? BUT I'LL PROLLY KEEP STICKING TO RECIPES AND TEAM UPDATES!)
(HE *MIGHT* COME ON AS A GUEST IF Y'ALL PROMISE TO *BE CIVIL*.)
PRESEASON IS WELL UNDERWAY AND CLASSES START NEXT WEEK... TRAINING FOR *MY LAST SEASON OF DIVISION ONE HOCKEY.*
LORD, I'M CAPTAIN THIS YEAR. CAPTAIN OF *THE SAMWELL MEN'S HOCKEY TEAM*.
AND BEFORE YOU GO CRAZY IN THE COMMENTS SECTION, I'M NOT PUTTING THAT MUCH PRESSURE ON MYSELF.
(...I THINK.)
IT'S JUST THAT I KNOW I HAVE THE CHANCE TO INSPIRE OTHERS *BY BEING OUT* AND LEADING THIS NCAA DIVISION I TEAM.
...SO HOW DO YOU BE A ROLE MODEL? HOW DO YOU EVEN BE A *GOOD CAPTAIN*?

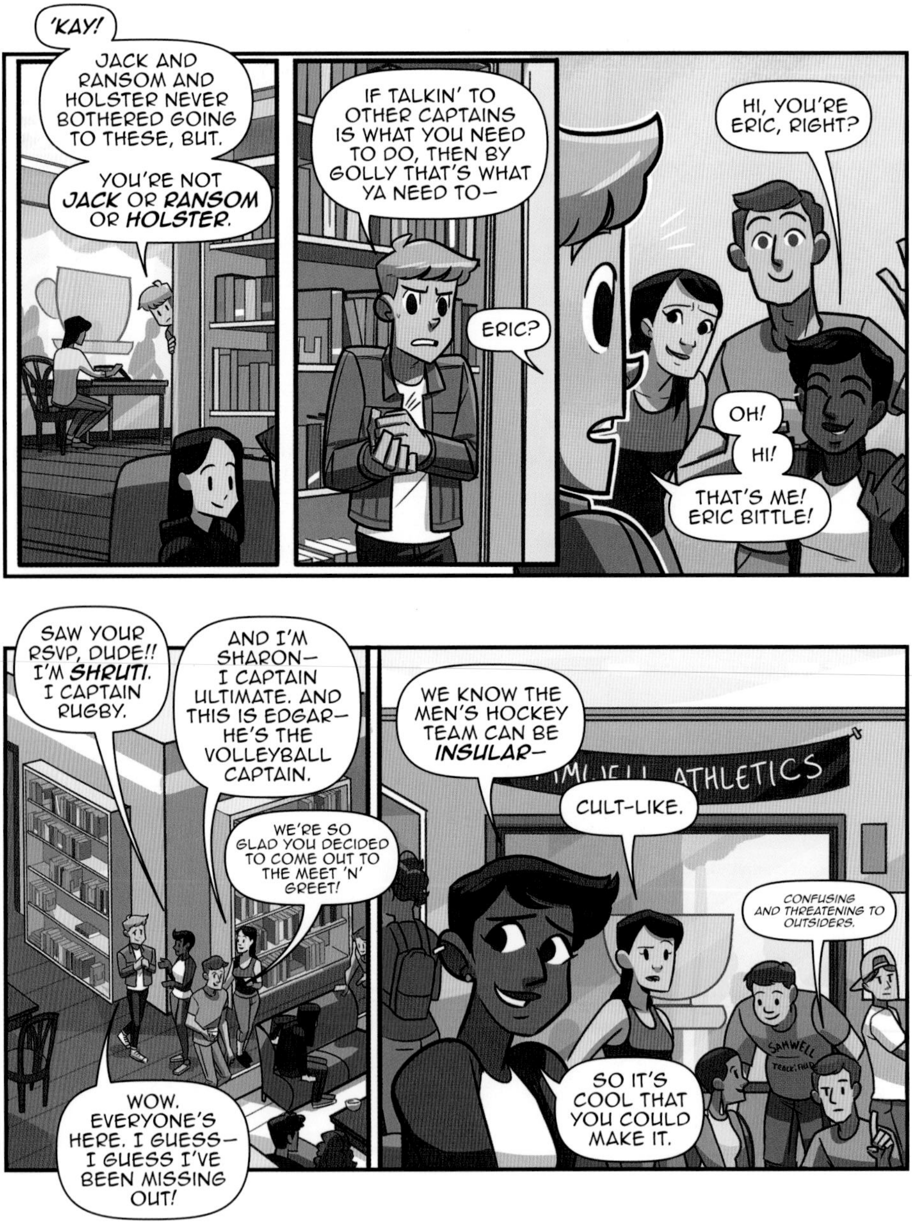
'KAY!
JACK AND RANSOM AND HOLSTER NEVER BOTHERED GOING TO THESE, BUT.
YOU'RE NOT *JACK* OR *RANSOM* OR *HOLSTER*.
IF TALKIN' TO OTHER CAPTAINS IS WHAT YOU NEED TO DO, THEN BY GOLLY THAT'S WHAT YA NEED TO—
ERIC?
HI, YOU'RE ERIC, RIGHT?
OH!
HI!
THAT'S ME! ERIC BITTLE!
SAW YOUR RSVP, DUDE!! I'M *SHRUTI*. I CAPTAIN RUGBY.
AND I'M SHARON— I CAPTAIN ULTIMATE. AND THIS IS EDGAR— HE'S THE VOLLEYBALL CAPTAIN.
WE'RE SO GLAD YOU DECIDED TO COME OUT TO THE MEET 'N' GREET!
WOW. EVERYONE'S HERE. I GUESS— I GUESS I'VE BEEN MISSING OUT!
WE KNOW THE MEN'S HOCKEY TEAM CAN BE *INSULAR*—
ATHLETICS
CULT-LIKE.
CONFUSING AND THREATENING TO OUTSIDERS.
SO IT'S COOL THAT YOU COULD MAKE IT.

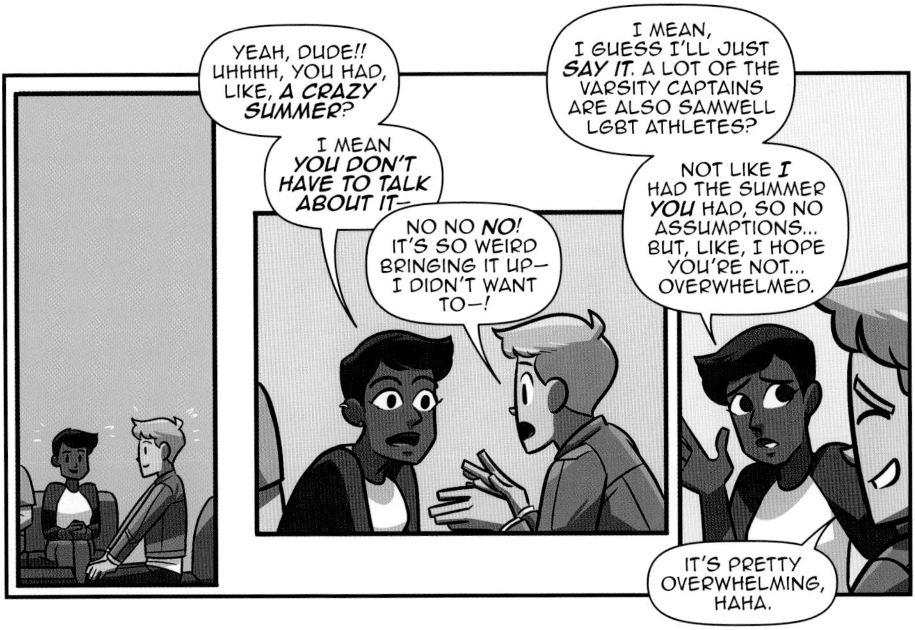
YEAH, DUDE!! UHHHH, YOU HAD, LIKE, *A CRAZY SUMMER*?
I MEAN *YOU DON'T HAVE TO TALK ABOUT IT*—
NO NO *NO*! IT'S SO WEIRD BRINGING IT UP—I DIDN'T WANT TO—!
I MEAN, I GUESS I'LL JUST *SAY IT*. A LOT OF THE VARSITY CAPTAINS ARE ALSO SAMWELL LGBT ATHLETES?
NOT LIKE *I* HAD THE SUMMER *YOU* HAD, SO NO ASSUMPTIONS... BUT, LIKE, I HOPE YOU'RE NOT... OVERWHELMED.
IT'S PRETTY OVERWHELMING, HAHA.

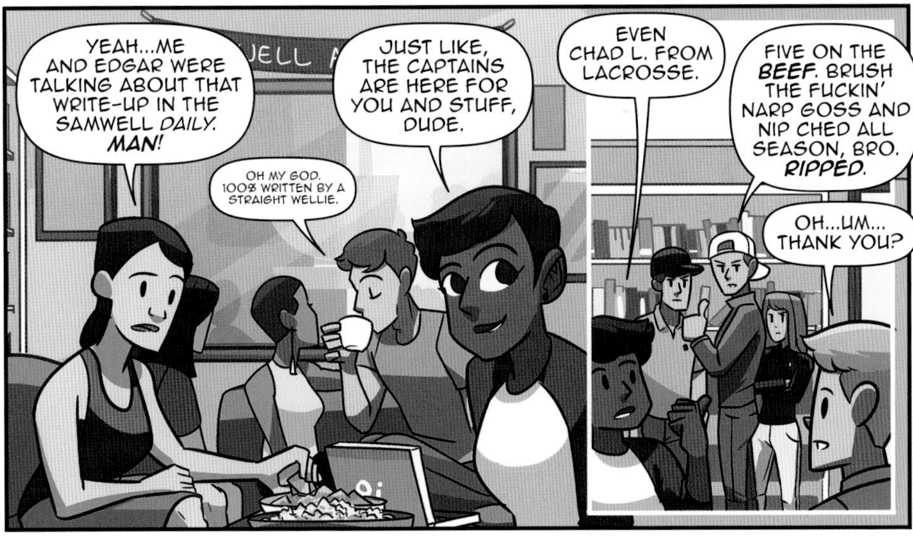
YEAH...ME AND EDGAR WERE TALKING ABOUT THAT WRITE-UP IN THE SAMWELL *DAILY*. *MAN*!
OH MY GOD. 100% WRITTEN BY A STRAIGHT WELLIE.
JUST LIKE, THE CAPTAINS ARE HERE FOR YOU AND STUFF, DUDE.
EVEN CHAD L. FROM LACROSSE.
FIVE ON THE *BEEF*. BRUSH THE FUCKIN' NARP GOSS AND NIP CHED ALL SEASON, BRO. *RIPPED*.
OH...UM... THANK YOU?

YOU GUYS SHOULD ALL COME OVER FOR A KEGSTER!! SAMWELL ATHLETICS EXCLUSIVE. I PROMISE THE HAUS ISN'T THAT HAUNTED.
OH MY GOSH, YES!!
UM, WAIT, DID THAT LOUD GUY WITH THE GIANT CHICLET TEETH GRADUATE YET...
OKAY. QUESTION. HOW DID THE FIRE OVER THE SUMMER START???
(CAN SOMEONE PLEASE EXPLAIN THE HOCKEY BRO LAX BRO RIVALRY? I CAN'T TELL MOST OF Y'ALL APAR-)
WHAT? THE SOCCER TEAM WISHES IT WAS THE GAYEST TEAM AT SAMWELL. PLEASE!
Annie's
WAIT. ERIC? WHERE DID THAT PIE COME FROM??

C

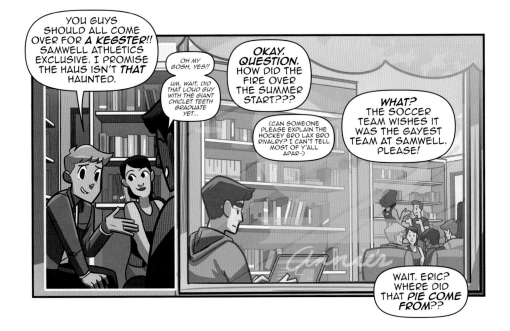

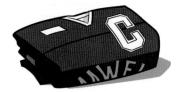

7

HAZE BY HAZEWEST: ROOKIE BLANKET

WEDNESDAY
WOW, BITS. SO YOU'RE GOING THROUGH WITH INITIATION?
OF COURSE! IT'S TRADITION.
AND AS A SENIOR AND CAPTAIN, THERE IS NOTHING MORE IMPORTANT TO ME THAN MAKING SURE NEW MEMBERS FEEL INCORPORATED INTO THE TEAM!
WELL, DON'T GO EASY ON THEM, BITS!!
THIS MIGHT BE THE ONLY CHANCE IN YOUR LIFE YOU GET TO BOSS AROUND A BUNCH OF JOCKS.
BOSSING AROUND A BUNCH OF JOCKS?
OH, LIL OL' ME?

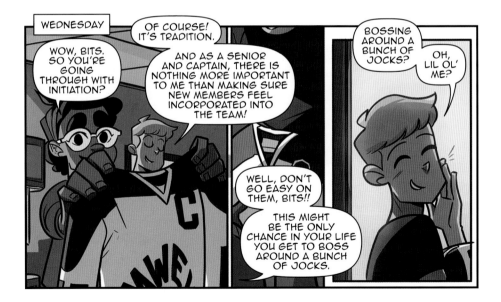

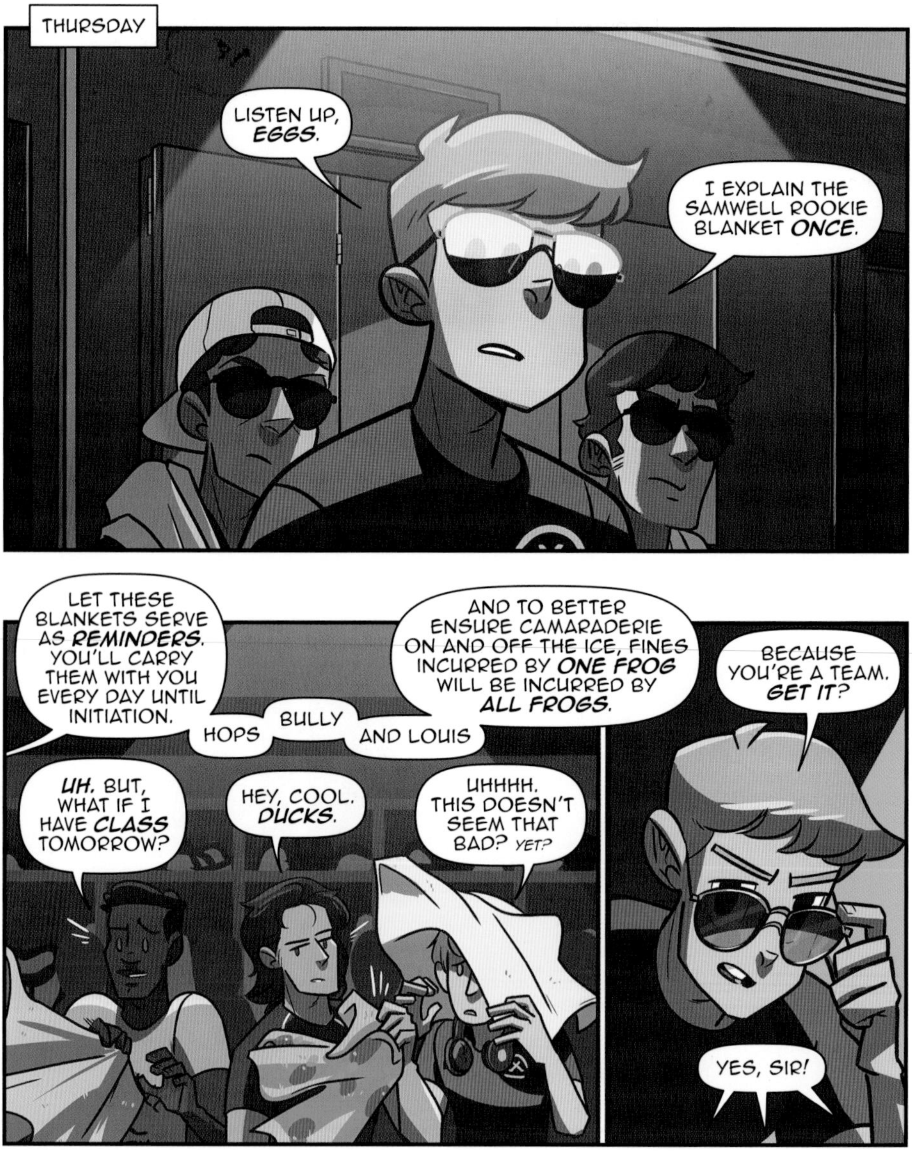
THURSDAY
LISTEN UP, EGGS.
I EXPLAIN THE SAMWELL ROOKIE BLANKET ONCE.
LET THESE BLANKETS SERVE AS REMINDERS. YOU'LL CARRY THEM WITH YOU EVERY DAY UNTIL INITIATION.
HOPS
BULLY
AND LOUIS
AND TO BETTER ENSURE CAMARADERIE ON AND OFF THE ICE, FINES INCURRED BY ONE FROG WILL BE INCURRED BY ALL FROGS.
UH. BUT, WHAT IF I HAVE CLASS TOMORROW?
HEY, COOL. DUCKS.
UHHHH. THIS DOESN'T SEEM THAT BAD? YET?
BECAUSE YOU'RE A TEAM. GET IT?
YES, SIR!

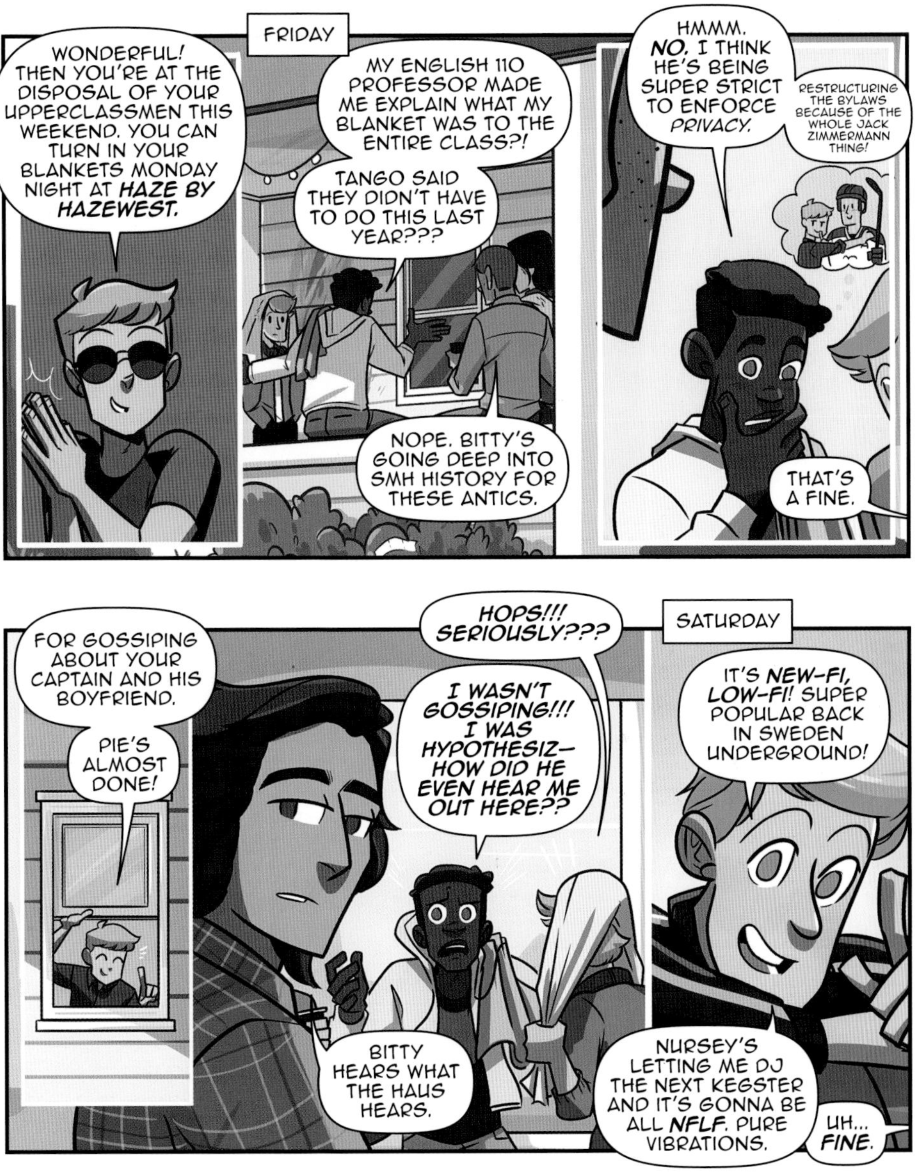
FRIDAY
WONDERFUL! THEN YOU'RE AT THE DISPOSAL OF YOUR UPPERCLASSMEN THIS WEEKEND. YOU CAN TURN IN YOUR BLANKETS MONDAY NIGHT AT HAZE BY HAZEWEST.
MY ENGLISH 110 PROFESSOR MADE ME EXPLAIN WHAT MY BLANKET WAS TO THE ENTIRE CLASS?!
TANGO SAID THEY DIDN'T HAVE TO DO THIS LAST YEAR???
NOPE. BITTY'S GOING DEEP INTO SMH HISTORY FOR THESE ANTICS.
HMMM. NO, I THINK HE'S BEING SUPER STRICT TO ENFORCE PRIVACY.
RESTRUCTURING THE BYLAWS BECAUSE OF THE WHOLE JACK ZIMMERMANN THING!
THAT'S A FINE.
FOR GOSSIPING ABOUT YOUR CAPTAIN AND HIS BOYFRIEND.
PIE'S ALMOST DONE!
HOPS!!! SERIOUSLY???
I WASN'T GOSSIPING!!! I WAS HYPOTHESIZ— HOW DID HE EVEN HEAR ME OUT HERE??
BITTY HEARS WHAT THE HAUS HEARS.
SATURDAY
IT'S NEW-FI, LOW-FI! SUPER POPULAR BACK IN SWEDEN UNDERGROUND!
NURSEY'S LETTING ME DJ THE NEXT KEGSTER AND IT'S GONNA BE ALL NFLF. PURE VIBRATIONS.
UH... FINE.

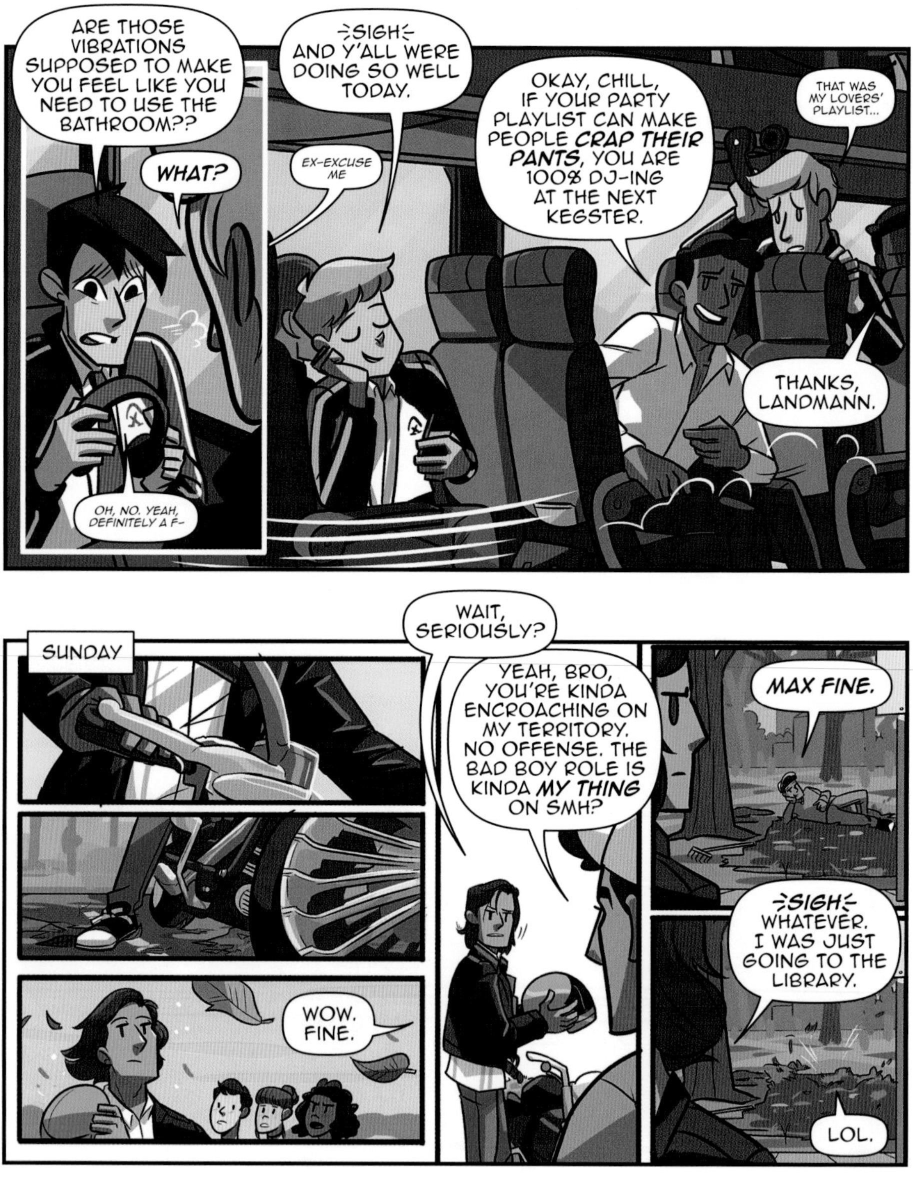
ARE THOSE VIBRATIONS SUPPOSED TO MAKE YOU FEEL LIKE YOU NEED TO USE THE BATHROOM??
WHAT?
OH, NO. YEAH, DEFINITELY A F-
EX-EXCUSE ME
=SIGH= AND Y'ALL WERE DOING SO WELL TODAY.
OKAY, CHILL, IF YOUR PARTY PLAYLIST CAN MAKE PEOPLE CRAP THEIR PANTS, YOU ARE 100% DJ-ING AT THE NEXT KEGSTER.
THAT WAS MY LOVERS' PLAYLIST...
THANKS, LANDMANN.
SUNDAY
WOW. FINE.
WAIT, SERIOUSLY?
YEAH, BRO, YOU'RE KINDA ENCROACHING ON MY TERRITORY. NO OFFENSE. THE BAD BOY ROLE IS KINDA MY THING ON SMH?
MAX FINE.
=SIGH= WHATEVER. I WAS JUST GOING TO THE LIBRARY.
LOL.

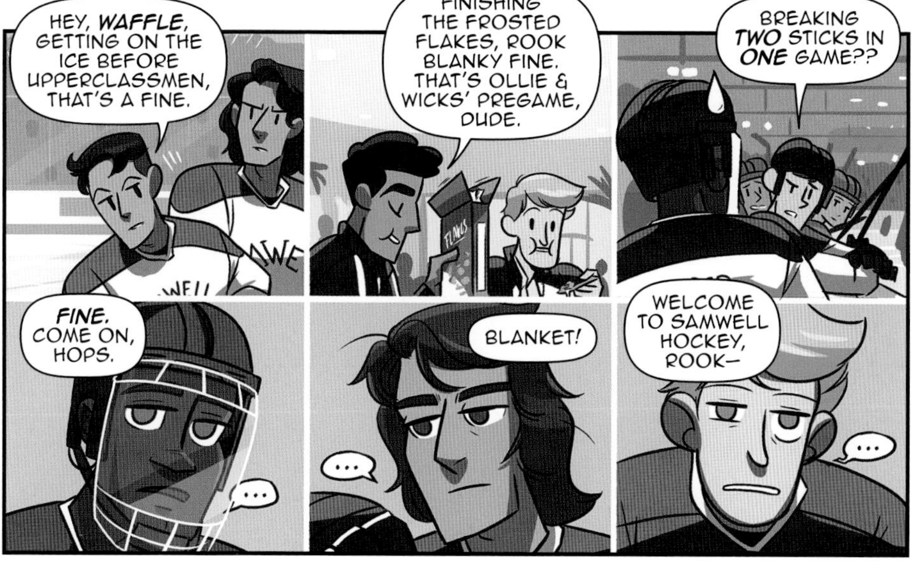
HEY, WAFFLE, GETTING ON THE ICE BEFORE UPPERCLASSMEN, THAT'S A FINE.
FINISHING THE FROSTED FLAKES, ROOK BLANKY FINE. THAT'S OLLIE & WICKS' PREGAME, DUDE.
BREAKING TWO STICKS IN ONE GAME??
FINE. COME ON, HOPS.
...
BLANKET!
...
WELCOME TO SAMWELL HOCKEY, ROOK—
...

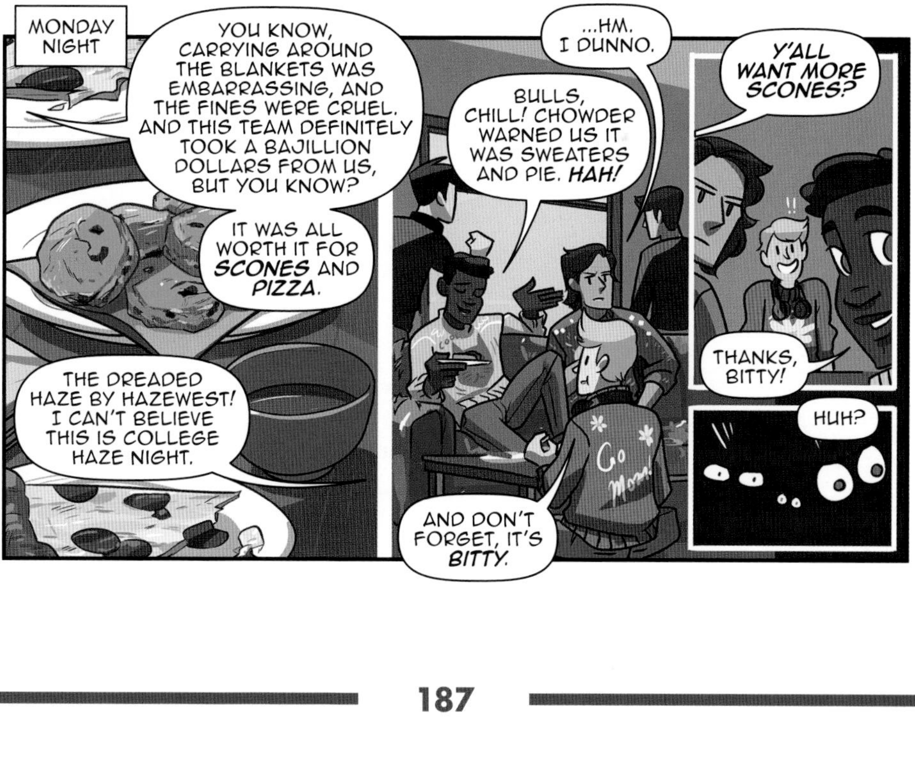
MONDAY NIGHT
YOU KNOW, CARRYING AROUND THE BLANKETS WAS EMBARRASSING, AND THE FINES WERE CRUEL. AND THIS TEAM DEFINITELY TOOK A BAJILLION DOLLARS FROM US, BUT YOU KNOW?
IT WAS ALL WORTH IT FOR SCONES AND PIZZA.
THE DREADED HAZE BY HAZEWEST! I CAN'T BELIEVE THIS IS COLLEGE HAZE NIGHT.
...HM. I DUNNO.
BULLS, CHILL! CHOWDER WARNED US IT WAS SWEATERS AND PIE. HAH!
AND DON'T FORGET, IT'S BITTY.
Y'ALL WANT MORE SCONES?
THANKS, BITTY!
HUH?

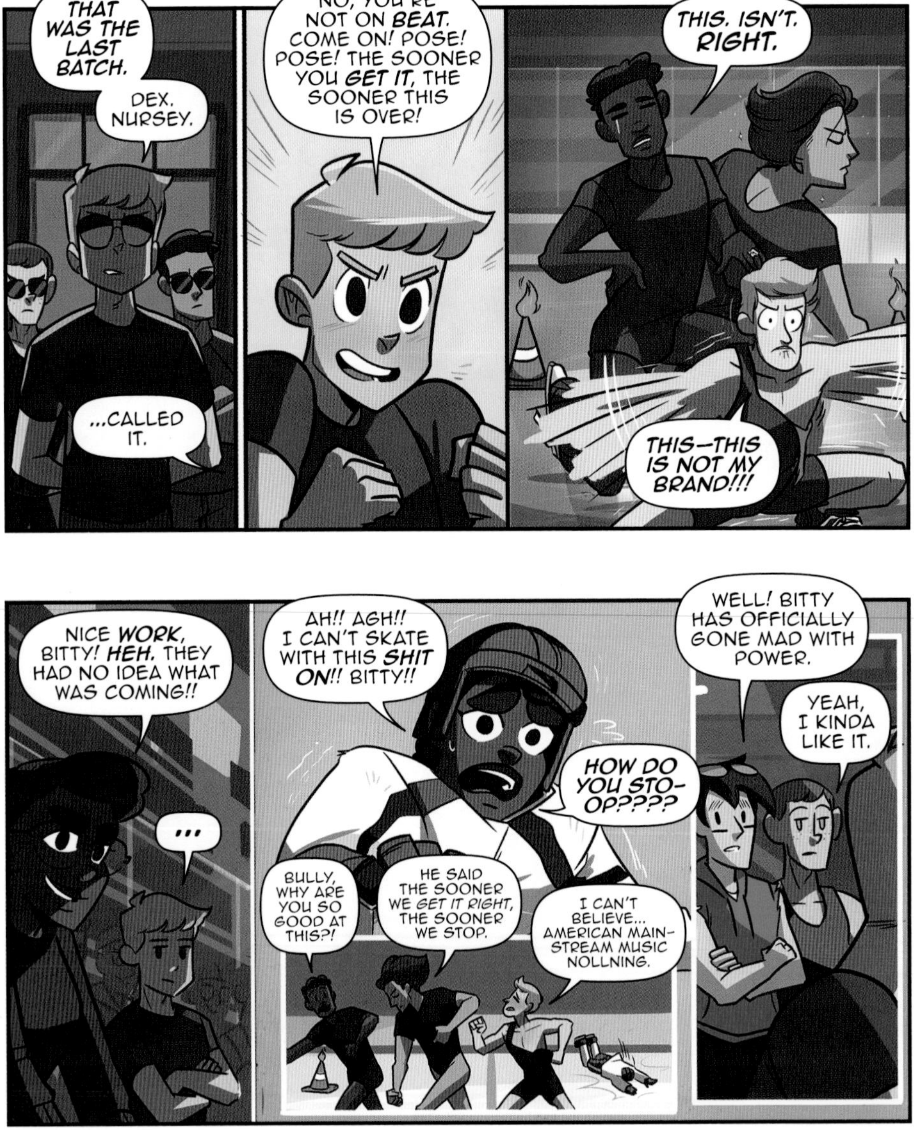
THAT WAS THE LAST BATCH.
DEX. NURSEY.
...CALLED IT.
NO, YOU'RE NOT ON BEAT. COME ON! POSE! POSE! THE SOONER YOU GET IT, THE SOONER THIS IS OVER!
THIS. ISN'T. RIGHT.
THIS—THIS IS NOT MY BRAND!!!
NICE WORK, BITTY! HEH. THEY HAD NO IDEA WHAT WAS COMING!!
...
AH!! AGH!! I CAN'T SKATE WITH THIS SHIT ON!! BITTY!!
HOW DO YOU STO-OP????
BULLY, WHY ARE YOU SO GOOD AT THIS?!
HE SAID THE SOONER WE GET IT RIGHT, THE SOONER WE STOP.
I CAN'T BELIEVE... AMERICAN MAIN-STREAM MUSIC NOLLNING.
WELL! BITTY HAS OFFICIALLY GONE MAD WITH POWER.
YEAH, I KINDA LIKE IT.

8

HAUS 2.0

IF I'M BEING TOTALLY HONEST, WE'VE BEEN DUE FOR AN INJURY.
NICE GOAL!
TOP SHELF, NURSE!
FUCKIN 'SWAWES—
HEY, THANKS FOR THE ASSIST, POINDEXTER!
YOU'RE LUCKY YOU DIDN'T BREAK YOUR NECK CRASHING THE BOARDS LIKE THAT, NURSEY.

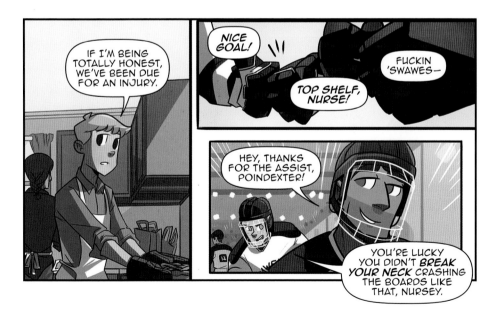

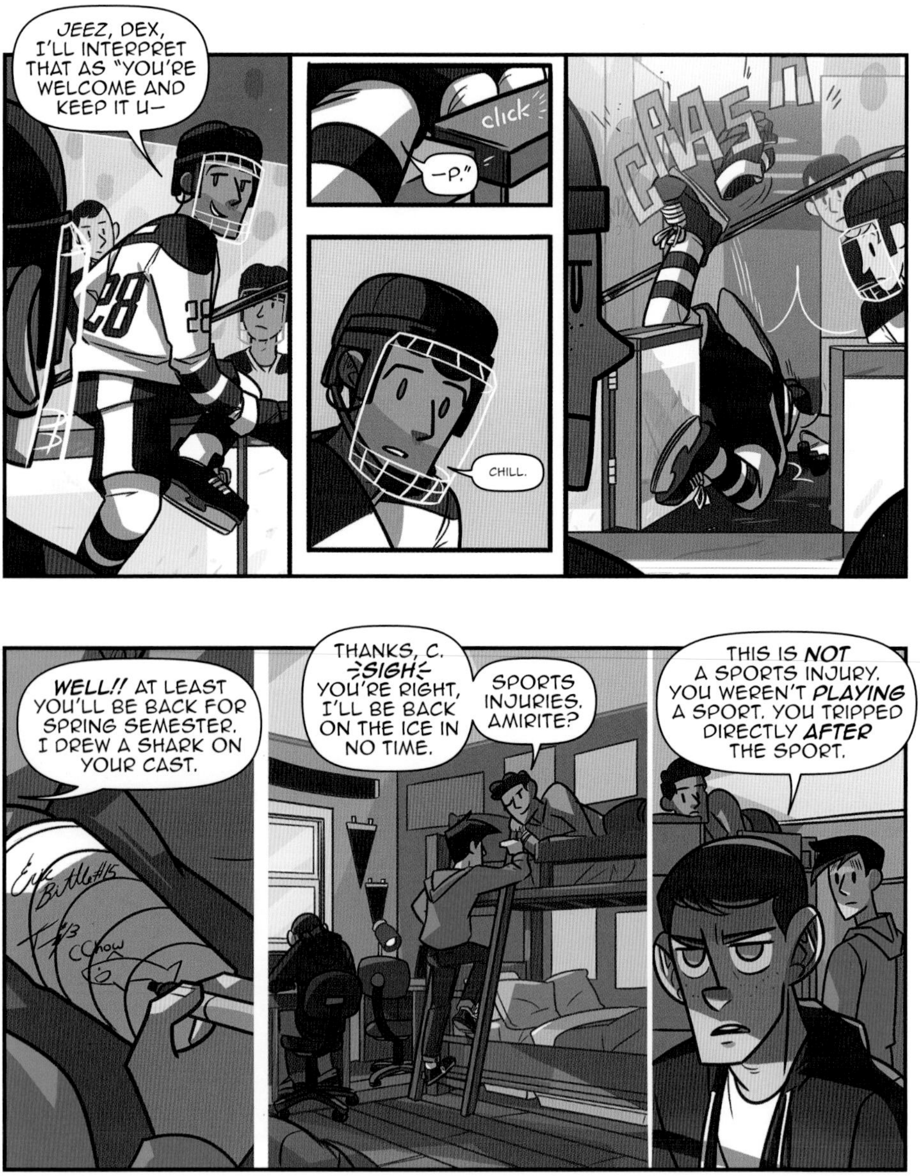
JEEZ, DEX, I'LL INTERPRET THAT AS "YOU'RE WELCOME AND KEEP IT U—
click
—P."
CHILL.
WELL!! AT LEAST YOU'LL BE BACK FOR SPRING SEMESTER. I DREW A SHARK ON YOUR CAST.
THANKS, C. *SIGH* YOU'RE RIGHT, I'LL BE BACK ON THE ICE IN NO TIME.
SPORTS INJURIES. AMIRITE?
THIS IS NOT A SPORTS INJURY. YOU WEREN'T PLAYING A SPORT. YOU TRIPPED DIRECTLY AFTER THE SPORT.

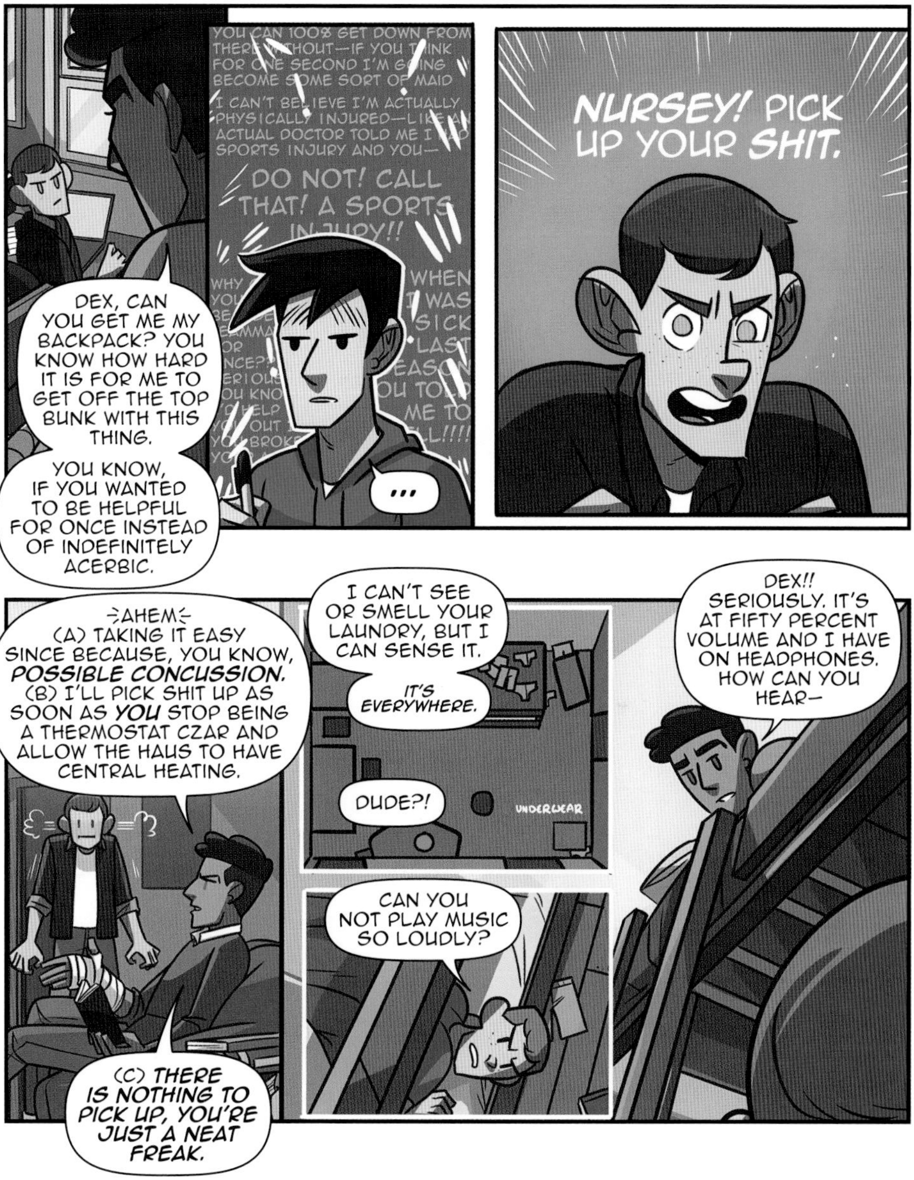
DEX, CAN YOU GET ME MY BACKPACK? YOU KNOW HOW HARD IT IS FOR ME TO GET OFF THE TOP BUNK WITH THIS THING.
YOU KNOW, IF YOU WANTED TO BE HELPFUL FOR ONCE INSTEAD OF INDEFINITELY ACERBIC.
YOU CAN 100% GET DOWN FROM THERE WITHOUT—IF YOU THINK FOR ONE SECOND I'M GOING BECOME SOME SORT OF MAID
I CAN'T BELIEVE I'M ACTUALLY PHYSICALLY INJURED—LIKE AN ACTUAL DOCTOR TOLD ME I HAD SPORTS INJURY AND YOU—
DO NOT! CALL THAT! A SPORTS INJURY!!
WHEN I WAS SICK LAST SEASON YOU TOLD ME TO
...
NURSEY! PICK UP YOUR SHIT.
AHEM (A) TAKING IT EASY SINCE BECAUSE, YOU KNOW, POSSIBLE CONCUSSION. (B) I'LL PICK SHIT UP AS SOON AS YOU STOP BEING A THERMOSTAT CZAR AND ALLOW THE HAUS TO HAVE CENTRAL HEATING.
(C) THERE IS NOTHING TO PICK UP, YOU'RE JUST A NEAT FREAK.
I CAN'T SEE OR SMELL YOUR LAUNDRY, BUT I CAN SENSE IT.
IT'S EVERYWHERE.
DUDE?!
UNDERWEAR
CAN YOU NOT PLAY MUSIC SO LOUDLY?
DEX!! SERIOUSLY. IT'S AT FIFTY PERCENT VOLUME AND I HAVE ON HEADPHONES. HOW CAN YOU HEAR—

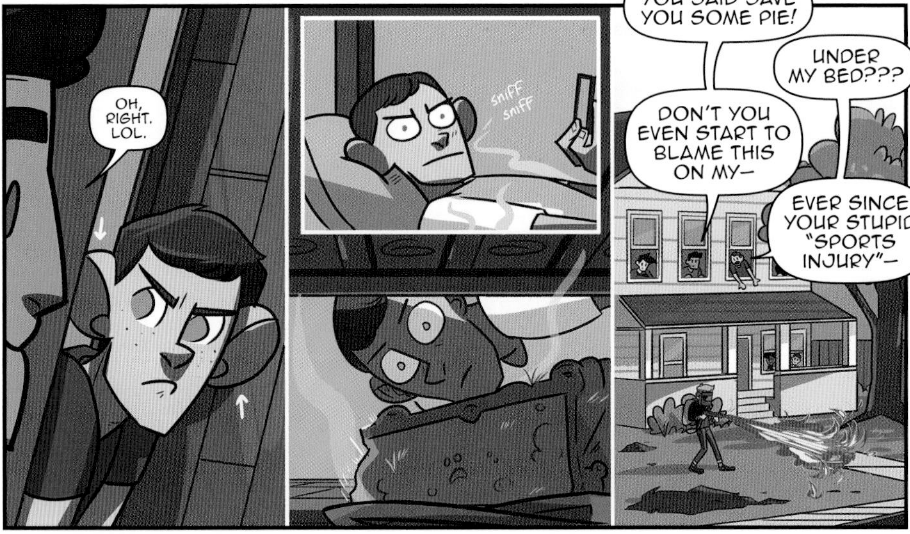
OH, RIGHT. LOL.
sniff sniff
YOU SAID SAVE YOU SOME PIE!
DON'T YOU EVEN START TO BLAME THIS ON MY—
UNDER MY BED???
EVER SINCE YOUR STUPID "SPORTS INJURY"—

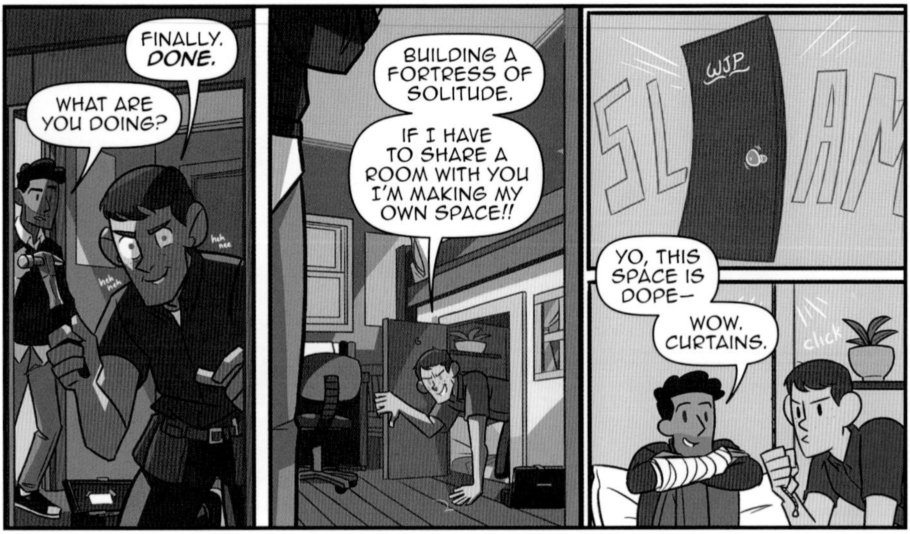
FINALLY. DONE.
WHAT ARE YOU DOING?
BUILDING A FORTRESS OF SOLITUDE.
IF I HAVE TO SHARE A ROOM WITH YOU I'M MAKING MY OWN SPACE!!
WJP
SLAM
YO, THIS SPACE IS DOPE—
WOW. CURTAINS.
click

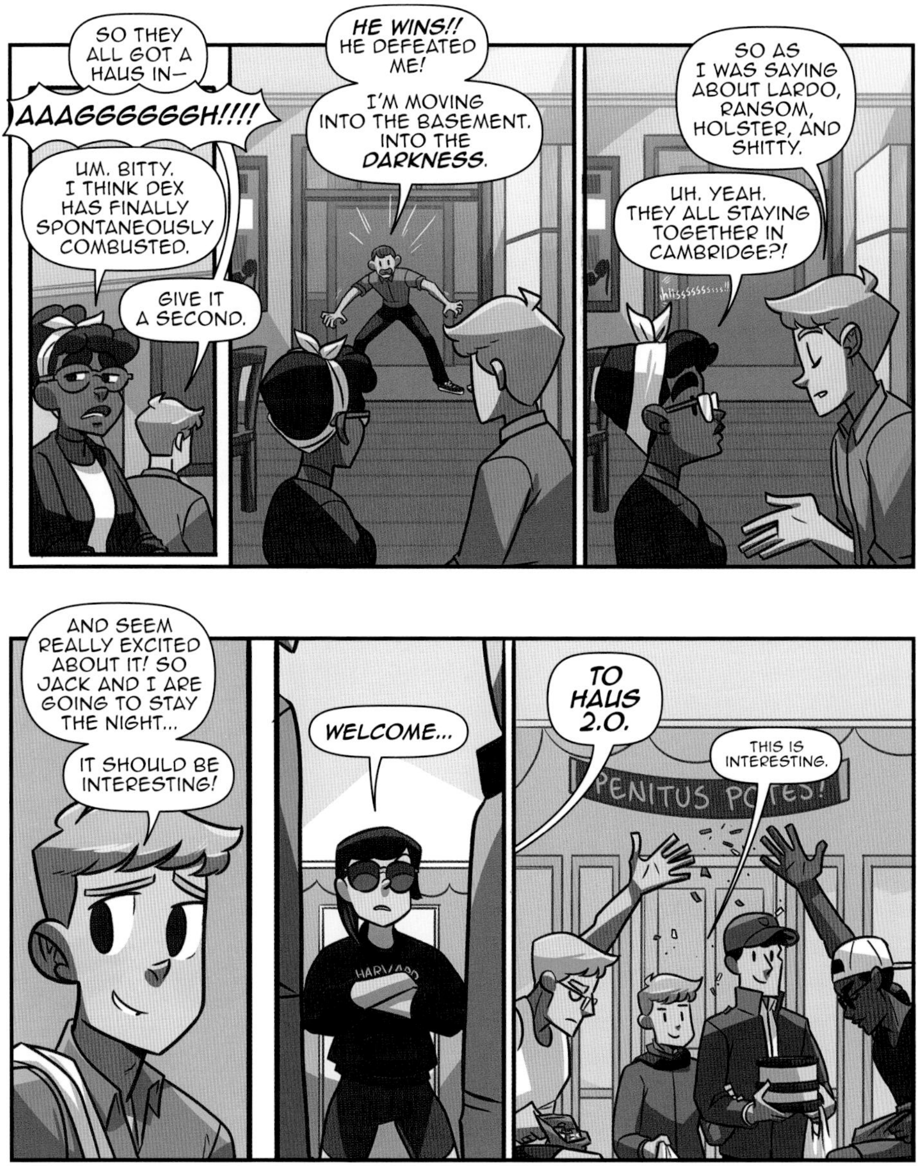
SO THEY ALL GOT A HAUS IN—
AAAGGGGGGH!!!!
UM. BITTY. I THINK DEX HAS FINALLY SPONTANEOUSLY COMBUSTED.
GIVE IT A SECOND.
HE WINS!! HE DEFEATED ME!
I'M MOVING INTO THE BASEMENT. INTO THE DARKNESS.
SO AS I WAS SAYING ABOUT LARDO, RANSOM, HOLSTER, AND SHITTY.
UH. YEAH. THEY ALL STAYING TOGETHER IN CAMBRIDGE?!
AND SEEM REALLY EXCITED ABOUT IT! SO JACK AND I ARE GOING TO STAY THE NIGHT...
IT SHOULD BE INTERESTING!
WELCOME...
TO HAUS 2.0.
THIS IS INTERESTING.

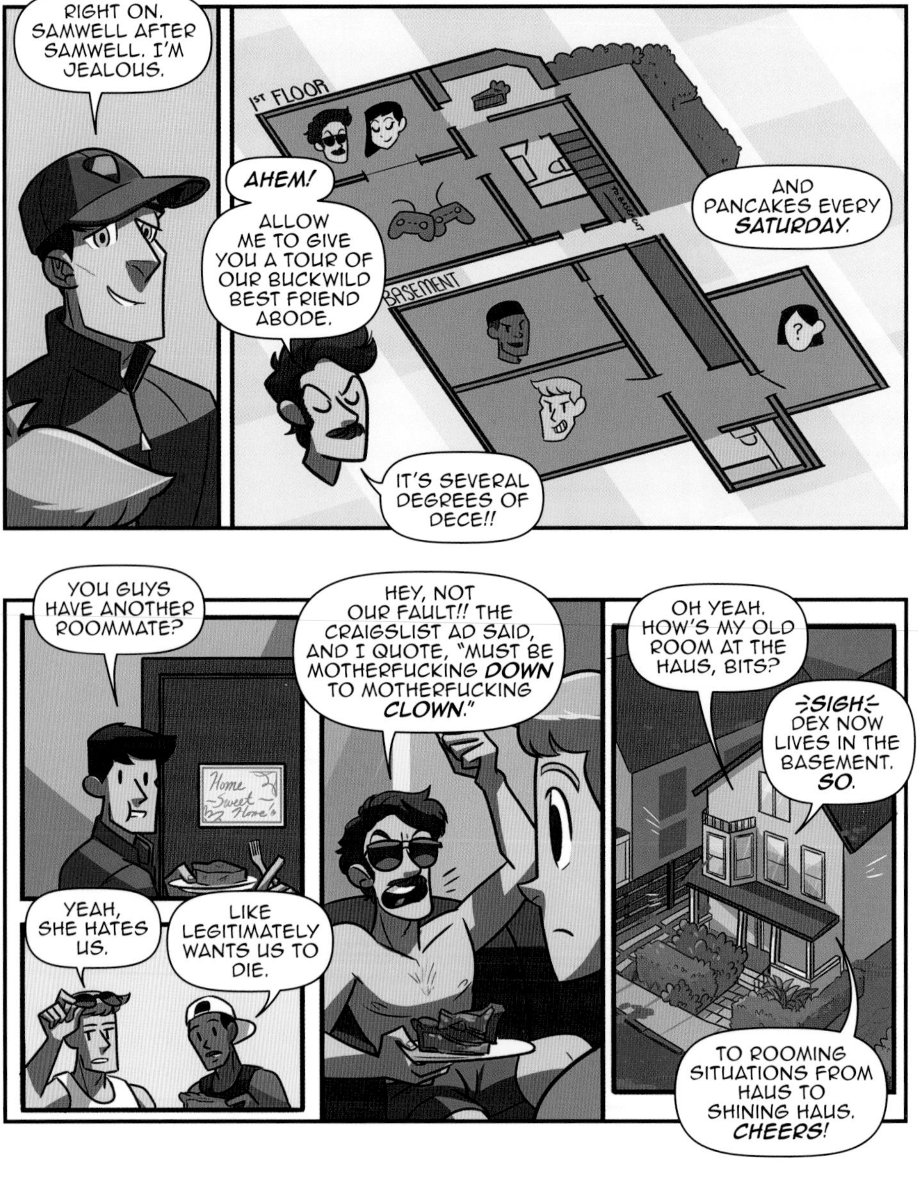
RIGHT ON. SAMWELL AFTER SAMWELL. I'M JEALOUS.
AHEM!
ALLOW ME TO GIVE YOU A TOUR OF OUR BUCKWILD BEST FRIEND ABODE.
1ST FLOOR
BASEMENT
AND PANCAKES EVERY SATURDAY.
IT'S SEVERAL DEGREES OF DECE!!
YOU GUYS HAVE ANOTHER ROOMMATE?
Home Sweet Home
YEAH, SHE HATES US.
LIKE LEGITIMATELY WANTS US TO DIE.
HEY, NOT OUR FAULT!! THE CRAIGSLIST AD SAID, AND I QUOTE, "MUST BE MOTHERFUCKING DOWN TO MOTHERFUCKING CLOWN."
OH YEAH. HOW'S MY OLD ROOM AT THE HAUS, BITS?
SIGH
DEX NOW LIVES IN THE BASEMENT. SO.
TO ROOMING SITUATIONS FROM HAUS TO SHINING HAUS. CHEERS!

9

WHISKEY

OH, JACK, IT'S **NOTHING**... IT'S JUST BEEN ON MY MIND LATELY...
WELL. SOUNDS LIKE IT'S SOMETHING, BITS, NOT NOTHING.
SIGH... CONNOR WHISK IS SAMWELL MEN'S HOCKEY'S TOP SCORER AND HE HATES ME. ***HIS CAPTAIN.***
AND I HAVE ***NO CLUE WHY.***
...BITS.

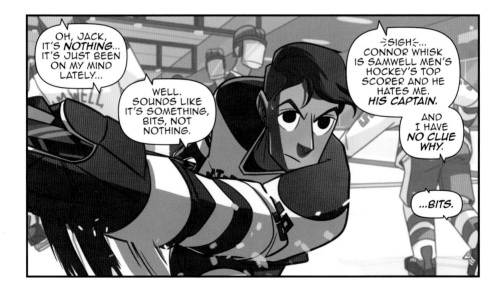

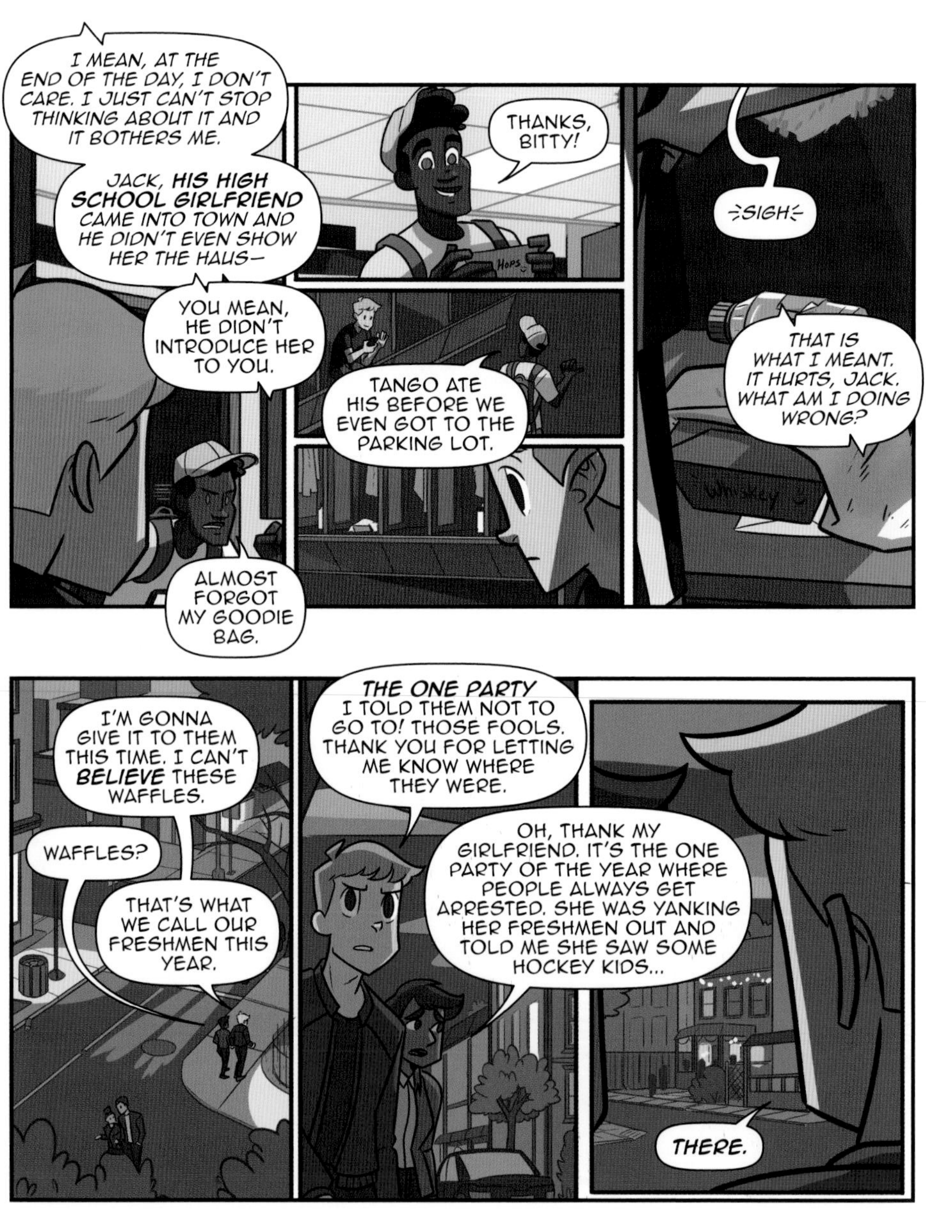
I MEAN, AT THE END OF THE DAY, I DON'T CARE. I JUST CAN'T STOP THINKING ABOUT IT AND IT BOTHERS ME.
JACK, HIS HIGH SCHOOL GIRLFRIEND CAME INTO TOWN AND HE DIDN'T EVEN SHOW HER THE HAUS—
YOU MEAN, HE DIDN'T INTRODUCE HER TO YOU.
ALMOST FORGOT MY GOODIE BAG.
THANKS, BITTY!
TANGO ATE HIS BEFORE WE EVEN GOT TO THE PARKING LOT.
SIGH
THAT IS WHAT I MEANT. IT HURTS, JACK. WHAT AM I DOING WRONG?
I'M GONNA GIVE IT TO THEM THIS TIME. I CAN'T BELIEVE THESE WAFFLES.
WAFFLES?
THAT'S WHAT WE CALL OUR FRESHMEN THIS YEAR.
THE ONE PARTY I TOLD THEM NOT TO GO TO! THOSE FOOLS. THANK YOU FOR LETTING ME KNOW WHERE THEY WERE.
OH, THANK MY GIRLFRIEND. IT'S THE ONE PARTY OF THE YEAR WHERE PEOPLE ALWAYS GET ARRESTED. SHE WAS YANKING HER FRESHMEN OUT AND TOLD ME SHE SAW SOME HOCKEY KIDS...
THERE.

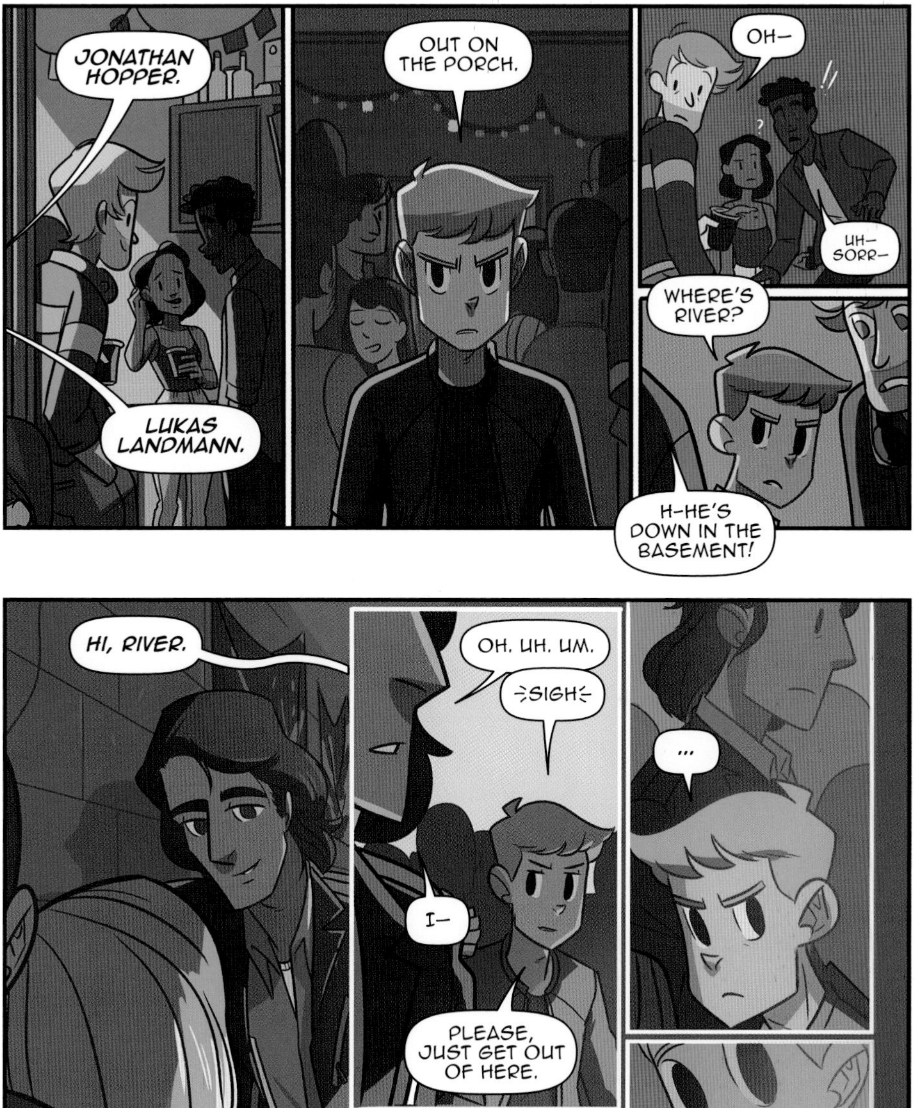
JONATHAN HOPPER.
LUKAS LANDMANN.
OUT ON THE PORCH.
OH—
UH— SORR—
WHERE'S RIVER?
H-HE'S DOWN IN THE BASEMENT!
HI, RIVER.
OH. UH. UM.
SIGH
I—
PLEASE, JUST GET OUT OF HERE.
...

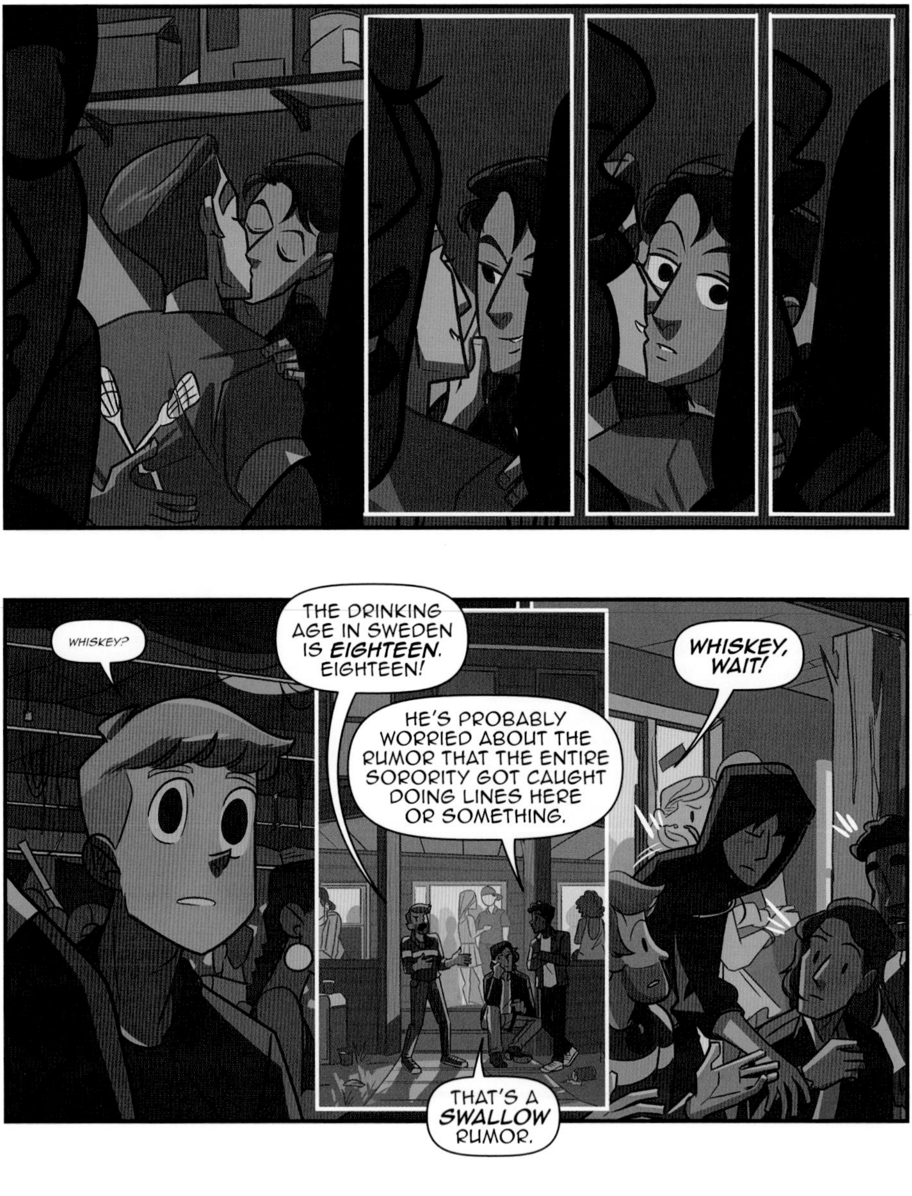
WHISKEY?
THE DRINKING AGE IN SWEDEN IS EIGHTEEN. EIGHTEEN!
HE'S PROBABLY WORRIED ABOUT THE RUMOR THAT THE ENTIRE SORORITY GOT CAUGHT DOING LINES HERE OR SOMETHING.
THAT'S A SWALLOW RUMOR.
WHISKEY, WAIT!

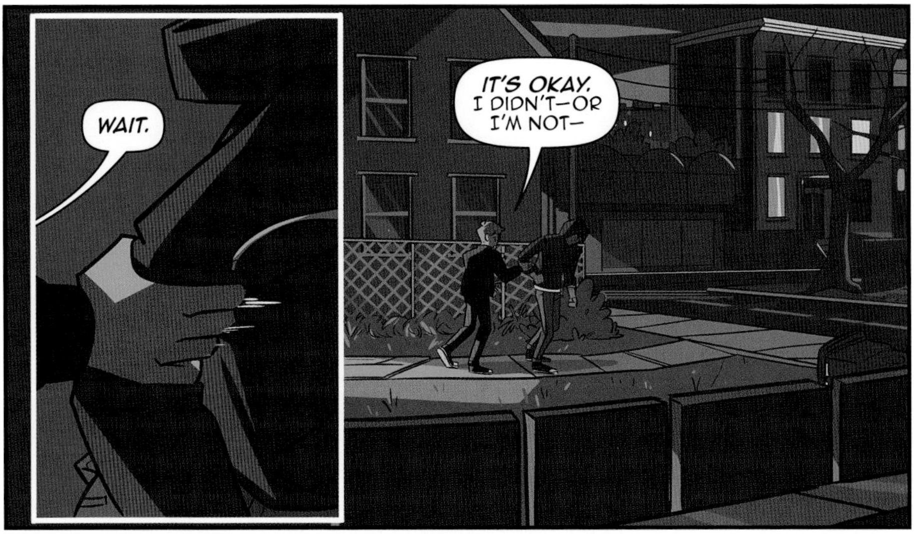
WAIT.
IT'S OKAY. I DIDN'T—OR I'M NOT—

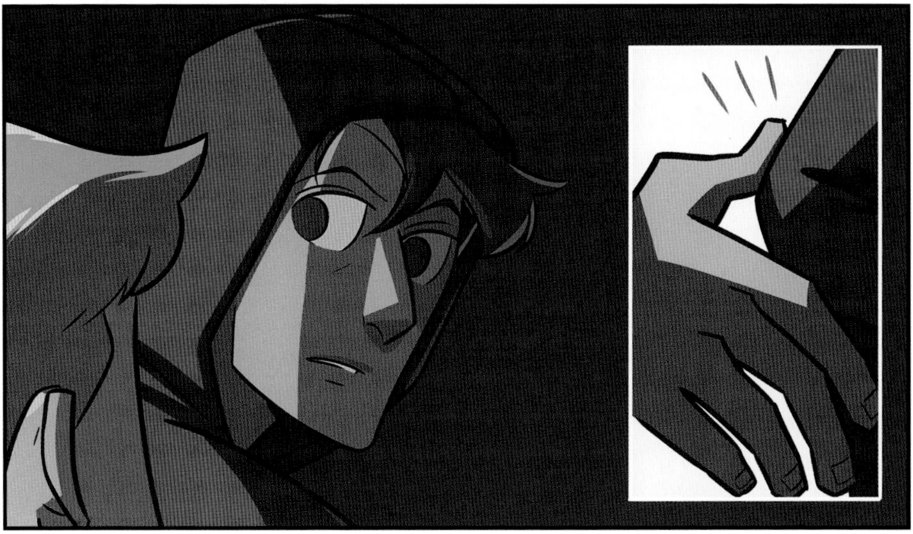

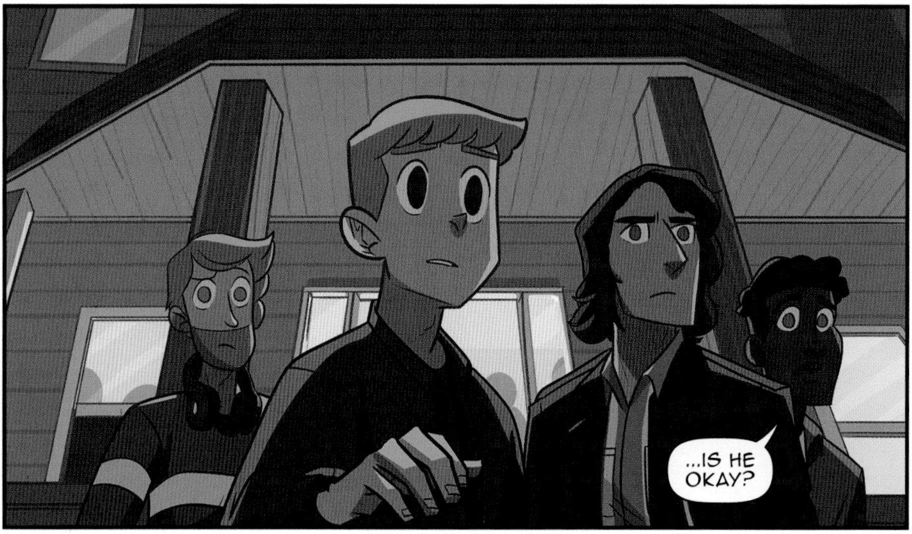
...IS HE
OKAY?

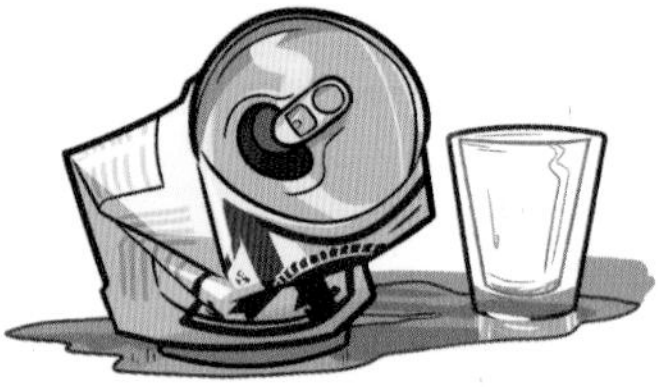

10

COACH — I

HEY, Y'ALL!
SAMWELL MEN'S HOCKEY IS READY FOR FAMILY WEEKEND!!

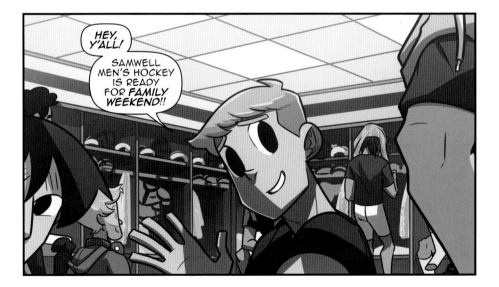

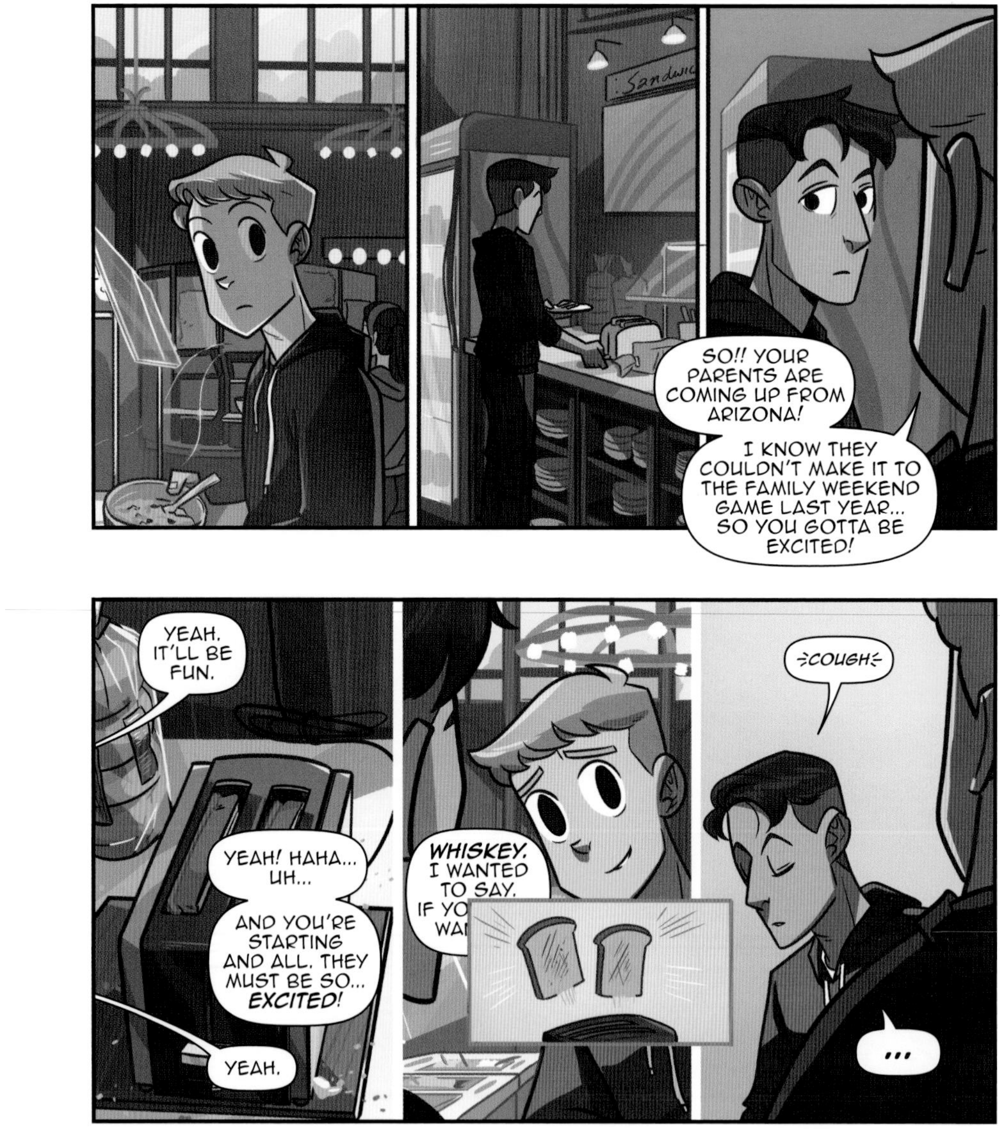
SO!! YOUR PARENTS ARE COMING UP FROM ARIZONA!
I KNOW THEY COULDN'T MAKE IT TO THE FAMILY WEEKEND GAME LAST YEAR... SO YOU GOTTA BE EXCITED!
YEAH. IT'LL BE FUN.
YEAH! HAHA... UH...
AND YOU'RE STARTING AND ALL. THEY MUST BE SO... *EXCITED!*
YEAH.
WHISKEY. I WANTED TO SAY.
COUGH
...

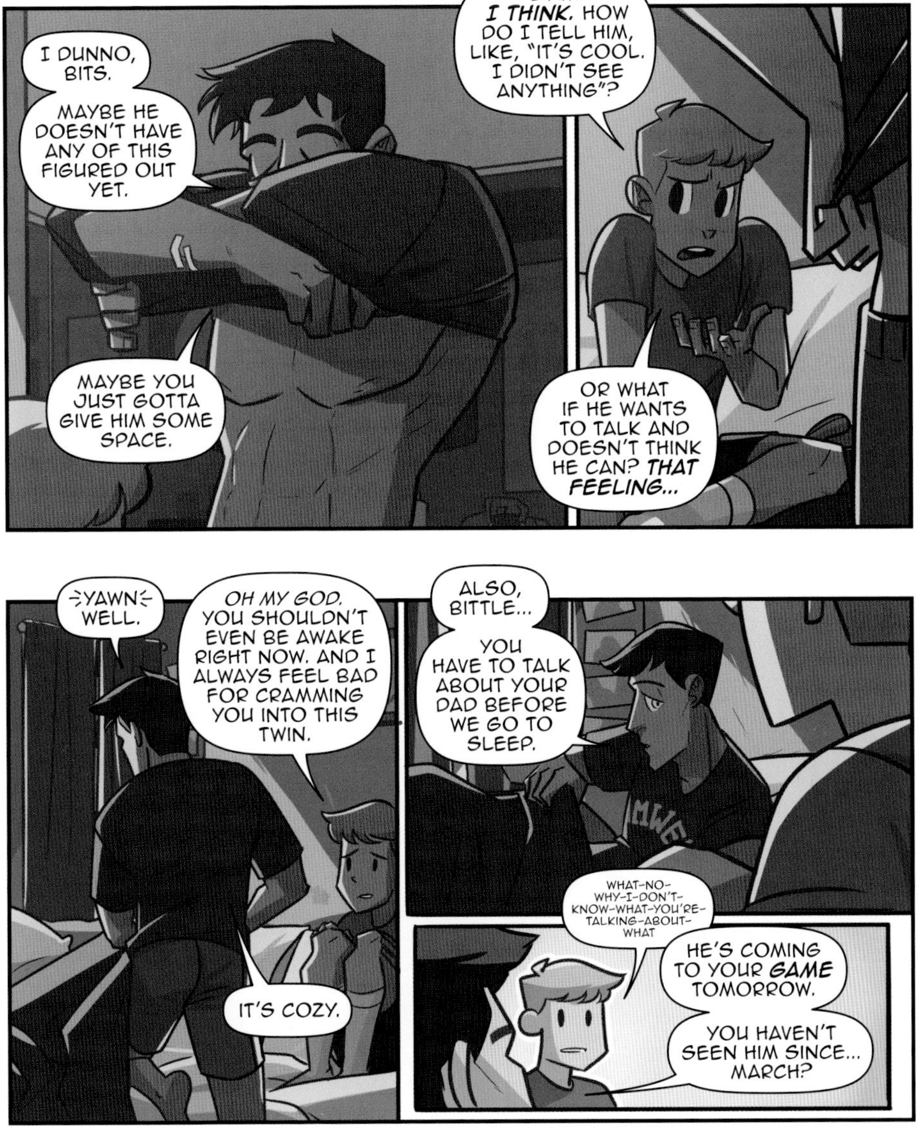
I DUNNO, BITS.
MAYBE HE DOESN'T HAVE ANY OF THIS FIGURED OUT YET.
MAYBE YOU JUST GOTTA GIVE HIM SOME SPACE.
I AM! *I THINK.* HOW DO I TELL HIM, LIKE, "IT'S COOL. I DIDN'T SEE ANYTHING"?
OR WHAT IF HE WANTS TO TALK AND DOESN'T THINK HE CAN? ***THAT FEELING...***
=YAWN= WELL.
OH MY GOD. YOU SHOULDN'T EVEN BE AWAKE RIGHT NOW. AND I ALWAYS FEEL BAD FOR CRAMMING YOU INTO THIS TWIN.
IT'S COZY.
ALSO, BITTLE...
YOU HAVE TO TALK ABOUT YOUR DAD BEFORE WE GO TO SLEEP.
WHAT-NO-WHY-I-DON'T-KNOW-WHAT-YOU'RE-TALKING-ABOUT-WHAT
HE'S COMING TO YOUR ***GAME*** TOMORROW.
YOU HAVEN'T SEEN HIM SINCE... MARCH?

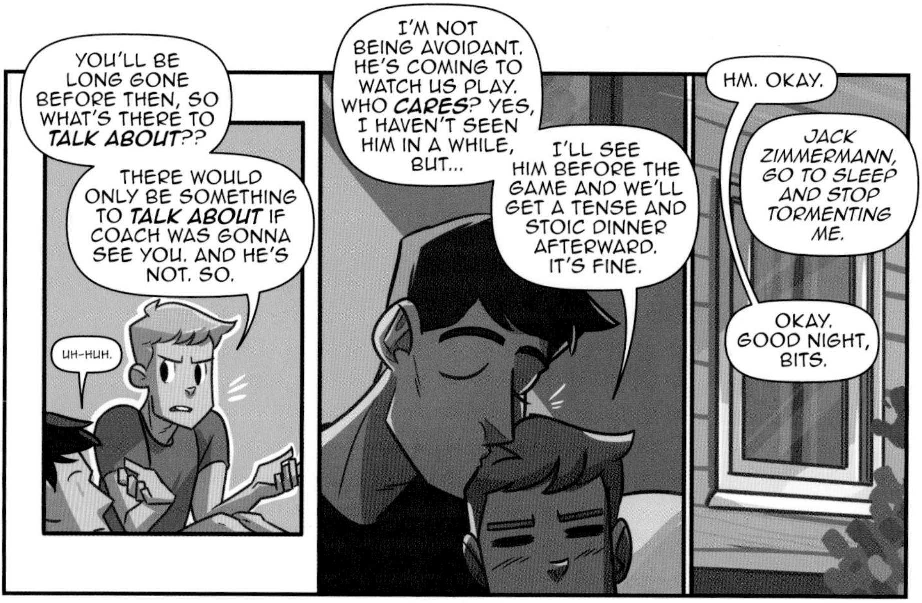
YOU'LL BE LONG GONE BEFORE THEN, SO WHAT'S THERE TO TALK ABOUT??
THERE WOULD ONLY BE SOMETHING TO TALK ABOUT IF COACH WAS GONNA SEE YOU. AND HE'S NOT. SO.
UH-HUH.
I'M NOT BEING AVOIDANT. HE'S COMING TO WATCH US PLAY. WHO CARES? YES, I HAVEN'T SEEN HIM IN A WHILE, BUT...
I'LL SEE HIM BEFORE THE GAME AND WE'LL GET A TENSE AND STOIC DINNER AFTERWARD. IT'S FINE.
HM. OKAY.
JACK ZIMMERMANN, GO TO SLEEP AND STOP TORMENTING ME.
OKAY. GOOD NIGHT, BITS.

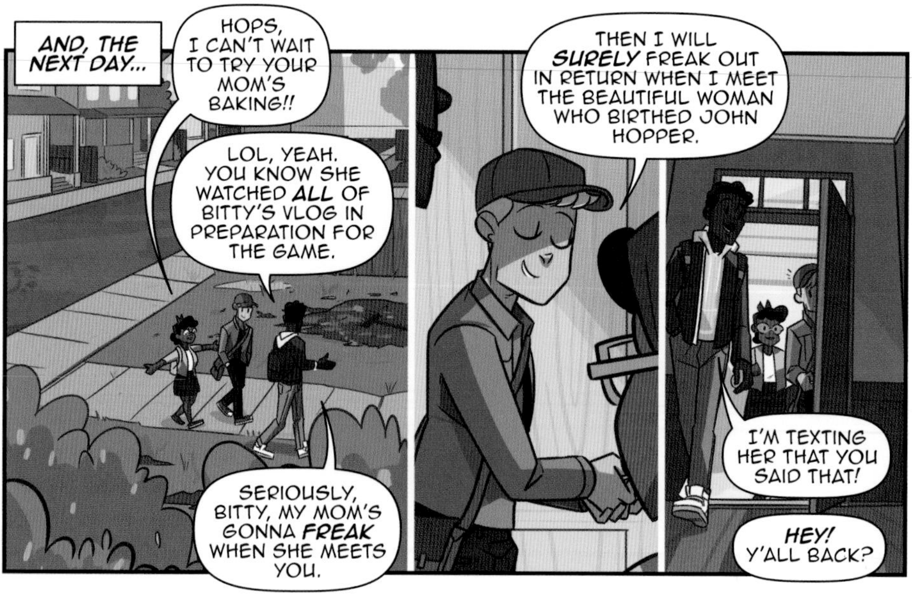
AND, THE NEXT DAY...
HOPS, I CAN'T WAIT TO TRY YOUR MOM'S BAKING!!
LOL, YEAH. YOU KNOW SHE WATCHED ALL OF BITTY'S VLOG IN PREPARATION FOR THE GAME.
SERIOUSLY, BITTY, MY MOM'S GONNA FREAK WHEN SHE MEETS YOU.
THEN I WILL SURELY FREAK OUT IN RETURN WHEN I MEET THE BEAUTIFUL WOMAN WHO BIRTHED JOHN HOPPER.
I'M TEXTING HER THAT YOU SAID THAT!
HEY! Y'ALL BACK?

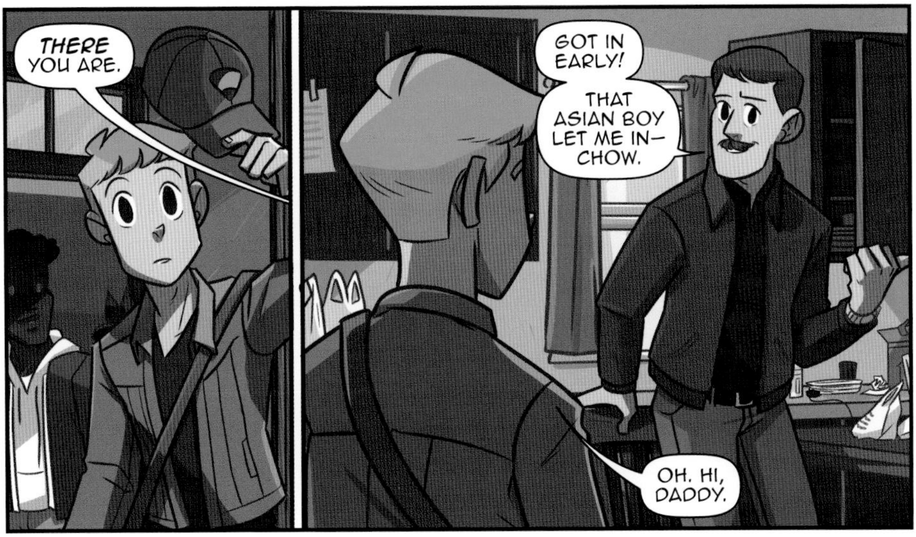
THERE YOU ARE.
GOT IN EARLY!
THAT ASIAN BOY LET ME IN—CHOW.
OH. HI, DADDY.

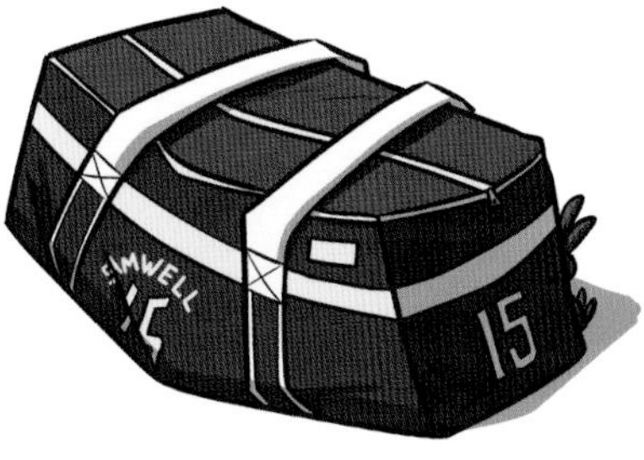
15

11

COACH — II

...TEXTED YOU AFTER CHECKING IN TO THE HOTEL—NO ANSWER, SO.
AND I THOUGHT IT WAS SILLY TO JUST SIT AROUND...
YOU KNOW, YOUR MOM SAID THIS WASN'T LIKE ANY OF THE FRAT HOUSES I'VE SEEN, AND, BOY, SHE AIN'T WRONG.
...
ARE THESE YOUR AUNT'S CURTAINS?

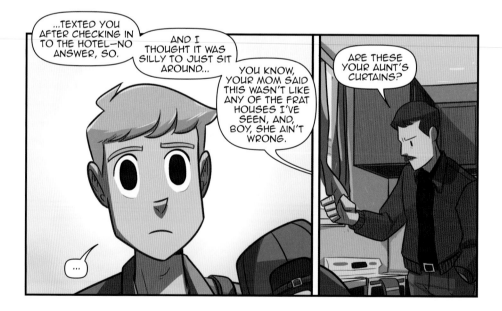

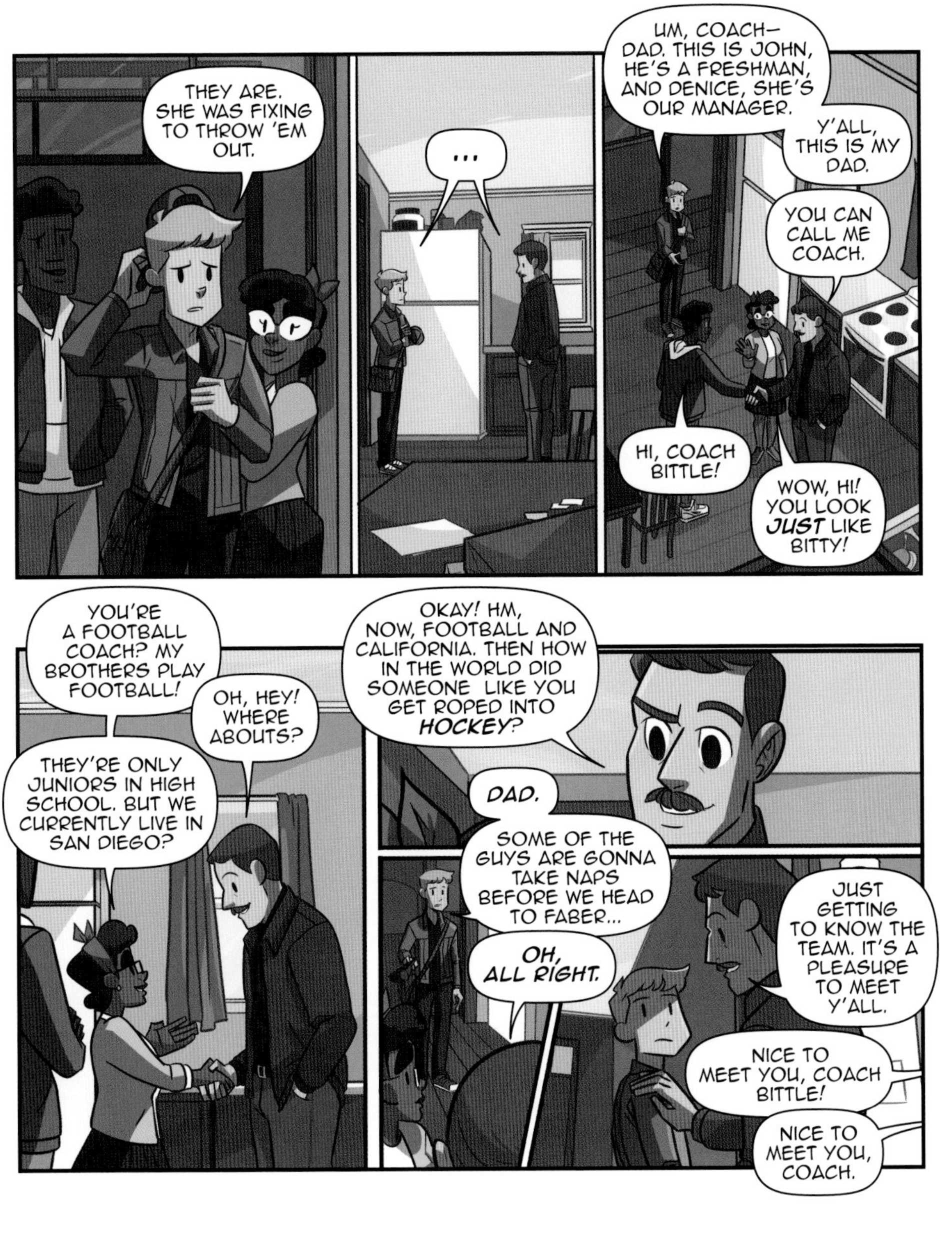
THEY ARE. SHE WAS FIXING TO THROW 'EM OUT.
...
UM, COACH— DAD. THIS IS JOHN, HE'S A FRESHMAN, AND DENICE, SHE'S OUR MANAGER.
Y'ALL, THIS IS MY DAD.
YOU CAN CALL ME COACH.
HI, COACH BITTLE!
WOW, HI! YOU LOOK JUST LIKE BITTY!
YOU'RE A FOOTBALL COACH? MY BROTHERS PLAY FOOTBALL!
OH, HEY! WHERE ABOUTS?
THEY'RE ONLY JUNIORS IN HIGH SCHOOL. BUT WE CURRENTLY LIVE IN SAN DIEGO?
OKAY! HM, NOW, FOOTBALL AND CALIFORNIA. THEN HOW IN THE WORLD DID SOMEONE LIKE YOU GET ROPED INTO HOCKEY?
DAD.
SOME OF THE GUYS ARE GONNA TAKE NAPS BEFORE WE HEAD TO FABER...
OH, ALL RIGHT.
JUST GETTING TO KNOW THE TEAM. IT'S A PLEASURE TO MEET Y'ALL.
NICE TO MEET YOU, COACH BITTLE!
NICE TO MEET YOU, COACH.

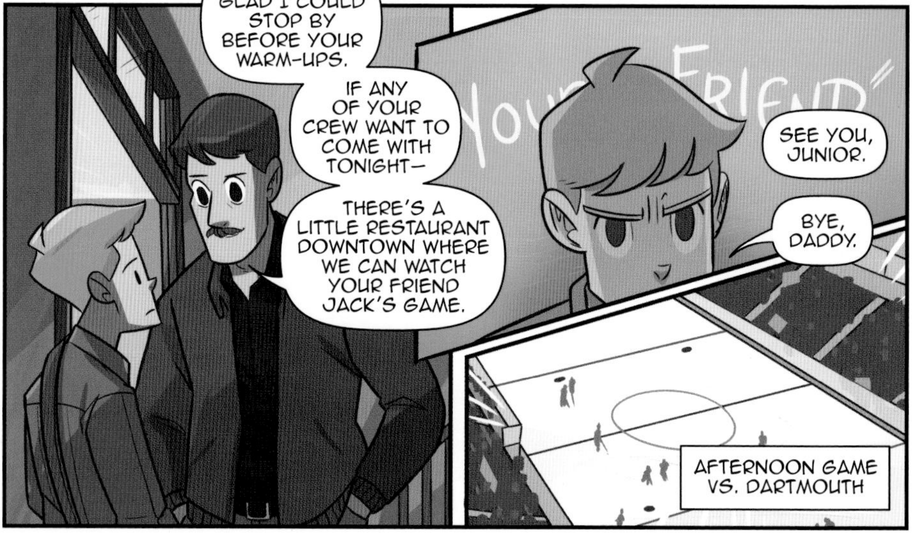
WELL, I'M GLAD I COULD STOP BY BEFORE YOUR WARM-UPS.
IF ANY OF YOUR CREW WANT TO COME WITH TONIGHT—
THERE'S A LITTLE RESTAURANT DOWNTOWN WHERE WE CAN WATCH YOUR FRIEND JACK'S GAME.
SEE YOU, JUNIOR.
BYE, DADDY.
AFTERNOON GAME VS. DARTMOUTH

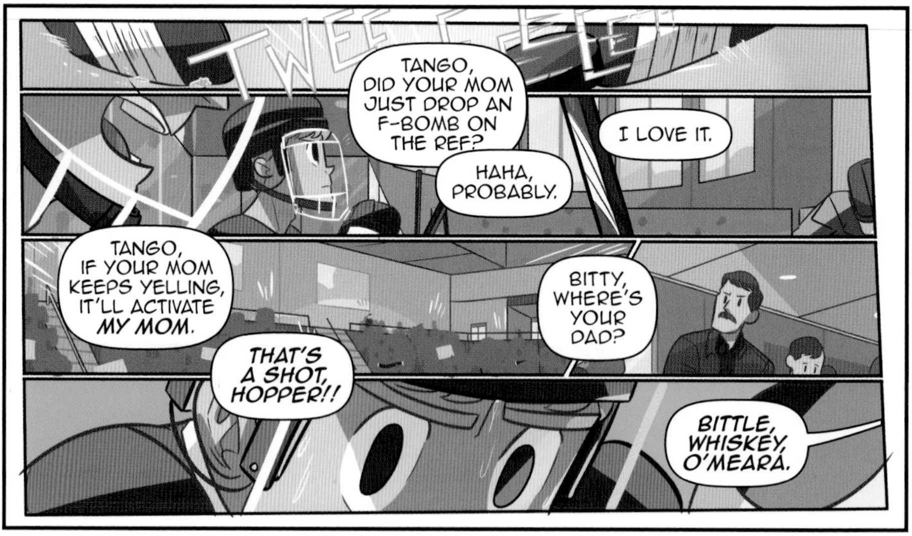
TANGO, DID YOUR MOM JUST DROP AN F-BOMB ON THE REF?
HAHA, PROBABLY.
I LOVE IT.
TANGO, IF YOUR MOM KEEPS YELLING, IT'LL ACTIVATE *MY MOM*.
BITTY, WHERE'S YOUR DAD?
THAT'S A SHOT, HOPPER!!
BITTLE, WHISKEY, O'MEARA.

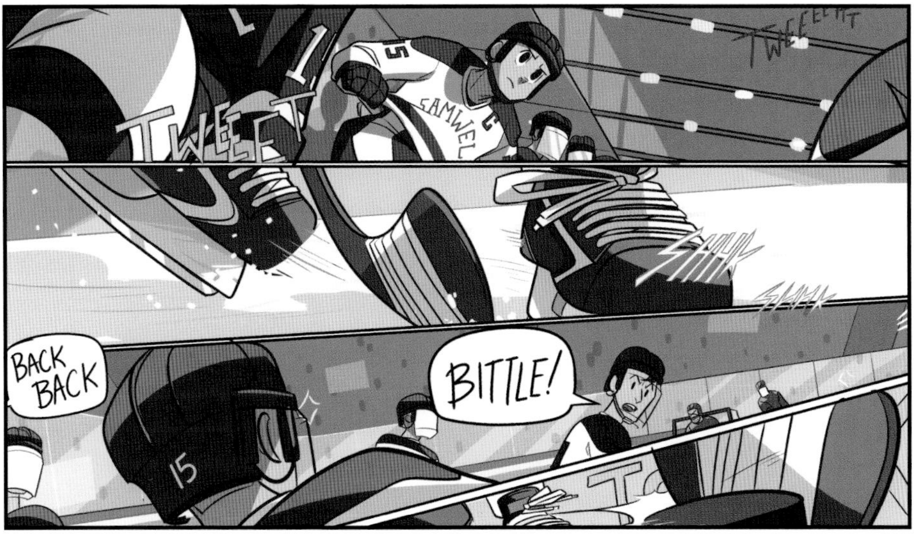
TWEET
BACK BACK
BITTLE!

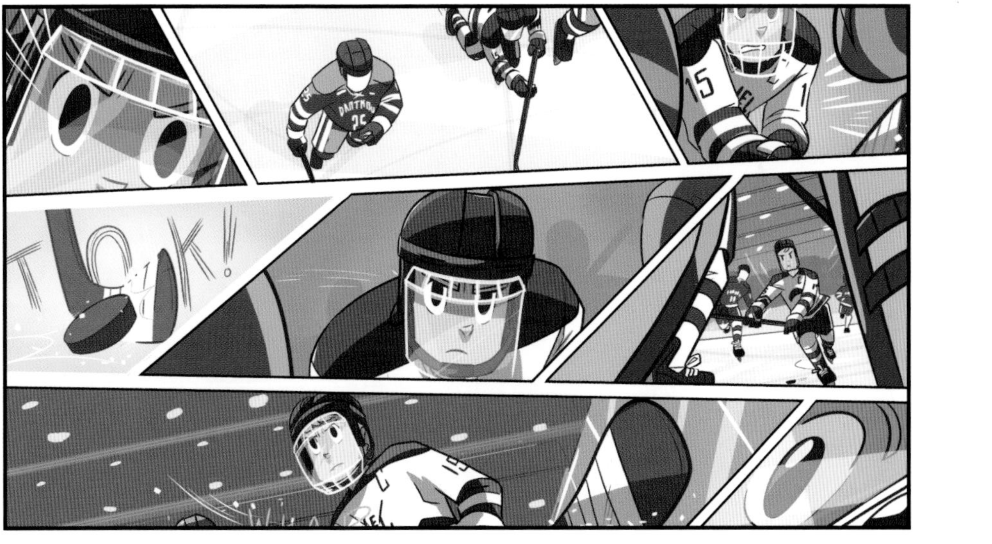
TOK!!

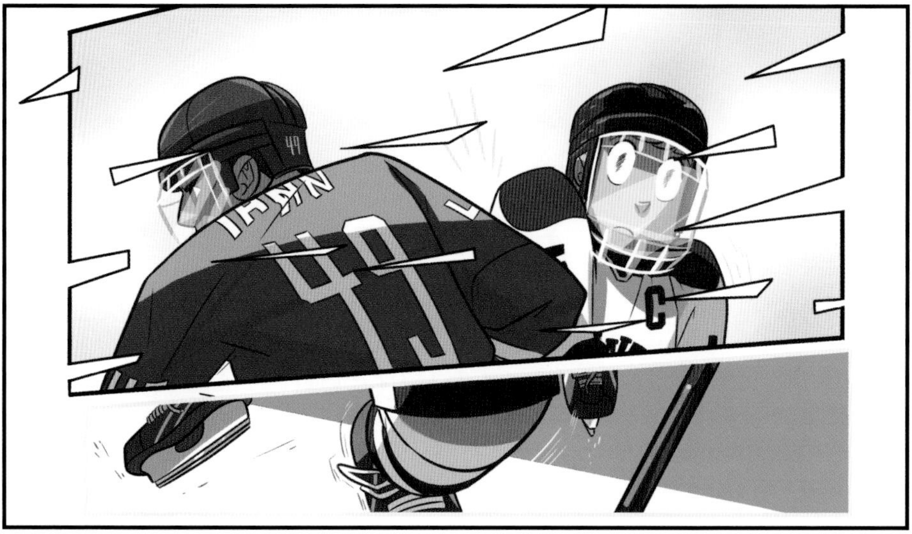

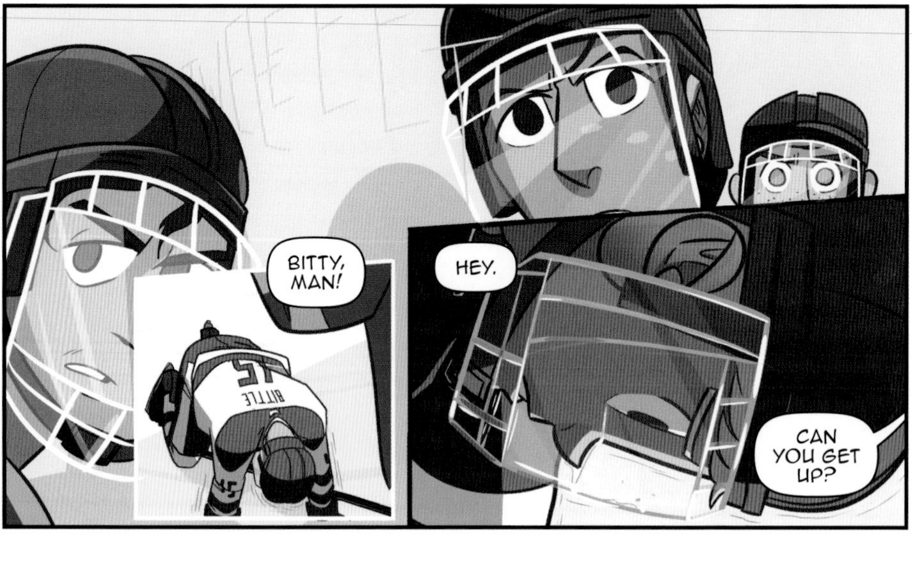
BITTY, MAN!
HEY.
CAN YOU GET UP?

12

COACH — III

TOUGH GAME BUT Y'ALL FOUGHT.
WHEW, 'SPECIALLY THOSE LAST TWO PLAYS.
WITH ERIC COMING UP THE BOARDS, YOU KNOW HE ***MAKES*** DECISIONS LIKE A COACH'S KID.
ONE REASON WHY ME AND HALL HAD HIM ON A LINE WITH JACK FRESHMAN YEAR.
HAH. ERIC, YOU KNOW... ***HE AND HIS FRIEND JACK***, THEY WORK TOGETHER.

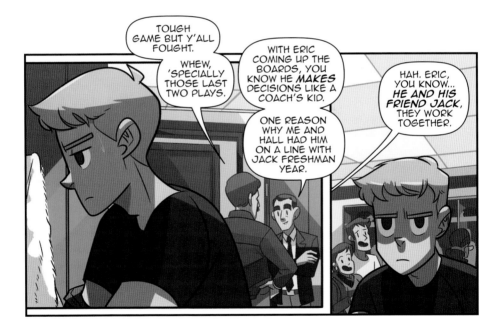

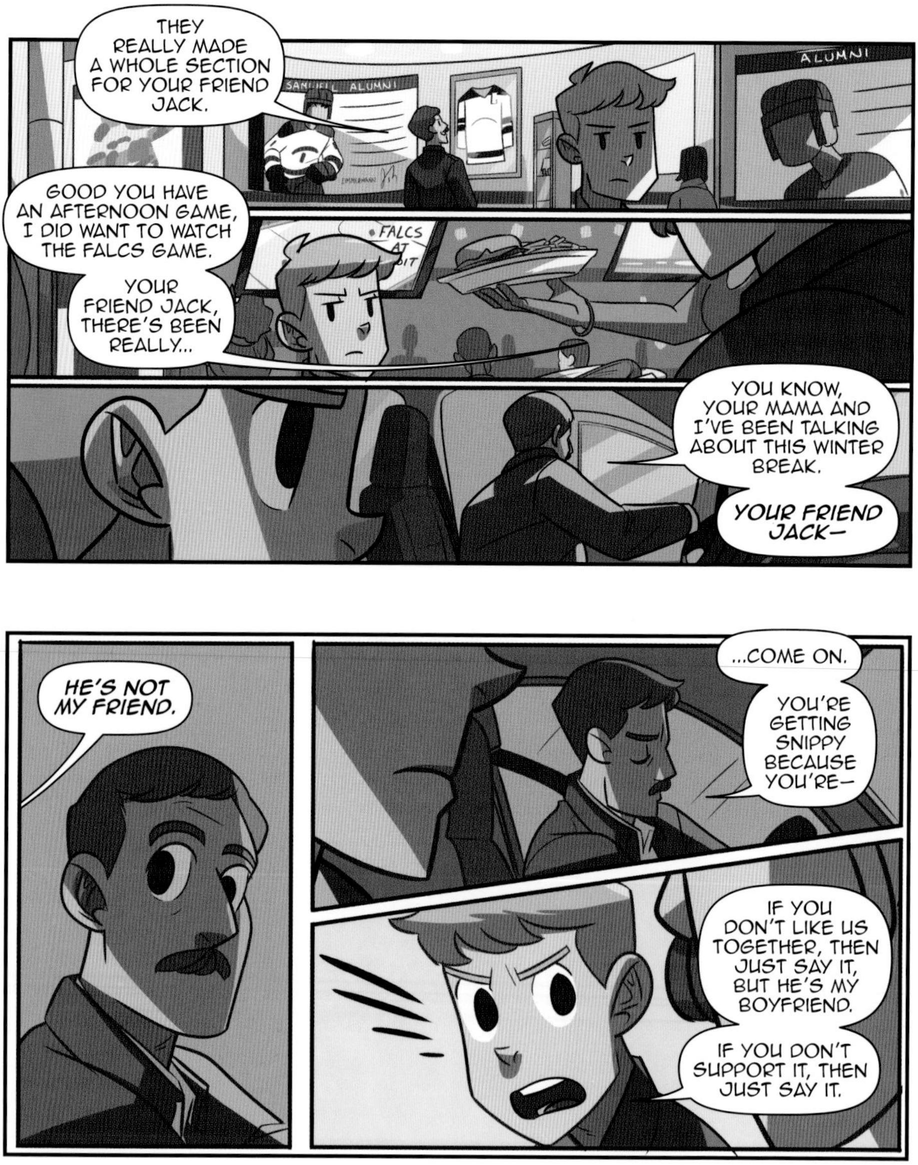
THEY REALLY MADE A WHOLE SECTION FOR YOUR FRIEND JACK.
ALUMNI
GOOD YOU HAVE AN AFTERNOON GAME, I DID WANT TO WATCH THE FALCS GAME.
YOUR FRIEND JACK, THERE'S BEEN REALLY...
YOU KNOW, YOUR MAMA AND I'VE BEEN TALKING ABOUT THIS WINTER BREAK.
YOUR FRIEND JACK—
HE'S NOT MY FRIEND.
...COME ON.
YOU'RE GETTING SNIPPY BECAUSE YOU'RE—
IF YOU DON'T LIKE US TOGETHER, THEN JUST SAY IT, BUT HE'S MY BOYFRIEND.
IF YOU DON'T SUPPORT IT, THEN JUST SAY IT.

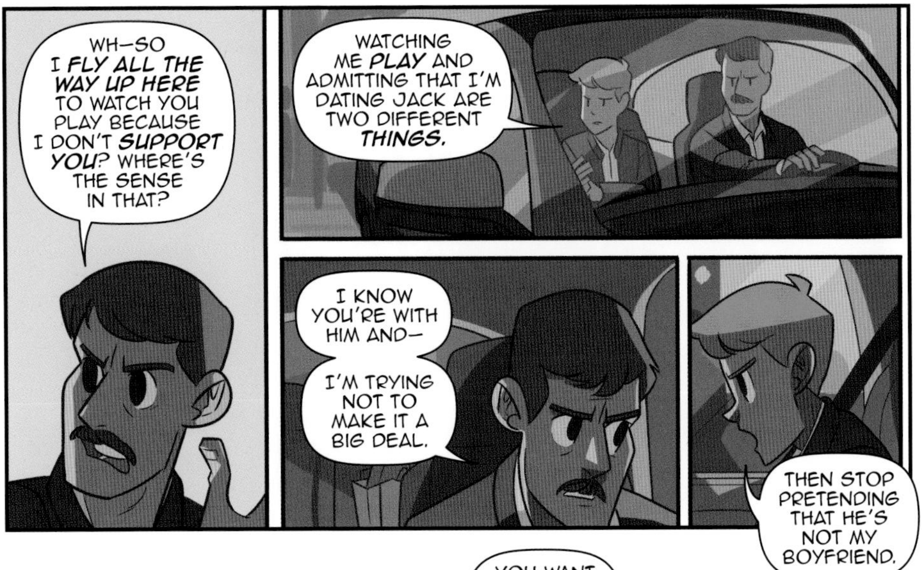
WH—SO I FLY ALL THE WAY UP HERE TO WATCH YOU PLAY BECAUSE I DON'T SUPPORT YOU? WHERE'S THE SENSE IN THAT?
WATCHING ME PLAY AND ADMITTING THAT I'M DATING JACK ARE TWO DIFFERENT THINGS.
I KNOW YOU'RE WITH HIM AND—
I'M TRYING NOT TO MAKE IT A BIG DEAL.
THEN STOP PRETENDING THAT HE'S NOT MY BOYFRIEND.

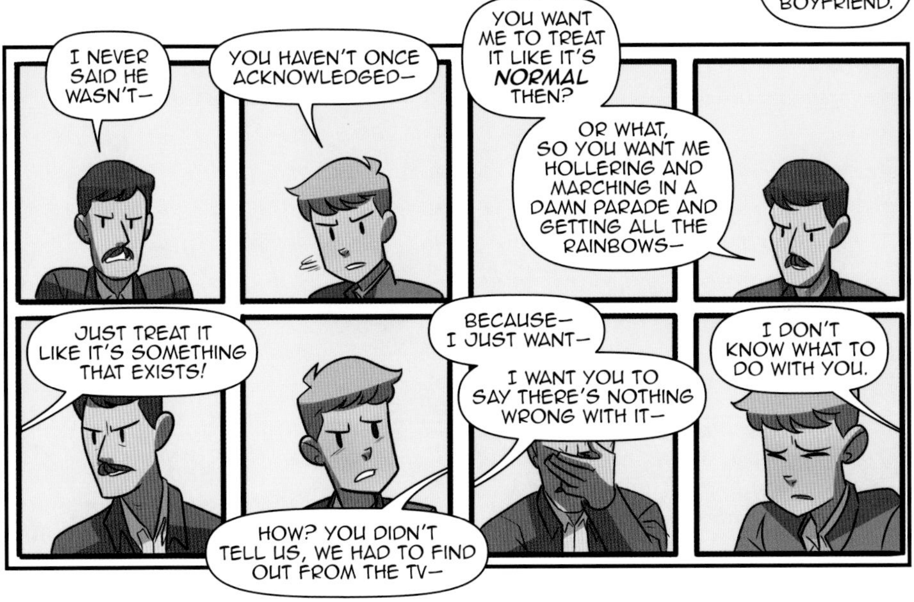
I NEVER SAID HE WASN'T—
YOU HAVEN'T ONCE ACKNOWLEDGED—
YOU WANT ME TO TREAT IT LIKE IT'S NORMAL THEN?
OR WHAT, SO YOU WANT ME HOLLERING AND MARCHING IN A DAMN PARADE AND GETTING ALL THE RAINBOWS—
JUST TREAT IT LIKE IT'S SOMETHING THAT EXISTS!
HOW? YOU DIDN'T TELL US, WE HAD TO FIND OUT FROM THE TV—
BECAUSE— I JUST WANT—
I WANT YOU TO SAY THERE'S NOTHING WRONG WITH IT—
I DON'T KNOW WHAT TO DO WITH YOU.

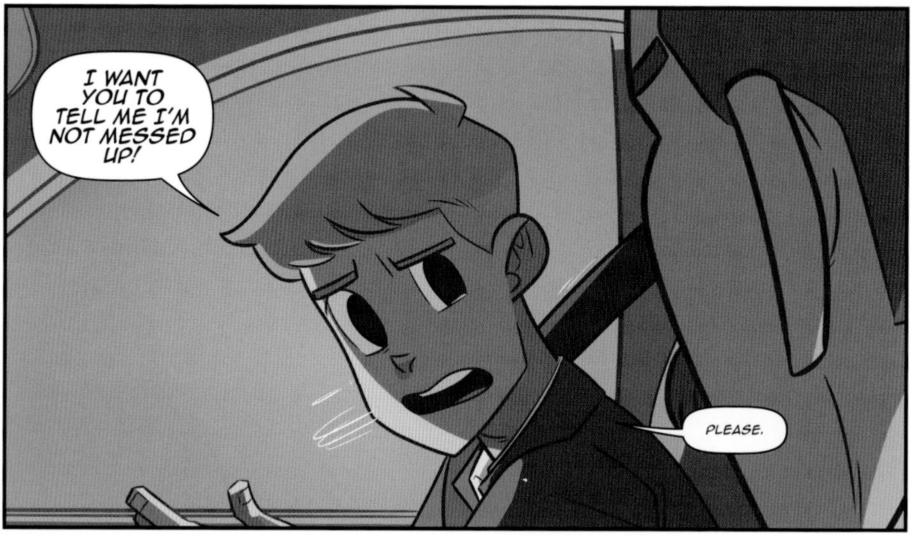
I WANT YOU TO TELL ME I'M NOT MESSED UP!
PLEASE.

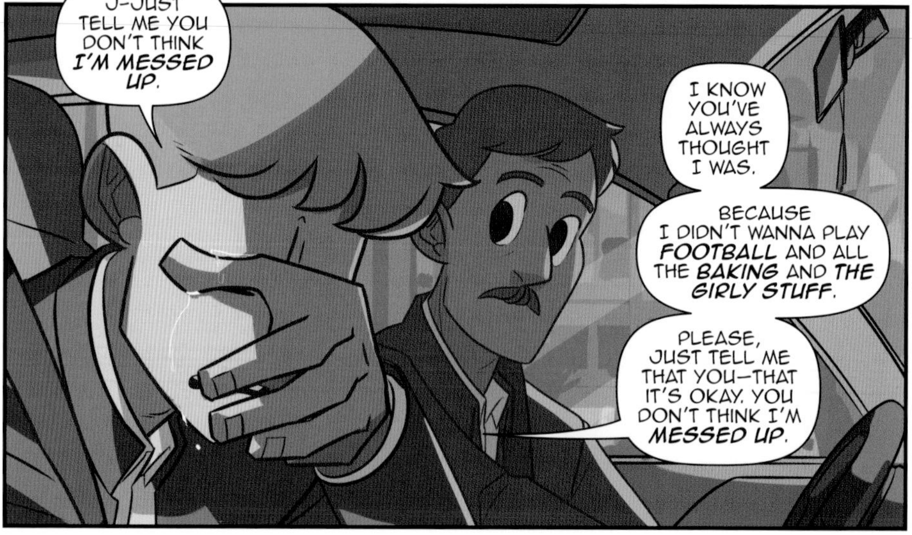
J-JUST TELL ME YOU DON'T THINK I'M MESSED UP.
I KNOW YOU'VE ALWAYS THOUGHT I WAS.
BECAUSE I DIDN'T WANNA PLAY FOOTBALL AND ALL THE BAKING AND THE GIRLY STUFF.
PLEASE, JUST TELL ME THAT YOU—THAT IT'S OKAY. YOU DON'T THINK I'M MESSED UP.

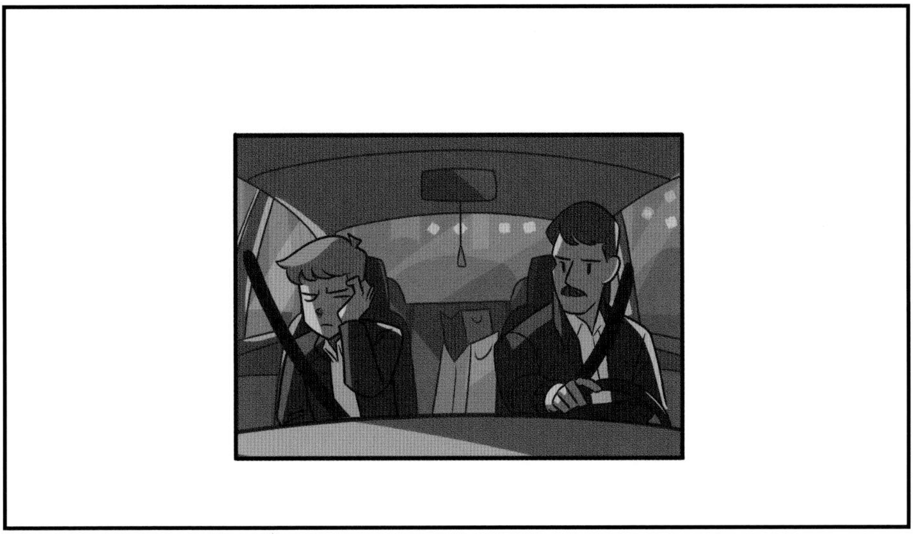

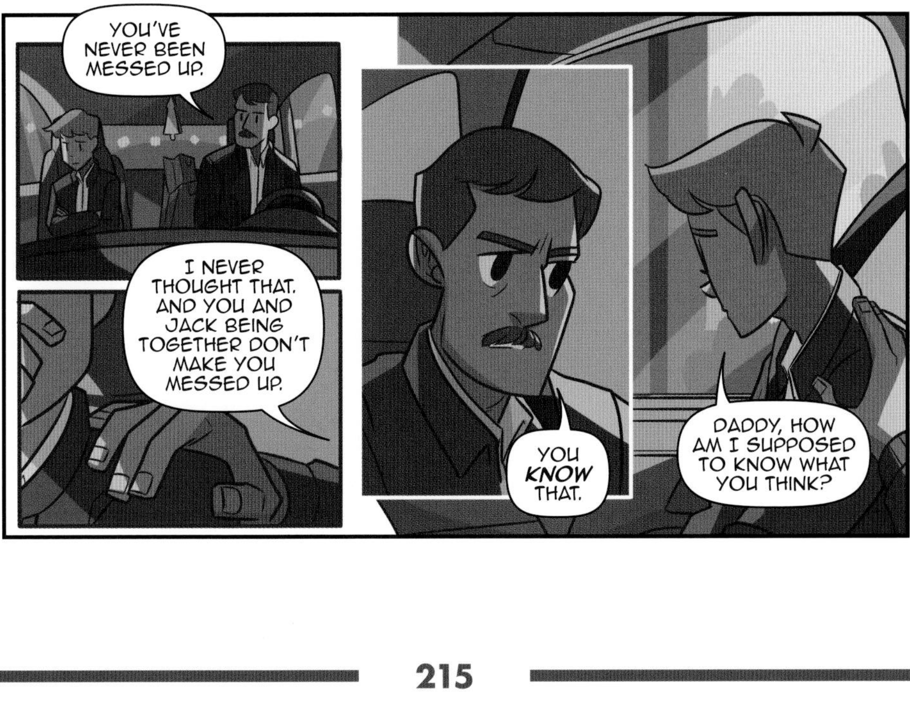
YOU'VE NEVER BEEN MESSED UP.
I NEVER THOUGHT THAT. AND YOU AND JACK BEING TOGETHER DON'T MAKE YOU MESSED UP.
YOU *KNOW* THAT.
DADDY, HOW AM I SUPPOSED TO KNOW WHAT YOU THINK?

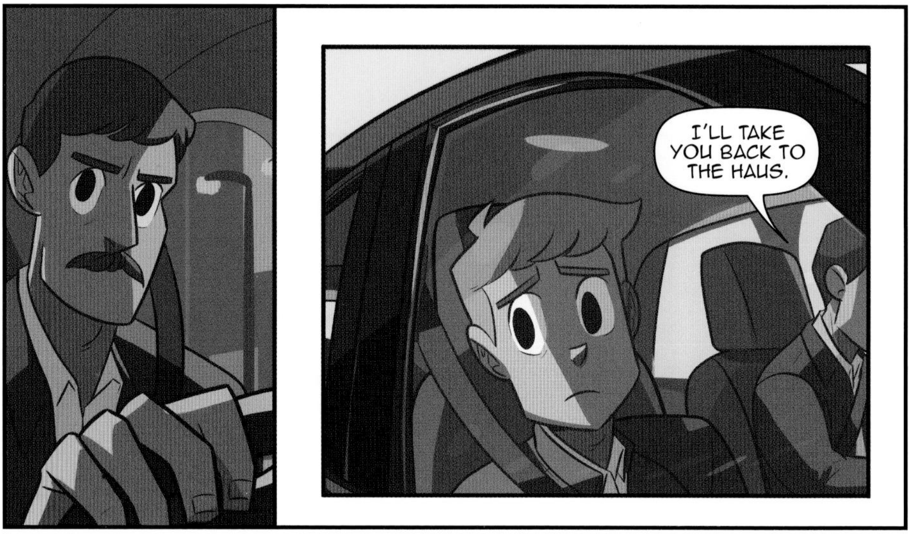
I'LL TAKE YOU BACK TO THE HAUS.

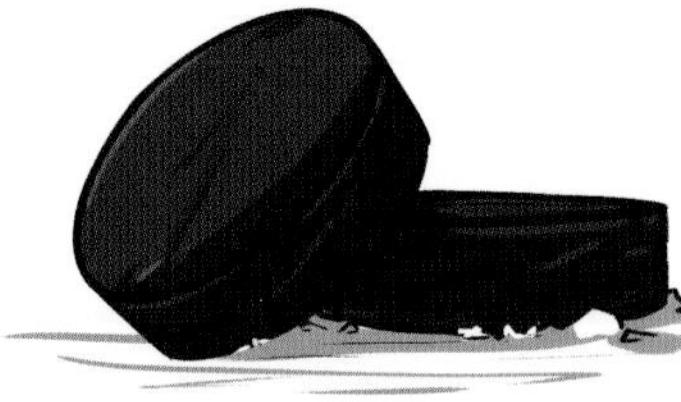

13

COACH — IV

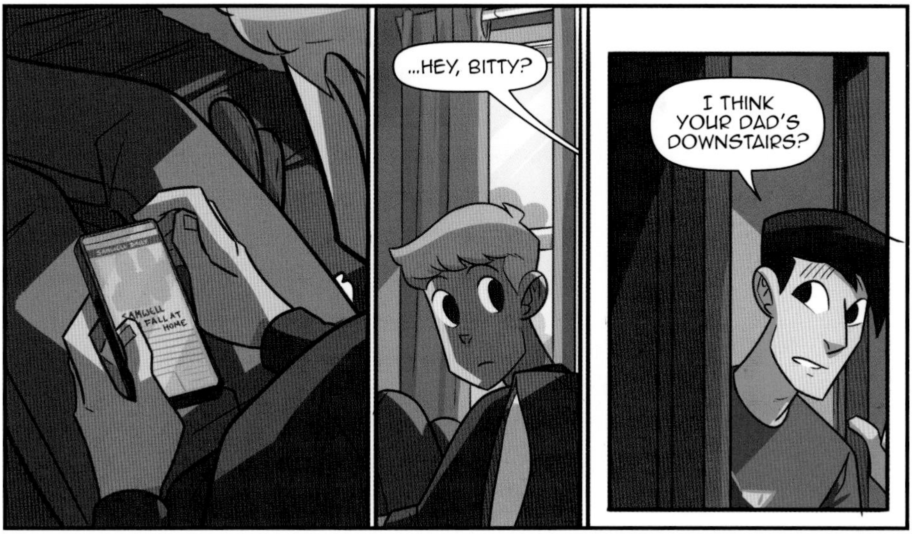
...HEY, BITTY?
I THINK YOUR DAD'S DOWNSTAIRS?

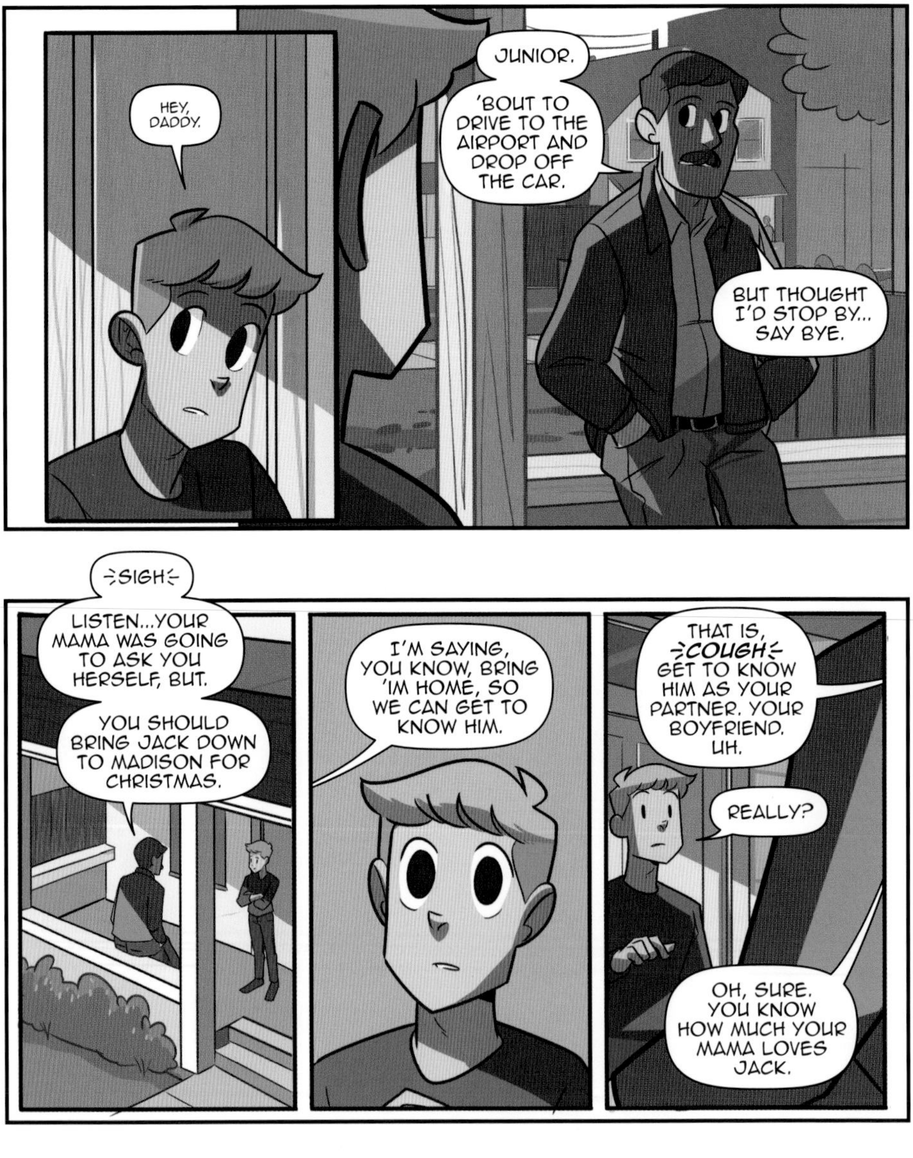
HEY, DADDY.
JUNIOR.
'BOUT TO DRIVE TO THE AIRPORT AND DROP OFF THE CAR.
BUT THOUGHT I'D STOP BY... SAY BYE.
⇉SIGH⇇
LISTEN...YOUR MAMA WAS GOING TO ASK YOU HERSELF, BUT.
YOU SHOULD BRING JACK DOWN TO MADISON FOR CHRISTMAS.
I'M SAYING, YOU KNOW, BRING 'IM HOME, SO WE CAN GET TO KNOW HIM.
THAT IS, ⇉COUGH⇇ GET TO KNOW HIM AS YOUR PARTNER. YOUR BOYFRIEND. UH.
REALLY?
OH, SURE. YOU KNOW HOW MUCH YOUR MAMA LOVES JACK.

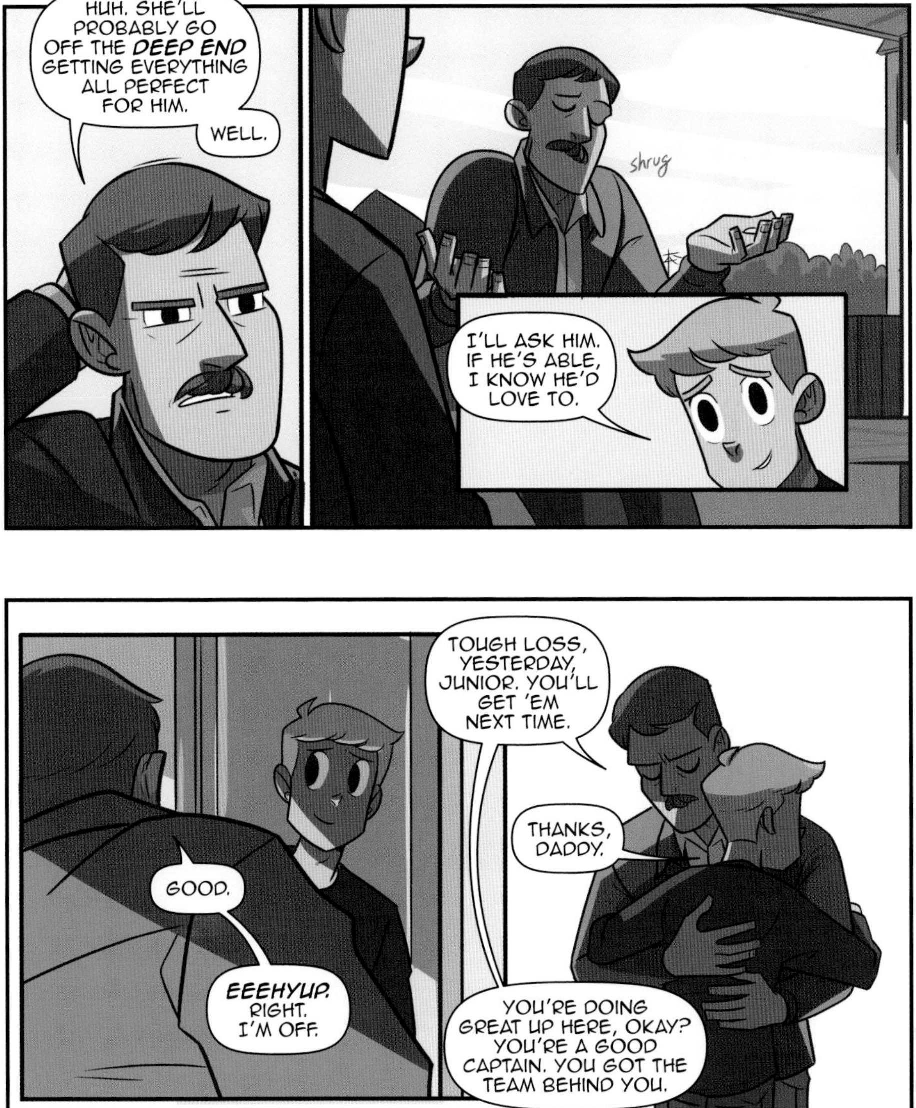
HUH. SHE'LL PROBABLY GO OFF THE ***DEEP END*** GETTING EVERYTHING ALL PERFECT FOR HIM.
WELL.
shrug
I'LL ASK HIM. IF HE'S ABLE, I KNOW HE'D LOVE TO.
GOOD.
EEEHYUP. RIGHT. I'M OFF.
TOUGH LOSS, YESTERDAY, JUNIOR. YOU'LL GET 'EM NEXT TIME.
THANKS, DADDY.
YOU'RE DOING GREAT UP HERE, OKAY? YOU'RE A GOOD CAPTAIN. YOU GOT THE TEAM BEHIND YOU.

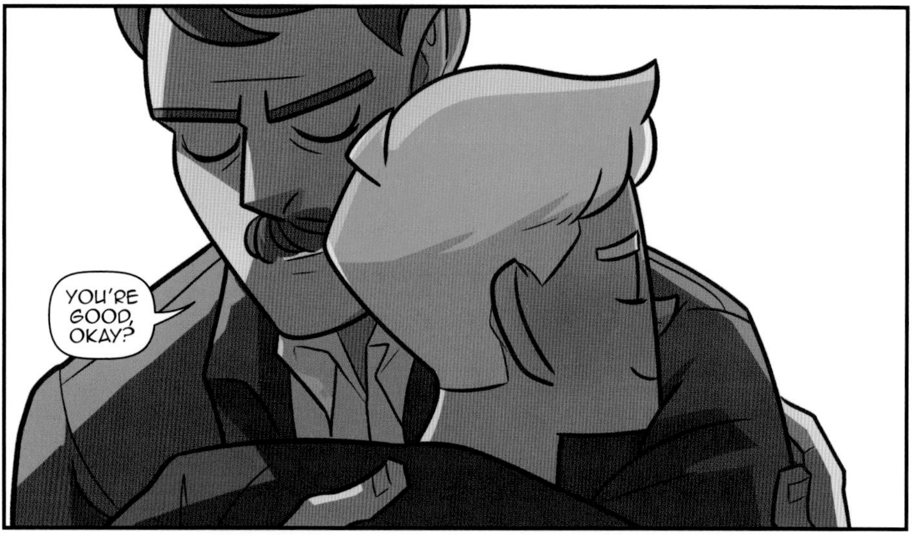
YOU'RE GOOD, OKAY?

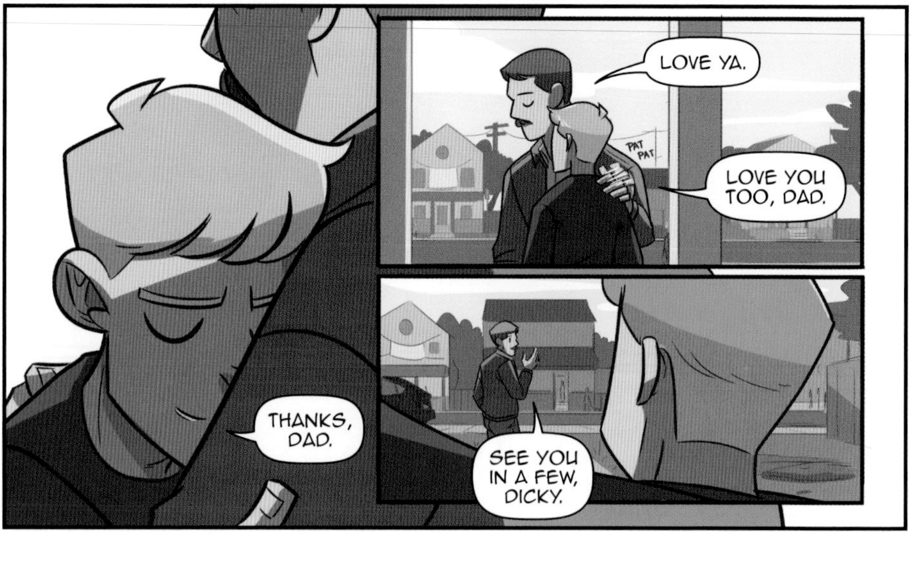
THANKS, DAD.
LOVE YA.
PAT PAT
LOVE YOU TOO, DAD.
SEE YOU IN A FEW, DICKY.

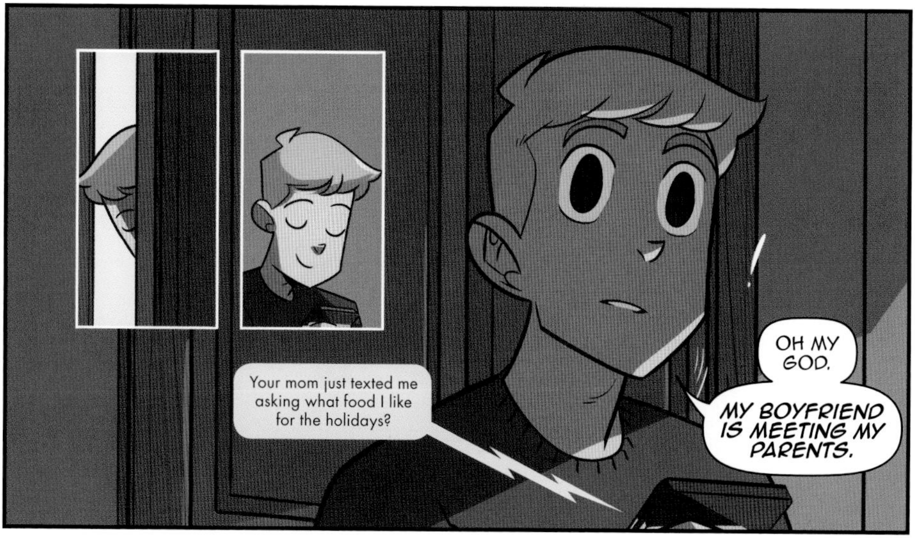
Your mom just texted me asking what food I like for the holidays?
OH MY GOD.
MY BOYFRIEND IS MEETING MY PARENTS.

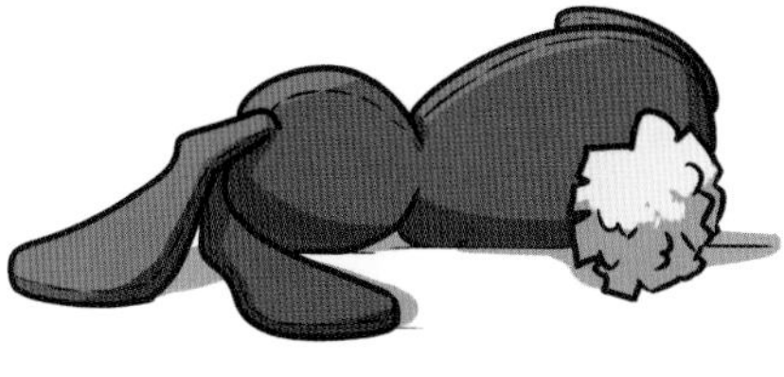

14

CHRISTMAS IN MADISON — I

WELL, Y'ALL. OUR LAST GAME OF THE CALENDAR YEAR IS TODAY.
T-MINUS FOURTEEN UNTIL I'M ON A PLANE DOWN TO GEORGIA.
HEY, ASK US HOW SAMWELL'S DOING IN THE STANDINGS!!
HOW'S SAMWELL DOING IN THE STANDINGS, MR. CHOW?
WE'RE HEADING RIGHT TO THE PLAYOFFS, BABY!!!!!
PRINCETON SUCKS!!
LOUIS, QUIT!!

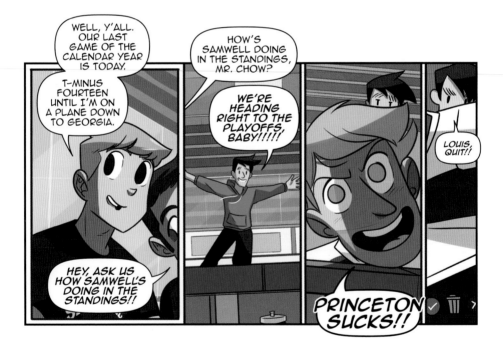

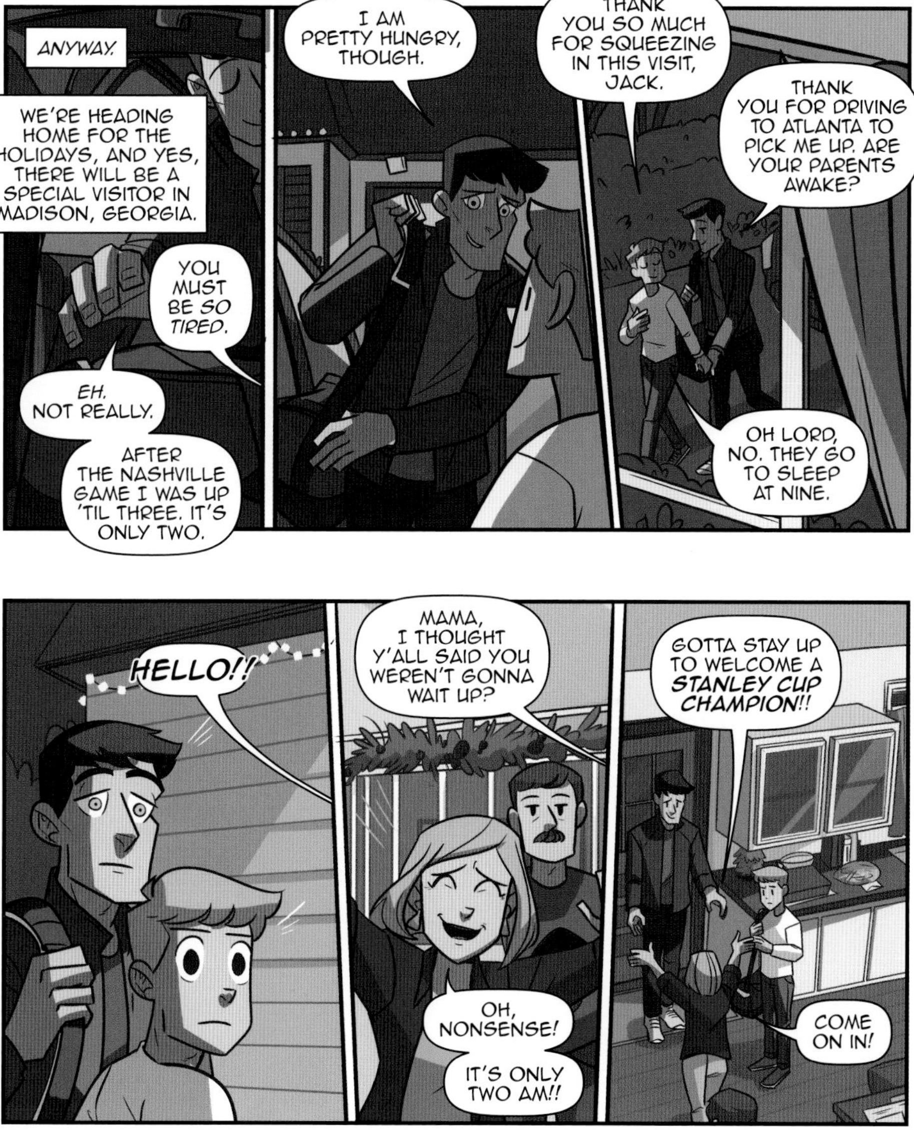
ANYWAY.
WE'RE HEADING HOME FOR THE HOLIDAYS, AND YES, THERE WILL BE A SPECIAL VISITOR IN MADISON, GEORGIA.
YOU MUST BE SO TIRED.
EH. NOT REALLY.
AFTER THE NASHVILLE GAME I WAS UP 'TIL THREE. IT'S ONLY TWO.
I AM PRETTY HUNGRY, THOUGH.
THANK YOU SO MUCH FOR SQUEEZING IN THIS VISIT, JACK.
THANK YOU FOR DRIVING TO ATLANTA TO PICK ME UP. ARE YOUR PARENTS AWAKE?
OH LORD, NO. THEY GO TO SLEEP AT NINE.
HELLO!!
MAMA, I THOUGHT Y'ALL SAID YOU WEREN'T GONNA WAIT UP?
OH, NONSENSE!
IT'S ONLY TWO AM!!
GOTTA STAY UP TO WELCOME A STANLEY CUP CHAMPION!!
COME ON IN!

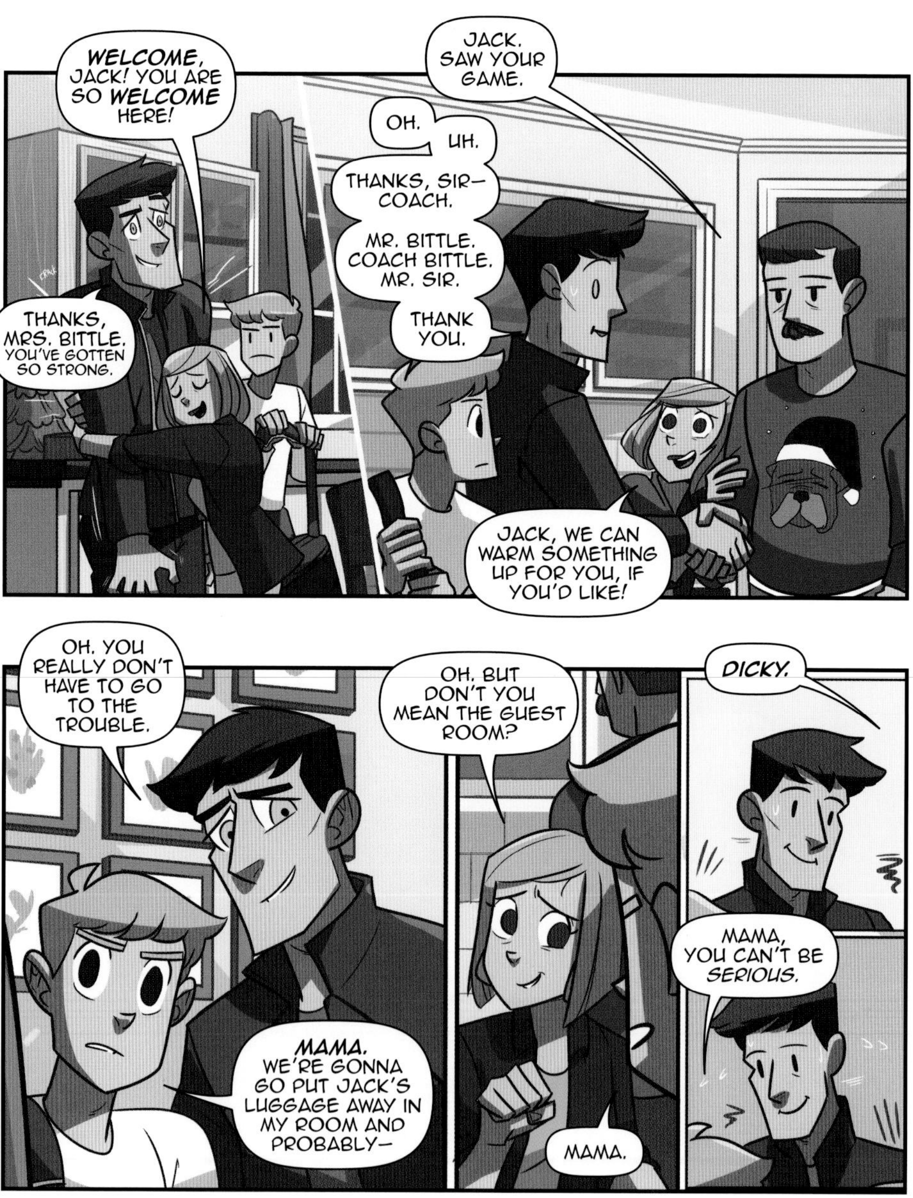
WELCOME, JACK! YOU ARE SO *WELCOME* HERE!
THANKS, MRS. BITTLE. YOU'VE GOTTEN SO STRONG.
JACK. SAW YOUR GAME.
OH.
UH.
THANKS, SIR— COACH.
MR. BITTLE. COACH BITTLE. MR. SIR.
THANK YOU.
JACK, WE CAN WARM SOMETHING UP FOR YOU, IF YOU'D LIKE!
OH. YOU REALLY DON'T HAVE TO GO TO THE TROUBLE.
MAMA. WE'RE GONNA GO PUT JACK'S LUGGAGE AWAY IN MY ROOM AND PROBABLY—
OH. BUT DON'T YOU MEAN THE GUEST ROOM?
MAMA.
DICKY.
MAMA, YOU CAN'T BE *SERIOUS.*

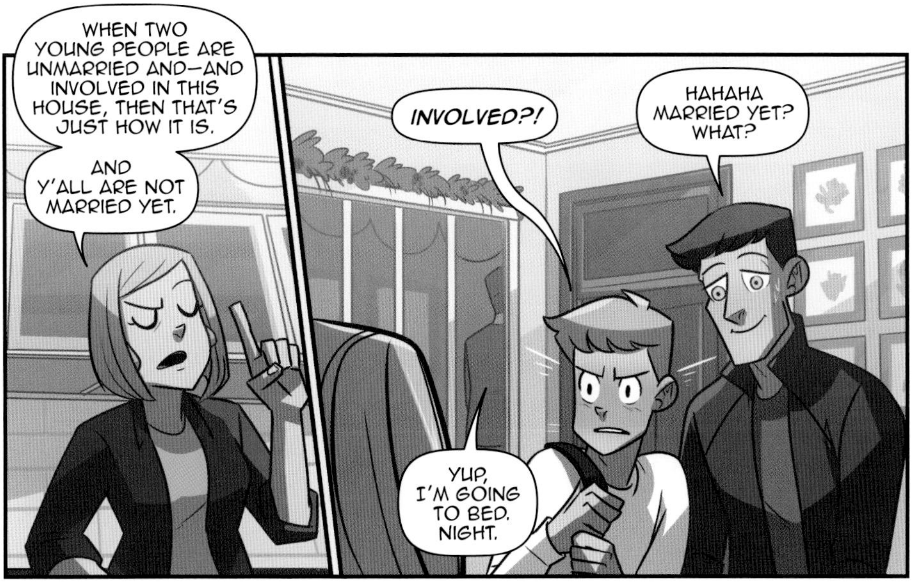
WHEN TWO YOUNG PEOPLE ARE UNMARRIED AND—AND INVOLVED IN THIS HOUSE, THEN THAT'S JUST HOW IT IS.
AND Y'ALL ARE NOT MARRIED YET.
INVOLVED?!
HAHAHA MARRIED YET? WHAT?
YUP, I'M GOING TO BED. NIGHT.

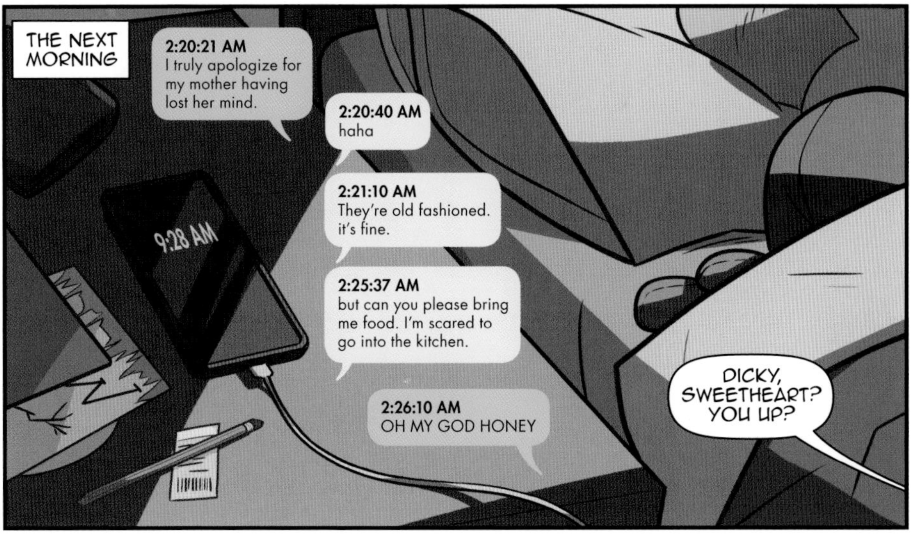
THE NEXT MORNING
2:20:21 AM
I truly apologize for my mother having lost her mind.
2:20:40 AM
haha
2:21:10 AM
They're old fashioned. it's fine.
2:25:37 AM
but can you please bring me food. I'm scared to go into the kitchen.
2:26:10 AM
OH MY GOD HONEY
9:28 AM
DICKY, SWEETHEART? YOU UP?

YAWN!
HEY, MAMA.
GOOD MORNING.
GETTING BREAKFAST READY BEFORE THE REST OF US MEN RUSTLE?
OH, THEY'VE ALREADY RUSTLED. JACK'S RUNNING ERRANDS WITH YOUR DADDY.
ISN'T THAT SWEET?

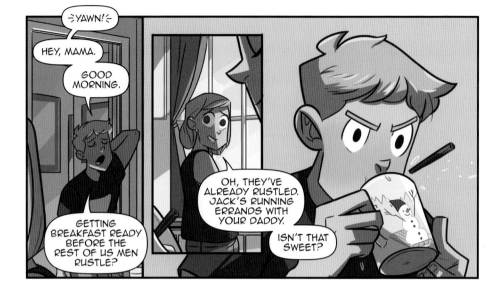

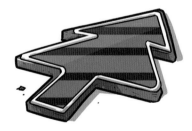

15

CHRISTMAS IN MADISON — II

IF YOU WANT A WOOD-GRAIN FINISH, THEN YOU WANT OLMAN'S. BUT THAT'S MAYBE A YEAR OF PROTECTION. DEPENDING ON FOOT TRAFFIC.
UH-HUH.
PRETTY SURE I CAN MAKE IT TWO YEARS.
ALL RIGHT, RICK, I'LL SEE YOU BACK IN THREE. HAHAH—
HAH, YOU TELL SCOTT TO QUIT RENTING THE ONLY DAMNED PRESSURE WASHER IN 27 MILES—

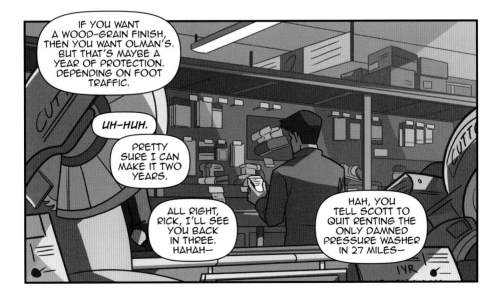

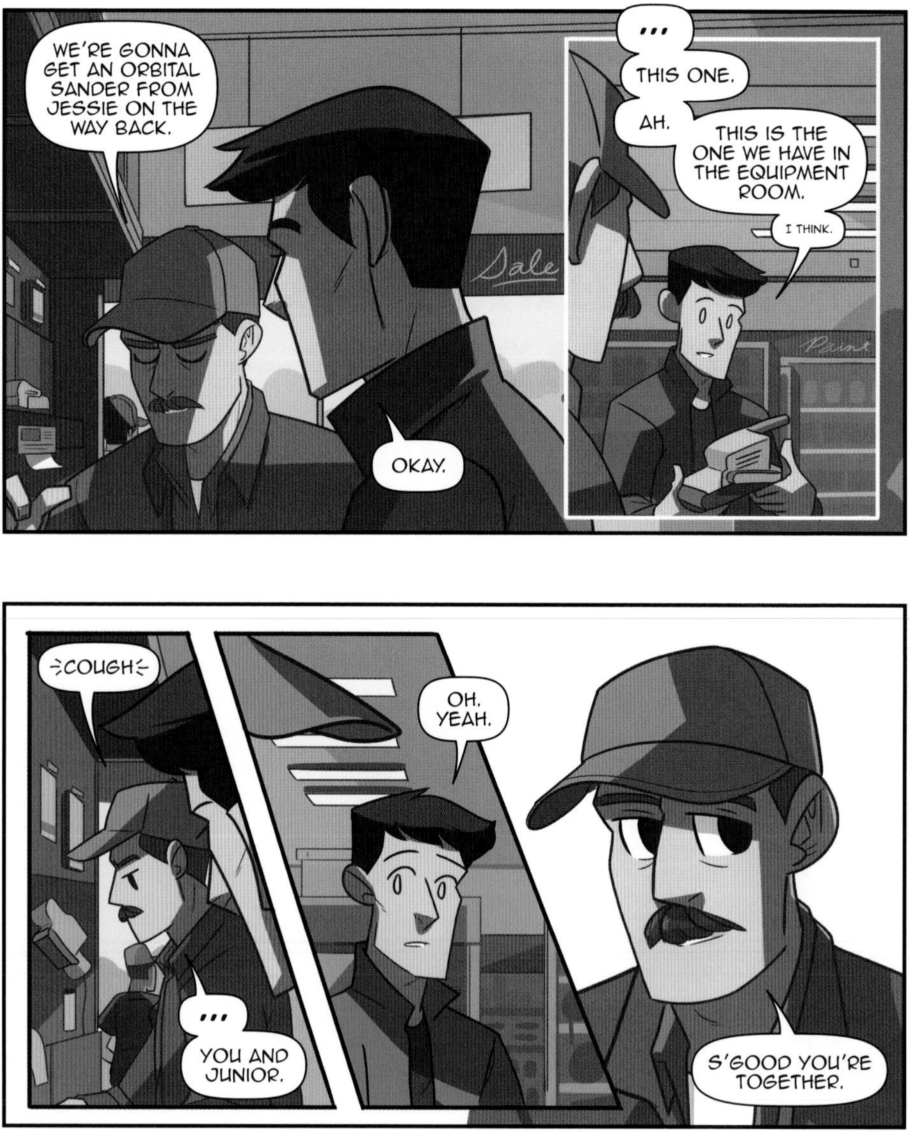
WE'RE GONNA GET AN ORBITAL SANDER FROM JESSIE ON THE WAY BACK.
OKAY.
...
THIS ONE.
AH.
THIS IS THE ONE WE HAVE IN THE EQUIPMENT ROOM.
I THINK.
-COUGH-
...
YOU AND JUNIOR.
OH. YEAH.
S'GOOD YOU'RE TOGETHER.

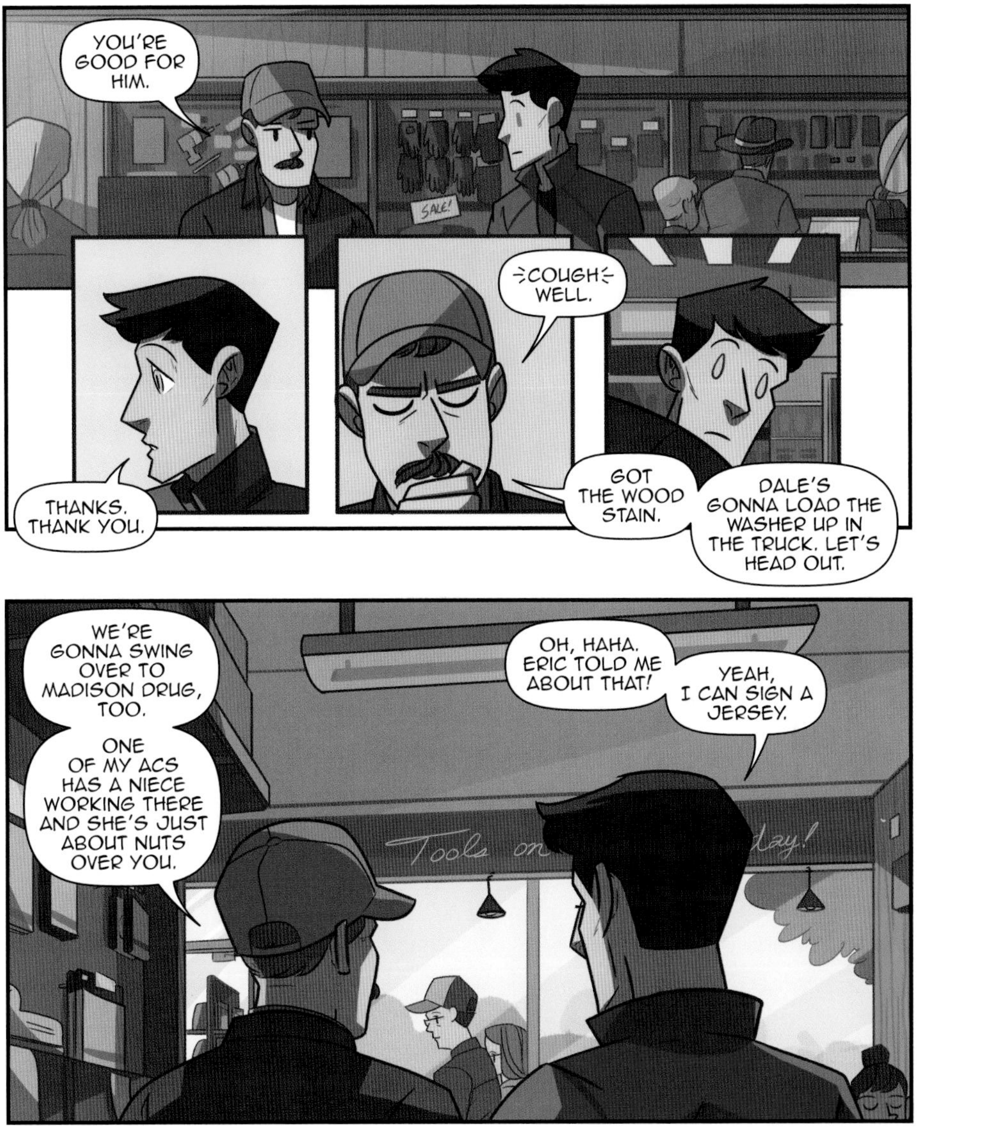
YOU'RE GOOD FOR HIM.
THANKS. THANK YOU.
-COUGH- WELL.
GOT THE WOOD STAIN.
DALE'S GONNA LOAD THE WASHER UP IN THE TRUCK. LET'S HEAD OUT.
WE'RE GONNA SWING OVER TO MADISON DRUG, TOO.
ONE OF MY ACS HAS A NIECE WORKING THERE AND SHE'S JUST ABOUT NUTS OVER YOU.
OH, HAHA. ERIC TOLD ME ABOUT THAT!
YEAH, I CAN SIGN A JERSEY.

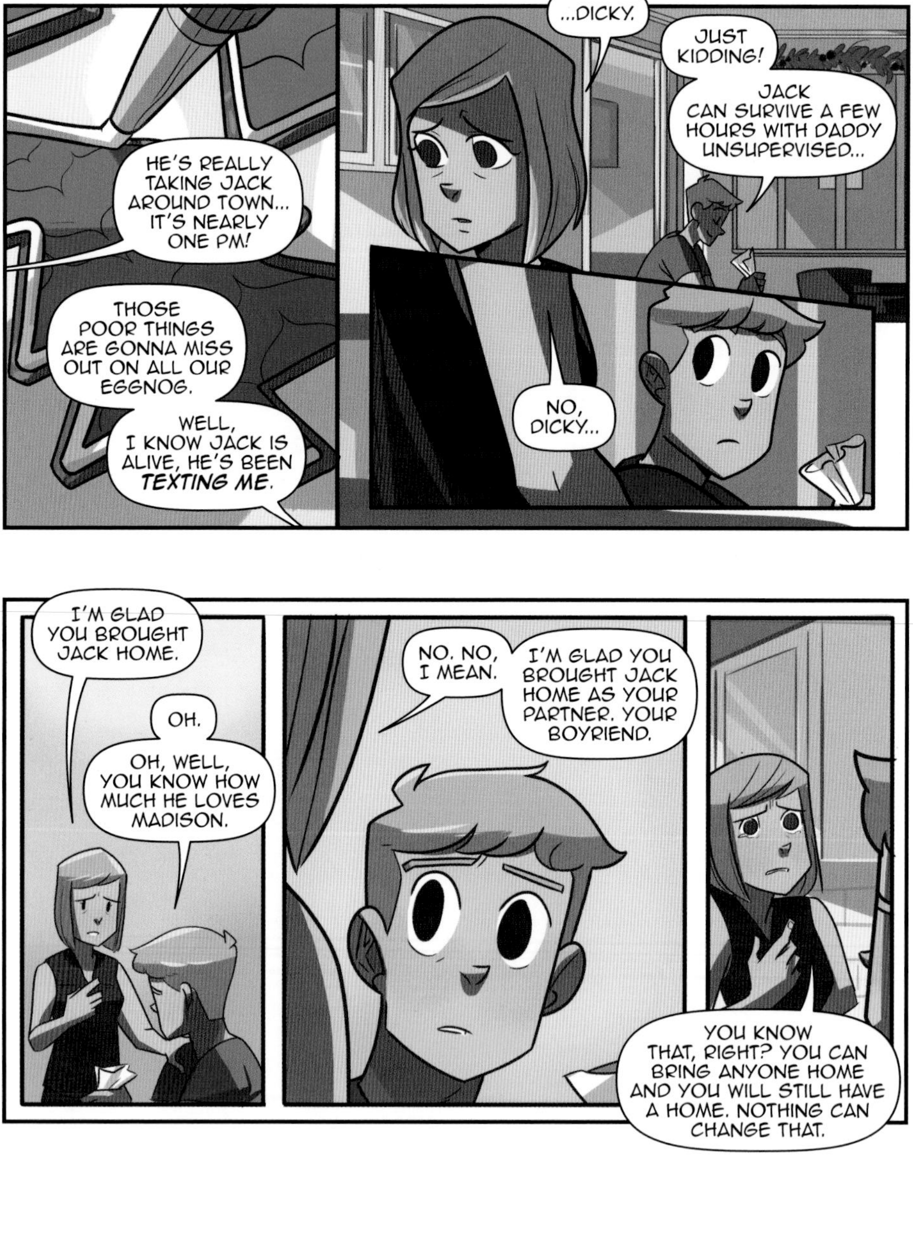
HE'S REALLY TAKING JACK AROUND TOWN... IT'S NEARLY ONE PM!
THOSE POOR THINGS ARE GONNA MISS OUT ON ALL OUR EGGNOG.
WELL, I KNOW JACK IS ALIVE, HE'S BEEN TEXTING ME.
...DICKY.
JUST KIDDING!
JACK CAN SURVIVE A FEW HOURS WITH DADDY UNSUPERVISED...
NO, DICKY...
I'M GLAD YOU BROUGHT JACK HOME.
OH.
OH, WELL, YOU KNOW HOW MUCH HE LOVES MADISON.
NO. NO, I MEAN.
I'M GLAD YOU BROUGHT JACK HOME AS YOUR PARTNER. YOUR BOYRIEND.
YOU KNOW THAT, RIGHT? YOU CAN BRING ANYONE HOME AND YOU WILL STILL HAVE A HOME. NOTHING CAN CHANGE THAT.

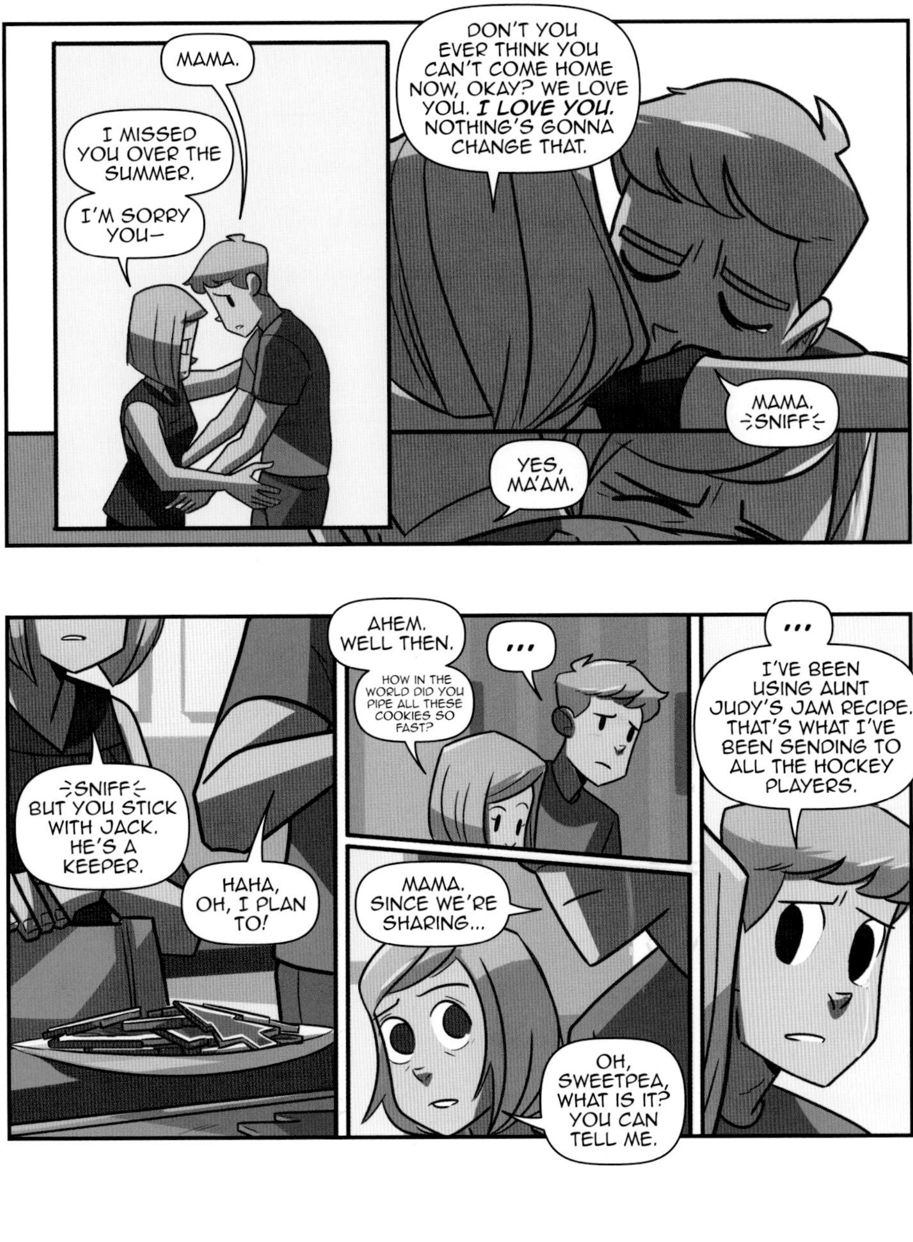
MAMA.
I MISSED YOU OVER THE SUMMER.
I'M SORRY YOU—
DON'T YOU EVER THINK YOU CAN'T COME HOME NOW, OKAY? WE LOVE YOU. ***I LOVE YOU.*** NOTHING'S GONNA CHANGE THAT.
MAMA. ⁼SNIFF⁼
YES, MA'AM.
⁼SNIFF⁼ BUT YOU STICK WITH JACK. HE'S A KEEPER.
HAHA, OH, I PLAN TO!
AHEM. WELL THEN.
HOW IN THE WORLD DID YOU PIPE ALL THESE COOKIES SO FAST?
...
MAMA. SINCE WE'RE SHARING...
OH, SWEETPEA, WHAT IS IT? YOU CAN TELL ME.
...
I'VE BEEN USING AUNT JUDY'S JAM RECIPE. THAT'S WHAT I'VE BEEN SENDING TO ALL THE HOCKEY PLAYERS.

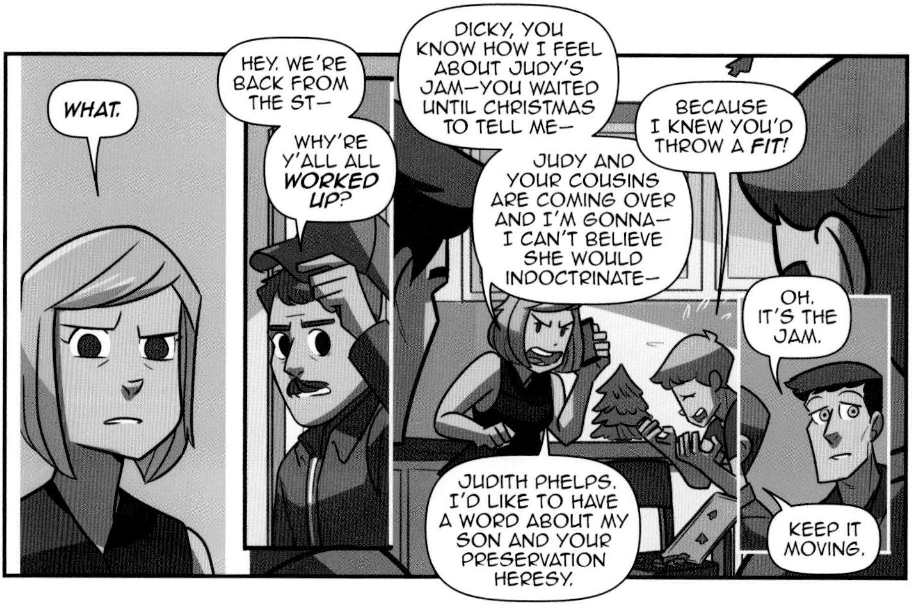
WHAT.
HEY. WE'RE BACK FROM THE ST—
WHY'RE Y'ALL ALL WORKED UP?
DICKY, YOU KNOW HOW I FEEL ABOUT JUDY'S JAM—YOU WAITED UNTIL CHRISTMAS TO TELL ME—
JUDY AND YOUR COUSINS ARE COMING OVER AND I'M GONNA— I CAN'T BELIEVE SHE WOULD INDOCTRINATE—
BECAUSE I KNEW YOU'D THROW A FIT!
JUDITH PHELPS. I'D LIKE TO HAVE A WORD ABOUT MY SON AND YOUR PRESERVATION HERESY.
OH. IT'S THE JAM.
KEEP IT MOVING.

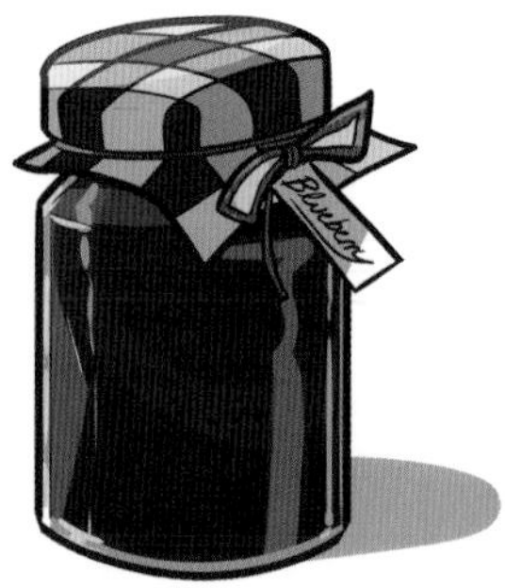

16

CHRISTMAS IN MADISON — III

SEASONS GREETINGS FROM MADISON, GEORGIA, AND HAPPY HOLIDAYS FROM SAMWELL HOCKEY AND THE PROVIDENCE FALCS!
SEND to GROUP
MY GOAL FOR THESE VERY SPECIAL HOLIDAYS? *STAY IN THE PRESENT.*
BUT THAT'S HARD WITH MY LAST SEMESTER AT SAMWELL STARTING IN DAYS. WELL!

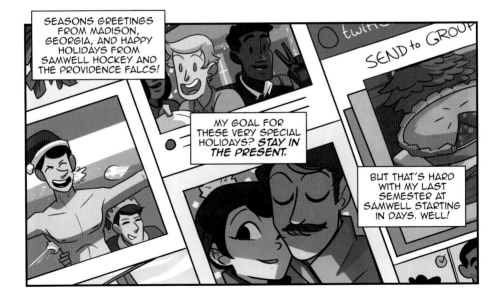

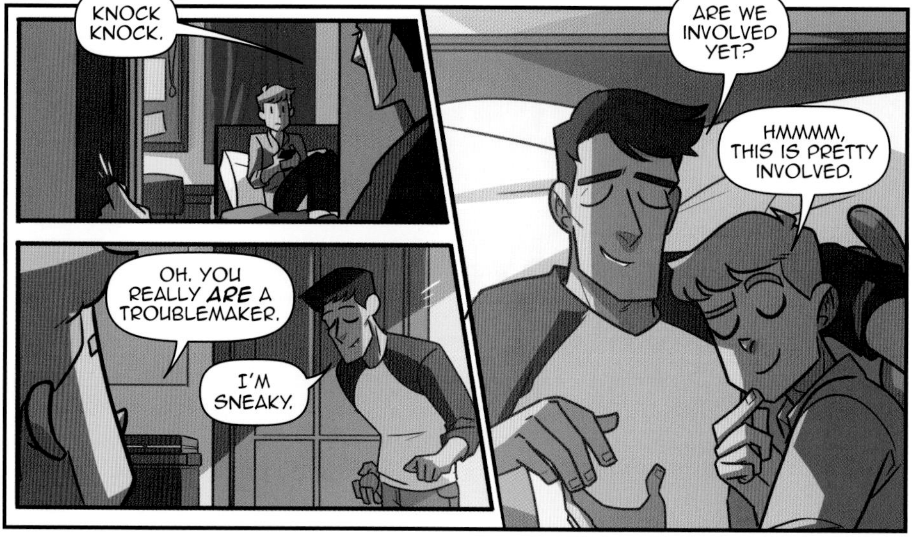
KNOCK KNOCK.
OH. YOU REALLY ARE A TROUBLEMAKER.
I'M SNEAKY.
ARE WE INVOLVED YET?
HMMMM, THIS IS PRETTY INVOLVED.

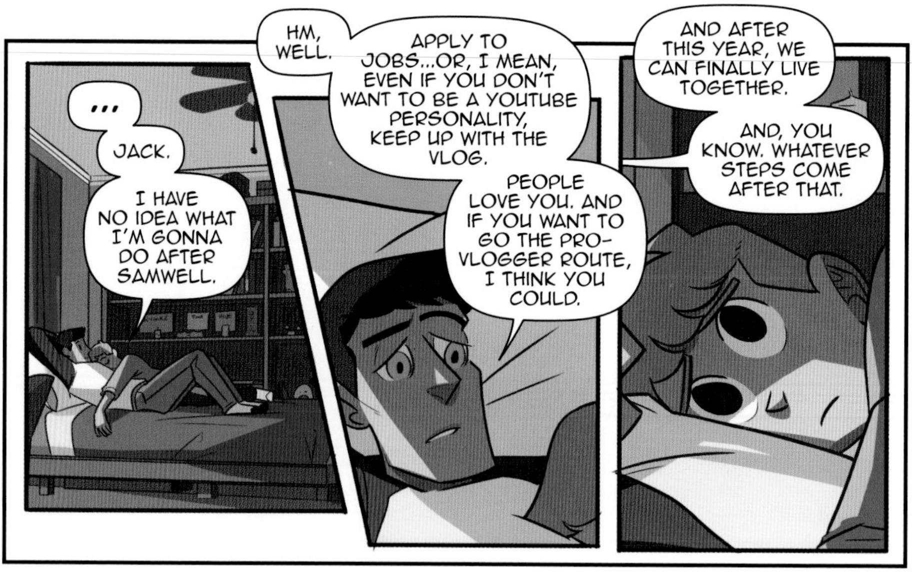
...
JACK.
I HAVE NO IDEA WHAT I'M GONNA DO AFTER SAMWELL.
HM, WELL.
APPLY TO JOBS...OR, I MEAN, EVEN IF YOU DON'T WANT TO BE A YOUTUBE PERSONALITY, KEEP UP WITH THE VLOG.
PEOPLE LOVE YOU. AND IF YOU WANT TO GO THE PRO-VLOGGER ROUTE, I THINK YOU COULD.
AND AFTER THIS YEAR, WE CAN FINALLY LIVE TOGETHER.
AND, YOU KNOW. WHATEVER STEPS COME AFTER THAT.

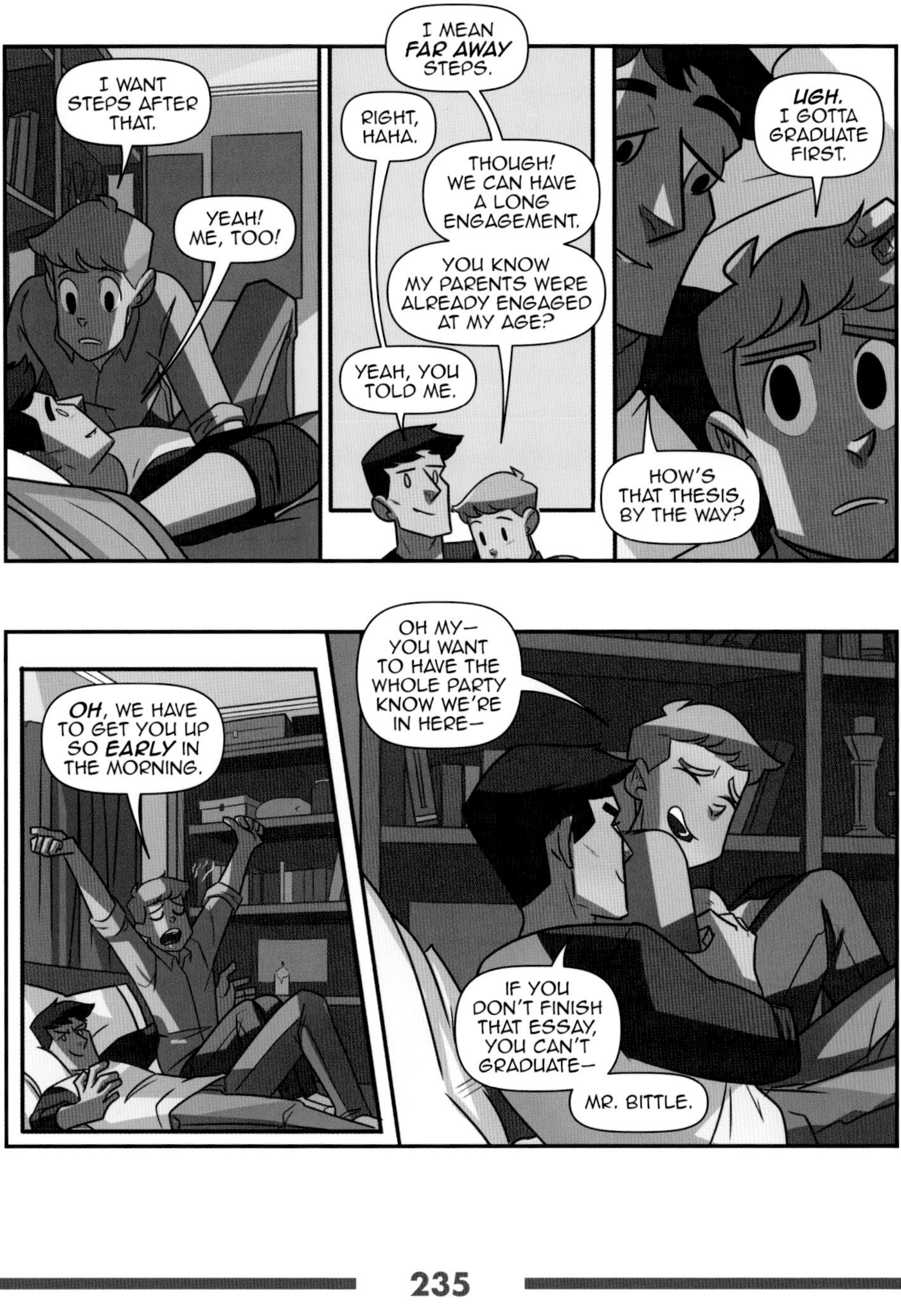
I WANT STEPS AFTER THAT.
YEAH! ME, TOO!
I MEAN *FAR AWAY* STEPS.
RIGHT, HAHA.
THOUGH! WE CAN HAVE A LONG ENGAGEMENT.
YOU KNOW MY PARENTS WERE ALREADY ENGAGED AT MY AGE?
YEAH, YOU TOLD ME.
UGH. I GOTTA GRADUATE FIRST.
HOW'S THAT THESIS, BY THE WAY?
OH, WE HAVE TO GET YOU UP SO *EARLY* IN THE MORNING.
OH MY— YOU WANT TO HAVE THE WHOLE PARTY KNOW WE'RE IN HERE—
IF YOU DON'T FINISH THAT ESSAY, YOU CAN'T GRADUATE—
MR. BITTLE.

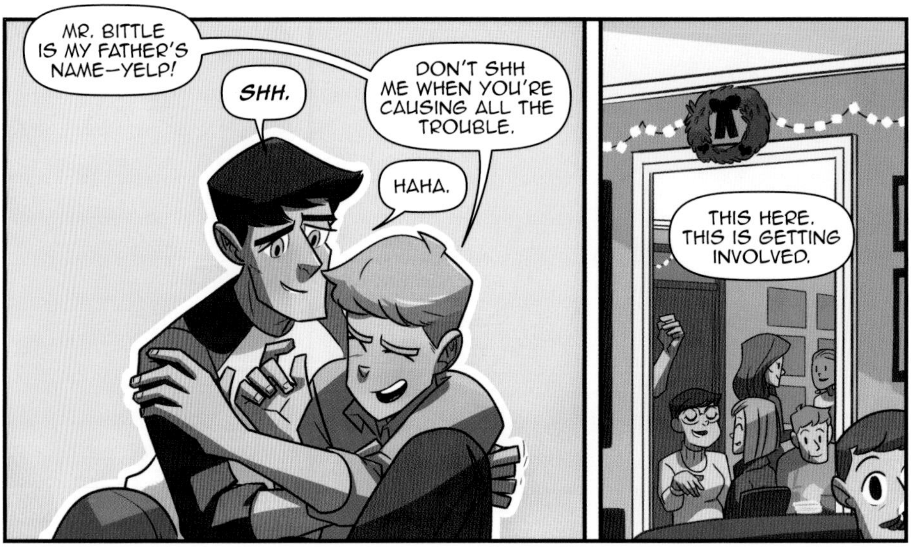
MR. BITTLE IS MY FATHER'S NAME—YELP!
SHH.
DON'T SHH ME WHEN YOU'RE CAUSING ALL THE TROUBLE.
HAHA.
THIS HERE. THIS IS GETTING INVOLVED.

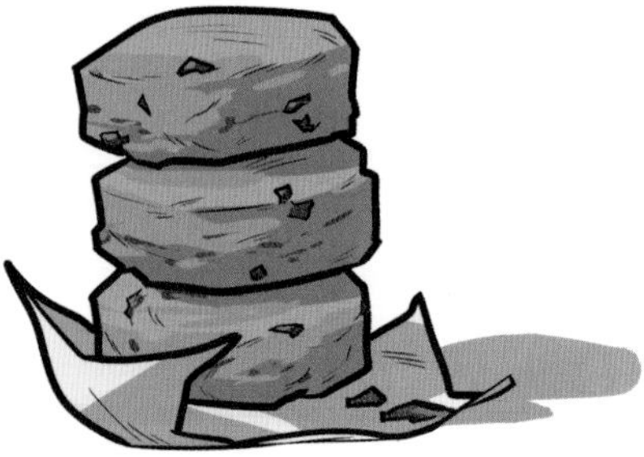

17

SENIOR THESIS

IT'S SPRING SEMESTER!
SO, MY TEAM IS A LITTLE WORRIED ABOUT MY PROGRESS ON MY SENIOR THESIS.
BLESS THEIR HEARTS.
FRANKLY, THEY'RE *OVERREACTING*.

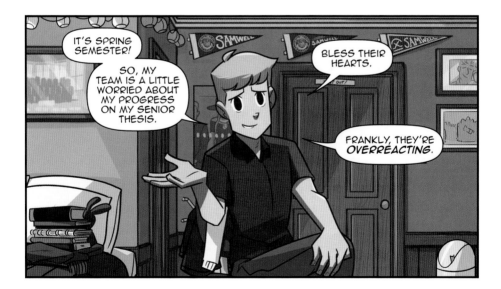

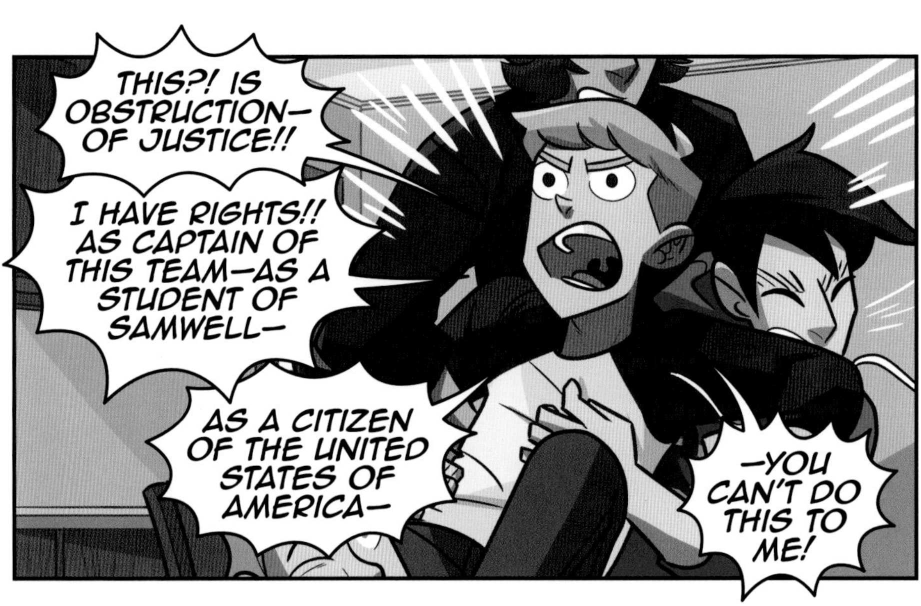
THIS?! IS OBSTRUCTION—OF JUSTICE!!
I HAVE RIGHTS!! AS CAPTAIN OF THIS TEAM—AS A STUDENT OF SAMWELL—
AS A CITIZEN OF THE UNITED STATES OF AMERICA—
—YOU CAN'T DO THIS TO ME!

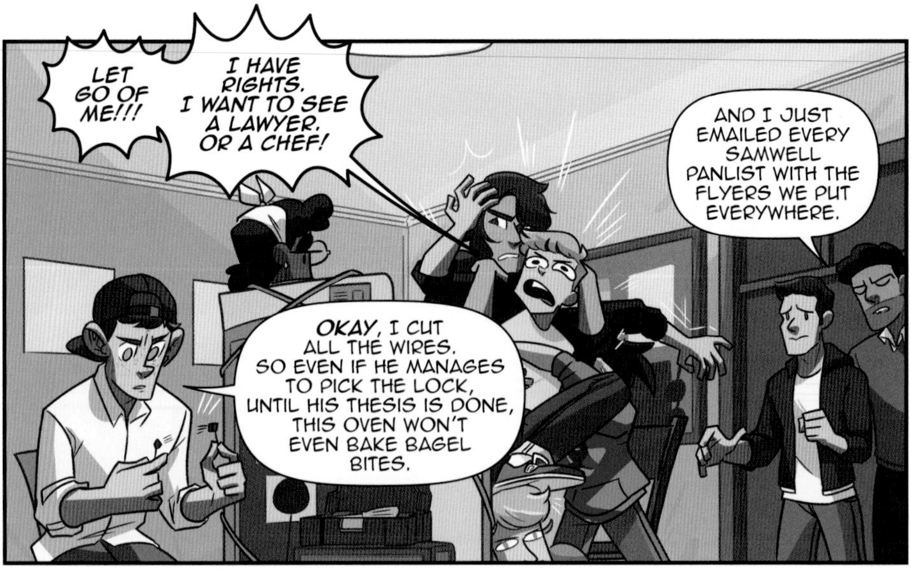
LET GO OF ME!!!
I HAVE RIGHTS. I WANT TO SEE A LAWYER. OR A CHEF!
AND I JUST EMAILED EVERY SAMWELL PANLIST WITH THE FLYERS WE PUT EVERYWHERE.
OKAY, I CUT ALL THE WIRES. SO EVEN IF HE MANAGES TO PICK THE LOCK, UNTIL HIS THESIS IS DONE, THIS OVEN WON'T EVEN BAKE BAGEL BITES.

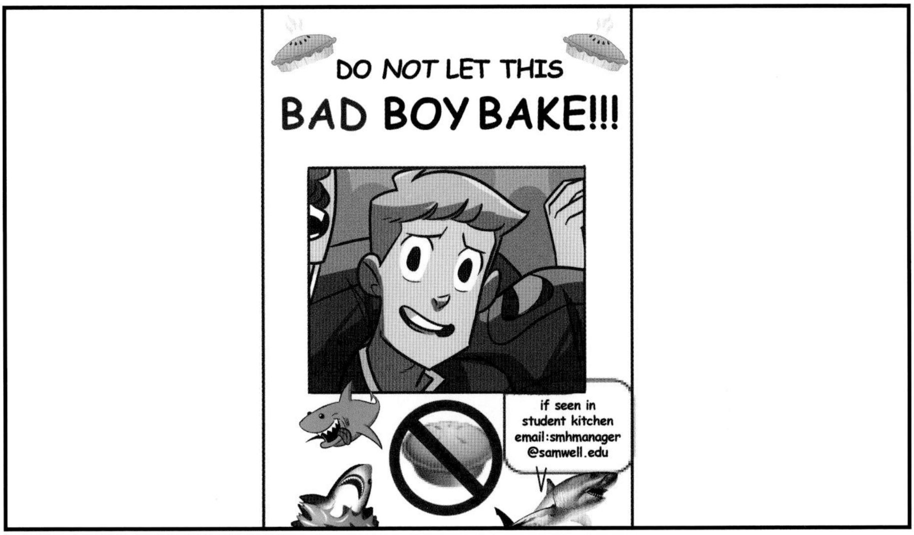
DO NOT LET THIS
BAD BOY BAKE!!!
if seen in student kitchen email:smhmanager @samwell.edu

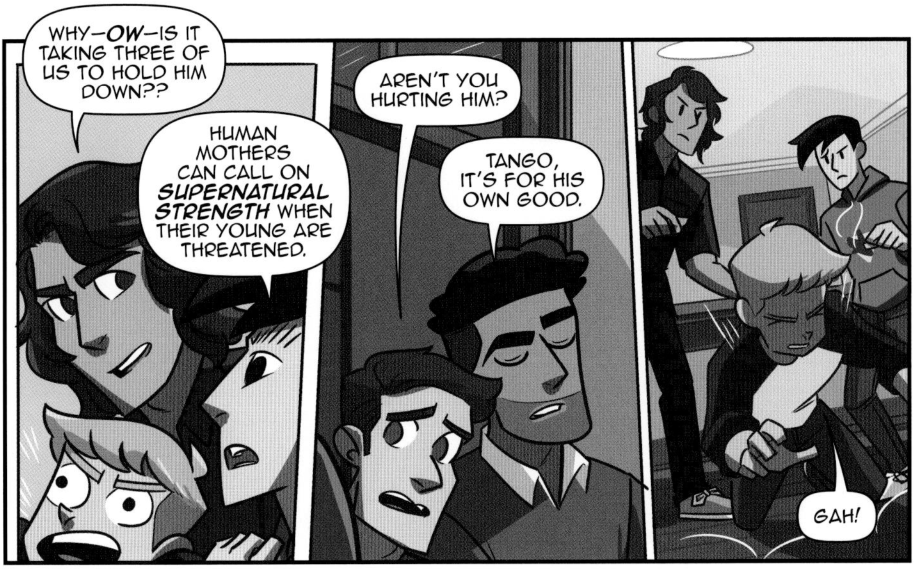
WHY—OW—IS IT TAKING THREE OF US TO HOLD HIM DOWN??
HUMAN MOTHERS CAN CALL ON SUPERNATURAL STRENGTH WHEN THEIR YOUNG ARE THREATENED.
AREN'T YOU HURTING HIM?
TANGO, IT'S FOR HIS OWN GOOD.
GAH!

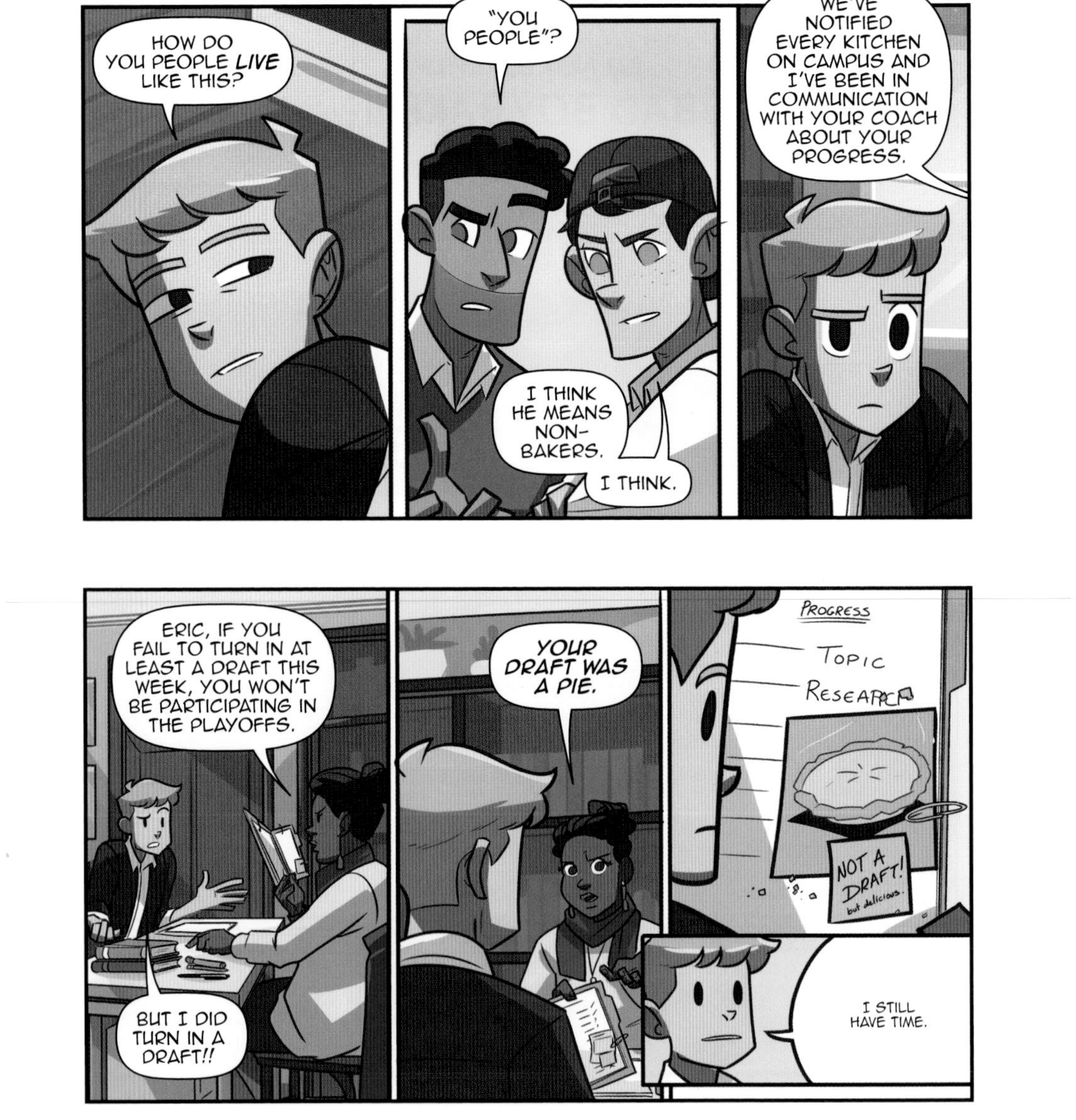
HOW DO YOU PEOPLE *LIVE* LIKE THIS?
"YOU PEOPLE"?
I THINK HE MEANS NON-BAKERS.
I THINK.
WE'VE NOTIFIED EVERY KITCHEN ON CAMPUS AND I'VE BEEN IN COMMUNICATION WITH YOUR COACH ABOUT YOUR PROGRESS.
ERIC, IF YOU FAIL TO TURN IN AT LEAST A DRAFT THIS WEEK, YOU WON'T BE PARTICIPATING IN THE PLAYOFFS.
BUT I DID TURN IN A DRAFT!!
YOUR DRAFT WAS A PIE.
PROGRESS
TOPIC
RESEARCH
NOT A DRAFT!
but delicious.
I STILL HAVE TIME.

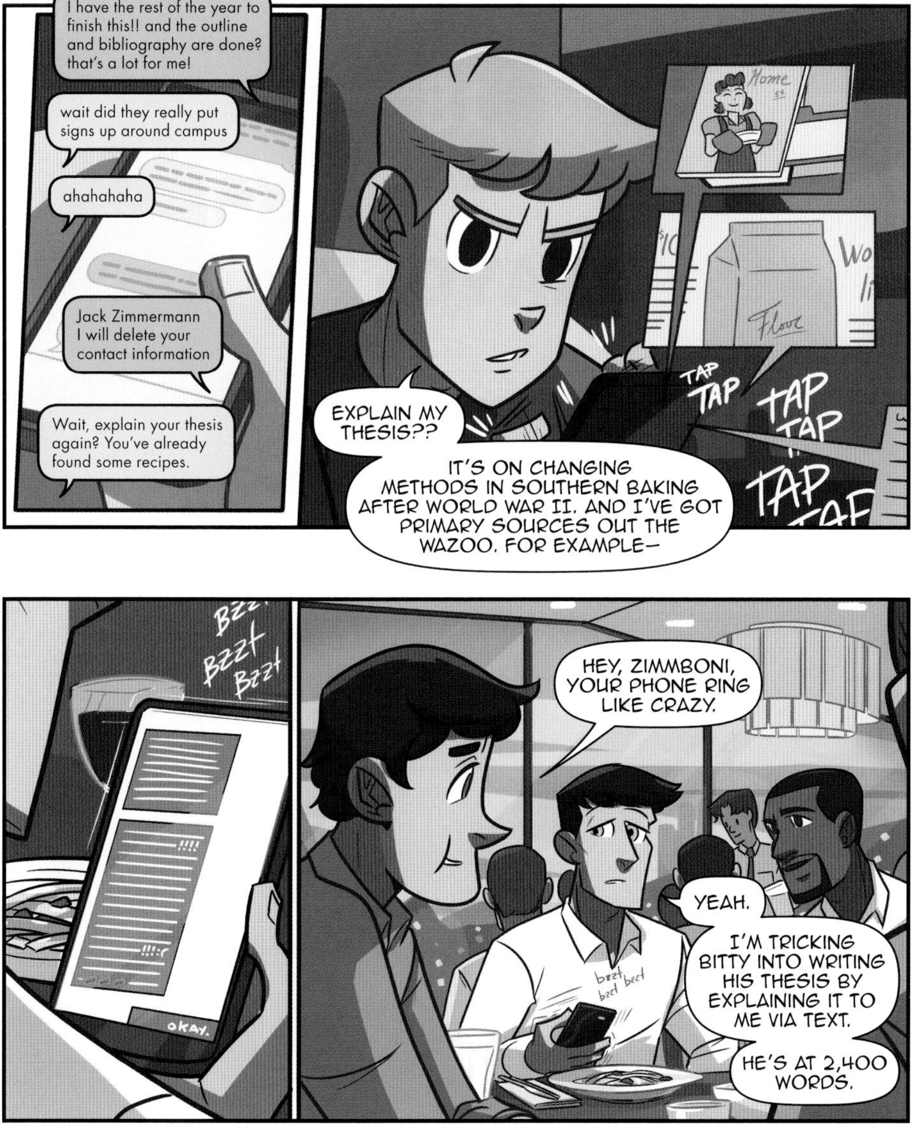
I have the rest of the year to finish this!! and the outline and bibliography are done? that's a lot for me!
wait did they really put signs up around campus
ahahahaha
Jack Zimmermann I will delete your contact information
Wait, explain your thesis again? You've already found some recipes.
EXPLAIN MY THESIS??
IT'S ON CHANGING METHODS IN SOUTHERN BAKING AFTER WORLD WAR II. AND I'VE GOT PRIMARY SOURCES OUT THE WAZOO. FOR EXAMPLE—
Home
Flour
TAP TAP
TAP TAP
TAP
BZZT BZZT BZZT
OKAY.
HEY, ZIMMBONI, YOUR PHONE RING LIKE CRAZY.
bzzt bzzt bzzt
YEAH.
I'M TRICKING BITTY INTO WRITING HIS THESIS BY EXPLAINING IT TO ME VIA TEXT.
HE'S AT 2,400 WORDS.

18

PLAYOFFS

ALMOST EVERY YEAR SINCE JACK ENROLLED IN SAMWELL, SAMWELL MEN'S HOCKEY HAS MADE IT TO THE NCAA PLAYOFFS.
WE'RE SAMWELL. IT'S ALMOST A GIVEN AT THIS POINT.
FIRST OUT CAPT
15
...

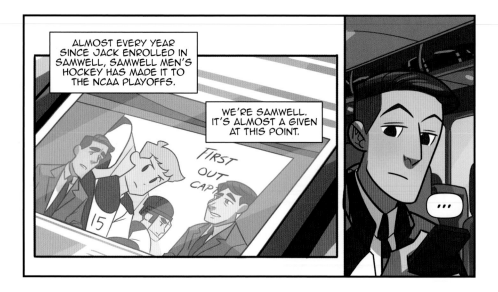

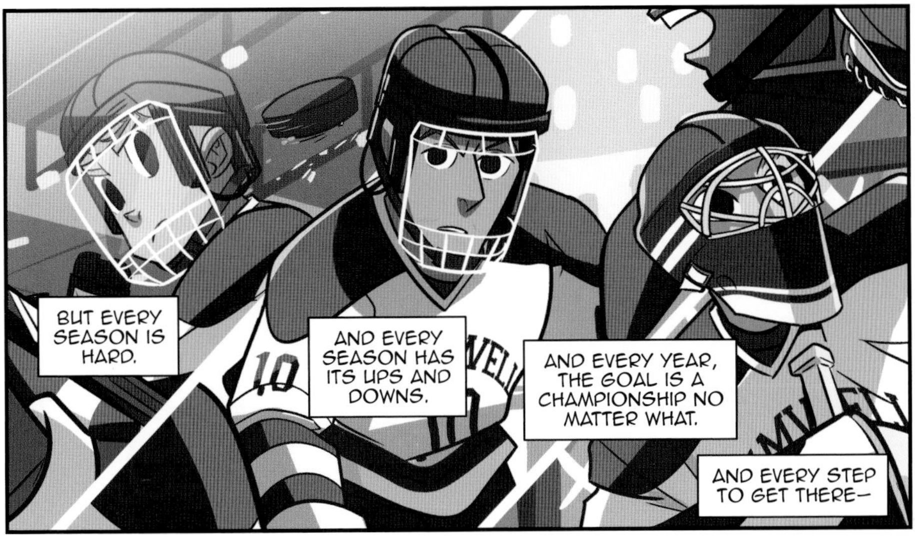
BUT EVERY SEASON IS HARD.
AND EVERY SEASON HAS ITS UPS AND DOWNS.
AND EVERY YEAR, THE GOAL IS A CHAMPIONSHIP NO MATTER WHAT.
AND EVERY STEP TO GET THERE—

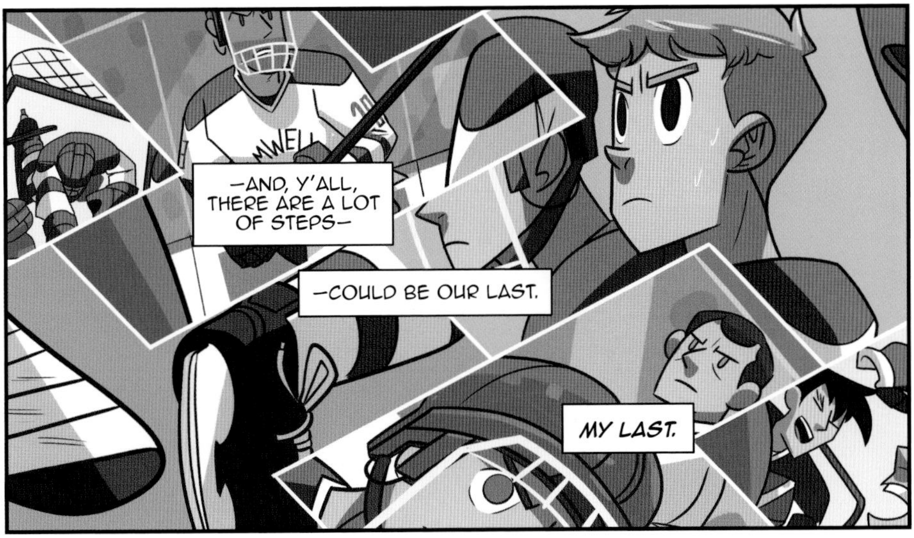
—AND, Y'ALL, THERE ARE A LOT OF STEPS—
—COULD BE OUR LAST.
MY LAST.

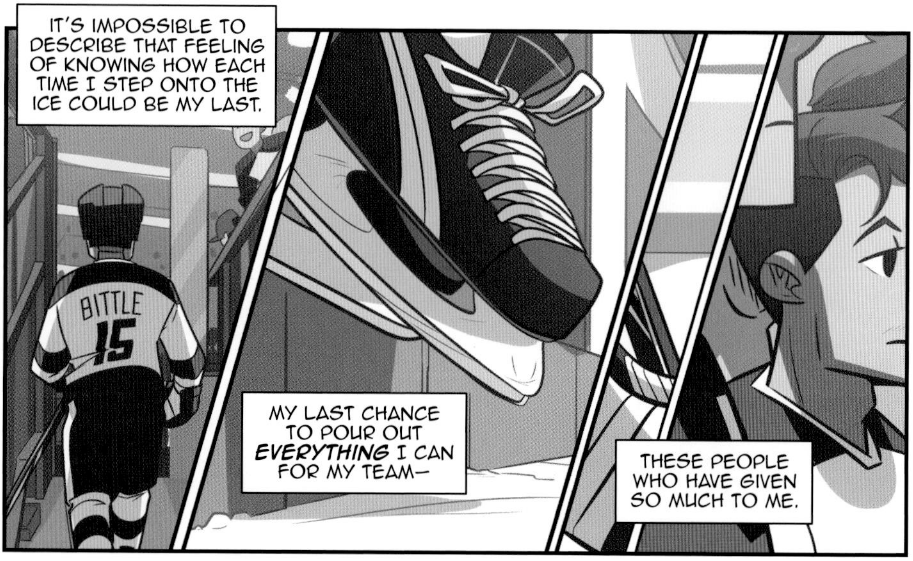
IT'S IMPOSSIBLE TO DESCRIBE THAT FEELING OF KNOWING HOW EACH TIME I STEP ONTO THE ICE COULD BE MY LAST.
BITTLE 15
MY LAST CHANCE TO POUR OUT ***EVERYTHING*** I CAN FOR MY TEAM—
THESE PEOPLE WHO HAVE GIVEN SO MUCH TO ME.

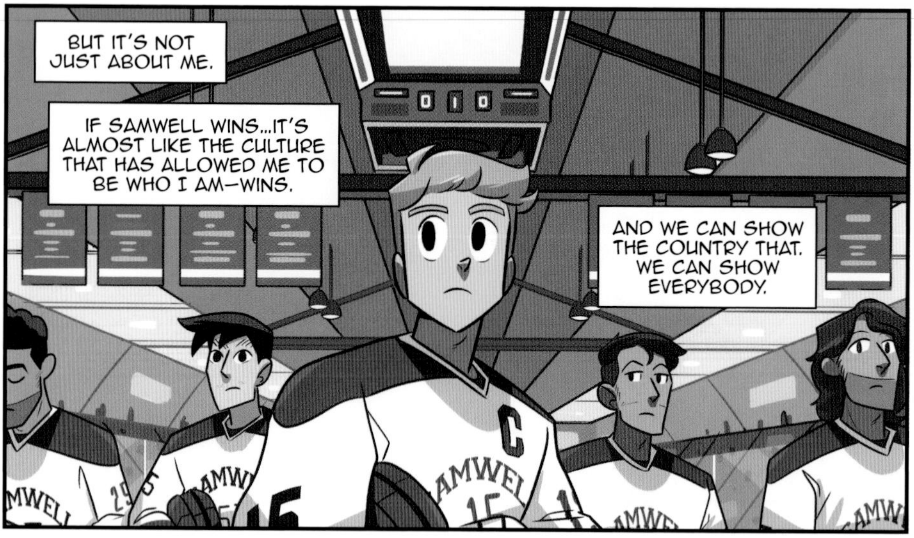
BUT IT'S NOT JUST ABOUT ME.
IF SAMWELL WINS...IT'S ALMOST LIKE THE CULTURE THAT HAS ALLOWED ME TO BE WHO I AM—WINS.
AND WE CAN SHOW THE COUNTRY THAT. WE CAN SHOW EVERYBODY.

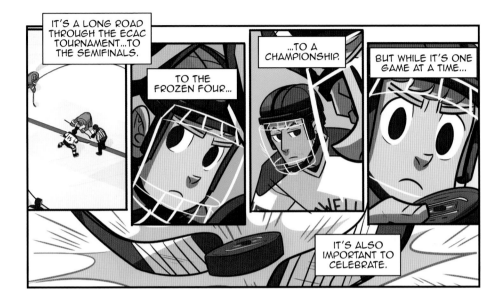

IT'S A LONG ROAD THROUGH THE ECAC TOURNAMENT...TO THE SEMIFINALS.

TO THE FROZEN FOUR...

...TO A CHAMPIONSHIP.

BUT WHILE IT'S ONE GAME AT A TIME...

IT'S ALSO IMPORTANT TO CELEBRATE.

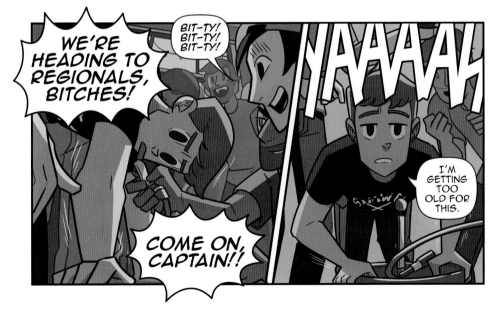

WE'RE HEADING TO REGIONALS, BITCHES!

BIT-TY! BIT-TY! BIT-TY!

YAAAAAH

COME ON, CAPTAIN!!

I'M GETTING TOO OLD FOR THIS.

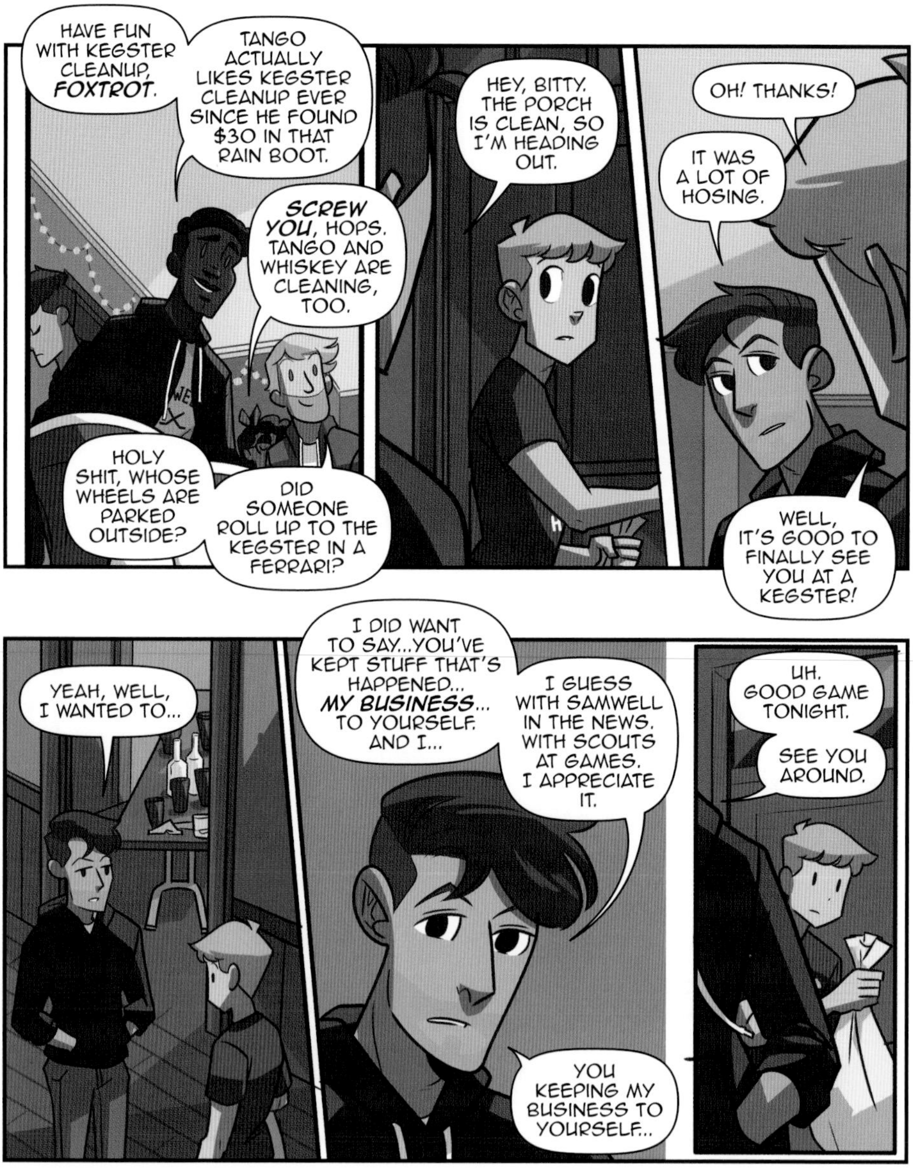
HAVE FUN WITH KEGSTER CLEANUP, FOXTROT.
TANGO ACTUALLY LIKES KEGSTER CLEANUP EVER SINCE HE FOUND $30 IN THAT RAIN BOOT.
SCREW YOU, HOPS. TANGO AND WHISKEY ARE CLEANING, TOO.
HOLY SHIT, WHOSE WHEELS ARE PARKED OUTSIDE?
DID SOMEONE ROLL UP TO THE KEGSTER IN A FERRARI?
HEY, BITTY. THE PORCH IS CLEAN, SO I'M HEADING OUT.
OH! THANKS!
IT WAS A LOT OF HOSING.
WELL, IT'S GOOD TO FINALLY SEE YOU AT A KEGSTER!
YEAH, WELL, I WANTED TO...
I DID WANT TO SAY...YOU'VE KEPT STUFF THAT'S HAPPENED... MY BUSINESS... TO YOURSELF. AND I...
I GUESS WITH SAMWELL IN THE NEWS. WITH SCOUTS AT GAMES. I APPRECIATE IT.
YOU KEEPING MY BUSINESS TO YOURSELF...
UH. GOOD GAME TONIGHT.
SEE YOU AROUND.

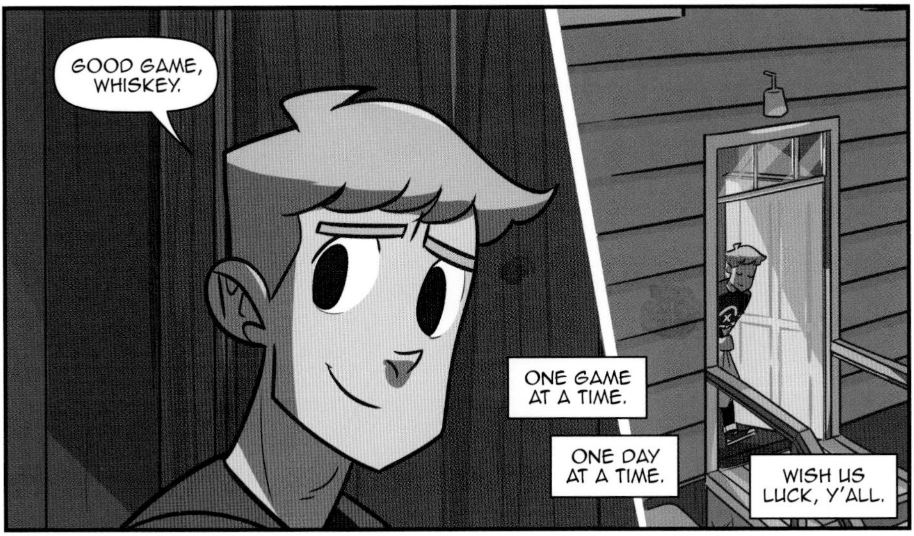
GOOD GAME, WHISKEY.
ONE GAME AT A TIME.
ONE DAY AT A TIME.
WISH US LUCK, Y'ALL.

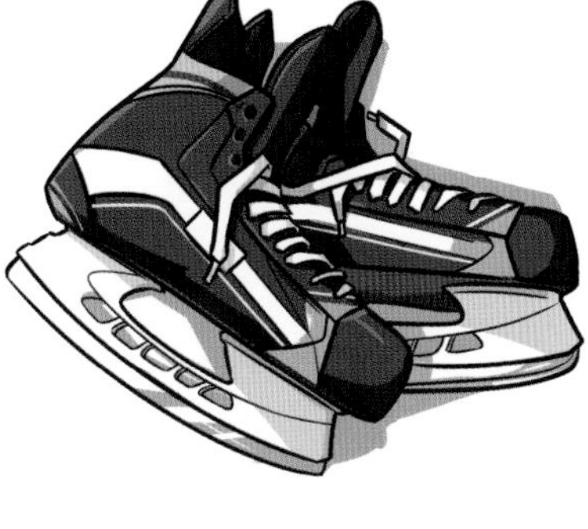

19

PARSE

AFTER THE KEGSTER...
HEY.
UH, HEY, SORRY IF THIS IS WEIRD.

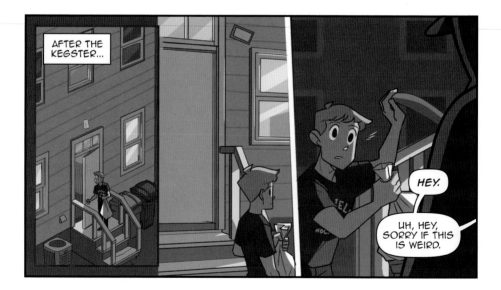

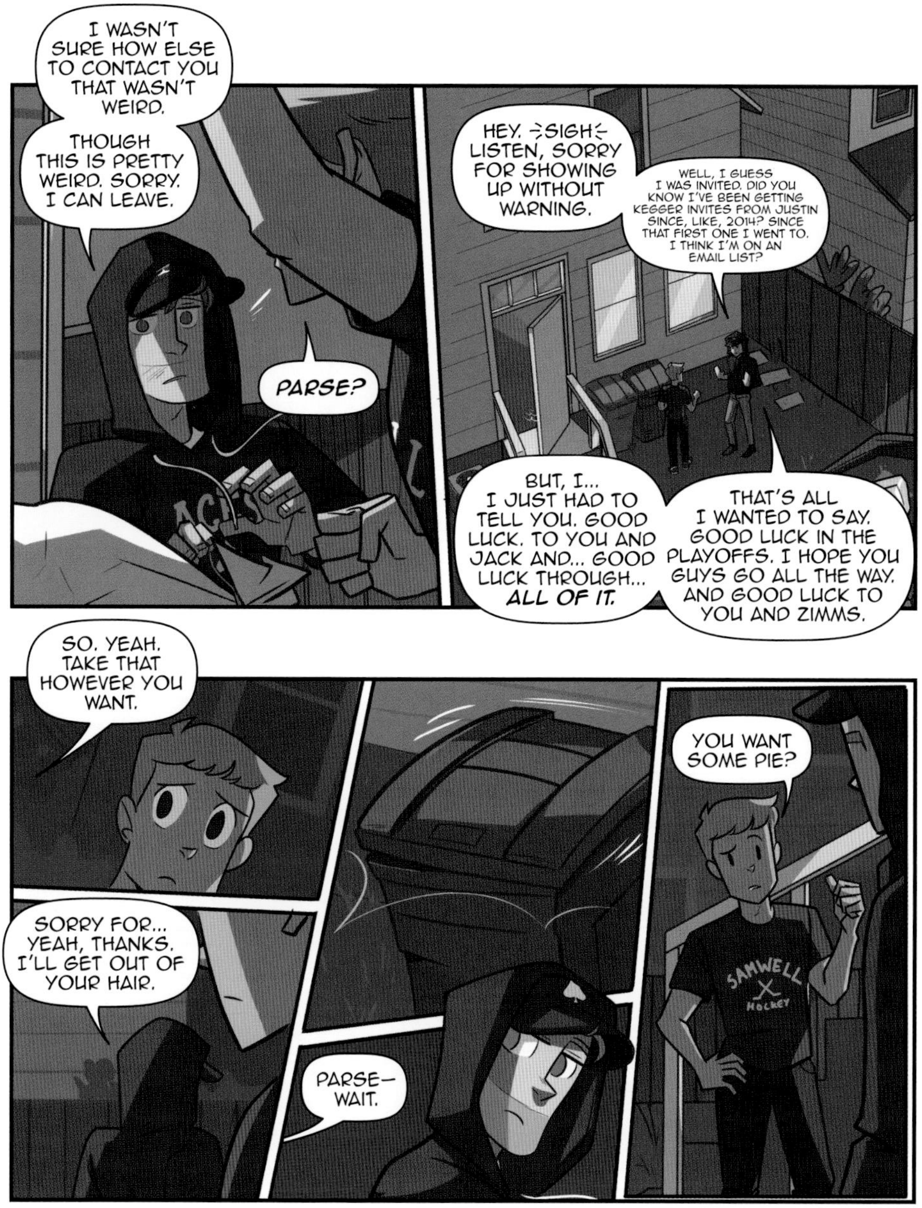
I WASN'T SURE HOW ELSE TO CONTACT YOU THAT WASN'T WEIRD.
THOUGH THIS IS PRETTY WEIRD. SORRY. I CAN LEAVE.
PARSE?
HEY. ⥱SIGH⥲ LISTEN, SORRY FOR SHOWING UP WITHOUT WARNING.
WELL, I GUESS I WAS INVITED. DID YOU KNOW I'VE BEEN GETTING KEGGER INVITES FROM JUSTIN SINCE, LIKE, 2014? SINCE THAT FIRST ONE I WENT TO. I THINK I'M ON AN EMAIL LIST?
BUT, I... I JUST HAD TO TELL YOU. GOOD LUCK. TO YOU AND JACK AND... GOOD LUCK THROUGH... ALL OF IT.
THAT'S ALL I WANTED TO SAY. GOOD LUCK IN THE PLAYOFFS. I HOPE YOU GUYS GO ALL THE WAY. AND GOOD LUCK TO YOU AND ZIMMS.
SO. YEAH. TAKE THAT HOWEVER YOU WANT.
SORRY FOR... YEAH, THANKS. I'LL GET OUT OF YOUR HAIR.
PARSE— WAIT.
YOU WANT SOME PIE?
SAMWELL HOCKEY

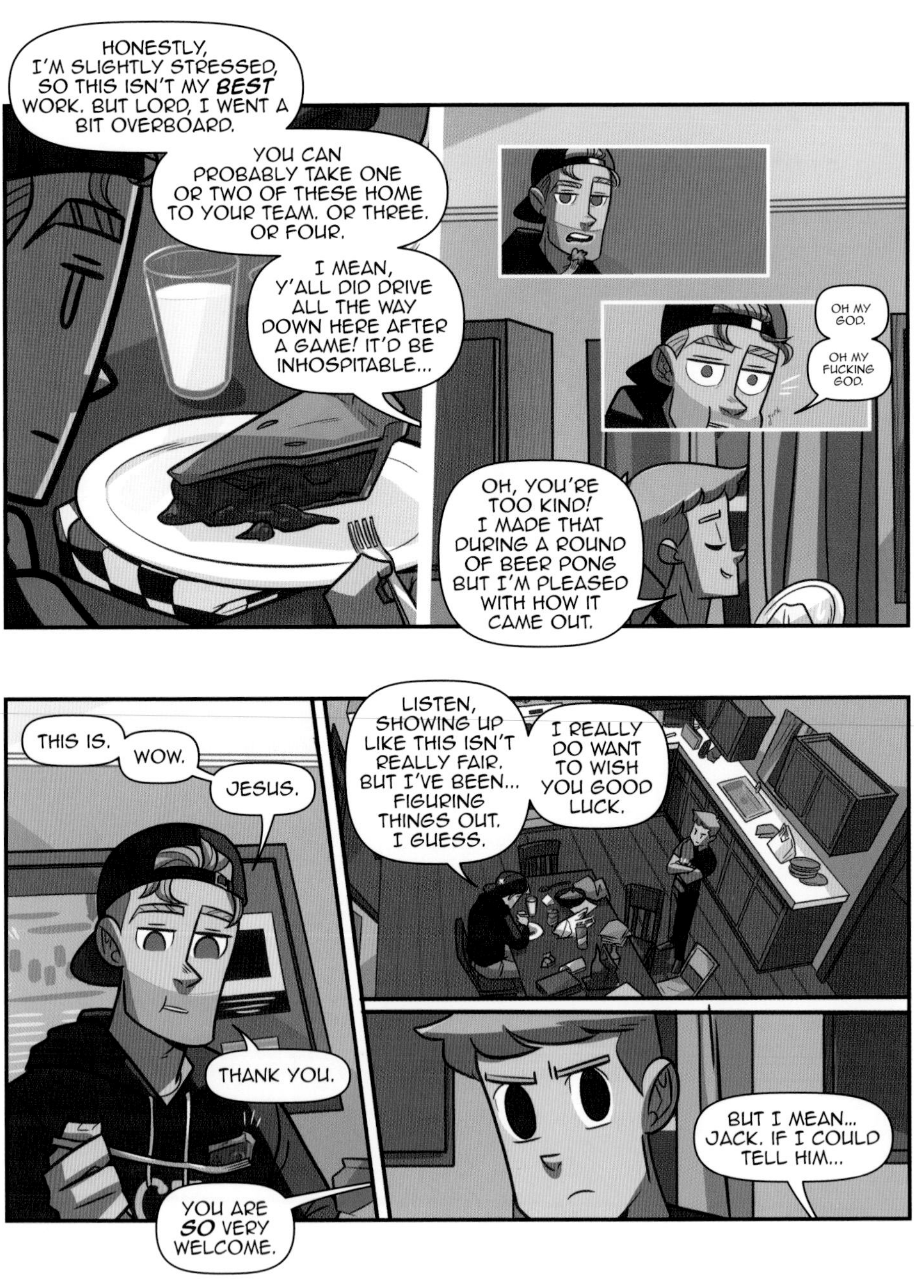
HONESTLY, I'M SLIGHTLY STRESSED, SO THIS ISN'T MY **BEST** WORK. BUT LORD, I WENT A BIT OVERBOARD.
YOU CAN PROBABLY TAKE ONE OR TWO OF THESE HOME TO YOUR TEAM. OR THREE. OR FOUR.
I MEAN, Y'ALL DID DRIVE ALL THE WAY DOWN HERE AFTER A GAME! IT'D BE INHOSPITABLE...
OH MY GOD.
OH MY FUCKING GOD.
OH, YOU'RE TOO KIND! I MADE THAT DURING A ROUND OF BEER PONG BUT I'M PLEASED WITH HOW IT CAME OUT.
THIS IS.
WOW.
JESUS.
THANK YOU.
YOU ARE **SO** VERY WELCOME.
LISTEN, SHOWING UP LIKE THIS ISN'T REALLY FAIR. BUT I'VE BEEN... FIGURING THINGS OUT. I GUESS.
I REALLY DO WANT TO WISH YOU GOOD LUCK.
BUT I MEAN... JACK. IF I COULD TELL HIM...

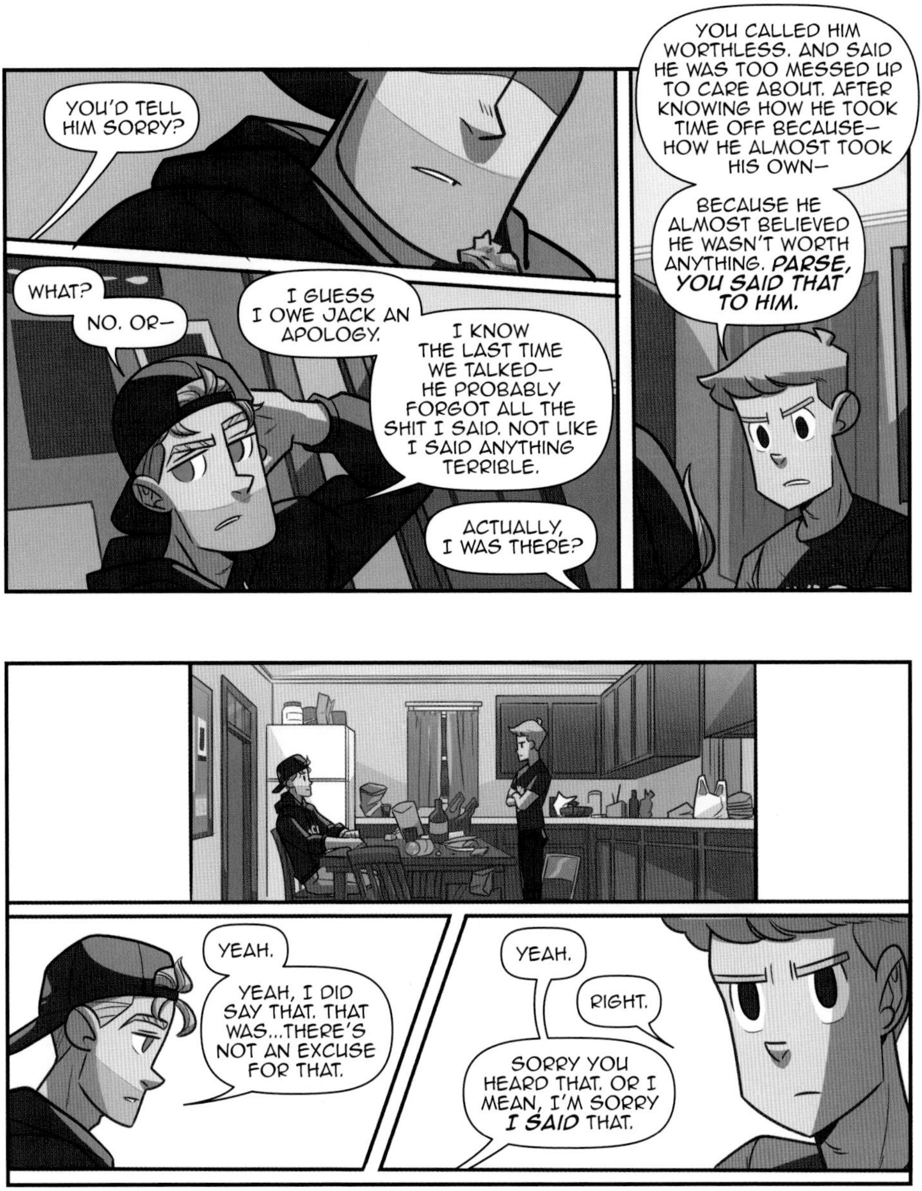
YOU'D TELL HIM SORRY?
YOU CALLED HIM WORTHLESS. AND SAID HE WAS TOO MESSED UP TO CARE ABOUT. AFTER KNOWING HOW HE TOOK TIME OFF BECAUSE— HOW HE ALMOST TOOK HIS OWN—
BECAUSE HE ALMOST BELIEVED HE WASN'T WORTH ANYTHING. ***PARSE, YOU SAID THAT TO HIM.***
WHAT?
NO. OR—
I GUESS I OWE JACK AN APOLOGY.
I KNOW THE LAST TIME WE TALKED— HE PROBABLY FORGOT ALL THE SHIT I SAID. NOT LIKE I SAID ANYTHING TERRIBLE.
ACTUALLY, I WAS THERE?
YEAH.
YEAH, I DID SAY THAT. THAT WAS...THERE'S NOT AN EXCUSE FOR THAT.
YEAH.
RIGHT.
SORRY YOU HEARD THAT. OR I MEAN, I'M SORRY ***I SAID*** THAT.

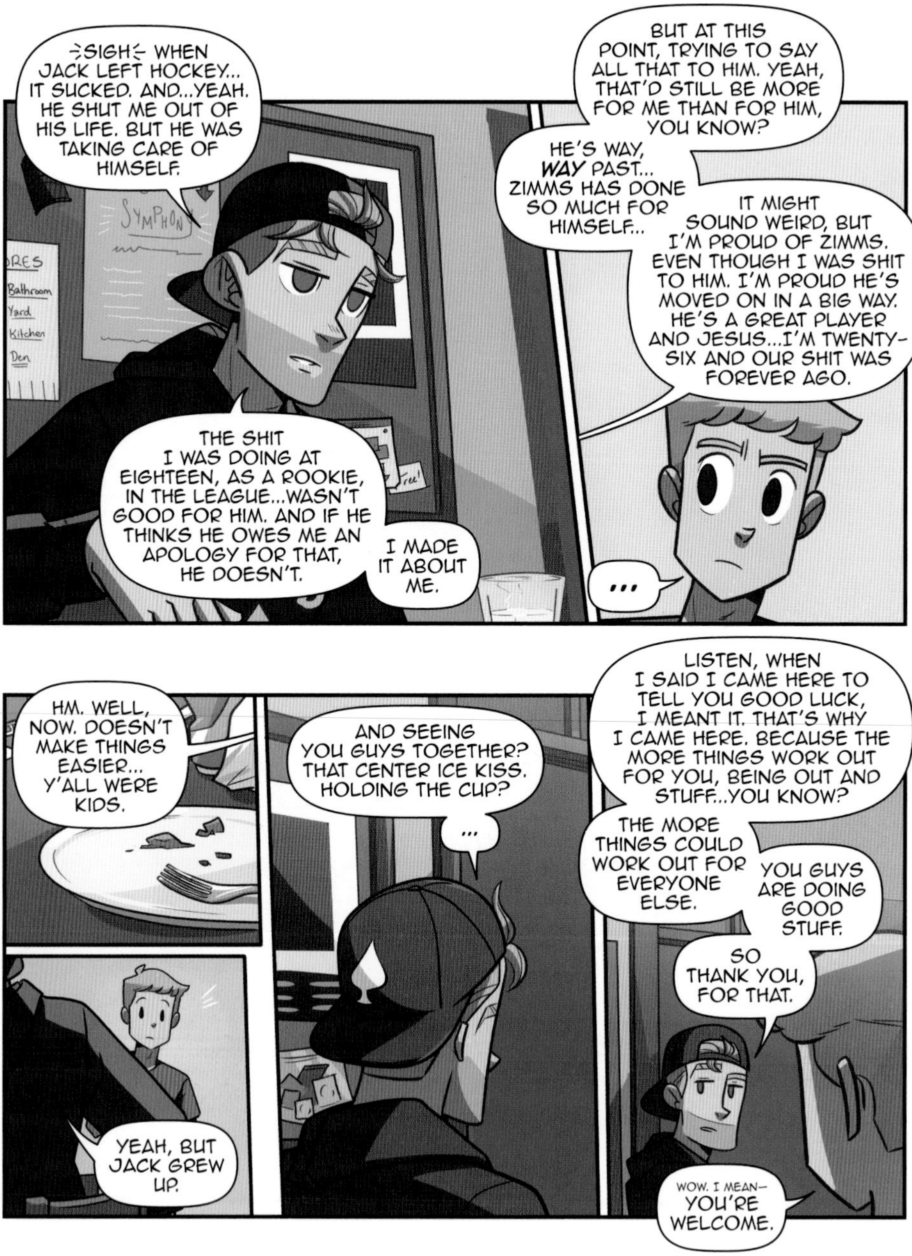

⁻SIGH⁻ WHEN JACK LEFT HOCKEY... IT SUCKED. AND...YEAH. HE SHUT ME OUT OF HIS LIFE. BUT HE WAS TAKING CARE OF HIMSELF.
THE SHIT I WAS DOING AT EIGHTEEN, AS A ROOKIE, IN THE LEAGUE...WASN'T GOOD FOR HIM. AND IF HE THINKS HE OWES ME AN APOLOGY FOR THAT, HE DOESN'T.
I MADE IT ABOUT ME.
BUT AT THIS POINT, TRYING TO SAY ALL THAT TO HIM. YEAH, THAT'D STILL BE MORE FOR ME THAN FOR HIM, YOU KNOW?
HE'S WAY, *WAY* PAST... ZIMMS HAS DONE SO MUCH FOR HIMSELF...
IT MIGHT SOUND WEIRD, BUT I'M PROUD OF ZIMMS. EVEN THOUGH I WAS SHIT TO HIM. I'M PROUD HE'S MOVED ON IN A BIG WAY. HE'S A GREAT PLAYER AND JESUS...I'M TWENTY-SIX AND OUR SHIT WAS FOREVER AGO.
...
HM. WELL, NOW. DOESN'T MAKE THINGS EASIER... Y'ALL WERE KIDS.
YEAH, BUT JACK GREW UP.
AND SEEING YOU GUYS TOGETHER? THAT CENTER ICE KISS. HOLDING THE CUP?
...
LISTEN, WHEN I SAID I CAME HERE TO TELL YOU GOOD LUCK, I MEANT IT. THAT'S WHY I CAME HERE. BECAUSE THE MORE THINGS WORK OUT FOR YOU, BEING OUT AND STUFF...YOU KNOW?
THE MORE THINGS COULD WORK OUT FOR EVERYONE ELSE.
YOU GUYS ARE DOING GOOD STUFF.
SO THANK YOU, FOR THAT.
WOW. I MEAN— YOU'RE WELCOME.

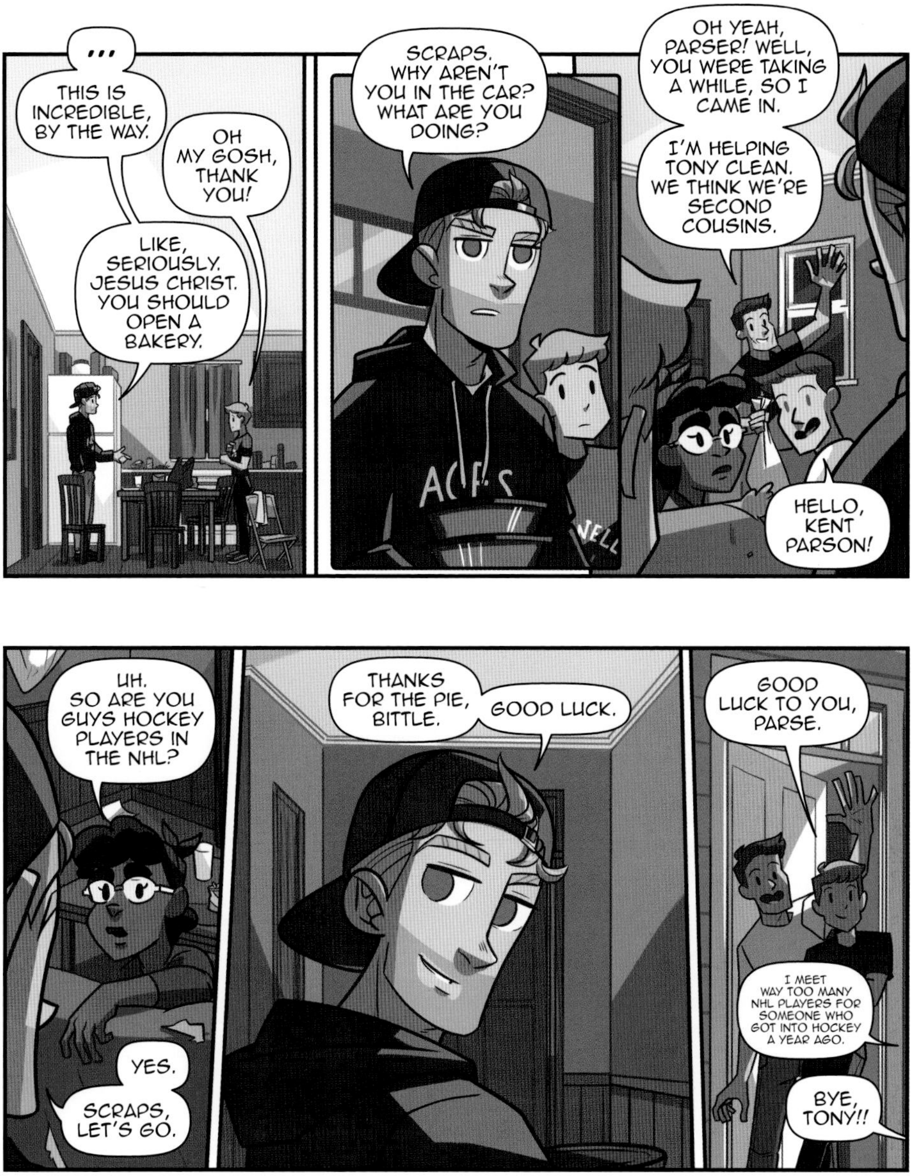
...
THIS IS INCREDIBLE, BY THE WAY.
OH MY GOSH, THANK YOU!
LIKE, SERIOUSLY. JESUS CHRIST. YOU SHOULD OPEN A BAKERY.
SCRAPS. WHY AREN'T YOU IN THE CAR? WHAT ARE YOU DOING?
OH YEAH, PARSER! WELL, YOU WERE TAKING A WHILE, SO I CAME IN.
I'M HELPING TONY CLEAN. WE THINK WE'RE SECOND COUSINS.
HELLO, KENT PARSON!
UH. SO ARE YOU GUYS HOCKEY PLAYERS IN THE NHL?
YES.
SCRAPS, LET'S GO.
THANKS FOR THE PIE, BITTLE.
GOOD LUCK.
GOOD LUCK TO YOU, PARSE.
I MEET WAY TOO MANY NHL PLAYERS FOR SOMEONE WHO GOT INTO HOCKEY A YEAR AGO.
BYE, TONY!!

20

SPOTLIGHT ON ERIC BITTLE

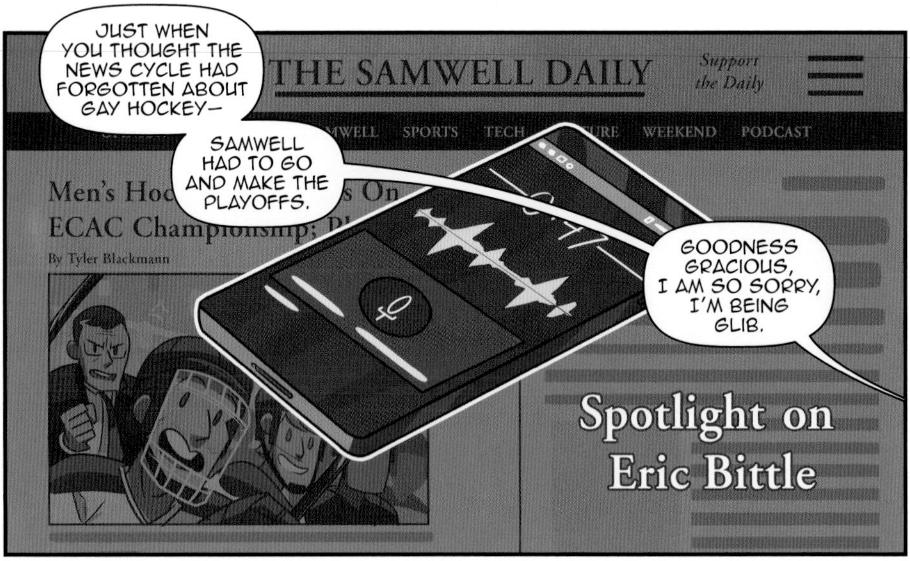

JUST WHEN YOU THOUGHT THE NEWS CYCLE HAD FORGOTTEN ABOUT GAY HOCKEY—
SAMWELL HAD TO GO AND MAKE THE PLAYOFFS.
GOODNESS GRACIOUS, I AM SO SORRY, I'M BEING GLIB.
THE SAMWELL DAILY
Support the Daily
SPORTS
TECH
WEEKEND
PODCAST
By Tyler Blackmann
Spotlight on Eric Bittle

The Samwell men's hockey team is no stranger to the NCAA men's ice hockey playoffs. Since Jack Zimmermann '15 joined the club in 2011, Samwell has enjoyed frequent appearances in the tournament every spring. But with this playoff appearance, another spotlight shines on Samwell hockey, and this light is trained on Eric Bittle '17, the current captain of the men's ice hockey team, who has been in the news for more than just sports. Bittle made headlines last spring when he and Zimmermann shared a history-making kiss at center ice after game 7 of the Stanley Cup playoffs. Now, leading Samwell men's ice hockey to his last NCAA tourney appearance, Bittle is officially the first openly gay Division I men's ice hockey captain in NCAA history.

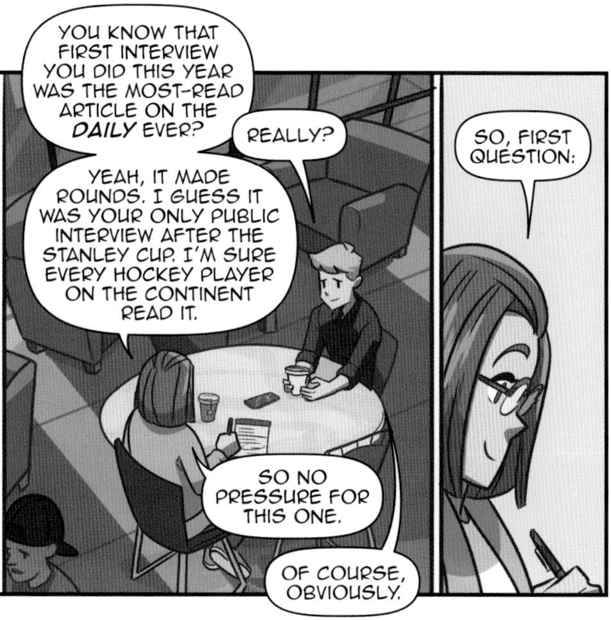
YOU KNOW THAT FIRST INTERVIEW YOU DID THIS YEAR WAS THE MOST-READ ARTICLE ON THE *DAILY* EVER?
REALLY?
YEAH, IT MADE ROUNDS. I GUESS IT WAS YOUR ONLY PUBLIC INTERVIEW AFTER THE STANLEY CUP. I'M SURE EVERY HOCKEY PLAYER ON THE CONTINENT READ IT.
SO NO PRESSURE FOR THIS ONE.
OF COURSE, OBVIOUSLY.
SO, FIRST QUESTION:

This is Samwell men's hockey's third time in the NCAA playoffs in four years and second time in the Frozen Four. How does this appearance feel different from past experiences?

Every journey to the playoffs has its own unique challenges, and this season has been no different. But I would definitely say the stakes are higher. I'd be remiss if I didn't attribute those raised stakes to my role as the first openly queer captain of a D-I NCAA men's hockey team, and what a win could mean for queer people everywhere. But other than my personal investment, I'd say we're putting in the same hard work Samwell puts in every year.

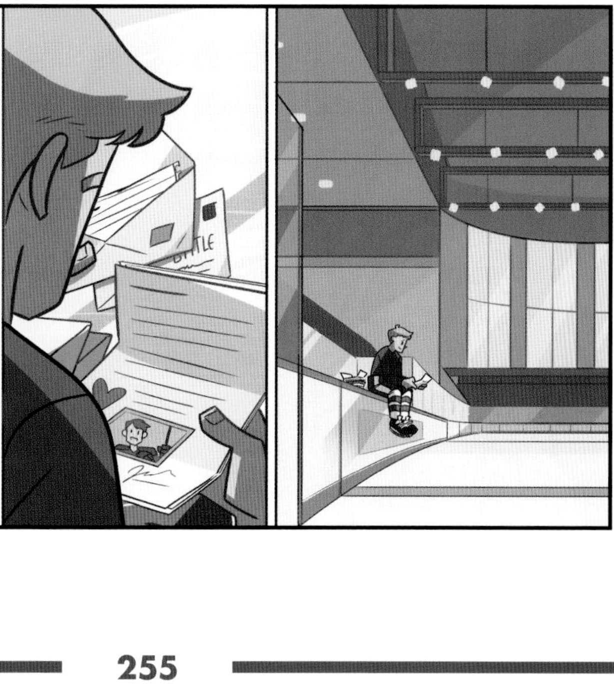

In your interview with the *Daily* this October, you talked about being a role model in two ways: as a captain and as a visible queer athlete. Now that Samwell is back on the national stage, your position as a leader has a much larger impact. As your season closes, what do you think you've learned about being a role model?

That it's hard. [*laughs*] As a captain, the number one lesson I've learned is that I'm mostly a teammate/linemate first and that I'm a captain second. It's my job to lead and motivate the team—to be a role model in some respects, but at the end of the day, each of us takes turns pushing each other and supporting each other. It's the same for every game, even a playoff match. And as an openly gay athlete...I think sometimes all you need to be a role model is to exist. To show it can work. Being a role model isn't about being perfect, it's giving an example of one way to live life successfully.

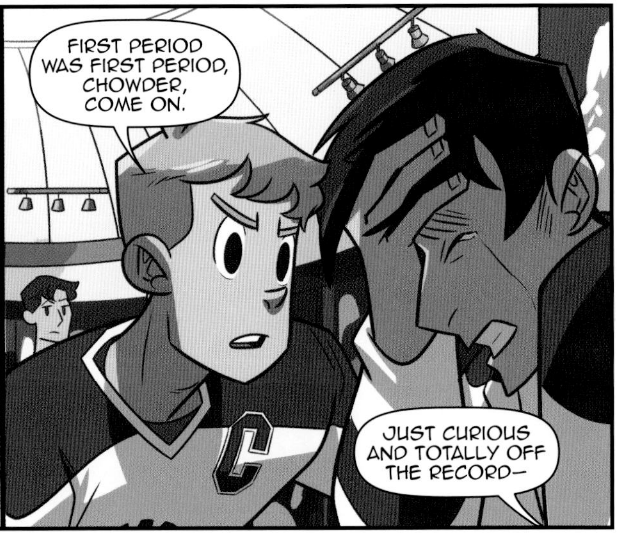
FIRST PERIOD WAS FIRST PERIOD, CHOWDER, COME ON.
JUST CURIOUS AND TOTALLY OFF THE RECORD—

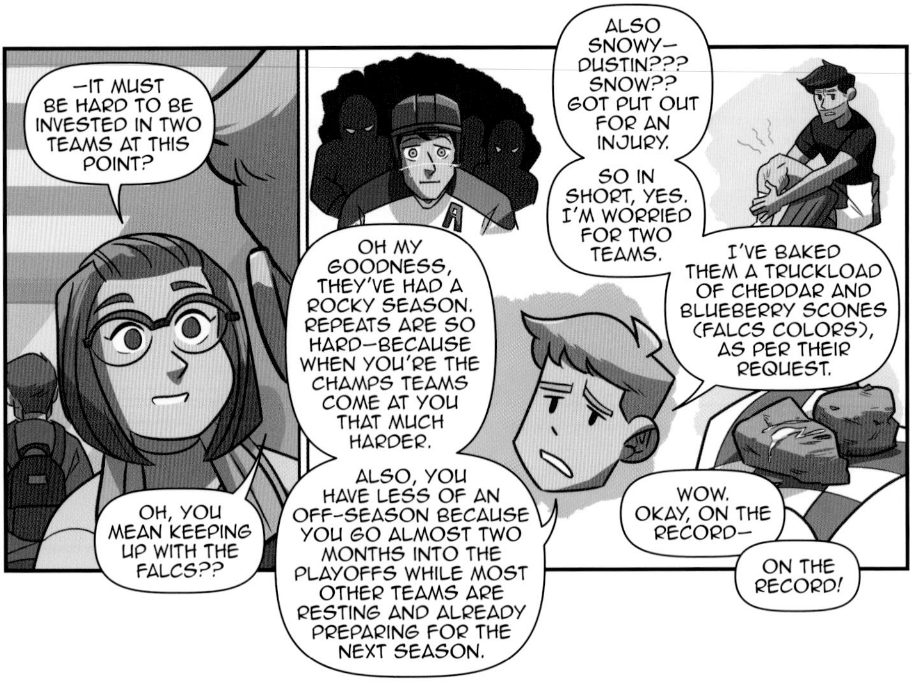
—IT MUST BE HARD TO BE INVESTED IN TWO TEAMS AT THIS POINT?
OH, YOU MEAN KEEPING UP WITH THE FALCS??
OH MY GOODNESS, THEY'VE HAD A ROCKY SEASON. REPEATS ARE SO HARD—BECAUSE WHEN YOU'RE THE CHAMPS TEAMS COME AT YOU THAT MUCH HARDER.
ALSO, YOU HAVE LESS OF AN OFF-SEASON BECAUSE YOU GO ALMOST TWO MONTHS INTO THE PLAYOFFS WHILE MOST OTHER TEAMS ARE RESTING AND ALREADY PREPARING FOR THE NEXT SEASON.
ALSO SNOWY—DUSTIN??? SNOW?? GOT PUT OUT FOR AN INJURY.
SO IN SHORT, YES. I'M WORRIED FOR TWO TEAMS.
I'VE BAKED THEM A TRUCKLOAD OF CHEDDAR AND BLUEBERRY SCONES (FALCS COLORS), AS PER THEIR REQUEST.
WOW. OKAY, ON THE RECORD—
ON THE RECORD!

Samwell men's hockey has been a welcoming space for you, but hockey is not known as the most inclusive sport. Playing against other teams, did you feel a change stepping out onto the ice this season?

In some ways yes, and in some ways no.

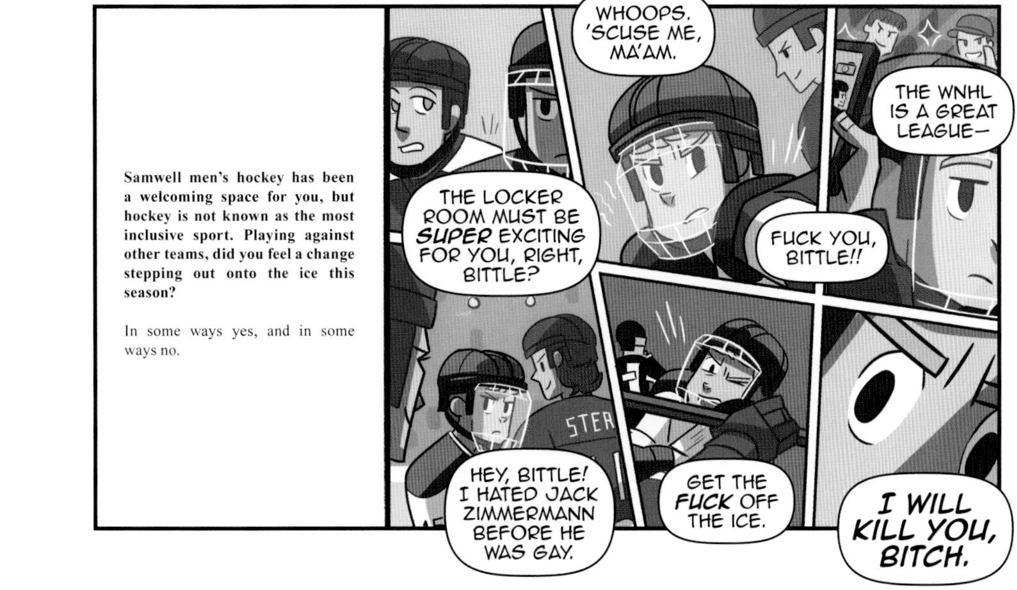
THE LOCKER ROOM MUST BE SUPER EXCITING FOR YOU, RIGHT, BITTLE?
WHOOPS. 'SCUSE ME, MA'AM.
THE WNHL IS A GREAT LEAGUE—
FUCK YOU, BITTLE!!
STER
HEY, BITTLE! I HATED JACK ZIMMERMANN BEFORE HE WAS GAY.
GET THE FUCK OFF THE ICE.
I WILL KILL YOU, BITCH.

More often than not, our opponents didn't seem to care—I was just another Samwell jersey in a play. You'll always get negative comments here and there, and people who target you, but I'm lucky to have teammates who have my back.

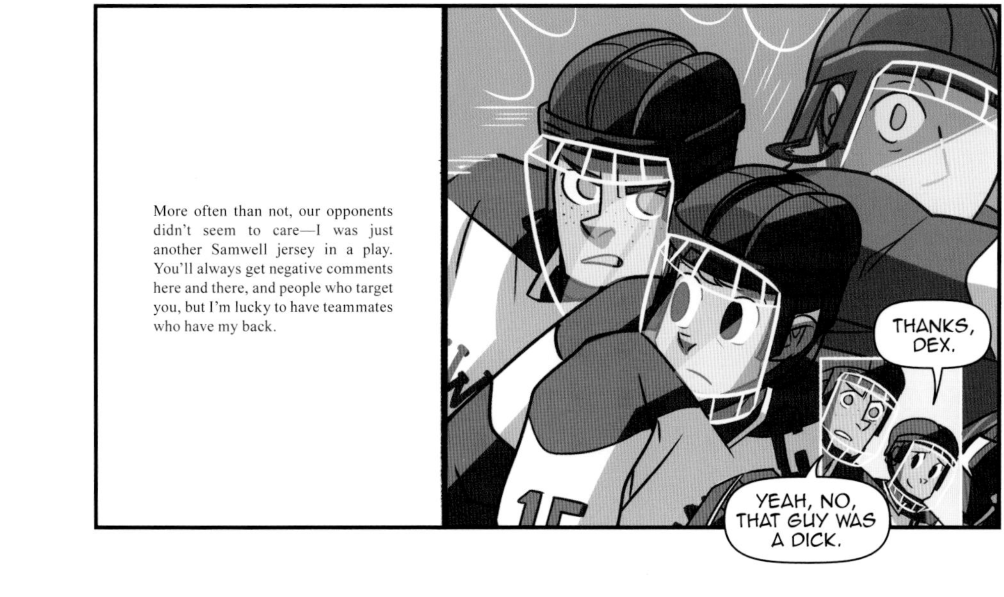
THANKS, DEX.
YEAH, NO, THAT GUY WAS A DICK.

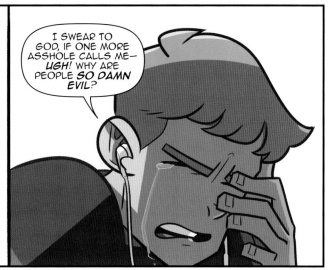

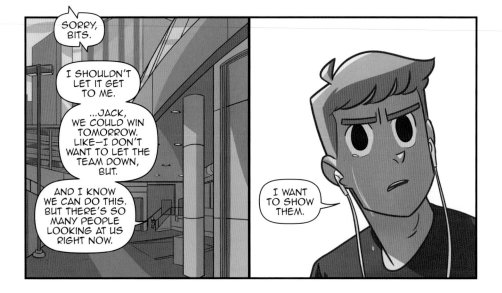

What makes Samwell a safe space for queer athletes? And Samwell men's hockey a safe space for you? How can other teams follow suit?

The culture was set way before I got here, and I hope I helped strengthen it. The type of homophobic or misogynistic talk you see in other locker rooms really gets shut down here. Even when I was a freshman some of the seniors would really be firm on that. I think some of the guys took that stance and everyone else followed suit. I think other teams just have to make that the norm. Which might be scary and might get you made fun of—but if everyone has a zero-tolerance stance on those types of comments, no one can complain.

Finally, any advice to queer athletes out there who might be reading this?

I SWEAR TO GOD, IF ONE MORE ASSHOLE CALLS ME— UGH! WHY ARE PEOPLE SO DAMN EVIL?

SORRY, BITS.
I SHOULDN'T LET IT GET TO ME.
...JACK, WE COULD WIN TOMORROW. LIKE—I DON'T WANT TO LET THE TEAM DOWN, BUT.
AND I KNOW WE CAN DO THIS. BUT THERE'S SO MANY PEOPLE LOOKING AT US RIGHT NOW.
I WANT TO SHOW THEM.

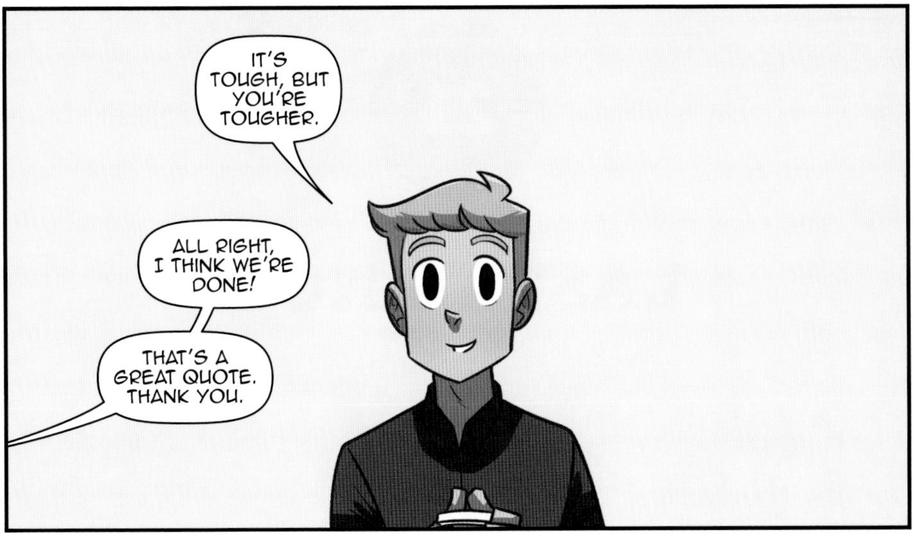
IT'S TOUGH, BUT YOU'RE TOUGHER.
ALL RIGHT, I THINK WE'RE DONE!
THAT'S A GREAT QUOTE. THANK YOU.

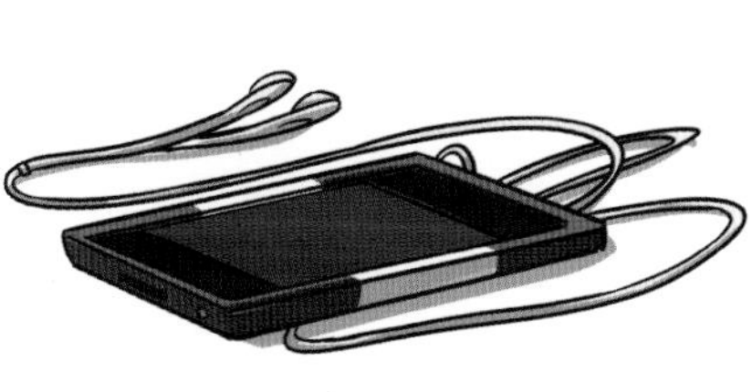

21

LAST DANCE

BITTLE
15
DO YOU KNOW WHAT A CHAMPIONSHIP WOULD MEAN TO ME?

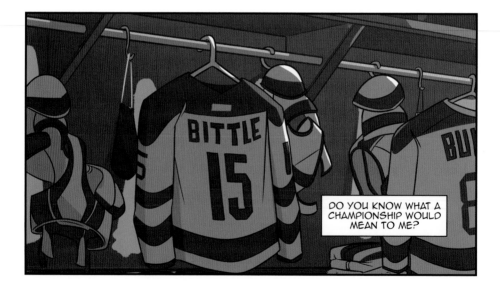

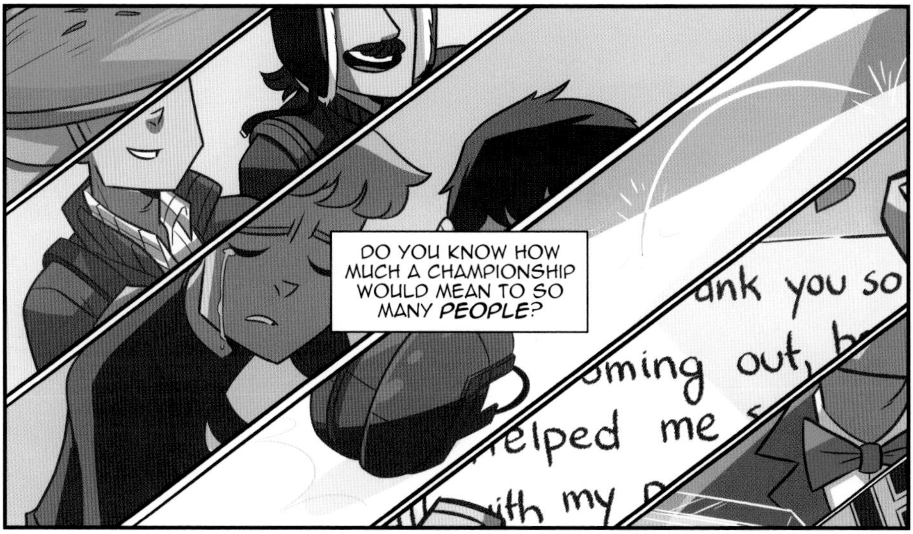
DO YOU KNOW HOW MUCH A CHAMPIONSHIP WOULD MEAN TO SO MANY *PEOPLE*?
ank you so
oming out,
elped me
ith my

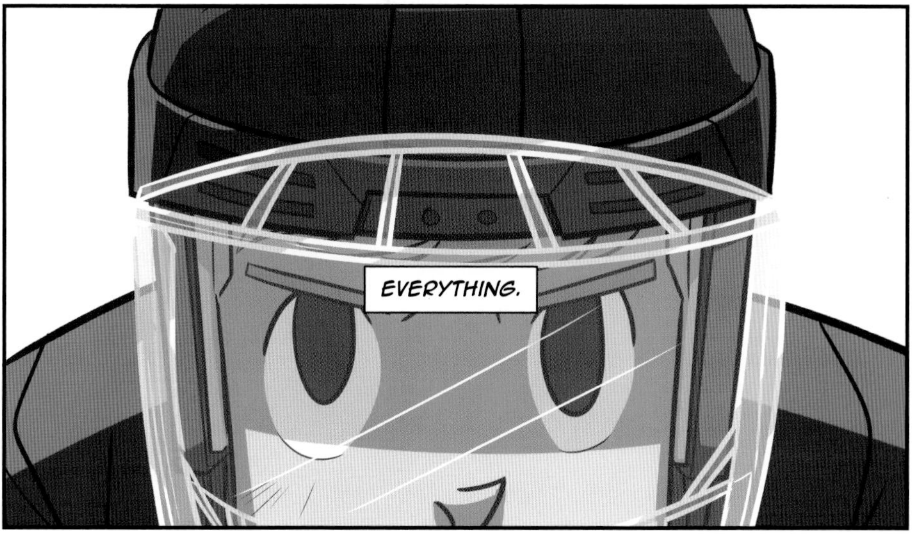
EVERYTHING.

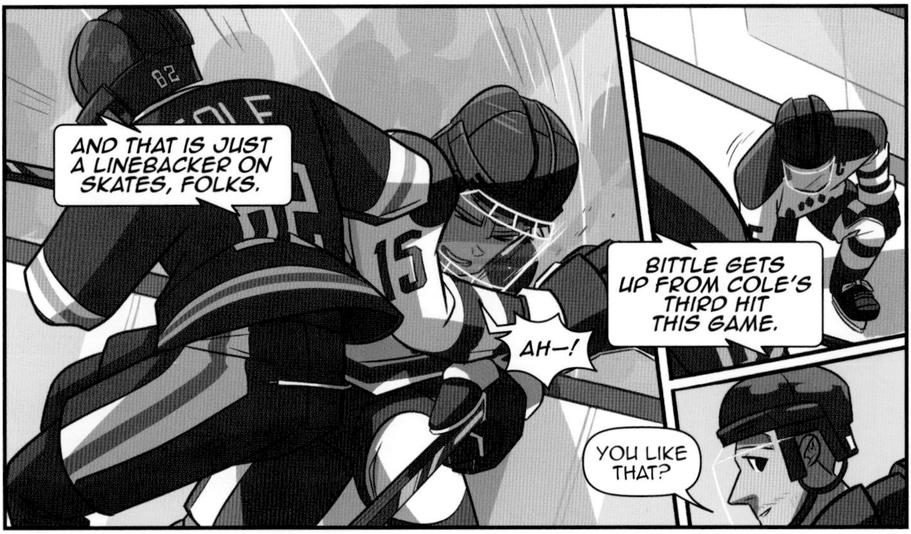
AND THAT IS JUST A LINEBACKER ON SKATES, FOLKS.
AH—!
BITTLE GETS UP FROM COLE'S THIRD HIT THIS GAME.
YOU LIKE THAT?

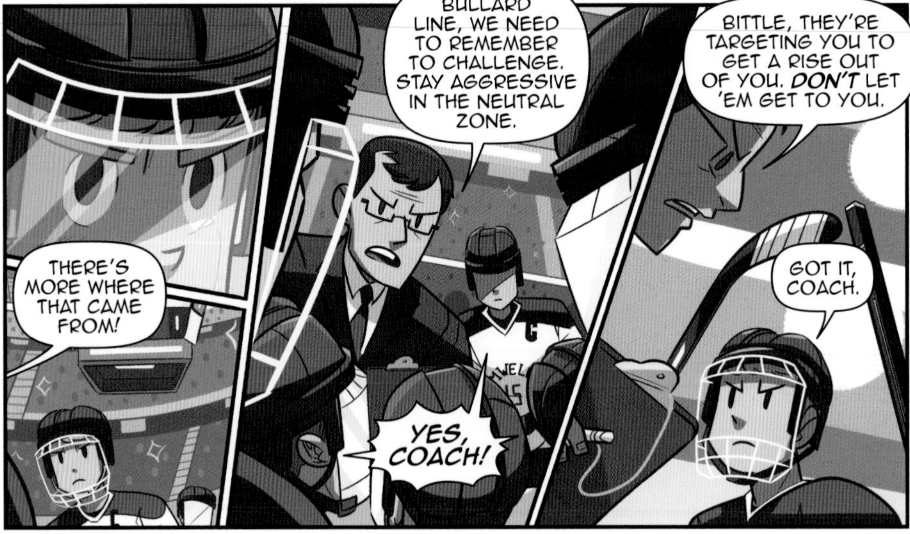
THERE'S MORE WHERE THAT CAME FROM!
BULLARD LINE, WE NEED TO REMEMBER TO CHALLENGE. STAY AGGRESSIVE IN THE NEUTRAL ZONE.
YES, COACH!
BITTLE, THEY'RE TARGETING YOU TO GET A RISE OUT OF YOU. DON'T LET 'EM GET TO YOU.
GOT IT, COACH.

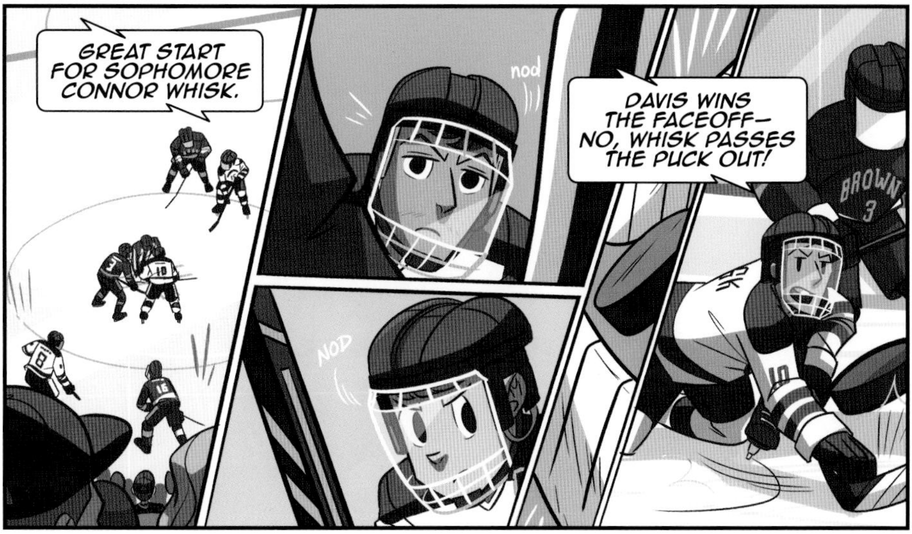
GREAT START FOR SOPHOMORE CONNOR WHISK.
nod
NOD
DAVIS WINS THE FACEOFF— NO, WHISK PASSES THE PUCK OUT!
BROWN 3

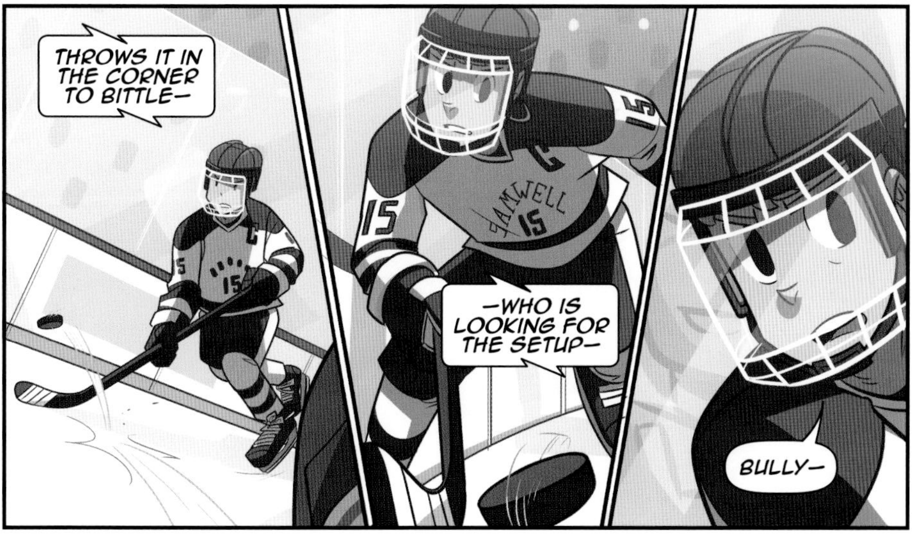
THROWS IT IN THE CORNER TO BITTLE—
SAMWELL 15
—WHO IS LOOKING FOR THE SETUP—
BULLY—

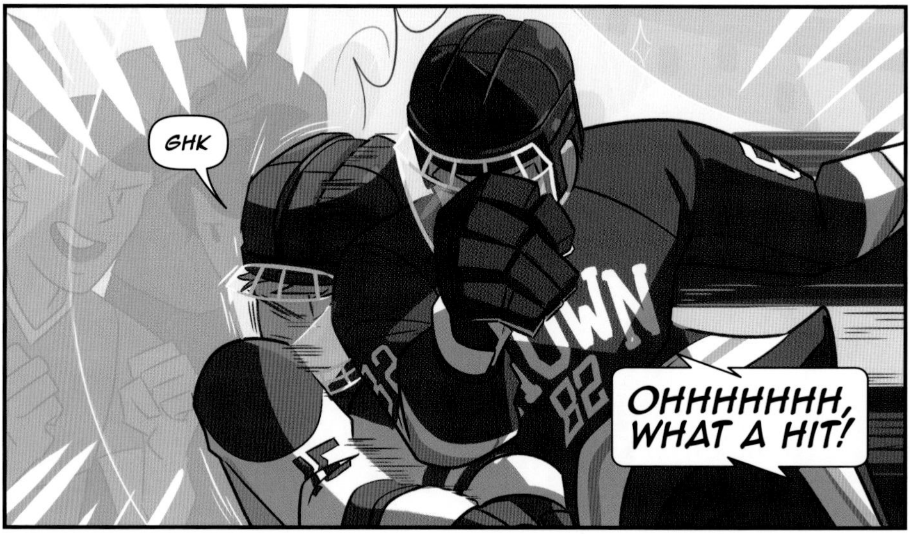
GHK
OHHHHHHH, WHAT A HIT!

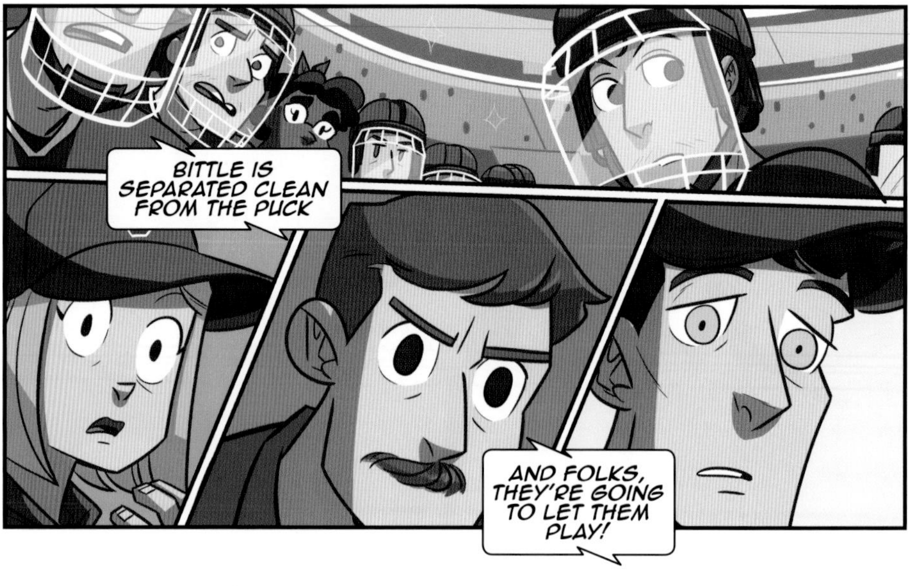
BITTLE IS SEPARATED CLEAN FROM THE PUCK
AND FOLKS, THEY'RE GOING TO LET THEM PLAY!

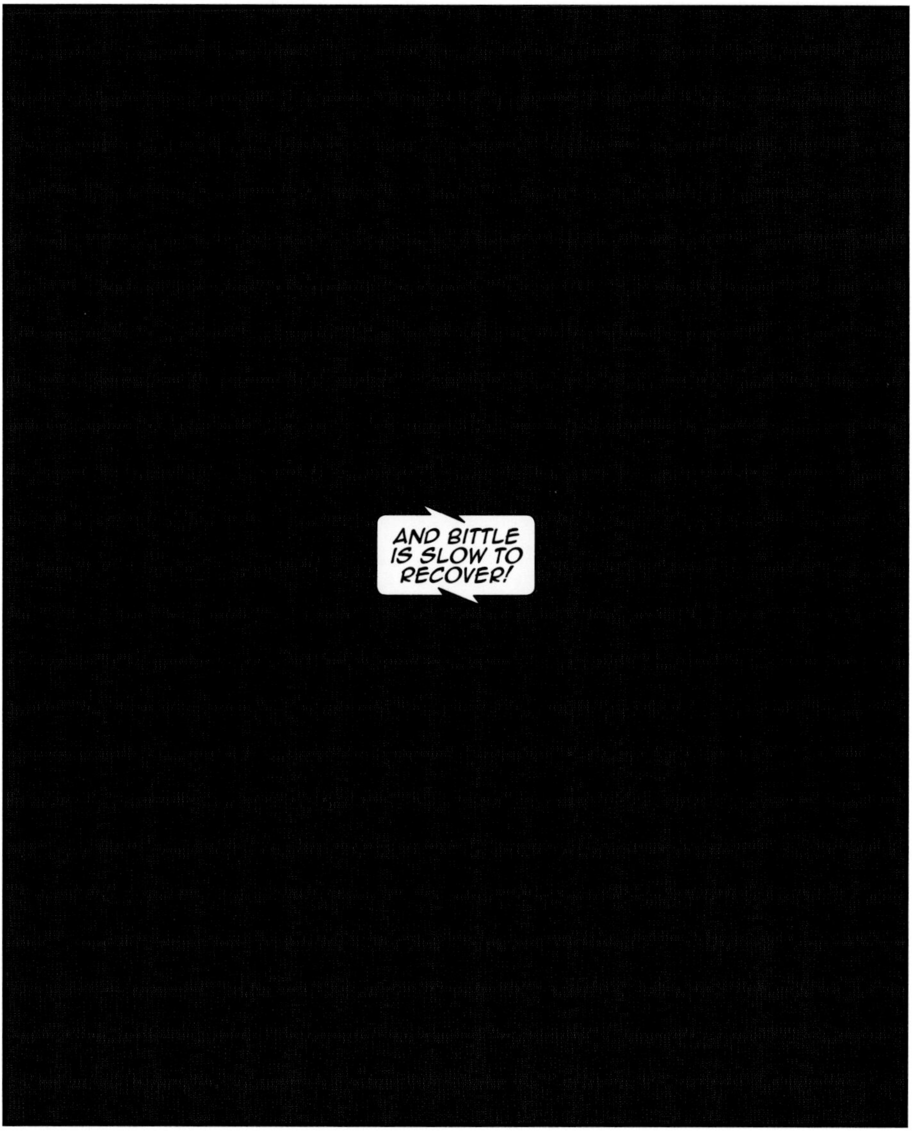
AND BITTLE IS SLOW TO RECOVER!

22

CHECK

TWEEET

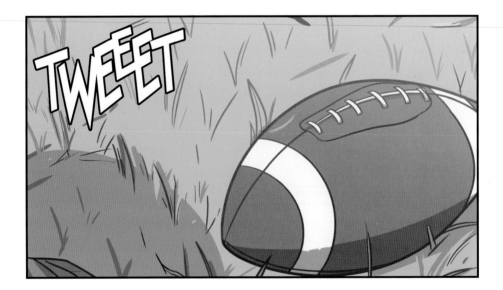

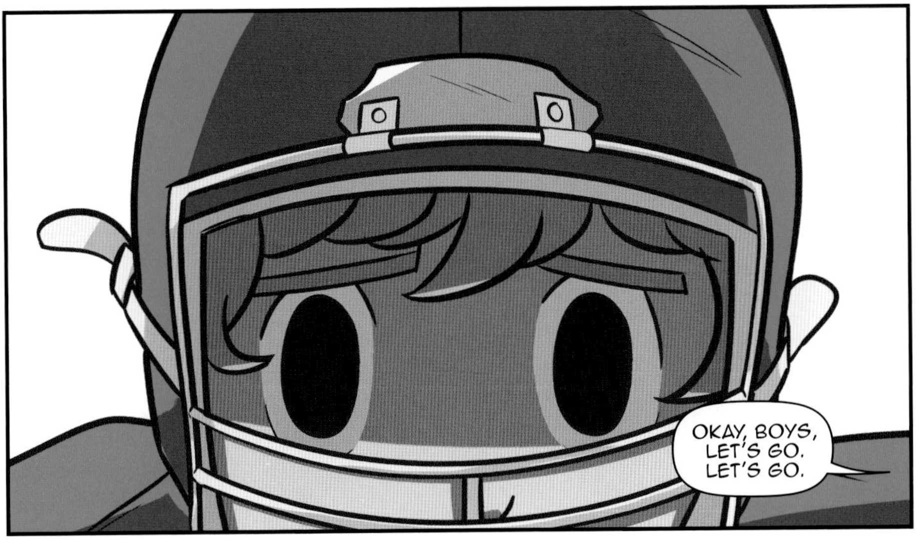
OKAY, BOYS,
LET'S GO.
LET'S GO.

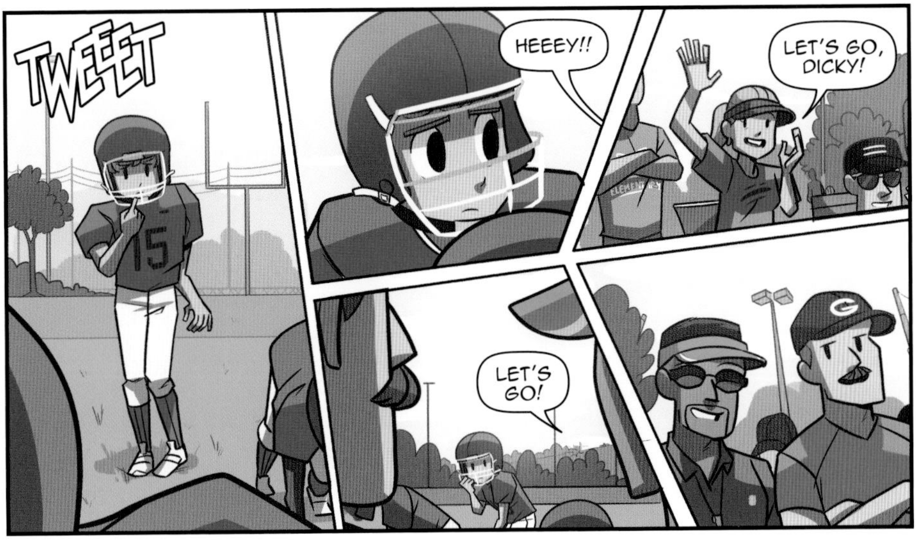
TWEEET
HEEEY!!
LET'S GO,
DICKY!
LET'S
GO!

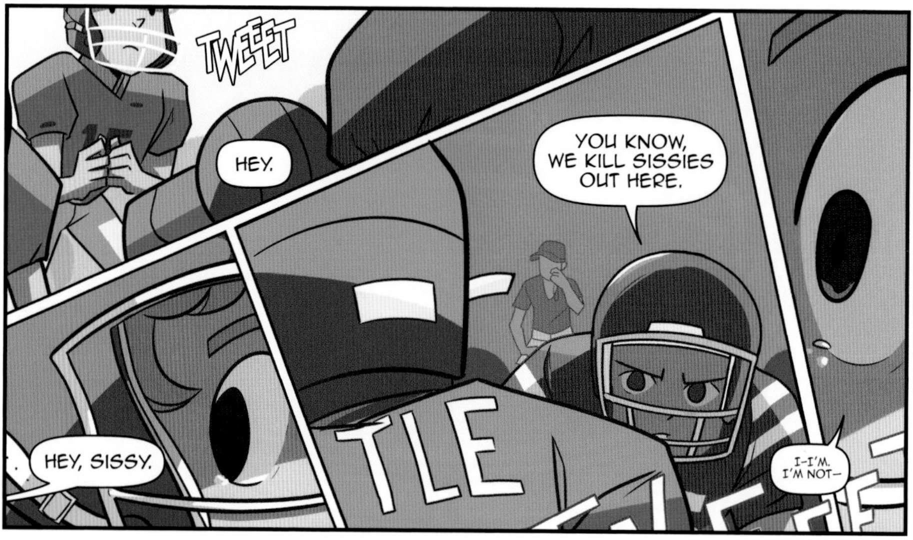
TWEEET
HEY.
YOU KNOW, WE KILL SISSIES OUT HERE.
HEY, SISSY.
I-I'M. I'M NOT—
TLE

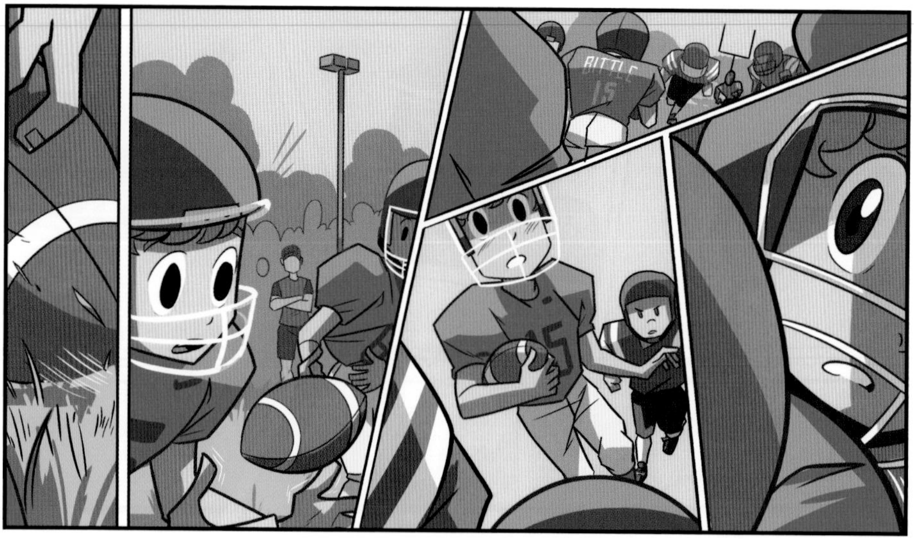
BITTLE
15

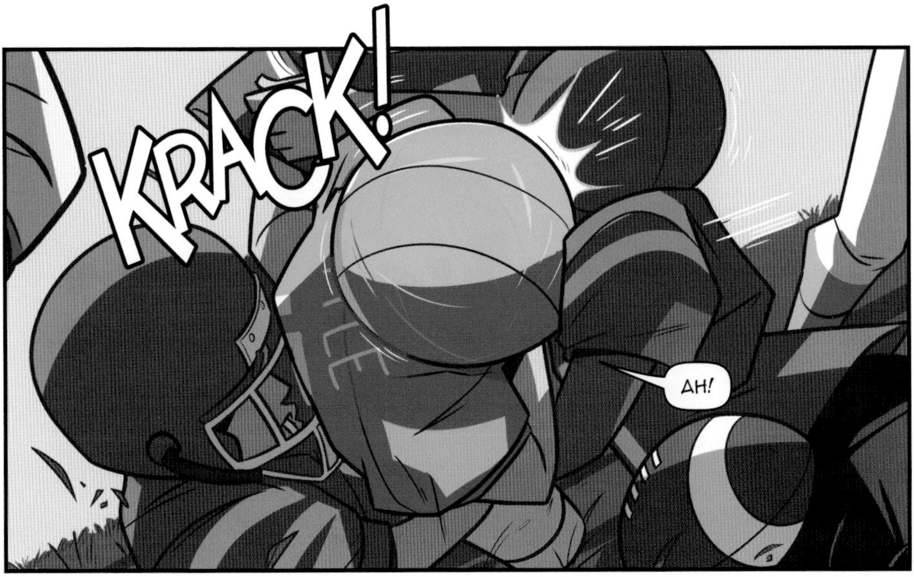
KRACK!
AH!

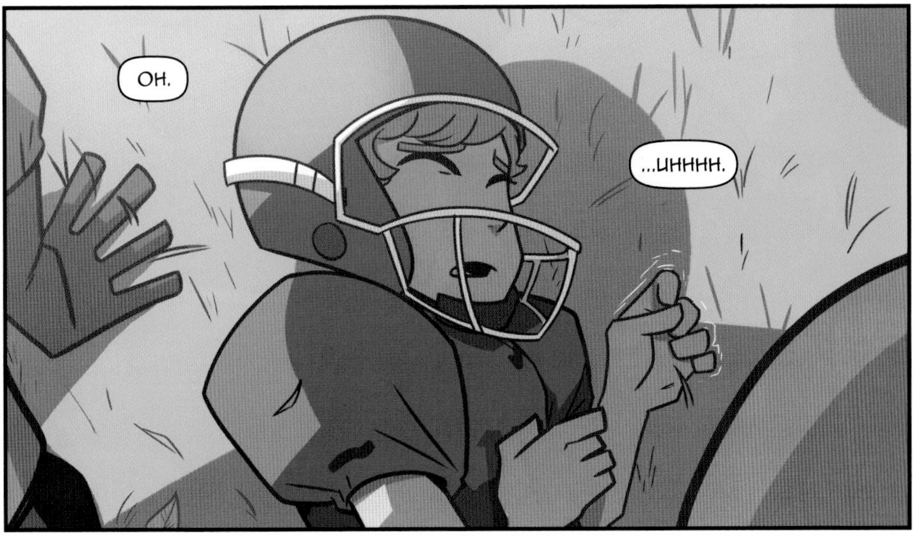
OH.
...UHHHH.

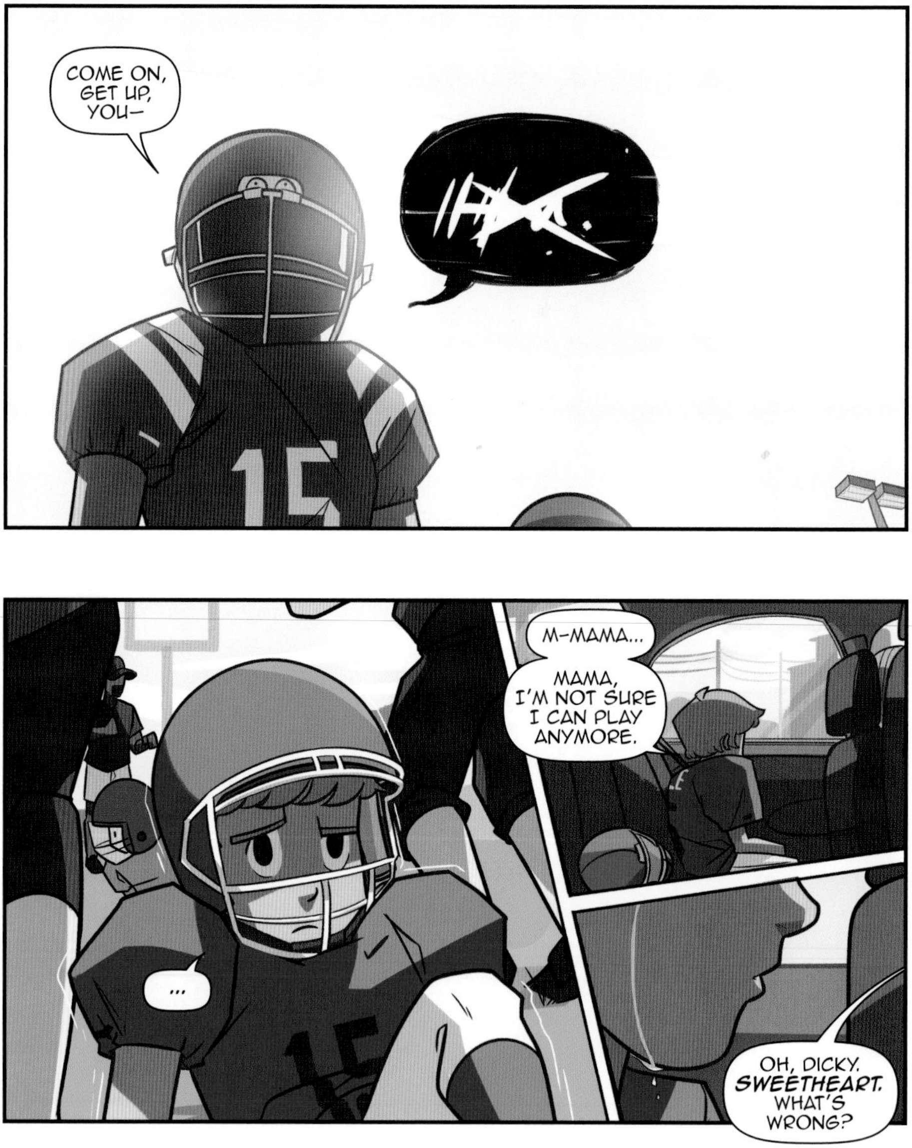
COME ON, GET UP, YOU—
M-MAMA...
MAMA, I'M NOT SURE I CAN PLAY ANYMORE.
...
OH, DICKY. **SWEETHEART.** WHAT'S WRONG?

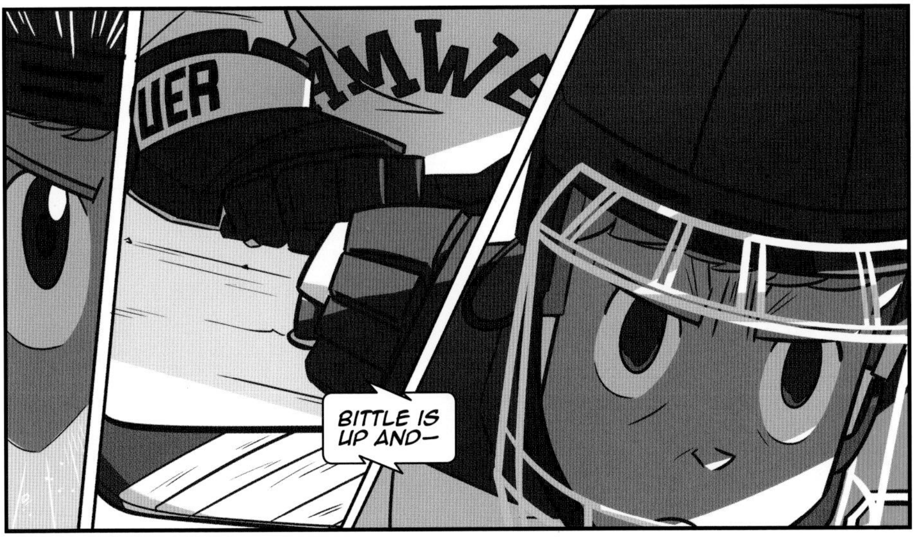
UER
BITTLE IS UP AND—

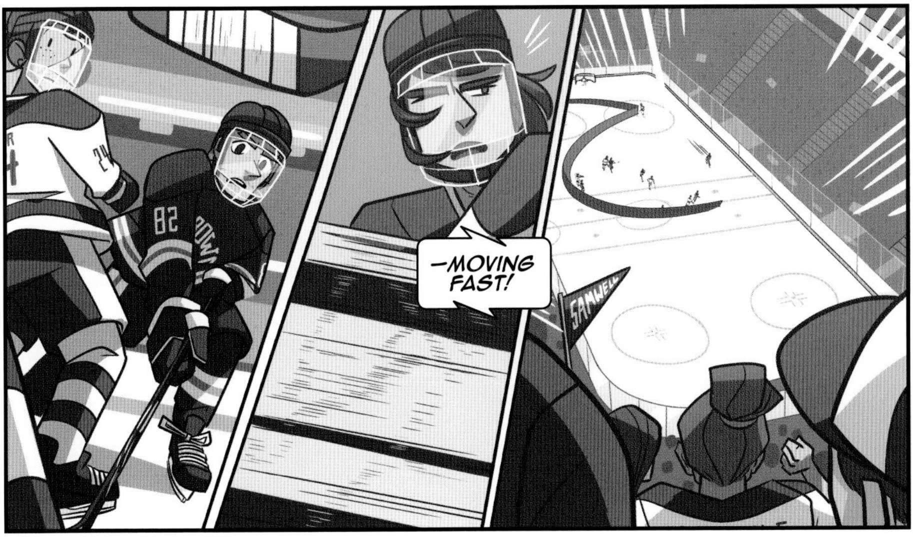
—MOVING FAST!

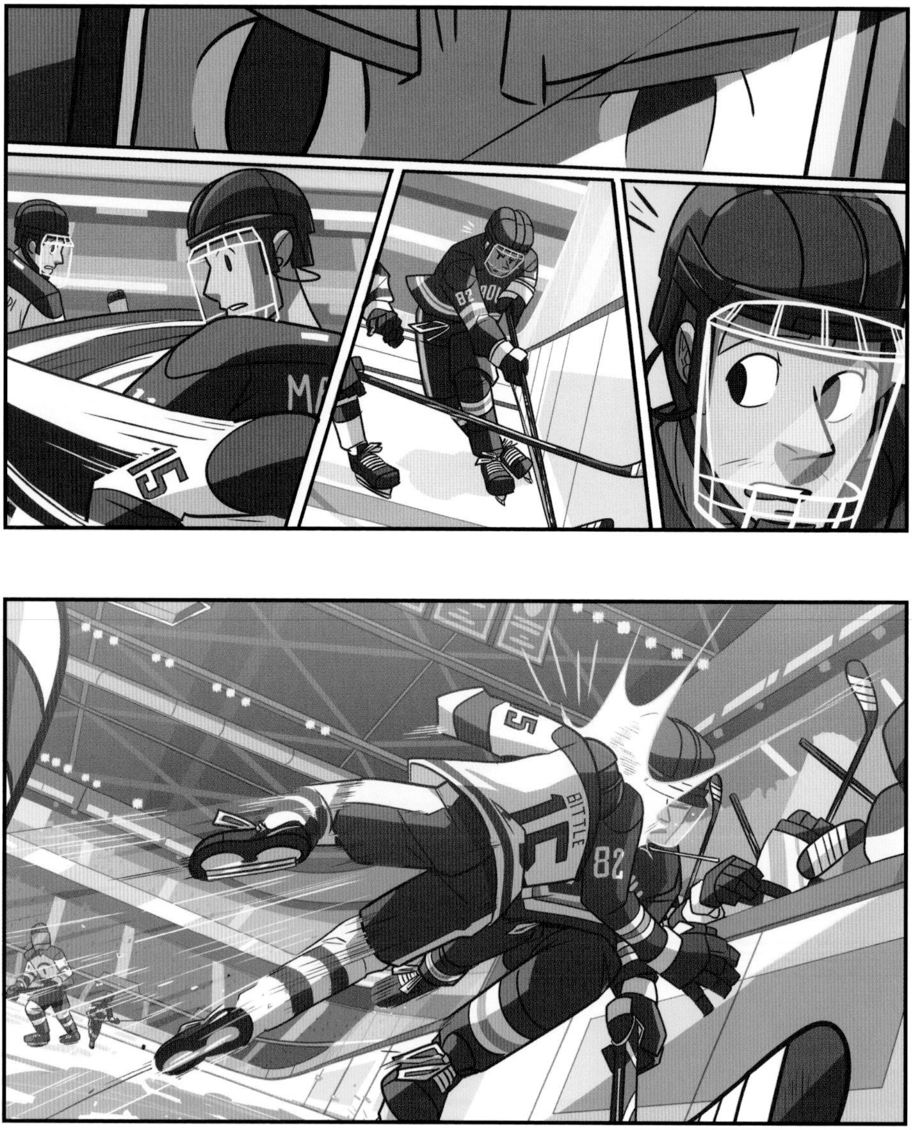
BITTLE

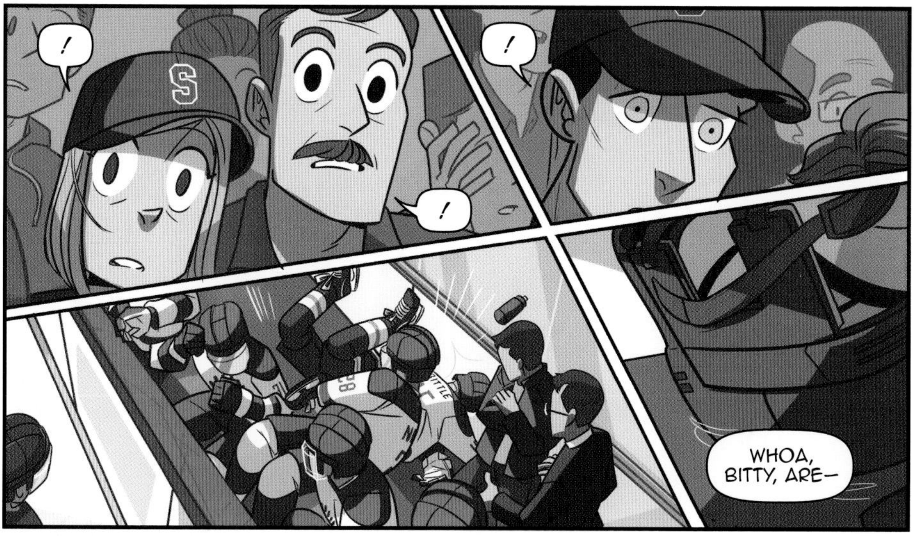
!
!
!
WHOA, BITTY, ARE—

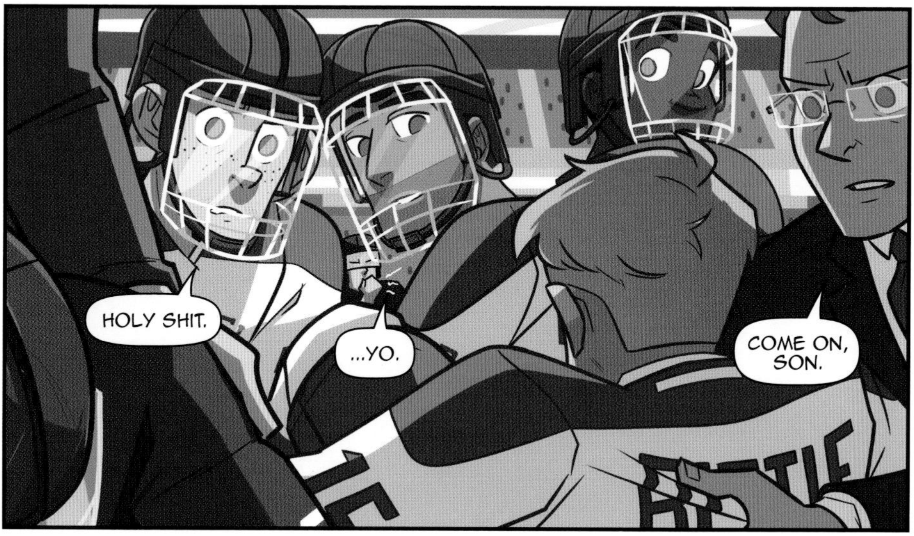
HOLY SHIT.
...YO.
COME ON, SON.

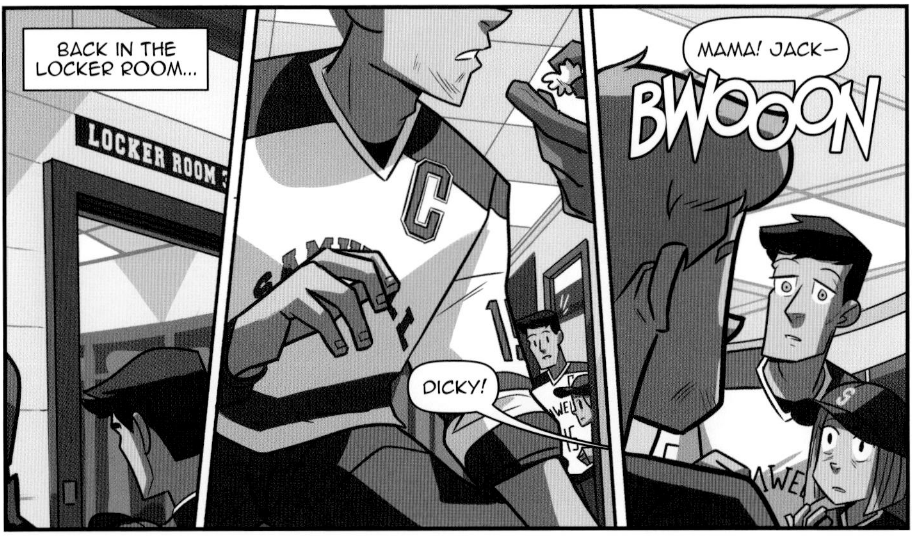
BACK IN THE LOCKER ROOM...
LOCKER ROOM 3
MAMA! JACK—
BWOOON
DICKY!

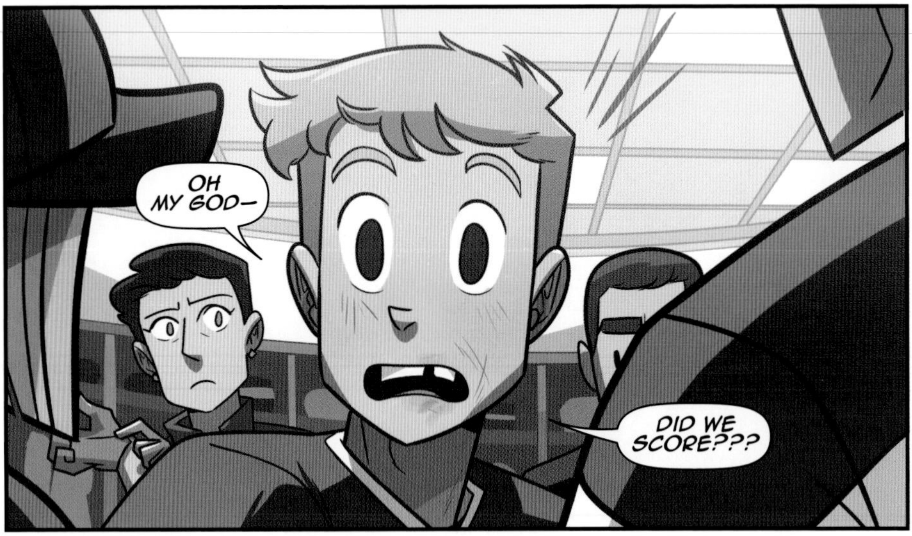
OH MY GOD—
DID WE SCORE???

23

DIBS

OH MY GOSH, Y'ALL.
SAMWELL UNIVERSITY NATIONAL CHAMPS
CAN YOU BELIEVE THEY ALMOST DIDN'T LET ME OUT ON THE ICE FOR THE CELEBRATION?

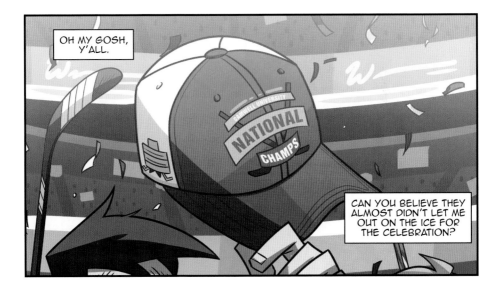

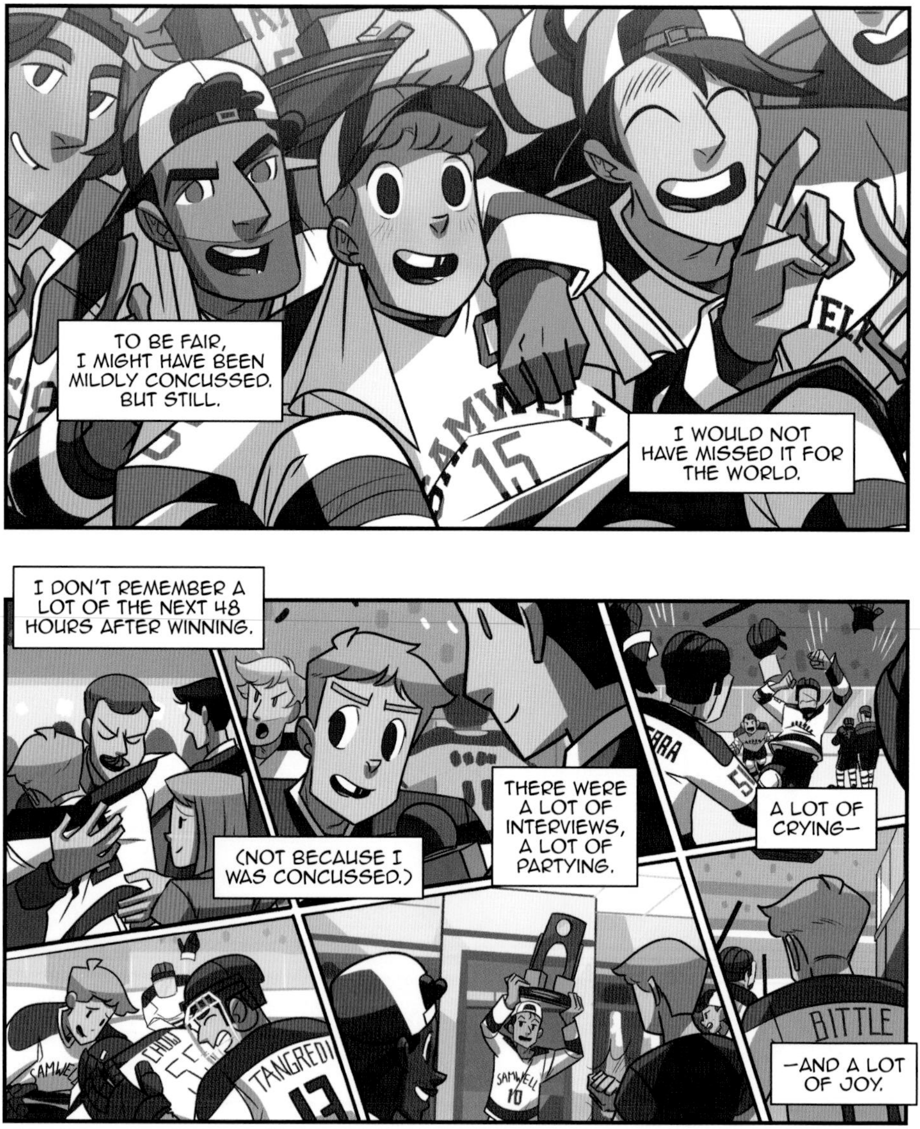
TO BE FAIR, I MIGHT HAVE BEEN MILDLY CONCUSSED. BUT STILL.
I WOULD NOT HAVE MISSED IT FOR THE WORLD.
SAMWELL
15
I DON'T REMEMBER A LOT OF THE NEXT 48 HOURS AFTER WINNING.
(NOT BECAUSE I WAS CONCUSSED.)
THERE WERE A LOT OF INTERVIEWS, A LOT OF PARTYING.
A LOT OF CRYING—
TANGREDI
13
SAMWELL
10
BITTLE
—AND A LOT OF JOY.

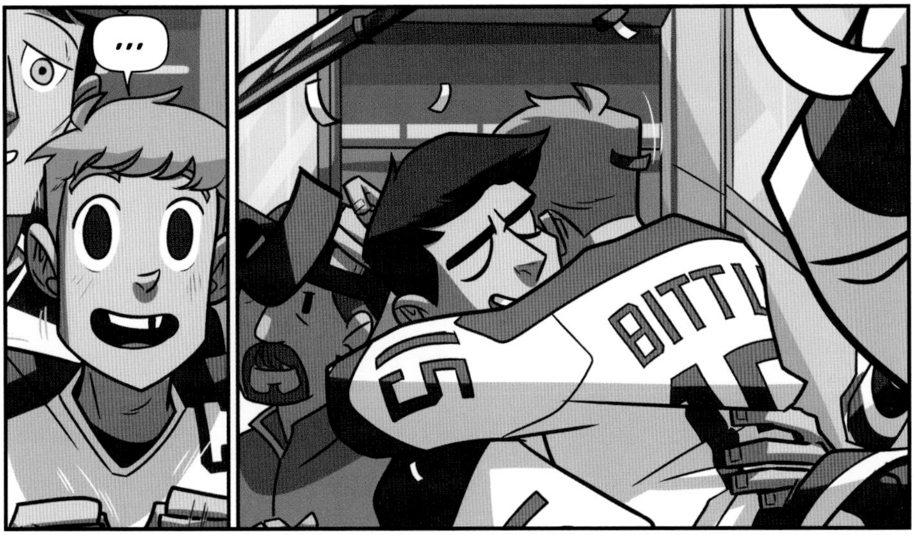
...
BITTLE
15

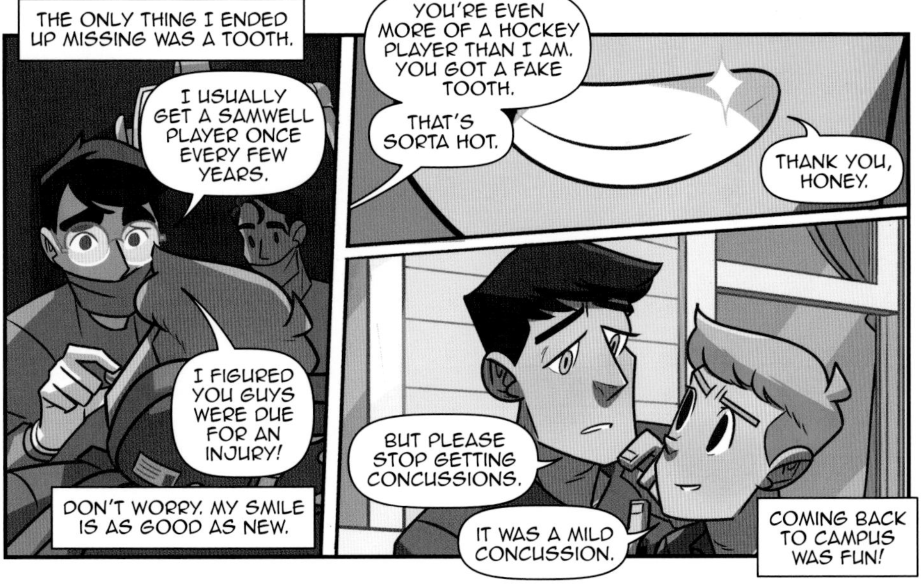
THE ONLY THING I ENDED UP MISSING WAS A TOOTH.
I USUALLY GET A SAMWELL PLAYER ONCE EVERY FEW YEARS.
I FIGURED YOU GUYS WERE DUE FOR AN INJURY!
DON'T WORRY. MY SMILE IS AS GOOD AS NEW.
YOU'RE EVEN MORE OF A HOCKEY PLAYER THAN I AM. YOU GOT A FAKE TOOTH.
THAT'S SORTA HOT.
THANK YOU, HONEY.
BUT PLEASE STOP GETTING CONCUSSIONS.
IT WAS A MILD CONCUSSION.
COMING BACK TO CAMPUS WAS FUN!

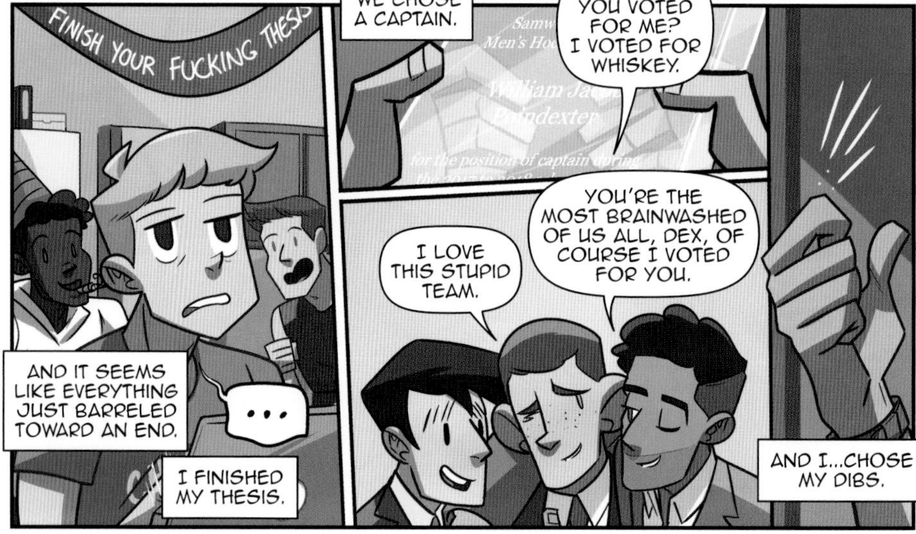
FINISH YOUR FUCKING THESIS
AND IT SEEMS LIKE EVERYTHING JUST BARRELED TOWARD AN END.
...
I FINISHED MY THESIS.
WE CHOSE A CAPTAIN.
NURSEY, YOU VOTED FOR ME? I VOTED FOR WHISKEY.
I LOVE THIS STUPID TEAM.
YOU'RE THE MOST BRAINWASHED OF US ALL, DEX, OF COURSE I VOTED FOR YOU.
AND I...CHOSE MY DIBS.

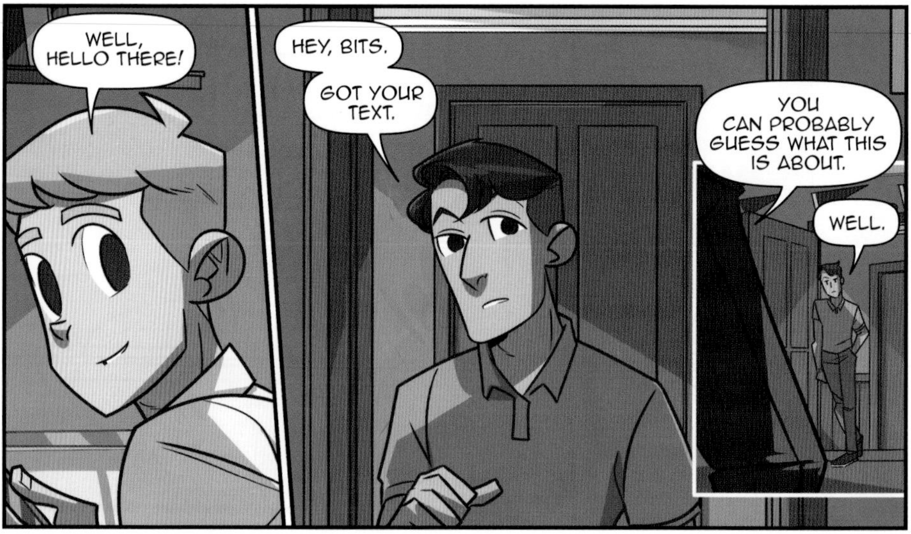
WELL, HELLO THERE!
HEY, BITS.
GOT YOUR TEXT.
YOU CAN PROBABLY GUESS WHAT THIS IS ABOUT.
WELL.

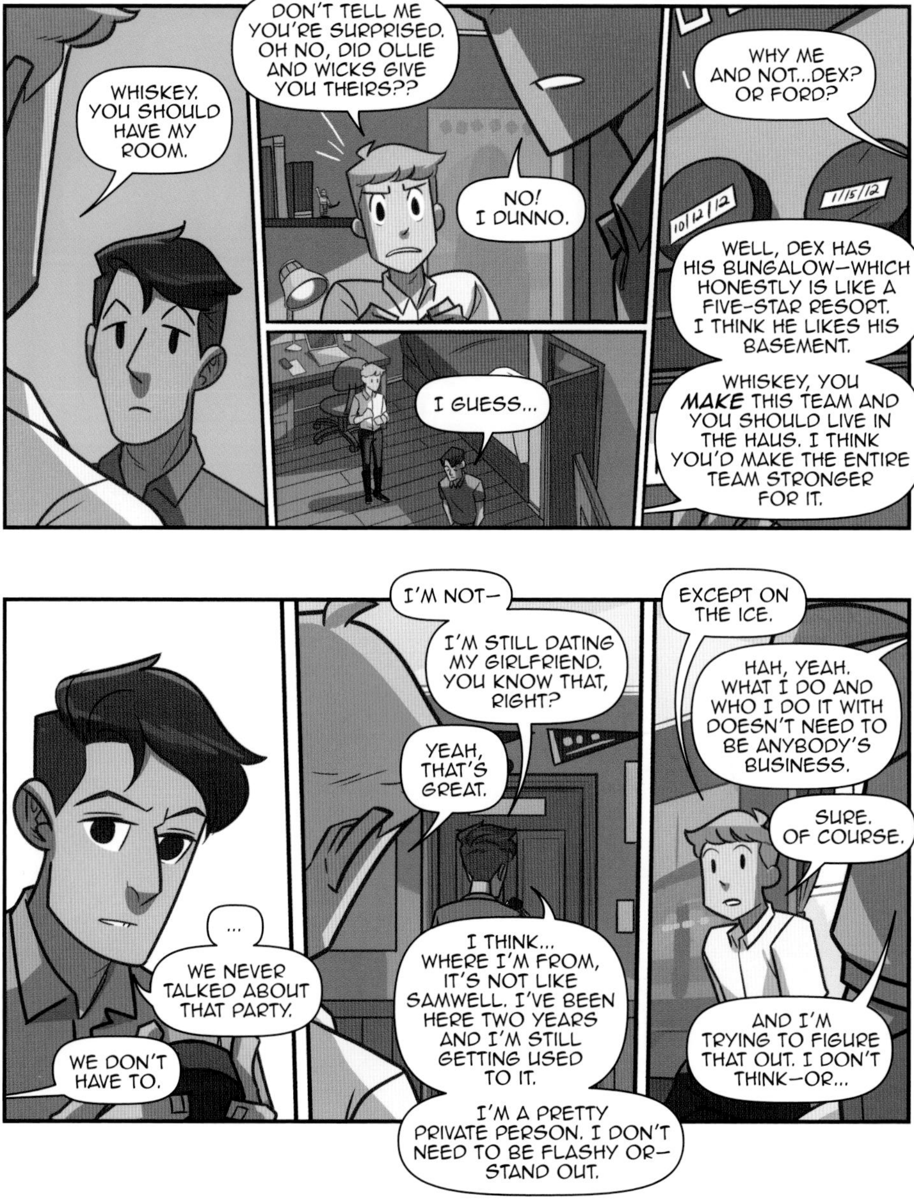
WHISKEY. YOU SHOULD HAVE MY ROOM.
DON'T TELL ME YOU'RE SURPRISED. OH NO, DID OLLIE AND WICKS GIVE YOU THEIRS??
NO! I DUNNO.
WHY ME AND NOT...DEX? OR FORD?
10/12/12
1/15/12
WELL, DEX HAS HIS BUNGALOW—WHICH HONESTLY IS LIKE A FIVE-STAR RESORT. I THINK HE LIKES HIS BASEMENT.
I GUESS...
WHISKEY, YOU *MAKE* THIS TEAM AND YOU SHOULD LIVE IN THE HAUS. I THINK YOU'D MAKE THE ENTIRE TEAM STRONGER FOR IT.
...
WE NEVER TALKED ABOUT THAT PARTY.
WE DON'T HAVE TO.
I'M NOT—
I'M STILL DATING MY GIRLFRIEND. YOU KNOW THAT, RIGHT?
YEAH, THAT'S GREAT.
I THINK... WHERE I'M FROM, IT'S NOT LIKE SAMWELL. I'VE BEEN HERE TWO YEARS AND I'M STILL GETTING USED TO IT.
I'M A PRETTY PRIVATE PERSON. I DON'T NEED TO BE FLASHY OR—STAND OUT.
EXCEPT ON THE ICE.
HAH, YEAH. WHAT I DO AND WHO I DO IT WITH DOESN'T NEED TO BE ANYBODY'S BUSINESS.
SURE. OF COURSE.
AND I'M TRYING TO FIGURE THAT OUT. I DON'T THINK—OR...

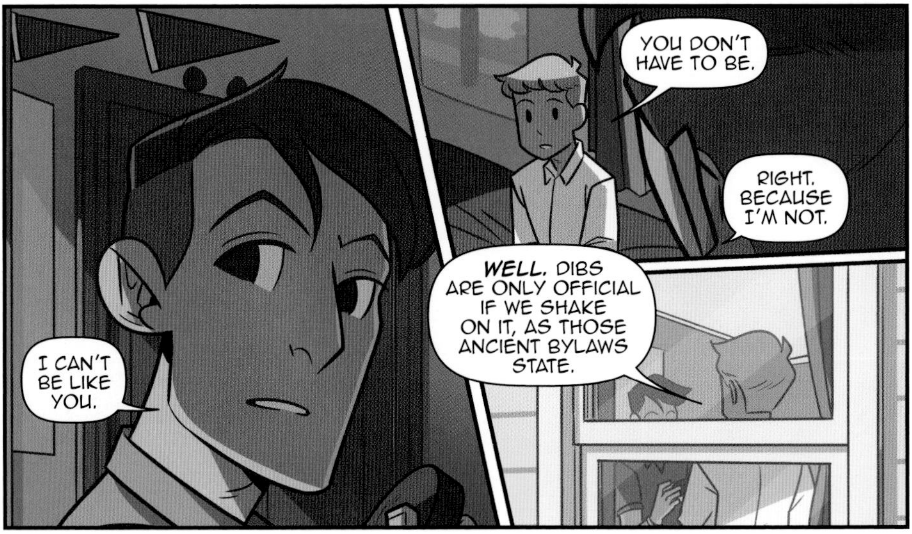
I CAN'T BE LIKE YOU.
YOU DON'T HAVE TO BE.
RIGHT. BECAUSE I'M NOT.
WELL. DIBS ARE ONLY OFFICIAL IF WE SHAKE ON IT, AS THOSE ANCIENT BYLAWS STATE.

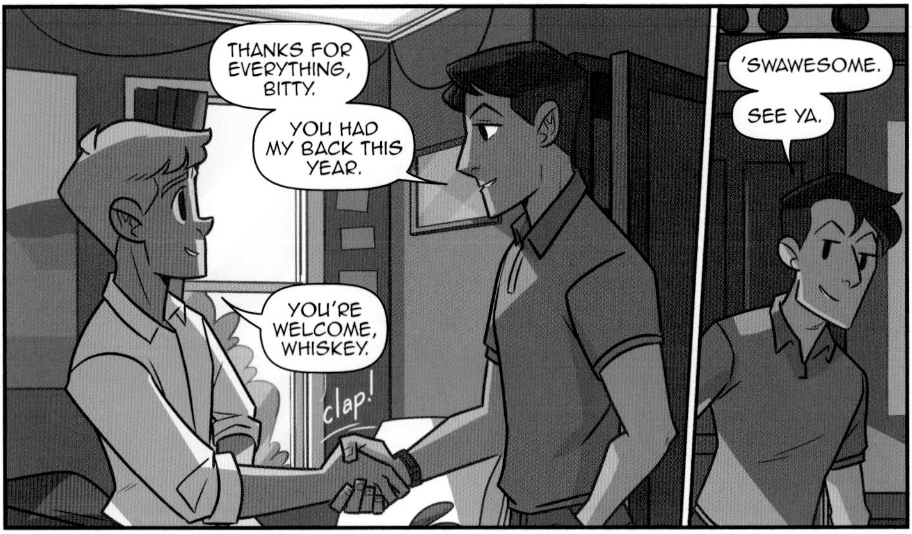
THANKS FOR EVERYTHING, BITTY.
YOU HAD MY BACK THIS YEAR.
YOU'RE WELCOME, WHISKEY.
clap!
'SWAWESOME.
SEE YA.

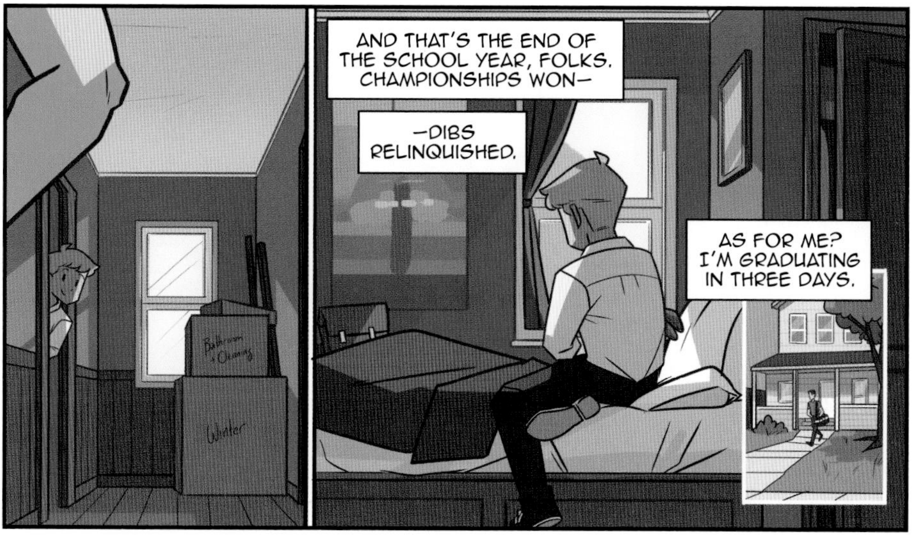
Bathroom + Cleaning
Winter
AND THAT'S THE END OF THE SCHOOL YEAR, FOLKS. CHAMPIONSHIPS WON—
—DIBS RELINQUISHED.
AS FOR ME? I'M GRADUATING IN THREE DAYS.

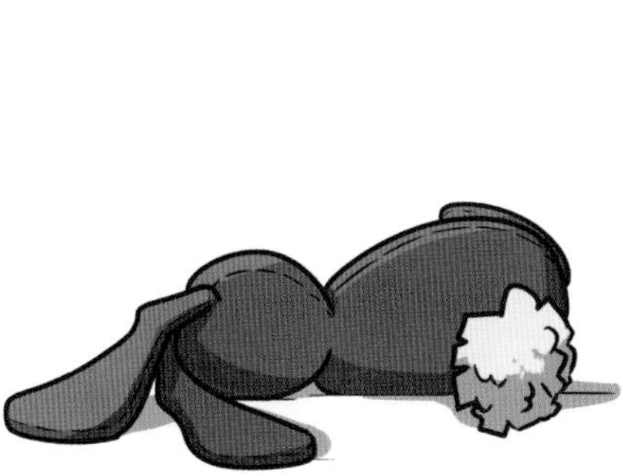

24

CLASS DAY

AND FINALLY...
"THE RACHEL GRAHAM MEMORIAL AND CLASS DAY PRIZE IS AWARDED TO THAT SENIOR WHOSE STRENGTH OF CHARACTER AND PERSISTENCE—
"SHALL BE ADJUDGED BY THE FACULTY TO HAVE PROVIDED LEADERSHIP FOR HIS OR HER FELLOW STUDENTS, INSPIRING THEM TO PRACTICE THE HIGHEST IDEALS FOR THEMSELVES AND OTHERS."
WE HONOR ERIC RICHARD BITTLE WITH THIS CLASS DAY PRIZE AND WELCOME HIM AS OUR STUDENT SPEAKER.

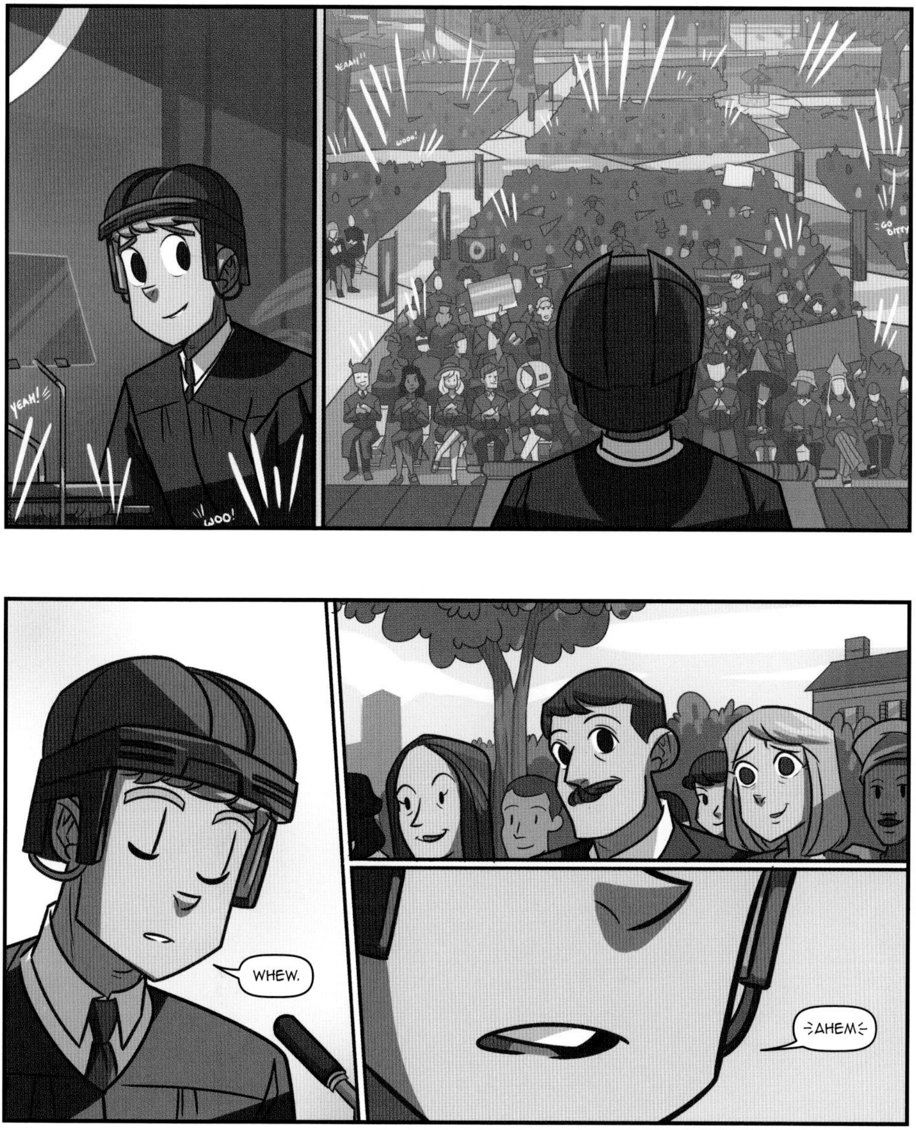
YEAH!
WOO!
YEAAH!!
WOOO!
GO BITTY
WHEW.
AHEM

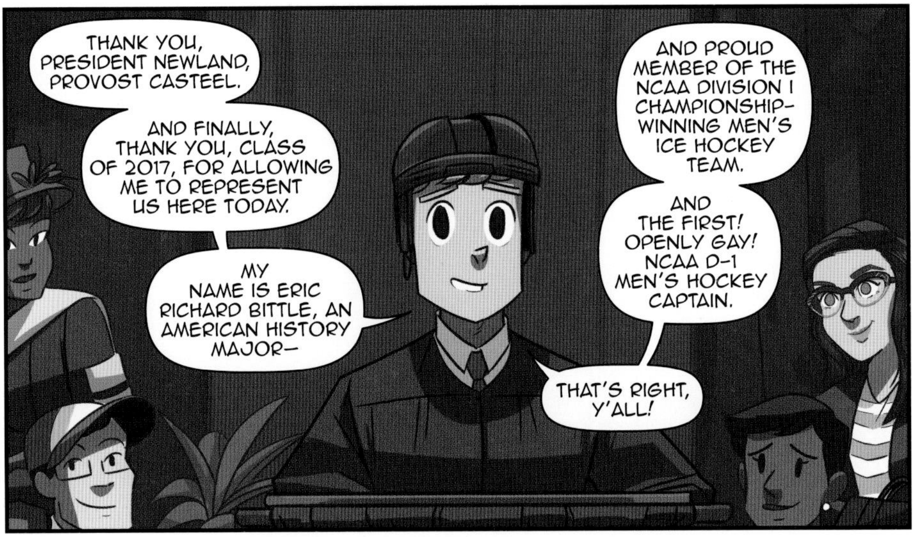
THANK YOU, PRESIDENT NEWLAND, PROVOST CASTEEL.
AND FINALLY, THANK YOU, CLASS OF 2017, FOR ALLOWING ME TO REPRESENT US HERE TODAY.
MY NAME IS ERIC RICHARD BITTLE, AN AMERICAN HISTORY MAJOR—
AND PROUD MEMBER OF THE NCAA DIVISION I CHAMPIONSHIP-WINNING MEN'S ICE HOCKEY TEAM.
AND THE FIRST! OPENLY GAY! NCAA D-1 MEN'S HOCKEY CAPTAIN.
THAT'S RIGHT, Y'ALL!

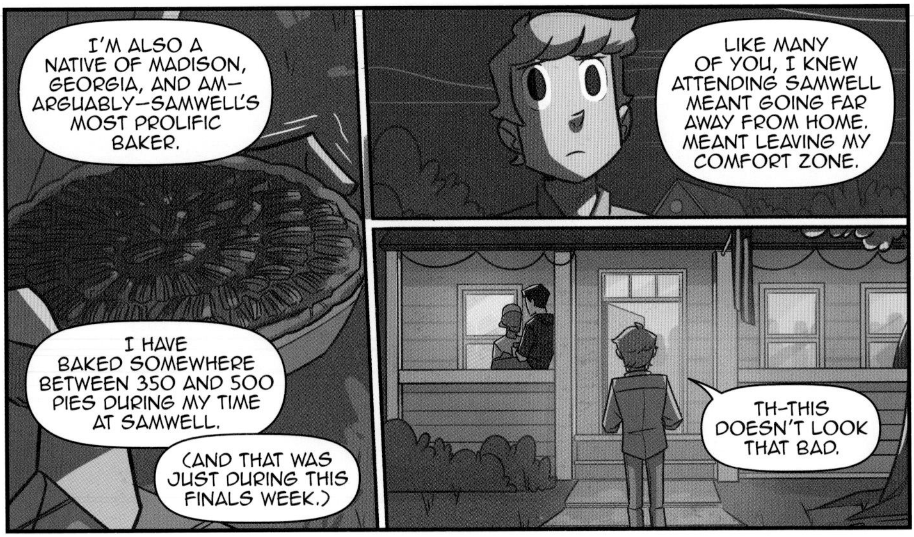
I'M ALSO A NATIVE OF MADISON, GEORGIA, AND AM—ARGUABLY—SAMWELL'S MOST PROLIFIC BAKER.
I HAVE BAKED SOMEWHERE BETWEEN 350 AND 500 PIES DURING MY TIME AT SAMWELL.
(AND THAT WAS JUST DURING THIS FINALS WEEK.)
LIKE MANY OF YOU, I KNEW ATTENDING SAMWELL MEANT GOING FAR AWAY FROM HOME. MEANT LEAVING MY COMFORT ZONE.
TH-THIS DOESN'T LOOK THAT BAD.

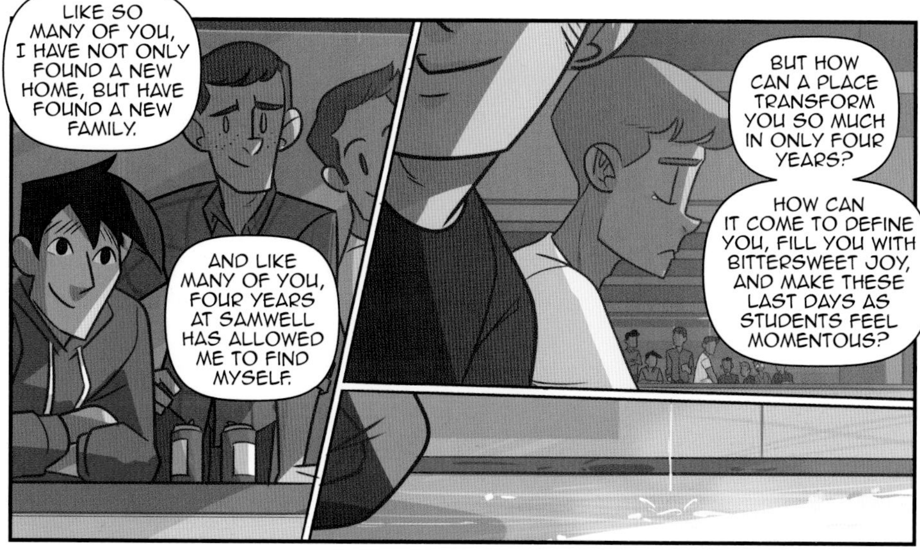
LIKE SO MANY OF YOU, I HAVE NOT ONLY FOUND A NEW HOME, BUT HAVE FOUND A NEW FAMILY.
AND LIKE MANY OF YOU, FOUR YEARS AT SAMWELL HAS ALLOWED ME TO FIND MYSELF.
BUT HOW CAN A PLACE TRANSFORM YOU SO MUCH IN ONLY FOUR YEARS?
HOW CAN IT COME TO DEFINE YOU, FILL YOU WITH BITTERSWEET JOY, AND MAKE THESE LAST DAYS AS STUDENTS FEEL MOMENTOUS?

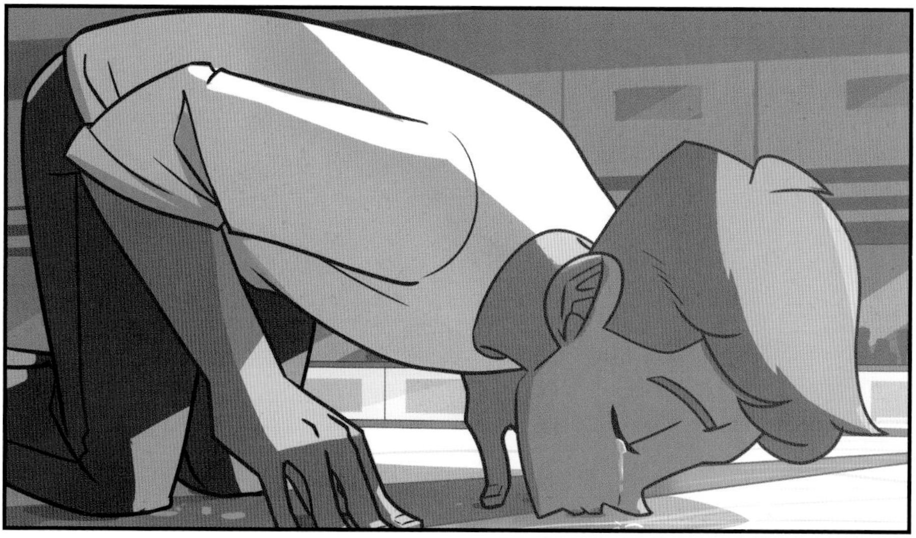

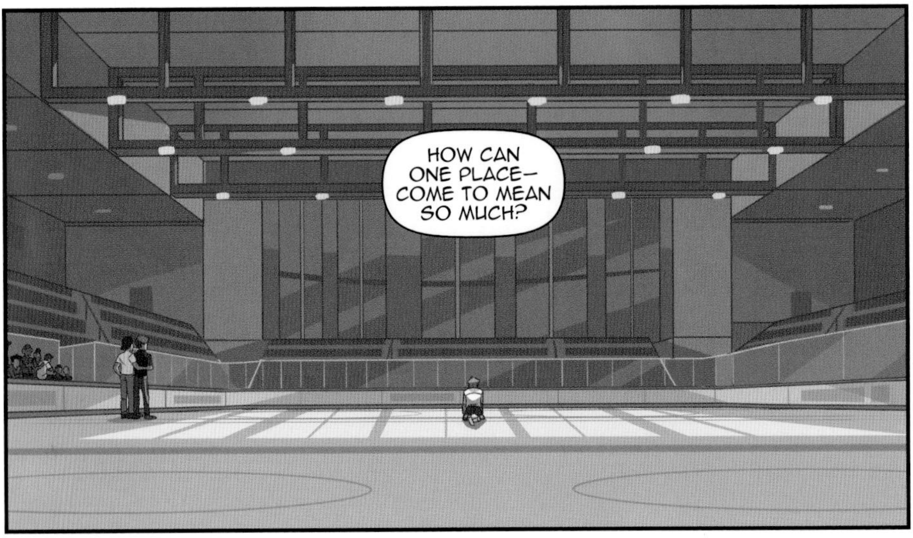
HOW CAN ONE PLACE— COME TO MEAN SO MUCH?

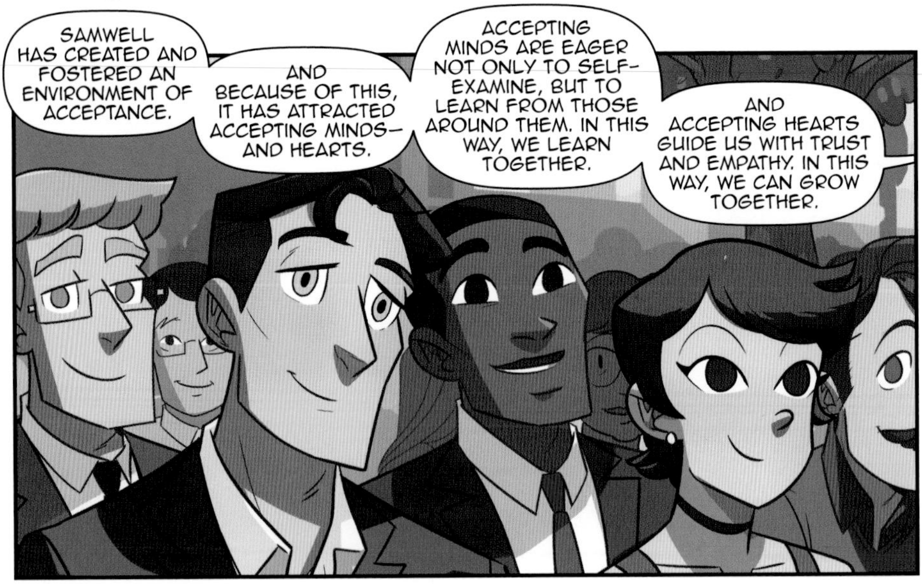
SAMWELL HAS CREATED AND FOSTERED AN ENVIRONMENT OF ACCEPTANCE.
AND BECAUSE OF THIS, IT HAS ATTRACTED ACCEPTING MINDS— AND HEARTS.
ACCEPTING MINDS ARE EAGER NOT ONLY TO SELF-EXAMINE, BUT TO LEARN FROM THOSE AROUND THEM. IN THIS WAY, WE LEARN TOGETHER.
AND ACCEPTING HEARTS GUIDE US WITH TRUST AND EMPATHY. IN THIS WAY, WE CAN GROW TOGETHER.

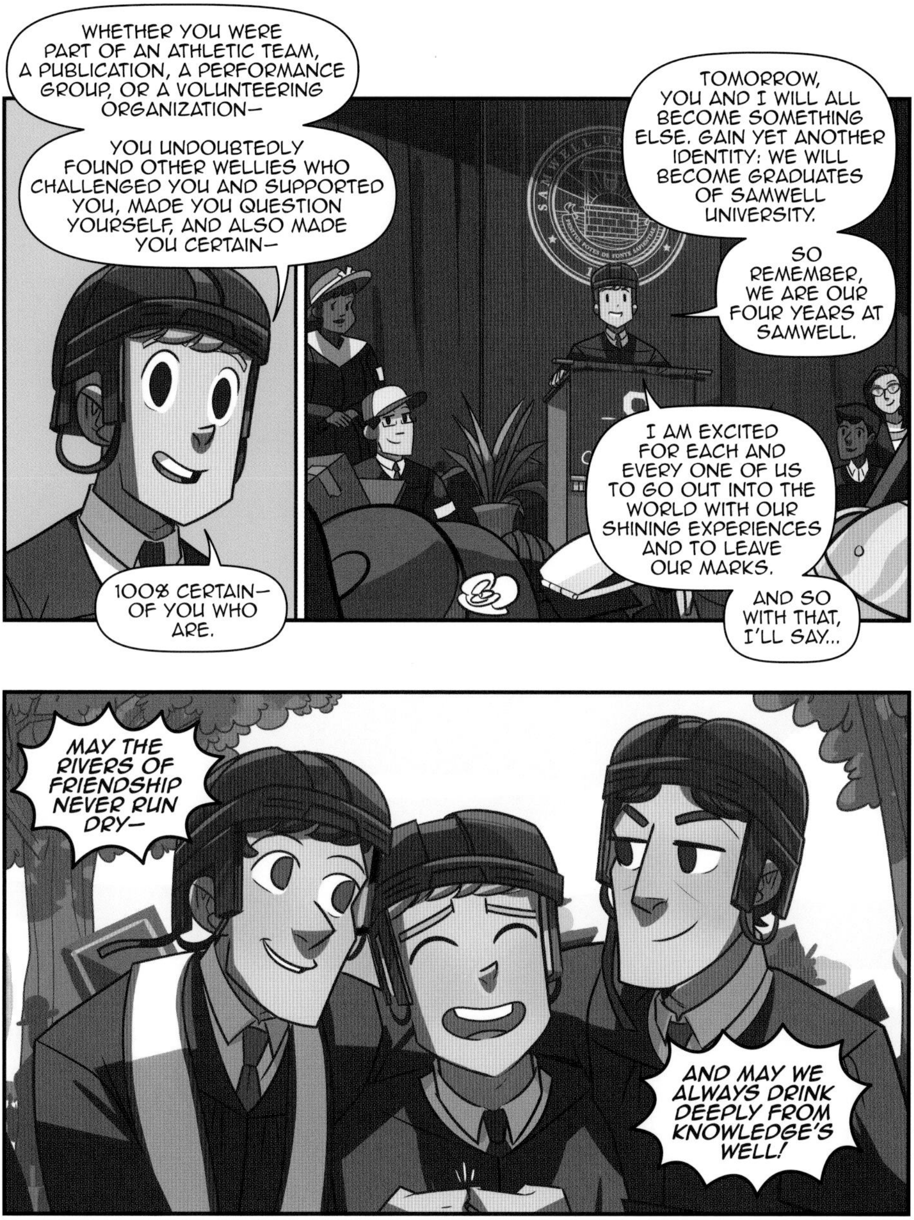
WHETHER YOU WERE PART OF AN ATHLETIC TEAM, A PUBLICATION, A PERFORMANCE GROUP, OR A VOLUNTEERING ORGANIZATION—
YOU UNDOUBTEDLY FOUND OTHER WELLIES WHO CHALLENGED YOU AND SUPPORTED YOU, MADE YOU QUESTION YOURSELF, AND ALSO MADE YOU CERTAIN—
100% CERTAIN—OF YOU WHO ARE.
TOMORROW, YOU AND I WILL ALL BECOME SOMETHING ELSE. GAIN YET ANOTHER IDENTITY: WE WILL BECOME GRADUATES OF SAMWELL UNIVERSITY.
SO REMEMBER, WE ARE OUR FOUR YEARS AT SAMWELL.
I AM EXCITED FOR EACH AND EVERY ONE OF US TO GO OUT INTO THE WORLD WITH OUR SHINING EXPERIENCES AND TO LEAVE OUR MARKS.
AND SO WITH THAT, I'LL SAY...
MAY THE RIVERS OF FRIENDSHIP NEVER RUN DRY—
AND MAY WE ALWAYS DRINK DEEPLY FROM KNOWLEDGE'S WELL!

25

FABER

SIGH

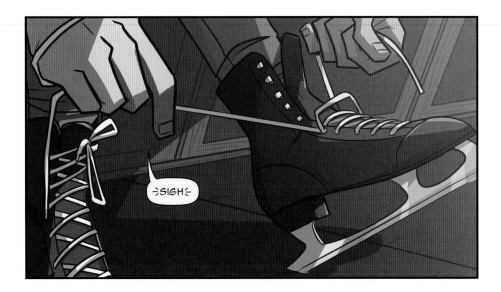

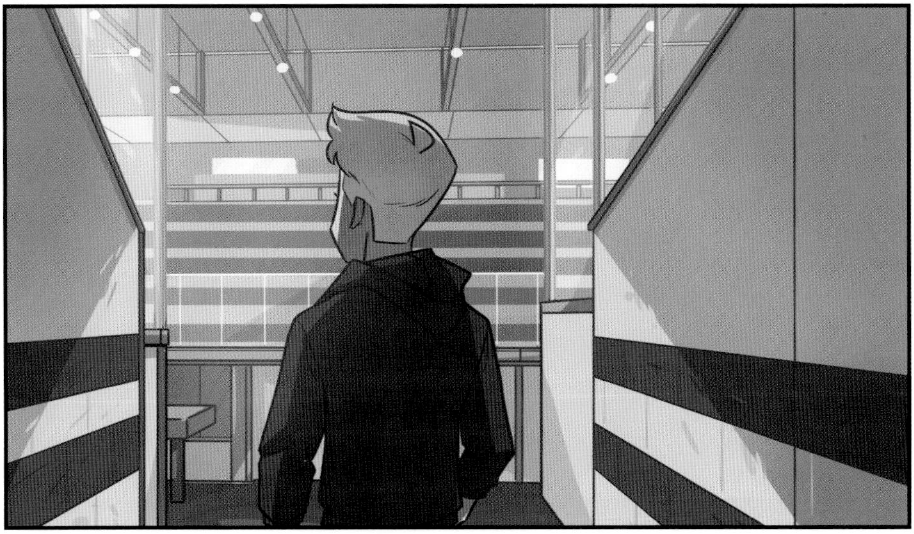

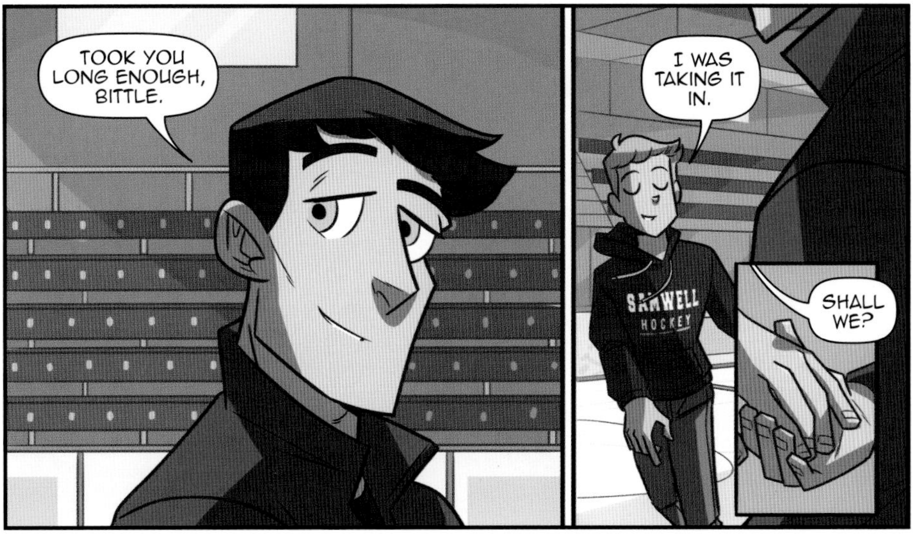
TOOK YOU LONG ENOUGH, BITTLE.
I WAS TAKING IT IN.
SHALL WE?

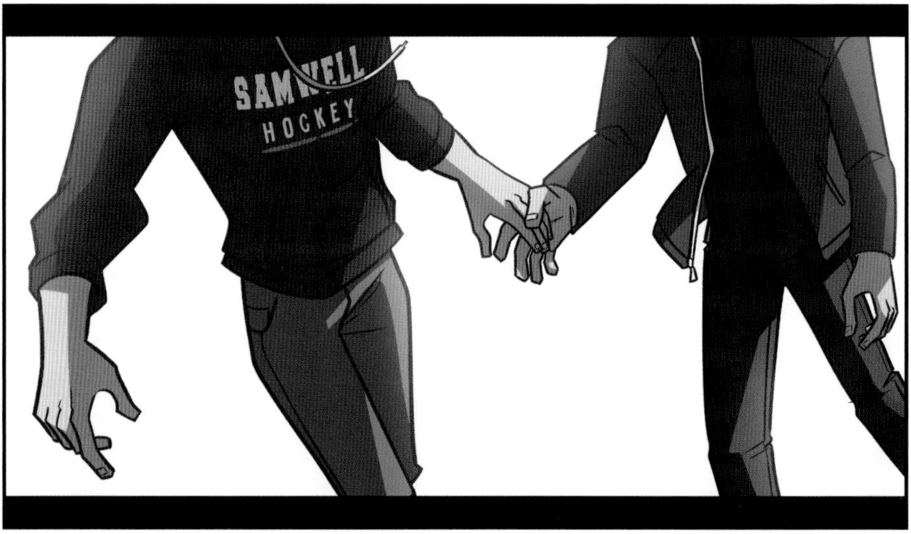
SAMWELL
HOCKEY

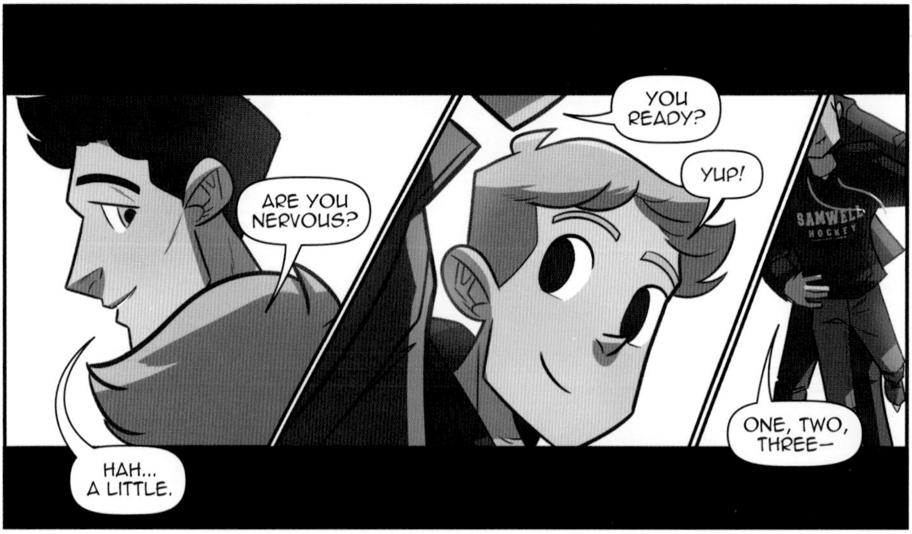
ARE YOU NERVOUS?
HAH... A LITTLE.
YOU READY?
YUP!
SAMWELL
HOCKEY
ONE, TWO, THREE—

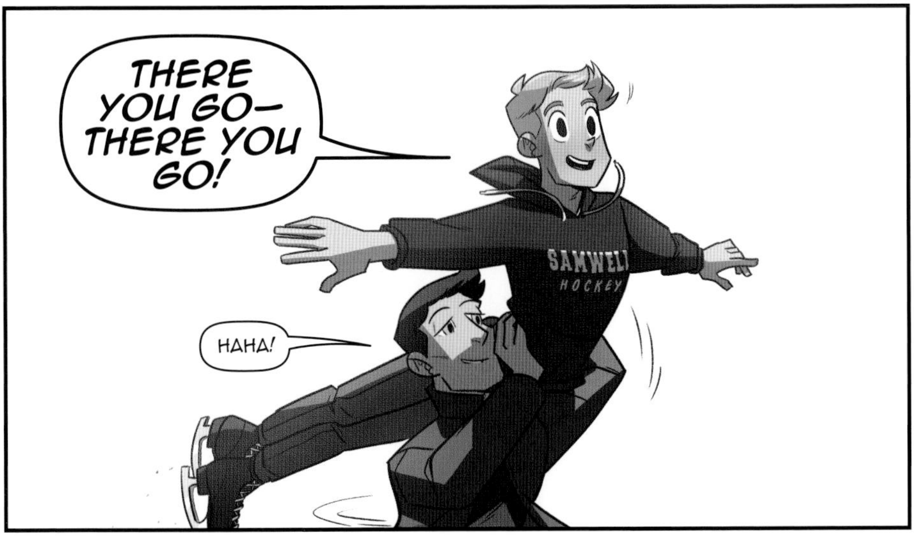
THERE YOU GO— THERE YOU GO!
HAHA!
SAMWELL HOCKEY

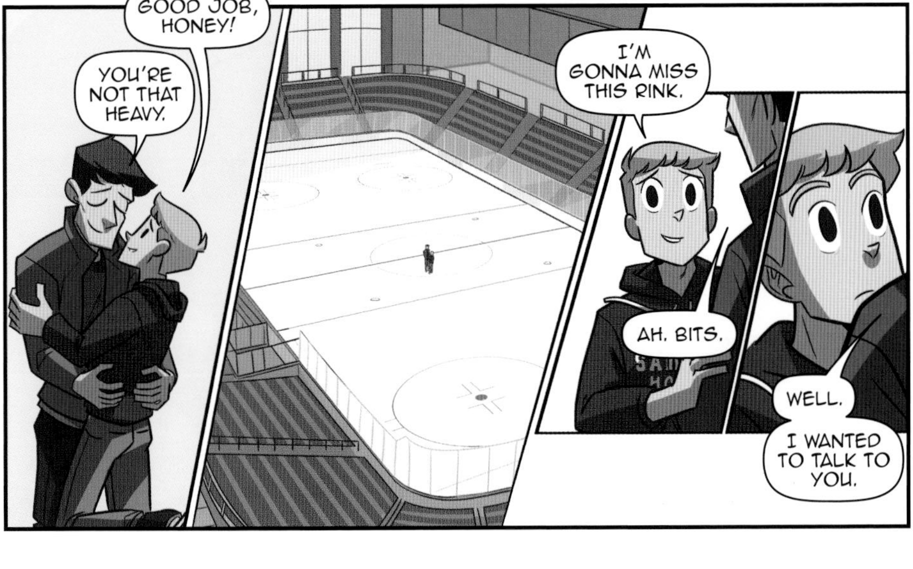
GOOD JOB, HONEY!
YOU'RE NOT THAT HEAVY.
I'M GONNA MISS THIS RINK.
AH. BITS.
WELL.
I WANTED TO TALK TO YOU.

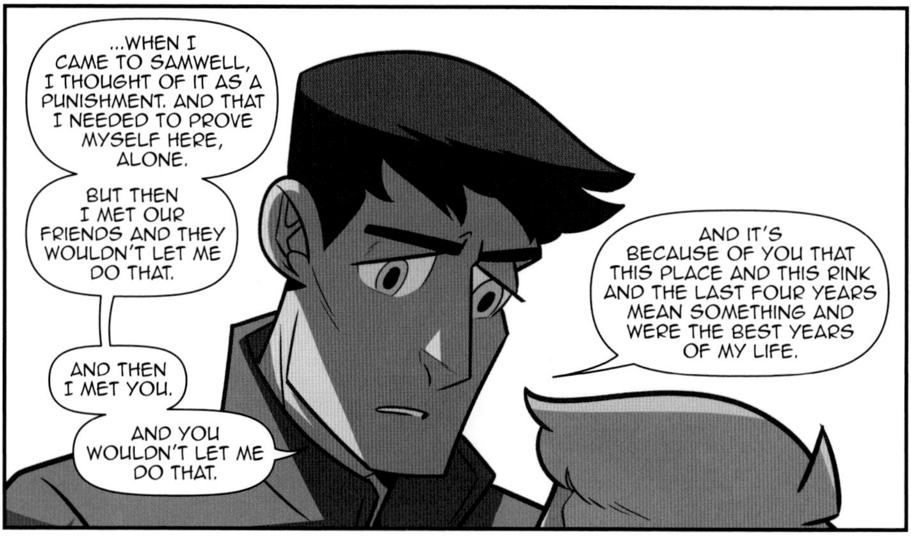
...WHEN I CAME TO SAMWELL, I THOUGHT OF IT AS A PUNISHMENT. AND THAT I NEEDED TO PROVE MYSELF HERE, ALONE.
BUT THEN I MET OUR FRIENDS AND THEY WOULDN'T LET ME DO THAT.
AND THEN I MET YOU.
AND YOU WOULDN'T LET ME DO THAT.
AND IT'S BECAUSE OF YOU THAT THIS PLACE AND THIS RINK AND THE LAST FOUR YEARS MEAN SOMETHING AND WERE THE BEST YEARS OF MY LIFE.

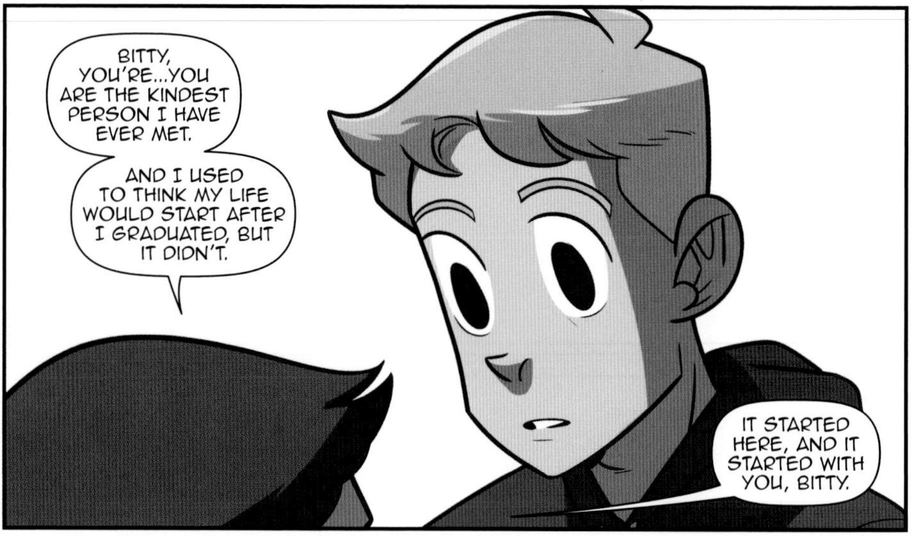
BITTY, YOU'RE...YOU ARE THE KINDEST PERSON I HAVE EVER MET.
AND I USED TO THINK MY LIFE WOULD START AFTER I GRADUATED, BUT IT DIDN'T.
IT STARTED HERE, AND IT STARTED WITH YOU, BITTY.

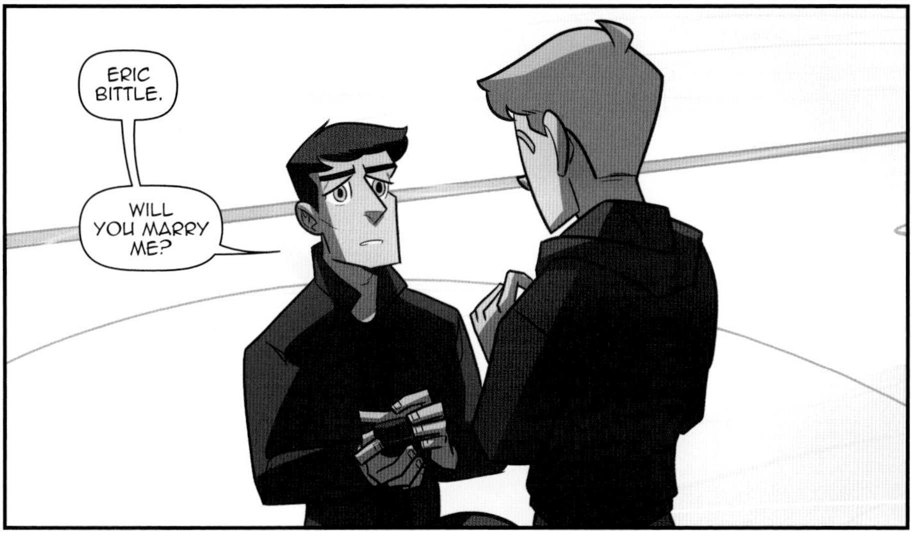
ERIC BITTLE.
WILL YOU MARRY ME?

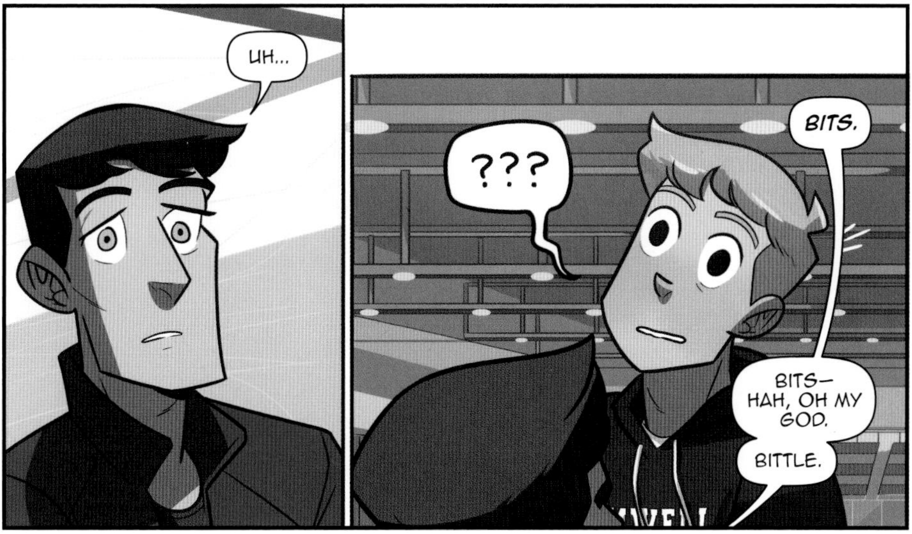
UH...
???
BITS.
BITS— HAH, OH MY GOD.
BITTLE.

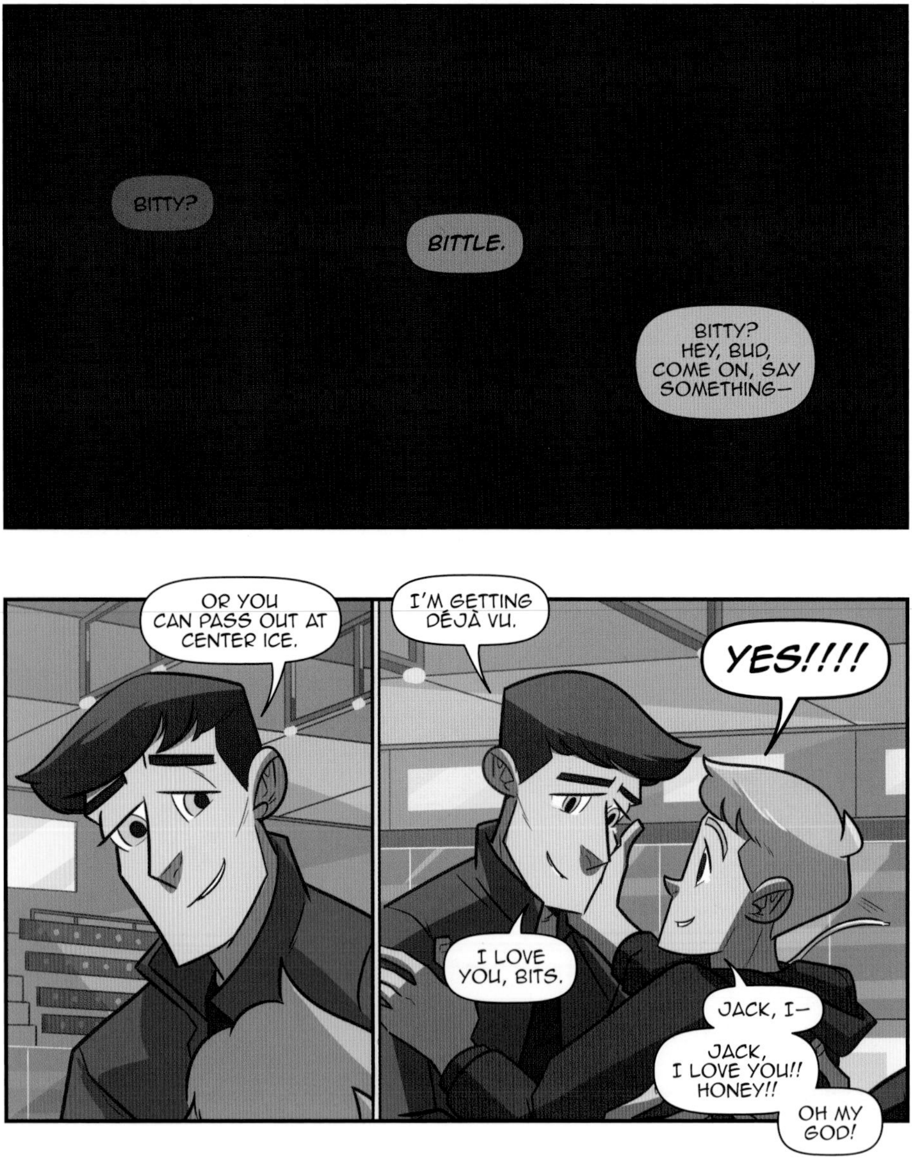
BITTY?
BITTLE.
BITTY? HEY, BUD, COME ON, SAY SOMETHING—
OR YOU CAN PASS OUT AT CENTER ICE.
I'M GETTING DÉJÀ VU.
YES!!!!
I LOVE YOU, BITS.
JACK, I—
JACK, I LOVE YOU!! HONEY!!
OH MY GOD!

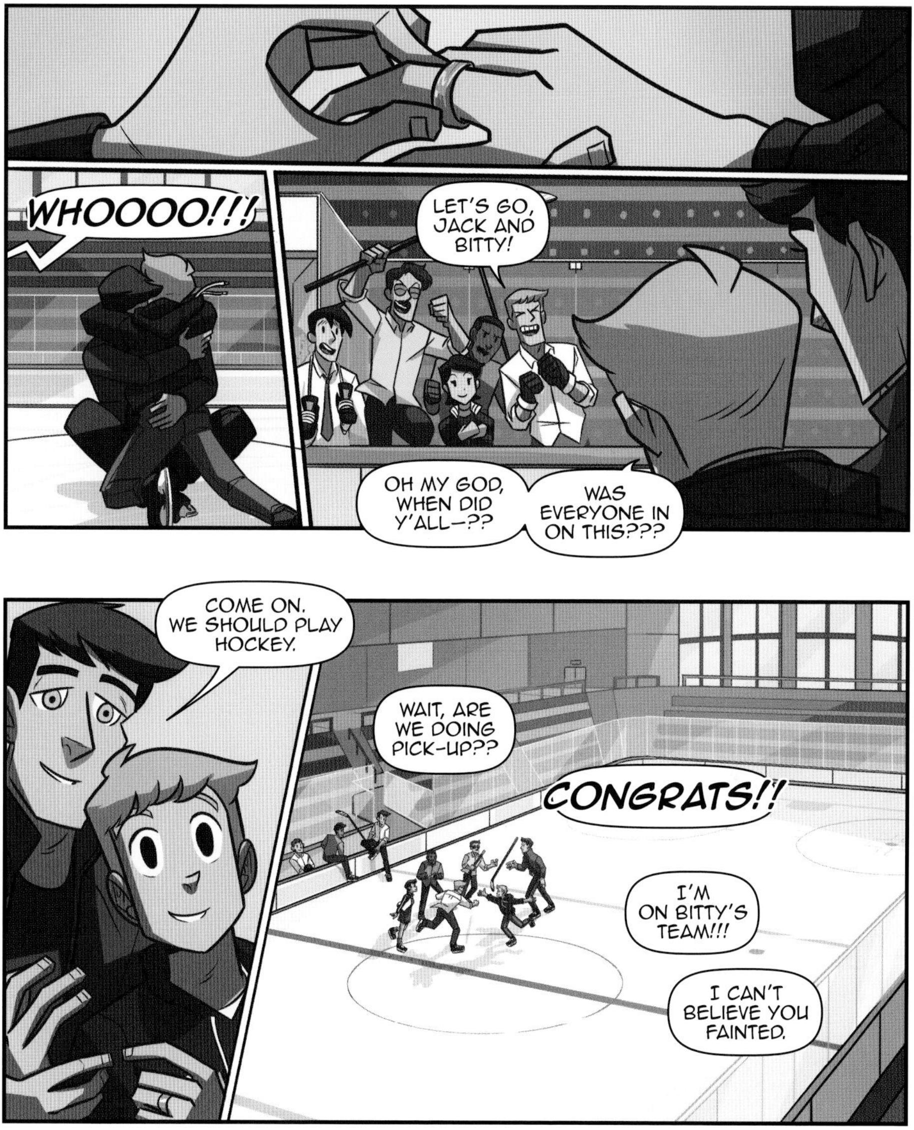
WHOOOO!!!
LET'S GO, JACK AND BITTY!
OH MY GOD, WHEN DID Y'ALL—??
WAS EVERYONE IN ON THIS???
COME ON. WE SHOULD PLAY HOCKEY.
WAIT, ARE WE DOING PICK-UP??
CONGRATS!!
I'M ON BITTY'S TEAM!!!
I CAN'T BELIEVE YOU FAINTED.

26

CHECK, PLEASE

OH, SHOOT, WAIT.
YOU GOT IT?
HMMMM YUP!

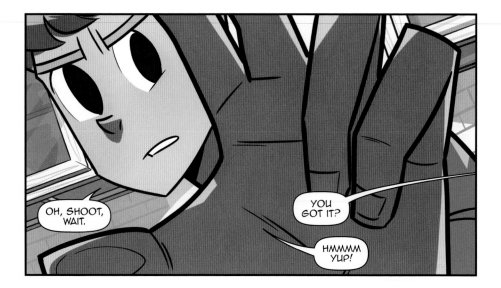

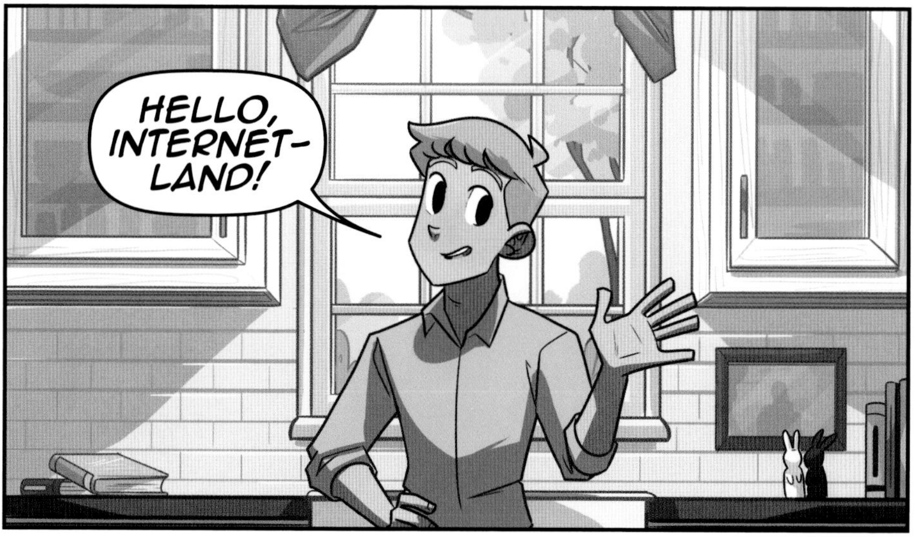
HELLO, INTERNET-LAND!

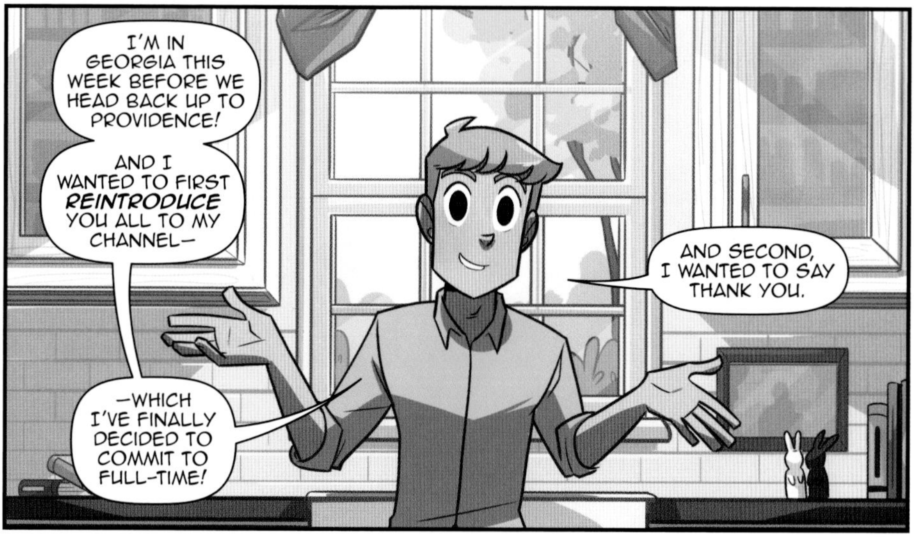
I'M IN GEORGIA THIS WEEK BEFORE WE HEAD BACK UP TO PROVIDENCE!
AND I WANTED TO FIRST REINTRODUCE YOU ALL TO MY CHANNEL—
—WHICH I'VE FINALLY DECIDED TO COMMIT TO FULL-TIME!
AND SECOND, I WANTED TO SAY THANK YOU.

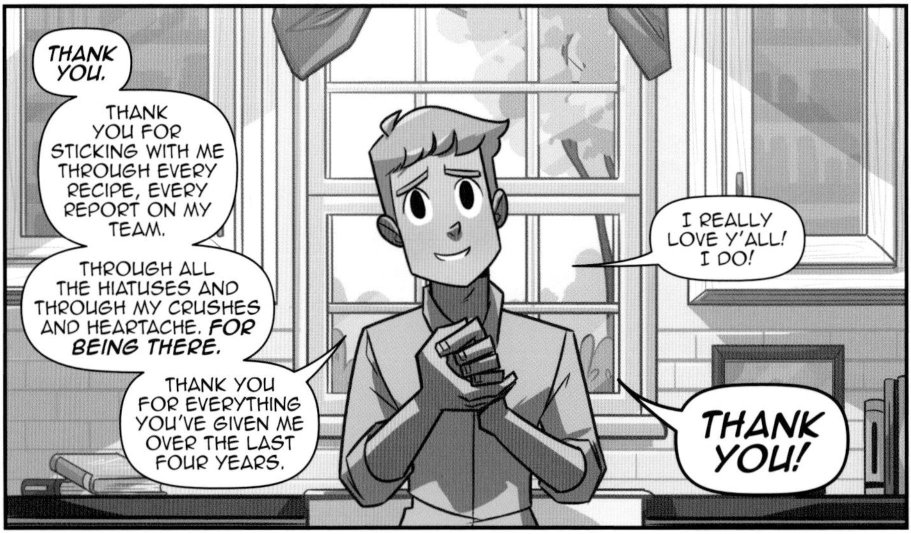
THANK YOU.
THANK YOU FOR STICKING WITH ME THROUGH EVERY RECIPE, EVERY REPORT ON MY TEAM.
THROUGH ALL THE HIATUSES AND THROUGH MY CRUSHES AND HEARTACHE. FOR BEING THERE.
THANK YOU FOR EVERYTHING YOU'VE GIVEN ME OVER THE LAST FOUR YEARS.
I REALLY LOVE Y'ALL! I DO!
THANK YOU!

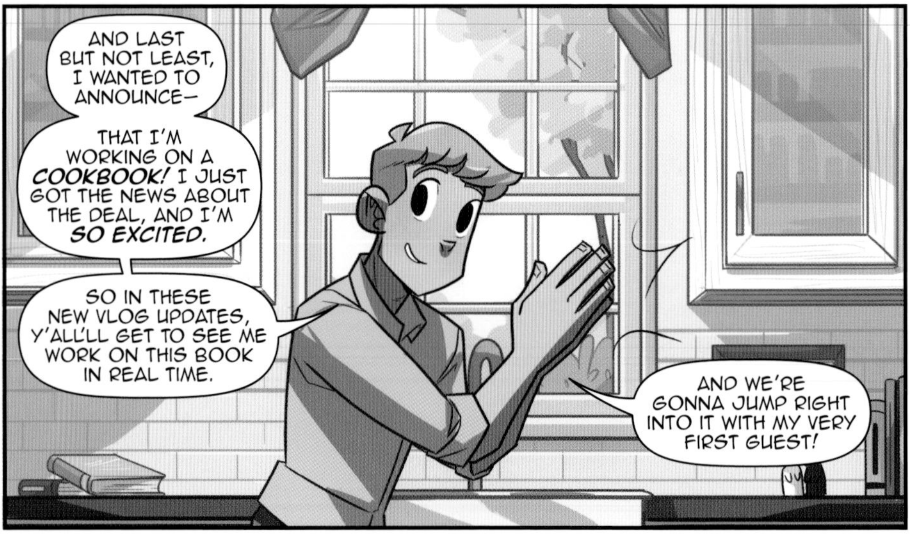
AND LAST BUT NOT LEAST, I WANTED TO ANNOUNCE—
THAT I'M WORKING ON A COOKBOOK! I JUST GOT THE NEWS ABOUT THE DEAL, AND I'M SO EXCITED.
SO IN THESE NEW VLOG UPDATES, Y'ALL'LL GET TO SEE ME WORK ON THIS BOOK IN REAL TIME.
AND WE'RE GONNA JUMP RIGHT INTO IT WITH MY VERY FIRST GUEST!

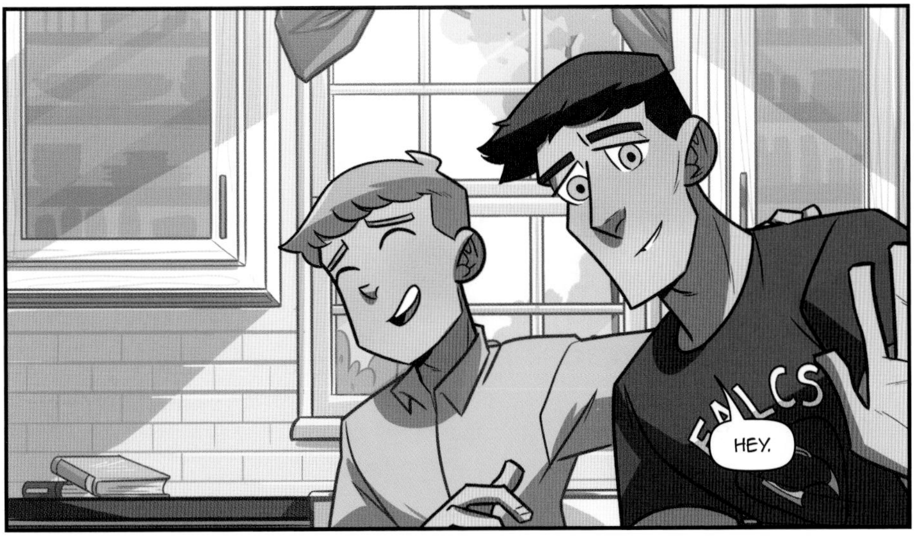
HEY.

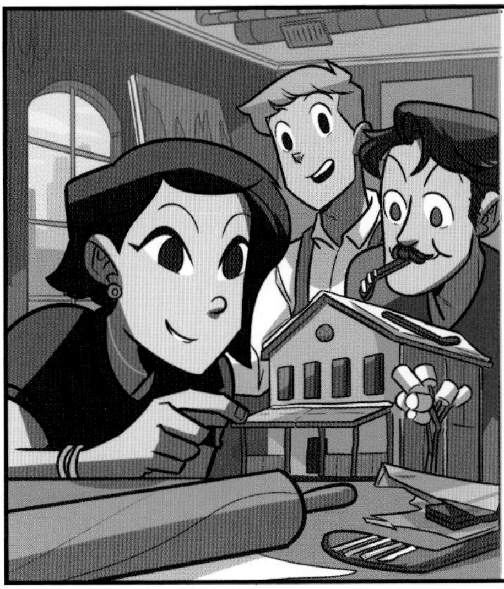

written & illustrated by

Ngozi Ukazu

with assistance from

**Johel Rivera,
Chelle Finkler,
& Tess Stone**

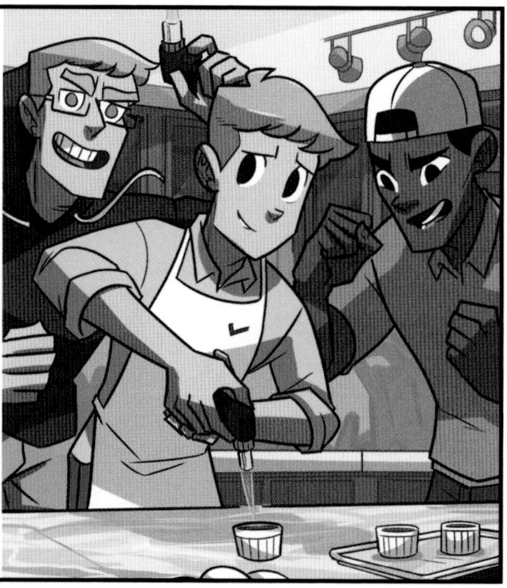

with special
thanks to

**Gale Galligan,
Max Ritvo,
Madeline Rupert,
Dave Valeza,
Rachel Young,
and Liam**

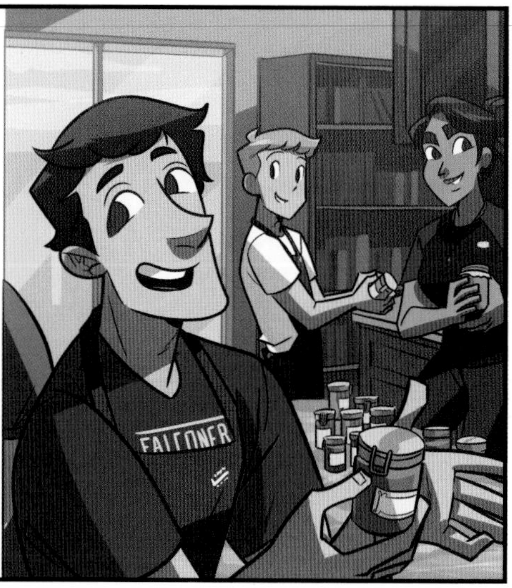

This story is dedicated to

my mom & my dad

**And to
every reader**

And to anyone who wants to thrive in a place where the world says they can't.

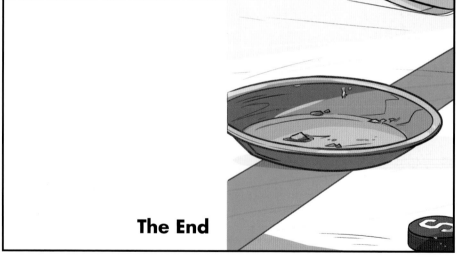

The End

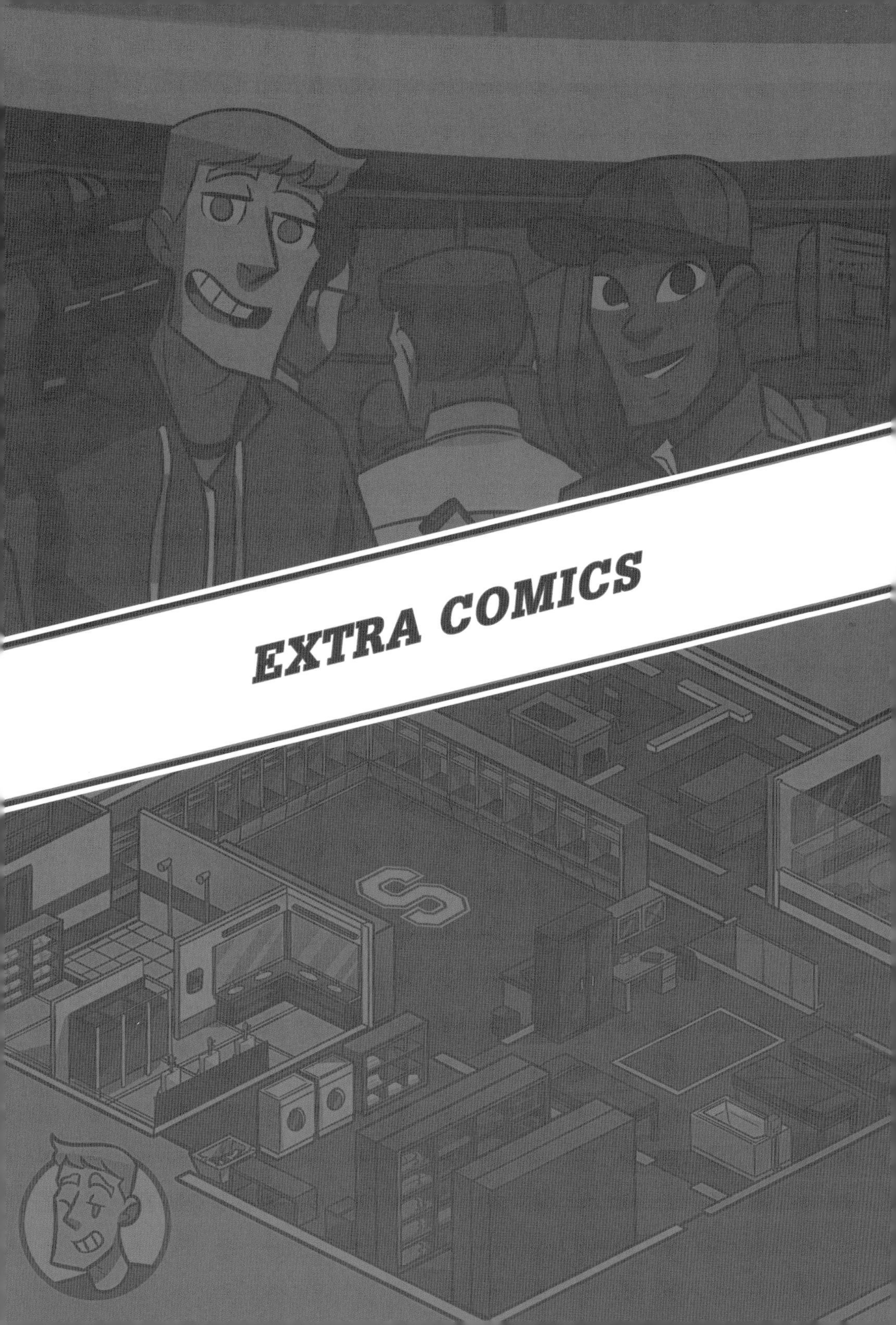

EXTRA COMICS

LOCKER ROOM

locker room, n.

1. The hallowed ground where the hockey
   player prepares for battle. What happens
   amongst the stalls—gross, heinous, or
   legendary—stays there.

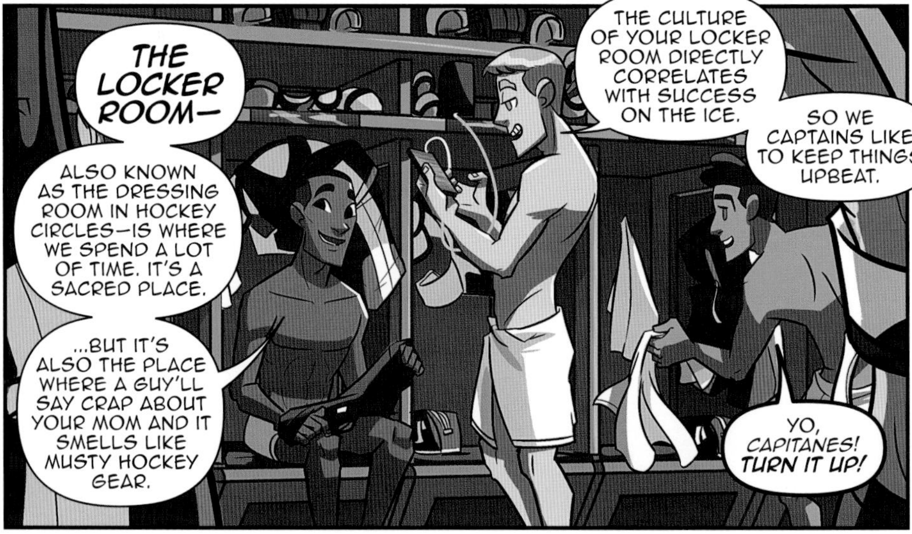
THE LOCKER ROOM—
ALSO KNOWN AS THE DRESSING ROOM IN HOCKEY CIRCLES—IS WHERE WE SPEND A LOT OF TIME. IT'S A SACRED PLACE.
...BUT IT'S ALSO THE PLACE WHERE A GUY'LL SAY CRAP ABOUT YOUR MOM AND IT SMELLS LIKE MUSTY HOCKEY GEAR.
THE CULTURE OF YOUR LOCKER ROOM DIRECTLY CORRELATES WITH SUCCESS ON THE ICE.
SO WE CAPTAINS LIKE TO KEEP THINGS UPBEAT.
YO, CAPITANES! TURN IT UP!

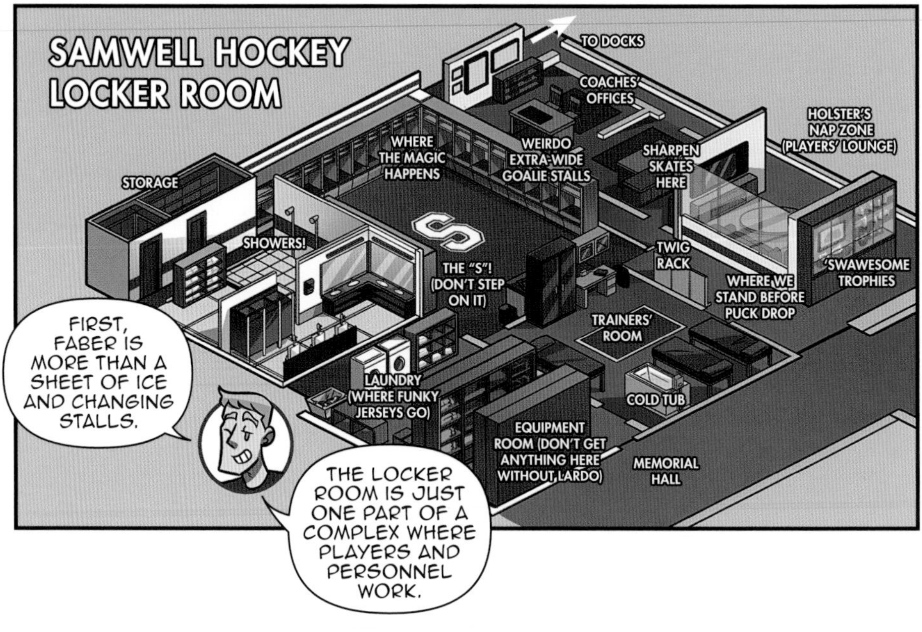
SAMWELL HOCKEY LOCKER ROOM
TO DOCKS
COACHES' OFFICES
HOLSTER'S NAP ZONE (PLAYERS' LOUNGE)
WHERE THE MAGIC HAPPENS
WEIRDO EXTRA-WIDE GOALIE STALLS
SHARPEN SKATES HERE
STORAGE
SHOWERS!
TWIG RACK
THE "S"! (DON'T STEP ON IT)
WHERE WE STAND BEFORE PUCK DROP
'SWAWESOME TROPHIES
TRAINERS' ROOM
FIRST, FABER IS MORE THAN A SHEET OF ICE AND CHANGING STALLS.
LAUNDRY (WHERE FUNKY JERSEYS GO)
COLD TUB
EQUIPMENT ROOM (DON'T GET ANYTHING HERE WITHOUT LARDO)
MEMORIAL HALL
THE LOCKER ROOM IS JUST ONE PART OF A COMPLEX WHERE PLAYERS AND PERSONNEL WORK.

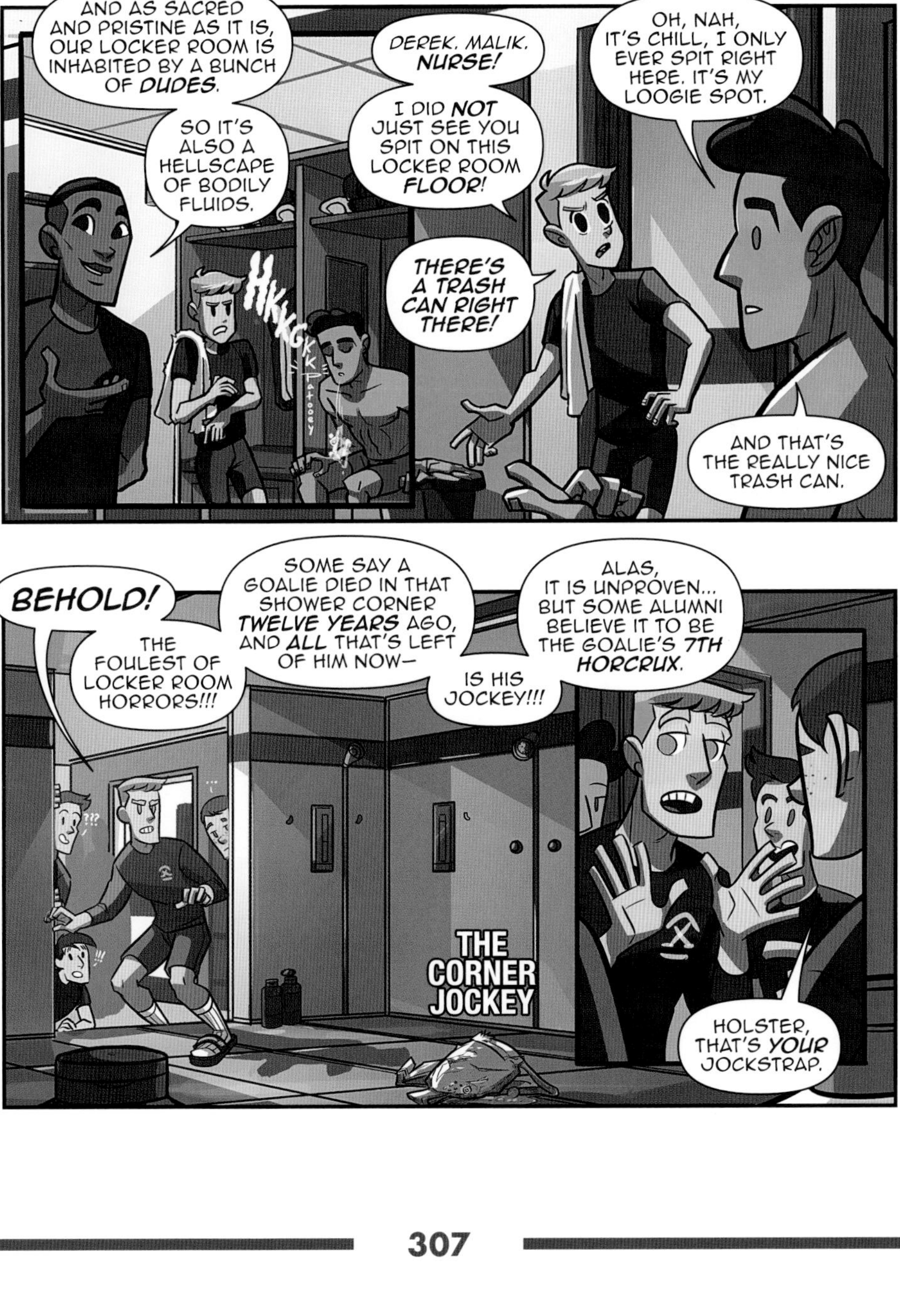
AND AS SACRED AND PRISTINE AS IT IS, OUR LOCKER ROOM IS INHABITED BY A BUNCH OF *DUDES*.
SO IT'S ALSO A HELLSCAPE OF BODILY FLUIDS.
HKKGKK
Patooey
DEREK. MALIK. *NURSE!*
I DID *NOT* JUST SEE YOU SPIT ON THIS LOCKER ROOM *FLOOR!*
THERE'S A TRASH CAN RIGHT THERE!
OH, NAH, IT'S CHILL, I ONLY EVER SPIT RIGHT HERE. IT'S MY LOOGIE SPOT.
AND THAT'S THE REALLY NICE TRASH CAN.
BEHOLD!
THE FOULEST OF LOCKER ROOM HORRORS!!!
SOME SAY A GOALIE DIED IN THAT SHOWER CORNER *TWELVE YEARS* AGO, AND *ALL* THAT'S LEFT OF HIM NOW–
IS HIS JOCKEY!!!
ALAS, IT IS UNPROVEN... BUT SOME ALUMNI BELIEVE IT TO BE THE GOALIE'S *7TH HORCRUX*.
???
!!!
THE CORNER JOCKEY
HOLSTER, THAT'S *YOUR* JOCKSTRAP.

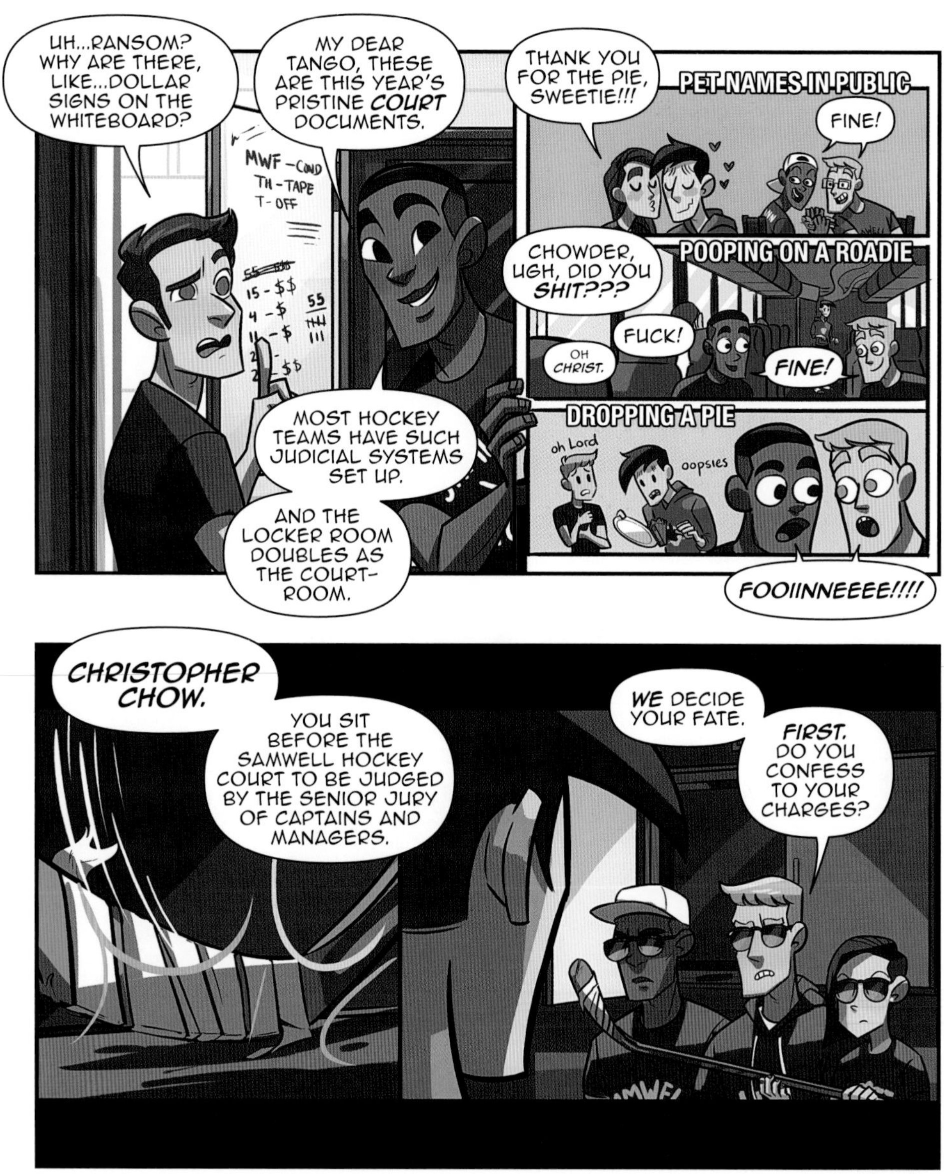
UH...RANSOM? WHY ARE THERE, LIKE...DOLLAR SIGNS ON THE WHITEBOARD?
MY DEAR TANGO, THESE ARE THIS YEAR'S PRISTINE COURT DOCUMENTS.
MWF - COND
TH - TAPE
T - OFF
MOST HOCKEY TEAMS HAVE SUCH JUDICIAL SYSTEMS SET UP.
AND THE LOCKER ROOM DOUBLES AS THE COURT-ROOM.
THANK YOU FOR THE PIE, SWEETIE!!!
PET NAMES IN PUBLIC
FINE!
CHOWDER, UGH, DID YOU SHIT???
POOPING ON A ROADIE
OH CHRIST.
FUCK!
FINE!
DROPPING A PIE
oh Lord
oopsies
FOOIINNEEEE!!!!
CHRISTOPHER CHOW.
YOU SIT BEFORE THE SAMWELL HOCKEY COURT TO BE JUDGED BY THE SENIOR JURY OF CAPTAINS AND MANAGERS.
WE DECIDE YOUR FATE.
FIRST. DO YOU CONFESS TO YOUR CHARGES?

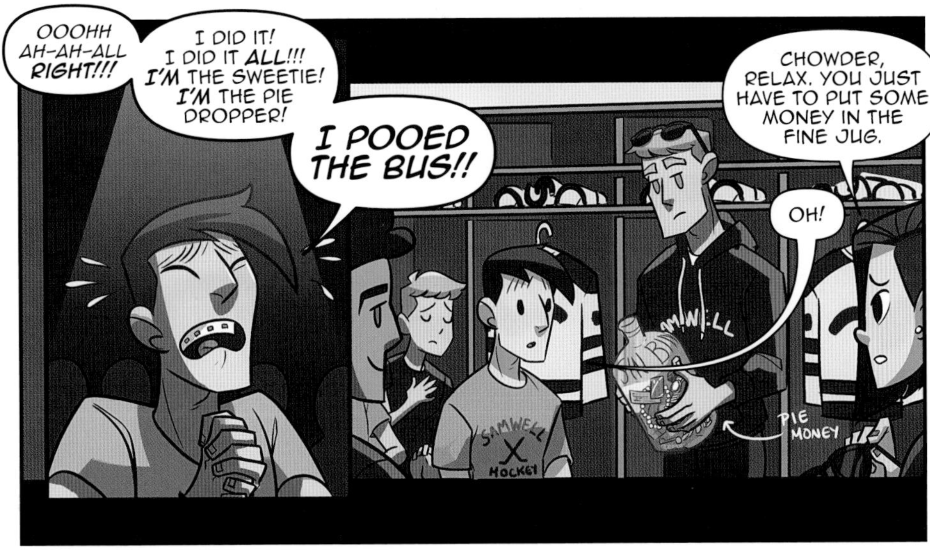
OOOHH AH-AH-ALL RIGHT!!!
I DID IT! I DID IT ALL!!! I'M THE SWEETIE! I'M THE PIE DROPPER!
I POOED THE BUS!!
CHOWDER, RELAX. YOU JUST HAVE TO PUT SOME MONEY IN THE FINE JUG.
OH!
PIE MONEY
SAMWELL HOCKEY

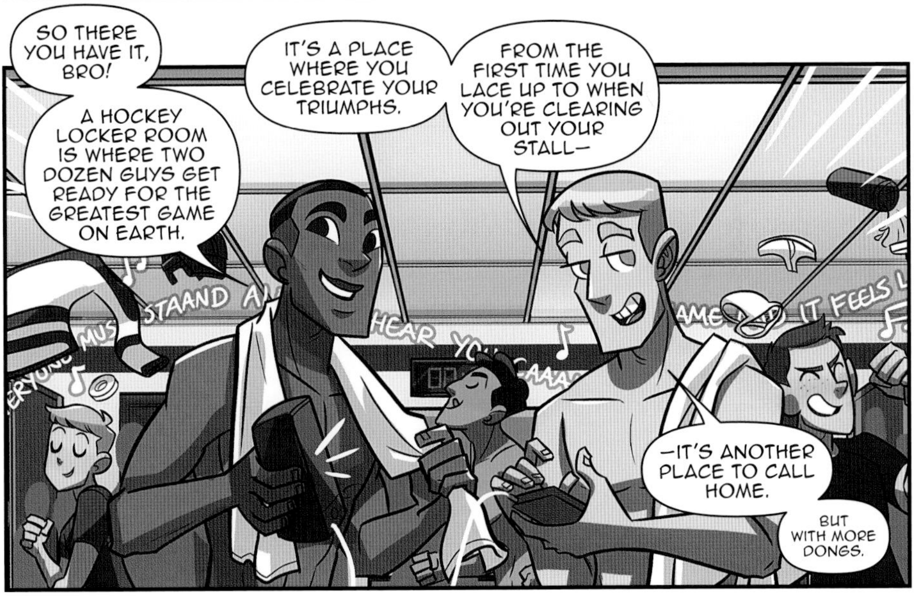
SO THERE YOU HAVE IT, BRO!
A HOCKEY LOCKER ROOM IS WHERE TWO DOZEN GUYS GET READY FOR THE GREATEST GAME ON EARTH.
IT'S A PLACE WHERE YOU CELEBRATE YOUR TRIUMPHS.
FROM THE FIRST TIME YOU LACE UP TO WHEN YOU'RE CLEARING OUT YOUR STALL—
—IT'S ANOTHER PLACE TO CALL HOME.
BUT WITH MORE DONGS.

HOCKEY SPEAK

hockey speak, n.

1. The reserved cadence, tone, and
   vocabulary used by hockey players
   during media appearances and
   moments of observed introspection.
   A modern cultural phenomenon.

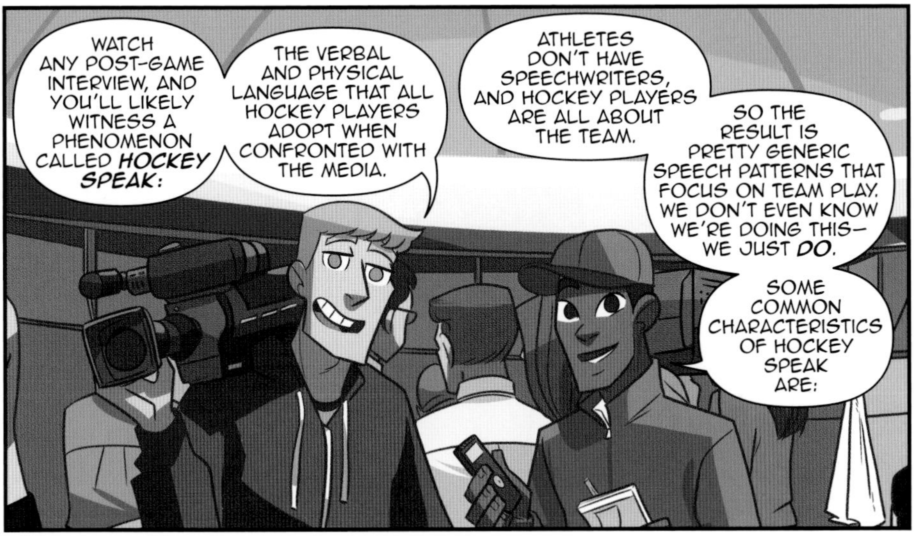
WATCH ANY POST-GAME INTERVIEW, AND YOU'LL LIKELY WITNESS A PHENOMENON CALLED *HOCKEY SPEAK*:
THE VERBAL AND PHYSICAL LANGUAGE THAT ALL HOCKEY PLAYERS ADOPT WHEN CONFRONTED WITH THE MEDIA.
ATHLETES DON'T HAVE SPEECHWRITERS, AND HOCKEY PLAYERS ARE ALL ABOUT THE TEAM.
SO THE RESULT IS PRETTY GENERIC SPEECH PATTERNS THAT FOCUS ON TEAM PLAY. WE DON'T EVEN KNOW WE'RE DOING THIS— WE JUST *DO*.
SOME COMMON CHARACTERISTICS OF HOCKEY SPEAK ARE:

HOCKEY SPEAK!

- A monotone
- Frequent sighing
- Use of top ten hockey catchphrases
- Interjections of "uh," "you know," "obviously," and "there"

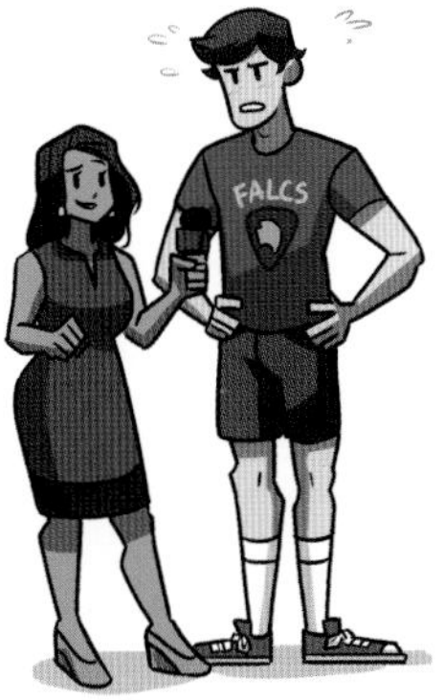
FALCS

- Immense physical discomfort. Torture.
- Spontaneous Canadian accent
- An empty stare that suggests an inner void
- Focus on team play. Go, team!!

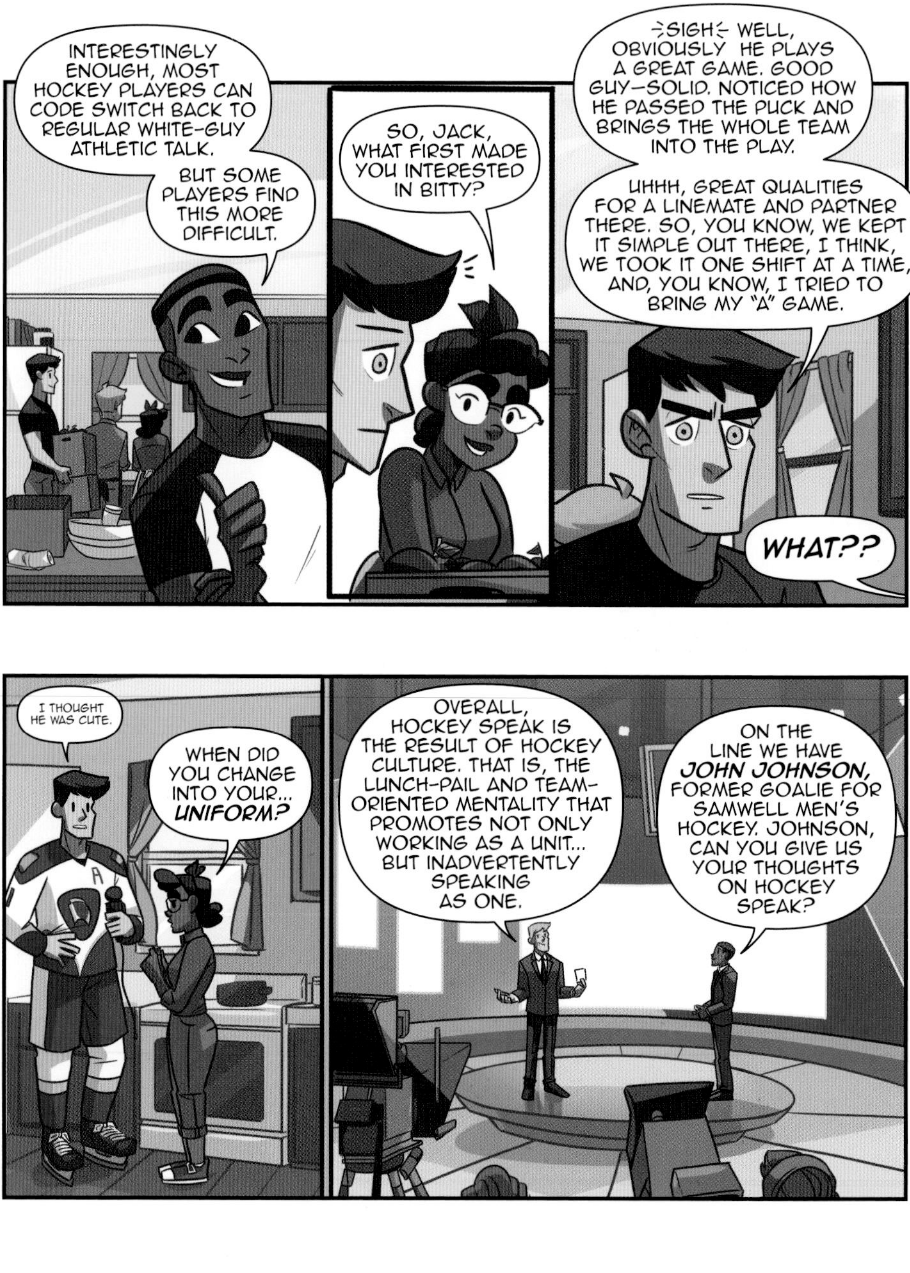
INTERESTINGLY ENOUGH, MOST HOCKEY PLAYERS CAN CODE SWITCH BACK TO REGULAR WHITE-GUY ATHLETIC TALK.
BUT SOME PLAYERS FIND THIS MORE DIFFICULT.
SO, JACK, WHAT FIRST MADE YOU INTERESTED IN BITTY?
SIGH WELL, OBVIOUSLY HE PLAYS A GREAT GAME. GOOD GUY—SOLID. NOTICED HOW HE PASSED THE PUCK AND BRINGS THE WHOLE TEAM INTO THE PLAY.
UHHH, GREAT QUALITIES FOR A LINEMATE AND PARTNER THERE. SO, YOU KNOW, WE KEPT IT SIMPLE OUT THERE, I THINK, WE TOOK IT ONE SHIFT AT A TIME, AND, YOU KNOW, I TRIED TO BRING MY "A" GAME.
WHAT??
I THOUGHT HE WAS CUTE.
WHEN DID YOU CHANGE INTO YOUR... UNIFORM?
OVERALL, HOCKEY SPEAK IS THE RESULT OF HOCKEY CULTURE. THAT IS, THE LUNCH-PAIL AND TEAM-ORIENTED MENTALITY THAT PROMOTES NOT ONLY WORKING AS A UNIT... BUT INADVERTENTLY SPEAKING AS ONE.
ON THE LINE WE HAVE JOHN JOHNSON, FORMER GOALIE FOR SAMWELL MEN'S HOCKEY. JOHNSON, CAN YOU GIVE US YOUR THOUGHTS ON HOCKEY SPEAK?

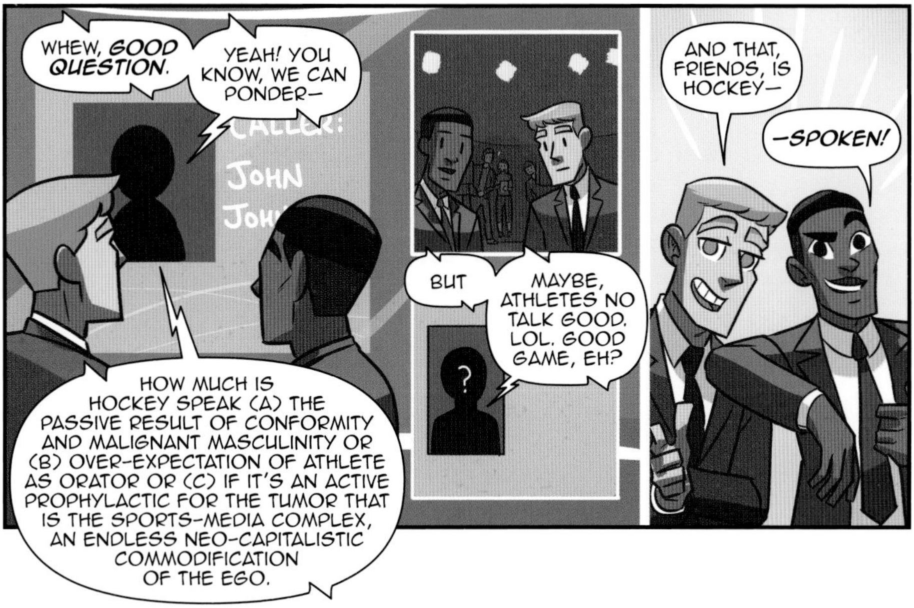
WHEW, GOOD QUESTION.
YEAH! YOU KNOW, WE CAN PONDER—
CALLER: JOHN JOH
HOW MUCH IS HOCKEY SPEAK (A) THE PASSIVE RESULT OF CONFORMITY AND MALIGNANT MASCULINITY OR (B) OVER-EXPECTATION OF ATHLETE AS ORATOR OR (C) IF IT'S AN ACTIVE PROPHYLACTIC FOR THE TUMOR THAT IS THE SPORTS-MEDIA COMPLEX, AN ENDLESS NEO-CAPITALISTIC COMMODIFICATION OF THE EGO.
BUT
MAYBE, ATHLETES NO TALK GOOD. LOL. GOOD GAME, EH?
?
AND THAT, FRIENDS, IS HOCKEY—
—SPOKEN!

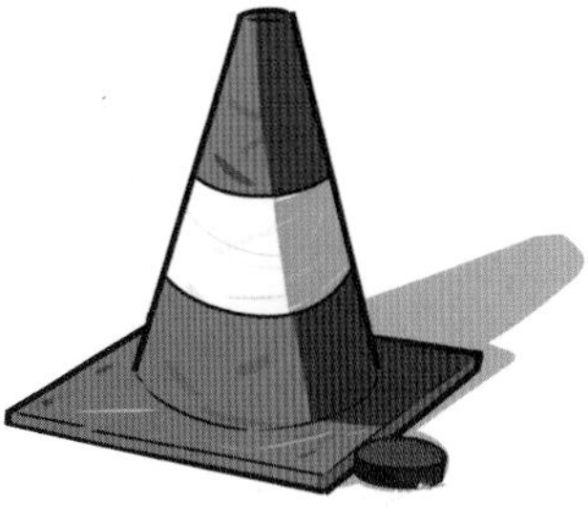

PRANKS

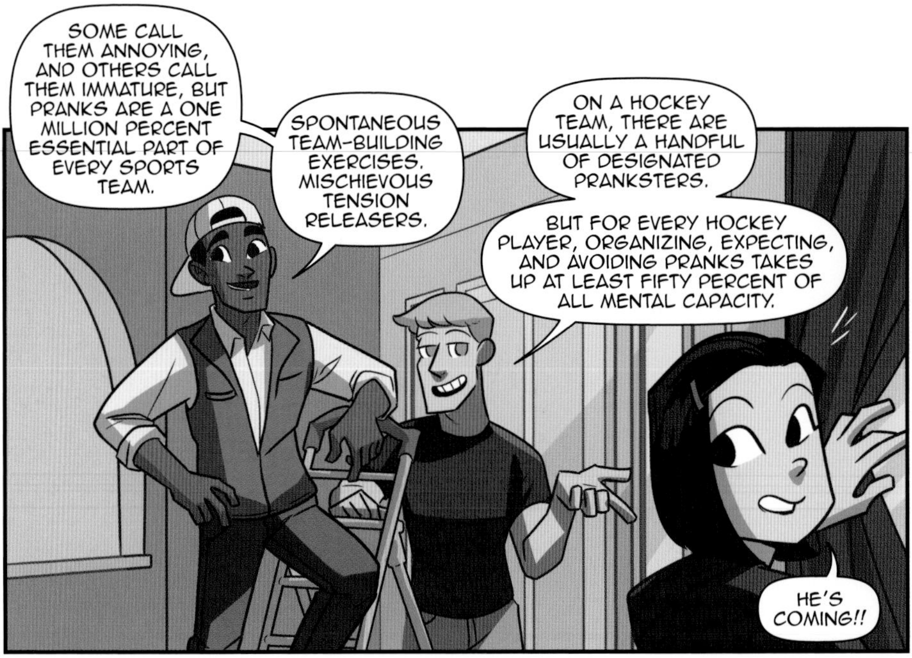
SOME CALL THEM ANNOYING, AND OTHERS CALL THEM IMMATURE, BUT PRANKS ARE A ONE MILLION PERCENT ESSENTIAL PART OF EVERY SPORTS TEAM.
SPONTANEOUS TEAM-BUILDING EXERCISES. MISCHIEVOUS TENSION RELEASERS.
ON A HOCKEY TEAM, THERE ARE USUALLY A HANDFUL OF DESIGNATED PRANKSTERS.
BUT FOR EVERY HOCKEY PLAYER, ORGANIZING, EXPECTING, AND AVOIDING PRANKS TAKES UP AT LEAST FIFTY PERCENT OF ALL MENTAL CAPACITY.
HE'S COMING!!

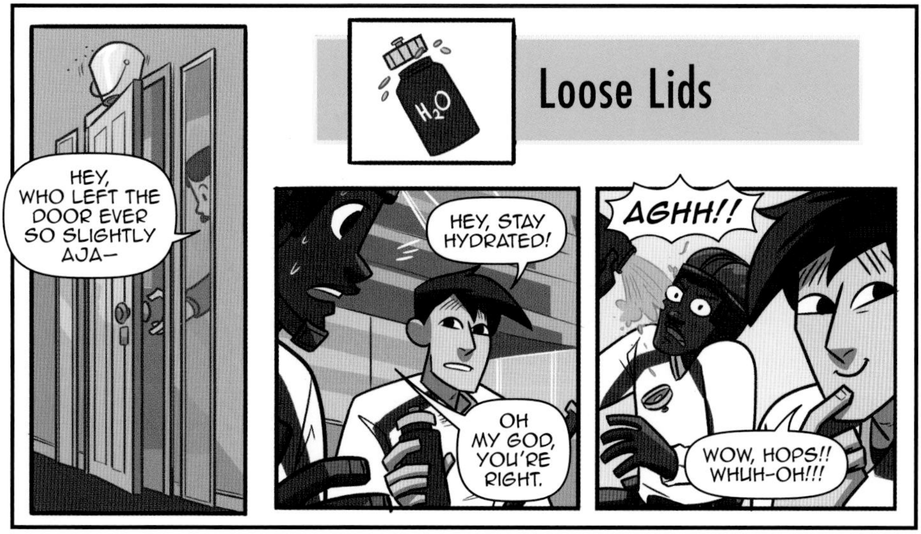
Loose Lids
HEY, WHO LEFT THE DOOR EVER SO SLIGHTLY AJA—
HEY, STAY HYDRATED!
OH MY GOD, YOU'RE RIGHT.
AGHH!!
WOW, HOPS!! WHUH-OH!!!

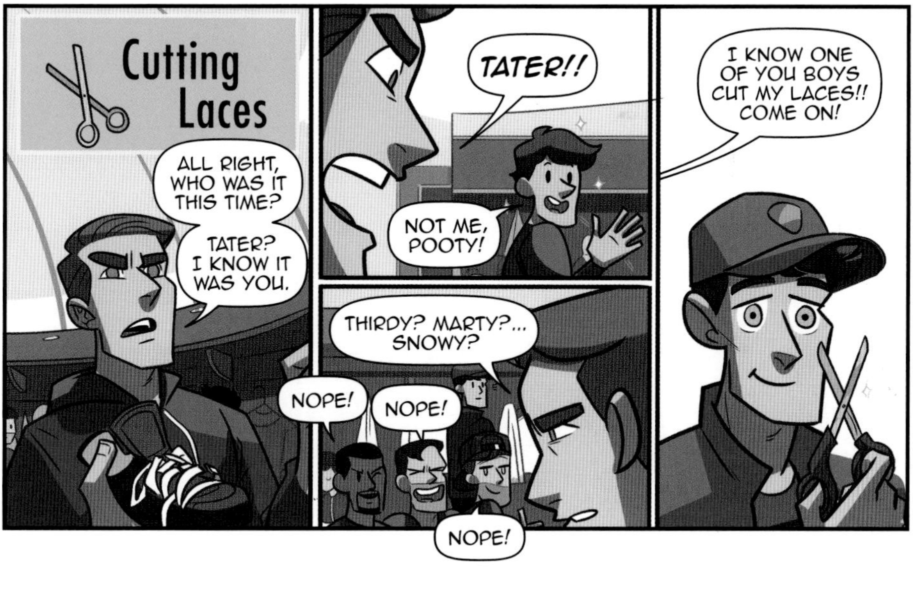
Cutting Laces
ALL RIGHT, WHO WAS IT THIS TIME?
TATER? I KNOW IT WAS YOU.
TATER!!
NOT ME, POOTY!
THIRDY? MARTY?... SNOWY?
NOPE!
NOPE!
NOPE!
I KNOW ONE OF YOU BOYS CUT MY LACES!! COME ON!

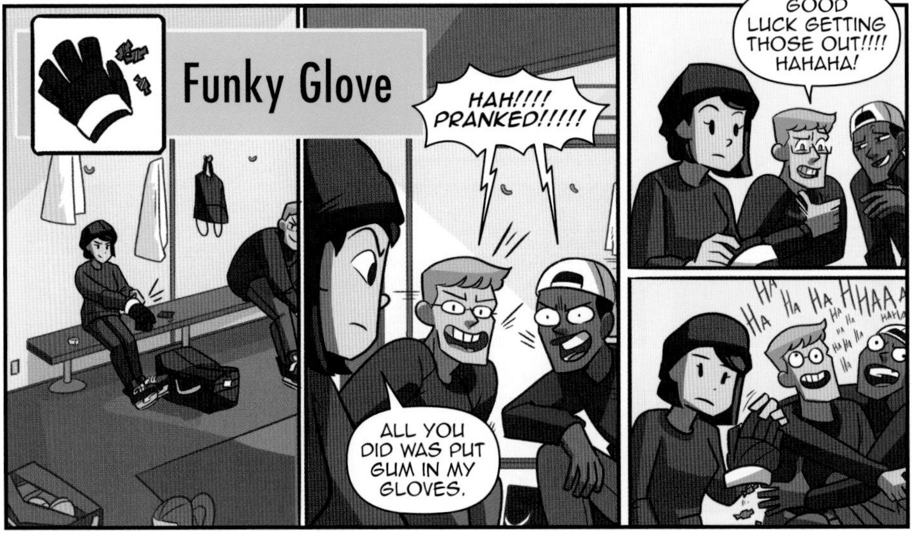
Funky Glove
HAH!!!! PRANKED!!!!!
ALL YOU DID WAS PUT GUM IN MY GLOVES.
GOOD LUCK GETTING THOSE OUT!!!! HAHAHA!
HA HA HA HHAAA

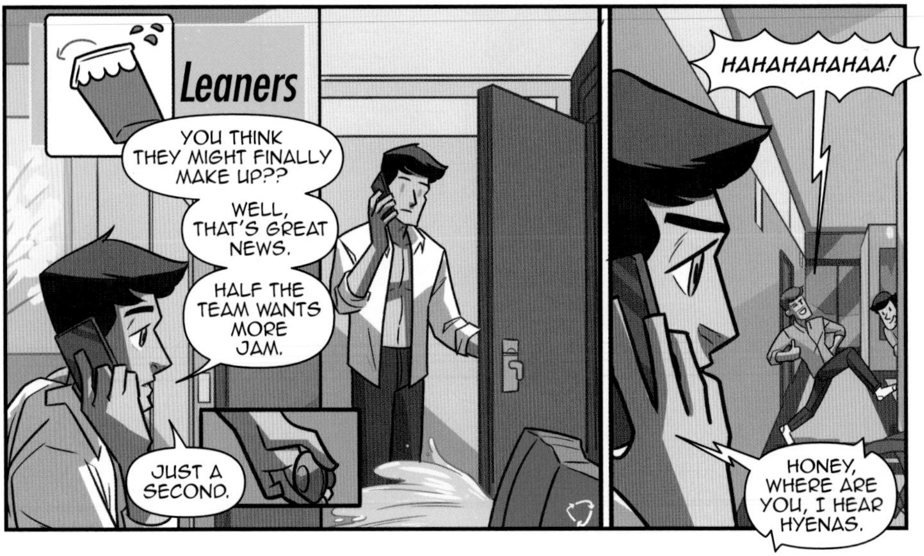
Leaners
YOU THINK THEY MIGHT FINALLY MAKE UP??
WELL, THAT'S GREAT NEWS.
HALF THE TEAM WANTS MORE JAM.
JUST A SECOND.
HAHAHAHAHAA!
HONEY, WHERE ARE YOU, I HEAR HYENAS.

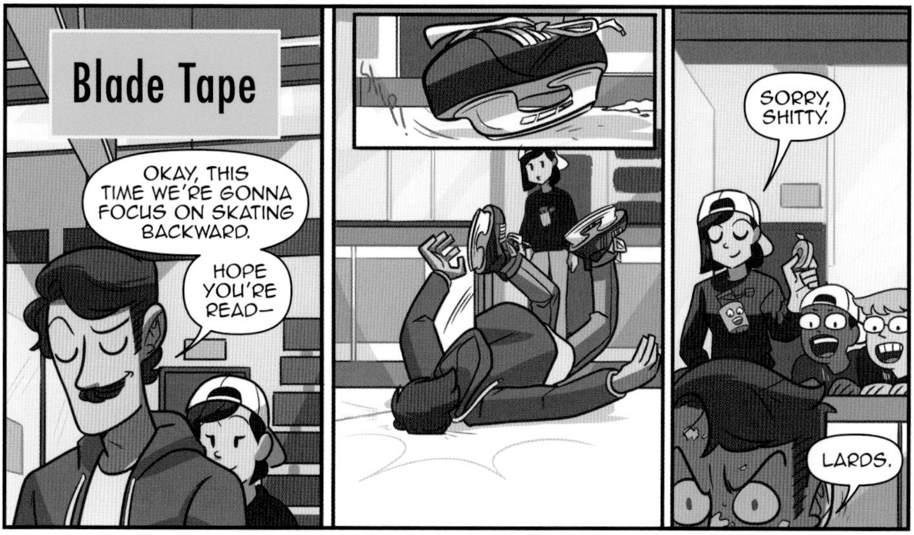
Blade Tape
OKAY, THIS TIME WE'RE GONNA FOCUS ON SKATING BACKWARD.
HOPE YOU'RE READ—
SORRY, SHITTY.
LARDS.

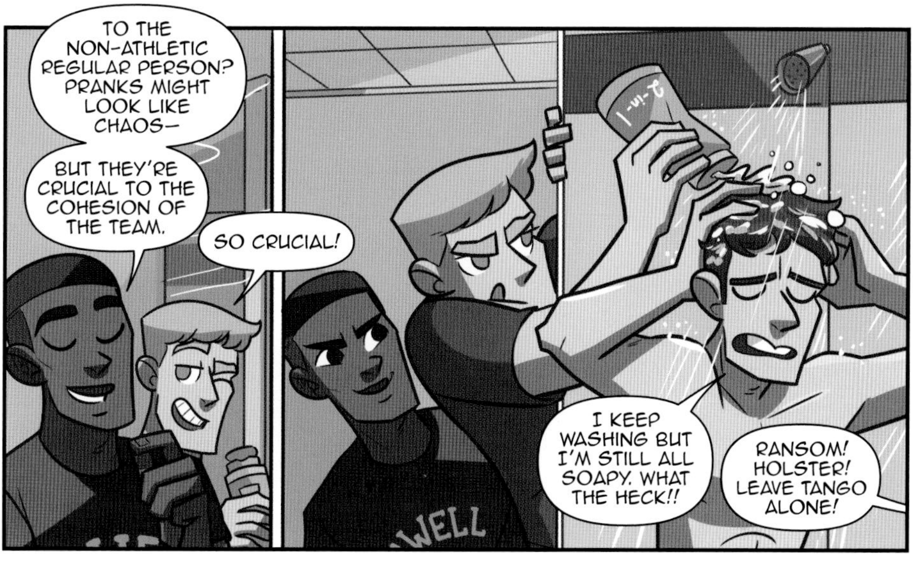
TO THE NON-ATHLETIC REGULAR PERSON? PRANKS MIGHT LOOK LIKE CHAOS—
BUT THEY'RE CRUCIAL TO THE COHESION OF THE TEAM.
SO CRUCIAL!
2-in-1
I KEEP WASHING BUT I'M STILL ALL SOAPY. WHAT THE HECK!!
RANSOM! HOLSTER! LEAVE TANGO ALONE!

TWEETS

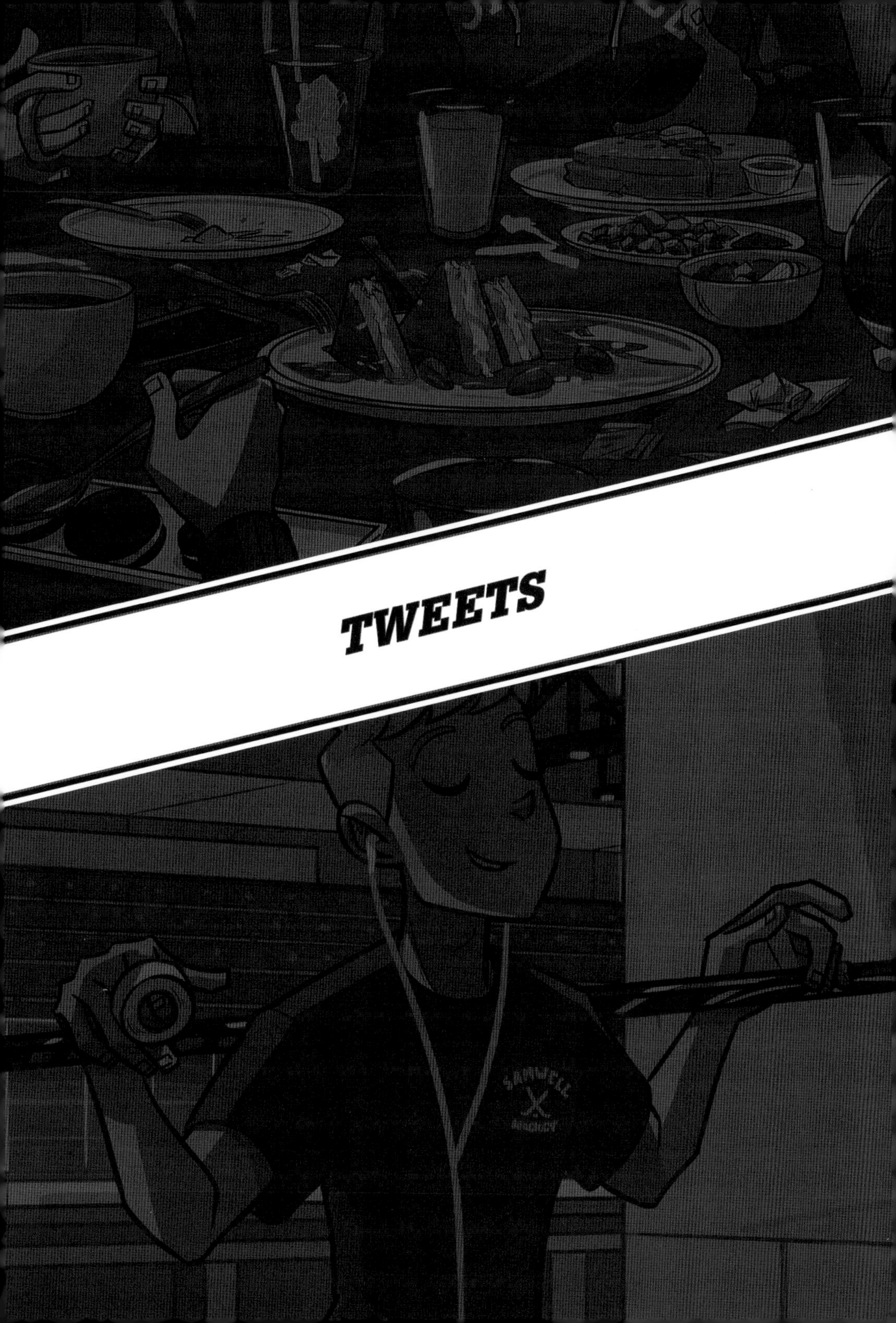

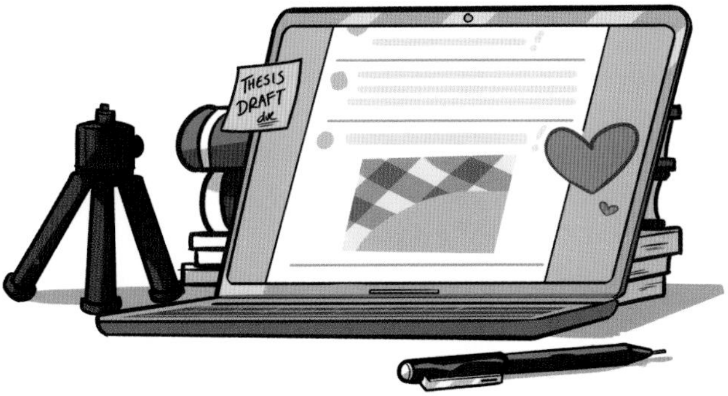
THESIS
DRAFT

SO. It turns out having a Secret NHL Boyfriend changes up how you tweet. First (when no one ***knows*** you're dating), it makes all your social media communication extremely vague. Second (when all of ***America*** knows you're dating), it makes you put your entire account on PRIVATE! But you've been keeping up with my vlog for all these years—I want to share my musings from my junior and senior year at Samwell with you! After all, Lardo, Rans, and Holster shouldn't be the only folks reading my tweets. Look out for a new (public!) account from me when my book comes out! ✓ ♥

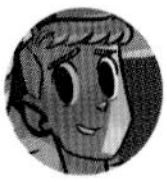

Eric Bittle @omgcheckplease · Thursday, August 27, 2015 | 3:12 PM
Well. It's about time I tackled my language requirement at Samwell. (Bonjour?)

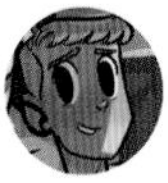

Eric Bittle @omgcheckplease · Friday, September 4, 2015 | 2:33 PM
Shitty just group texted us a picture of his study carrel in the library w/ the caption "JUST MOVED IN!!!!" ;~; Let this law student survive.

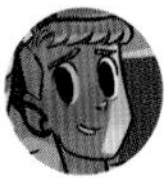

Eric Bittle @omgcheckplease · Friday, September 4, 2015 | 6:23 PM
Rans: how come jack hasn't introduced us to mashkov yet? he owes us! right??
Holster: he totally owes us. hashtag Mashkov kegster 2015

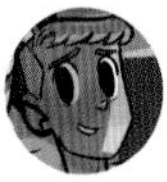

Eric Bittle @omgcheckplease · Friday, September 4, 2015 | 8:04 PM
Rans: I bet he's SO good at pong
Holster: and probably like a tank
(R&H still talking about Alexei Mashkov)

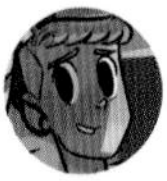

Eric Bittle @omgcheckplease · Monday, September 7, 2015 | 2:33 PM
We're getting a visitor later today!!!!! so I HAVE to finish these PIES.

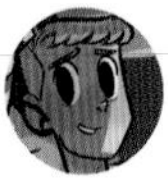

Eric Bittle @omgcheckplease · Monday, September 7, 2015 | 2:57 PM
Ransom: oh BRO BRO maybe he'll bring Mashkov
Holster: [LOUD GASP] TEXT HIM

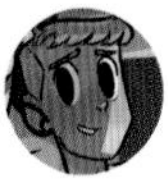

Eric Bittle @omgcheckplease · Monday, September 7, 2015 | 4:46 PM
Jack: Yeah, Tater wanted to come. Ah, mashkov. That's what we call him.
Ransom and Holster just said "Tater" in unison, completely in awe.

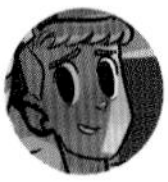

Eric Bittle @omgcheckplease · Monday, September 7, 2015 | 5:12 PM
Jack: The biggest change is probably my diet. Less pie.
This boy still thinks he's hilarious.

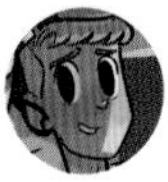

Eric Bittle @omgcheckplease · Thursday, September 10, 2015 | 4:20 AM
merci...more like lord have mercy i just want to go to sleep and stop learning nouns

---

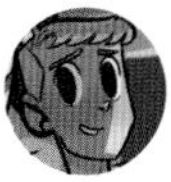

Eric Bittle @omgcheckplease · Thursday, September 17, 2015 | 6:20 PM
SMH group text
Ransom: yo why haven't we met Mashkov yet?
Jack: maybe after the game
Ransom: oh fuck
Jack: no promises
Ransom: ???????????

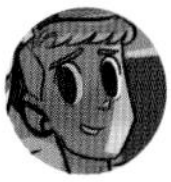

Eric Bittle @omgcheckplease · Thursday, September 17, 2015 | 6:23 PM
Ransom: what if he's lame
Ransom: haha impossible

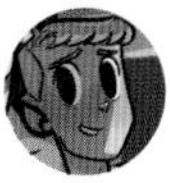

Eric Bittle @omgcheckplease · Wednesday, September 23, 2015 | 9:51 PM
My mother LOVES Shitty's new haircut by the way. Every time I mention it to her she sighs and goes "you know, thank goodness."

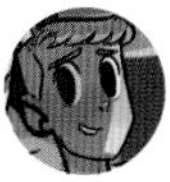

Eric Bittle @omgcheckplease · Friday, October 2, 2015 | 1:11 AM
Me and Lardo just Skyped Shitty! Who actually just Skyped jack. Who Chowder apparently texted before running into me in the hall. #connected

---

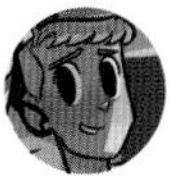

Eric Bittle @omgcheckplease · Friday, October 2, 2015 | 1:14 AM
Shitty: Also, Jack Zimmermann has a fucking girlfriend and he's being cagey about it and it's driving me NUTS

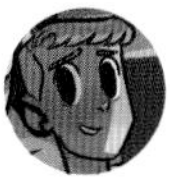

Eric Bittle @omgcheckplease · Saturday, October 3, 2015 | 2:58 PM
Tango: ...that pie was...like, really good. Do you like cook a lot or something?
Oh my God. Well. Bless his heart.

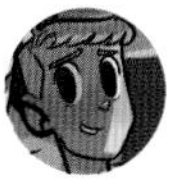

Eric Bittle @omgcheckplease · Sunday, October 4, 2015 | 2:02 PM
ahem A Tango Follow up
Tango: Bitty should be on TV!
Chowder: Yeah!!!!
Tango: I mean on a TV show.
Chowder: ...Okay!
????

Eric Bittle @omgcheckplease · Friday, October 16, 2015 | 8:26 PM
Re: The Great British Bakeoff!!
Holster: Sweet. I thought I was running out of TV.
Me: Sit down, Tango. You need to be educated.
Tango: huh?

Eric Bittle @omgcheckplease · Friday, October 16, 2015 | 8:27 PM
....And Whiskey, of course, has something else he needs to do. I get it. He doesn't like baking.

Eric Bittle @omgcheckplease · Monday, November 2, 2015 | 1:14 AM
What do I have to do to get Whiskey to spend some time with us? Seriously.

Eric Bittle @omgcheckplease · Tuesday, November 3, 2015 | 9:43 AM
Also, Whiskey said I had a "pretty great shot" after practice. First thing that tadpole's said to me in days! I should be so relieved. These tadpoles are so different from my frogs.

Eric Bittle @omgcheckplease · Wednesday, November 4, 2015 | 7:10 AM
Team Bfast: Post-Grad Employment
Ransom: what if I did consulting
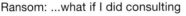
Nursey: you'd be totally soulless and working for the man
Ransom: ...what if I did consulting

Eric Bittle @omgcheckplease · Wednesday, November 4, 2015 | 8:15 PM
I love that Shitty has a naturally curious mind but I really wish he'd, uh, quit trying to figure out who Jack is dating. They're best friends but—privacy? Boundaries?

Eric Bittle @omgcheckplease · Thursday, November 5, 2015 | 3:35 AM
I hate being away from the people I need most. I'm not that strong. Or I know I can and should be stronger. But.

Eric Bittle @omgcheckplease · Thursday, November 5, 2015 | 3:41 AM
There's so many things I can't do and can't say. So many secrets and it's so unfair. I'm just going to finish this pile of flashcards and go to bed.

Eric Bittle @omgcheckplease · Thursday, November 5, 2015 | 1:46 PM
Good job last night, Falconers.

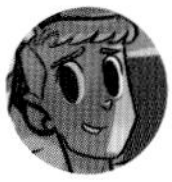

Eric Bittle @omgcheckplease · Thursday, November 5, 2015 | 4:51 PM
Hanging out in the kitchen
Lardo: well.
Lardo: gotta start looking for a new team manager
Dex: W-WAIT YOU HAVEN'T STARTED TRAINING SOMEONE

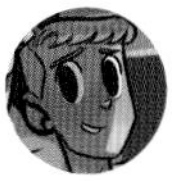

Eric Bittle @omgcheckplease · Thursday, November 5, 2015 | 4:51 PM
Dex: they have to know our schedules—practice times, game times—GAME DAY PROCEDURE—locker room rules, equipment organization, THE BYLAWS
This is amazing. He's really freaking out.

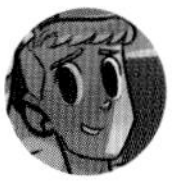

Eric Bittle @omgcheckplease · Thursday, November 5, 2015 | 4:56 PM
I think lardo could assuage his fears,
But she's enjoying this

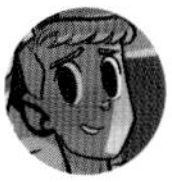

Eric Bittle @omgcheckplease · Thursday, November 5, 2015 | 4:59 PM
Chowder: helloooo! Mmm!!! are those brownies??
Dex: lardo's looking for her replacement
Chowder: i don't want a brownie anymore :((((

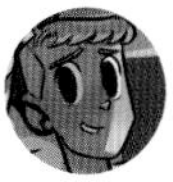

Eric Bittle @omgcheckplease · Thursday, November 5, 2015 | 5:02 PM
Nursey: oh shit brownies
Chowder: Lardo's finding another manager for us!
Nursey: augff! Aawwwff larffo!

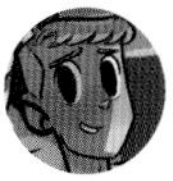

Eric Bittle @omgcheckplease · Friday, November 13, 2015 | 8:50 PM
Chowder's interior design approach is "What would happen if the San Jose Sharks gift shop exploded?"

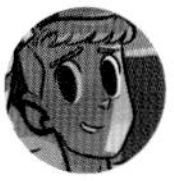

Eric Bittle @omgcheckplease · Sunday, November 22, 2015 | 1:22 PM
Waiting for the boys at Jerry's with Jack. (Yes, it's true, they serve brunch.)

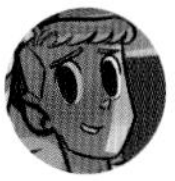

Eric Bittle @omgcheckplease · Sunday, November 22, 2015 | 1:31 PM
When you tell your teammates about your SO because you trust and love them.
And they respond with an endless torrent of chirps. #SMH

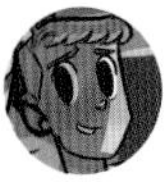

Eric Bittle @omgcheckplease · Tuesday, November 24, 2015 | 9:02 PM
- SMH Group Text -
Shitty: Sooooooo
Shitty: heard Bitty's new piece is slammin'
Ransom: lol oh ya bro
Ransom: Bitty's got mad wheels

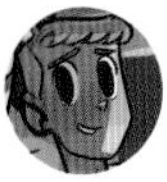

Eric Bittle @omgcheckplease · Tuesday, November 24, 2015 | 9:07 PM
Jack: This is a Samwell hockey record
Jack: Chirps lasting longer than the ones re: Holster & Esther S.
Shitty: HooAOHAHFUCK
Holster: ... Jack

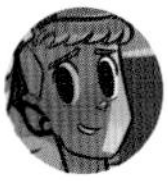

Eric Bittle @omgcheckplease · Tuesday, November 24, 2015 | 9:08 PM
Jack: :)
Holster: Don't fucking smiley face at me when you threw me under the bus
Holster: why you come for me like that, man?

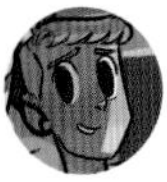

Eric Bittle @omgcheckplease · Tuesday, November 24, 2015 | 9:13 PM
Nursey: whos ES
Jack: i'll write you an email
Holster: AN EMAIL?? REALLY??
Holster: I DIDN'T EVEN START THIS

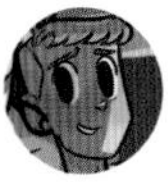

Eric Bittle @omgcheckplease · Friday, December 4, 2015 | 12:54 AM
Dear Bittle's followers,
Bittle has exams and needed help studying for them. He revoked his Twitter privileges until he passes French.

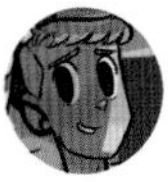

Eric Bittle @omgcheckplease · Friday, December 4, 2015 | 12:55 AM
And reviews for his HIST exam. And finishes his essay for prof. Atley's Indep. study.

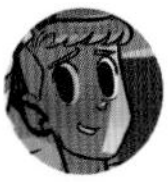

Eric Bittle @omgcheckplease · Friday, December 4, 2015 | 12:56 AM
He says "Sorry, y'all! Gotta buckle down!...I'm gonna regret this."

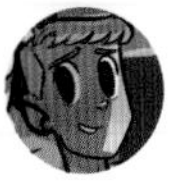

Eric Bittle @omgcheckplease · Friday, December 4, 2015 | 12:56 AM
He will be fine. He promises to study hard. Thanks.

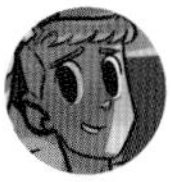

Eric Bittle @omgcheckplease · Monday, December 7, 2015 | 1:02 PM
Have been told to tweet "#GoPVDFalconers".

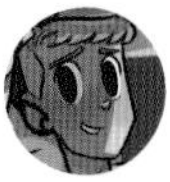

Eric Bittle @omgcheckplease · Thursday, December 10, 2015 | 10:51 PM
Update: studying well, excited for jam in GA...Aunt Judy's jam.

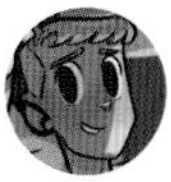

Eric Bittle @omgcheckplease · Saturday, December 12, 2015 | 7:26 AM
Epikegster planning. #Epikegster

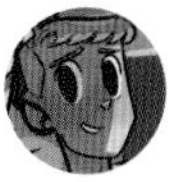

Eric Bittle @omgcheckplease · Wednesday, December 16, 2015 | 4:02 AM
Samwell has one more game left in 2015. #samwellhockey

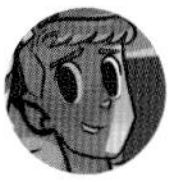

Eric Bittle @omgcheckplease · Wednesday, December 16, 2015 | 4:04 AM
Overall doing good .PCT
all games: .583
conference: .500
The boys can build up momentum. #samwellhockey

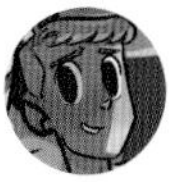

Eric Bittle @omgcheckplease · Wednesday, December 16, 2015 | 4:05 AM
We always have a good showing in the spring. #samwellhockey #samwell

---

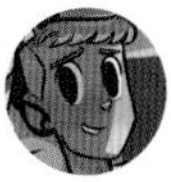

Eric Bittle @omgcheckplease · Wednesday, December 16, 2015 | 4:06 AM
Bittle's up late for a paper due tomorrow at noon.

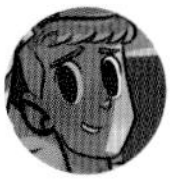

Eric Bittle @omgcheckplease · Wednesday, December 16, 2015 | 4:11 AM
Will pass on encouragement, thanks!

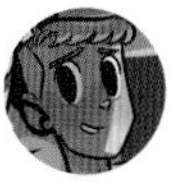

Eric Bittle @omgcheckplease · Wednesday, December 16, 2015 | 3:26 PM
Good play but tough losses.

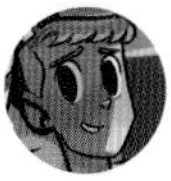

Eric Bittle @omgcheckplease · Wednesday, December 16, 2015 | 4:22 PM
Finish that paper, Bittle! Let's go! Home stretch. French next.

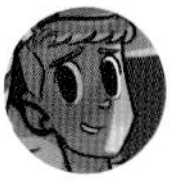

Eric Bittle @omgcheckplease · Thursday, December 17, 2015 | 8:23 AM
Presentation finale.

Eric Bittle @omgcheckplease · Thursday, December 17, 2015 | 9:07 AM

DONE!!

 Eric Bittle @omgcheckplease · Thursday, December 17, 2015 | 9:13 AM

I would like to thank my very incredible ghost-tweeter for keeping everyone updated!

 Eric Bittle @omgcheckplease · Friday, December 25, 2015 | 5:45 AM

Merry Christmas, y'all!

 Eric Bittle @omgcheckplease · Saturday, December 26, 2015 | 12:33 AM

- SMH Group Text -
Jack: Excited for boxing day.
Holster: Jack you do this joke every year.

 Eric Bittle @omgcheckplease · Monday, December 28, 2015 | 9:35 PM

Dex: hey, Tango, what're you thinking about majoring in?
Tango: hm.
Tango: CS seems pretty easy so far
Dex: [spits out pie]

 Eric Bittle @omgcheckplease · Monday, December 28, 2015 | 9:37 PM

Chowder: What about you, Whisk—
Whiskey: Economics.
Whiskey: I figure I'm playing hockey or doing finance so.

 Eric Bittle @omgcheckplease · Monday, December 28, 2015 | 9:40 PM

Chowder: wow, so you think that'll be fun? Or cool?
Whiskey: [shrug]

 Eric Bittle @omgcheckplease · Monday, December 28, 2015 | 9:41 PM

I've never seen someone communicate "my decisions are practical, efficient, and probably hereditary" in a shrug

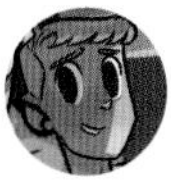

Eric Bittle @omgcheckplease · Sunday, January 3, 2016 | 11:24 PM

- SMH Group Text -
Lardo: officially posted the app for new team manager
Holster: well
Rans: wooow
Nursey: yo
Chowder: :(
Jack: good luck

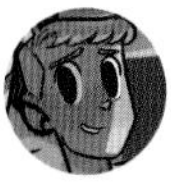

Eric Bittle @omgcheckplease · Sunday, January 3, 2016 | 11:25 PM

Dex: How many rounds of interviews are you doing?
Dex: I think four is a reasonable number.

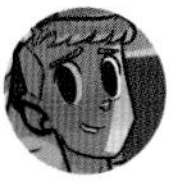

Eric Bittle @omgcheckplease · Monday, January 4, 2016 | 1:18 AM

- SMH Group Text -
Nursey: Yo, Bitty do you remember any French?
Jack: no.

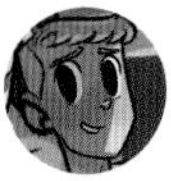

Eric Bittle @omgcheckplease · Monday, January 4, 2016 | 1:28 AM

Me: I can speak for myself, Mr. Zimmermann.
Jack: Well.
Jack: Not in French.
Shitty: HAH.

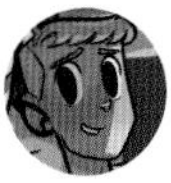

Eric Bittle @omgcheckplease · Tuesday, January 5, 2016 | 1:07 PM

Walking Out of Faber
Nursey: Dex, man, even if our next manager isn't great we can look out for ourselves.
Nursey: [topples down stairs]

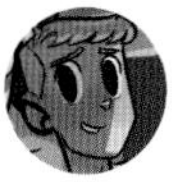

Eric Bittle @omgcheckplease · Wednesday, January 13, 2016 | 9:18 PM

- SMH Group Text -
Jack: Anyone watch the #SOTU?
Ransom: I'm studying and Canadian.

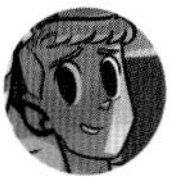

Eric Bittle @omgcheckplease · Thursday, January 14, 2016 | 3:05 PM

Whenever I need to use an accented "é" I honestly just Google Beyoncé and copy/paste. #ThoughtsDuringLecture

---

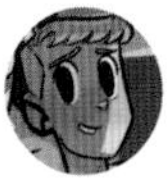

Eric Bittle @omgcheckplease · Sunday, January 17, 2016 | 3:28 AM

Overheard at a Samwell kegster:
Girl 1: This is like, nice for a frat Haus
Girl 2: You should see the ones in TX
Girl 1: I mean but curtains

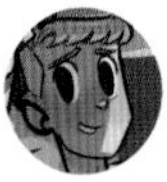

Eric Bittle @omgcheckplease · Wednesday, January 20, 2016 | 1:55 PM

I haven't had the chance to talk to this girl yet, but Lardo is training a new manager!

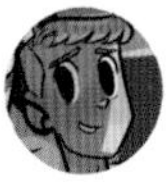

Eric Bittle @omgcheckplease · Thursday, February 4, 2016 | 9:21 AM

Overheard From Across The Hall
Lardo: Chowder. There's white people hair in our shower drain.
Chowder: HOW??????

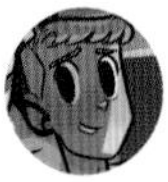

Eric Bittle @omgcheckplease · Thursday, February 4, 2016 | 10:22 AM

- Busing our breakfast Later-
Chowder: You know? Maybe it's because we're both dating white people?
Lardo: ....mmmmoh yeah.

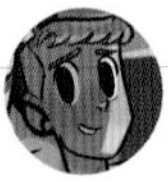

Eric Bittle @omgcheckplease · Thursday, February 4, 2016 | 4:12 PM

Ford: And what's Kent Parson like?
Me:
Me: He's a hockey player.

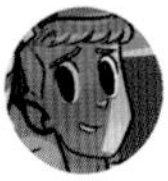

Eric Bittle @omgcheckplease · Sunday, February 14, 2016 | 7:50 PM

And happy birthday Derek Nurse! You being born today kind of explains everything

---

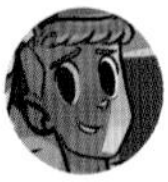

Eric Bittle @omgcheckplease · Monday, February 15, 2016 | 8:10 PM

Nursey: Guess how many cards I got today, Poindexter?
Dex: [a long sigh]
Dex: Like 20.
Nursey: Eight. One was from my mom.

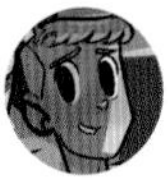

Eric Bittle @omgcheckplease · Monday, February 15, 2016 | 8:11 PM

Ah, Dex tried to hide that laugh but there's pie everywhere.

Eric Bittle @omgcheckplease · Tuesday, March 1, 2016 | 6:53 PM

Lardo's coaching Ford! Personally? I'd teach the finer workings of Samwell hockey anywhere but on that upholstered cesspool we call a couch, but I trust Lardo.

Eric Bittle @omgcheckplease · Tuesday, March 1, 2016 | 6:55 PM

Lardo: And if someone's late you just write it down. If someone doesn't show let RH know.
Ford: RH. RansomHolster. Got it.
Lardo: 'swawes.

Eric Bittle @omgcheckplease · Tuesday, March 1, 2016 | 6:57 PM

Ford: Right. I get that it's positive? But why do you guys say 'swawesome?
Me: You'll find something weirder to worry about soon enough.

Eric Bittle @omgcheckplease · Wednesday, March 2, 2016 | 2:22 PM

Nursey: Hey, Las Vegas is playing Providence tonight.
Dex: Uh oh. Jack versus Parse.
Dex: I'm obvs rooting for Jack but that should be good.

Eric Bittle @omgcheckplease · Thursday, March 3, 2016 | 9:30 PM

NHL players like pie—but also mason jars filled w/ jam prepared according to an old family & aunt-perfected recipe. (A lil bird told me.)

Eric Bittle @omgcheckplease · Thursday, March 3, 2016 | 9:31 PM

But when your #friend asks you to make a batch, does he mean enough for his team? Does that include the coaching staff?

Eric Bittle @omgcheckplease · Wednesday, March 16, 2016 | 6:15 PM

Dear Lord the SMH group chat
Lardo: I need to beat Alexei Mashkov at beer pong.

Eric Bittle @omgcheckplease · Wednesday, March 16, 2016 | 6:17 PM

Jack: haha he's serious about that.
Lardo: then why has it taken so long
Lardo: time and place
Shitty: yessss that's my girl

Eric Bittle @omgcheckplease · Wednesday, March 16, 2016 | 6:18 PM

Tater is literally twice the mass of Larissa Duan.

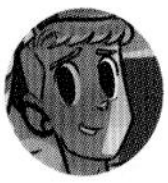

Eric Bittle @omgcheckplease · Wednesday, March 23, 2016 | 3:42 PM

JAM IS IN DEMAND. The situation: A friend of a friend got hold of my aunt's jam, & now a good portion of a pro. hockey team is on a jam (or pie) waitlist. Odd.

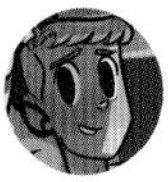

Eric Bittle @omgcheckplease · Friday, March 25, 2016 | 1:12 AM

Coach: How's school?
Me: My GPA's at [OMITTED], meeting w/ my American Studies adviser on my thesis
Coach: History?
Me:
Me: Pie history.

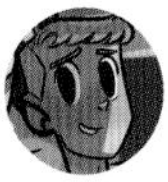

Eric Bittle @omgcheckplease · Friday, March 25, 2016 | 2:29 PM

Holster: what ever happened to the better bitty's butt thing or whatever?
Ransom: oh the bureau? i'm not saying we achieved goals but.

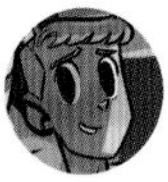

Eric Bittle @omgcheckplease · Friday, March 25, 2016 | 2:33 PM

Ahem Though not much has changed I feel more confident in my assets. It was about bettering the bitty and not the booty all along.

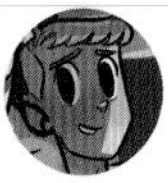

Eric Bittle @omgcheckplease · Friday, March 25, 2016 | 6:19 PM

Ford is a natural. She just sent an email out to the team. Good CHOICE, Lardy-lards!

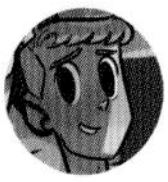

Eric Bittle @omgcheckplease · Wednesday, March 30, 2016 | 12:28 AM

Half a dozen teams are already guaranteed a spot in the NHL playoffs. The Falconers just joined them #GoPVDFalconers #PVDFalconers #GoFalcs!!!!

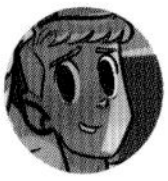

Eric Bittle @omgcheckplease · Wednesday, March 30, 2016 | 12:31 AM

- SMH Group Text -
Lardo: you did it you did it you did it you did it you did it you did it you did it you did it you did it you did it you

---

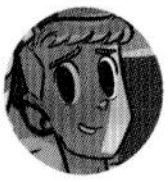

Eric Bittle @omgcheckplease · Tuesday, May 3, 2016 | 3:12 PM

Alice: We'll hit the ground running next year with that thesis!
Me: Yup! I'm going to bake so many pies!!
Alice: child

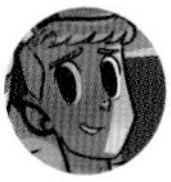

Eric Bittle @omgcheckplease · Thursday, May 5, 2016 | 9:39 AM

We had an awful lot of "scheming" going on last year for my birthday. I love a surprise every now & then, but I'm glad things seem normal?

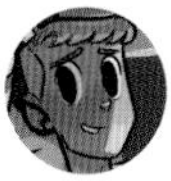

Eric Bittle @omgcheckplease · Thursday, May 5, 2016 | 9:52 AM

So. Sometimes when Holster hugs you he'll lift you clean off the ground.

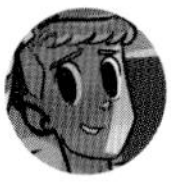

Eric Bittle @omgcheckplease · Thursday, May 5, 2016 | 12:33 PM

Oh my goodness, everyone is so excited today!!! Dex just gave me the biggest hug!!!!! Right off the ground!! He's usually more reserved?...Aw, I'm tearing up.

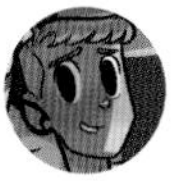

Eric Bittle @omgcheckplease · Thursday, May 5, 2016 | 12:36 PM

I mean—We were in the middle of the crosswalk at the bridge? He couldn't even wait! A car honked at us, but they don't understand my team.

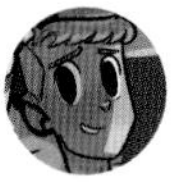

Eric Bittle @omgcheckplease · Thursday, May 5, 2016 | 1:46 PM

OKAY WHAT

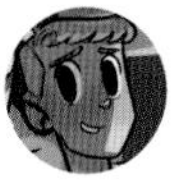

Eric Bittle @omgcheckplease · Thursday, May 5, 2016 | 1:47 PM

I just saw Nursey on River Quad w/ his classmates??
Nursey: ya just a sec
Nursey: Happy Birthday Bitty
NURSEY: [PICKS ME @OMGCHECKPLEASE UP]

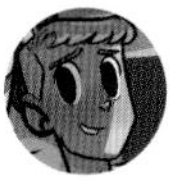

Eric Bittle @omgcheckplease · Thursday, May 5, 2016 | 1:50 PM

Wellie: oh my god MOVE i have to turn in this ESSAY
Nursey: haha you need a hug too?
Me: >:(((((

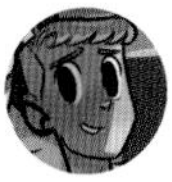

Eric Bittle @omgcheckplease · Thursday, May 5, 2016 | 1:52 PM

...I haven't even seen half my team today

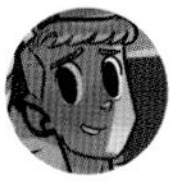

Eric Bittle @omgcheckplease · Thursday, May 5, 2016 | 3:35 PM

Whiskey: Hey, Bitty
Whiskey: [picks me up]
Whiskey: See ya

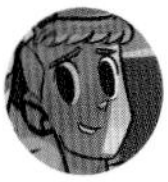

Eric Bittle @omgcheckplease · Thursday, May 5, 2016 | 3:50 PM

THE GROUP TEXT!!!!!

Holster: Bitty, want to meet for coffee? A lil pick-me-up?

Nursey: I duno bits seems so uplifted today

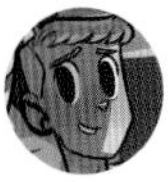

Eric Bittle @omgcheckplease · Thursday, May 5, 2016 | 3:51 PM

Which one.....

Which one of those boys...................................idea was this......

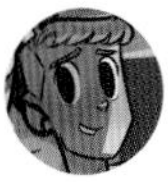

Eric Bittle @omgcheckplease · Thursday, May 5, 2016 | 3:52 PM

I have to swing by the rink to meet up with Coach Murray—if Lardo is there, she'll illuminate me.

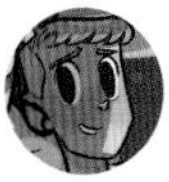

Eric Bittle @omgcheckplease · Thursday, May 5, 2016 | 4:05 PM

Well I just.

Apparently Chowder was working with the goalie coach today.

Chowder: BITTY!!!!!!!!!!!!!!!!!!

Me: [runs]

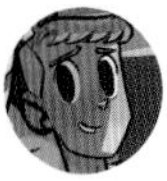

Eric Bittle @omgcheckplease · Thursday, May 5, 2016 | 4:06 PM

Chowder: [after putting me down] there ya go!

Chowder: I was worried you'd lock yourself in your room!

Chowder: Have a nice birthday!!!!!!!

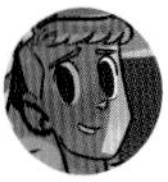

Eric Bittle @omgcheckplease · Thursday, May 5, 2016 | 5:16 PM

Me: Lardo! I—

Lardo: Hold on.

Me: No.

Lardo: Yes.

Me: You can't.

Lardo: Lol brah.

Lardo: You're not the first

Lardo: not the last

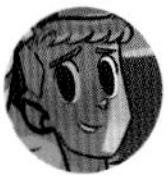

Eric Bittle @omgcheckplease · Thursday, May 5, 2016 | 5:35 PM

Tango: hey

Tango: [picks me up]

Tango: i'm just following orders

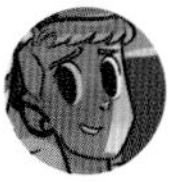

Eric Bittle @omgcheckplease · Thursday, May 5, 2016 | 7:01 PM
I hope they're not planning anything crazy downstairs. I specifically requested NO KEGSTERS for my 21st.

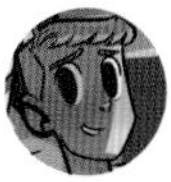

Eric Bittle @omgcheckplease · Thursday, May 5, 2016 | 8:31 PM
Y'all, they baked for me.

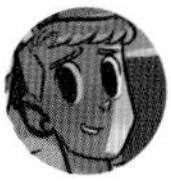

Eric Bittle @omgcheckplease · Friday, May 13, 2016 | 3:37 PM
Tango: well, I gotta go, but I wanted to say bye, Bitty.
Tango: Bye, Bitty. I had a great year!
I'm gonna cry.

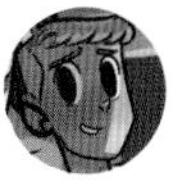

Eric Bittle @omgcheckplease · Wednesday, May 18, 2016 | 6:10 PM
We're on our way to Providence! (And they're already setting chairs up on River Quad.)

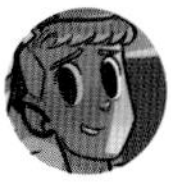

Eric Bittle @omgcheckplease · Sunday, May 22, 2016 | 12:28 PM
I'm so proud of my teammates and can't wait to celebrate their accomplishments this weekend. <3 Congrats Samwell 2016!

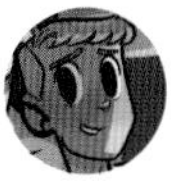

Eric Bittle @omgcheckplease · Tuesday, June 7, 2016 | 12:28 AM
#GoPVDFalconers!!

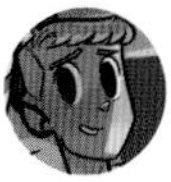

Eric Bittle @omgcheckplease · Monday, June 13, 2016 | 8:56 AM
OKAY LOCKED

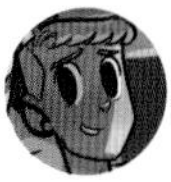

Eric Bittle @omgcheckplease · Monday, June 13, 2016 | 8:56 AM
ME AND JACK KISSED ON TV

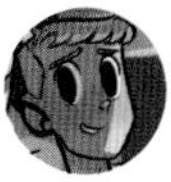

Eric Bittle @omgcheckplease · Saturday, June 18, 2016 | 10:31 AM
The last 5 days have been joyous, insane, chaotic and if i'm being totally honest—mildly terrifying. Thread forthcoming. Lord in heaven.

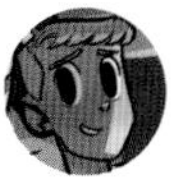

Eric Bittle @omgcheckplease · Saturday, June 18, 2016 | 10:31 AM
First, I put my Twitter on private a few days ago. Because? ....Y'all, I was getting overwhelmed. If you're still following this account, it means I still *WANT* you following it...

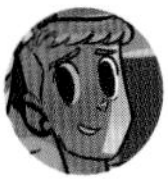

Eric Bittle @omgcheckplease · Saturday, June 18, 2016 | 10:32 AM

(I did a LOT of unfollowing. If you're wondering who all can see this, it's anyone who has lived/is living in the Haus and a handful of baking mutuals. LOCKED DOWN.)

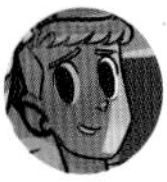

Eric Bittle @omgcheckplease · Saturday, June 18, 2016 | 10:32 AM

Second, I...don't know when I'll unlock this account. If ever. But for now I just want to tweet about me and Jack and SMH and the cup and baking and avoiding my parents

---

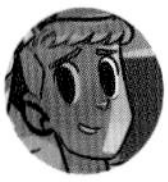

Eric Bittle @omgcheckplease · Saturday, June 18, 2016 | 10:33 AM

Third, I came out to my parents. Kind of. Anyway pie.

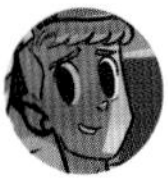

Eric Bittle @omgcheckplease · Sunday, June 19, 2016 | 4:19 PM

AND FINALLY I CAN TWEET ABOUT THE FALCS. ONE of WHOM is my BOYFRIEND. JACK ZIMMERMANN. Another of whom is living in my boyfriends condo? ALEXEI MASHKOV.

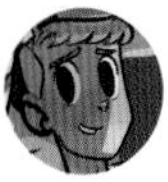

Eric Bittle @omgcheckplease · Sunday, June 19, 2016 | 4:20 PM

I'm an active member of 5 distinct group chats however. And since many of you are members of those group chats, forgive me for tweeting less.

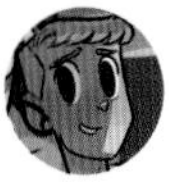

Eric Bittle @omgcheckplease · Saturday, July 2, 2016 | 11:01 AM

I cannot believe that the Stanley Cup will be in this derelict frat den in a matter of minutes. I am so proud. Haus Sweet Haus!

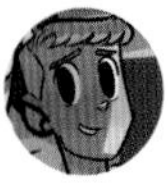

Eric Bittle @omgcheckplease · Saturday, July 2, 2016 | 12:08 PM

Shitty: Jack
Shitty: Will you please sit in the cup.
Jack: Ah. That's okay

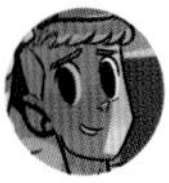

Eric Bittle @omgcheckplease · Saturday, July 2, 2016 | 12:19 PM

Lardo: Tub Juice in the Cup?
Ransom: Tub Juice in the Cup?
Holster: Tub Juice in the CUP?!?
Shitty: TUB JUICE IN THE GODDAMN CUP!!!

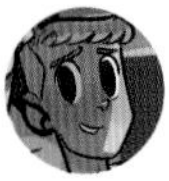

Eric Bittle @omgcheckplease · Saturday, July 2, 2016 | 9:19 PM

Well, the Haus is on fire!!!

Eric Bittle @omgcheckplease · Sunday, July 10, 2016 | 10:17 AM

I'm in Providence!

Eric Bittle @omgcheckplease · Sunday, July 10, 2016 | 10:23 AM

I love my boyfriend. How did I spend an entire year VAGUE TWEETING about him. Why didn't y'all stop me. Lord, how tacky.

Eric Bittle @omgcheckplease · Monday, July 11, 2016 | 3:25 PM

Hockey Champion Jack Laurent Zimmermann: I think I'm gonna make an instagram
Me: !!!
HCJLZ: And learn Photoshop
Me: I'm calling the police

Eric Bittle @omgcheckplease · Sunday, August 7, 2016 | 6:00 PM

Lord in heaven, school starts in a week and I owe 18 hockey players—only 40% of whom are falcs—SEVERAL jars of jam.

Eric Bittle @omgcheckplease · Monday, August 8, 2016 | 11:11 AM

The Real Secret For This Secret Twitter: I'm using my aunt's jam recipe. I'm using my Aunt Judy's Recipe and my mother must NEVER know.

Eric Bittle @omgcheckplease · Monday, August 8, 2016 | 11:14 AM

@lemonitswed. Good Question. Back when they were teens, my aunt revamped my grand-moo-maw's recipe and entered the county fair. TO COMPETE WITH MY MAMA.

Eric Bittle @omgcheckplease · Monday, August 8, 2016 | 11:14 AM

My mama had won last year, but aunt judy claims it was 'cause a judge had a crush on my mom? But this year they TIED.
By a HAIR. AND!!!!

Eric Bittle @omgcheckplease · Monday, August 8, 2016 | 11:15 AM

My mama borrowed the only copy of my grand-moo-maw's handwritten jam recipe? And claims that Aunt Judy stole/destroyed it. Aunt Judy denies this...I don't know who to believe.

Eric Bittle @omgcheckplease · Monday, August 8, 2016 | 11:19 AM

the jam feud is the culmination of a decade-long teenage sibling rivalry and southern women weaponizing food preparation.

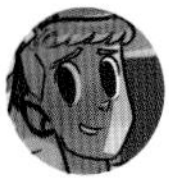

Eric Bittle @omgcheckplease · Saturday, August 13, 2016 | 7:23 AM
Have you met me and my boyfriend's unexpected injured NHL roommate Alexei Mashkov.
Tater: I move back to my house after summer! No worries!
Zimmboni and Pie. Good recovery!

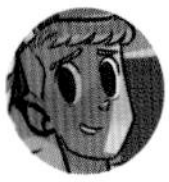

Eric Bittle @omgcheckplease · Tuesday, August 16, 2016 | 1:53 PM
I would never have guessed that Ford, Tango, and Connor would be such good friends, but these frosh groups are unpredictable now, aren't they?

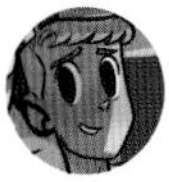

Eric Bittle @omgcheckplease · Tuesday, August 16, 2016 | 1:56 PM
I've broken it down this way: Ford navigates, Whiskey keeps things calm, and Tango keeps things moving. It's really rather sweet. :)

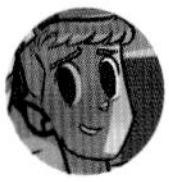

Eric Bittle @omgcheckplease · Thursday, August 18, 2016 | 5:38 PM
Imagine being a freshman on the Samwell men's hockey team and entering into the chaotic media aftermath of your captain kissing Jack Zimmermann on national TV.

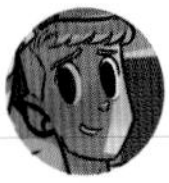

Eric Bittle @omgcheckplease · Saturday, August 20, 2016 | 6:10 PM
Imagine being the caPTAIN OF THE SAMWELL MEN'S HOCKEY TEAM AND ENTERING INTO THE CHAOTIC—

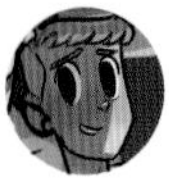

Eric Bittle @omgcheckplease · Wednesday, August 24, 2016 | 11:34 AM
@lemonitswed @justincoco91 Why did y'all avoid the captains meetings? I need an answer other than because SMH is an insular cult. I already know this!!

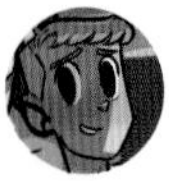

Eric Bittle @omgcheckplease · Wednesday, August 24, 2016 | 11:35 AM
@lemonitswed @justincoco91 Listen, I'm actually going to go to the varsity captains meeting. I need gay friends.

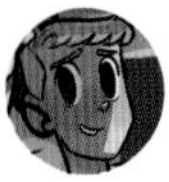

Eric Bittle @omgcheckplease · Wednesday, August 24, 2016 | 1:03 PM
Gays attained.

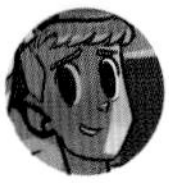

Eric Bittle @omgcheckplease · Wednesday, August 24, 2016 | 7:31 PM
@ducksducksducksducks @shrutitootie Twitter give me a lesbian flag emoji now, you cowards.

Eric Bittle @omgcheckplease · Monday, October 3, 2016 | 8:45 PM

SORRY SORRY SORRY! For the lack of tweets!! After the start of OUR season and JACK'S season things got hectic. Nursey broke his ARM. Ugh!!

Eric Bittle @omgcheckplease · Monday, October 3, 2016 | 11:16 PM

And now I'm mostly tweeting to avoid becoming enraged because I have to get these freshman OUT of this party.

Eric Bittle @omgcheckplease · Tuesday, October 4, 2016 | 3:06 AM

I think I'm having the worst night I ever had at Samwell.

Eric Bittle @omgcheckplease · Wednesday, October 12, 2016 | 6:52 AM

I cannot stress how important it was for me to be able to choose when I came out and to who. I don't take that lightly.

Eric Bittle @omgcheckplease · Wednesday, October 12, 2016 | 6:53 AM

And, for me, I needed to feel comfortable. It's scary. There's never a rush, but finding people who you trust and accept you is important.

Eric Bittle @omgcheckplease · Wednesday, October 12, 2016 | 9:15 AM

And I just found out my mom can't make it to family weekend so it's just going to be my dad.

Eric Bittle @omgcheckplease · Saturday, October 15, 2016 | 12:02 AM

Late night walk to Murder Stop N Shop because I have no self-preservation and I need to stress bake 3 pies

Eric Bittle @omgcheckplease · Monday, October 17, 2016 | 3:26 PM

Visit with Coach: 3/5. We yelled at each other and I cried, but we had a hug that lasted more than 3 seconds and Jack is coming to Madison???

Eric Bittle @omgcheckplease · Monday, October 17, 2016 | 4:27 PM

MY BOYFRIEND IS MEETING MY PARENTS ALDFJA;JF;

Eric Bittle @omgcheckplease · Thursday, October 27, 2016 | 8:08 AM

Tuning right on in to Twitter for the inside scoop on the PROVIDENCE FALCONERS HALLOWEEN PARTY.

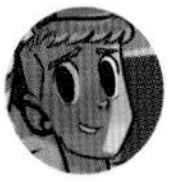

Eric Bittle @omgcheckplease · Thursday, November 17, 2016 | 1:04 PM

Listen, I'm not tweeting about politics. I can't. I'm just focusing on hockey and baking and my team.

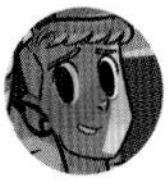

Eric Bittle @omgcheckplease · Monday, November 21, 2016 | 9:14 AM

Anyway glad I'm staying in Samwell for Thanksgiving. :^)))) I'm pretty sure I'm suffering from mild depression.

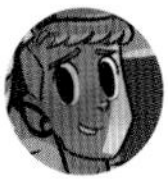

Eric Bittle @omgcheckplease · Thursday, December 22, 2016 | 12:35 PM

Jack, getting into my car at Hartsfield-Jackson. "It's two days from Christmas and it's 78 degrees outside." Welcome to Georgia you sweet Canadian nomad.

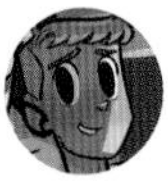

Eric Bittle @omgcheckplease · Saturday, December 24, 2016 | 10:32 AM

I TOLD MY MOTHER ABOUT THE JAM AND NOW THERE ARE CHRISTMAS TREE COOKIES ON THE CEILING.

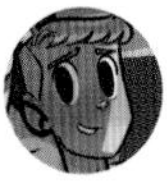

Eric Bittle @omgcheckplease · Saturday, December 24, 2016 | 10:35 AM

@lemonitswed - WE WERE SHARING, BIRKHOLTZ
@ducksducksducksducks I'll make sure Jack gets some hi-res photos. It's still up on the ceiling. Definitely art.

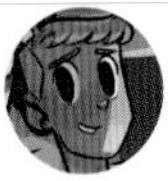

Eric Bittle @omgcheckplease · Sunday, December 25, 2016 | 9:35 AM

Merry Christmas!! Jack worked up the courage to hug me in front of my dad and no one died, so HAPPY HOLIDAYS

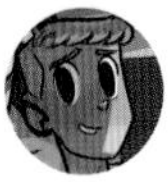

Eric Bittle @omgcheckplease · Sunday, December 25, 2016 | 4:35 PM

You know, kudos to Jack and my dad for having an hour long conversation about soccer. They only talk about sports, history, and rock/country music.

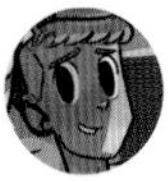

Eric Bittle @omgcheckplease · Sunday, January 1, 2017 | 12:15 AM

Happy New Years!!!

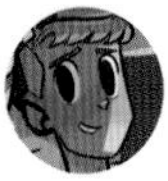

Eric Bittle @omgcheckplease · Friday, January 13, 2017 | 7:00 AM

Hi, I'm back to vent and muse please join me I feel like there's an entire genre of Jock that is probably-bi guys who have no idea what to do with their sexuality

---

Eric Bittle @omgcheckplease · Friday, January 13, 2017 | 7:03 AM
I realize that everyone has 110% the right to live their lives however they want? But I don't think that one's frustrations with their OWN sexuality—

Eric Bittle @omgcheckplease · Friday, January 13, 2017 | 7:04 AM
Should manifest as disdain for those who feel comfortable in themselves. And that's my tweet. Samwell jocks figure yourselves out. I'm sick of it.

Eric Bittle @omgcheckplease · Tuesday, February 14, 2017 | 8:55 AM
Nursey: Singing Valentine's. Pft. A cappella culture is lowkey lame
Bully: I like a capella
Nursey: i mean it's lame but in a cool way, obviously. So cool.

Eric Bittle @omgcheckplease · Wednesday, February 15, 2017 | 7:43 AM
For a Belated Valentine's Day Gift, Jack drove down to have dinner with the team and the Haus

Eric Bittle @omgcheckplease · Wednesday, February 15, 2017 | 7:47 AM
Because the greatest gift this man can give me is inflicting small, surreptitous but potent amounts of PDA on this hockey team.

Eric Bittle @omgcheckplease · Sunday, February 26, 2017 | 8:12 PM
My friends and family are beginning to become "concerned" about my "lack of progress" on my "senior thesis" and while I appreciate their concern it is most unwanted thank you.

Eric Bittle @omgcheckplease · Monday, February 27, 2017 | 7:30 PM
Hi, it's Jack. Bitty needs to revise his senior thesis. Actually he needs to turn in a draft and then revise that. He's unbelievably behind.

Eric Bittle @omgcheckplease · Tuesday, February 28, 2017 | 7:31 PM
Bitty thought it would be a good idea to change his password until he's done. I'll send updates over the next few weeks.

Eric Bittle @omgcheckplease · Wednesday, March 15, 2017 | 7:54 AM
Samwell's doing well in the playoffs. Some nail biters, but they're pulling through. Bitty had a goal and an assist yesterday against Quinnipiac.

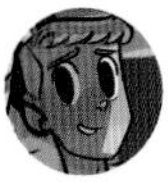

Eric Bittle @omgcheckplease · Wednesday, March 15, 2017 | 7:55 AM

@lemonitswed - i track everyone's stats. He's my boyfriend. You wish you had SO Stats, Birkholtz. =)

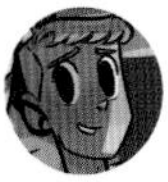

Eric Bittle @omgcheckplease · Friday, March 3, 2017 | 7:58 AM

He's baking while supervised. =) He's nearly done!

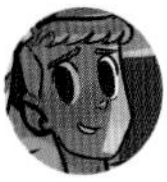

Eric Bittle @omgcheckplease · Tuesday, March 28, 2017 | 9:20 PM

Samwell makes the FROZEN FOUR!

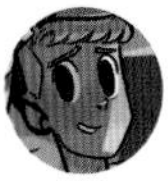

Eric Bittle @omgcheckplease · Monday, April 3, 2017 | 11:21 PM

OKAY!!!! Y'ALL!!! I'm FREE. I've finished my draft and even revised it and am a step away from turning in EVERYTHING.

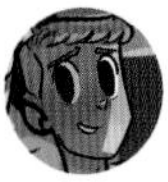

Eric Bittle @omgcheckplease · Monday, April 3, 2017 | 11:23 PM

And I wanted to share the news...I was asked to give THE Senior Closing Speech at Class Day!! Graduation speech!!!

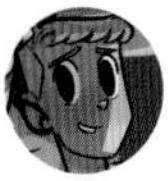

Eric Bittle @omgcheckplease · Monday, April 3, 2017 | 11:29 PM

Lord in Heaven, I have so so so many things to say about this place. I just hope I don't CRY.

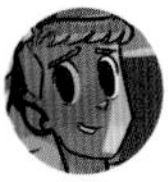

Eric Bittle @omgcheckplease · Saturday, April 15, 2017 | 12:03 AM

THE SAMWELL MEN'S HOCKEY TEAM IS THE NCAA NATIONAL GODDAMN CHAMPS!!!

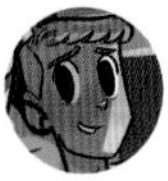

Eric Bittle @omgcheckplease · Saturday, April 15, 2017 | 12:06 AM

WE ARE OUT AND WE ARE YELLING ON THE BUS. AND I'M OVER 21 I CAN DRINK LEGALLY.

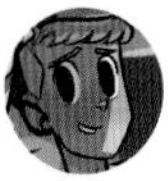

Eric Bittle @omgcheckplease · Saturday, April 15, 2017 | 12:07 AM

AND I MAY HAVE LOST A TOOTH.

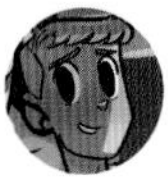

Eric Bittle @omgcheckplease · Sunday, April 23, 2017 | 4:15 PM

There's something about Dibs. The Haus. Kissing the ice. And all of the traditions we have in SMH. If I had known how much they would affect me…

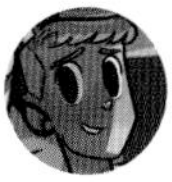

Eric Bittle @omgcheckplease · Sunday, April 23, 2017 | 4:15 PM

I just love this team. this school. this Haus. my time here. I'm 100% revising my Class Day speech and getting misty eyed. Samwell.

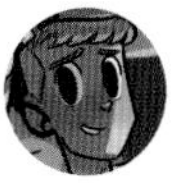

Eric Bittle @omgcheckplease · Thursday, April 27, 2017 | 6:45 AM

So big, big, SECRET news, y'all!......I've decided to make a public twitter account while keeping this one locked. Because?

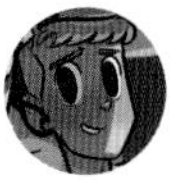

Eric Bittle @omgcheckplease · Thursday, April 27, 2017 | 6:47 AM

I MAY HAVE A BOOK DEAL IN THE WORKS!!! After graduation!! A COOKBOOK. That ties in to my vlog???? I MIGHT ACTUALLY HAVE A JOB!!!!! I'm getting an AGENT???

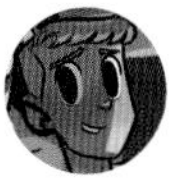

Eric Bittle @omgcheckplease · Friday, May 19, 2017 | 9:46 AM

Mama and Coach are officially in Samwell for Class Day, Graduation, and for meeting BOB AND ALICIA.

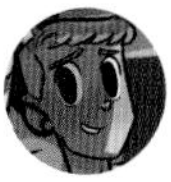

Eric Bittle @omgcheckplease · Friday, May 19, 2017 | 9:47 AM

So so so sorry if I'm not around. I'm running all over this campus like a chicken with my head cut off. My thesis was approved by the by!

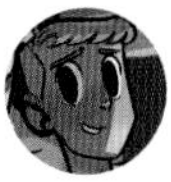

Eric Bittle @omgcheckplease · Sunday, May 21, 2017 | 8:23 AM

For posterity: At MY graduation, Jack seems even more nervous for me than I am? Honestly, so sweet....I mean, my speech was yesterday? Very odd.

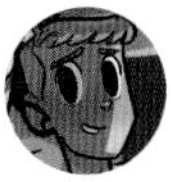

Eric Bittle @omgcheckplease · Sunday, May 21, 2017 | 8:27 AM

The Zimmermanns weren't able to make it to Class Day, but they made it down to Samwell for commencement! Bob and Alicia are such dolls! My mama is SO nervous.

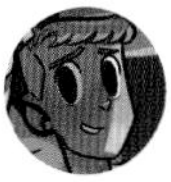

Eric Bittle @omgcheckplease · Sunday, May 21, 2017 | 10:04 AM

Yes, my name is Eric Bittle and I am tweeting while waiting in line for commencement because I'm a fool overwhelmed by emotion.

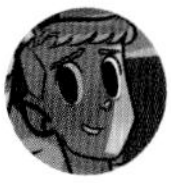

Eric Bittle @omgcheckplease · Sunday, May 21, 2017 | 10:05 AM

I love this place. I love Samwell. I love my friends. I love my team. I love this place. I loved this place. I love this place. I'm still a Samwell student for another hour.

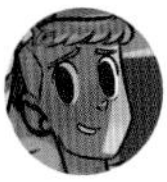

Eric Bittle @omgcheckplease · Sunday, May 21, 2017 | 10:06 AM
Four years passed by so quickly. And I grew so much. I said it in my speech yesterday. I am who I am because of this place. And y'all, I'm crying.

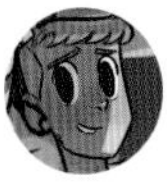

Eric Bittle @omgcheckplease · Sunday, May 21, 2017 | 10:08 AM
It's hard to type because I learned to love myself because of the love of my teammates and boyfriend and professors and friends and parents and family.

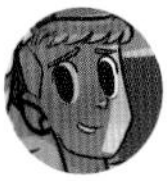

Eric Bittle @omgcheckplease · Sunday, May 21, 2017 | 10:09 AM
I learned to stop being afraid because of my time here and the love I felt here. I am who I am because of this. I'm so thankful. Thank you all.

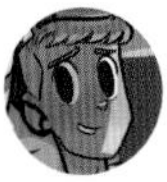

Eric Bittle @omgcheckplease · Sunday, May 21, 2017 | 12:48 PM
Diploma in hand. Samwell Alum!! :-)

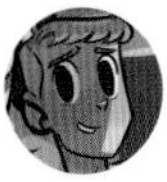

Eric Bittle @omgcheckplease · Sunday, May 21, 2017 | 1:35 PM
On our way to lunch and my life has changed forever.

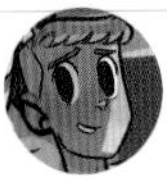

Eric Bittle @omgcheckplease · Sunday, May 21, 2017 | 2:30 PM
I realize I just became a college graduate but MORE IMPORTANTLY
Jack: Mom, have you seen Shitty?
Alicia: Oh Byron? He found his old philosophy professor
Jack: Wait what?
Holster: wait
Ransom: wha
Lardo: The S stands for Sterling if you're wondering about that too

---

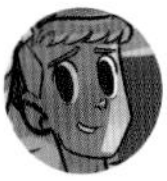

Eric Bittle @omgcheckplease · Sunday, May 21, 2017 | 2:31 PM
BYRON STERLING "SHITTY" KNIGHT. I'm going to EXPIRE.

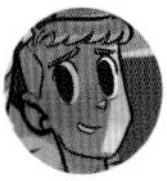

Eric Bittle @omgcheckplease · Sunday, May 21, 2017 | 2:32 PM
Confronting Shitty at lunch and Shitty: B.S. Knight? B.S.? You guys know I'm full of shit.

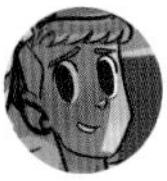

Eric Bittle @omgcheckplease · Sunday, May 21, 2017 | 3:01 PM
Oh my goodness, Jack is so nostalgic. He asked the operations guy at Faber if he could skate there one last time. I'm down!

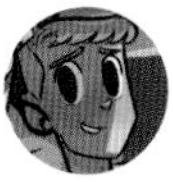

Eric Bittle @omgcheckplease · Sunday, May 21, 2017 | 3:58 PM

....I'm engaged.

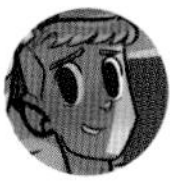

Eric Bittle @omgcheckplease · Sunday, May 21, 2017 | 4:01 PM

This boy. My fiancé.

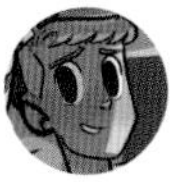

Eric Bittle @omgcheckplease · Sunday, May 21, 2017 | 8:17 PM

MY FIANCÉ!!!

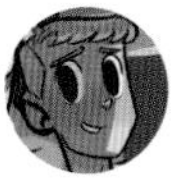

Eric Bittle @omgcheckplease · Wednesday, June 7, 2017 | 9:46 AM

Um. So I'm in Canada for the first time? I'm at Jack's parents' house! And it's delightful!...But I'm actually....making a summer resolution to try and use my Twitter less? And then only tweet for my public account?

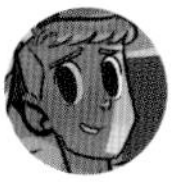

Eric Bittle @omgcheckplease · Wednesday, June 7, 2017 | 9:46 AM

BUT Answering all of your post-engagement questions: 1.) He asked me. I would've asked him but he beat me to it. 2.) He did get down on one knee

---

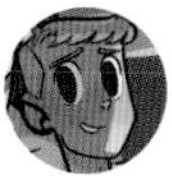

Eric Bittle @omgcheckplease · Wednesday, June 7, 2017 | 9:48 AM

3.) He was EXTREMELY NERVOUS APPARENTLY 4.) My mom SCREAMED about it even though Jack had talked to my mom about it? And most importantly, 5) I FAINTED

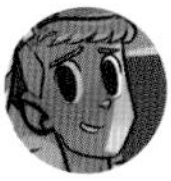

Eric Bittle @omgcheckplease · Wednesday, June 7, 2017 | 10:04 AM

But we're off! Jack is showing me his old stomping grounds, and then we'll be back in time for some dinner made by Bad Bob Zimmermann? And after that?

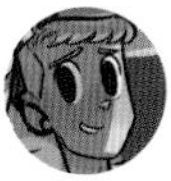

Eric Bittle @omgcheckplease · Wednesday, June 7, 2017 | 12:00 PM

Well, I think I'll bake a pie. <3

Copyright © 2020 by Ngozi Ukazu
Published by First Second
First Second is an imprint of Roaring Brook Press,
a division of Holtzbrinck Publishing Holdings Limited Partnership
120 Broadway, New York, NY 10271

Don't miss your next favorite book from First Second! For the latest updates go
to firstsecondnewsletter.com and sign up for our enewsletter.

Library of Congress Control Number: 2019930756

Hardcover ISBN: 978-1-250-17949-4
Paperback ISBN: 978-1-250-17950-0

Our books may be purchased in bulk for promotional, educational, or business use.
Please contact your local bookseller or the Macmillan Corporate and Premium Sales Department
at (800) 221-7945 ext. 5442 or by email at MacmillanSpecialMarkets@macmillan.com.

First edition, 2020
Edited by Calista Brill and Kiara Valdez
Book design by Molly Johanson and Chris Dickey
Printed in China

Paperback: 10 9 8 7 6 5 4 3 2 1
Hardcover: 10 9 8 7 6 5 4 3 2 1